JULIA'S CHILDREN

JULIA'S CHILDREN

A Norwegian Immigrant Family in Minnesota (1876-1947)

by

Margaret Chrislock Gilseth

"Then the Lord answered Job out of the whirlwind, and said: Hast thou commanded the morning since thy days, and caused the dayspring to know its place?" Job 38:12

St Charles, Minnesota

Library of Congress Catalog Card Number: 87-72390
ISBN 0-9619327-1-6

PRINTED IN THE UNITED STATES OF AMERICA
BY DAVIES PRINTING CO., ROCHESTER, MINNESOTA

ACKNOWLEDGMENT:

The author wishes to acknowledge the immeasurable help and sustaining support of her husband, Walter, in the preparation of this book. Other persons whose help she wishes to acknowledge are: Carl H. Chrislock, Gerald Thorson, David Wood, John Brownell, Louise Kjosa, Rosemary Klein, Norma Craighton, Francis Goodrich and Keith Dyrud. Book design by Mary Craighton Shrode.

Dedicated to the memory of
my father and my aunt,
presented here as
Henrik and Anna

FOREWORD

The migration of an estimated 35,000,000 human beings from other parts of the world—including some 850,000 from Norway—to the United States in the century between 1825 and 1925 ranks as one of the great folk movements of history. Nor is it a saga completed. Following restriction of immigration in the 1920s, most observers assumed that so far as the United States was concerned, emigration-immigration was past history. The assumption was, of course, mistaken. Since the end of World War II, and particularly since passage of the 1965 Immigration Law, immigration again has become a major factor in the contemporary American experience; and although most of our new Americans are of non-European origin, many of the patterns linked to the earlier immigration are resurfacing.

Contrary to simplified popular wisdom, the hard-working "worthy" 19th century immigrant did not necessarily "live happily ever after" in the New Land. This was as true of Scandinavians as of other groups. More typically, the adjustment process was difficult and traumatic. Overall, economic opportunity was open to those possessing the job skills required by the expanding American economy; but that economy manifested a uncomfortable habit of moving unpredictably from boom to bust and back.

The tendency of immigrants to settle in neighborhoods inhabited by their countrymen was a source of mutual support; but social and cultural conflicts that had festered in the old home frequently divided immigrant neighborhoods in the New Land. Above all, there was the inexplicable loneliness rooted in separation from a cherished homeland. Becoming wholly "American," whatever that may ultimately mean, could not be accomplished in a few years or even a generation.

For many years American historians have focused their talents on the emigration-immigration story, and more recently their European colleagues have joined the quest. It goes without saying that the contributions of both groups have been invaluable. It is useful to know something specific about the factors that "pushed" Europeans and others out of their homelands, and the "pull" factors that lured them to the United States. Likewise, it is important to learn which classes were more prone to emigrate than others, and how well American social mobility accommodated the ambitious immigrant—insofar as this can be ascertained on the basis of available evidence. Immigrant roles in religion and politics are other areas that historians have illuminated to our advantage.

However, by the very nature of their discipline, historians can rarely go beyond the "macro" level of the immigrant experience. Except in those rare cases where comprehensive family records provide an adequate primary source foundation, they have only a limited ability to interpret the impact of immigration on ordinary individuals. This opens an arena of opportunity for the creative artist, particularly the novelist. Most library shelves include an impressive array of novels based on the immigrant experience. As might be expected, all are not equally useful in broadening our understanding. Some take as their starting point unexamined myths, while other are placed within a carefully researched historical context.

Julia's Children, the story of a Norwegian immigrant family, clearly falls within the latter category. The author began by acquiring an intimate familiarity with the works of historians, and followed this up with a thorough investigation of the surviving records of the family whose experience provided the inspiration for her story. She then went on to exercise her impressive talent as a literary artist to create characters who are both believable and interesting, and consistently functioning within the context of their time. The result is a book of considerable merit that should attract a variety of readers.

Carl H. Chrislock
Professor of History, Emeritus
Augsburg College
Minneapolis, Minnesota

PART ONE (1876-1885)

ROOTS IN NEW SOIL

Chapter 1

Very early in the morning of an August day in 1876 Arne Aslakson stepped out of his cobbler shop. For most of the night the little Norwegian settlement of Wanamingo, Minnesota, had been steeped in moonlight.

The cobbler hadn't slept well. The cool morning air was a balm after being in his stifling bedroom on second floor. He must be the first one up; no one would be stirring in the street at this hour. Although the moon was still shining, fewer and fewer stars could be seen. The houses and shops of the little town were still dark silhouettes.

As he moved out into the road he was caught up in the enchantment of this early hour. The smell of ripening wheat and the buzz of a million crickets from the surrounding fields penetrated every crevice. It was as if the fields were taut with the vibrating string of the Hardanger fiddle, and Fossegrimen, shy of mortals, was fiddling away in the distant woods.

The modest buildings on either side of him seemed larger now than they were in broad daylight. To his left was the general store, so alive by day, neighbors greeting one another with loud voices, laughter, and gossip. Now it stood serene, its door closed, only some pickle barrels were entrusted to the open porch. Every hitching post was idle.

To his right stood the residence of Nils and Julia Kristian. Julia was always the last one in the town to go to bed, her's being the only lamp to come off the shelf in summer. If she weren't carding and spinning, she would be reading. No one there was stirring yet, but it wouldn't be long. As soon as the sun was up, Julia would be slipping out the back door with her milk pail to the pasture directly north of their house.

Across the street from their home rose the Kristian blacksmith shop. The big door was wide open. No wonder. the place needed cooling off. No man Arne knew sweat as profusely as Nils Kristian as he trotted back and forth from anvil to forge and back to anvil to hammer away at red-hot metal. He would take time off if some one wanted to talk. Then he would come out into the open, lifting his leather cap and wiping his forehead with a big, blue handkerchief. A smile would be on his face as he waited to hear a customer's latest joke, a bit of gossip, or even a complaint. Arne held Nils as his best friend, almost like a brother, since Arne had left all his own relatives behind in Norway.

Scarcely to be noticed, as buildings and trees began taking on color and distinction, daylight was on its way. Birds were starting their morning songs although there were fewer robins now. Arne missed them as they seemed to leave in late July after nesting and raising their young. This morning, however, he heard one or two leading the chorus.

Arne turned to his left and walked up the street to the south. He stopped when he reached the corner where another street came in from the east. Beyond the houses stood a newly-built blacksmith shop. Nils Kristian had merely laughed when Arne had mentioned that competition was just around the corner. As it turned out, Tollefson, the new neighbor, was a horseman and spent much of his time shoeing horses.

Arne continued walking south. At the very edge of the town's south end the villagers had built their one-room schoolhouse. It hadn't been occupied during the summer months, and now a sea of dry grass alive with crickets surrounded it. During the slack season on the farms, newcomers from Norway enrolled alongside of the children, hoping to learn the English language. Arne himself hadn't had any formal schooling here in this country—immigrants were just too busy for that—and he hadn't cared much. During the twenty or so years he had been here in America he had picked up enough words to get along. In this town one could almost forget the world of English if it weren't for the Yankee strangers passing through and what went on in that little schoolhouse.

The moon had become white as a china saucer. Across the street the five-room hotel that accommodated the Yankee strangers was framed in pink with the coming of dawn. On the open front porch a row of chairs stood empty. Even now, in his mind Arne could hear out among the villagers how the English-speaking salesmen interrupted the flow of the Norwegian language.

A mourning dove sent out a long call as melancholy as the horn of a Norwegian fishing boat far out at sea. Although the call seemed to come from the other end of the world, Arne knew the bird must be sitting somewhere on a farmer's fence or even as close as a branch in one of the town's maples or cottonwoods. Mourning doves were mysterious. Sometimes he fancied they called to him from his old home in Norway where as a boy he used to hear their call, as it were from the other side of the mountain.

A rooster crowed. He abruptly turned around and walked back to his own door. He didn't want to meet any of his town folk just yet. They would perhaps wonder at his prowling around before sunrise.

Now daylight was assured, light enough to begin working after he had made himself some coffee and looked in on Inga, his wife.

Arne lived in the back half of the cobbler shop, mainly one room with a cook stove and a cupboard at one end, and a door leading to a pantry, now converted into a tiny bedroom, at the other. The occupant of this bedroom was his invalid wife, Inga. It had just enough room for her narrow bed and an armchair; fortunately it had a window. Not far from the door was a steep stairway which led to a low, second story that was divided into two rooms. Arne slept in one, the other was left for storage.

Arne was just finishing his coffee when through his screen door he saw Julia Kristian approaching. Quickly he took the dirty dishes off the table and wiped the oilcloth.

"Morn, Julia. *Du er så snil å komme,"* he said as he pushed open the door to let her in. She was carrying a pitcher of milk in one hand and a jar of perserve in the other.

"Morn. Hvordan er Inga?" Julia set the jar and the pitcher on the table.

"She looks like she's sleeping, but she does that so much of the time now. I think it is good we get her up every day."

"I thought perhaps she would drink some of this fresh morning milk. I made plum butter yesterday. I brought you some. Nils sure likes it."

"You are so kind, Julia."

"Shall we get Inga into her chair?" Julia never loitered.

"We must keep trying to do our best," Arne replied mournfully as they moved through the door into the tiny bedroom. "See, she grows more lifeless every day. It is hard to imagine what she cares about anymore or what she understands."

"I'm sure she knows us and would tell us a lot of things if only she could."

They filled the chair with pillows and moved it slightly so that the patient would have full benefit of the window. Locking hands under her and behind her shoulders, together they lifted Inga out of her bed and into the chair. Her eyes were open now and remained open as her head rested on the propped pillow. How mechanical it all was! The eyes were open now because they were supposed to be open, and when she was returned to bed they would automatically close. Every morning Arne was troubled, and every morning Julia was reassuring. It was always the same.

"I'll try and get her to eat a little," Julia said. "Anna is watching the cradle while I'm gone. Nils tells me you are so busy with harnesses these days."

"Busier than I want to be."

Julia's offer to feed Inga gave Arne a mixed feeling of relief and guilt. He should be feeding his wife; it shouldn't be left to the neighbors. He followed Julia out of the tiny room leaving Inga where they had put her.

"I know she appreciates all that you do for her, Julia, and I thank you for helping me."

Julia was already pouring fresh milk into a cup. She knew her way around here as well as she did her own kitchen. Hesitating a moment, Arne could think of nothing better to do than to move through the door into his shop. Julia would let herself out.

Work had been piling up. There was so much for one man to do, and he wasn't young anymore. Nils had said he should get himself a helper, but who would he find to stir around with him in this shop? He knew it was a mess, but it was his mess. He knew where everything was, but how would anyone else?

Two jobs were pressing. One was the alteration of a harness for Bernt Kvam, who was coming into town today. What this town needed was a harness shop. Working with leather did not automatically make him a harnessmaker; he was a shoemaker.

The second job was tailoring a pair of shoes for little Anna Kristian whose fifth birthday was tomorrow. He took delight in this project—if only he had more time. Julia frequently gave him things, beautiful woolen stockings for winter, a warm quilt to put over Inga's knees when she sat in her chair. But it wasn't merely wanting to return these unusual kindnesses. Anna was a lively child, and he loved to see her eyes light up and her feet dancing. He was sure she suspected nothing. He had measured her foot about a month ago, and she had thought it was all in fun.

He checked the harness for the final time and draped it across the pegs near the door. Now for the shoes—he hoped he would have time enough to get all the buttons sewed on. Julia, of course, would get out her thimble and coarse thread and do the job if he ran out of time. But that wouldn't be right; a gift should be complete and as perfect as possible.

He leaned to the left and pulled open the supply drawer, deep with notions of every kind: spools, laces, gold tacks, even round, flat cans of polish and bottles of half-used solutions. This part of the job didn't interest him much. Why did women have to button; couldn't they just as well lace? He preferred to rivet eyelets.

As he worked, a dread settled over him. Inga was certainly failing. It had been almost four years since the paralyzing stroke. That, of course, is a long time to be living completely helpless. It was getting harder and harder to get her out of bed and into her chair. And her hair was almost gone. A woman's pride is her hair, they say. Inga now wore a nightcap all the time. She was losing her appetite, too. She wouldn't feed herself with her good hand as readily as she once had. And her eyes had been changing! They were glass eyes, now, big glass eyes—so much dull white where the lower lids had sunk away in wrinkles. And how faded the irises! They had been a delightful saddle brown that went with reddish hair and freckles. Today they were the color of wheat. He would touch her cheek. The skin was soft, strangely like a baby's, but, of course, that, too, was unhealthy.

He began to wonder, how long? This fall? This winter? Julia had said he should ask the minister to come and give her communion. He felt uncomfortable around religious people, ministers—not Julia, she was religious, too, but of a different sort. Arne was not a churchgoer.

There was that disturbing question raised by these Haugeans: "Are you saved?" He had never been exactly sure what that meant, and they made it sound so urgent and so ultimate. What Arne couldn't understand was how come a loving God would destroy his creatures. Wouldn't He then be acting in the same way as wicked people? Should he fear God as he would an evil man? "Being saved," they said, was being forgiven, being sure that God would not destroy them. Julia was always talking about "being saved." He wondered why a person as beautiful as she should need to be afraid. And, now, poor Inga? Who would have anything but pity for her?

He had one button left. He got up and went to the window and looked across to the blacksmith shop. Nils was out there talking with two farmers. Returning to his stool, Arne resolved to join them, even now they were taking time for stories. He would tell Nils that Bernt Kvam's harness was ready. Maybe Nils would bring him across to Julia for forenoon coffee. That would be good, a cup of coffee.

Chapter 2

"Poor Greta, she'll never go to sleep if you keep pushing her and kicking her with your feet. You're naughty today, Henrik."

Little Anna Kristian was in her usual corner rocking the cradle of her baby brother. She was sitting on the bottom step of the steep stairway that led up to the family's sleeping rooms. This was Anna's playhouse, a cove roomy enough for Henrik's cradle.

Anna stopped the rocking. Something must be done. Her baby brother wasn't going to let her dolly sleep. Greta was a stuffed stocking with unraveled black yarn flopping around her head. The heel of the sock served as a face, having black button eyes and nose, and a mouth embroidered in red. Anna rescued Greta and held her lovingly.

Suddenly she shook the doll in front of Henrik's face.

"Look at her, Henrik, her eyes are wide open. She'll never go to sleep."

The chubby child in the cradle shrieked with glee. Few things she did ever brought on a laugh like that. And who wouldn't laugh at such a doll! Her eyes never slept, her wide smile never went away and her silly nose was so flat.

But Greta couldn't help how she looked. Anna smoothed the green calico dress her dolly wore and patted the wooly, black hair. She wrapped her tenderly in one of Henrik's diapers and laid her down on the second step of the stairs.

That done, she turned her attention back to the cradle. Her baby brother was better than a dolly any day. She reached her finger toward him and he quickly grabbed it and grinned between plump cheeks. She wished he'd laugh out loud again. Tickle him? No, she must never do that, her mother had cautioned, such laughing wasn't good for him. Anna looked over at Julia who was kittycorner across the room busy with her kettles on the stove.

Henrik drew up his foot and put his toe into his mouth. How could he do it? She couldn't. Suddenly she remembered the names of all the toes. She pinched the little one, *Titill,* the next, *Tåtill,* next, *Spilleros,* then *Mufrenfru,* and finally the grand climax, *Store Gubbe*

Hesten! She pulled teasingly at his big toe, then she let him jerk it away. There it went into his mouth again.

Anna saw that her mother was putting out cups and saucers for forenoon coffee. She set a plate of molasses cookies on the center of the red-checkered oilcloth together with cream and sugar. Soon Papa would come through the door with his friends.

Anna left her corner and skipped to her mother.

"Why does Papa call me *Lille Mor* all the time?" said Anna, anticipating her father's presence. She knew the name was endearing and she loved the attention.

"Well, you are a little mother aren't you? You have been with Henrik all morning, ever since I went to Arne's."

Anna wanted to hear this and felt happy. She ran to the window to see how many men were coming in for coffee. There were two windows facing the street, one on each side of the front door. She pushed aside a white curtain.

"It's only Papa and Arne," she announced, looking back at her mother. "Bernt Kvam is driving off in his wagon. He's laughing and waving at Papa and Arne."

As the two men came to the door, Anna ran back to her seat at the bottom of the stairs. Papa and Arne were laughing too loud to pay attention to anyone as they let the screen door slam. They went straight for the chairs and pulled up next to the red tablecloth. Mama didn't seem to care what was so funny. She simply poured hot coffee into two of the cups and placed one in front of each. Mama never listened to foolish talk. Now she turned to the back of the stove where she was kneading bread in the big wide pan. Mama did talk to Papa and Arne over coffee often, though. She told them what she read in the newspaper, but not today.

"I heard a joke last week, too, about plowing," Nils said.

Arne wiggled a little closer to the table. He poured coffee into the saucer to cool.

"One day a newcomer asked his neighbor, 'How will I make a furrow straight over such a long field?' 'Oh,' replied the neighbor, 'just aim for a tree, a post, or something like that.' The newcomer started out. Soon the neighbor noticed that the furrow was taking off through the middle of the field. 'What in the world is he eyeing for?' Up ahead was a cow moving slowly across the pasture."

The laughter that followed was contagious, and Anna giggled to herself in her corner. It was fun when people laughed even though she didn't always understand what was so funny. Was this to be the end of the foolish talk? Anna hoped not.

"And that Bernt Kvam," Arne began after a swallow, "thinks he is going to plow deep with that new plow of his. Why, I knew a man one time who plowed so deep he wore out the brim of his hat in the stubble!"

Papa's laugh made him jerk in his chair. His eyes misted now, almost like tears.

"Naw, you Arne, that's entirely too much!" Papa said, shaking his head.

The fun was by no means over. It would go on until all the cookies were gone except one. As Anna watched, she noticed how tall her father sat compared to Arne. Papa's hair was heavy and dark and his beard moved up and down when he talked. Arne sat small and stooped, with hardly any hair, and no beard to speak of. Papa put his head back and laughed real hard; Arne just bent forward, his whole body shaking, and the sound that he made was more of a wheeze than a laugh.

Finally Papa stood up indicating that both men would soon be leaving. Arne, however, still sat and was squinting around the room.

"Anna?" he said as he caught sight of her in the corner. "Come here, Anna."

Anna rushed forward. She climbed into his lap without hesitation because Arne could make her laugh, too.

"When is your birthday?"

"Tomorrow!"

"Tomorrow, and how old will you be?"

"Five. And I'm going to have my picture taken in my new dress!"

"No! Then the shoes will have to be ready, too, won't they?"

"Shoes!" Anna almost leaped out of his lap. She remembered the day he had measured her foot. He had really planned to make her a pair of shoes!

"Well, we'd better get back and see." Arne let her slip down and then stood up and pushed his chair back under the table. "*Mange takk,* Julia."

Anna clung to Arne's arm with both hands as they went next door. She loved the smell of leather. She also liked to pick up the curled chips of leather from the floor around Arne's stool.

She danced into the shop ahead of him. She looked first at the chips around the stool and then up among the shoes on the shelf behind the big machine.

"Can you find them, now?"

She caught sight of a pair of girl's shoes, high shoes with shiny black buttons.

"There!"

"Hold on! We'll have to see if they fit first."

Without being told she climbed into the tall chair where people always sat in Arne's shop when they were to try on boots. Her feet didn't touch the floor so she swung them frantically.

"Does your mother have a button hook?" He reached into the cigar box on his bench to find one.

"Oh, yes, of course."

He propped a wooden box under her feet and helped her on with the left shoe.

"I know how to button shoes."

"You do?"

"See." She grabbed the hook and put it through the lowest button hole and pulled the button through.

With delight Arne watched her, her tongue sticking out of the right side of her pretty mouth. Like her father she had a broad forehead and dark hair that tended to curl, and her eyes had the same lively intelligence. Her nose was rather small, pointed and upturned enough to expose the nostril. Her mouth was large and expressive. Arne was fascinated by the likeness between father and daughter.

"So tomorrow you go to Zumbrota?"

"Yes," she said, looking up. "I'm going to hold the baby while Mama holds the reins. And we're going to visit Mrs. Ringstad. She lives in a great, big house."

"And you will go to the picture studio?"

"Oh, yes, and I'll be wearing these shoes!" She jumped onto the floor, with both shoes buttoned all the way to the top. "Have you ever had your picture taken?"

"Yes."

"What did they do to you?"

"The photographer points a black box at you, about this big," replied Arne. "Then he throws a black cloth over himself and looks at you through the window in the box."

"What will I do?"

"You'll just smile the way you want to look in the picture."

She never knew about Arne, whether to believe him or not, but he had told the truth about the shoes. She looked down at them again, wiggling her toes inside. They were just like Mama's!

"Well, I guess they fit," Arne said, winking at her.

"Oh, they do!"

"Then sit down again and let's take them off. It's not your birthday yet." He bent down. Getting women's shoes off was as bad as getting them on. He drew one shoe off and handed it to her. He marveled at a child's foot, so small and firm.

"They smell good," she said, watching him. She wished she could have kept them on. The old ones looked so shabby!

"Now take your new shoes home to your mother." He handed her the prize.

"Oh, thank you, Arne, thank you! I'm sure you're the best shoemaker in the whole world! Goodbye."

As she rushed out, she knew he was still standing in the doorway, but she was too excited to turn and wave. New shoes! She could hardly wait until tomorrow!

Chapter 3

Julia hadn't been away from Wanamingo for two years except for the family's weekly trips to church three miles away. Late last summer she might have made this seven-mile trip to Zumbrota if she hadn't been pregnant with Henrik. She had been cautious then. Following Anna's birth Julia had had two miscarriages, one in the seventh month, leaving her weak and dismayed. It was hard to bury the still-born child so fully developed. Dark days followed.

Today, before leaving she was taking time in a rocking chair to let her baby nurse. He would be much easier to manage if he got his fill. Henrik was a good baby. From the moment he had been conceived he had brought a new vitality to his mother. He had such a robust will to live.

Nils had gone out after breakfast to the pasture to get Lady, the small, white horse he had recently purchased from a stranger. Being train-shy she was no good in city traffic. She was just the horse for Nils, however, who had now finished repairing a little buggy wrecked in a run-away. "This rig is just right for you, Julia. You'll look so fine."

Anna had run out the door a few minutes ago to join her father. She had been disappointed when she saw her new dress folded away in her mother's traveling bag. But she was wearing her new shoes.

The wooden box filled with cheese sat on the kitchen table. She had just finished wrapping the cloth-covered chunks in newspaper to insulate them against the heat of an August day. This summer their two cows had yielded full pails making it possible for her to make butter and cheese to sell. From the rocking chair she again figured what it might bring in trade at Lett's General Store—quite a bit she should think. She did have a small roll of bills in her draw-string bag, however. She hoped she wouldn't have to use too many of them.

Henrik was satisfied. She smiled as she put him down again in his cradle, then quickly went for her bonnet. She stood before the oval mirror above the roller towel as she tied it on. She had tried to soften the look of her hair, not pulling it quite so severely into a pug. Still she was not quite like a city woman, but she knew it was all right to be from the country if one knew how to speak and act.

Next she picked up the wooden box, grabbed the light shawl she had laid out for herself and proceeded through the door.

As she turned at the corner of the house, she saw the rig ready and waiting.

"Lift me up and let me pet her nose, Papa," Anna was asking.

"She'll get you to Zumbrota and back," he said, lifting her up to greet the white mare.

"Maybe I could hold the lines sometimes, too." The velvet nose was warm against her fingers.

"She's gentle, Lady is, but you must do as Mama says. Help her all you can."

"Oh, I will."

Seeing Julia, Nils put Anna down.

"Under the seat might be cooler than the carriage box," she said, handing the box to Nils.

She went back to the house as quickly as she had come and returned with her traveling bag and the baby over one shoulder.

"Lift me up on the seat, Papa. Mama says I am going to hold Henrik."

"Our *Lille Mor,*" said Nils, lifting her up onto the spring seat. Julia placed the baby in her arms.

"You'll get tired before long, holding that plump child, but we'll stop and rest. I hope it doesn't get too hot."

Julia raised herself up onto the seat and took the reins.

"Goodbye then, Nils. I hope to be back before dark."

"Goodbye. Greet the Ringstads."

"Goodbye, Papa." Anna couldn't free a hand to wave.

"Happy Birthday," he called, holding aloft his big hands as they drove out of the yard.

Lady was trotting beautifully now and the little carriage moved rapidly along the dry trail. It was quite easy to go the seven miles to Zumbrota, do one's business, and return home in a single day. The morning dew as it evaporated before the sun gave out a fragrance of soil and wild sweet clover. Julia noticed the fields; some of them were already in shocks, sheaves of grain stacked against each other. In the distance she saw a reaper waiting in Ole Bakken's field. When the dew dried away, the cutting would begin again and men would follow the machine, tying bundles with strands of straw.

Nils had had more work to do since these new reapers came into use—it was an exciting time for him. It was almost as if he had invented the machine himself. Farmers for miles around came to him. They knew he could fix anything. Some claimed he could make better and stronger parts to replace broken ones, and it didn't take long either. At mealtime he would bring the waiting men across to eat. Julia never quite knew how many she would have for dinner, but that was all right. She had a good man. Not everyone was as fortunate as she.

Times were good and wheat was becoming a very important crop. Two years ago, Goodhue County was declared the banner county in the United States for wheat, averaging forty bushels to the acre. How excited the men had been telling about the 655 wagons which had stood in line at Red Wing, waiting to unload their wheat! There were things about this country to get excited about, and often she was caught up in the enthusiasm of her husband.

Julia was brought back from her thoughts by two violent sneezes.

"Bless you, Anna. You cannot be taking cold. It must be the dust."

Anna merely turned a sad face toward her mother with nothing to say. Julia noticed that a cloud of dust was being tossed up by Lady's trotting feet. There was an inch-deep layer of dirt as fine as flour on the road.

At Sophie Ringstad's they would clean up. Julia had planned to stop and visit there before going to the studio with Anna. Sophie was an old friend she had known in Wisconsin long before either of them had married, and Julia would feel at home even if the Ringstad house was more elegant than her own.

It was wheat that was bringing Johan Ringstad his wealth. He had been in the milling business for several years, getting his start along streams in Wisconsin and finally coming into Goodhue County. The mill at Zumbrota had prospered beyond expectation, turning out a good grade of flour. Nils had told Julia a rumor that Johan was planning to open a bank. Johan Ringstad had done well in this country, that couldn't be denied, and Sophie was fortunate to have married so well. Sophie's maiden sister Bertha lived with them. She had a dressmaking studio in the Ringstad residence. It was a pity that Sophie and Johan had no children.

Julia looked again at Anna and decided she had better stop. Henrik was waking up and becoming a bit of a problem for his sister. Seeing a tree just ahead, she drew up the reins and brought Lady to a stop. She wound the reins to the catch and climbed out of the buggy. She took the baby out of Anna's lap.

"What a load you are!" she said as she peeled off the shawl.

"He is!" agreed Anna as she stood up, preparing to jump down.

Julia watched her daughter making it out of the buggy by herself.

The grass beneath the tree was soft and green. Julia put young Henrik on the ground. It felt much cooler here than in the buggy out in the open sun. Julia removed her bonnet to let the cool air reach her temples. Anna's lay on the buggy seat; she had dropped down beside her brother.

As Julia looked at the two of them, she remembered that the photographer spoke English.

"*Kan du si* 'Good afternoon'?"

Anna sat up quickly and looked at her mother in surprise.

"What?" The words sounded strange.

"Good afternoon." She repeated the English words slowly with a pause between syllables.

Anna shook her head. It sounded foolish.

Julia repeated it several times. Then she began nodding and smiling as if speaking to the photographer:

"Good afternoon, Mr. Sloan."

"Good afternoon, Mrs. Kristian. How are you today?"

"I am fine, thank you. Mr. Sloan, this is my daughter Anna."

"Good afternoon, Anna."

"Good afternoon."

Anna's eyes widened in surprise. *"Jeg vil ikke!"* said the child jumping up and pulling at her mother's skirt to stop her.

"You must learn to speak English," Julia said. "English is the language of this country. We all have to know English. There are others here besides Norwegians, you know." Julia looked into her daughter's face with a seriousness the child couldn't ignore. "Say it after me. 'Good afternoon'."

"Goo—daff—ta—noo," Anna stammered, hurriedly covering her face.

"Don't hide your face—smile! You are saying *'God dag'* to the man. Again, Good afternoon."

"Good after—noon." She smiled, imitating her mother.

"That's fine, Anna!"

"I can say it. Good after—noo—oon." She skipped around the tree repeating the words several times. Julia smiled at her daughter, knowing that the day would come when Anna would speak better English than she.

"We are more than half-way now," said Julia. "I think Henrik can sit between us for the rest of the ride."

Seeing that her children were secure in the seat beside her, Julia clicked her mouth and tapped the reins. Lady was happy to be moving again. She had stood long enough bobbing her head and lifting her feet against the flies.

The buggy rolled along at a good clip. At the top of the next hill they would see Zumbrota. This town had been settled by Yankees who migrated from Massachusetts. Julia considered them unusually fine people. They had built their church, a beautiful structure like ones they had known in New England, within five years of their arrival. And the sale of liquor was forbidden; she thought that a wise ordinance.

"When are we going to eat?" Anna spoke up suddenly.

"Not too long now. Sophie will be expecting us. I mailed her a letter last week. She knows you will be hungry. Wait nicely and be sure you say thank you." Julia began to feel a bit uneasy. She would have to nurse Henrik almost immediately upon arriving. Sophie wasn't used to the routine of children.

They were passing houses now. As they turned the next corner, she saw the two evergreen trees in front of Sophie's house. Arriving, Julia drew back on the reins and Lady came to a halt.

No sooner was Julia down with Henrik in her arms than Sophie came, unhurried, through the front door. Anna stared. She wasn't wearing an apron. This was a beautiful lady with red hair dipping across her temples in soft curves. The red hair shone in the sun. She was not ordinary like Anna's mother who wore her hair pulled severely back from her forehead.

"How good to see you, my dears. I got your letter," she called as she came down the walkway. When she reached the buggy she put out her hand to Anna.

"So this is Anna. You're a big girl now," she said in a lively, clear voice. "You must be tired riding such a long time."

Anna continued to stare but suddenly realized she must answer when spoken to. She smiled as nicely as she could and said, "No, Aunt Sophie." Holding Sophie's hand, she stood up and jumped to the ground.

"And look at this little man!" Sophie laughed as she patted Henrik's cheek. He was not taken in her arms, however, as babies usually were received when taken visiting.

"Your horse will be taken care of," she said turning toward the house. She ushered her guests up the walk. "Don't worry about a thing. We must have a cup of coffee. And the children, they must be hungry, too."

Sophie opened the tall front door. *"Vær så god."*

"I think we need to wash our faces," began Julia after glancing around a brief moment.

"You may go upstairs. In the first room there is water in the pitcher," said Sophie, pointing up a stairway with a railing of polished oak, the steps turning at a right angle into the rooms above.

Anna stopped on every other step to gaze across the railing into the parlor.

"Go on, Anna. We'll be down again soon, and then you can look around."

With this Anna came to life and ran up the stairs, almost stumbling, it wasn't the same as the steps at home.

"Now may I wear my new dress?"

"Your face first, my dear." Julia poured water into the large, gleaming white basin. Such fine needlework on the towels!

Sophie was waiting at the bottom of the stairs when Anna appeared above, wearing the birthday dress. It was made of white voile, the bodice full of soft tucks. It had a high neckband edged on both sides with lace. Beginning below the elbow, the sleeves were tucked like the bodice and reached to the wrists. The skirt was very full and fell in soft folds almost to the tops of her high shoes. At the waist was a wide sash. Anna started down the steps.

"My dear Anna, what a lady you are becoming!" Sophie held out her hand to meet her.

"Mama made it for my birthday," Anna said, smiling with pride. "And Arne made my shoes."

"Arne?"

"Yes, Arne is my friend." She was surprised Sophie didn't know who Arne was.

"Come, Bertha," called Sophie. "See what a beautiful dress Julia has made for Anna."

Out of a room hidden under the stairway emerged a lady quite a bit taller than Sophie with a tape measure around her neck. Her hair was brown and piled on top of her head. She was wearing glasses. Anna hadn't seen many people with glasses.

"My, I should say that is beautiful!" Bertha bent close and felt of Anna's skirt.

Julia followed Anna down the stairs with Henrik on her arm. Julia observed her daughter. No, she wasn't shy like so many immigrant children were, who seldom got away from their homes.

Leaving her guest to Bertha, Sophie disappeared for a moment seeking out a little, blue, plush box in the top drawer of the dining-room buffet. She returned quickly.

"Anna, one more thing you must have now that you are so dressed up."

Anna turned from Bertha in surprise. Sophie was holding something behind her back. Did she want to play "Which hand do you want?" Not quite. Anna was given the little box.

"Open it, my dear," coaxed Sophie.

It was a box which could snap back on your fingers. She was careful.

"Mama, a locket!"

"Let's put it on. It will be just beautiful worn on this dress," said Sophie as she reached for the locket and undid the clasp. "See?" She moved behind Anna and put it on.

"Thank you, Aunt Sophie. It is beautiful!" Anna's chin went down on her chest. She raised the locket on her thumb and looked at it a long time. It was hard to believe it was to be her very own!

Julia knew that jewelry meant a great deal to Sophie. What could make her happier than to give a little girl a locket! Julia stood wondering if it was pity she felt for her friend just now.

"Come, let us sit around the table and have a bite to eat. We will have dinner before you go to the studio, but now you must be hungry traveling as you have. *Vær så god!"* Sophie moved with her guest into the dining-room where plates of bread and jam, doughnuts, and frosted cookies awaited them.

After drinking a glass of milk and eating a frosted cookie, Anna wandered into the parlor, which had intrigued her immediately upon entering the house. She walked on a carpet as soft as grass only it was red and was bordered around and around with flowers. There were chairs with red pillow seats. Dared she sit in one? She leaned into a chair just to get the feel. And there was an organ like one in church.

What finally caught Anna's eye was a life-size picture of a girl in a gilded frame supported by an easel about a foot from the floor. The girl wasn't smiling—Anna thought she looked sad—but she was pretty. Her hair had been curled and she wore a ring on her finger. The picture went down to the girl's lap so Anna couldn't tell about her shoes. Her dress was like her own with tucks and lace. The girl wore a locket, too, like the one she had been given. Anna fingered for her own and brought it out on her thumb again to compare.

Anna wanted to rush to her mother and ask whether her picture would be big like this and stand on the floor. But she decided not to when she saw how busy talking the grownups were. Most pictures were high on the wall, or small in albums, but this one was just right for her to look at. She continued to stare until the girl almost became alive, and Anna thought she was beginning to smile. The lace curtain at the window moved with a tiny breeze and it almost seemed as if the girl noticed.

"Anna." It was her mother's voice. "What are you doing?"

Anna turned around, startled. She didn't know how long she had been standing there.

"I'm here, Mama." She started back to the dining-room, where the rest were still sitting.

"You were looking at that picture, weren't you?" Sophie had been clearing the table but now came to meet Anna. They both returned to the picture. "That girl is Inga, my youngest sister. She is dead now. This is her confirmation picture."

"She is very pretty," whispered Anna.

Julia, catching the conversation, moved into the parlor rocker and began nursing Henrik.

"I remember her," Julia put in. "She was very frail, wasn't she?"

"Yes, she was. She died of consumption. It was so hard on Mother." Sophie's face became sad, like the girl's.

Anna turned away from the easel. She decided she didn't want her picture in a big frame. Just a small one—one she could run and show Papa and Arne when she got home. That girl was dead. Anna moved over to her mother's chair and felt secure again, leaning against her mother's shoulder. Henrik was opening and closing his eyes as he nursed.

"Bertha, we ought to show Anna the doll," said Sophie, who loved entertaining guests and had a long list of conversation pieces.

A doll, did Anna hear a doll?

Anna followed Sophie past the staircase and through a little hallway with a door leading to Bertha's dressmaking studio. Bertha had already opened the door.

Anna looked around. There was an open sewing machine near a window and a table covered with brightly colored scraps of cloth and rumpled paper patterns. On the opposite wall was a bench. This, too, was covered, but with bolts of gingham and half-finished sewing. There was certainly no place to sit down. A doll, where? She spotted it propped on a soft pillow at the far end of the bench. It was a doll with a shiny white face, blue eyes, and pretty red lips. Its hair was shiny like the face, only very black. She was dressed in an elegant pink dress, tucks, sash, and lace—nothing lacking. Her hands were like her head, and so were her feet, which were painted to look as though she wore buttoned shoes. Anna ran quickly toward the doll and knelt down beside it. She wanted to pick it up.

"Let's just look at it, shall we?" said Bertha.

"Its head, hands, and feet are made of china, like your mother's good cups and could break very easily," explained Sophie as she picked up the doll for Anna's inspection. "See, her body is made of cloth stuffed with sawdust. Bertha made the body and attached the china head, forearms, and legs." She held the doll high up in front of her. "And best of all, she dressed her. Now take the doll, ever so carefully, and show it to your mother."

"Look, Mama!"

Sophie and Bertha stood behind Anna, smiling and waiting for Julia's response.

"Have you ever seen the like! Isn't she beautiful? Where did you get that lovely head, Bertha?" asked Julia.

"I saw it in a catalog at Lett's Store and they ordered it for me."

"I'm sure it was very expensive."

"It's fine china," Bertha nodded.

As Anna and Sophie returned to the sewing room with the doll, Anna decided that dolls in beautiful houses needed to be nicer than the one at her home.

"Do you have a dolly?"

"I can throw my dolly. Her name is Greta and her head is stuffed with quilt cotton. Mama made her. Greta has yarn hair made from an unraveled stocking."

"How nice."

"Oh, she isn't really so nice, but I love her."

When Julia returned after leaving her sleeping child on a bed upstairs, she saw Bertha busy setting the table for dinner. She spread out a heavy, linen tablecloth, their fine china and glassware, and their highly polished silverware. Julia felt embarrassed. Surely they must know that she and her two children were, after all, common folk and, furthermore, this was a weekday.

Should she offer to help? Instead she sat down in the parlor rocker again after removing Anna from it. It didn't seem right for a little girl to be amusing herself on this family's furniture.

Suddenly everyone heard the front door latch. It signaled the coming of the man of the house.

Julia saw the entry from where she was sitting, how he closed the door behind him and hung his stiff black hat on the tree. Having done that, he straightened before its mirror and patted his meager strands of hair.

"How nice of you to come, Julia. We have been looking forward to your visit ever since we got your letter." He came toward her offering his hand. He was heavier than Julia remembered him, and he wore a black mustache, too pretentious for her taste.

"Thank you, we're happy to be here," said Julia pressing his hand. "We've had such a good time visiting already."

"And you are Anna!" He bent down around Julia. His gold watch chain which reached from pocket to pocket across his dark vest dangled forward.

Anna immediately came out of hiding and went into a surprising little curtsy. "Hello, Uncle Johan."

Of course Johan was not Anna's uncle, or Sophie her aunt, but Julia had decided that such titles were more respectful and appropriate than simply letting her children use first names for adults, and the Ringstads took to it. Johan didn't pick her up this time and spin her around the way he used to do. Could it be the dress, the curtsy?

"You look very pretty today, my little sweetheart."

"It's my birthday".

"Yes, we know that," he announced as he glanced toward the dining-room where Bertha and Sophie were bringing in their platters and serving dishes. "That's what this celebration is all about."

He swung back to Julia. "Too bad Nils cannot be with us."

"You know we are in the middle of harvest," Julia said to this man in a white shirt with a bow tie. "It keeps the blacksmith busy, too."

"I shouldn't wonder. The new reaper working well?"

"Indeed, The farmers are very excited about how quickly a field gets done. But there are breakdowns sometimes and parts to be mended."

"Nils is an inventor himself," Johan picked up on what she was saying. "I hope he gets patents on ways he finds to improve breaking parts. He could be rich some day."

"Nils?" Julia smiled in disbelief.

"Why not? This is a great country, wide open to new products and new inventions."

The women signaled the parlor folks that the table was ready and Johan ushered forward his guests. *"Vær så god."*

Julia watched her daughter. Anna consented with a smile when Bertha tied a dish towel over her dress. During the meal she answered brightly when spoken to and remained quiet while adults visited. She ate everything on her plate.

"Come," signaled Johan to Anna. "It's time to cut the cake."

Anna willingly climbed into his lap. Together they cut generous pieces and soon Anna was going back and forth with plates for the guests. Julia's daughter was endearing herself. Such lavish attention for one day; it couldn't hurt, could it?

With the meal, the birthday festivities were over, but Julia and Anna had still the trip about town. Johan took Julia's box of cheese to the store on his return trip to the office.

"I believe the baby will sleep a little longer," said Julia. "It would be nice if I could leave him with you." Sophie looked helpless for a moment. "What will I do if he cries?"

"He's usually good natured when he wakes up."

"Just run along. We'll do just fine."

Richard Sloan had his photography studio in the parlor of his home. Julia and Anna entered quietly, responding to a "Walk In" sign in black and gold letters on the window of his front door. Anna knew that here her mother would talk English to the man. There was no one in the entry, so they stood side by side just waiting. Anna thought the smell was funny, not like anything she had smelled before, not like leather, not like soapmaking. And there wasn't the usual stairway. But to the right was an open door into the parlor which had a window in the ceiling. Anna bent forward without leaving her mother's side and looked in. Under the window stood a chair, a carved chair like the minister's in church. Would she have to sit there? Her feet would dangle like in Arne's shop. And there were very black curtains hanging around; Anna wondered why they were black.

"Good afternoon, Mrs. Kristian."

"Good afternoon, Mr. Sloan."

"How are you today?"

"Just fine, thank you. Mr. Sloan, this is my daughter Anna."

"Good afternoon, Anna."

"Good afternoon," Anna smiled, then glanced at her mother for approval. It went as Mama had said. English wasn't so hard; she would learn it. She would certainly know the language of the country.

Mr. Sloan began talking very quickly in English, so it seemed to Anna that her mother even looked like a stranger as she spoke to him.

"He wants you to stand beside the chair and rest your hand on the chair arm," said Julia, becoming familiar again.

Mr. Sloan guided Anna and posed her with elaborate gestures. He was indeed strange, thought Anna, and he muttered, too, in English. Soon the box was rolled out, yes, just as Arne had said—he hadn't been fooling.

"Now you must stand very still," said her mother. "Remember you have your hand on the chair arm. Don't move your feet. Hold your head up. (Mr. Sloan had his hand under her chin.) Now listen carefully, Anna. You must not move at all until we tell you we are finished. Now smile just a little."

Mr. Sloan went under the black cloth as Arne said he would. She felt a shaft of light shining down through the window in the ceiling. No, she must look only at the box—keep smiling, don't move even if your foot itches. No, don't move. When would they say it was over? Was she still smiling? She was smiling at Arne out of a picture—she was smiling at Papa. She thought for a moment that she might jerk as Henrik did sometimes in his sleep. No, she wouldn't move. She realized suddenly that she had been blinking her eyes—eyes had to blink. She wasn't sure, but she thought she was swaying. No, she wouldn't move. Her picture would be smiling as she was doing now. She hoped her shoes would be on the picture, all of her. She thought about her feet in new shoes. How big they felt right now! No, she wouldn't move.

The black cloth flew into the air as Mr. Sloan jumped out from behind the box. "Done!" he said, his arms in the air. "And you are a good girl." He rubbed his hands together with satisfaction. Anna knew what he had said; her mother didn't need to translate.

Mr. Sloan disappeared for a while and Anna kept watching for him to return with her picture. When he did return he said that the negative was fine and that he would send the picture by mail.

That would certainly be a long time. Arne hadn't told her she wouldn't get her picture right away. How did she even know that this funny man really did take her picture?

Anna trudged slowly at her mother's side on the way to Lett's General Store. They climbed the steps up to the porch where two men were sitting on a long bench. This store was like Clarence Haroldson's in Wanamingo, only much larger.

Anna hung against the counter while her mother became that stranger again. Things were piling up on the counter as the clerk kept running back and forth bringing the items Mama wanted. With each item Anna hoped it would be the last.

She tried walking around the store looking at things, but nothing seemed to take shape for her. At one point the proprietor took a peppermint stick out of a glass jar and gave it to her. She thanked him in Norwegian, but he didn't seem to mind; he simply walked away behind the counter.

The last item on Julia's list seemed to take the longest of all. She was hesitating over a bolt of white sateen cloth. It was rather expensive and she needed quite a bit. If she bought this it would be more than the amount she had gotten for the cheese, but she thought in this case Nils wouldn't mind if she did take a little cash from the roll of bills in her bag. Feeling Anna leaning against her side, she quickly made up her mind.

"I'll bring the rig around here shortly," she said as she pulled the drawstring on her bag.

"Very well," the clerk smiled. "These parcels are yours."

As all idle eyes were on Julia and Anna as they left, the clerk said to the proprietor, "That woman speaks good English for a Norwegian. One can't talk with most of them."

Chapter 4

The sun was still high in front of them as Julia and her children were on their way home to Wanamingo. Lady's good clip assured Julia that the trip would not take long. Henrik, who had slept most of the day, was leaping on his mother's lap. Beside them sat Anna, sound asleep against Julia's unsteady shoulder.

The rhythm of the wheels was finally having a soothing effect on Henrik; the squirming ceased and he contented himself watching the flocks of little grey birds rise out of the road in front of Lady.

Julia's thoughts returned to the eight yards of white sateen among her parcels. She felt uneasy. It wasn't like buying backing for a piece quilt however she looked at it. Buying lining for a coffin while its occupant was still alive seemed a bad omen. But she wanted something nice and new for Inga; Haroldson's store had nothing suitable.

Julia remembered how Inga had been failing. This morning they had not gotten her into the chair—it was too early—unless Arne had been determined enough to do so and had sought help from someone else. The look of Inga's eyes distrubed her. What was going on behind them? Julia was sure she had already taken leave of this world—no desire anymore, no visible response to anything. How long had it been since she fed herself or feebly squeezed Julia's arm with her one good hand? Julia was distressed, too, as she thought about eternity so close to Inga's door. Was she a child of God? How good it would be to know! Julia had read scripture for her many times, had prayed aloud and sung hymns. Inga had never said she was saved, although she had gladly accompanied Julia to the Ladies Aid Society and attended church services on festival days with the Kristians. For the past four years, of course, Inga had not been able to utter a word. She must be fair to Inga; God in His mercy would be the Judge. She began to pray for Inga, but her prayer was interrupted.

Lady was going down hill, and the buggy wanted to roll faster than Lady would permit. Julia caught a hold of the slack reins just as Henrik began squirming again. She let the child raise himself on his feet and supported him with her free hand as he looked over her shoulder. She hoped he wouldn't wake his sleeping sister.

Henrik was a lively child, Julia found, always anxious to see out into the wide world. He would be like the uncle he was named for, all right. Julia's youngest brother had been her constant companion during childhood; he was six and she was ten when they had crossed the great ocean between Norway and the new land. It was this brother, too, who had drawn her later from her home in Dane County, Wisconsin, to this community of Wanamingo, in Goodhue County, Minnesota. He and his wife had acquired land here after his service in the Union Army. Living near one of her own family was not to be for long; Henrik died two years later. He had never been weak or ill, but a brutal shoulder wound during the war shortened his life. To fill the aching void left by his death, Julia named this child Henrik.

When they reached the bottom of the hill, Henrik wanted to sit facing front again. As Julia turned to give way for him, she noticed the dust they had stirred still spinning in a coil up the hill. That must have been what had fascinated her little son.

Lady was climbing a long hill. Julia saw the road rising in the distance. She watched the agile motion of their city horse. It was hard for her to imagine Lady in a panic, train or no train. But there would be a train soon in Zumbrota. She remembered Sophie telling her that Johan was building a grain elevator to have ready when the railroad came through. There had been talk of a railroad for three or four years now, and money for it had been raised locally. This would be interesting news for Nils and his farmer friends; no need to go all the way to Red Wing with their loads of wheat. But Lady wouldn't appreciate the railroad, she who was now so proudly conducting them home.

Julia's thoughts went back to Sophie. Sophie was naturally happy about the prospects of Johan owning an elevator, but Julia had detected a void in the heart of her old friend. Was Sophie a woman to be pitied? Certainly not. But Julia had to conclude that her feelings were that of pity.

The road was following the river. They passed the mill where the big waterwheel ground flour for the settlement folk from their own wheat. Julia was suddenly reminded of Inga's brother Gunder, who used to work here. Did he know of his sister's condition? Families had a disturbing way of losing track of one another in this vast country. Julia's brother's wife and child had returned to her parents in Wisconsin after his death, and she hadn't seen them since.

Reaching the vicinity of Wanamingo, Julia noticed Ole Bakken's field was all in bundles. Men were still out there putting together shocks. The sun was on its way down now, and there would be a long twilight, a chance to finish loose ends and bring the working day to a halt. Long summer days were nice that way.

A rooster darted out of Lady's path. They were already in town and passing Tollefson's blacksmith shop. They rounded the corner into the Kristian yard without the slightest tug on the right rein. Lady needed no signal. Nils was on hand to assist Julia, but wasn't jovial. Looking closely at him Julia knew things were not right.

"Dr. Grønvold was here today," he began. "Arne went for him this morning when Inga wouldn't wake up."

O Lord what has happened? Julia said to herself. She remembered the eight yards of cloth.

"He borrowed Joseph Tollefson's team and buggy and brought the doctor back within an hour."

"Is Inga awake now?" Julia hadn't moved from the buggy.

"No, Julia, she is in a deep sleep, so says Dr. Grønvold. She is about gone."

Certainly this had been expected for a long time, but she was shocked nonetheless. Soberly they attended to the children, the parcels, and the horse. Neither of them spoke for a long time. Anna, who was now quite awake, wondered at the silence and the sad faces of her parents but thought it best not to ask questions. She was told to mind Henrik, who had been dropped against his will into the cradle.

Julia hurried next door. Arne was sitting by the bed as Julia arrived. He seemed relieved that she had come and rose to meet her.

"Well, I guess we won't have to lift her into the chair anymore," he said, his eyes watery enough to spill tears. "It's best for her, Julia, if she goes soon. She doesn't know anything now; she's not suffering." He seemed anxious to talk.

"*Stakkars* Inga," said Julia coming forward and making a feeble attempt at smoothing the quilt.

"We have done what we can, Julia." Arne hadn't stopped talking. "I brought the doctor here. Did Nils tell you?"

Julia nodded.

"And it is a good thing I did, even if he couldn't do anything for Inga."

Julia was puzzled.

"Because Ole Bakken almost lost his hand this afternoon in that new reaper of his. Dr. Grønvold just happened to be here when the men brought him in from the field. And do you know, since he could sew him right away he thinks the hand will be saved! He spent almost two hours in your kitchen sewing those smashed and bleeding fingers. Petra Haroldson helped him by keeping water boiling and giving him towels and whatever he asked for. That Grønvold is a marvel, I tell you!"

"Of that I am sure," Julia said, trying to absorb all Arne had told her. She returned to Inga and patted her pillow.

Arne, who had been on his feet while he told this extraordinary news, sank down again beside the bed. Julia thought he looked exhausted.

"I'll come back again soon, Arne," she said, trying not to appear to be running away.

"It's all right," he said weakly. "I'll call you if there's any change."

Julia hurried back to her own house. Grasping at her were sharp misgivings she couldn't explain. Maybe it was wrong for her to have been gone today.

She worked at the tasks at hand as if relieved to be doing something useful. Anna was put to bed after she had drunk a glass of milk while sitting on her father's lap. He listened, of course, to comments on her day. But when she didn't see the usual luster in her father's eyes, she let go of her desire to talk. Henrik fell asleep while being nursed again, he and his mother in the familiar rocking chair.

Arne appeared in the doorway as Nils was lighting the lamp. His face was grave.

"No change. You folks just go to bed. We've done all that we can."

"Good night, then, Arne. We are here if you need us."

"Good night."

Silence followed. The lamplight caused large shadows around the little kitchen. Julia was the first to speak.

"Have you thought about the coffin?"

"Yes. I have the pine boards. It's just a matter of sawing and nailing." Nils' healthy face looked pale to Julia.

"I bought cloth for the lining today. I had to pay cash for it. It was more expensive than I had figured."

"Never mind that. I'm glad you are so thoughtful."

"I'll fill the bottom with fresh grass and cover it with the sateen. The lining of the sides and lid will look like a quilt tied with yellow yarn. I'll make a pillow, too, of the sateen and edge it with a ruffle."

Nils stood nodding as she spoke. His mind, she was sure, was on measuring and sawing.

"Will there be time, I wonder, to do all this?" Julia broke into a question.

"We'd better begin tonight. I'll light the lantern, and we will go across to the shop. I'll show you what I have in mind."

They made their way across the road, Nils carrying a lantern, and Julia following in the swinging circle of light. The smell of iron was potent in the heat of the shop, and tonight there was a suffocating dampness. They walked to the far end, brushing by the huge bellows of the forge to reach the stairway to the carpenter shop. As Julia climbed, she saw a few feeble coals still glowing down in the firebed. Nils hung the lantern on a high peg at the top of the stairs. He showed Julia his boards, then began measuring. The sound of his saw ripped against the quiet of the night. Julia watched the curls of wood dropping from his plane into the shadows. She turned to leave. Now that she knew the measurements she could begin her task.

"I will give it a coat of dark varnish," he said.

"That will be nice, and perhaps a little gilt for the edges." Having answered, she made her way down the stairs.

Crossing the road, she glanced at the cobbler's house. The coffin must be completed soon—a dead body in August must not be made to wait burial. She hoped Arne wasn't seeing Nils' lantern.

They both worked until midnight. Nils didn't stop until he had brushed on the varnish; it would be dry by morning so Julia could work with the lining. Julia had the cutting and quilting done as Nils set his lantern beside the lamp on the kitchen table.

"You must be tired, my dear," said Nils as he watched her fold away her work. "It has been a long day for you."

There was no change in Inga's condition for three days. Then, on the morning of the fourth day, Arne appeared in Julia's kitchen just as Julia was finishing the ironing. Keeping the stove going to heat the irons made the room unbearably hot. Julia could tell by his large eyes that a change had occurred. He told her that Inga had stopped breathing—it was as simple as that. He had stood at the window holding the curtain aside, wondering momentarily if it might rain. When he turned and glanced toward the bed again, he discovered she wasn't breathing! Julia returned the iron to the stove, glanced toward Henrik asleep in the cradle, and rushed with her friend to his wife's bedside. It was true, Inga was gone.

The whole community knew at once that a death had occurred. Petra Haroldson arrived to help Julia bathe and dress the body, while Nils dropped his work and stayed close to Arne, helping him with all arrangements.

The next day Inga was buried. Friends gathered first at the Aslakson living quarters behind the cobbler's shop, a little room that became overcrowded. Everyone wore black formal clothes. The day was hot and humid; if it hadn't been for harvesting, the area could have used some rain. Men were wiping their foreheads with large white handkerchiefs, while women feebly attempted to fan themselves with theirs. The minister stood next to the open coffin with a Bible and read Psalm 91: Because you have made the Lord your refuge, and the Most High your habitation, no evil shall befall you, no scourge come near your tent.

Doubt pierced Julia's consciousness again. Had Inga made the Lord her refuge, and Arne? O Lord have mercy on us! How low the ceiling suddenly seemed. A prayer couldn't possibly ascend. And people were continuing to push through the low door. Inga's brother, Gunder, should have been among them, but he wasn't.

Anna stood at her mother's side, not daring to ask any questions. She knew that this was no time to distract her mother. The people around Anna were so tall and all in black. Her mother had let her wear her new dress, which was white. That was strange. Shouldn't she, too, be wearing black? She stood in her new dress with her gold locket and her new shoes, but no one noticed them now. She remembered Arne. Where was he? It was easy to see her father since he was so tall—but Arne. Still clutching her mother's skirt, she strained until she finally saw him. But was this really Arne? He wasn't wearing the rumpled, faded shirt open at the neck, or the big brown apron of his trade. Now he stood so quiet in a black tailored suit with a stiff white collar and tie. A wet comb had plastered his thin, disheveled hair to his head, making him seem smaller than ever. He was sad. Anna wanted to run to him, as if that would make him change back to the good friend she knew. But, no, she mustn't. The other men were dressed like Sunday, too. She had seen many men in clothes like these, but never Arne.

She was curious about Inga, who was lying in a chest with the lid lined like a quilt. Julia had hurriedly told her two things that day, although she had asked no questions. "Inga has gone to heaven to be with Jesus."—and a little later, "Inga is asleep and won't wake up anymore in this world." Anna had heard folks say that Inga was dead. That was somehow right—dead. But Inga didn't look much different than she had ever looked. Anna wasn't sure but that she might wake up if they tried hard enough to wake her. They weren't trying, so she guessed that she wouldn't wake up after all.

A strange smell began disturbing Anna, not the clean smell of leather she associated with Arne's shop. It must have been the heat that made it smell that way. Her forehead was wet, and her upper lip.

After the minister was through praying, people began parting to the sides of the room, and Anna saw her father and five other men lift the coffin off the table and carry it out to the waiting wagon. The horses were whipping their tails against the flies. The shrill scream of a blue jay came from a near-by tree. Inga was in the chest. Anna knew that and felt uneasy. Soon Inga would be in the ground, like the others, with a gravestone over the place they would put her. She was sure Arne didn't want to put Inga in the ground. It was as if all these people were doing this to Arne, and she didn't like it at all.

Arne had told Anna once that Inga was a beautiful lady before she got old and sick; that she walked into the woods and picked berries the way other women did and that she wore pretty bonnets and dresses. Now she wondered if Arne had been fooling. Inga wouldn't have been Inga if she hadn't sat still in that chair, never talking or laughing. That was how Anna knew her. And now she was dead and in the chest.

Anna fidgeted with her locket. Suddenly she remembered the girl in the big picture frame at Sophie's house. She was Inga, too, but another Inga, young and beautiful, who also was dead. Dead like Inga—in a chest like this Inga. And again, she didn't like it.

But, next thing she knew, she was sitting between her parents on the buggy seat. Her father held the reins and Henrik sat on his mother's lap. She felt secure now; she was so close to them both. She didn't want her father to step out of the buggy, which she was sure he would do when they got to where they were going.

Julia glanced at Anna. How sober she was, how adult! But could she possible know what all this was about? She wanted to explain to her about the Last Day when all who were asleep like Inga would wake up and if they were saved would go with Jesus into His Kingdom. But it was somehow too complicated and would perhaps lead to more questions than it would answer for a child of five. Julia was uneasy about what the child might be wondering and not daring to ask.

At the Wanamingo Lutheran Church and cemetery on a hill one mile north of town a large group of people were gathered for the funeral of Inga Aslakson. Townsmen had closed their shops, farmers had halted their reaping, and housewives had let their ironing wait. Men were tying their horses to the hitching posts while women were making the long step from the buggy to the ground, careful not to catch their long skirts. They waited as long as possible outside the church door; inside it would be hot indeed. Soon they saw the procession coming up the hill, a coil moving through a cloud of dust. This was a signal for the women and children to move in and seat themselves on the left side of the aisle. The men waited longer getting in just before the pallbearers took the coffin off the lead wagon.

Anna watched her father and the other men lift the coffin to their shoulders. They walked twenty paces to the church door and up the steep steps. Anna grew increasingly uneasy as she saw the awkward slant of the chest, with Inga inside, as the bearers proceeded up to the entry.

The interior of the church was depressing. Anna immediately pushed close to her mother as they seated themselves, as if this would prevent contact with the others around her. Why should people she knew frighten her? It seemed as if they were betraying the friendship they had once had toward her. Now the women she knew were holding hymnbooks in front of them as if this were what life was all about, and she had been fooled. When the song ended, they looked neither to left nor right but held those books reverently as if waiting quietly for the next time to sing.

A fly settled on the back of Mrs. Haugen's bonnet. She doesn't know it's there, imagined Anna. Soon it left and settled on Mrs. Hegvik's shoulder. Momentarily Anna was aware that there were many, many flies, and one could hear them buzzing everywhere in the heat. The window by her pew was full of them. Her mother didn't like flies and neither did she. Henrik was asleep. She looked at his plump cheeks. If a fly settled on him, she would chase it away. Then Anna saw her father stand up tall. He slowly went to the chest and opened it so the quilt appeared again. He then began ushering people past the coffin, each acquaintance pausing a few seconds. When it was all over they would talk about Inga, and the memory of her in her coffin would remain for years. Soon it was Anna's turn to leave the pew. Her shoes felt stiff as she moved along. She hoped it was true that Inga would stay asleep. She mustn't wake up now. Anna wanted her to be dead.

As she got closer to the front, she recoiled at the staggering heat and the unclean smell she had noticed at Arne's house earlier. Henrik lay asleep on his mother's shoulder just ahead of her, and her mother was dabbing a handkerchief to her eyes with her free hand. Why were the women crying? She felt a stone in her own throat, too, and wondered why she was going to cry. It was her turn to look. She hadn't realized Inga's nose was so big. Was it really Inga? As she turned to follow her mother, she caught sight of Arne in the front pew—the strange Arne who sat with his head bowed and his idle hands limp in his lap. The stone in her throat felt harder. She hurried to catch up with her mother, even if it was only a few steps.

Soon her father closed the chest for the last time with his hammer, tapping nails into the four corners. The quilt covered Inga. It wouldn't be so bad if they weren't going to put her in the ground. Anna felt funny in her stomach, but she wouldn't tell her mother. The flies were buzzing again at the window; someone ought to open it and brush them out.

Soon she and her mother were moving again, ever so slowly, and Henrik was still asleep. Finally she was out on the steep steps. The sunlight momentarily blinded her. Two steps more and a cool breeze blew against her face. She took a deep breath. She moved along with the people much easier now, noticing that crickets were singing in the grass and that a little gopher scampered and disappeared into his hole. The people were still very sober and quiet; they weren't finished yet. They were making a grave here, out in this bright sunny world on a late summer day. Anna watched a blue jay flying from the fence to a tree and back to the fence. Three cows with big, curious eyes were staring at the people across the fence.

When all the buggies were coming back from the church, Anna sensed it was time to be happy again. The people were smiling and talking at last. Julia and the other women had prepared a good meal in Julia's kitchen and served it outside around the Kristian's house and the cobbler's shop. They gathered after the horses had been put away and benches brought. Anna was now able to let go of her mother's skirt and frolic among her friends.

Chapter 5

"I need to take a grain sack to school today, Mama." said Anna as she was finishing her breakfast. She wasn't late, but she sounded in a hurry.

"What in the world for?" Julia was finally sitting down to eat.

"Martin has finished the tree house, and all we need is a door. I haven't furnished anything for it yet. Martin told me to bring a sack."

"Does Mr. Starr approve of such goings-on?"

"He does. He can't help us much, but he watches us. Maybe he never built a tree house when he was a boy. Please, Mama, I need a grain sack."

"Ask Papa."

"I already have. He told me to ask you."

"All right, I'll take a look in the barn."

Julia returned with a sack that had holes beyond patching.

"And Mama, Mr. Starr is coming here after school today. He told me to tell you." She kissed her mother and ran out the door.

In September of 1880, when Anna was nine years old, a new schoolmaster came to teach the village school. He had come from Massachusetts to Zumbrota with his older brother, who was beginning a law practice there. He was known by the townsfolk as a Yankee with a good command of English. Since English was so important to the future of immigrants, they considered themselves fortunate. He had a room in the Kjos Hotel across from the school and hadn't as yet been seen much in the town. The townspeople considered Julia to be the one with whom he would communicate, the one who had the talent for hospitality.

Enrollment had increased these past three years. Adult enrollment had grown since there was a steady in flux of newcomers who wanted instruction in English, but their attendance was sporadic, depending entirely on slack times in the busy world of making a living in the new land. The school, of course, was primarily for the community's children, whose number had also increased. Not only were there more children from the farms, but the village had also grown by two large families, the Mundahls and the Veblens. Melvin Mundahl was a harness maker, someone whom Arne welcomed above all. There were four lively children in the Mundahl family: two boys, Martin and Iver, and a girl Mari, who were of school age, and a boy of four. Rolf Veblen opened a second general store across from Tollefson's Blacksmith Shop. He was a tailor by trade and left the management of his store to his two oldest sons, keeping a back room equipped as a tailor's shop. The Veblens had four daughters: Agnes, Josie, Emma, and Magda, and one son, Gesli, of school age.

The school bell rang four times a day from its tower, almost as formidable as a church bell. This meant a reluctant return to lessons. The playground noises stopped, and a spell of quiet duty fell across the whole town as the echo of the bell died away.

The one-room school, set back twenty paces from the street, had three steps going up to its door. The door opened into a cloakroom where coats hung limp on pegs assigned to each child. The one classroom had six windows, all alike, three regularly spaced on the south wall and three on the north. In the front of the room was a raised platform on which stood the teacher's desk. To the left of it was a potbellied, wood-burning stove. The room was permeated with chalk dust, not only from blackboard use, but also from pupil slates. Dust particles danced in the shafts of sunlight pouring in the south windows on sunny winter days. There were several double desks in straight rows for the older pupils. These had smooth, slanted tops with grooves for holding pens and holes for inkwells. The younger children were seated on benches, each child with a slate for writing and figuring. Paper was scarce and could be used only for advanced penmanship. English prevailed in this place. Even the playground games were those with English limericks rooted in Yankee culture.

Julia spent part of the afternoon making *krumkaker* because her pastries set aside for guests were running low. Furthermore, the fire, comforting on this cool October day, was just right for the krumkake iron. She rolled each flat cake into a scroll as it came off the iron, putting it on a serving plate as she went along. When she finished she would put the surplus away in a tin box on the pantry shelf.

Mr. Starr had visited Julia twice before, the first time when he had been hired, and the second when he had wondered what to do about badly needed books and supplies. Julia was impressed with him. He knew a great deal, of that she was sure, and she liked his quiet dignity. She believed there is a fine difference to be made between authority which is wielded merely for convenience and that which is benevolent. She felt he was good to the children as well as being strict with them.

As she checked her tea kettle to be sure there would be boiling water for Mr Starr's tea, Anna flung open the door and entered with Mari Mundahl. The girls eyed the *krumkaker*, but knew better than to ask for one. They were not guests. If they were truly guests dressed up and sitting like ladies around the table that would be different.

"There are apples on the steps going down to the cellar," Julia reminded Anna. "You and Mari can each have one. And will you let Henrik play with you while I visit with Mr. Starr? Henrik is outside now, but he gets lonesome playing alone."

"Yes, of course. He can play with Lars. Mari has to mind him. Come, Mari." Mari followed Anna upstairs, where Anna would change her clothes. Julia saw to it that even the starched cotton apron which fit over the wool serge dress would stay clean as long as possible. The girls were out of the house in no time, closing the door behind them.

Soon a gentle knock was heard on the door. Tying on a clean white apron, Julia went to answer it. On the way she cleared her throat; it would be English now.

"Good afternoon, Mr. Starr. So good of you to come. How are you?"

"Good afternoon, Mrs. Kristian. I am fine, thank you. And you?"

"Oh, I am fine. Come in and sit down. I have hot water for tea. Surely you would like some."

"Thank you. I would like a cup of tea."

Julia was reaching for his hat when she noticed the book.

"Here is a novel I brought you. After our last conversation I thought you might like to borrow it. It comes from the Zumbrota Public Library. Did you know Zumbrota now has a free-lending public library?" He handed her the book so she could see the title. Julia saw *Little Women*. "Remember I told you about Louisa Mae Alcott, the young woman from Boston who is becoming quite famous as a writer?"

"Yes, yes indeed. I am delighted."

"You said most of your reading are books in Norwegian."

"Yes that is true. I do read English, though. I am certain I will enjoy this." She paged through it briefly. "Thank you so much. You are very thoughtful. Please sit down."

She laid the book down gingerly at the place she had set for herself at the table and proceeded to pour water into the teapot. Although she preferred coffee, she would drink tea today.

Mr. Starr was a tall, slender young man with a very sharp, clean-shaven chin. His hair, what there was of it, was auburn. His forehead seemed vast because the top of his head was bald. His eyes were round as grapes in their sockets, and shone as they caught the light. They were light brown eyes that changed expression readily. When the eyes grew dark, Julia imagined that no child would challenge that grave expression. As he talked, she noticed he raised his brows, causing four or five straight furrows across his forehead.

She poured the tea into his cup. "There, now, have some pastries. We call these *krumkaker*." She passed the plate to him.

"Thank you. You eat these by unrolling the scroll, I presume," he said as he decided against biting into one end.

Julia nodded and smiled, afraid that an audible response to the question might embarrass him.

"Do you know you have a very intelligent little daughter?" he continued after he had mastered the Norwegian pastry. "She always finishes her numbers first—and correctly. She memorizes very readily, too."

It was Julia's turn to be embarrassed, and she lowered her eyes. "Yes, I have suspected as much," she said modestly. "It is a gift to be thankful for."

"Indeed," he agreed, lifting his eyebrows and making the furrows. "I marvel at many of the little girls. They do better than most of the boys. That shouldn't be the case, should it?"

"I think they are simply more inclined toward school. They like nothing better than reading stories and drawing pictures." There the matter rested.

"There is considerable excitement these days at recess." He had finished the *krumkake* and reached for his teacup. "A tree house is being constructed in the tallest of the maple trees. Martin Mundahl seems to be in charge. The younger children at first paid little attention, playing at their own games. But now, when it is almost finished, everyone is excited. Anna has always had a hand in it. The boys readily take advice from her, even if she is younger and a girl at that. And, of course, when I'm not around they speak Norwegian." He smiled and shook his head. "Oh, I encourage English on the playground, too, and it goes very well if we play formal games. But they grow tired of them sometimes. Building a tree house is more fun at the moment."

"Anna asked for an old grain sack this morning. It was to be a door. She said you approved the tree house." Julia lifted the lid of the teapot to see if she needed to replenish hot water.

Since the tone of her voice was not threatening, not questioning this irregularity, he felt comfortable to continue.

"Indeed. It is a worthy enterprise and it is completely carried out by them. I'm truly amazed at it. I thought the project would have been abandoned somewhere along the way. But they were persistent." His eyes in their shallow sockets glistened. "They brought pieces of lumber from home. The pile became higher. I saw little girls carrying the dinner pails while their brothers carried boards on their shoulders. And some of them walked several miles. Martin had the hammer. Where they got the nails is a guarded secret. They have a ladder going up the trunk so that even the littlest pupil can climb into it. It's marvelous!" Julia wondered when the intensity in his face would begin to fade.

"They are children of Norwegian immigrants," laughed Julia, letting him know she enjoyed the story. "Have another *krumkake,* and let me fill your teacup." Julia held the plate in front of him sensing that this was a moment she could break in as a good hostess.

"Thank you. I like these very much."

Julia refilled the teacups and poured more hot water into the teapot. Her guest peeled the pastry scroll apart, fascinated as much by this as by tasting and eating.

"I'm curious, Mrs. Kristian," he said at length. "Where did you study English?" He glanced at the book he had brought, beside her on the table. Surely this question wouldn't embarrass her now, and he was vitally interested. This country with its influx of immigrants was a source of perplexity, so many babbling tongues across the land. And here was this unusual woman.

"I came with my parents from Norway when I was ten years old, along with my two brothers, one older and one younger than I. This was in 1845. We settled among other Norwegians in Dane County, Wisconsin. I learned English in the village school, although I have to admit it was very limited. I taught what I knew to my younger brother. This was a good way to practice it, and it helped him, too. When I was fourteen—after confirmation in our church young people are considered adults—I got a job doing housework for a well-to-do family in Madison. Before long I became the governess of their three children. How could one do this job without learning quickly how to speak the language? The children taught me—how much I learned from them! They loved to have stories read to them. This I did. Of course, the stories weren't very difficult to read, but I read them over and over out loud to myself before I went to sleep at night. They were charming stories. I hadn't heard any of them before. The children knew the stories almost word for word before they were read to them, and they would correct me when I mispronounced a word. I worked here for almost eleven years watching these children grow up. As they became older, they shared their school work with me, and I read all the stories in their readers. They were very bright children, Mr. Starr; I couldn't have had better teachers." Julia sensed that his deep interest was giving her fluency. She surprised herself.

"That is most interesting, most interesting!" He put stress on the word "most" and his eyes thanked her.

"A little more tea?"

"Thank you." He took two or three sips while Julia wondered what more he might ask. He looked thoughtful.

"And what will happen to your own language—I am supposing you think of Norwegian as your own—in a new land, far from the shores of Norway? I'm thinking of the importance of one's mother tongue, isn't it difficult to..." The vertical line between his eyebrows deepened and he searched for a way to make clear what he was asking.

Julia laughed to let him know she understood perfectly. "Our Norwegian is becoming infested with English. Why, every time Nils comes home from Red Wing or Zumbrota he has slipped another English word into his Norwegian. Newcomers find this very distressing, but we find it rather amusing."

Her listener wasn't amused, and she felt chagrined. She would try again.

"I am meaning, of course, the language of the common people—the way we talk. We seem to be developing our own dialect here in this country, we Norwegians." She heard in her mind the various dialect of Norse country folk, but wasn't sure she could make him understand that.

"Vernacular, I believe, is what you mean. Vernacular language?" he smiled comprehendingly.

"Yes, vernacular, indeed, that's it." But that wasn't all there was to it. Fine Norwegian was important to her; she must give him the right impression. "We Norwegians hear our language at its best when our ministers preach to us on Sunday mornings. And the language of hymns and scripture is alive in us. We have begun a Norwegian parochial school, taught by a seminary student, here during the summer to teach our children to read Norwegian and to memorize the catechism. These things do not change. We have brought with us our church. The first colonists did that, too, did they not?"

"That is true, Mrs. Kristian," he nodded.

The conversation seemed to have culminated. Mr. Starr took out his watch from his vest pocket, snapped it open, and sought the time.

"I'm afraid I must go now," he said returning the watch. "I have thoroughly enjoyed my visit. Thanks for the tea and the kru—, pastry that was so delicious."

"You are welcome," said Julia smiling as she rose to bring him his hat. "Do come again. I will begin reading the book this very night, and we can talk about it next time you come."

"Thank you, I will be happy to come again." He lifted the latch and let himself out.

Chapter 6

Julia had finished whitewashing the walls and ceilings of her two upstairs rooms, and the pungent fumes of lime pervaded the place. There was a reason for all this. If one could name the dire enemy mortally feared by fastidious women like Julia, it was bedbugs. They must not be permitted to live in the walls.

She was now on her hands and knees scrubbing the floor. The floor boards must not be stained with lime droppings, but must have their own natural whiteness. She had a bar of lye soap and a foot-long, stiff brush in her bucket. The floor was getting clean. She glanced with approval at the first square she had tackled, which was quite dry now. Squares were being added as she worked her way toward the stairway, each in a different stage of dryness. The pleasure would come when she could bring in the mattresses filled with fresh straw. She had carefully gathered it from Ole Bakken's wheat field last harvest and stored it until now in the barn, together with the sheaf of grain reserved for the birds on Christmas Eve. The curtains were washed and starched, ready to be hung up. Then, of course, the long scatter rugs. How white they would be after their boiling in lye soap! She had her big copper kettle that rested on three stones over an open fire for this job.

Julia used the outdoor kettle for many things all summer long, even now into late autumn. Its most frequent use, of course, was heating water and boiling clothes on washdays, but it had other uses. She boiled plums in season, straining them through a cloth, the first step in making preserve. She could do the same with apples too. And grapes. Her vines had yielded such abundance this year that she had used the copper kettle for the initial preparation of jelly. She had invited all her neighbor women to take home juice, filling their containers with the rich purple liquid from the kettle. Now, surely, there was grape jelly in every pantry in town. Julia was proud to own the big copper kettle. Next week the kettle would do its last job of the season, heating large quantities of water for butchering. It would be the first week in December, and soon the snow would fly. She didn't appreciate the day when all tasks must be done indoors. Heating water was not the same when done in the kitchen, and washday then was not her favorite day of the week.

She moved to another square, pausing a moment to fasten a pin in her hair. She felt her pug unraveling as a result of her vigorous activity. She slid from square to square without rising, since she hated to have her tucked-up skirt coming down into the soapy water.

But what was nice about all this, be it thorough housecleaning, butchering or baking, was that it all climaxed in Christmas. Whether she scrubbed, ironed, or stirred her batter, anticipation of the Holy Season gave inspiration.

Floors like these really improved with scrubbing, she decided as she wrung out her rag for the last time. Next she would tackle the stairway with the same vigor.

"We've come for coffee, Julia." It was the loud voice of her blacksmith husband. Who would he have with him this time?

"I'll come. I have the stairs left to scrub, but it can wait."

His wife's voice came a bit louder than Nils had expected, but he understood as he caught sight of her uncovered legs near the top of the stairs. The men faced the window and took off their coats. Julia untacked her skirt, letting it fall to her ankles. She left her bucket on the top of the stairs and hurried down to wait on her husband. Out came the cups and saucers and molasses cookies. She glanced around quickly to see who had arrived with Nils. It was Ole Bakken.

"When did you say you would butcher?" Ole began as he reached for the cookies. He took two.

"Monday. The weather should stay reasonably cold this late in the year." Nils always used lots of cream in his coffee.

"I suppose Julia will be making that good *pølsa* again. Clara's was good, too, after getting help from you." He looked around for Julia, hoping to ingratiate his hostess. She had momentarily disappeared.

"Clara can do so many things well," said Julia upon returning. She poured a cup of coffee for herself and sat down at the table. She had already brushed some order into her hair and had tied a clean apron over her tattered skirt.

During a moment of silence she noticed Ole's hand, the one with red scars, holding the coffee cup. It was nimble and useful. She remembered Arne's account of the accident which took place four years ago.

"Don't stare, Julia," laughed Ole. "You know I'm certainly lucky to have this hand." He put the cup down and held his hand up on display. "If it hadn't been for that clever Norwegian doctor, I would have a stump like all the rest who have had such accidents. Machinery is a good thing, but it had mutilated many of us, too. It was right here in this kitchen that he saved it, and you missed out on all the excitement." Ole had a conversation piece to last him the rest of his life.

Nils seemed in a mood to let him keep talking, and Julia simply nodded and smiled.

"You know," he went on, "It is important that doctor and patient talk the same language. Those Yankee doctors think we're stupid. I wouldn't want to go to any of them. I knew a man not long ago, Karl Swenson, who was treated by one of those in Rochester. Well, he'd been sick for many days. He couldn't piss. It was pretty hard for him to tell the doctor what was wrong, and I shouldn't wonder but what he was embarrassed, too, with a Yankee doctor. One had to give those doctors credit, though. He was able to empty the man's bladder with a hollow needle. Imagine that! It was awful stuff that came out, a mixture of blood and pus. Of course, this helped relieve the pain, but the infection had gone too far, and the man died." Ole cleared his throat hoping to hold the attention of his listeners for a moment longer. He had a point to make. "Now, if he had had a Norwegian doctor like Grønvold, he might have gone to him a lot sooner. I don't know." Suddenly he felt his point wasn't worth pursuing further. "I guess we never know."

"We are fortunate to have Grønvold only five miles away. That is closer than Zumbrota," put in Nils.

"We can really understand why you appreciate Grønvold so much," said Julia at length.

"The hand is pretty red, but a man like me wears gloves most of the time." He winked at Julia, thinking the women would naturally be revolted at the sight of such scars.

"Your hand is useful." There was reprimand in Julia's voice. "There is no shame, nothing to hide. We must only be grateful."

There were snowflakes in the air Monday morning. In the Kristian's backyard a brisk fire burned under the copper kettle. The logs were glowing cylinders shooting flames as the wind swept between the firm stones. Plenty of wood had been piled for the job, and a barrel of water was ready for the refill as hot water was required. Clouds of steam rose from the kettle into the frosty air.

Another barrel under a frame and pulley was ready for dunking the carcass of the hefty hog that had been routing all summer and fall. But not until he had been properly slaughtered, and the blood drained into the large bread pan set aside for blood sausage would he thus lose his hair. Skill was required to judge just how many hog-sloshings in the scalding water were necessary to make for easy scraping. Nils left this decision to Arne.

Supplying sharp knives was Nils' role, leaving the cutting to his adept wife. It was too cold to do the cutting outdoors, so the carcass, split in half like a pea pod rid of its insides, was brought inside and laid on the kitchen table. The cuts intended to be eaten fresh were carried back outside to be frozen and stored in a sturdy wooden box with a prayer that the cold weather would hold. The side pork slabs were salted down in large store jars. The head was thrown into the copper kettle to be boiled free of its flesh, meat that would make up a cold loaf known as *sylte,* or head cheese. Lard would be rendered in the oven from skin and other scraps. The intestines were washed and made ready for sausage casings. The feet were sliced lengthwise and put to boil in salted water on the kitchen stove as the first step toward pickled pig's feet.

It was afternoon before Julia got back to the blood, and it was imperative to give it immediate attention. *Blod pølsa* was a delicacy toward which no one could be neutral. Either it was the prize of the slaughter, or it was repulsive because of its base ingredient, blood. Julia always made it, not only because she wouldn't waste a thing, but also because Arne felt so well rewarded when he was given a sausage or two to take back to his own kitchen.

She filled an oblong copper boiler—the one used for heating water and washing clothes during the winter months—about half full of water and put it on the stove. She then made a thin batter of the blood by mixing flour with it and adding seasoning: salt, allspice and ginger. The batter was then poured into cloth bags about twelve inches long and four inches wide and fastened securely at the top with needle and thread, leaving ample room for the sausage to expand. The bags were dropped into the boiling water and left to cook for two hours. One of these sausages would be kept hot and served for supper; the others would be put in a cool place and later brought out to be sliced and fried in butter, preferably for breakfast.

"I see there is coffee on the stove. Why don't you stop and drink a cup with me," said Nils as he returned from his last errand outside.

"I have just one bag left to fill. I'm so glad to get through with the *blod pølsa.* Tomorrow I'll grind the sausage and fill the casings and also make the *sylte.*" With the remaining red and sticky string, Julia stitched the last bag closed and dropped it into the boiler with the others. She hurried to the kitchen pump to wash the blood off her hands. "Where's Arne? Maybe he'd like some coffee?"

"He'll be along. I left him watching the hog head in the kettle. It's almost done, I think. It can be left in the kettle as it is and brought inside later, can't it?" Nils went to the door to call his friend.

"Yes," Julia said. "I'll get the cups out as soon as I have wiped off the table."

Arne smelled the rendering pork skin the minute he stepped into the kitchen. He pulled open the oven door thinking he might find a piece of skin crisp enough to eat. "Not yet?"

"I'm afraid you'll have to wait. It takes a while." said Julia. "Just see, Anna will ask the same question when she gets home and sniffs her nose around here."

"So, I'm not the only one," laughed Arne.

It was December 23, the eve of which was known as *Lille Julaften* among Norwegian immigrants. Julia was finishing some last-minute baking. As a rule she would have all her pastries made by this time, but she thought the box or Christmas baking intended for the *prestegaard* (parsonage) was a bit skimpy. She was making the queen of Norwegian pastries, *berlinerkranser,* the little cookie shaped like a wreath and decorated with sparkling crystals of sugar.

Henrik was leaning hard against the kitchen table, his knees on a chair, watching his mother. She was creaming the sugar and butter together in a bowl. He wondered why this took so long. He was waiting for the time she would crack the two hardboiled eggs. He wanted to take the shell off, but she wouldn't let him try—his hands wouldn't be clean enough. But he would be given the white part of the egg; she always gave him the white part after she had let the firm yellow ball drop into her batter for further creaming. With a little salt, how good it would be!

"Here you are," she said.

Henrik reached for the salt shaker. He knew he wouldn't be allowed pepper, so he didn't ask. Highly spiced foods weren't good for children.

"May I go with Papa to the woods today?"

"Have you talked to him about it? Maybe it will be too far for you. You might not be able to keep up with him."

He had turned five in November and was beginning to lose those baby cheeks, and his arms and legs had become longer.

"It's not far, Mama. Do you remember where the little Christmas tree is? Papa says we will cut it this year. He said I should ask you if I could go along. May I, Mama?" He shifted restlessly.

"The little tree?" They had discovered the little fir tree while cutting firewood several years ago.

"May I go with him, Mama?"

"If he wants to take you, that's fine," she said finally.

The frown on the freckled face turned to a grin, and the oven door opened to receive a pan of *kranser*.

Nils came through the door. He had snow on his boots.

"Mama says I can go with you," blurted the small boy as he ran to his father's side.

Papa didn't answer. He wasn't smiling.

Nils took off his mitten and reached in his jacket pocket. He drew out a letter and held it toward Julia. "From Norway. I heard from Ditmar today."

"Your mother, is she worse?" Julia read her husband's face. His mother hadn't been well.

"She is gone, Julia. She died on the twenty-ninth of September."

"Your mother, oh, Nils." She went to him leaving her baking utensils. She took the letter.

"Now I'll never see her again." He removed his heavy jacket and hung it on the back of a kitchen chair. He sat. "I suppose I have known all along I wouldn't, but now... now it is so final."

Henrik wandered around to the other side of the table and looked across at his father. Was Papa going to cry? The man had dropped his head into his hands. His mother sat down beside Papa. She had finished reading the letter.

"That's the way it is with us emigrants," said Julia. "Of course we had to leave dear ones behind."

"I said my goodbye to her years ago," said Nils, raising his head and looking at his wife. "I left home... left home... and my poor mother stood there so sad! 'God go with you,' she said."

Everything had changed! A wave of uneasiness engulfed the small boy as he listened. There was something very wrong about Papa. He shouldn't have left his own mother because now she was dead, and he would never see her again. Henrik went and stood beside his mother's chair. He dropped his head against her shoulder. Her arm encircled him even if she was still talking to Papa.

"We must write a letter right away," Nils said finally. "And you must help me, Julia."

Nils rose slowly. "Henrik, get your coat. We will go."

Henrik pushed closer to his mother. He didn't reply.

"You thought he might not keep up with you, is that why you sent him to ask me whether he could go?"

"No, no," replied Nils. He put on his coat and reached for his mittens.

The mother's arm still encircled the boy.

"He's got strong legs now," she continued. "Take him along."

Henrik wanted to stay with his mother.

"Haven't you good strong legs?" She was withdrawing her arm, but she still looked at him. She was smiling.

He nodded and went for his coat, cap, and overshoes.

Every Christmas Eve, Arne would go to the cemetery on the hill and put an evergreen branch and a candle on the grave of his wife. Julia had seen him at Haroldson's store this morning buying a candle, and knew also that Nils had given him a bottom branch from the tree he and Henrik had brought from the woods yesterday. This was not a custom she had ever heard of, either here or in the old country, and she often wondered where Arne got this beautiful idea. She supposed it was a kind of family observance. Inga had been his only family here. He thus tenderly remembered her on this night when all the families the world over are close to one another. What if there were a custom somewhere? What if there were cemeteries ablaze with hundreds of tiny lights that would burn until they finally collapsed in the snow? Julia saw in her fascination this beautiful sight like a sky full of stars on the holiest night of the year. She admired Arne for placing his one star. It gave her satisfaction to think that Arne would be with them around their family table this evening. She stirred the cream she had just poured into a kettle on the stove. It must come to a boil, but must not scorch. She was beginning the *fløtegrøt* (cream porridge), the first course of the festive meal.

"Mama, may I go with Arne to the cemetery?" Anna appeared at the door quite out of breath.

"Close the door, my dear," said Julia feeling the chilly gust fill the room. Last she knew, Anna was out sliding with the Mundahl children. The clock said ten after four.

"Did he invite you to go with him? He has always gone by himself on Christmas Eve. Are you sure he wants you to go with him?"

"He does, Mama. He does! He wants me to see how beautiful it is when the stars come out on Christmas Eve."

"He said that?"

"Yes," said Anna with intensity. She wasn't taking off her wraps, not even her mittens.

"All right. And you bring him back here with you. He'll be with us tonight, you know."

"I know. I will, Mama." Another cold gust came as the door opened and closed.

The sun was a blaze of fire in the southwest as the two friends headed north on the snow-covered road, well trampled by horses' hoofs and sleigh tracks. The trees were stark silhouettes from their trunks and heavy branches to their far-flung twigs. The stillness was broken only by the rhythm of boots crunching in the snow. The sun was rapidly becoming redder, and the clouds just above the horizon on every side were absorbing the same hue as if to sustain the warmth for a further moment before the icy night crept forth.

The two spoke very little as they walked along. Anna sensed that Arne had his own special thoughts, and she would not disturb them. She thought about the stars. When would they come? The sun would have to set first. You could look straight at the sun now; it was a ball the color of a rose. Anna ran ahead a few paces, then stared into the sunset while Arne caught up. How warm the sky looked, but how nippy the frosty air was!

"The sun is really red tonight isn't it, Anna," said Arne keeping his usual pace and reaching her before she expected him.

"Oh yes. It must be because it's Christmas Eve. You said the stars would come." Anna was enchanted.

"On our way back you'll see. Look, the sun is slipping away. It goes down so fast this time of year."

Anna thought that the snow had even been a little pink before the sun set, but now it was becoming white again, even a light, light blue. She ran ahead of Arne, up to the middle of the bridge that crossed the Zumbro River. She wanted time to check the stream. How black the water was, but it flowed over the old familiar stones. There were little animal tracks on the snow here and there near the water. A fallen log was as black as the water, and last summer's weeds were crisp stalks, many of them bent and crippled.

Soon they were walking up the hill together. How big the church looked, and how tall the steeple, stark like the trees against the faint lavender sky! Anna thought she knew what holy meant. This was a holy night.

As they reached the grave, Arne stood a long moment before he bent down to lay the evergreen. Anna shared the moment with him, knowing that what he was about to do he would do very slowly. He made the candle stand in the snow beside the evergreen branch. There were no swirls of snow adrift, no wind at all. The candle would stand a chance of staying lit for quite a while. Arne scratched a match and lay it against the slender wick. Slowly it took light, a bubble at first, then a flame straight upward. Arne rose. He and his little friend fixed their eyes on the fragile candlelight as it shone against the approaching darkness.

After a long moment, Arne turned. The time had come to go back. After ten paces they looked back. The candle was still burning. Ten paces more and it was a star on the ground, gleaming out of the ice. They turned again at the bridge. They were leaving the tiny star behind. How far away it seemed, and how much deeper the darkness had become!

Just as they crossed the bridge, a little animal scampered up from the river, crossed their path, and disappeared into the darkness of the woods.

"What was that?" blurted Anna. She hadn't meant to break the silence.

"A little jack rabbit, maybe; he hopped like one." Arne pointed out the track, small black dots evenly spaced across the blue snow. He stared in the direction the little creature had taken. "Did you notice? Was he wearing a red cap?"

"I don't know," whispered Anna. The enchantment she had felt all along kept her from even suspecting that Arne might be fooling her.

"My goodness, I almost thought I heard the little tinkle of his bell!"

"What? Who do you think it was?"

"*Julenissen.* You know the kind of elf who comes down the mountain in Norway with gifts for children."

"Really? Do you think so?" Anna wanted it to be so, very badly.

"Here in Minnesota? No. I don't thing there are any *nisser* here in America. They live only in the mountains of Norway." His voice was sad. The crunching rhythm began again.

"Tell me about *nisser*?"

"Hasn't your mother told you about *nisser*?"

"No," Anna answered impatiently.

"They are little elves with long beards that come around the home places in Norway. Many times they are looking for a handout. Some of them are kind and fun, and some are mean and full of tricks. People put a bowl of milk or *grøt* out if they suspect one to be around. They often stay for weeks at a time in the barn with the animals. If a peasant finds his tools scattered or broken, he knows a mean one is around. He would then make mighty sure never to miss putting food out, lest he do worse tricks. But most of the time they are helpers. If anything got lost around the place, a good *nisse* would see to it that in the morning the lost article would be lying right in front of your nose."

"Do they come into the house, too?"

"Not as often, because they are very shy creatures. Funny thing though, they have a preference for cats. They often share the same bowl, that is, if the cat feels like being friendly. If they come into the house, it would be to an attic or storeroom where they could easily hide. They sleep a lot."

"You don't think there are any *nisser* in Minnesota? You thought you saw one, didn't you?" Anna was insisting them into existence.

"Well, I don't know how they'd have gotten here," he said slowly. "Unless..."

"Unless what?"

"They have come as stowaways in those big trunks the newcomers bring with them. *Nisser* often climb into chests, if they are ever left open you know."

"You might have seen one just now, then?" Anna tried hard to picture a red cap with a bell on what really looked like a jack rabbit.

"It perhaps was a little animal who lives in the woods, but it is Christmas, and one never knows about these things." His eyes were surely twinkling, Anna surmised, as she looked at the dark form of her friend beside her on the road.

"The stars! Look, Anna, the stars are coming out. Over there, and over there!" Arne was making another of his abrupt stops and was pointing rapidly in all directions.

Anna began walking in circles with her face to the sky. It was true. The more intensely she looked, the more of them she saw. They were special stars, these, because it was Christmas Eve. Since she and Arne had left the bridge, the sky and the ground seemed the same color. Now the sky was a much deeper blue, like a velvet dress.

"Look how big that one is!" she cried, pointing east. She thought she saw Bethlehem beneath it, but Arne would think she was fooling, so she simply repeated, "Look Arne!"

I'm so glad you took this walk with me!"

They were almost back among the houses now, and crystal-clear lamps shone through the windows.

"I hear the church bell." Anna stopped. "Shhsh, listen."

They both turned in the direction they had come and held their breath. Unmistakably it was ringing, reaching the two in waves that came toward them, struck them, and passed beyond them, as ocean waves might.

Behind them were the villagers coming out of their houses, filling the street, being struck by the wave that had just passed beyond Arne and Anna. Christmas Eve was here! The holy season was arriving across the snow and under the stars.

Other church bells than the one on the hill? Yes! Between the loud tones were church bells from farther away.

"Lands!"

"Minneola!"

"Aspelund!"

The people were calling out names of neighboring churches, as they were sure a new bell had joined the others. A few seconds of silence held sway after the bells had stopped ringing, then a burst of cheer arose and people called, *"Glade Jul!"* to each other as they re-entered their homes.

"Come Arne. Mama said I was to bring you home with me." She put her mittened hand in his and drew him onto the path leading to her house. Through the window they saw that Henrik was wearing the new sweater Mama had made for him.

Chapter 7

Like most Minnesota winters, January 1881 was frigid with big drifts of snow everywhere. A goodly supply of wood had been piled outside each dwelling in Wanamingo, and no one was in immediate danger from the cold. Paths were quickly shoveled where people needed to walk, and houses were banked to the windows with snow to keep out drafts. However, days were getting longer. People comforted each other with this thought as they must have done in the old country where darkness could consume twenty or more hours a day.

The Kristian house was kept warm by the cook stove in the one main room which served as kitchen, dining room, and living room. There was a second downstairs room opposite the front door, which at this time served as a storeroom, a place where Julia could stow away her *rokk,* her loom, her churn, her washtub, or whatever equipment couldn't be standing out in the open. It was also an overflow pantry. The door was usually closed so little heat would be lost to it. The stove was near the wall between these two rooms, and its stovepipe went through the first-floor ceiling and up through the second floor into the brick chimney. Besides the heat the stovepipe would yield, considerable warmth rose through the open stairway.

The Kristians all slept in the large room above the stove. Another small bedroom upstairs served as a storeroom for trunks they had brought with them. Overnight guests were not a rarity, however, and the little room saw frequent use.

This particular winter Hans Mentvedt, a steady boarder, occupied the room. He was one of a growing number of unattached men who did itinerant farm labor during spring, summer and fall, but needed a place to stay during the winter. Julia agreed to take him in, in exchange for doing chores such as caring for the animals, splitting wood and keeping the house supplied with firewood and water. Nils had also outfitted him with winter clothing at considerable expense.

Hans was a big man. Anna marveled at his huge sheepskin coat as it hung on its peg, and at the deep caverns of his boots, which were left beside the stove when he went to his room. He was a tolerable worker but didn't particularly like chickens; at least this is what Julia concluded. She took care of them herself, bringing boiled potato peelings and hot water to their separate quarters in the barn. The chickens did not lay many eggs during the winter; surviving the cold was itself an accomplishment. Julia had lost only two of her flock of nearly twenty. And, of course, she milked the two cows. No man, not even Hans, could be expected to do that.

Hans never said much. He slept in a chair when he came in from the cold, unless it happened that Nils brought men in for coffee. Then he was capable of boisterous laughter at whatever stories ensued. Nils and Arne discovered they could tease him; he loved to be the center of attention and didn't mind having a little fun poked at him.

Julia did manage to get him to change clothes when she asked if she might wash his dirty ones. For this she considered herself fortunate, because he had a reputation for being filthy, and she knew he slept in his clothes. But she couldn't curb his appetite. While Julia was concerned about the boarder eating her poor, Nils was joking about the many pancakes he could eat at a sitting and calling him *Mat Hans.*

Hans was tolerant of Henrik, who spent a lot of time in the barn with the animals. Henrik watched his friend clean the barn and carry hay. Soon he wanted to help. They filled the woodbox together and shoveled snow. Hans encouraged the small boy to be proud of his muscles and to attempt new feats of climbing and jumping. Another point in his favor, according to Julia, was that he did not leave when she brought out the Bible for family devotion, but sat attentive and seemed absorbed.

This was a year for skiing. Nils had made a pair of maple skis for Anna. She was big enough now for a pair of her own. Henrik and little Lars Mundahl were learning on barrel staves. Their turn for real skis would come when they were taller, maybe at age eight or nine. The younger children would wade through snow until they reached a gentle slope towards the river, not too far from the town. Here they would ski or slide on sleds made in their fathers' shops. There was, however, another more challenging slope where the older children and adults went. It was a descent towards the river from the opposite direction and was known as Sande Hill.

"Let me go with you," Anna called to Martin and Iver Mundahl as she saw them heading off toward Sande Hill.

"That's no hill for girls. Stay with Mari. Watch Henrik and Lars."

Their reply was what she expected . Boys were like that.

"Have you seen my new skis? Papa just finished making them. I'll let you try them."

They stopped and waited while she hurried toward them. She wasn't quite used to the skis yet. They seemed so long.

"Let's see them," began Martin. "Papa said your father makes awful good skis. Think he'd make us a pair?"

"I don't know. It takes a long time to get them really smooth. And getting them to curve up at the front—that takes days and days. You have to soak them in water so they will bend. Then they must dry." Anna was pleased with her attentive audience. She knew now that she was accepted in their company.

They continued their trek toward the bridge. She was just as good as Iver, if not as good as Martin. The skis had been freshly waxed, and the glide was better than she had ever felt under her feet before. Would she dare go down that steep hill? She was in for it now. Maybe she could sit on them first, putting them side by side to form a toboggan. She wished, now, that Mari had come so she would have support against the boys.

Finally they reached the summit of the slope and the brave skiers looked at one another.

"You first, Martin," said Anna, who wanted him out of the way when her turn came.

"Watch me, then. See how I do it," he replied with self-assurance.

Anna thought his skis went mighty fast; the slope looked longer and steeper than she had expected.

"You next, Iver," Anna commanded. "You've done this before. I haven't."

Iver fell before he was a third of the way down. But he didn't hurt himself in the slightest. If she fell she would be no worse off than he.

"Bend your knees," called Iver as he saw her start, passing on the advice of his older brother.

Anna felt her cheeks stinging and her eyes watering. Never had she flown like this. She managed to stay on her feet longer than Iver; she was at least two-thirds of the way down before she fell. She picked herself up and waited for Martin, who was on his way up.

"Lean forward when you feel like falling," he advised, shifting his skis from one shoulder to the other. The walk up could be tedious if one weren't anticipating another run down better than the first.

"I didn't know I was going to fall. It happened so fast. How can I tell myself to lean?"

"You did good, Anna, really you did," said Martin, man to man.

No sooner had he spoken those beautiful words than Anna felt a little twinge of pain just below her shoulder blades. She shifted her skis to her other shoulder as she had seen Martin do. She wanted badly to stand the whole way down. If she could go two-thirds of the way, why couldn't she go the rest of the way?

"Watch me again," said Martin. "See how I lean." He was off with a flair of confidence.

"Good luck," said Iver when he saw she was about to follow Martin without waiting for him.

Oh, it was like flying! She felt the water forming in the corners of her eyes as she kept her attention on the skis. She was a *Valkyrie,* that's what she was! Arne had told about how those maids rode on horses and flashed light through the sky. Her feet were even now in stirrups, and light flashed from the brilliant snow as she flew.

Finally she was slowing down. Her skis were taking her farther than Martin's had taken him. These beautiful skis! She stopped just at the edge of the river bank. She looked back up the hill. Two long ribbons lay on the slope, ones she had made. She couldn't believe it! She saw Martin now, almost at the top. He would certainly see how far her skis had taken her.

She bent over to pick up her skis. There was the twinge of pain again. She managed to get the skis to her shoulder and walk a few paces, but there it was again. She shifted her skis to the other shoulder and looked up the hill. It was a terribly long way. Maybe she should get on her skis and go here along the river instead, until she reached a suitable place to cross. Yes, she knew where that would be, just a little ways from here. She didn't care what the boys would think. She had gone farther than Martin, hadn't she? She dropped the skis heading them toward home. She pushed her toes into the straps. Why was she leaving Martin and Iver like this? Was it because the hill was too steep? No, there was the twinge again, she couldn't ignore it anymore.

When she reached home, her father was standing out in the yard watching for her.

"How goes the skiing?" he called when she was close enough to hear.

"So much fun, Papa," she called, quite out of breath. "Thank you for the best pair of skis in the world!"

"Can you stand up on them?"

"Of course. I went down the big slope and stood the whole way!" The twinge hadn't gone away yet, but it would.

"I've always known you could ski." His eyes twinkled under his heavy brows. Making Anna's skis had been his project during the cold week after Christmas. He was sure that maple was a better wood than pine. He had heard of pine skis here in America, but they couldn't be much.

Anna wiped the snow off the undersurface of her skis with her mitten and stood them up against the house. Then she went in.

"Is Henrik with you?" Julia was rolling together some stockings that had finally dried.

"No. I was out on the Sande Hill today on my new skis. I can ski the big slope now, Mama, really I can."

"That is good. And Henrik will soon be along with Mari and Lars?"

"Yes."

"It is Saturday, and we must have our baths before supper. I don't want it to be too late. Hans is out doing chores. He won't be in for some time."

"Please start with Henrik, not me. I'll go and call him." She was out the door.

Julia brought in the washtub and set it somewhat out of sight on the side of the stove opposite the stairway. She lay out a washcloth and towel. She glanced out the window wondering how long it would take for Anna to find Henrik. She went for her book; she would read until they got back.

When Henrik suspected why his mother wanted him right away, he was very reluctant to leave the snowy world and go in with his sister. His mother would dig in his ears and splash soap in his eyes. Besides, it meant he couldn't go back outside, lest he catch pneumonia. But there was no way of successfully resisting. That he knew.

When the two children entered, their mother was ready for them. She put down her book while the children's coats went up on their proper pegs.

Anna climbed into the washtub when her mother lifted Henrik out and began rubbing him vigorously with the towel. Satisfied that the small boy would continue the rubbing, she poured more hot water into the tub from the kettle on the stove. Anna stood hunched on one side and watched.

"That's enough. Don't make it too hot." Anna wasn't happy about a bath either, but she felt a bit more adult now that she could ski the Sande Hill, and was determined not to show childish agitation.

"Here, I'll wash your back," said her mother as Henrik was almost dressed. "Stay near the stove, Henrik. Your hair is still wet."

The scrubbing began with the back of her neck and then her shoulders. Anna wished her mother wouldn't rub so hard. She gritted her teeth.

"Did you fall out there, Anna?" Julia felt a lump beside Anna's spine just below the shoulder blades. A swelling, maybe, but it felt more like bone.

"Only once, and I didn't hurt myself." Her mother had put her finger on the sore spot. She always found out sooner or later.

"There is a little bump here. Does it hurt?"

"A little when you touch it like that."

"It may go away. Hurry before you get cold. Your clothes are on the chair."

The next morning the Kristian family went to church as usual. They were not members of the congregation on the hill north of

Wanamingo, but of Aspelund, a church about four miles to the northwest.

Julia was troubled to notice that Anna was not her usual self. She wouldn't let Henrik touch her. They always bantered and shoved each other when they had a chance. She seemed to be cold and hunched herself deeply between her parents in the little cutter. Usually she preferred to sit on the edge of the seat with most of herself out in the open taking in the whole world. She squirmed with discomfort in the church pew. No, there was something wrong.

"We will go to Grønvold," Julia announced when they were seated and ready to go home from church.

"What is it, Julia?" asked Nils in surprise. She definitely hadn't discussed something with him.

"I want him to look at Anna's back. I'm not sure if it is serious, but I won't rest until he sees her. We're only a mile or so from his house, so this is a good time."

"But it's Sunday, Julia," returned Nils, who was now directing Lady onto the road.

"I don't think he keeps the Sabbath," said Julia, surprising Nils with her brusqueness. "But he's a good doctor. I'm sure he won't mind."

Nils headed west. Julia must have good cause when she got that firm-set mouth. He looked for Anna, who had sunk almost out of sight behind him. Her back, he reflected, had she hurt her back skiing? O God, forbid!

Julia got out of the cutter at the immigrant doctor's house, walked up the neatly shoveled path to the door and knocked. He was at home, sure enough, and motioned to them to come in. Nils directed Lady into a driveway where a hitching post was readily available. He lifted his children out of the cutter. He hadn't lifted Anna for a long time, and now she held him tightly for the brief moment it took. Anything wrong with Anna? Nils was not prepared for it.

Momentarily forgetting the twinge in her back, Anna was overcome with curiosity as she walked into the doctor's house. While coats were being hung on the pegs in the entryway, she edged toward an open door and found herself looking into the parlor. There on a sofa under a heavy woolen blanket lay an old man. Being in the doctor's house, he must be very, very ill. He opened his eyes. Anna wondered if he heard the talking in the hall. The eyes were taking a long time to focus. They must have been seeing things in a far-off world.

"Come in here," said Dr. Grønvold, motioning his guests into the parlor. "I want you folks to meet Paul Hjelm Hanson. Surely you have read some of the pieces he has written in our Norwegian newspapers."

"So this great man is a friend of yours," said Nils as he quickly approached the sofa.

Henrik watched the men shake hands, his father's dark brawny hand grasping the thin, white one with its bulging blue veins.

"Very pleased to meet you," said Julia when it was her turn to shake his hand. So this was the gifted journalist who had influenced her people by promoting the acquisition of homesteads in the Red River Valley rather than settlement in the rapidly-growing cities. She, too, had agreed with him. She remembered rumors about him, that he was exiled from Norway because of his radical views, and most likely he was a freethinker. This gave her pause for she sensed that he had a fatal illness and was not too far from his day of reckoning. She was momentarily distracted from Anna's complaint. Then the doctor spoke.

"Come, Mrs. Kristian. You and the child you spoke of will go upstairs to my infirmary, and we will leave Nils to visit with Paul." He gestured Julia out as quickly as he had brought her in.

Anna was ushered across the red carpet of the parlor and up the stairway which was beautiful like the one she had seen at Sophie Ringstad's. She was brought into a room full of strange-looking things. There were glass cabinets full of bottles, another full of books, and a table covered with unfamiliar silverware, or might they be tools. Then, there was a tall chair that swung around rather than rocked, and a narrow table, or was it a bed?

"Undress her, and we'll take a look," the doctor said as he began stirring around in this room of his.

"Come, Anna," said Julia. "He will take a look at your back. Don't be bashful now. He's a doctor."

Anna became limp and said nothing. The twinge was there. It had been there when she woke up this morning, was there when she sat in church and when she rode in the cutter. She let her mother undo her dress and all the buttons on her clothing.

The doctor sat in a chair with the child's back in front of him and began running his fingers up and down her spine. Julia watched him as he felt the lump. He was taking quite a while.

"Does it hurt there, right there?"

"Oh it does," cried Anna holding back on a shriek.

"Here, put this blanket around her," he said, handing Julia a white blanket. He put on his reading glasses and pulled a book out of the shelf. After what seemed a long time, he found what he was looking for and closed the book conclusively.

"She had a collapsed vertebra. This is caused by tuberculosis—not of the lungs, you understand, but of the bone."

He watched Julia turn pale. He was frightened himself. He had escaped until now treating a case like this, and for some unknown reason these cases had become more prevalent.

"What we must do is to see to it that it doesn't deteriorate further and interfere with the spinal cord. By all means, we must protect the spinal cord."

"So it isn't due to a fall or injury?"

"No. We don't know what causes tuberculosis of the bone any more than we do consumption, but it is not contagious in the way consumption is. We can pretty safely say that."

Anna huddled against her mother, trying to comprehend some of this. No, she hadn't hurt herself when she fell yesterday. It was pretty bad though, because the doctor's eyes measured her up and down, and what he said disturbed her mother.

"Julia, I have to give you credit for bringing her right away. She would have been paralyzed sooner or later. That is the truth." He kept bringing the fingers of his own two hand together. "A collapse like that could easily pinch the spinal cord, and that would be all it would take and she'd never walk again."

"I must say I am a bit frightened, Doctor. I had a strong intuition that I shouldn't put off coming to you, so we are here even if it is Sunday." Julia was trying to smile.

"We must get her off her feet. She must be kept very still. Nothing must jar that area. I'll come home with you. Nils may be able to rig up a bed for her." He was looking around the room for a stretcher. He wouldn't risk her walking down those steps. "You have the cutter, don't you? I'll take my sleigh so she can lie down while going home."

Lie down? She didn't need to lie down. It was only a little twinge. He couldn't be meaning it. Why yesterday she had flown! Nothing could be so terribly wrong—or could it? Anna felt trapped in this room. It wasn't a comfortable place, and the doctor wasn't a jovial person. She liked men who would laugh and tell stories. Why had her mother brought her here? She was full of resentment.

She was carried out the door on a stretcher, fully dressed and covered with a buffalo robe. Henrik was astonished.

"Isn't Anna coming with us, Papa?"

Nils was as perplexed as his son. He was given few details about what was discovered in that upper room, only immediate instructions.

"She is, but Dr. Grønvold is bringing her in his own sleigh. Mama will ride with Anna, so you and I will have the cutter to ourselves. Come." He lifted Henrik into the cutter and with Lady led the way back to Wanamingo. The little brother looked back to make sure the doctor's sleigh was bringing Anna.

"Did you meet with an accident?" asked Arne. He and Hans had spotted the returning cutter and had gone out to meet them.

"No, not an accident. We have a very sick girl, though." Nils was not himself. He was directing things at hand with an unnatural intensity. "You can help carry her in."

"Eighteen months to heal? You mean she will have to lie on this board for eighteen months? That's longer than a broken leg! Why that's...!" Nils was shouting. He could not control himself.

Dr. Grønvold had told Nils he wanted to see him out in the blacksmith shop. There he had laid out specifications for a bed to fit the curve of her spine. In it she would be kept absolutely rigid. If some means could be devised for raising the bed to a more vertical position, that could be done. She wouldn't slide, because her feet would be set well against the foot of the bed.

"This isn't just a broken bone, Nils." The doctor spoke almost in a whisper, as he didn't want this man to yell. "Tuberculosis is a difficult thing to eradicate. A healthy young body like that of your daughter stands a chance if all the rules I specify are carried out."

"Have you known cases like this before?"

"I have, and the patient has been saved from paralysis. We must try, Nils. I am now beginning to think about a brace so she can move some parts of her body without disturbing her back. She's growing, too. Being so rigid does have its problems. You are a clever man, Nils. Maybe we might be able to devise a brace to fit her."

After spending several hours at the Kristian house, the immigrant doctor was on his way home. His horses, that had the reputation of being the fastest in the country, sped along through fresh snow, and it was still snowing.

What a terrible thing to happen to such a beautiful child! The impact of what had transpired since noon on this January Sunday was just beginning to dawn on him. He marveled at the trust these people placed in him. It was almost frightening. He had worried for a moment that Nils would balk; he had seen such disbelief in his eyes. And might he not have ground for it? He had just finished making her a pair of skis, and she had been out on Sande Hill—pretty good for a girl. And on the next day he was told that her spine was collapsing and that she must be on a board for eighteen months. Might he not have insisted, naw, it is just a bruise, or even a broken bone that will heal in a matter of weeks? Or, wait and see? How many times he had encountered this attitude: Suffer with it awhile and the reward for endurance would be relief. His fellow Norwegians, they were that way. And how devastating it would have been in this case!

He saw the child on the rigid board. He had prescribed it and even been proud to have accomplished such a cast. But wasn't it, after all, an instrument of torture? Julia had thought so, but tried to smile. The child had submitted. Submitted! What is there with children, anyway? He had instigated this, and they had accepted. Was he worthy of such trust? He shivered in his big coat.

He was so alone. All he had were his books. No one to consult with, no one to reinforce his judgments. If only he could talk over this idea of a brace with one of his own profession—there were problems with it. Could such precise work be done by a blacksmith?

He was on the home stretch now and saw Aspelund Church, a silhousette in the snowy dusk up ahead. He remembered that the Kristians were Aspelund people. They belonged to Østen Hanson's church, Haugeans. They were unpretentious pietists like their hero Hans Nielson Hauge, Norway's renowned reformer who articulated the corruption in the State Church. The Doctor believed this country existed for such dissenters, a place for fresh institutions that would not be encumbered by corruption. That's what he and his friend, Paul, had talked about so often since he had come to him. The doctor shuddered again when he thought of his homeless, dying friend. Not all become rich here, contrary to what many like to believe.

As he passed the church yard, it occurred to him: Østen Hanson might be willing to bury his friend when the time came. Even if these Haugeans were straightlaced, they had an appreciation of freedom because they needed it for themselves. How ironic it was that there should be two Norwegian Lutheran churches within a mile of each other in this country, one Haugean and the other Norwegian Synod, a transplant of the State Church of Norway. Since Paul was among those who had rejected the State Church, Holden's Rev. Muus couldn't be expected to bury such a man. He passed both Holden Church and its parsonage. He was almost home.

As his horses pranced toward the carriage house, happy to be home, the doctor sighed, attempting to cast off his heavy spirit. But the most compelling burden, the sober face of the child Anna continued to flash across his consciousness. Although he was not a praying man, in the innermost recesses of his heart he felt that this child needed more than the skill he could bring her. Her parents would pray, there was no question about that, and their prayers would be heard. He was convinced that if anyone could move the Almighty it would be a Haugean. The snowflakes continued to fall on him as he walked toward his door.

Chapter 8

Anna woke her mother nearly every night by crying out in her sleep. Her voice was foreign and strange. It frightened Julia that Anna sounded so unfamiliar. As time went on these cries took on supernatural proportions in Julia's ears, troubling her more and more.

It was after midnight on one of these nights, a raw cold night in early March, that Julia rushed to awaken Anna. She wished she could pick up the whimpering child, but the rigid bed would not permit it, so she stroked the moist forehead and lifted the wet curls from her temples. Although the child returned to sleep quickly, as she usually did after these disturbances, Julia remained restless and chose to wrap herself in a quilt and sit for a while in a chair.

A persistent anguish had hung for weeks over Julia's spirit. It was a morbid foreboding that couldn't be shaken, try as she would. There was no where to look but into the darkness. She had experienced this before. In fact, it was like an old enemy showing its all-too-familiar face at unexpected times, but always whispering like a ghost catastrophe and death. These visitations of dread were as old as Julia herself, and sometimes she attributed them to the old Norse tales of trolls and giants from which she thought she had been vindicated by civilization, by coming to this new land, and certainly by her faith in God.

She noticed Anna's head drop to one side as she slept. Sometimes children smile in their sleep, beautifully, but she knew Anna wasn't smiling. Something hurt too much. How she wished she could take her place! There was a terrible injustice in that her own two limbs were so agile and her child's so rigid. Waves of guilt came over Julia, as though it were in her power to right this injustice and wasn't doing anything about it. What was to be done? What was there to do? She heaved a heavy sigh. There was never any answer—never. How tired she was!

Soon her head began to nod, and she caught it in a jerk. She thought it best to go back to bed, but clung for a moment longer to the comforting quilt. Her head dropped for a second time.

"Don't let any troll take away your little sister!" It was the voice of Hovda Besta calling to her far down the lane, where seven-year-

old Julia was leading little Beret. It was that familiar hoarse voice, all right, straining to make itself heard.

Julia awoke with a start. Poor old Hovda Besta. Certainly she was not coming to trouble her now. She could trouble a girl of seven with the troll legends—that was very long ago. *But—little Beret had died within a month of that day, hadn't she?* Troll revenge? That mortal fear of childhood! But the morbid foreboding she felt now was identical with the dread she had felt then, wasn't it? That same oh-so-familiar enemy! *Evil had entered this house, too!* She recognized the premonition! Her heart froze.

She got out of the chair and went to the window. Frost giants were here, too, in America, billowing larger and closer than she could ever remember them, those invincible giants that even the gods could not conquer. There were no mountains in this country where they could live in remoteness; here they clamored over one's very dwelling.

She clutched the quilt more tightly and continued to stare out the window. She caught sight of a star for one brief moment. Dear God... Dear God...

Why wouldn't her prayers reach the Throne of Heaven? They never got beyond the end of her tongue, and she gave up before she got started. Punishment, it must be punishment! She must settle down and recognize why this affliction had come. God has his reasons. He cannot just tap her on the shoulder like this and she not respond in penitence and grief over her sins. The shoulders sank in weariness. She couldn't collect her thoughts.

Nils awoke. He saw Julia standing by the window, the quilt trailing down her back to the floor.

"Julia, come. The child is asleep now, isn't she? Come to bed, Julia. You mustn't take cold."

A few days later Julia announced to Nils as he came in for morning coffee, "I'm going to the parsonage today. Petra Haroldson will be here with Anna. Mr. Starr will come after school, and she will have tea for him."

"I'll have the cutter ready for you," he said without hesitation. The strain was beginning to show on her face. He grieved for her as much as he did for his child. She had such deep religious feelings, he wasn't sure he really understood her. Was it good to be so religious, he wondered? He felt he knew only how to stand by and be kind.

"I really don't know how long I'll be gone, but I'll surely be home before dark." She climbed into the cutter and took hold of the reins. Lady was ready to go.

"Everything will be fine here. Greet the Hansons," he called after her. He headed back to his shop.

The Norwegian immigrants were for the most part Lutherans, but they were not all of the same predilection. Even in the small village of Wanamingo, people were not members of the same Lutheran church. The little church on the hill to the north belonged to a synod known as the Norwegian-Danish Conference, which grew out of the conviction that in this new country the church should not be encumbered by an elaborate hierarchy but should be in keeping with this new land of free institutions. Julia, who read with interest the issues that arose in American Lutheranism, had a high regard for this church, but it was not her own.

While in Wisconsin, she had been brought up in a Lutheran group known as the Haugeans, followers of Norway's Hans Nielson Hauge, a laypreacher who deplored the lack of spiritual warmth and inner life for the individual in the State Church. Because of his criticism of the established church, his followers met with persecution in their own country and looked to this new land as a place of freedom, even as the earlier Puritans had.

Finally there was the Norwegian Synod, the church as the immigrants had known it in their established parishes in Norway. There was a right way things were to be done, decreed ways, that would give a security to one's life if carried out. The rituals of baptism, confirmation, marriage, and burial were carried out with dignity. There were three such congregations to which people in Wanamingo belonged. Julia's high regard for the church included a deep respect for this synod, too, in that it contributed greatly to preserving for Norwegian-Americans a substantial part of their culture. She, however, found little spiritual comfort from her Norwegian Synod sisters. They never spoke of spiritual matters, as if to do so would be to deviate from the memorized doctrine, the last word regarding things spiritual. "We don't weep, we who belong to Rev. Muus," one of her friends from Holden Congregation had told her once. Religion was a matter of the heart for Julia, and she had a hard time refraining from judging these people, thinking they had not had a real spiritual experience.

The cutter was moving through soft, wet snow. The midday sun in March was potent. Spring would soon be here. There was comfort in that.

The youngest of the Hanson children was rolling snow into huge balls as Julia rode into the yard. A big snowman stood guard at the gate. No sooner had she passed this sentinel than she spotted the Reverend himself pushing the makings of another snowman ahead of him.

"So it is Julia Kristian arriving in her prim little cutter. How are you today?" He hurried toward her, clapping the snow out of his big, black mittens. Next to his small boy, he looked exceedingly tall.

"Fine, thank you," Julia responded, finding it easy to laugh a little in the presence of this warm, fun-loving man. She pushed aside the robe that covered her knees and stepped out of the cutter.

"It isn't every day one can make snowballs," Østen Hanson said as he drew Lady toward the hitching post. "Simon has been waiting so long to make snowmen. And I needed to lay aside my reading for a while to get a little fresh air. So you caught us, Julia."

"It's such a beautiful day one shouldn't stay inside," said Julia, glancing over the yard. Its snow was all rumpled with the activity of the children and their jovial father.

"Mrs. Hanson is in the kitchen churning butter, I do believe." He escorted her up the path to the house.

"I have come to see you," said Julia, coming to the point. "But, of course, I will be happy to visit a moment with Mrs. Hanson, too."

"Fine. We can go right through the dining room and into my study."

Østen Hanson had come from Norway at the age of fifteen and had lived for a time among Haugeans in Wisconsin. He took a homestead here and soon found himself preaching, since there was no minister. This was not unusual for Haugean laymen to do. When he was twenty-five he became an ordained minister. He was self-educated, spending hours every day reading from a wide range of subjects, but mainly historical and theological works. He sought out learned men, eagerly discussing with them what he had read. One such person was his neighbor, the Norwegian Synod minister of Holden Church, B.J.Muus, a graduate of the University of Oslo. Østen Hanson was an engaging person, successful as a preacher and highly respected by his peers.

He pulled up a chair for Julia near the little woodburning stove that heated his study. He threw two more pieces of wood into the fire and drew up his own chair.

"How is Anna?" he began, suspecting that what Julia had on her mind would have a direct connection with what was happening to her child.

"She is doing as well as can be expected, under the circumstances," Julia began. "She's unusually patient during her waking hours. She enjoys company—people lift her spirits. But the nights are the worst. She has nightmares that cause her to wake up screaming. This is particularily distressing, as I don't know what I can do for it. I always rush to see that she is fully awake, then she whimpers and goes right back to sleep. It's always the same, night after night. We have dark clouds hanging over us, Rev. Hanson."

Her eyes had grown darker and seemed deeper set than usual. He simply nodded slowly as he listened.

"Ever since this happened, I have had dark thoughts. Is God punishing us for something? Sometimes I feel as if I have grasped onto what that something might be, but before I can use my head to examine it, it vanishes into thin air. Then I begin searching among my past deeds and thoughts lest there be something left unconfessed. The search leads into frightening corners of doubt. Then I search through our marriage relationship. Might there be something there that is displeasing to the Lord? This leads into worse darkness, because then I begin blaming Nils and finding fault with probably the kindest man on earth. What evil way are we to turn from? I have no answer for that, only the terrible realization that something is very wrong." She paused with her eyes on the floor. The sticks of wood caught fire and crackled in the stove.

"You no doubt have prayed," he said in a voice almost inaudible.

"My prayers never go up. They are uttered and stay choked inside of me. The more I pray the more choked I become. I look at Anna and think what a miserable mother she has that cannot send up acceptable prayers in her behalf. I count on prayers of other Christians like yours, Rev. Hanson, not on mine."

There was another long pause. She lifted her eyes from the floor, searching his face for a response.

"Julia, you are a very intelligent woman. Perhaps that is why you are so quick to decide things. It seems that you have decided that this affliction is a punishment, that God is somehow displeased with you, and you don't know why. Why are you so quick to decide that this affliction is punishment for some specific sin? Of course you must have read the answer Jesus gave his disciples when they asked concerning a blind man: Who sinned, this man or his parents, that he was born blind?"

Julia nodded vaguely.

"It was not this man that sinned or his parents, said Jesus, but that the works of God be made manifest. If these are the words of Jesus, why do you decide that your affliction is due to some sin you have committed?"

"I don't know. I guess I am too frightened to believe such words might apply to me." Julia wondered why she had been so inconsistent in her thinking. What he was saying was so simple. Why hadn't she thought of that?

"Suffering is too deep for us. We cannot grasp its meaning. You have tried hard, Julia, to grasp the meaning of your present suffering. You are like Job." He reached for his Bible and turned several fragile pages. "Listen to what the Lord ended up saying to Job:

> Where were you when I laid the foundations of the earth, declare if you have understanding...have you commanded the morning since your days and caused the rising sun to know his place?

That's one for you, Julia, who are so quick to decide things. Can you command the morning?" He laughed a bit as though he were teasing her. She understood and smiled.

"Who are we to even begin to understand the Almighty. We'd better be humble and recognize our limitations." He put the book back on the desk and put the palms of his hands together. "There are things we do know, however."

Julia felt blue sky above her head. Clouds may gather again, but she wouldn't forget this moment of clearing. "I believe I know the rest," she said with a smile.

"I'm sure you do. Haven't we Haugeans been preaching the Gospel of God's mercy and love toward us even when we were yet sinners? You must not sit in those dark corners of fear, you who know so well the Gospel." He was delighted with her smile. She didn't lack understanding. "The Lord is strong in your defense, that's really all you need to know, isn't it?"

"It is, truly."

"We are all praying that Anna's back will heal. The healing power in a young body is God's own miracle. His power is everywhere and always strong in our behalf."

"I will remember that when I pray—even while I am praying the miracle is taking place." She looked on her counselor with gratitude.

"Grønvold is an outstanding doctor. We should thank God for him. I hope that those of us who benefit from his skill and devotion to his work will not judge him too harshly simply because he doesn't sit in a church pew. I tell you, Julia, only God knows what is in a man's heart."

"I have the highest regard for Dr. Grønvold," Julia hastened to say. She knew how strongly Rev. Hanson felt about judging others, and also what a tendency there was among Haugeans to do just that.

After chatting briefly with Mrs. Hanson, Julia settled in the little cutter with Lady up ahead eager to bring her home. Her heart was lighter. A shaft of hope had pierced the gloom. Clouds may billow again, but now they wouldn't be invincible. How Haugeans loved to quote this Bible verse: *All things work together for good to them that love God.* She could hear them now. And, *God's power is everywhere, strong in our behalf, Julia.*

The next morning, Henrik didn't go with Hans to the barn because he was intrigued by what his sister was drawing on her slate. How quickly she did her sketching!

Nils had designed a stand for Anna's rigid bed so that it could be drawn up into a diagonal position. Now she could watch her mother work in the kitchen, look out the window or read a book. Since she could freely move her arms, her father had also designed an adjustable writing board with clamps that would hold a book or slate.

"Thor went to visit in the land of the giants." Anna, happy to have an audience, began telling Henrik the story behind the picture she was sketching.

"Did he take his hammer with him?" asked Henrik.

"Oh yes. He wouldn't dare go there without it." Anna made her voice sound menacing, and she quickly drew a hammer on one corner of the slate. "And he had his magic belt." She hurriedly drew one on his body, as the idea had just occurred to her. "And his iron gloves." A few strokes of her chalk made the hands look as though they wore gloves.

"Were the giants bigger than Thor?" asked Henrik, who thought of Thor as a giant.

"Oh yes. Just wait and you'll find out how big they were." Her voice was commanding and her eyes wide. "Thor with two companions started out in search of giants to kill. Because he was carrying his magic hammer, he was sure he could kill any giant that came along. Pretty soon they got tired. They ate some food from their provisions and began looking for a place to sleep. Soon they saw a big building with wide-open doors like Papa's shop. Well, they went in and lay down, and soon they were asleep. But, it wasn't long before they felt an earthquake."

"What's an earthquake?"

"The ground begins to shake. The building was so shaken that they were scared for their lives. Thor got up and went outside. As he staggered about he realized he was walking around a great big giant lying on the ground."

"Where were the other two companions?"

"They were still in the building, only they had scrambled into another room. Thor was so frightened when he saw how big the giant was that he didn't throw his hammer. Then he found out what caused the earthquake: The giant began to snore again!"

"Naw!"

"Yes. And do you know where they had been sleeping? Inside the giant's glove! And the other two were still sitting and shaking inside of the thumb. Thor had to hurry and get them out." Henrik's face was very close to his sister's now.

"Did the giant wake up?"

"He did indeed. And he looked around for his glove. The giant talked friendly and seemed pleased that they had come to visit in his land. But when he fell asleep the next night, Thor decided he'd better use his hammer and kill him, because he knew that giants were enemies and this one couldn't be trusted either. He threw his hammer with such force that it made a dent as big as the hammer right in the giant's skull. Do you think he died?"

"I don't know," Henrik whispered.

"No, Sir. He woke up and said, 'An acorn fell on my head!' "

"Where did you hear such stories?" Julia, who had been busy kneading bread, came toward them with flour on her hands.

"Arne tells Mari and me stories sometimes. He has a hammer he calls *Mjolner*. We wondered why, and he told us all about Thor."

Anna wondered at her mother's apparent disapproval. "They are fun stories, Mama."

"I wonder," said Julia scornfully. "Haven't you some nicer stories in your own reading books? Henrik, why don't you put on your coat and go outside for a while. Anna shouldn't get so excited."

Henrik was disappointed. Now he wouldn't know until later how Thor escaped from the country of the giants.

"Why shouldn't I get excited, Mama?" Anna wondered about her mother's anxiety.

"You need to stay calm and rest," said Julia evasively. The haunting screams she heard at night from Anna were still on her mind. This was difficult to talk to a child about, particularily a sick child.

Thor, to Julia, was a vestige of heathenism, of the darkness that flanked the Norsemen even after the enlightenment of Christianity. Giants had been closing in on her even now, hadn't they, that dark dread that could only follow those old stories? It wasn't to be wondered at that Haugeans, at least those she knew, put a taboo on such stories.

Anna tried to rest as her mother suggested, still wondering why she shouldn't get excited. There were times she simply could not understand her mother. There couldn't be anything wrong with being happy? She suddenly realized that her mother seldom laughed these days. She guessed her poor mother was just getting tired taking care of her and that it was she who needed rest.

Anna heard her father stamp the wet snow off his boots outside the door. Her heart leaped.

"How's my pet?" he said as he hung his jacket on a peg.

"I'm fine. I was drawing on my slate until Mama told me I'd better rest."

Nils glanced at Julia. "Do your arms get tired, then?"

"Oh no. I think the writing board is wonderful. You are so clever, Papa. When will the brace be ready?"

"Now, Anna, it will be a while before we get to that," put in Julia, setting a cup and saucer on the table for Nils.

"I know that, Mama, but why can't I look forward to it? My feet aren't paralyzed. I'll be walking when I get my brace."

Julia felt a surge of remorse at having put a damper on Anna's expectations, but it was just that she couldn't bear the thought of seeing a disappointed child if things didn't turn out as expected. Dear God, may things work out, she cried in her heart as she put the molasses cookies before her husband. The Lord is strong in your behalf, Julia, she heard Rev. Hanson saying. Nils poured half a pitcher of cream in his coffee. Julia smiled.

"Anna, you keep us all going with those wonderful hopes of yours," said her mother. "Want a cookie?"

"Yes, please."

"I'm going to Zumbrota today to get another size bolt. I think I have figured out how to make your brace adjustable. That's what Dr. Grønvold is so concerned about. If it isn't adjustable it is impossible to get it fitting right. All I need now is the right size bolt."

"I wish I could go along and see Sophie and Johan," said Anna, pretending that this could indeed be possible.

"I'll stop in and see Johan at the bank. Imagine, he owns a bank! I'll greet them for you."

After the evening meal of salt pork and potatoes, followed by Bible reading and family devotion, Henrik got ready for bed. He undressed by the stove, folding his clothes neatly on a chair. He drew off his shoes and placed them beside those huge boots, those giant's boots that belonged to Hans, who had just gone up the stairs to his room. Now Henrik would find out from Anna how Thor escaped from the land of the giants, if he could only stay awake until they carried her up. It's funny how he hadn't noticed much lately that she couldn't walk.

Anna heard the anvil ringing louder than she had ever heard it before. What can Father be making that he strikes the anvil so hard? She ran as fast as her legs would carry her, only to stop abruptly at the large door. Her father looked strangely tall. And his arms striking those heavy blows on the anvil—weren't they unusually long and thick?

"What are you making, Papa?" she called from the doorway. But it wasn't her father. The huge man lifted his cap off a crop of red hair and looked at her. Sparks were flying, not from the forge, but from his eyes. Thor, she whispered to herself, it's Thor! He came toward her with a sheepish smile.

"You know who I am, don't you?" he began. "I am grateful to your Papa for the use of his shop. I don't like to intrude on folks, you know, but I needed badly to mend the buckle on my belt."

"Your belt, your magic belt?" Anna's curiosity brought her closer. He has good manners, she decided.

"Yes, I had to get out of my sky chariot and get my belt fixed. If I didn't have my belt securely buckled, I wouldn't have more strength than you have." He laughed as he turned again to the forge.

Anna saw the belt lying on the floor behind him, stripped of its buckle. It was wide and colorful and had the most beautiful embroidery she had ever seen. "Who embroidered your belt?" she asked, wondering why she had this easy relationship with someone as awesome as Thor.

"Freya. Do you know Freya? I saved her once from becoming the wife of a giant."

"Yes, I know."

"Your Papa must be a good blacksmith," he said as he gave two heavy blows to the anvil. "His anvil is of unusual steel. Otherwise it would not hold up under my hammer."

"Your hammer?" Anna came closer, her eyes wide with curiosity.

"Yes."

"Your real hammer?"

"Yes. What do you mean, real? I have but one hammer and use it for everything. You see I have no sword. I only have my hammer."

"Yes, yes, I know. Arne was right," she muttered as she gazed in astonishment at the unusual mallet.

"Arne? Who's he?"

"My friend."

"Does he know me so well, then?"

"Oh yes, he was the one who told me about you. He knows you better than anyone else in this town."

"Really? I have heard that most Norwegians forget about me when they move to America."

"Arne remembers lots of things like *nisser, valkyrie*—many things like that. He has even named his favorite hammer *Mjolner* after yours. He's a cobbler, you know, and has lots of tools."

"Sorry I'm not able to meet your friend. I'm sure I would like him. I'll tell you what I'll do. I'll make his hammer magic so it will never fail to hit its mark. What do you think about that?"

"Wonderful!"

"And, my dear, what could I do for you?"

"I would like to go to *Valhalla*. You are there often, I presume?"

"Oh yes. In fact I will be going there now as soon as my buckle is fixed. But why do you want to go there?"

"I want to ride on one of those flying horses. Since I'm just a little girl, I don't suppose I could be a real *valkyre,* but I'd like one fast ride."

"You shall have your wish since you are a little American girl who knows the good friend of her ancestors."

"But you will bring me back here, won't you?" she said with apprehension. "Promise?"

"I promise. You will find youself standing here right beside your papa's anvil." He had finished now and was fastening the buckle. She had never seen such a big buckle. It covered his whole stomach. She'd have to remember that when she sketched him again on her slate.

As they walked out the big door of her father's shop, they were no longer in Wanamingo. Anna saw a huge castle that looked like ice shining in the sun.

"Here we are, my dear," said Thor as he set a stride she almost had to run to keep up with.

"So you want a ride. We'll go to the stable then."

They turned toward a building like Tollefson's livery barn, only ever so much larger. It was filled with stalls bedded with straw that shown like gold and smelled like goldenrods. The horses were shiny black; she'd thought they'd be white like Lady. As they were standing in the stable door, Thor gave a whistle and suddenly a groom stood before them.

"This is a little girl from America. I have brought her here because she knows us. I promised her a ride on one of those steeds." He put his hand on her head the way Johan Ringstad would do, and Anna felt secure, even in this strange place, with such a friend.

"There are some *valkyrie* leaving immediately. Here they come."

Ten maidens appeared just as she had imagined them, with armor as shiny as looking glass.

"Come," said one. Before she knew it, Anna was snatched up and was off.

"Did Thor tell you where to leave me?" she called to the maid who held her securely on the swift animal.

No answer.

"...where to leave me...where to leave me," she kept calling out as she found herself not heading into the sky, but falling, whirling round and round like a feather. "At my papa's anvil... Papa's anvil!"

"Wake up, Anna, you are dreaming." Her mother was bending over her. "You were screaming, Anna. Are you all right?"

Anna sighed deeply. It would have been all right even if you hadn't woke me up, Mama, she breathed to herself. Thor would have kept his promise.

Chapter 9

Johan and Sophie Ringstad came to visit almost immediately upon receiving Nils' invitation. They had hesitated to come earlier, after they had heard the news of Anna's illness, wondering if it would be the right time for such a visit. Anna's condition upset poor Sophie every time she allowed herself to think about it. By the time they were actually at the Kristian's door, her apprehension had reached dark proportions.

"You are shaking," whispered Johan as he helped her down from the buggy, hoping to prevent her having to step into the deepest mud. It was early April.

"How good of you to come," Nils called as he rapidly approached them from the shop. "I'll put your horses away. Just go along into the house."

"Hello, Nils," Johan and Sophie both responded.

Having relinquished his team to Nils, Johan gave his full attention to his wife and the box he was bringing. He carefully guided Sophie to the split logs that lay across the ditch. The last of the snow was melting and only a few dirty ice patches remained. In the ditch a tiny stream of water ran, but there was evidence that it had been much larger and swifter.

"Be careful, my dear," he said taking her hand as she stepped from the logs onto the stone walkway.

"I'll be all right," she said as much to herself as to him.

The door opened before they reached the step and Julia appeared. She had just combed her hair and was wearing a white apron. Sophie thought she was thinner.

"Come in, come in," she called. "We have been waiting for you. How are the roads? The snow has certainly gone fast. The ground is awfully wet." Julia had seen them through the window as they drove up. In no time at all, she made herself and her "one room" presentable.

After embracing Sophie and shaking Johan's hand, Julia drew them into the house. Anna's bed, upon the child's insistence, had been tilted up so she could see the door.

"Aunt Sophie! Uncle Johan!" Anna called to them the moment they came through the door. She reached out her arms, which seemed disproportionately long.

Sophie was stunned! Her limbs began to tremble, and for a moment she thought she was going to faint. She saw before her an Egyptian mummy in its case, tilted on display as it would appear in a museum. She had seen such a thing in books. Only here, the head was of a beautiful, pale princess, and the mummy was alive, waving its arms. She would let Johan greet the child first. He was stronger than she.

"Anna, my child!" Johan moved unhesitatingly in her direction. He leaned forward and let her kiss his cheek. He stroked her hair. "Its been a long time since I saw my girl," he went on, warmed by the light in her eyes.

"My poor little Anna!" Sophie made her move toward the child. Anna put her arms around Sophie's neck and smelled the fragrance of her beautiful red hair. She held her as long as she felt she could, but finally released her. She saw tears on Sophie's pretty face.

"I'm soon going to walk, Aunt Sophie. Papa is making me a brace," said Anna cheerily, hoping that Sophie would soon smile. No one she knew was as pretty as Sophie, no sound as nice as her laugh.

"Poor little one," Sophie began to mutter, drawing her lace-bordered handkerchief from the cuff of her sleeve. She turned aside dabbing at her eyes. Her shoulder jerked, betraying a sob. Julia went to her and led her across the floor toward the door leading to the back room.

Johan watched Anna's disappointment and felt awkward. "You must forgive Sophie. She'll come and talk to you soon. She loves you very much, Anna. She feels bad because you are sick."

I made her cry, thought Anna with a rush of bewilderment. She saw still how Sophie's pretty nose had become red, and how a tear had rolled off the end of it before she had freed her handkerchief.

"We brought you some oranges," continued Johan, groping for something to bring a change into the face of his young friend. He waited for her to turn her face in his direction, then lifted a paper bag from the box he had set on the table. "See how nice and big they are." He held one up. "Lett's Store just got a new shipment."

"We have oranges only at Christmas time." Anna was smiling again. "They are so good."

"The whole bag is yours," said Johan with a sweeping gesture of relief.

Anna looked around for Henrik. She thought he was around somewhere, shy in a corner, perhaps. That would be like him. Did Johan mean that she would get them all and Henrik none? She was suddenly realizing that being sick meant you would get smiles and presents you wouldn't get otherwise. It was kind of nice to know the whole bag was hers, but she would be kind. She wanted to give Henrik one.

"Henrik," she called. "Come."

"Well, if it isn't Henrik. If you hadn't been hiding I would have seen you," said Johan as the boy approached his sister. He felt he had to make verbal amends for not noticing Julia's other child. He smiled and wagged his head toward Henrik.

"I wasn't hiding," said Henrik quite innocently, happy at last to come out of the corner.

"You can have an orange, Henrik. Take one." Anna sounded like his mother.

"Thanks." He reached for the golden fruit handed to him by Johan, then withdrew quickly, biting away the first of the peeling.

"I want to show you how I can multiply," said Anna, deciding now to make use of Johan's undivided attention. "See my writing board and slate over there? It fits here. Would you bring it?"

"Your papa must have figured this all out," said Johan as he brought the board, curious as to how it fit together.

"Oh, yes." She clamped the slate into place and reached for the chalk. "You know how clever he is."

"I believe you are as smart as he is." Johan wasn't used to making conversation with a child, but he was doing his best. He pulled up a chair beside her.

"Mr. Starr—do you know him? He comes and teaches me every day. I know the multiplication tables real well now." She put several numbers on her slate to prove her newly acquired skill.

"Mr. Starr. I know his brother very well. Very fine people." Johan felt as though he were talking to an adult. There was a pause as the fingers made numbers while the lively mind made calculations.

"There. See if that is the right answer." She drew a line under the answer with a flourish.

"I'm sure it must be," replied Johan, not sure whether he was required to go through the calculations. Julia and Sophie saved him the trouble by returning.

"Mama, Uncle Johan gave me a whole bag of oranges," exclaimed Anna, quite ready to give up numbers for a while. Sophie was smiling.

"I should hope you thanked him."

"Thank you, Uncle Johan." Anna wouldn't risk letting anyone think she wasn't grateful. "Will you peel one for me, Mama?"

"Let me," said Sophie. She had regained her composure. The child was certainly the little girl she had known, someone she loved and could do nice things for.

Anna watched Sophie's clever fingers prying loose large caps of peeling, exposing those juicy segmemts ready to be separated into bite-sized pieces.

"Aunt Bertha sent a doll for you." Sophie plunged immediately into another pleasant thing she could do for her little friend.

Anna suddenly saw Bertha's sewing room and the china doll sitting on a pillow. "A china doll?"

"Yes, indeed." Sophie began rustling in the box that Johan had carried in. "She had been making these ever since she found out where to send for the heads. Lett's Store has had her dolls on display for a long time and sold several."

She brought out the doll from its tissue paper wrapping. Yes, it had the same shiny white face, blue eyes, and rosy red lips. The black hair was china, too, and shiny like the face. The doll was fully clothed in a red checked dress with a long gathered skirt and a wide sash at the waist. Down her back hung a matching bonnet. From her dainty wrist hung a tiny umbrella of the same material. Anna wondered if it would really open.

"Oh, Aunt Sophie, I'll take very good care of it." Anna reached out her arms and took the doll, holding it up in front of her. Then she glanced around, wondering whether Henrik was watching. Would they give him something, too? But he wasn't sick. He would have to wait until he got sick. She drew the doll to herself and returned Sophie's smile. Right now she thought her own smile was as pretty as Sophie's.

"Thank you. Tell Aunt Bertha thank you. No girl in my school has such a beautiful doll!"

Sophie beamed with satisfaction.

Anna had no sooner handed the doll to her mother for safe keeping than it was Johan's turn again. Anna noticed he had his fingers in his vest pocket, and thought at first he was taking out his watch. But, no, he was holding a little, blue, plush box like the one that held her locket.

"I was at the jewelry store the other day and found this ring." Johan opened the little box with the spring cover and held it in front of Anna. "It's a sapphire. See the stone. It's called a sapphire. Only a real gem would be good enough for my girl."

Anna felt her eyes blink. Could anything be lovelier than the doll? She looked intently at the stone as she had been told to do. She saw a deep blue chip of glass. But she knew it wasn't glass; it was something very expensive. Was it really blue? It seemed to change to purple right there in the box. She felt her eyes blink again as she looked into Johan's face. His eyes were big and gleaming like Mr. Starr's, and she knew he must love her very much. She felt a tear escape near the side of her nose, and she hurriedly wiped it away with the back of her hand.

"Here, let me put it on your finger. It should fit your finger. There, see? Just right." He slid the cool metal band onto the ring finger of her left hand. She shuddered a little. Why? Now she wore a ring like the dead girl, Inga. Anna saw behind her eyes the picture that stood on the easel in the Ringstad parlor.

The moment of anxiety was broken by her mother. "That is really too much." Her mother's voice surrounded Anna with security. "It is really very kind of you, but..."

"Oh, no, nothing could be too much. We are really very fond of Anna." It was Sophie now, rather than Johan, who met the objection.

Anna took courage once again to look at her hand. She lifted it before her and rubbed her little finger against the ring as she had seen Sophie herself do to the ring she was wearing.

"I like it very much," said Anna, tilting her head as she focused on the gem. Why shouldn't she want a ring?

Henrik, who had stood with his knees on a chair behind the rest, looking at the doll that had been put in the middle of the table, now quickly got to his feet and circled the group until he stood safely behind Anna's bed. Here he might catch sight of this new development without being noticed. He really didn't like the way Anna flaunted her fingers in the air. Now, maybe, she wouldn't want to tell him stories anymore.

After Sophie had wiped the last dish following the evening meal, the Ringstads left for home. There was just enough daylight to last most of the way. The days were really getting longer now.

Anna was being carried across a huge pasture. She felt vaguely frightened. There might be a bull among the grazing cattle. She knew that women picking plums had to be careful if they entered a pasture. But there seemed to be no cows, and all was very quiet except for the brushing sound of trouser legs, made by those who carried her.

"Soon we will get you to Jesus and He will do a miracle." It was Sophie's voice. Was she one of the carriers? Surprising!

"It is a long way," Anna found herself saying. "How far have we come?"

"All the way from Zumbrota, but we'll soon be there."

"Where is there?"

"To a building that has a stairway to the roof."

Anna remembered a picture from a book: a flat roof that could open up a door and let a bed down. And there would stand Jesus, himself, with his long beard and his beautiful white robe. Yes, and all the people would see how he could make lame people walk. It was really nice of the Ringstads to be bringing her to this house.

It was getting a little darker now, but surely they would get there soon. The wind was blowing and her mother, if she were here, would want her to be covered with the pieced quilt. The wind was louder now, tangling her hair and blowing into her ears. She felt the rhythm of the feet that were carrying her and the rise and fall of the knolls they were crossing. Soon she became agitated.

"Put me down," she found herself calling out.

"Hush, my child," said Sophie. "We must have patience—and faith if we expect Jesus to help us."

That was true, Anna remembered. Jesus had said, "Your faith has made you whole."

Soon her bed tilted severely, and she knew they were going up the ladder. She wanted to shout, "Don't drop me," but she would have faith.

Finally all the feet came to a halt and her bed was resting on the roof. Hinges squeaked like her cellar door. She wondered about ropes. Did they have ropes as in the picture? They needed ropes, she was sure of that. No ropes? They would drop her without ropes!

Suddenly she felt herself mercilessly dropped and her rapid descent began. She had her eyes wide open staring up through the hole. It was a well! They had dropped her into a well! She remembered the boards, she had been warned never to go near, behind the old vacant house. Under them was a dangerous well. Now she saw Sophie, way up there where the boards were, looking after her. Sophie's face was full of terror, and her red hair was blowing wildly in the wind.

"Poor little one," she called. The lace hankerchief finally covered her eyes, and she turned away and disappeared.

"Sophie! There were no ropes. No ropes!" She tried to call out that Jesus wasn't here, but she couldn't pronounce his name.

"Aunt Sophie! Aunt So..."

"Wake up, Anna, you are dreaming." It was her mother again surrounding her with security.

She sobbed and stayed awake longer than usual. What is real is better than dreams, she was willing to admit.

"You're quite a fine lady with that expensive jewelry," said Arne the next morning as he lingered to talk to Anna after having forenoon coffee with Nils.

"Have you seen my ring?" Anna held out her hand as a lady would to a gentleman.

Arne kissed her hand as a gentleman would to a lady. Then he examined the ring more closely. "It's like a princess would wear."

Anna smiled. The enchanted world Arne always brought to her filled her with anticipation. "How is *Mjolner* behaving these days?" Anna had often wondered whether Thor's promise to her was ever kept.

"Better than ever. Sometimes I even think my hammer is magnetized. What else can explain its action unless it would be its name."

I knew it, said Anna to herself. If she told Arne her dream, it would spoil the magic.

Arne caught the wistful glint in her eyes and knew it would be a good time for a story. He wasn't in a hurry to get back to the shop. Julia was outdoors feeding the chickens; he felt more comfortable when she wasn't around.

"Let me draw *Balder* on my slate," Anna began, pointing toward the writing board. She knew she had Arne's undivided attention. "He must have been very handsome compared with his brother Thor."

"Sure was," said Arne, attaching the board and clamping the slate.

"Tall and straight." She began sketching. "White hair." She shaded the top of his head with the side of her chalk. She finished by making lines that radiated from his face as from the sun. "There. How do you like him?"

"That's him, all right."

"Tell me more about him, please?"

"He lived in a beautiful place that shone like heaven, and nothing bad could ever enter that place. One day, strange as it may seem, he began to have bad dreams. Balder became so unhappy about these bad dreams that..."

"Arne, what are you telling her?" Julia had just entered through the back door with a pail of fresh water from the pump. Her voice was loud enough to frighten Arne, who had not seen her enter. She was removing her coat.

"A fun story, Mama," Anna put forth quickly. "Please don't stop him!"

Arne wanted no confrontation with Julia. He grabbed his jacket that hung over a chair.

"No, Arne, don't go," pleaded Anna.

"I forgot that Jens Berg said he'd stop in this morning for the shoes he wanted half-soled."

He opened the door, and much to his consternation, Julia followed at his heels. She had grabbed her shawl on the way out and was clenching it around her as much from anger, he was sure, as from chill. The cold wind tore at her hair.

"Arne, I must talk with you." She stopped him a few steps outside the door. Arne wouldn't escape this time!

"Yes, Julia?"

"I want you to stop telling Anna those awful stories. Don't you know she wakes up screaming with bad dreams every night? What could be worse than you telling her about Balder? Don't you know any better? And she tells these stories to Henrik, too, and she draws awful pictures on her slate." Words were coming out of a deep well inside of Julia. "You're not civilized, Arne. You keep bringing up those old stories. I can't understand how you, who have lived among Christian folks for so long, can coddle those tales of darkness!"

Arne's mouth dropped open as though he were going to speak, but no words came. He felt warm tears welling in his eyes, and his legs began to shake.

"No more of this, I'm warning you, Arne. You may come in with Nils for coffee, but leave Anna alone, do you understand?" Julia saw the little cobbler cringe and felt assured she had gotten her point across.

Arne glanced helplessly at the blacksmith shop across the road, then made a pretense at nodding toward Julia. He didn't straighten up again even as he entered his door.

Chapter 10

Arne crept back into his shop after his encounter with Julia, anguished as if he had just seen his favorite animal die. There was just nothing to be done about it. It must simply be buried. No amount of regretting would undo what had happened. And one couldn't grieve either, because it was just an animal, nothing to make a fuss about. Just take up the spade. In a few days it would all be forgotten.

He returned his jacket to its peg on the wall. He blew his nose violently into a grimy, blue handkerchief drawn from his back pocket, then folded it systematically, as habit would have it, and put it back. He laced his fingers and wrung his hands. "Yes, where was I," he sighed aloud. The half-soles had been cut and the underside of the shoes prepared for them. All that was left was to slip the shoe onto the iron foot and put the two together. He struggled to focus his thoughts. Where were his tools, the right nails? He put on his apron. He couldn't return to work without his apron. He felt in the pocket and found the nails. He sat down at his bench.

Most people didn't mind when he entertained children with stories. He couldn't believe Julia would react so intensely. It must be her religion again. He shuddered with a feeling he couldn't explain. Could there be evil in those old stories? Naw, they were only stories, one couldn't take them for more than fun. Of course they weren't true. Did she think he believed them the way she believed her Bible? She had said he was uncivilized. How outrageous!

This wretched thing would be hard to bury. He felt a terrible sense of loss. A vital friendship had been virtually destroyed, snuffed out! How awkward would be the coming days!

And they hadn't all been old Norse tales he had told to children either. Julia might have approved of the story he had told to a little boy on the boat coming from Norway. Had that really been any different?

He saw again the pale little boy, so soon to die, whom he had carried up on the deck. He had suggested to the mother that the boy needed fresh air and sunshine, so he was bundled up in a shawl.

The child was surprisingly light considering that his legs dangled over Arne's forearm.

He had propped the child beside him up there, sheltering him from the salty wind. At least here they both could breathe.

"So you are Peter. That is a very good name."

"Do you really think so?"

"I do. It makes me think of Peter who was a disciple of our Lord. Once a wicked king put him in prison with a big stone wall around it. Shall I tell you the story?"

"Yes, yes, do." The boy had turned his head inside the shawl and smiled at him.

"The stone wall had a big gate that was locked tight. No one could go through it, since only the jailor had the big key. One night, when everyone in the jail was sleeping, an angel came to Peter and said, 'Get up on your feet.' Peter did as he was told and his chains fell off. 'Put your shoes on and dress yourself,' said the angel. Again Peter did as he was told. He thought he was in the middle of a dream. Then they walked right out the door. Soon they came to the big iron gate. It opened by itself! 'What a pleasant dream,' thought Peter."

"Was Peter dreaming?"

"What do you think?"

"I don't know."

"Listen. When they got out into the street of the city, the angel simply disappeared, and there was Peter, free to go where he pleased."

"Did he wake up then?"

"He was awake all along, I guess. Don't you think so?"

Three days after that, the ship's carpenter made a rude coffin for the boy and put sand in it. Arne remembered the burial at sea, the boy's mother standing there so forlorn. She was shivering in the shawl, the same shawl in which he had carried the boy. And Inga, yes, dear Inga had put her arm around the woman.

Arne's brother-in-law, Gunder Rossing, had talked Arne into leaving Norway and going to America. Inga and Arne had just been married, and Gunder was happy with his new relative.

"Think what that new country must be like, Arne. If you want to farm, you can just set your plow and go straight over those prairies. And if you want to carry on as a shoemaker, better yet. There will be many people to make shoes for. You will be much in demand. And me, Arne, think how they will need millers. I might start my own mill on a new site, on a stream where no mill has ever stood. Inga is a good girl. She won't say no. She would be happy where you are. Let's do it, Arne. We won't be sorry, you'll see."

Why he had ever listened to Gunder, Arne would never know. He had never been discontented in the old country. Oh, yes, he supposed they had been poor, but a living had been made by his father in the cobbler's shop, and he had learned that trade early.

Here in America were no mountains to give that all-encompassing security. Mountains were comfortable, predictable, when one had grown in their presence. They responded routinely to changes, be it to the position of the sun, morning to evening, to weather, cloud-cover to clear, or to the seasons, summer to winter. He remembered how they were snow-capped, how they yielded fresh streams tumbling over pebbles, rocks and boulders. Then there were the deep fjords full of fish. He supposed one got tired of eating fish all the time, but what about pork? Is that any better? Arne figured it was the absence of the mountains and fjords that troubled him most about this country, and in retrospect they had taken on intangible meanings he couldn't express even in his thoughts.

His mind returned to Anna. How she listened to his stories! He was suddenly conscious of holding *Mjolner* in his hand. It was striking its mark every time. He heaved a deep sigh, as if it were an overloaded shovel of dirt that would hasten the burial of the hurt.

So he, Inga, and Gunder had crossed the ocean. The wind often blew in the wrong direction and it took nine weeks to reach Quebec, Canada. The food in their trunk had turned moldy in spite of the attempts to dry the contents after every soaking storm. How well, after all, that little ship had taken those storms, creaking and tearing, but never collapsing. And three people died, including the little boy. The trip had made Inga sober. He had discovered something deep about Inga on that trip. From then on she was less frivolous and more wise and understanding. She had even become resigned to being childless. "It isn't easy for mothers with young children in this country, Arne," she would say. At these times he knew she was hiding a deep void. Not having children, of course, might have been another reason why this country didn't seem right to him.

He began to think about Gunder, big and handsome as he was. How had he fared? He remembered how much easier it had been for Gunder to walk behind the wagon on the last stretch of the journey than it was for him. The driver of the wagon, whom they and another family had hired, insisted that the women and children ride with the trunks and the boxes and that the men walk. Gunder, was he still keeping up, he wondered?

Gunder, upon their arrival in Wanamingo, joined the mill operating on the Zumbo River just east of town. This mill was three years old, and business had been growing rapidly as the farms were becoming established. After some years, however, Gunder learned of a new mill coming up in Faribault. It used a new process to mill a purer type of flour which would yield a better price on the market. He made several trips there, becoming more and more excited about the "shaking sieves" as he called them. Finally he announced one day that he was going to join the La Croix milling operation and was gone. Then in early spring two years later, Gunder suddenly appeared in Wanamingo. The La Croix mill on the Straight River had closed because a flash flood collapsed the dam and destroyed the bridge leading to the mill. "No, we won't rebuild," Gunder explained. "We will go instead to Minneapolis! A miller there wants to install La Croix's shaking sieves."

Arne remembered that day. His brother-in-law was robust as iron and had a rash enthusiasm which the little town soaked up. Wheat and flour-milling—of course they went together. At that time only Inga seemed unaffected—he will never have a wife and family. And shortly after that, how long Arne couldn't accurately perceive, she had had her stroke and carried her concern for her brother into her silence.

And the worst of it was, Gunder never wrote letters or established an address. If he were in a small town like Faribault, where he could easily be known, a message could reach him. But Minneapolis was different. Gunder had never known what happened to his sister.

Arne swung away from his bench. Jens Berg's shoes had been successfully half-soled and had lots of good wear left in them. Arne greased them thoroughly and set them on the shelf. As he wiped the grease off his hands he looked over toward Nils' blacksmith shop. He wondered how long he could stay out of Julia's kitchen. He shuddered.

He began checking his supplies. Maybe he needed more leather, and he was low in thread.

Gunder. He kept returning to his mind. He remembered how shocked the surrounding country had become, reading about the mill explosion in Minneapolis. The roof of the Washburn Mill, weighing hundreds of tons had been sent flying five-hundred feet straight in the air, where it cracked into millions of pieces and fell as ghastly rain. It was a while before the dead were accounted for—only eighteen. It seemed unbelievable, but it happened after seven in the evening, and most workers had gone home. Arne had seriously wondered if Gunder were among the dead, but this fear had been laid aside when all the killed had been identified and the list published in the Minneapolis newspaper. Nevertheless, he hadn't heard from Gunder—and this was how long ago? Two years. He had toyed with the idea, then, of making a trip to Minneapolis to find him. But he dreaded the thought of being among total strangers, mostly Yankees, and had put it off.

But now, yes, now he could go, he should go. He stopped short! He felt a chill in the palms of his hands. He decided not to order supplies right now. He would need all the money he had. There were no immediate orders to fill. Of course, when the farmers got started in the fields he got harness jobs, urgent repair jobs. Mundahl had more business then than he could handle, no matter, this was the time. He went to his ill-kept desk and began searching through the pigeonholes.

The next morning, Nils looked up just as he was dropping a hot billet into the water bucket. The steam partially obscured his view, and he hardly believed what he saw. Arne stood before him dressed in his formal suit, which he so seldom wore. Nils hadn't seen him in it, that he could remember, since Inga's funeral. Or was this a stranger?

"I've come to say good-bye, Nils. I am going away for a while. Please give these shoes to Jens Berg who will be in town today, maybe." Arne put a package wrapped in newspaper down on the workbench behind Nils.

"Naw, I can't believe it. Where are you going?"

"You know I've been wondering what has happened to Gunder. I haven't heard from him for a long time."

"You're leaving now when spring is coming? Are you crazy?" Nils drew off his gloves and approached his friend. There must be more to it than looking for Gunder. That was only an excuse. Arne was good at finding excuses.

"Nils, I am reasonable enough. Can't a man take a trip when he wants to?"

"I suppose." Nils wouldn't push the issue. He could see Arne was serious.

"Say good-bye to the family for me." Arne's voice was unfamiliar.

"Why don't you go over now and say good-bye? Julia and Anna are both in the house."

"No, I mustn't keep Rolf Veblen waiting. I will ride as far as Zumbrota with him. He has an errand there."

"You won't see Julia and Anna, then?"

Arne turned quickly, avoiding Nils' question, and disappeared amazingly fast through the wide door. Nils followed and watched his friend climb into the waiting buggy. Arne didn't look back, and Nils didn't wave. As they drove away, Nils looked at the locked door of the cobbler's shop and wondered when it would open again. There is a sad heart behind all Arne's storytelling and laughter, Nils decided as he returned to his forge. Why hadn't he stopped at the house? Maybe he wouldn't be gone so very long at that. Maybe a week or two.

When it was dinnertime, Nils entered his house.

"Arne left town with Rolf Veblen. He won't be around for a while," Nils began immediately telling what troubled him. He hung up his jacket and went to the wash basin.

"What?" Julia held the bread plate and potato dish in her hands a long moment before setting them down on the table.

"He was all dressed up. He said he was going to Minneapolis to look for Gunder."

"That's noble of him. He's talked of doing that for two years." Julia covered her initial shock. People have to do what they must do.

"But he didn't say good-bye," Anna called out in agitation.

Nils went to her and put his two hands on her two cheeks. They smelled clean, but the odor of the forge was on his clothes.

"He told me to tell you good-bye. He wouldn't forget that." He glanced at Julia who bore this with indifference. "He had Rolf Veblen waiting. His team was ready to go."

"When will he come back?" asked Anna. The sound of the child's voice gave Julia a turn.

"He didn't say. Maybe not very long. It's my guess he'll not stay away very long. He's not very fond of strangers."

Nils sat up to the table.

"Where's Henrik?"

"Right here, Papa." Henrik was on his tiptoes, wiping his hands on the roller towel. He ran to his chair and sat in it.

"Let me eat later, Mama," Anna said almost inaudibly.

A team of swift-moving horses came to an abrupt stop in the road in front of the house.

"Who can that be?" Nils was out of his chair and putting aside the curtain from the window. "It's Dr. Grønvold!"

"I wonder if he has had dinner." Julia quickly assessed her kettles.

Nils went out to welcome the good doctor and take care of his team.

Anna came to life. With every visit her doctor paid, she raised her hopes. He came to free her legs and to exercise them. At first it had been very painful, but that only meant that she was not paralyzed. And Papa had the brace ready, or almost ready. Today, perhaps? She felt the roots of her hair tingle.

Having put on a clean, white apron, Julia went to the door to welcome her guest.

"I thought maybe that clever father of yours had by now solved the problems we had with the brace, so I got in my buggy and headed for Wanamingo." The doctor removed his cap, revealing unruly hair above his ears.

He approached his young patient. The small, sharp eyes and the severe dimple in the chin had often held terror for Anna, but she had gotten used to him. He had warm hands and knew how to help sick people.

"Hello, Dr. Grønvold," she called out.

"You take good care of her, Julia. I can see that."

Anna continued to smile. She was glad he was so pleased with her.

"Won't you have some dinner with us, Dr. Grønvold?" said Julia, already setting another place at the table.

"Thank you, Julia. I don't mind if I do."

"You've had a busy morning?"

"Always busy." He suddenly noticed Henrik waiting patiently at the table. "You're hungry, young man. We shouldn't keep you waiting. Here comes your father."

Both men pulled up their chairs.

"And the big one, where is he, Henrik?" He took a piece of meat from the platter Julia held out to him.

"You mean Hans?" Henrik looked at his father. "He's gone."

"He hired out for spring's work over on the south prairie," added Nils.

Anna wasn't listening to the conversation, and neither was she eating. Her mother had honored the request—or had it been more convenient to let her wait? Anna wondered how it would feel to stand, to expect her two feet to hold her up. She wondered how it would be to put one foot ahead of the other and walk. Some months ago she wouldn't have given this a thought, she would have known. But now she wasn't sure. "She'll have to learn to walk all over again," Dr. Grønvold had said the first time he came by to exercise her legs. She wondered how it would be to lift her foot over the threshold and stand outside. She would go out into the road and look up and down. She would go next door to Arne—no! He would have to wait now to see her with her brace. So it would have to be. She felt a wave of impatience. It was taking them a long time to finish eating.

Chapter 11

Arne and Rolf spoke very little as they rode side by side in the buggy on the way to Zumbrota. Rolf turned frequently toward his friend but found him completely lost in thought. How extraordinary! He had looked forward to this trip. The cobbler was full of stories, so entertaining. Rolf began the conversation.

"Where are you going, then, Arne?" He hadn't expected to see him all dressed up.

"To Minneapolis," was the short reply, no more.

"Have you heard from Gunder, then?"

"No, but I will look for him. It's been awhile."

"He is often spoken of. Lots of people remember him."

That had been the end of it. Arne had no desire to talk, and Rolf wouldn't press him. The heads of the good horses were bowing as they walked, and occasionally one would raise his tail and let his droppings fall on the road.

Rolf had a good team, well-made harnesses, and an expensive buggy. Arne was not envious by nature, but he often reflected on how certain people succeeded in this country. Although Veblen's store had competition at the outset in the small community, it had prospered. Arne thought he was doing better than Haroldson's, and, as a tailor, Rolf had more business than he could handle. Who would have thought that? Yes, he guessed it was a great country. There were opportunities if a person had a little luck to go with it.

Arne put his finger into his shirt collar. His clothes were tight, even his shoes were tight. A wave of discomfort came over him that was more than tight clothes. He felt like a stranger even to himself. Why was he riding in Veblen's buggy like this, going to Zumbrota? Was he really going to Minneapolis? Why? He was going to find Gunder. It was commendable to find Gunder. But he had hardly ever thought about Gunder until yesterday. And no one had talked him into leaving. It was his own decision.

The buggy rolled on, mile after mile. Distances were great here compared with Norway—towns were far apart, with prairie and wilderness between. There were many cultivated fields now, but these only depressed him. A person was seldom to be seen unless he happened upon the road. Was it broad stretches like this that made him uneasy? He wasn't sure how it could be that.

How would he act now that he was to move about in large towns, first of all Red Wing and then the cities farther north? He shuddered at the thought of projecting the image of a Yankee gentleman. No. Then why was he wearing these clothes? He would be as good as the next man. In this country one man was the same as the next, everyone knew that. There was no need to feel uncomfortable on that score. The next? Who was the next person who he was as good as? He wasn't sure.

"Thank you, Rolf, for the ride," said Arne as he stepped down onto the street in Zumbrota. "You have done me a great favor."

"It is nothing. Glad to have company," replied Rolf as he secured his horses at the hitching post outside Lett's Store. He watched his friend climb the steps up to the entrance. He would undoubtedly be looking for someone going to Red Wing. What has gotten into him? Rolf shook his head and went about his own business.

"Attorney Starr will be leaving this noon for Red Wing. He would like a passenger. He intends to spend a few days there." Mr. Lett was giving Arne the information he was seeking.

"That's fortunate for me," replied Arne, trying to hide his uneasiness. Starr, yes, he knew his brother, Wanamingo's schoolmaster—not a total stranger, then.

It occurred to him that Zumbrota had a daily stage, but he didn't inquire further. He climbed into a rig even more expensive than Veblen's an hour later.

"So you're on your way to Red Wing," began the amiable young attorney, who looked very much like his brother.

"Yes," replied Arne awkwardly, wondering why he was in a position where anyone would ask him where he was going.

"You are going to visit someone there?" continued the self-assured voice in perfect English.

"Yes, I have a brother-in-law in Minneapolis. I am going there." He heard in dismay his attempts at the language of the country.

"Oh, so you are going farther. It's nice this time of year. Riverboats have been moving for several weeks now."

Soon both men settled in with their own thoughts. It wasn't merely a problem of language; Arne seemed to want it that way.

The first stretch of road out of Zumbrota was relatively level but already suggestive of rolling hills up ahead, and they both knew that finally there would be deep valleys and rising bluffs. They rolled into long stretches of wilderness; one might wonder at the first road makers who cut their way through the thick wood and found places to ford the rivers. At one point in among the giant trees, Arne spotted a settler struggling manfully to clear a farm for himself. It looked impossible. Gunder, your description of simply sinking a plow on flat prairie isn't quite true. No, not quite. The rhythm of the buggy wheels and the soft creak of good leather put the two men even deeper into reverie.

There were patches of wildflowers near the trunks of tall trees and along the edges of little brooklets. Lavender crocuses, snow-white bloodroots, purple violets, and golden-yellow buttercups were not escaping Arne's notice. He admired the modest courage of such delicate plants to come forth, tiny and fragile, amid greedy tree seedlings. Out of the soil rose an elemental fragrance, rainwater absorbed and sought out by a myriad of rootlets. A heady breeze tossed the branches of trees, alive and healthy with tiny leaves tender to the sun. Winter was past. The wind's song was becoming tempered with soft, wafting easiness. It was indeed music, rising and receding, awesome and soothing, not like the compulsive rhythm of turning buggy wheels. Arne wondered why he couldn't decide right now that it was precisely here he was going. It was nice here. The road was constantly curving around hills, yielding a new tableau at every turn. The sky, exceedingly high above their heads, drove billowy white clouds. Sometimes the movement of the rig would stubbornly counter the clouds; at others it would flow with them. But most of the time the clouds would simply float over from left to right. As summer would progress, these woods would become too deep with foliage to admit sunlight, but as yet the moving billows could shadow the world momentarily and cause renewed anticipation of sunlight.

Soon the horses had to be content with steep climbs and long declines where the buggy had to be held back, the pole raised against disaster. Red Wing would soon be reached; the bluffs were rising in front of them. One couldn't be sure of distance, however. Bluffs were farther away than they seemed. No need to become impatient yet.

What had been going on in the mind of the other, each of the men would never know. Arne supposed his benefactor had his mind on complicated legal matters; land claims, he knew, could be sources of real trouble among settlers, and someone must clarify the law. But Arne was hardly interested in such issues and asked no questions. The lawyer, not sure how much English his traveling companion knew, silently wondered at the slight little Norwegian at his side. He didn't look like one who was consumed by visions of an enterprise of his own in this land of opportunity. Why bother him with questions?

"I'll be staying at the St. James Hotel. Perhaps I could drop you off there." Mr. Starr had broken the long silence at last.

"Thank you. That will be fine."

The sun was setting as Arne stepped out of the buggy at Red Wing. The huge bluff on the east end of town was glowing with the late rays of the sun. Arne stood a long time on the boardwalk outside the hotel, gazing at the closest thing to a mountain he had seen in this country. It stirred memories of his arrival in Minnesota, but it stirred something deeper than that, something he would not even try to surface.

Everyone for miles around talked about Barn Bluff. Many had seen it at a great distance while approaching on a steamer, as Arne had, knowing it marked a point of landing. The French had given it its name, La Grange, but it was now translated Barn. It was a bold rise, higher than the others along the river, and stood quite alone on the water's edge. It was flat on top, inviting ambitious climbers to view the new land for miles in any direction. Arne was no climber, however. He wanted to stand in its shelter to revere its very presence, as generations of Indians must have done before him. The glow was turning a deeper yellow now, and soon the bluff would relinquish its hold on the sun's warmth.

Someone on the bustling walkway bumped into Arne, bringing him back to the reality of the town, the need to seek information about steamers, and most likely to find lodging for the night. He hadn't thought about food; it wasn't often he went a whole day without food. Now perhaps that, too, was necessary.

"A steamer heading north is due here early in the morning," the hotel proprietor told Arne. "But surely you will take the train. We all travel by train these days. The one to Minneapolis leaves at 9:56 in the morning."

The train? Arne hadn't thought about the train. Certainly people traveled by train these days. Would he go by train?

"Do you want a room and meal?" asked the proprietor, seeing this hesitant little fellow about to walk away.

"I do, I do." Arne turned his attention back to the desk and nodded.

After he had gotten his room and eaten his meal for the day, Arne was out in the street again. Yes, of course, the railroad. It wasn't in his concept of the town. He walked the short distance to the river front, looking for the boat landing. Now there were railroad tracks to cross. The rigid iron tracks followed the water, as far as he could see, in both directions. He had not figured on this, but, of course, every form of travel follows the river. He saw an impressive new building; it must be the railroad station. But a person could still choose to take a steamer, couldn't he? Arne's uneasiness grew more intense with this new development. Well, all that would be dealt with tomorrow. He returned to the street in front of the hotel.

A restlessness drew him up and down the boardwalk. There were people loitering about. Spring had drawn them out. Although it was chilly, anticipation of coming summer evenings kept them out later than usual. There were noisy rivermen among the more sedate traveling men, and quaint characters one could only suspect were peddlers who would head out in the morning carrying their huge packs, or, if prosperous, with a horse and wagon. There were Indians, or most likely, half-breeds, who were inclined to take on the ways of the white man, watching from the sidelines. Arne listened for the sound of his mother tongue. Hearing none, he decided to enter a saloon.

Three or four Swedes in a group close to the entrance were talking loud and laughing heartily. If he found no Norwegians, he might settle for a word with them. Slowly he made his way behind the people lined up at the bar. The odor that invaded his nostrils told him he didn't wish to be served just yet; he wasn't a drinking man and the thought of a glass of ale was revolting. He stopped short of reaching the other end. He heard what he wanted to hear: *Halling* dialect! He would break in.

"So there are some Norwegians in town, too," Arne began when he sensed his chance. "I heard those loud Swedes down there and began to wonder."

The two men from Hallingdahl turned around, and Arne quickly decided they were brothers.

"We are constantly surrounded by Swedes," said the one who wore a shabby dark suit that was too tight for him.

"So you live in Vasa Township?"

"Not hard to guess, is it?" continued the same stout fellow. "I am Bernt Fjelset and this is my brother Sjur who has a farm among them. I am on my way north to Minneapolis, where I work. I have just spent the winter here, but now I must go back. And you?"

"Arne Aslakson, from Wanamingo," He shook hands with his new friends. "So one of you is a farmer and the other a businessman." He noticed that the brother who hadn't spoken yet was wearing a new overall jacket.

"You might say that," continued the one who talked. "I am connected with the railroad in the business of building elevators. No, I'm not a builder. I hire people. I go looking for strapping newcomers who are eager to work." His voice had become louder.

"So this is good-bye for the summer."

"Yah, you might say so. Tomorrow I must stop at the tailor for my new suit, then get on board the 9:56. And you?"

"I'm heading north tomorrow, too. I have in mind to take the steamer in the morning."

"A packet? You don't mean it. Those slow-moving, bad-smelling boats? They don't take many passengers anymore, you know."

"Then I suppose I, too, must board the train."

"You can't imagine how much faster you'll get there. You're going where?"

"To Minneapolis. I intend to find my brother-in-law. He hasn't visited or written for quite awhile."

"So," nodded the man, who now anticipated a traveling companion. He wouldn't question him further just yet. There would be time.

"You've been in this country quite awhile?" Arne turned his attention toward the farmer who so far hadn't done anything but smile.

"For twelve years. I took land in 1869." The farmer's voice was as robust as his brother's "I'm doing fine, as far as that goes. It's heavy sledding, but I manage to clear a bit more every year. Come, have a drink with us."

"Don't mind if I do," Arne lied. He entered the slot the two men had made between them.

"So, we will be leaving tomorrow on the 9:56, you and I. Let's drink to it."

Arne felt a heavy arm draped over his shoulder.

"To the 9:56!" said Arne, bravely taking a swallow of his drink. The bitter liquid was worth it now that he had made an acquaintance.

Arne was awake early. Because the train he and his friend were boarding wouldn't leave for many hours, he decided to be on hand for the docking of the riverboat the proprietor had said was arriving early. He heard it. The boat whistle was echoing among the bluffs as the steamer left Lake Pepin. People still responded to it and a small crowd was gathering. No, he supposed they weren't passengers. Many of them, of course, were there waiting to load or unload cargo, but there were also the bystanders who had watched many a riverboat come and go. Was this curious crowd of onlookers dwindling these days, he wondered?

The whistle blew a second time, and a faint cloud of smoke curled into the sky.

Among the bystanders close to him was an Indian woman with two small children, one on her back and one at her side. Her coal-black hair hung in two long braids, and her dress was of coarse brown cloth with a border of beads at the hem. She clenched a shabby shawl, fringed in red, that covered both her and the child on her back. The infant was asleep, resting his chin on the mother's shoulder. The little girl at her side was dressed like her mother, except her shawl was merely a triangular piece of cloth fastened in front with a safety pin. Arne stared; he wasn't used to seeing Indians.

The little girl stared at Arne; no one had taught her it was rude to stare. There must have been a twinkle in Arne's eye because the little girl smiled.

Who were these Indians anyway? Withdrawing his eyes from the child, he let them sweep along the opposite bank of the river. There was a reservation around here someplace where a tribe of Mdewakantons lived. Arne conceived of Indians as people out of mythology. Chiefs like Scarlet Wing and Wacouta were a kind of god, with painted faces and wearing strings of beads and feathers. He pictured them as going on journeys, too, as the Norse gods did, and bringing back scalps. That was peculiar. But real people who wore shawls with fringes, who used safety pins, who joined a crowd to watch a steamer stop so early in the morning—this he had never imagined.

The packet had mostly cargo; he saw very few people walk off. There was no crushing crowd as there had been when he landed here as a newcomer; now there was only the lifting, carrying, and tossing of heavy crates onto the dock. He noticed two Negroes among the boat hands, powerfully strong, lifting unbelieveable loads. They looked into no faces, and no one looked into theirs. They had been slaves, Arne knew, but he was uncomprehending. They were no more real to Arne than the mythological giants forging iron in mountain caves.

After the steamer had blown its whistle and entered again into the channel, Arne moved toward the big, new railroad station. He looked around for the Indian woman and her children, but they had disappeared. His attention now shifted from the river's mainstream, the bearer of loads, to the iron tracks that lay at its side.

The apprehension he had felt earlier returned. He reached the station early and sat down on one of the crisp new benches on the platform. There was cargo activity here, too, but none of the usual shabbiness. Here loads rolled along on brand new, freshly-painted wagons, in a style all their own.

"So here you are. You're one of those people who believe in being on time, aren't you." Bernt had arrived. Arne promptly rose and followed him into the station. Bernt's suitcase was almost trunk size, and Arne assumed his new suit of clothes was carefully folded inside it, because he was still wearing the tight one.

"You said it. Always wake up early. I had a good breakfast and had nothing much else to do, so here you have found me."

Having purchased their tickets and seen their cases placed among the others on the little dray wagon, they joined the knot of people on the far end of the platform. Heads were straining in the direction of the coming train. Some travelers snapped open pocket watches. Arne felt uncomfortable among these anxious people. He wondered why everyone appeared in such a hurry when this mode of travel was the fastest ever conceived.

"Do you expect any 'strapping newcomers,' as you call them, coming off here?" asked Arne, attempting casual conversation.

"No, I don't. Besides, we have to get on ourselves. There will be no time for me to watch those who get off," said Bernt, thinking that his companion didn't seem to understand that this was not a slow-moving boat where comers and goers could look one another over.

"Do you have a place to stay when you come to Minneapolis?" Bernt asked.

"No, that I haven't," answered Arne. He did not want to admit how much this very thing worried him. "I suppose you are well acquainted up there."

"That I am. Your brother-in-law, where do you expect to find him?"

"He is a millhand," Arne hesitated. "It may take some time."

"That it might. I know where you could stay at the outset, though. It is an avenue where not a few Scandinavians stay, and it is not very expensive. I have hired many Norwegians and Swedes who have stopped there before going elsewhere."

"That is fortunate for me," replied Arne. "I certainly will rely on you in this matter." Arne felt a sense of relief, but it was quickly displaced by terror—that with a shrill steam whistle and a rumbling sound that shook the earth. The locomotive sped past the waiting passengers before coming to a stop. Arne heard a rush of steam up ahead.

"Come," said Bernt, grabbing Arne's arm with an urgency that quite overwhelmed the little cobbler. "They don't wait very long, you know."

He put his foot cautiously on the step placed by a trainman—was he black?—who stood beside it with his hands behind his back.

"Watch your step, watch your step," he kept repeating.

Arne was glad Bernt was with him, but he resented the way he was being shoved.

"Here we will sit," said Bernt after the two had pushed up the aisle. There were two places, beautifully upholstered with moss-green plush. Bernt decided that Arne should sit by the window.

The locomotive bell stopped ringing, and the shrill whistle blew; the train was beginning to move. A wave of uneasiness came over Arne, and he did his best to conceal it. Those little iron wheels on those mighty-narrow, raised tracks were rolling faster and faster. Along with a strange vibration was a rhythmic clicking that began to get on his nerves. And it was no comfort to look out the window, either. There the fixed landscape was set into motion. Trees flew by, rock walls, boulders—it made him dizzy. It was safer not to look. This was altogether unnatural. Humans were never intended to move at such speed.

"This is, of course, your first train ride, isn't it?" Bernt sensed his companion's tenseness and wanted to put him at ease. "It's quite safe, you know."

The steam whistle blew occasionally as they went along. Warnings, Arne imagined. The sound lingered mysteriously behind, echoing in the hills. It seemed an intrusion by the gods.

Chapter 12

Butterfly, Butterfly, turn around,
Butterfly, butterfly, touch the ground,
Butterfly, butterfly, show your shoe,
Butterfly, butterfly, twenty-three to do.

It was Anna's voice heard over the twirling rope and the scuff of toes on the ground. Mari Mundahl was jumping a rope turned by Agnes and Josie Veblen.

It was a day in May and the sun shone warm on Anna's shoulders as she sat on a bench outside her house. She wasn't walking much yet, but she could move short distances without her legs trembling. Dr. Grønvold had put her into the brace that April day he had stayed for dinner. Julia had wrapped the sharp-edged metal with yards and yards of carpet rags from a huge ball prepared with other intentions but exceedingly appropriate now. Dr. Grønvold had told Anna that she would get over the feeling of being like jelly, and he was right. She had been sitting out here for quite a while now without even a chairback on which to rest her shoulders. The school term was over, happily bringing back her friends for longer periods of time.

Salt, pepper, mustard, cider, vinegar!

That signaled the turners to increase the speed of the rope, and Mari finished her performance with a quickened beat and a leap out of rope range.

"Say the lines for me," cried Agnes. "I'm next!"

Mari, red-faced and breathing hard, grabbed the end of the rope Agnes had dropped, and Anna again began the singsong.

Julia stood out of sight in the doorway, listening. She was conscious of the intensely blue sky and life stirring in the soil. A wave of fresh spring air reached her nostrils, reviving lost particles of memory deep within her; the freedom of a little girl to run and play, the lightness of limb, the warmth of the sun on loose-flowing hair. Although the words were English, it mattered little; the new land was yielding the same joys to little girls as the old. For now it was Anna out there, her foot moving with the singsong rhythm, and her body bowing at the waist. How she had picked up! Spring with its rush of new life had brought vitality to the ailing child, too. Nothing was much the matter today. She slipped inside and returned to work.

"Let's play the game Anna can play," shouted Mari as Agnes bowed away from the twirling rope, whose rhythm slackened and died.

"I'd like that," said Anna, sobering a bit as she pushed her hand against the bench to raise herself.

The game was to be "Draw a Bucket of Water." Mari carefully grasped Anna's two hands and drew her forward a few steps. They paused a moment in this position while Agnes and Josie clasped their hands across those of Mari and Anna. Cautiously they swayed as the game called for, back and forth:

> Draw a bucket of water
> For my lady's daughter.
> One in a rush,
> Two in a rush,
> Please, little girl, bob under the bush.

At the signal "bob" all bowed their heads in and raised their arms up without unclasping hands. The arms were then brought down around the waist of each companion. Thus drawn together, Agnes and Josie felt the uncomfortable fact of Anna's brace, a reminder that their friend must be treated with care.

Suddenly the sound of hoof and harness announced a buggy in the Kristian driveway. The girls dropped their hold, and all four stared in the direction of the visitors.

"Anna, is it really you out here playing with your friends?" It was Rev. Østen Hanson. He fastened the reins and hurried to her.

"It's me, Rev. Hanson," said Anna, holding Mari's hand. "Good day. I am quite well now."

Nils and Julia came from opposite directions to greet their pastor, but he scarcely noticed them.

"You certainly look well." He saw the rope. "Don't tell me you girls have been skipping that rope."

"Oh, yes, we have. All except Anna. But she counts and calls for us." said Mari.

"She keeps us playing fair," said Agnes.

"She can play 'Draw a Bucket of Water,' " put in Josie.

"Let's see," said the minister.

They went through the motions of the game again, but with much livelier singing. The audience had increased by two as Julia and Nils stood waiting upon their guest.

"What a marvel!" said Østen Hanson as he turned toward the parents, who ushered him through the open door of the house.

The sun had made them blind to the little room, and the ceiling seemed to weigh down upon them. They left the door open.

The minister got to the point of his visit. "I want to give you the news about Grønvold's friend, Paul Hjelm Hansen. He died this morning."

Julia felt a rush of dread. She saw again the Grønvold parlor and the extended hand she had clasped in a handshake. Now he had passed into eternity.

"We met him once at Grønvold's house," said Nils.

"I wasn't aware that you had met him."

"Oh, yes, I visited with him while the doctor checked our Anna. He was feeble then, but his mind was certainly alert."

"He had been failing ever since he came to Grønvold last winter. It seems he came there to die. I believe he was quite alone in this world and with very little means." Rev. Hanson watched Julia as he spoke. She had a way of pursing her lips when in serious thought.

"What a pity to be alone in the world," Julia began speaking, "He who has certainly been so highly thought of among our people. You say he had no family? No one?"

"He left Norway possibly as an exile. He had been together with the dissenter, Marcus Thrane. People with such radical leanings, as you know, either chose America, where the political future looked brighter to them, or were exiled as agitators. And, his being a journalist, it isn't hard to believe. How he knew Christian Grønvold is harder to say. It must have been back in Norway."

"Most likely," said Nils. "Grønvold would do that for an old friend."

There was a long moment of silence. The three of them were a still-life tableau in Julia's kitchen.

"He was sitting on a bench in the orchard enjoying the blossoming trees when he dropped over," Rev. Hanson said at length. "Grønvold said Paul was a poet at heart, and he thought the place of passing very appropriate."

"He had great talent," said Julia, raising her eyes and looking beyond her two listeners. "I am sure Grønvold was not far wrong when he called him a poet. We have read with great interest his descriptions of the Red River Valley country. No wonder many of our people have gone there to live due to his influence."

"Grønvold wants to have his friend buried at Aspelund." Rev. Hanson spoke slowly, studying Julia's face. She gave no evidence of wanting to question him, so he continued. "Maybe Holden is too much the Church of Norway with which Grønvold and his friend had differences—no unbelievers in their sacred soil. But, be that as it may, at least he is not expecting Muus to bury this man. What can we do?"

Nils and Julia were quietly waiting. They knew what their minister's decision would be.

"I don't want to judge him an infidel, God be his Judge." The wall clock ticked. The pastor paused a long moment. "The beautiful thing about this man was his convictions concerning religious freedom."

"You granted Grønvold's request?" said Nils.

"I did."

"That's good." There was another long pause.

"I want you folks to come to the service."

"We will."

"At one o'clock tomorrow."

They rose and moved back outside into the freshness of this May day. Anna and Mari were chatting on the bench. The minister was in no hurry as Nils and Julia followed him to his buggy.

"What farmer has time to come to town on a day like this?" said Rev. Hanson, catching sight of a wagon approaching from the north, the direction he soon would be going.

"There is someone coming, all right," replied Julia, not too surprised.

"It looks like Lars Monson's team," said Nils. "Poor Lars has had a lot of bad luck. He comes to town more often than he wants to with a dragging harness or a broken piece of machinery. He doesn't seem to have much talent for fixing things himself."

"Is that the *Vossing* family that lost two children a year ago...from...was it diphtheria?" Julia shaded her eyes. "I remember Marie Dokken telling about them. She tried then, as a neighbor, to be of some help. They keep to themselves pretty much, don't they, Nils?"

Nils nodded. "His farm is stony. He tills land that gives meager yields—some of the last land to be claimed—too sandy. It isn't all perfect, even in Goodhue County."

"That is true," said the minister. "We won't all be rich."

The wagon was now in full view. On the spring seat beside the farmer sat a boy of eleven or twelve, holding in his arms a bundle wrapped in a brown shawl. It was certainly a baby; the boy was so protective. The wagon came to a stop across the road in front of the blacksmith shop. Another boy, quite a bit younger and not visible until now, had been riding at the end of the wagon, dangling his feet. He quickly jumped down, preparing to follow his father.

"Hello, Lars," called Nils, now sure it was Monson.

The farmer approached and removed his hat. He was taller than he had seemed on the wagon seat. His hair and beard were a sandy red, and his nose was flecked with tiny veins.

"This is Rev. Hanson," said Nils. "And, of course, my wife Julia."

Lars Monson shook hands with the minister and then with Julia. His movements were slow, almost hesitant. "Rev. Hanson, I am pleased to meet you. And Julia, good-day to you. Nils I have known for sometime. You are a good man as well as being clever." He didn't smile. He kept nodding. "I have come to you as a person needing help."

"Yes, you are among friends, Lars." encouraged Nils.

"I have lost my wife." He lowered his eyes and paused. "She took ill suddenly with a very sharp pain in her stomach which lasted for a night and a day." He lifted his eyes and looked toward his blacksmith friend. "She is dead, Nils."

"We feel for you, Lars, my wife and I," said Nils.

"May God be with you," added Rev. Hanson.

"My children are without a mother. Mrs. Dokken said you were a good woman, Julia. She said that if I asked you, you might take care of the baby for me."

The young boy who stood close to his father clung a bit tighter to his arm, never taking his eyes off the three adults talking there.

"That I can do," said Julia without hesitation.

Lars retained his composure with considerable effort. "We buried her yesterday from Minneola church. We have two children buried there, you know. Mrs. Dokken has taken care of our little Sarah these last three days, but now she must be excused as she has one of her own coming very soon."

"You have two fine boys. What are their names?" asked Nils.

"Alfred," Lars said, nodding toward the one still sitting in the wagon. "And Oscar, here. They will remain with me. They are very good boys."

"I'm sure they are," replied Julia, looking at Oscar, who quickly turned his head. "And little Sarah..." Julia finally made a dash toward the boy on the wagon. Østen Hanson had already crossed the road and made the acquaintance of the oldest boy. He was holding the child while the boy climbed down.

"See this beautiful child, Julia," exclaimed the minister, tilting the bundle and exposing a rosy-cheeked infant.

Julia took the bundle and began unwrapping. "She must be warm rolled up so tight. You take good care of your sister, Alfred."

Alfred, now on the ground and relieved of his burden, smiled at Julia. "She slept most of the way."

Julia finally freed the child's arms and legs. The little girl was perhaps six months old. Her face was mostly rosy cheeks, but a pair of eyes stared unabashed into the world.

Anna and Mari were not oblivious to what was happening. Anna wanted to go closer and take in the whole conversation, but she knew her mother would only send her back to the bench. Mari was too well-mannered to dash into another family's affairs, and remained beside her friend. But when the baby was drawn from the shawl, it was too much for both.

"Mari, go, then come back and tell me." Anna gave her friend's shoulder a shove.

"No."

"Please, Mari. They won't notice you."

Mari crossed the road at a safe distance and found a place where she could listen without being seen.

"It is much to expect of you, Julia, taking care of my child like this. I have no idea what arrangements I will be making to keep my family together, so I cannot tell you how long it will be before I will be able to take care of her myself. But—" He took his eyes off the baby in Julia's arms and gazed into the distance.

"She'll be fine with me. It isn't hard to love an infant, Lars. She will be a blessing to us."

Mari hurried back over the route she had come and stood breathless before her friend with the startling news. "Your mother is going to take care of that baby, Anna, that pretty baby!"

"Really?"

"Yes. The man can't. He has no wife, I guess... something like that."

Anna couldn't sit still. She would go and stand beside her father. This was a family affair. She need not be left out. Mari could come, too.

Østen Hanson finally took leave when Julia and Nils invited the Monsons into the house. As he sat in his rig, he heard in his mind Julia saying," She'll be a blessing to us." He was proud of such a woman. Her strength and goodness were known for miles around. He wouldn't be surprised if that child would grow up right there with the Kristians—and that could be nothing but fortunate.

As he rolled along mile after mile, he was gratefully aware of how much easier traveling conditions had become. There was no more fear of sinking in the mud, and it was too early for dust. *And the sound of the (meadowlark) is heard on the earth. Song of Solomon.* He smiled. This day had been edifying.

Who could be buried in the sacred soil of the church cemetery, and who should not? It was controversial, there was no question about that. He had wanted reinforcement for his decision to bury Dr. Grønvold's friend; that was why he had planned this visit with Nils and Julia. We are not to judge what is in a man's heart: that had been his premise, one that he felt they understood. He knew Julia to be reflective, one who struggled honestly with her conscience. If she raised no issue, he would feel assured. She was one from whom a person could draw strength when action needed to be taken. She had given him strength.

He had grown tired of church controversies so often churning in his head—words, phrases, counter words, counter phrases. But action, deeds—there was something to be said for deeds being more meaningful than words. And, come to think about it, his soul had been refreshed by deeds this day. Julia Kristian had taken in a motherless child and Christian Grønvold had given comfort to a dying friend.

The road ran along the river now. The water was higher and faster than usual. It had been a wet spring.

And wasn't it truly remarkable how well Anna was getting along? How many cases like that has Dr. Grønvold treated? Probably this was the only one he had ever encountered. What courage of one's convictions it must take to invoke such drastic measures when symptoms seem so relatively minor. How fortunate for the immigrant community to have such a doctor! He thought about Julia. Anna's illness had not been easy for her, but now she must certainly feel rewarded. And Nils, the quiet partner of both wife and doctor—how seldom he spoke, but how good he was!

The road had veered away from the river now, and freshly prepared fields lay black on both sides of the road. If one looked closely, one might see that the wheat sprouts were coming out of the ground. He couldn't help but think how young these fields were, how recent had been the struggle with stumps, rocks and deep, deep sod. He remembered how he had come and taken his homestead along with the others. There was exhilaration in working such land knowing it is one's own, and passing something as permanent as land to one's children.

But there was something greater about this country, and he wondered if this was fully grasped by all his fellows. This country meant freedom for all who sought it, needed it. Haugeans could thrive here without the humiliation they suffered in the old country. There were fresh fields for new ideas here, without the threat of exile. Then, too, the lines of social distinction were nonexistent, and if they were evoked, the result would be ridiculous. Imagine his being called the bishop of the Hauge Synod! He laughed out loud at the thought of anyone calling him that. The free air breathed here even made it possible for the university-educated, properly-ordained Rev. Muus to associate seriously with him, the lay preacher made minister. What else could make that happen? It was something that had to do with this new land. Of course, no one knew better than he the conflicts there were in the church. But somehow equal footing was possible here which hadn't been the case in the old country. Who recognized the supremacy of the State Church of Norway here? Religious freedom was a wonderful thing!

He was almost home. He saw his church against the blue spring sky. Tomorrow he was to bury Paul Hjelm Hansen. Had this country been an answer to a vision for Paul Hjelm Hansen? If so it would be fitting to give him decent burial in its soil.

Chapter 13

"This is a remarkably clean room," said Arne as he hung up his suit coat on one of the hooks behind a drawstring curtain which served as a closet. "No bedbugs, I shouldn't think."

"I agree with you," said Bernt. "Believe me, this is not usual in rooming houses on Washington Avenue. It must be that you are lucky."

"I wouldn't say that exactly, I've never regarded myself as lucky. I hope I didn't speak too soon about bedbugs." Arne checked along the mopboard in a dark corner by the night stand. "I believe I could smell them if they were here."

"I must leave you, Arne, my friend. It is getting late. My landlady will be looking for me. I wrote and told her I was coming. I'm glad we found this room for you. My best to you. I hope you will locate your brother-in-law without much trouble. Here is my address should you want to look me up."

Arne followed his friend into the long hallway and down to the front door.

"Good-bye then, Bernt. You have proved to be a very good friend. Many, many thanks for your help."

"You are very welcome. We may see each other again."

Arne watched Bernt as he disappeared among the people on the street. He wanted to leave the rooming house door open, but guessed it was better to keep doors closed when one is in a city. Arne wondered why the hallway was not as clean as his room. Cobwebs laced the corners and lint balls rolled with the current of air stirred by the opening of doors. Was it boiled cabbage he smelled? Perhaps a mixture of that and stale tobacco.

He reached his room and continued to check its furnishings. There was a table opposite the bed with two chairs up to it. A lamp with a crystal-clear chimney was in its holder above the table. By the window was an armchair with a large, red pillow in the seat. Finally he decided to sit in it. He was becoming conscious of how exhausted he was.

The cobbler from Wanamingo had come a long way in two days. Each moment, since he had left, had rolled forth something new, and more often than not, unpredictable. As he sat in the chair, clutching the arms with unrelaxed fingers, the events of this day rolled again.

The train, finally coming to a stop, brought a kind of relief to Arne, but sights through the window worried him. The many railroad tracks side by side with cars sitting at random on them, the two and three-story warehouses with their rows and rows of windows, the smokestacks with smoke darkening the blue of the sky; he was indeed coming into an alien world. Bernt wasn't talking as the two of them hustled out of their seats; there was an uncomfortable determination on his face.

There were throngs everywhere. Where had they come from? Some pushed past him, while many others just milled around in confusion. Among the dispersing people outside the station were wagons and rigs of every description, from dray wagons pulled by several teams of horses to expensive, fringed surries. Feeling intensely awkward, Arne struggled to follow Bernt, whose trunk-sized suitcase was now in the hands of a taxi driver. They were being led to a single-horse buggy. There was no way of escaping the people. Arne looked to his right. Someone was walking in stride with him, carrying a suitcase just as he was, a total stranger indifferent and silent. He looked to his left. There was another fellow human just as oblivious to him as the one on his right. He heard tongues as foreign as his own bombarding him in snatches, too rapid for comprehension, if he were indeed required to comprehend. He wasn't used to ignoring the presence of others, whoever they might be.

Having climbed into the taxi, Arne was attracted to the agile little horse who sprang forward without hesitation. He might not have needed the blinders. He eased in and out among slower-moving wagons and around parked ones. Hooves clattered on the hard dirt street; so hard it was from the constant flow of traffic that only faint traces of wheel ruts and hoof tracks remained. Gusts of wind, channeled between the buildings, swept up fine dust from the hard surface, as a blizzard would sweep snow from hard drifts, stinging the face and watering the eyes. As they rode along, the sun became a huge, blood-red ball hanging over the city, soon to drop unnaturally into the horizon. One might wonder if it would return again for another day.

Realizing that he was sitting in the dark of his newly acquired hotel room, Arne considered lighting his lamp. But he decided against it, letting himself sink deeper into the armchair. The street noises and the street lights reached him through the window. He vaguely listened to voices of drivers spurring on their horses. He watched patches of light move across the opposite wall.

"We'll eat at Ellas's," Bernt had said, as they stepped out of the taxi, indicating a small cafe across the street before entering the rooming house. It had clean, blue-checked curtains guarding the windows. They were served the meal of the day: corned beef and boiled potatoes and sour, gray bread. Bernt had eaten heartily, but Arne wasn't hungry. Now he wished he hadn't eaten what was on his plate.

Arne got out of the armchair. It was a bit uncomfortable after all. The events of the day were overwhelming him, and he needed to rise out of the ocean of his thoughts. He lit the lamp. He must make himself at home. The room, now full of shadows created by the lamplight, was his. He paced awhile searching for his former self. He wondered if the old easiness, which seemed to have been left behind, would return when he had stayed in this place—in this room—for awhile. He desperately hoped it would. Whoever cleaned here cleaned like Julia.

There was a knock at the door. Arne stopped abruptly and hesitated. Of course, he must open it. He moved cautiously until he had his hand on the knob.

"Yes?" he said in English.

In the doorway stood a young woman. She was much too plain to be a woman of the streets. Upon seeing him she became bewildered, and her eyes scanned the room behind him.

"I'm sorry," she said finally. "I was thinking someone else was here. You just move in? Are you a friend of his?"

Recognizing this Norwegian girl's halting attempts at English, Arne gladly shifted to his native tongue.

"Come in and have a seat."

She promptly entered and took a chair beside the table.

"Thank you. You speak Norwegian." She smiled at Arne, who hadn't taken his eyes off her. Closer to the light, her face impressed him. Her cheeks were round and fresh, and her mouth, wide in a smile, exposed straight, white teeth. Her hair was drawn up into a knot, but not as severely as Julia's. Her eyes were innocent and engaging. The smile with which she had returned the greeting faded quickly.

"Yes, I'm from Hallingdahl, as you may well hear." Arne was almost jovial trying to bring back the smile.

"You just moved in here, then?" She remained sober.

"Yes, I'm new to the city. A friend of mine, Bernt Fjelset, brought me here. He's not the one you are looking for, is he?"

"No," she said, giving up hope. She stared into the lamplight on the table before her. "He just packed up and left, I guess," she said at length. She glanced around the room, seeing none of his things.

"He was a good friend of yours?" Arne was touched by her disappointment.

"He was." She studied Arne's face for a moment and continued. "I really thought he cared for me. He had lived here as long as I have. He treated me like I belonged to him. He paid my rent. He bought food and I prepared it. I washed his clothes and cleaned this room."

She tossed her hands above her head and brought them down on the table in front of her. Arne hoped she wouldn't cry.

"It is very clean in this room," he put in quickly. "In fact, I was quite amazed. I'm very sorry that I should be the one to open the door for you instead of your friend."

"I believe you are kind," she said. "I shouldn't have counted on his staying here forever. People come and go in places like this. I should have known."

"How long have you been here?"

"Since last July, I left my husband just as harvest began. He is a very cruel man," she said with fierce emphasis. "He beat me. I wasn't sure but that he might kill me. He drank. I suppose that was really the trouble, and it kept getting worse. I packed food and a few other things in a bag and took my baby with me. I caught rides with farmers. I guess they wondered who I was and why I was traveling like this, but few asked questions. And they were kind. I reached the city and was completely overwhelmed! That was when Iver found me and put me up in this rooming house."

"Don't you have parents in this country you could go to?" Arne was becoming bewildered by this girl's predicament. She seemed more of a child now than a woman.

"Yes, but my father is a severe man, too. Not cruel, you understand, but he would say, 'Your duty is with your husband. You must not act like a child.' "

"So you have been here for close to a year. And Iver, as you called him, was he here until now?"

"That is the way it is." She studied Arne as if he might have an answer.

He simply nodded. With this room as clean as Julia's house had come a responsibility he wasn't prepared to handle. His shoulders drooped and he stared absently at the floor.

"You mustn't trouble yourself," she said at length. "You perhaps have troubles of your own." She posed as a willing listener.

"I have come to Minneapolis to find my brother-in-law Gunder Rossing. He is a millhand somewhere. I haven't seen him for a number of years."

"You have no idea where? This is a big city. It might take a long time. People get lost in places like this." Her eyes were round and sober.

He nodded again.

"I will cook food for you if you want me to. I will wash your clothes and clean your room if you would like?" The words came eagerly as if only her intensity upon them would bring an affirmative answer.

"No, no, no, I wouldn't want you to do that," said Arne quickly, startled enough to sit straight in his chair.

"You wouldn't?"

"I couldn't let you do that."
"Why not?"
All Arne could do was shake his head emphatically.
"Well, then, I'd better go," she said finally. "I am sorry I bothered you. We will be friends though, won't we? I'll bring my little daughter to see you. Wouldn't that be all right?"
Arne was on his feet, ready to show her to the door. "That would be fine. Do that."
"Good night."
"Good night."
Arne closed the door and turned in upon his room once more. He paced round and round the little table, circling the light. He shook his head again and again. He finally decided it must be bedtime. Tomorrow would be another day. He didn't dare to think about it. He poured some water from the pitcher into the washbowl. Bending over, he splashed water on his face with cupped hands. He did it once, twice, three times, then grabbed for the towel. The wash brought a sweet wave of relief. He carefully folded the towel and hung it where he had found it.
For many days—he scarcely knew how many—Arne wandered in the vicinity of the mill at St. Anthony Falls, the biggest and the closest. He watched and listened as he made his way along the street. There were many idle men like himself just having arrived, perhaps, or more likely waiting for a job, or looking for someone else. He hadn't figured it out. As he frequented certain streets, he would run into the same person the next day, and the next. These were silent men and he never felt like intruding. He had Gunder in mind. He reserved all for him.
At the end of the working day, Arne would sit on a bench outside a little saloon in the center of traffic. He kept an alert eye as the millhands came, many of them passing very near him as they entered for their draft of beer. It was impossible to mistake a millhand, as they were coated from head to foot with fine flour. Their arms dangled as they walked, and Arne pictured them as having tossed sacks all day. Frequently one would shove his cap up and scratch his head, and Arne knew they all must itch. He stayed until he was satisfied that none of them was the person he was looking for.
When he returned to his room, Melva would knock and invite him to her quarters for a meal. The first evening, she had enticed him with potato dumplings that had a nice piece of salt pork in the center of each. And he smelled fresh bread. He was sure it would not be sour or gray. Arne was impressed; he couldn't refuse. As he entered, he noticed that she had a small cook stove instead of a heater, such as the one in his room. He had hardly found a chair before her year-old daughter toddled out of a corner and placed two chubby hands on his knee. It became a ritual for the little one to sit on his lap before the meal, and she immediately sought out the watch in

his vest pocket. Arne held the gold timepiece across her little ear, and a rapt smile glowed from the eager face.

One day—perhaps a week had gone by—Arne ran across Bernt.

"Well, my good friend, it is good to see you again," said Bernt, drawing him out of the mainstream of sidewalk traffic. "How are you faring, then?"

"I'm still around as you can see. I have not run across my brother-in-law yet. I visit this area every day and stay until the saloons fill up, but no luck yet."

"Haven't you inquired in the mill office? They surely would know who work for them." Bernt was surprised at Arne's ineptness.

"I guess I'll have to do that after all," Arne concluded, glad that his friend had some advice.

"By all means, do that. And if you find out he isn't there try other mills. There are several smaller mills that have sprung up along Minnehaha Creek about ten miles southwest of here. One I know is Minnetonka Mills."

"Of course, that is sensible advice. I'm much obliged to you, my friend."

"How are your quarters at the rooming house?"

"Most fortunate. I have a cook, Bernt. You can't believe what I'm going to tell you." Arne went on to tell all about the knock on the door that came after Bernt had left, about Melva Fosse and her child across the hall. She cooked his meals, washed his clothes and cleaned his room. He explained how another fellow named Iver had had all these advantages and that he, Arne, had in a sense inherited them from a former occupant.

"You don't say," said Bernt in a tone that embarrassed his friend.

"She's a plain country girl." Arne wanted to correct any false impression he might have given Bernt. "I pay her rent, you understand, and give her money for the food she prepares."

"She won't stay a country girl very long in a city like this," Bernt predicted. "When you leave, Arne, will the next occupant be as decent as you? Hardly. She'll learn what all young women learn to do here if they expect to eat and live. No question about it."

"I suppose you are right. You know more about the city than I do," said Arne as he watched the flow of humanity passing in front of him.

"Good luck to you, Arne," said Bernt at last, slapping his big hand on Arne's stooped shoulder. "Do as I say about inquiring at the mill office."

"I will. Thank you, Bernt, and good luck to you."

They parted. Arne now had courage to do what he had known all along he must do. He wasted no time. He cautiously crossed many railroad tracks to reach the office. His inquiry sent a clerk to a file drawer. He had been frightened of this place with its formidable smokestacks, tall elevators and fast-moving trains, but here he stood. It was hard to believe that such a simple thing as milling should become such a huge operation. It hadn't been like this in Norway, or even on the Zumbro. The clerk returned, shaking his head.

"Not now, and not at any time according to our records. No name like Gunder Rossing."

Arne nodded. The clerk waited, not sure the man before him completely understood—these foreigners, you know.

"Thank you," said Arne turning slowly in the direction of the door.

"You're welcome."

The next day Arne made plans to go to Minnetonka. He told Melva she should not expect him to return for two or three days. It might even be longer. If he found Gunder, surely they would visit awhile.

There were passenger coaches among the railroad cars he had seen in the vicinity, but he knew so little about trains and decided he could afford to play the part of a gentleman. So he engaged a rig.

The Minnetonka Mill wasn't small either. As he approached, he saw two, large smokestacks and several big buildings, including an elevator thirty or more feet high. The mill itself was a gable-roofed building at least three stories high, located on the south bank of the creek. And, of all things, there was a conveyor that spanned the stream from the mill to the elevator. Railroad cars stood waiting on both sides of the creek. Surrounding the mill there seemed to be a village, or perhaps, these houses, all alike, were cabins of mill workers.

Arne looked around, wondering where the office might be. He dismissed the rig, deciding he would take a chance. He headed for a two-story building not far from the elevator, just north of the main operation.

It was a cooper shop, where barrels were made to supply the shipping needs of the mill. He entered slowly through the wide door. He had little fascination for milling, but barrel making was different. He knew the process and what constituted a well-made, long-lasting barrel. He stood aside for a moment adjusting his eyes after the bright sunlight.

"Are you looking for someone?" A worker holding a stave in his hand took Arne by surprise.

"Good afternoon. As a matter of fact, I am," said Arne, feeling awkward using English. "I'm looking for Gunder Rossing."

"Joe, come here," shouted the worker holding the stave. "Some one is here asking for Gunder."

Arne stared into the far corners of the shop. The men who worked here knew Gunder.

"Joe!"

"Yes, I hear," came a voice from the middle of the room. "Wait just a minute, I have almost finished."

"Joe will be with you soon." The worker returned to his task.

The shop was rich with the smell of moistened wood. There were barrels, dozens of them, stacked inside the doorway to his right. Everything in America was done on a big scale. Where was Gunder? He doubted that Gunder worked here; what he knew was milling. "Someone is here asking for Gunder," the man had said. Why hadn't he been sent to the mill area?

"I'm Joe Harding, and you are...?"

"Arne Aslakson."

A broad-shouldered man stood before Arne in the coarse smock of his trade. He didn't shake hands immediately. He washed his hands by pouring water from a bucket into a basin outside the wide door. He dried them on a large towel that hung from a nail above the basin. He threw the used water into the dusty driveway.

"Come," he said after shaking hands. "I will take you to my cabin. We will talk there."

Arne followed. There was something about this stranger who knew Gunder that worried Arne. Sharing mutual acquaintance was usually a jovial matter. This was just the opposite.

"You are a relative of his?" Joe began.

"Yes, I am his brother-in-law. My wife Inga was his sister." Having to use English made this fact seem unfamiliar even to Arne.

"You don't know, do you, that he is dead?"

"No, no, I didn't know." Arne looked into the stranger's serious eyes. They clutched him, there was no escape.

"I'm sorry to be the one to tell you this."

A long moment passed. A locomotive blew its whistle. A train was approaching.

"How long ago was this?"

"About a month, early May."

"He worked in the mill, didn't he?"

"Yes. He came here after the big Washburn Mill explosion. Many came here looking for work then. Gunder was one of the eighteen needed to run the mill. He lived with me here in this cabin."

The locomotive was bringing empty boxcars. They joggled along because there was no weight in them.

Gunder, not just you and your helper doing cozy jobs, one farmer at a time. There were many of you all living in cabins just alike.

"But he was never well as long as I knew him. He had a terrible cough. It's no wonder, breathing all that dust. He kept losing weight, and try as we would, we couldn't get him to eat much. 'You can't work if you don't eat,' we told him."

The locomotive began switching. One never could understand the way cars were left and cars were taken. The brakemen would simply wave their huge gloved hands.

Gunder, you had good lungs. Remember how we ran those miles, you and I, behind that wagon when we first came to America? You hardly panted; I was almost dead. You had a wonderful appetite, Gunder. It doesn't sound like you at all.

"He never said much about where he came from, and we were never sure how well he could talk English. We had two Swedes here for a while, but they left to go logging. We saw a livelier side to Gunder while the Swedes were around. We thought Gunder would go with them. But no, he had always been a miller, he said. When they left he became pretty silent."

The locomotive seemed far down the track now, but the quickened spurts of power indicated that the engineer was still switching. He must hook the full boxcars.

Gunder, you were robbed of your own language. You didn't know that would happen, did you, when you made that fine speech to me as we left the old country.

"Did he ever mention his sister?" asked Arne.

"No."

"Did he leave anything?" Arne glanced around the cabin trying to picture it as Gunder's place. It made no sense at all.

"Yes, his watch. You should have his watch." The broad-shouldered man went to a chest drawer and took out a gold watch the size of a silver dollar attached to a coarse-linked gold chain. He handed it to Arne. "What money he had was used for his burial, I guess. The company took care of that, since no one claimed the body."

The locomotive was returning for the full boxcars. The last of the quickened throbbing echoed off into the wilderness.

Gunder, where is the mill you wanted on a fresh stream where no one yet had raised a mill? The company buried you—the big company. I should have been here, I know. But I didn't realize... didn't realize...

Joe saw the drooping head of Gunder's relative. He hoped he'd be man enough not to weep, but he wasn't sure. He looked at the clock on the wall.

"You could get back to the city with the train men. The 4:25 will be leaving shortly."

"That is a good suggestion," said Arne. He placed Gunder's watch in the inside pocket of his coat.

"I'll see to it." The cooper rose from his chair and moved toward the door.

The locomotive was standing on the main track, releasing steam sporadically. Outside the cabin Arne waited for his travel arrangements to be made.

Beyond the railroad tracks, on the south side of the mill, he saw the receding wilderness. Pigeons stayed around, but he wondered about the other birds. Among the white clouds of early summer was black smoke from the towering stacks.

Gunder, not enough good air for you here. No miller should suffocate, Gunder.

Chapter 14

President Garfield assassinated at the railroad station in Washington, D.C. "I am a Stalwart and Arthur is president now!" cried the assassin after he shot the president in the back. The president's condition is grave. He is fighting for his life.

This tragedy occurred July 2, 1881. The news, simply that the president had been shot, reached Wanamingo at a Fourth-of-July celebration in Bakken's grove, just east of town. A man on horseback from Zumbrota brought the news to the flat wagon, tacked with flag bunting, just as the minister from Minneola was beginning his patriotic speech. The people who had gathered for a good time left in silence; even the horses pulling the carriages had drooping heads.

Two days later, the people in the little village gathered around Julia, who could read and interpret an English newspaper article better than anyone. No, the president may still be living; the message at the grove had given the impression he was dead. After the reading each returned to his or her place of work, and life went on as usual.

Julia went to the meadow north of the house to make haycocks out of the stand of grass and clover Nils had cut with the scythe the day before. The yield was greater than she had expected, and there was a lot of hay to be lifted with her fork.

So another president lay dying. Julia wondered if Garfield could still be alive. The newspaper article hadn't given much hope—Lincoln had died the next morning. The assassin called himself a Stalwart. (Stalwarts were an Eastern faction of the Republican Party who had failed to nominate their candidate for the presidency in 1880.) There had been disappointment among some New York politicians over Garfield's cabinet appointments—this she had read about. Now assassination? Julia wanted to believe that government was carried on by gentlemen who respected each other and held the law of the land in high regard. But, of course, it would take just one disgruntled man with a gun to perform this deed.

Julia undid the ties of her bonnet and gave her face and neck the benefit of the breeze. It was a hot day. High clouds sailed in the sky, causing shadows to move one after the other across the meadow. Julia found herself waiting for the next shadow, a sweet relief from the sun.

She remembered the news of President Lincoln's assassination. No sooner had the people become jubilant that the terrible war was over than word of Lincoln's death fell like a pall. Less than a week apart. How the people wept, and she among them! She had wondered why God could permit such a thing to happen. And the war had been so cruel. Julia's two brothers had been soldiers in separate Wisconsin regiments. She remembered Henrik's severely wounded shoulder and how he had been sent home after initial treatment in one of the crowded, makeshift hospitals. Julia could still see the horror on her mother's face as the wound was laid bare for her attention. Henrik was never to regain strength in his left arm, and surely this wound shortened his life. Her other brother, who was almost ten years older than Henrik, had fared better. He returned with a sound body and continued to be a source of strength to the family. Julia suddenly realized she hadn't seen him in a long time, even if he was only as far away as Red Wing.

She put her fork aside and let herself drop into a haycock for a moment of rest. She wondered why she was always in such a hurry to complete each of her tasks, only to start another. No, she should stop sometimes; pausing could make a moment eternal, an island in the restlessness of temporal life. A little field mouse scampered in the stubble. This was his home. What a pleasant home! She let herself become conscious of the fragrance of clover and the warm, prickly hay beneath her. But she hadn't forgotten the president who had been shot. *Guide this country, O God, the shaky affairs of men. Teach us gratitude. Open our eyes that we may truly see that thou art good.*

The moment belonging to the eternal passed, and she was up with her fork again.

But the cause was just. Paul had said that. Slavery was inhuman and barbarous, civilized people enslaving the black race, how intolerable! But many said the Negroes were inferior human beings. Julia could not understand how they could be inferior since they had souls. She had read that they made good Christians, with genuine childlike faith. Children of God treated like work animals by other children of God? Never! When Julia thought of this she was exceedingly proud that her two brothers had fought in this war of liberation. But the tragedy of the bloodshed—so many strong young men gone! And the leader, too, had died—like the Savior, he was. So now another president had been shot. At this moment, was he still alive?

"Is that her way down there in the hayfield?" asked Arne, lifting his cap and scratching his head. "She'll never see us with that bonnet on. Women's bonnets are like harness blinders, Nils." Arne was home now, talking to his best friend.

"Henrik, Go and tell your mother Arne is back," Nils called to the boy, who was tinkering with the wheel of his little wagon. The boy took a second look at the man he thought was a stranger and then fled in the direction of the meadow.

"Nils, this is Melva Fosse and her little daughter, Ellen. I brought them with me from Minneapolis."

"Pleased to meet you," said Nils, extending his hand to the modest creature.

"Good day," she said with a smile, showing her beautiful teeth. "Ellen, smile at the man. He is Uncle Arne's friend."

Nils looked at Arne and back at the young woman. "A relative of yours? Gunder's . . . ?"

"No, no, I guess you might say I'm an adopted uncle." Arne had a mild twinkle in his eye and made quick little nods with his head.

Suddenly Arne noticed that Nils was looking toward the house. He turned. There stood Anna. Upon recognizing her old friend, she put out her arms and dashed forward as rapidly as the old brace would permit.

"She's on her feet, Nils! I hardly dared to hope . . ."

"Arne, see how well I am!" she called as she came. "You were to be the first one I would visit when I could walk outside, but you were gone!"

Arne felt a wave of sweetness sweep through him. He was at home and this was Anna.

"My dear Anna!" He put his two hands on her shoulders and looked into her face. "You're no longer locked in that . . . that mummy case. You can wear shoes again. How marvelous! I'll make you a pair!"

"Thank you, Arne, but don't make any rash promises. I never know when you are fooling."

Arne laughed louder than he had in a long time. "You know better than that. You know I mean it when I say I will make you a pair of shoes. And it's your birthday soon. See, I don't forget."

Anna suddenly became aware of the smiling woman who stood behind Arne. She was pretty. Who was she?

"Oh, you must meet Melva," said Arne, noticing the surprised look on Anna's face. "And her little girl, Ellen."

"How do you do?" Anna used English. Even if the woman smiled, she was still a stranger.

"I am glad to meet you, Anna. Arne has told me about you and all his good friends here." Her dialect was definitely from *Sogn*. She continued to smile.

Anna stared. She forgot to smile. What was this woman doing here? She was perhaps just a visitor and would soon leave. Suddenly she remembered her manners and with a wee little smile bowed slightly.

"Hello, Ellen," Anna responded with genuine warmth. "I have a little sister you would love to play with."

"What's that?" said Arne.

"Yes, I have a sister, you wait and see." said Anna, remembering that Arne knew nothng about Sarah. "Mari, Mari!" she called. Mari didn't know Arne was back. "Mari, come and bring Sarah!"

Mari, another of Arne's friends, came out of Anna's house, carrying the newly acquired sister.

"Sarah is the youngest of Lars Monson's children," Nils explained. "He lost his wife about a month ago. You remember Lars, the *Vossing* north of here."

"Yes, I do. So Julia has another to care for. Julia hasn't changed. I can see that already."

"No, she never hesitates when she is needed," replied Nils modestly.

Without stopping to wash or don a white apron, Julia hurried to the small knot of people standing in the road between the house and the blacksmith shop.

"It looks like I have come back just in time to help you with the haying," said Arne to Julia. "Or, am I too late?"

"Welcome home, Arne. We have all missed you." Julia shook his hand warmly.

"Thank you. I can't tell you how glad I am to be back!" The old hurt in his heart was completely gone, and he again stood in the presence of the best woman he knew.

"And this is Arne's friend, Melva Fosse. He brought her and her little daughter, Ellen, with him from Minneapolis," said Nils.

"I would like to help you with the hay," said Melva.

"Thank you," said Julia, quite surprised. She was certainly no city girl. "Come in. Perhaps we can have some afternoon coffee. Are you folks hungry?"

No one really answered. The men went their way toward the shop and the women into the house.

"Do you want to come with us, Ellen?" asked Anna. She and Mari had decided to go to Mari's yard to play.

The tiny girl all but disappeared in her mother's skirt. Melva lifted her up and held her.

"Not just yet, I guess," smiled the new woman. "Come back later, then she might."

"I looked for Gunder," Arne began as he and Nils stopped just short of entering the shop. "I searched for weeks, it seemed. I looked for him among the millhands at St. Anthony Falls. When I found out he wasn't there, I went to Minnetonka Mills on the Minnehaha

Creek. There I learned from the man who shared a cabin with Gunder that he had died."

"Gunder is dead, then?"

"Yes, that is what I found out. How I wish I could have found him earlier. It is lonesome to think he should go without any of his family around."

Nils received this news with his eyes lowered to the ground. After a pause, he lifted them and looked at Arne.

"How was it? Was he sick a long time?"

"They said he died of a lung disease. He coughed a lot. Dust. You can't imagine how big those mills are, Nils. How can anyone who works in such a place get away from dust? It killed him, Nils."

"It's very sad to hear that," said Nils, lowering his eyes again.

"Everything becomes so enormously big in this country, Nils. There can't be just a mill on a stream. It grows into an entire town. Things are put out by the hundreds, whether it be barrels, harnesses, shoes, or carriages. Railroad trains carry enormous loads, and crews of men do nothing else all day but load freight. Where is it all going? Where will it all end? The farmers are no different, adding as many acres as possible for wheat fields." Arne drew closer to his listening friend, looking at him with eyes larger than Nils remembered them.

"I'm sure what you say is true, Arne. Nothing hinders growth here. In the old country there was always a lack of something—never enough land." Nils thought he understood what Arne was saying.

"But for people like Gunder who do the work—see what happens to them?" Arne turned away for a moment, then returned. "It was a shameful death, in this virgin country, to breathe dust until you die."

Nils sympathized with Arne, but did not quite share his bitterness.

"Maybe he would have been smarter to stay right here the way you and I have done."

"You are right there, my friend," said Arne with a tone of finality. "The city is not a good place for our people; I know that now."

"You're not the first to say that. I agree with you."

"For example, Melva Fosse. She was living in a rooming house alone. No family. How long do you think she would have stayed the decent girl she is if she hadn't been given the opportunity to return to the country?" Arne was trying to convey to Nils what he had learned from Bernt.

"You brought her out of the city? She belongs to no one?"

"No one. She had left her husband that beat her. She didn't dare go home to her own family, either, because they believed she belonged with her husband."

Arne looked at Nils for approval but saw only surprise.

"You found yourself a housekeeper, is that it?"

Arne was embarrassed. He needed to justify himself. He told the whole story from beginning to end.

"She needs good womenfolk. What better place than next door to Julia?"

Nils nodded and smiled a little. Arne tried again.

"Nils, I don't crave a woman in my bed, if that could be what you are thinking."

"Naw," said Nils. He thought it inappropriate to laugh, knowing that what had just been said took courage for a man like Arne. "You have a kind heart, my friend, and she is very fortunate. Fortunate for her child, too, I would say."

Several days after Arne's return, Mari and Anna were sitting on the schoolhouse steps. It was a place they used to share secrets away from their parents and other listening adults. In July school was not in session.

"I don't like her very much," said Anna, "But Ellen is a dear little girl. I've nothing against her."

"Melva? You don't like her?" said Mari quite surprised. "She's pretty and she even turned the rope for us one day when we were playing in the yard. She's nice."

"I don't mean she isn't nice," returned Anna. "She just doesn't belong here, that's all. I thought she was just a visitor who would go away after awhile."

"Anna, just think about all she does. She helped your mother with the hay and even thought it was fun. And the way she cleaned Arne's house. Just think how glad that made him." Mari was sitting with her chin in her hands and her elbows on her knees, pausing briefly as she listed virtues. "And—don't forget she is minding Sarah along with Ellen right now so we can run and play."

"I know. I guess I should be ashamed of myself, but it is the way I feel and I can't help it."

"Maybe you are wishing you could do more things? You'd like to cock hay yourself, wouldn't you? Maybe that is why you don't like Melva?"

"How can you say such a thing! You're my best friend, Mari. How can you think of saying anything as mean as that!" Anna stamped her feet awkwardly from her sitting position on the steps.

"All right, I'm sorry if I hurt you. I was only trying to understand why you don't like Melva."

"It's impossible to like everyone in this whole wide world," Anna continued, trying hard to reconcile her feelings. "I don't hate Melva. I might even like her a little bit."

"Let's not worry about it then," said Mari, who jumped off the bottom step, prepared to move on.

"Do you think the president is still alive?" said Anna, delaying. It took her longer to get on her feet.

"I hope so. I prayed for him, did you?"

"Of course."

Since Julia planned to spend the entire afternoon attacking weeds in the garden, Anna was left with the responsibility of giving her father and whoever else might be around afternoon coffee. Sarah was still with Ellen and Melva. Mari had gone home. It was Papa and Arne as usual.

"So you're really going to put together a threshing rig," said Arne, looking like himself again with his blue shirt open at the collar.

"Yes, that is what I am planning," said Nils with his country's optimism.

"Those steam engines cost money," Arne said, pouring the hot coffee into the saucer.

"Of course I'll have to find someone to go in with me on it. Might it be you?" Nils laughed.

"Naw, not me. I'm quite content with shoemaking."

After a moment Arne looked around for Anna, who had been pouring their coffee. She had taken a molasses cookie off the plate and withdrawn to the window. "She must come over after we have finished our coffee."

"I have an idea what you are up to, Arne," said Nils. "You haven't much time this year. You've been fooling around taking trips. But I think you'll make it."

Upon hearing this, Anna turned around quickly. She wanted to fly next door immediately. The coffee was still hot. That's right, drink it out of saucers.

Arne's shop smelled the same as it always had, although Anna hadn't been there for goodness knows how long. She watched Arne reach for his apron.

"Are you going to marry her?" She spoke while his back was turned.

The words rattled the whole room, and he was barely able to tie on his apron.

"No," he managed to say. "Whoever gave you that idea?"

"No one. I just wondered why you brought her, that's all." Anna kept her eyes on the floor. She knew what his eyes would be like—sharp and black—and she didn't want to see them.

"She's my housekeeper and a very good one. You know how bad things get for me. Don't you think I need a housekeeper?" Arne looked at this child with her drooping head and her almost-too-straight body. Was she growing up and becoming difficult like all women?

"Anna, look at me. I had a wife once, and I loved her very much, as you must know. I'm sure I'll never love anyone but Inga. Don't you know that?"

Anna believed him. He was more earnest than she had ever seen him, and it frightened her a bit. She wondered if she had hurt him. But she had to know.

"Come now, let's not talk foolishness," Arne continued, moving busily around the room, searching for some way to get rid of misgivings. "Your legs won't dangle now, so I won't have to use the footstool."

"You might," laughed Anna. "I sit pretty straight and far back in a chair. And I'm not really very tall yet, am I, Arne?"

"I'll bet those feet have grown, though."

"I have big feet like my mother."

Anna backed awkwardly this time into Arne's special chair. Arne remembered when she had gone knees first.

"How could you leave on a journey without your hammer, and your belt of strength?" Anna grabbed Arne's apron and gave it a twist. She grinned, hoping he would recognize the clue to the fun they always had together.

"It was a mistake, I'll have to admit that," said Arne. "I missed my belt more than I did my hammer, though. It wasn't easy. One feels strange when he's not wearing what he is used to wearing. I was weak."

"Did you meet *Grid*, then?"

"*Grid at Geirrodsgard?* She who lent Thor her belt of strength and her iron gloves?" Arne watched Anna's growing delight. "Oh, yes, she was there all right. There is always some one on a journey that can help you out."

"Did you see *Vidar?*"

"No." Arne paused, wondering what to make of this.

Suddenly he quit measuring and pulled a big box from under the workbench. "But see. You know, don't you, how all these years I have been saving scraps of leather from toes and heels?" He put his hand into the leather shavings and brought them up in handfuls, letting them fall again into the box.

"Vidar had thick soles." Anna quickly remembered the story. "So saving toe and heel scraps even here in America brought you luck?"

"It must have, otherwise how could I go on a far journey without my hammer?" Arne shoved the box back and returned to measuring Anna's feet for the birthday shoes.

"Did you see *Skidbladner, Frey's* ship? I heard you were near the Mississippi River." Anna was not about to stop the fantasy.

"Well, it's hard to say," Arne mused. "If dwarfs—that is *Ivald's* sons—had made the sailing vessels I saw, they wouldn't have put those ugly smokestacks on them. You know, Anna, on my journey I saw so many smokestacks. The train engines had them, the mills had them, the boats had them—and your father is going to have one on his threshing rig!"

"If the dwarfs didn't make them, who did?"

"That, I'll admit I don't know. But one thing I do know: there are whistles that go with the smokestacks. They might have been forged by dwarfs. I'm not sure. But they might very well do such a thing. The steamboat has a whistle and so does the locomotive."

"And Papa's threshing rig?"

"I believe so. We'll have to wait and see."

Arne wrote the last figure on his pad and put his hand out to his young friend.

"Old Arne will be busy now for a few days," he said as he walked her to the door.

"Arne?"

"Yes?"

"Do you think the president will live?"

"It's hard telling."

PART TWO (1885-1906)

WHEAT FIELDS

Chapter 1

Instead of walking on the road, Anna decided to cut through the pasture along a cowpath. She was returning home, having brought coffee and sandwiches to her father and his crew, who were building a new bridge across the Zumbro River.

Before too many weeks the threshing season would begin, and getting back and forth across the river with his heavy rig would become an urgent matter for Nils. The long beams had become more porous and rotten each year in the three seasons he had been moving his rig from place to place, and now he couldn't risk another crossing without major bridge repairs. He couldn't imagine horses uprooting a steam engine should it become intrenched in the riverbed. Now steel beams prepared in his own blacksmith shop were being hauled to the site to be set with cement into sturdy rock walls.

Bringing afternoon coffee to the men pleased Anna since it meant a chance to drop her knitting, a miserable task especially on sunny summer afternoons. Because the coffee in the tin pail would get cold very quickly, she needed to hurry to the men, but on her way home she could take her time. The cowpath was shadier than the road, and there were familiar stopping places.

She lingered at a thorn-apple tree. The marble-sized fruit was already red, in fact, it was red even out of blossom. Now the apples were hard and bitter, but by fall they would be mealy and tart, leaving a tingle on the tongue. They were no earthly good, her mother had said, no one she knew ever picked them. Suspecting it to be bitter, she sampled one anyway. The taste was bad; she should have known better. A squirrel scampered into an oak tree. "The acorns are still green, no treat for you today either," she retaliated.

Anna left the thorn-apple tree and set her lunch basket and tin pail down on a grassy knoll where several round, white stones were pushing out of the green sod two to three feet apart. Every time she passed this way she would take a rest on the biggest one. Sitting on the hard surface now, her knees together and her feet spread apart, she soon grew lost in the movement of the billowy cumulus clouds. She fancied a sheep trying to leap up higher, and a little chick straying from the brood. But wasn't the whole cloud bank a bed for the white, full-bearded giant who lay asleep under a feather tick? Soon he began to tear apart, held together only by a mist that thinned slowly until it was as fine as a spider's web.

There was a time when she fancied these as characters in Arne's tales. But these days she avoided bringing those stories to mind. It seemed a bit childish now to rush in on Arne as she once had. Sarah could do that. Furthermore, Anna didn't think he was telling those stories anymore. She supposed there was something not quite right about them after all, even if she hadn't figured out just what. But she did know that remembering her delight in them made her blush with a strange sense of shame.

She threw off her bonnet. She let the cool breeze blow through the curls at her temples. She wore a bonnet oftener now that she was a lady. At fourteen she was seen by others as a lady even if she seldom felt like one. Being a lady meant having finished the eighth grade, having been confirmed at church, and having become full-breasted and as tall as one was meant to be. Indeed a fourteen-year-old could pass for an eighteen-year-old, and that could mean marriage, even.

With the breeze through her hair she watched the sleeping giant sever completely. Enough for cloud watching, she went into her usual game of hopscotch. She got on her feet and jumped from the big stone to the next and to the next until she had touched all eight without missing. Then she repeated the routine, leaving out one each time until she was back on the big stone. Now it was hers. She had won the big stone many times by this method.

When she had won it, it was time to go on up the cowpath. As she went for her things, she was distracted by a cluster of yellow snapdragons. She hadn't seen them yet this year. She rather liked their odor, not sweet-smelling like roses, but rather like the smell of cookie spices. When she was six or seven she might have picked a fistful, but she decided against it now, ladies didn't carry weeds in their aprons, besides, the wagon bringing supplies to the men at the bridge was passing on the road.

Had she been seen playing hopscotch on the stones? She seized her bonnet and enclosed her head. "That Kristian girl acts like a child, doesn't she?" Anna conjured up make-believe gossip about herself until she felt a wave of something she was beginning to understand as embarrassment. It was different from childish shyness; it could be there even if one were all alone.

Back on the path after the wagon was safely out of sight, she pushed off her bonnet again and let it hang down her back. Following the cowpath as it made a slant up a hill, she stopped and looked down, wondering where the cows might be. There were four of them now. Bessie was the grandmother of the tiny herd and also the lead cow that brought the others behind her, one after the other, up the path to the barn. Anna was often sent by her mother to bring the cows home, and she would usually find them in the far end of the pasture, clustered in the shade. She guessed her mother still thought cows were women's work so Henrik was never sent, and she was glad of it. It was a time she could disappear down this hill alone, playing her games and dreaming her dreams.

But her mother would never let her do the milking. She swung the tin pail fiercely as she continued her tramp along the hillside. Anna didn't really understand why her mother wouldn't let her. Maybe it was the result of the time she wore her brace, or when she gradually quit wearing it. Did she think the cow would kick and she would land on her spine? "You're delicate, Anna, let your mother do the milking." Delicate, delicate, how she resented that word! It reminded her of Aunt Sophie. She didn't know why, but she no longer cared to be like Aunt Sophie. She never wore the sapphire ring anymore. It remained set in the satin-lined plush box under all her clothes in the bottom drawer of the dresser upstairs. She kept seeing that sapphire ring on the finger of the dead girl in the picture in Aunt Sophie's parlor—Aunt Sophie's dead sister. In fact, the older Anna got the more intense the memory of the portrait on the parlor easel became. In a far corner of her mind was buried a dread—of what? Death, perhaps? She refused to drag it out and articulate it. No, it was too painful.

Looking behind her once more, she saw the cows, far down on a sunny green knoll. They knew it was not time to go home yet. Three of them were lying down chewing their cud and the fourth one, just standing like a statue. Her next few paces brought her to the top of the hill and within sight of her house.

Among the men in Nils' crew was Peder Olson, a newcomer, who had arrived last year in time for threshing. He was the twenty-two-year-old son of Nils' nearest neighbor in the old country, a neighbor who had been very interested in coming to America with Nils but had decided against it, thinking himself too old. But here was his son! Nils was delighted. And there wasn't a thing this young man couldn't do. He was one-hundred percent reliable. That was why Nils had made him fireman for his steam engine, for Peder instinctively knew how to watch that gauge. There needed to be enough heat to keep the steam power up so the grain separator wouldn't clog, but not so much that the operation would be in danger. Nothing was more frightening to steam threshers than the thought of an explosion. Also there was the danger of fires set by sparks from the firebox dropping into the dry straw and stubble. Now Peder could be entrusted to watch both. And he was so much like his father—to Nils he was unmistakably familiar. Julia was just as pleased with Peder as Nils. He had occupied the Kristians' small guest room for almost a year now. He was a clean young man. He never drank, chewed tobacco, or used bad language—a good example for Henrik, who now was ten.

The threshing always began with Ole Bakken's crop, the closest to home. The steam engine and the separator had stood idle for a long time exposed to weather changes in a lean-to shed next to the blacksmith shop. With luck the machinery would run smoothly at once, but, then again, it could balk in defiance and need any number of unforeseen repairs. Who could know how the separator would act when it received the first bundles of the season? It was good that it was stored near the blacksmith shop; that way Nils was ready for the challenge without particular anxiety.

No one could be happier that threshing was beginning close to home than Henrik and his pal, Lars Mundahl. When the rig would move to outlying farms, his father would be gone, Peder would be gone, and the whole crew for weeks. But it took several days at Bakkens, threshing the grain out of the shocks brought in on wagons from the field, and he and Lars could be right in the middle of it. They anticipated the drivers giving them permission to take the reins when the empty wagons returned to the field, and riding back to the separator again on the bulging-high loads. And since Hans Mentvedt was the driver of the grain wagon, which was equally as much fun, Henrik was sure his old friend would willingly accept them, and even let them hold sacks.

Already he could hear the warning: "Don't go near that belt!" That belt was the twisted figure eight that stretched unbelievably far between the engine and the separator and moved rapidly over the big wheels that spun so fast their spokes were a whirling blur. They would respect that warning, or better, they would respect the danger. They needn't be told.

"We'll take Henrik with us tomorrow when we fire up the engine," said Nils at the supper table the second evening of the season. "So if he's gone when you get up, you'll know where he is."

"Very well," said Julia. "But come back here for breakfast. Clara need not be bothered then. She'll have enough with the dinner and supper, not to mention morning and afternoon coffee."

"Clara's a good cook," said Nils. "That's more than we can say about some of the women on our run."

"Don't you wish you could go?" Henrik shot an arrow in Anna's direction.

"Don't act so smart, little brother. I might be there, too, helping Clara Bakken." Anna looked over at Peder who she was sure would smile in approval.

Henrik felt no humiliation. He knew Anna would much prefer to catch rides, the way he and Lars would do, than to pour coffee and swish the flies off the sandwiches. Funny how grown-up she tries to act. That's girls for you.

Before it was light the next morning, Nils woke his son from a deep sleep.

"Come, we must go," he said. "Peder is up already."

Henrik slapped the top of his head and jumped up. He found his clothes in the dark, wiggled into his overall and snapped the suspenders. He moved carefully until he found the stairway, then, half slid until he reached the bottom step where his shoes were waiting. He slipped them on and hurried outside without tying the laces. Once outside, he bent down and tied them in front of the two men who were waiting for him.

As the three of them headed toward the stubbled field, a number of stars were still in the sky, but an expectation of dawn was caught in every hedge, post and gate. One scarcely knew where the light was merging from since there was no sign of the sun except for a faint streak in the east above a band of clouds. Nils was beginning to anticipate those dark, chilly mornings in late autumn when the fireman would carry a lantern to the rig. Then the large, cone-shaped grain stacks would loom in the field together with the machinery. Today there were no stacks; bundles would be fed into the separator from wagons loaded in the field.

Henrik kept astride the two men as they sloshed through the heavy dew. Their pants legs were soaking wet, but they could feel nothing through their greased work shoes. Henrik heard a rooster crow.

The engine had cooled overnight and could be touched safely anywhere. Peering into the huge cavity of the firebox, Henrik saw a tiny spark from yesterday's fire flicker out. Peder filled the dark hole with straw and lay a match to it. He pampered the little flame by blowing, then clanked the iron door shut. Soon smoke and sparks flowed from the stack into the morning air. Henrik watched the gauge. It would take a while for the needle to wiggle, but the straw was burning all right. Henrik heard the crackling flames drawing a draft, and soon there would be gurgles of steam.

Nils walked toward the separator, running his hand along the huge belt as he went. Anxious to explore, Henrik jumped down and let Peder watch the gauge. It had a ways to go before they would go home for breakfast.

First Henrik checked the tank wagon, which looked like a large barrel on its side. Plenty of water had been brought from the river to start off the morning. He climbed onto the seat and pretended he was on his way to replenish the water supply. A strange mist was rising out of the river bed as he looked down the trail to the Zumbro. Lars' big brother Martin would be the water driver this year, and Henrik wondered if he would let Lars and him ride along. He hoped so, but brothers could be stubborn.

"Come, Henrik," Nils called from the separator. He was carrying the grease bucket as usual.

Henrik was at his father's side in an instant. He listened intently to his father's instructions while staring at the shiny green grease. He always had an urge to taste the stuff, but it didn't smell good.

He had often stuck his finger in the bucket and wiped it off on his overall, but he wouldn't do that now.

"Under that wheel is a cup that needs grease. Take this stick and fill it. You can crawl under and reach it better than I can."

The boy eagerly got down on his hands and knees in the sharp stubble. He was taking orders from the boss of the rig just like all the other men were soon to do.

When these early morning tasks were done, the two men and the boy followed the dewy trail they had made through the stubble home for breakfast. As Henrik thought about sitting down at the table, he remembered the look Peder gave Anna, the evening before, at supper when he was supposed to have been humiliated.

"You like my sister, don't you?" he said suddenly to Peder at his side.

Peder looked back for Nils who was a safe number of paces behind. "Why yes, shouldn't I?"

"Sure, but she's no lady if you think she is. She's a kid like me."

"You don't say. Maybe she's growing up and you don't know it."

"Naw." Henrik knew the real Anna. That wouldn't change.

In planning his crew this year, Nils had hired an extra man, a "spike pitcher", who would stay in the field and give help to the wagon drivers as they filled their racks with bundles. If he proved a good worker, he would be used as a "stack pitcher" later in the run. This new member of the crew was a Red Wing Seminary student whose hands were a little too soft, Nils thought, but they would toughen in painful stages. Julia was glad that Nils had a job for this worthy young man, and she took great interest in conversing with him. His name was Sivert Lunde.

Henrik and Lars had ridden out with the first wagons of the day and were watching the men tossing bundles high into the wagon racks, their three-pronged pitchforks being polished more brightly bundle after bundle. The men worked fast—they didn't have time to talk much—and Henrik and Lars knew better than to bother them. The boys felt important, however, when they were permitted to go in front of the horses and guide them forward as the pitchers moved from shock to shock.

Henrik was having trouble keeping his straw hat on in the wind, so he decided not to ride in on the loaded wagon, but instead to talk to Sivert, who would be resting a few minutes before the next wagon arrived.

"It's windy," began Sivert, sensing Henrik's difficulty. He stuck his fork in the ground and slowly took off his right glove.

"I guess my hat's too big," said Henrik, glad that the new spike pitcher had started the talking. He swung the new straw hat in his hand as he approached Sivert.

"Don't worry. Maybe the band can be tightened a bit. Give it here." Sivert took the hat and looked it over. "I'll bet your mother could tighten this a little by undoing it here and shortening the band a bit."

Henrik took back the hat without replying. The suggestion was no remedy for now.

"Your mother tells me you read a lot," Sivert began again. "She says you folks are subscribing to an English newspaper because you are interested in what's going on in the world. Is that right?"

"It's true," Henrik said matter-of-factly, feeling a bit shy, becoming the subject of conversation. "I guess I read English a little better than Norwegian. I'm going to be in fifth grade when school starts this fall."

"You must be a smart boy."

"Oh, I don't know. Lars is smarter than me in some ways, though he doesn't care to read like me."

Henrik waited while Sivert examined his sore hand.

"Do you like going to school in Red Wing?" Henrik had seen pictures of monks huddled over large open books, but he wasn't sure Sivert was exactly like that.

"I do, certainly." Sivert spoke with renewed interest upon this question. "Let me tell you how I happened to become a student for the holy ministry."

Henrik, chewing on a wisp of wheat, was more than ready to listen.

"I was called. I got a call from God." He let the words sink in for a moment to create the right mood. Henrik continued chewing. "I was sitting in church one Sunday morning in my home congregation, where I was confirmed. On the altar of that church is a white statue of Jesus looking down into the world and reaching out his hands."

Henrik nodded. He had seen this same statue in his own church.

"I was sitting there and the people were singing *Hvor Salig er den Lille Flok.* When we came to the second verse: *Min Jesus er jeg en af dem? Vil du meg kalde din?* The statue seemed alive. The Lord spoke to me. He said, 'If you love me, you will go and preach wherever I send you.' The Lord was speaking to my heart." The seminary student saw his young audience of one, wide-eyed in surprise. He was inspired to continue. "The Savior's eyes were like those that looked at Peter as he was coming out of Pilate's hall. What could I say but, 'Yes, Lord.' I didn't want to grieve His Holy spirit. For that, there is no forgiveness, you know."

Henrik felt uncomfortable. His eyes were no longer on Sivert. He fingered his hat round and round, keeping his eyes on the round. Suddenly he felt Sivert's hand on his shoulder.

"Don't be one to grieve the Holy Spirit, young man." There was a menacing warning in the voice of the man who towered over Henrik.

There was no time for questions. The wagons were coming. Henrik heard them bouncing along without looking up, and soon he was relieved of the weight on his shoulder.

"Whoa!" shouted the driver as he pulled alongside Sivert and Henrik.

Henrik watched the glove being drawn quickly over the hand that had touched him, and the fork being jerked out of the ground. Henrik's anxious glance toward the wagon told him Lars was not with this rack. He was glad. He wanted some moments to be alone.

He started toward the field road where two more wagons would be coming soon. As he trudged, he felt the roots of his hair swelling and the palms of his hands prickling. That was an icy stone in his chest. He sighed many times hoping it would go away.

Grieve the Holy Spirit—no forgiveness for that—the statue had talked. Henrik was beginning to identify with the story, and as he did so his tongue became wooden and dry.

In the upstairs bedroom in Henrik's house was a picture by a Dutch painter named Rembrandt of Jesus being taken from the cross. It had hung there as long as Henrik could remember. He had spent hours looking at this picture and knew all the melancholy details. He felt sorry for the limp Jesus who had left blood stains from his hands and feet on the places where he had been nailed on the rough boards. Jesus had been killed. He was dead. The people were taking Him in a white sheet and would soon carry Him away to a grave. There were times he had stared at this picture until he thought Jesus' eyes were opening. His child heart had overflowed with pity. His mother had told him the story. She said He was the Savior of the world, that He could have saved Himself and even brought down a host of angels to rescue Him, but he didn't. He wanted to be the Savior of the world. He died for all of us, she said, even for him, Henrik, so we might be forgiven and go to heaven when we die. That the crucified one could have spared Himself and didn't, touched Henrik even more. He wanted to tell him, "Please save yourself, don't suffer so." But he knew this wasn't right. We were supposed to watch Him suffer and say, "Thank you, Jesus, for saving us." Anna had told him she said thank you to Him every day, and he should, too.

Had those Jesus eyes, which he had imagined opening, seen him? Had He said something, too, that he had not heard? He stumbled but caught himself, as his foot sank in a gopher hole hidden by the stubble. Sivert had heard the statue speak, hadn't he? No, if he were to be entirely honest, he knew that statues didn't talk and that the picture only caused him to imagine. Imagination was not for real. Even he, a boy of ten, knew that. If this was so, then Sivert was just telling what he imagined. But he believed what he imagined. He was becoming a minister because he didn't want to grieve the Holy Spirit!

Grieve the Holy Spirit—no forgiveness. This thunderbolt stunned the boy. No forgiveness meant ultimate darkness and death. Henrik couldn't articulate what that was; he trembled only, with a fright that captured his whole being. He hadn't heard of "no forgiveness" before, but he had sensed a deep seriousness in the voices of religious people who talked about being saved as if it were, after all, uncertain. And now he was caught unaware in this awful uncertainty.

A wagon with Lars holding the reins was almost upon him.

"Where are you going?" called his friend, surprised to see him on the road toward home.

"Just waiting for you," he managed to shout as he jumped onto the back of the moving wagon, grabbing hold of the boards of the rack. He climbed in, ran the length of the wagon, and stood beside his friend. He felt better now. Poof! Maybe he should be like these farmers, or like his papa who had no worries except real ones, like getting the steam engine to run and the separator working right.

"You drive awhile. I'll climb up and sit on the rack at the back." Lars waited until Henrik had forced his hat firmly on his head.

The pitchforks began to move, and the bundles were filling the four corners of the rack. There was a way to build a load, the boys had been told. Henrik fastened the reins and dropped to the ground as he was signaled to guide the team forward. He wondered if horses were aware that the load was getting heavier. To Henrik they were patient creatures, worthy of admiration and respect. He patted a velvet nose and felt the warm breath on his fingers. Before long he looked and saw to his surprise that the load was ready to go.

"Come, kid, if you want to ride back with me," called Oscar Hammar, who was already in his load, untying the reins and turning the wagon around.

Henrik caught hold and clawed his way to the top. The wagon joggled slowly across the uneven field. Soon they would get onto the well-worn field road where they could move somewhat faster.

Henrik flopped into the center of the load, kicking his feet in, to keep his balance. Poof! He was a farmer today. He was still shrugging away, the ugly feeling diminishing. His sighs drew in their wake fresh surprises of wheat flavor and odors he could attribute only to the obedient horses and the axle grease in the hubs of the wagon wheels. A surge of good feeling finally returned. Things were all right, after all.

The horses slowed as the reins guided them close to the separator for unloading. Henrik was proud of them for not being frightened by the hum of the machinery.

Oscar was now standing in his load with his pitchfork ready to drop bundles into the feeder. Henrik would have to get out of the way.

There went his hat! Suddenly all the men were laughing as he began looking around for it. Then he saw the last of the red band disappearing into the teeth of the separator.

Poof! So now he wouldn't have to carry it anymore. If these men laughed, Papa would, and Peder would. And he would have something funny to tell Lars who was riding on the load just behind him.

Chapter 2

The wedding day was set. Melva Fosse was going to marry Sigurd Veblen, the oldest son of Rolf Veblen, the tailor who also owned a general store. As his tailoring business had reached full-time, Rolf Veblen left the management of the store to his two grown sons, Sigurd and Albin. Sigurd had built a new house just east of town for himself and his bride.

Melva, since the day she arrived in Wanamingo, had looked after the needs of Arne, her benefactor. The shoemaker's house was the cleanest in town and his oven warm with fresh baking. Melva's daughter, Ellen, surrounded by the security of the home Arne provided, had blossomed to the age of five.

Prompted by Julia's advice and reinforcement, Melva had again established contact with her parents. From them she learned that her drinking and often violent husband had been killed in a runaway on the way home from town. The wagon battered into a fence post; the horses broke loose, and the man was thrown into a ditch, hitting his head on a rock. Melva was filled with remorse; certainly her leaving him hadn't improved his condition, but then she had left for the sake of her child and herself, hadn't she? She drew strength from Julia. Arne was right; Melva needed womenfolk like Julia.

And now, of course, she was free to marry. She was quick to recognize the interest the young store proprietor showed in her every time she came to buy groceries. He sought her out the minute she entered and let Albin wait on others. He winked at her as her coffee was being ground and watched with fascination as she tasted the pickled herring he offered her from his kegs. He had never known anyone with a smile like hers, honest and clean, and those straight, white teeth.

Almost everyone in the town was interested in the romance between these two handsome people. He would certainly be a good provider and she a good wife. She was an excellent housekeeper; she had proved that. The people watched with interest the new house coming up, and many of them helped in the building of it. Gossip? Yes, there had been some curiosity about Melva, what her past had been and why she so readily chose to live in the cobbler's house. But her openness quelled all rumors. She delighted the community with her choppy *Sogn* accent, and she chatted freely with whoever it might be. They shared her grief regarding her first marriage and her husband's tragic death, because she willingly talked about it with a pervasive innocence. And Julia was her stanch supporter.

Arne's life had gone as usual, but greatly eased by having help. Ellen and Sarah were a source of delight, even as Anna had been, but he still cast longing eyes in Anna's direction. No one could quite replace her, and now she had grown out of his reach. He accepted Melva's plans to marry as any devoted father would have, and he was glad she was not moving away. Yes, she would still clean his house and bring him fresh bread every week although he said that would be too much to expect.

The marriage would take place this coming Sunday after the regular worship service at the church north of town. This church suited Melva, as it seemed to be Arne's preference—his Inga was buried there—although he never attended. Melva attended regularly, however, with her little girl at her side. Marriages among members of this church usually took place after the regular service because the minister was not a resident. He came all the way from Rochester, and only one Sunday a month.

On the day before this important event, Anna and Mari were peeling apples just outside the kitchen door of the Kristian house. Julia had decided to make *Eple Grøt* (Apple Pudding) for the dinner that would follow Melva's wedding since there was such an abundance of apples this year, and it would be a very practical dessert to make for a large crowd. The guests would include everyone, those who attended the ceremony and those who didn't. No one would be excluded. Julia had two peelers and could engage others if she needed them. And she had plenty of sour cream, which would be thickened with flour to pour over the sugared and spiced apples. And she made provisions for sweet cream, too, which would be whipped for topping when the time came.

"I watched Melva peeling apples one day," chatted Mari to Anna as the paring knives were dropping spiral lengths, of red skin. "And do you know what she told me? If you take the peeling of a whole apple and swing it around your head three times and let it drop on the floor it will form the first initial of the man you are going to marry. And she proved it—really she did! She threw the peeling right there. And can you imagine it? The peeling formed a perfect S."

"That is a good trick," admitted Anna as she plumped the handle of her knife against the pan in her lap. "Do you think it always works?"

"It did for Melva, didn't it? S stands for Sigurd." Mari smiled to herself and looked absently into the air. "Why don't you try it," she burst out.

"Me? I don't dare. It might not turn out to be Martin. You know how I feel about him," said Anna glumly.

"I know. Even if he is my brother I think he is getting mean. He treats us both like we're silly girls. He has no right." Mari was peeling vigorously again.

Anna began on another apple. She worked slowly and carefully. She would try at least to have the peeling of the whole apple intact.

"Go ahead, Anna. Whoever you marry will be nicer than Martin if it doesn't turn out to be an M."

"One, two, three!"

The peeling plopped on the ground and the girls dropped their knives and pans and rushed to it. No, it didn't look like an M, no matter what direction one tried to look at it.

Julia was in the kitchen making doughnuts. The hot fat received the freshly-shaped dough with thirst. They bubbled and sizzled. The oven was hot enough for pans of *Eple Grøt,* and the stove top was kept free of spatter, since *lefse* would be made shortly, when Petra Haroldson arrived to assist. Making doughnuts was a hot job for this day in late summer, but doughnuts were the best pastry Julia could think of to go with afternoon coffee, which would be served to the departing guests before they went home to their chores. Then, too, she could send a pan of doughnuts over to Clara Bakken to help feed the threshers.

But Julia's thoughts were not on wedding preparations or food for threshers at the moment as she flipped the doughnuts. They were on Henrik. He was becoming a serious boy. He read a great deal and occasionally asked her profound questions she never suspected he was capable of asking. Maybe he will want further education, a profession, perhaps. Red Wing Seminary? The Ministry? She hardly dared get her hopes up for that. She had been no Hannah of the Old Testament praying for a son that she might give him to the Lord. Could it be that he had an aptitude in this direction after all? But then there was the complicated matter of a "call from God." She must leave this matter in His hands. Now Sivert evidently had a sense of "Call"; he seemed very dedicated. Julia found talking to Sivert stimulating. Although there was an immaturity about him, he was interested in his studies and could answer many of Julia's questions. Her constant reading opened many avenues of curiosity and left in their wake gaps she could fill only by talking to seminary students, or with such students as Nils would hire. But Julia also felt sorry for Sivert. She wondered how this young man would fare among the threshers who were indeed strong and good but whose language could be rough and whose manners crude.

Julia lifted the last doughnut from the hot lard and let it drip for a moment from the fork. Anna was just as avid a reader as Henrik, Julia recognized. She had read all the books the little village school could afford. Strange that both her children should be like her in that respect.

Doughnuts filled the big bread pan to the brim. Julia washed the mixing bowl with water from the tea kettle and wiped it swiftly, making it ready for the *lefse* dough. She carried out the kettle of hot fat and swished the stove top with a wad of newspaper to ready it for the sheets of rolled-out *lefse*. She shoved another oak stick into the stove. She knew just how much wood it would take to maintain the right heat for this delicate operation.

At this moment, she noticed Anna and Mari chatting over their peeling. Perhaps they were almost finished? No, they fool around too much to be done yet. Yes, Anna. She should really be given music lessons. Everyone agreed she had a beautiful singing voice. It might not be impossible to get a reed organ now that Nils' threshing was bringing in more money. After all, if the Veblens could give lessons to Agnes and Josie, why not the Kristians to Anna? Mattie Skaar would appreciate more pupils in Wanamingo, too, since she came all the way from Zumbrota. Besides, Anna wasn't strong, not suited for heavy peasant work, and she had talent. There was no question about that. Perhaps they should think about sending her to a ladies' seminary. And she must find a good husband, too, someone who would take good care of her. But it was a bit early to worry about that.

She went to the door to check on the apple peelers. She caught the peeling-over-the-head game and chuckled to herself. See, they are thinking about beaus. Never too early, the silly girls. There were a few unpeeled apples left; she would have to give them more time.

"Here are the boiled potatoes," said Petra, coming in the front door and putting her kettle on the table beside the mixing bowl. "I brought some flour. Have you seen the bride today? I suppose she is putting the finishing touches on her dress. Won't she be a beautiful bride?"

"She's a good girl," said Julia. "That's better than being pretty."

"Yes, of course." Petra wasn't surprised Julia would see it that way.

Julia felt of the kettle. "They're nice and cold. Who helped you whip them? They look so nice and smooth."

"I'm pretty strong, don't forget."

Enough flour and lard was added to the whipped potatoes to make the dough consistent for rolling. Julia made balls of the dough and Petra began wielding the rolling pin.

"We've finished. See here. It made that much." It was Anna pushing a huge kettle of peeled apples ahead of her through the door. "Now can we go over to Veblens and see the bridesmaid dress?"

Julia took the kettle from Anna and set it down. "Go if you must, but don't stay all day. There is much yet to be done."

Mari and Anna quickly washed their hands outside at the wash bench used by the men and dried them on the towel hanging on a peg. Agnes, who had come to hurry them along, watched impatiently.

"Magda is going to wear a lace collar Melva crocheted. It's beautiful! Melva is wearing one almost like it instead of a veil. She intends to carry lavender, pink and white asters."

They ran through the store to the living quarters at the back.

"Come in here," motioned Agnes, indicating the tailor shop. "The dress is hanging in here."

Anna and Mari had never been in the tailor studio before. The Veblen children had been warned never to trouble their father at tailoring lest they disturb a client being measured for a garment. Agnes was sure of herself now, however, and all three of them entered.

There was the big sewing machine, larger, to be sure, than the one Anna's mother had. And there was the headless manequin wearing a coat without sleeves. Anna moved about slowly, passing a full-length plate-glass mirror. She hadn't expected to see herself. Quite forgetting why she had come here, she turned slowly and studied her own appearance. At home the mirrors permitted one to see only head and shoulders. This was something new. Yes, she had a full enough bust, not such big hips, but big enough. Suddenly she caught a glimpse of the profile of her back. Could she believe what she saw? There was an ugly hump! Where other people were indented between the shoulder blades, she had something protruding! She hadn't thought about the brace for a long time. It must have been three years since she quit wearing it. Now the whole dreadful experience raced before her: the rigid splint, the dreams, the brace, the painful hours of learning to walk. Now she was marked, marked for life! She was one with a hump—a hunchback! And no one had told her. They had all been looking at her, but no one told her she was deformed! A surge of resentment welled up, choking her.

"Anna, Anna, you came to see the dress, didn't you? Why do you stare at yourself like that? Melva and Magda should be looking in the mirror, not you, not yet anyway."

Anna wanted to turn and run, to find a place to go and cry, but she must not show her feelings. She moved closer to the girls who were examining a linen dress.

"It's beautiful," she managed to say.

"See the gorgeous lace collar?"

"Uh-hum."

Emma, Agnes' older sister, suddenly stood in the doorway. This Veblen girl was not as attractive as her sisters and usually kept to herself. She was awkwardly heavy, and her large face covered with pimples.

"Agnes, are you bringing the whole town over here? Can't these girls wait until tomorrow?" Emma's voice had an unpleasant rasp that made Anna uncomfortable.

"Don't be grumpy, Emma," said Agnes, moving her guests out ahead of her.

Anna caught herself staring at Emma. I'm ugly just like she is, she thought. No one will want to marry me either. "I hope we didn't disturb anything." Anna spoke, trying to smile at Emma. She wanted to make up for the stare and her unkind thoughts.

They moved quickly back through the store and out into the street. Anna fled from Mari and Agnes with astonishing haste.

"Whatever got into her?" said Agnes.

"I can't imagine."

Anna passed the women busy making *lefse* in the kitchen and went upstairs. She flung herself on the bed and stuck her face in a pillow. She wanted to cry, but tears wouldn't come. She was too alarmed to cry. This must be thought about first, then maybe tears. Mother had always insisted she was delicate, but Anna hadn't realized this meant deformity. And her father, who had the habit of calling her "his pet"—was he feeling sorry for his little hunchbacked daughter? And all her schoolmates—what about them? Why hadn't they teased her as Iver was teased about his big ears, or Emma, who was fat? All her schoolmates had been stone silent. If they had laughed behind her back, she would have known. They couldn't fool her. But silence! It must be too dreadful to talk or tease about! And Mari, her best friend. Why hadn't she mentioned it? She should have, if she truly was her best friend. I'll bet she knows why Martin likes Agnes better than me, but she won't say, will she? Anna was screaming inside. Henrik is the only one who is innocent! He wouldn't see something like that. All he ever wanted was for her to tell him stories. Lately it had been reading to him what he couldn't quite manage himself. Little brother was all right! She suddenly wished he were here. No, she didn't. She would have to explain why tears—tears—tears—. They came at last. There followed long, exhausting sobbing.

"Where is Anna?" called Mari through the open door to Julia and Petra around the stove.

"Isn't she with you?"

"No, she ran home ahead of us." Mari turned slowly and left.

Anna crept down the stairs when she knew it was time for her to help with dinner. Seeing that her mother had stepped outside, she hurried to the wash basin and splashed water into her eyes. She wiped them on the roller towel, hoping they would not be red. She chose not to look in the oval mirror. It hung too high anyway.

"Anna, where were you? Mari came looking for you."

"Upstairs, just upstairs."

"We're terrible busy today. Don't you feel well?"

"Mama?" Anna came to her mother. "Mama?"

Julia saw a face swollen from crying.

"Yes, Anna?"

"Mama, why didn't you tell me I became a hunchback?"

"A hunchback, you say? You are no such thing. Whoever gave you that idea?"

"You wouldn't tell me, would you. I had to find out for myself."

"Whatever do you mean?"

"I saw myself, Mama, in Rolf Veblen's tailor shop. He has a full-length mirror."

"Forevermore!"

Julia saw Anna's chin begin to quiver. "Anna, my dear," spoke Julia putting her arm around her daughter. "You have a little bump where your trouble was, but it is nothing. You certainly are no hunchback."

"Why have I gone around this long with people looking at me and I not knowing about it?"

"Because it is *nothing,* that's why. When you wear your usual tucked-in waists, no one ever sees it."

Julia felt Anna relaxing a bit against her side.

"How thankful we are that you are well and active. You might have been chairridden, you know."

"Yes."

"You are growing up, Anna. Naturally you think about how you look to others. And that is good. Papa and I don't tell you how beautiful you are for fear you will become vain. But you are beautiful enough, far prettier than your mother."

"I wish I could believe that I'm pretty."

"You can. Your mother never tells lies."

Anna smiled.

"No one for dinner except you and me?" Anna suddenly realized the men were all threshing. What good fortune.

Julia felt relieved. Anna had quick mood shifts like this and they meant the turmoil was eased, if not resolved.

By sundown, most of the preparations for the wedding had been completed and nearly everyone in the little town was caught up in the growing anticipation.

"Anna, take Arne his suit. I have just finished cleaning and pressing it. And here, the shirt, too. It's worn so seldom it was hard to get the yellow out of it, but it turned out whiter and stiffer than I thought it would. Melva was far too busy to fuss with this." Julia draped the garments over Anna's arms.

Anna was glad to get out of the house for a while; she had been trying her best to do intelligently what her mother singled out for her to do.

"My dear Anna, you are doing a great favor for your old friend," said Arne, opening the door. "You coming over like this. I suppose I'll have to wear this monkey outfit again, I hope it's not too bad a fit. I'm not shaped the way I used to be. Come in, come in!"

Anna remembered how he had looked at Inga's funeral, in this suit and topped off with combed wet hair. "I know how you feel," she said with conviction. "I, if you don't mind, like you better in your apron."

Arne remembered how she had called the apron his magic belt, but somehow he felt inhibited from mentioning it. That merriment had been so long ago. He wished he could say something that would entice the light into her eyes. He draped the suit over the big chair.

"You're growing up, Anna, you're quite a lady. I always knew you would become a beautiful woman. You are becoming prettier every day. You have your father's features, and he's a handsome man, I tell you. But you must smile—that's what makes you pretty. You must smile!"

"I hope you're telling me the truth."

"You know I am. I'm not fooling now. If I were a young man I know what young lady I would be courting."

Anna caught sight of the dismal little hammer that once had been *Mjolner*. But it would be cruel to think it had lost its magic.

"I hope we will always be friends," said Anna, smiling as nicely as she knew how.

She had no sooner said the words than a painful longing swept over her. She wanted to throw her arms around him and cry, but, of course, this was out of the question.

He was standing close to her, as he did to all with whom he spoke seriously. He reached out and stroked her hair. She put her hand on his shoulder. No, this was no time for tears. She smiled again.

"Some day soon there will be another who will discover how truly nice you are." His eyes gleamed into hers as intensely as she remembered them when he told his old Norse stories. She was caught again in his spell.

"Arne, you are so kind. I don't believe a kinder man ever lived, except, perhaps for my papa."

Surely good friends are forever, Anna thought as he withdrew his hand and returned to the object of the errand.

"Thank your mama. The suit looks like new."

"I sure will," said Anna, going toward the door.

"Good-bye, then."

"Good-bye."

The next day, the people were out in front of the church after the regular worship service, impatiently waiting for the time the wedding ceremony would begin. The expensive surry arrived with Rolf bringing the Veblen women in their finest attire. Certainly they were eyed by many of the female onlookers. The second rig brought the three male members of the wedding including the groom. The Veblens were members of Minneola Church, and it looked out of place for them to be driving in on these premises on a Sunday.

While Nils was shepherding Arne, Julia attended Melva in the church as she removed her shawl and bonnet and placed the intricately crocheted neck piece over her linen dress. Ellen was to carry a basket of fall flowers, asters mostly, but also two huge, red dahlias. She stood in the doorway watching the people and waiting for the basket that would be her responsibility. At last she saw it coming. Magda was carrying it, together with the bride's and her own bouquet.

"They're here, Mama," called Ellen.

Melva and Ellen took the front pew on the left side of the aisle while Julia went out to the crowd, a signal that the bride was ready. The groom then entered, followed by the bridesmaid and the best man, the men taking their places in the front pew on the right side. Finally the minister appeared in the doorway, signaling the guests to come in. After the immediate families had entered, the women filled up the pews on the left side and the men the right. Anna watched as her father, Henrik, and Peder took the pew directly across the aisle from her.

The minister entered the chancel and motioned for the bride and groom to come forward. The ceremony was short; his exortations had been made in his sermon of the day, although the groom had not been in attendance to hear it.

Anna sat at the end of her pew, taking advantage of her chance for good viewing. Some people say weddings are sad, she reflected, but she didn't think so. A wedding is the fulfillment of a girl's dream, a strong, handsome person to love her forever. Yes, Sigurd was handsome. Girls could very well envy Melva.

She looked across the aisle. There sat Peder at the end of his pew. His eyes caught her glance and he smiled. She wasn't used to having people smile at her in church, especially not a young man, but she nodded slightly and returned the smile.

She was too shy to sustain it and looked away as quickly as she felt it expedient. He did look at her often, didn't he? Even in Church! Or, maybe all Norwegian newcomers are like that, she mused. No, she was almost sure he had more smiles for her than for anyone else. P—that's it! P! His name is Peder! She felt her heart beating and her face turning red. Could it be? No, he knew her as a kid like Henrik, a mere child loping around the house and scarcely acting like a lady. But something told her not to settle for that exactly. Hadn't Arne noticed she was becoming a lady and a pretty one at that? No, not really. The hump was still on her back—that had to be reckoned with, didn't it? P for Peder. He was certainly liked by the rest of her family and she like him, too. Dared she look again? she stole another look across the aisle. He was facing straight ahead now. Of course he was handsome. No one could deny that.

The marriage vows had been spoken and the married pair were turning around ready to follow the minister on their march down the aisle. They were now facing their friends. The little flowergirl, swinging her basket, darted behind her mother, ready to walk between the two couples. The radiant smile of the bride flooded the church with sunlight, and the people beamed back. How glad they all were for her, she with that unhappy past! Ellen was sober and bent on her task. She smiled, however, when she saw Anna close to the aisle.

The immediate families followed. Arne walked singly like a pilgrim in black, looking neither to left or right. He was getting old, people said, and didn't he look strange in that stiff, white shirt? He was kind, Arne was, and people respected him.

The Veblens, too, were strangers to this church, but very familar in the town. The Veblen women nodded and smiled as they went, bringing a relaxed atmosphere to the people still in the pews. No one talked to his neighbor, however, until the door of the santuary had been reached.

The wedding feast was laid out on a long table on the north side of the Kristian house. People came knowing nothing good would be spared, all those delicacies that were not everyday fare. But there was no liquor—understandably no liquor. Melva had had enough of drunkenness and Julia, of course, would have nothing at all to do with trafficking alcohol. If anyone in the town didn't know this, someone would be quick to tell him. There was plenty of coffee and apple cider, however, and all manner of people were welcome: those just passing through, threshers idling away the Sabbath, or tramps who may have gotten wind of the feast.

Anna and Mari were busy running back and forth with platters of *kringle, lefse,* and *potet kake.* Anna couldn't wait to tell Mari her secret. They smiled and sighed as they met each other coming and going.

"Meet me at the cellar steps when its's our turn to eat," called Anna at one point of passing. She knew that the outside cellar doors would remain open all day as the cold cider was being carried up. It was the most private place she could think of where they could still be considered helping, if anyone noticed.

"Mari, I think I know who P is," said Anna settling deep out of sight on the middle step. She held a plate of food on her lap.

"No, really? Who?" Mari was making sure the step she was to sit on wouldn't soil her dress.

"You're interested, huh?"

"Of course, tell me!"

"Peder."

"Peder. You mean your father's man... threshing... fireman?"

Anna nodded, earnestly awaiting Mari's response to this startling discovery.

"I don't know, Anna."

"What do you mean, you don't know?"

"He's kind of old for you, isn't he?"

"Old?"

"He's always with the older men, isn't he?"

"But that's because he's a newcomer. He isn't more than a year or so older than Martin, I'm sure. And besides, why shouldn't I like someone slightly older than myself?"

They heard footsteps and fell silent. Another crock of cider was taken up and again they were alone.

"He's a son of Papa's friend back in Norway. That would make him the same age as a cousin, wouldn't it? He isn't old like you think, Mari."

"How old is he?"

"I haven't asked." Anna took a bite of *lefse* with brown sugar rolled up in it. She wondered herself now exactly how old he might be. "But the reason he seems older than most of the guys is that he talks Norwegian all the time. We use English sometimes when we talk, so maybe he prefers to be with Papa and his friends who talk only Norwegian."

"You might be right."

"Mari, I'm going to teach him English," said Anna with sudden decision. "He wanted me to help him last winter during the time he was in school, and I did, some. But if I help him more, really help him..."

"Maybe."

"Mari, aren't you happy for me?"

"Of course. I even think he is nice. He is handsome and certainly a good worker. Papa says the most important thing a husband must be is a good provider."

"I grant you that. But, you think he is handsome?"

"I do."

They had finished eating and drank the last of the cider in their cups. Anna got on her feet.

"Come, we have to help gather dirty dishes."

Chapter 3

It was hot and humid in the Ringstad parlor. Try as she might, Sophie had been unable to keep it closed against the heat of the July afternoon. The red rug made itself even more potent by the damp musty odor it yielded into the stale air. Lace curtains hung at the windows in front of shades drawn more than halfway down. Morbid gossip and wive's tales were coming from the dining room, where pale women were sipping well-sugared coffee and nibbling on paper-thin rosettes.

Anna, as when she was five, was standing in front of the same easel portrait of Inga, Sophie's dead sister, Inga. The sad little smile was still there, and the ring, too. What a burden on Anna's memory had been that fragile hand with the ring! A little breeze moved the lace curtain at her left. Had Sophie opened the window after all? Anna expected the girl in the picture to notice, but she didn't. No life at all. The sad smile was frozen there. She was dead.

Maybe I ought to join the others, sighed Anna. She hated these stifling associations with middle-aged women. As she turned and walked halfway across the room, she wondered again about the window—was it open? Instinctively she turned back upon what she had left. The breeze had become a fierce gust, and the curtains were reaching far into the room. What had become of the picture? It had disappeared and in its place was the full-length mirror from Rolf Veblen's tailor shop. She saw herself in it! No, not me, I'm not going to die, she told the mirror. The curtain at the window collapsed in response as if to say, so be it—so be it.

Anna awoke. Her nightgown felt damp. It had not been a pleasant dream, but, after all, only a dream. One could be thankful it was not true. She threw her arms outside the covers, turned over, and returned to sleep. No more dreams for the rest of the night. By morning the apparition had almost totally faded from her consciousness, as did most of those dark dreams on the theme of death.

As early in the spring as such a piece of freight could be safely transported, a new reed organ arrived at the Kristian residence. Nils had agreed with Julia that they could afford it now, and Anna would be given her chance to learn music. Mattie Skaar, the spinster from Zumbrota who rode in once a week in her little single buggy, had taken on an additional pupil. Leaving her horse and buggy at the Tollefson livery stable, Miss Skaar made her rounds, carrying her music portfolios. She was highly respected by the populace, who were glad that such cultural advantage was available to them.

Anna was fast becoming Mattie's best student. She was never bored with finger exercises, as were some of Mattie's other, less imaginative pupils. Anna enhanced the scales with new life. Little Sarah, who was almost five, was in the habit of standing close at hand during Anna's lesson. Mattie wanted to tell her to leave but never quite felt comfortable doing it. Julia should by rights have removed the curious child, but she never did. She was glad Sarah showed this interest. In her own home, Sarah was entitled to learn what she could.

Rev. Hanson had been right in predicting little Sarah's future that spring day five years ago when her troubled father had put her into Julia's arms. She was growing up in the Kristian family. Her father, Lars Monson, the *Vossing,* came in with Nils for meals sometimes but seemed to pay little attention to his daughter. He only smiled and nodded at her foster parents, relieved that everything was still going well. Running his hilly farm, now with the help of his two sons, continued to overwhelm him, and he couldn't be bothered with affairs of womenfolk. Julia accepted this as a matter-of-course and nothing disturbed the close-knit relationship of Sarah to her adoptive family.

Anna recognized eagerly Sarah's interest in playing the organ and begrudged no time in helping those plump hands acquire agility. "Now let's sing the song, shall we?" Julia heard from her busy corner, then Sarah and Anna would join their voices to the melody of the keyboard. What could have delighted Julia more?

The organ was always going these days when Nils came in with his companions for coffee. This was well and good, and he was proud, but finally, since the organ was so close to them, Anna was instructed not to play at such times. One day Julia heard Nils tell Peder and Arne that he intended to build an extension to the house, a parlor, so to speak, for the organ. It would have a bay window like Sigurd Veblen's house, and the room where they sat would remain a kitchen. Of course! Julia was glad the idea had occurred to Nils, and this summer would be a good time for such construction, since there were several young men around who wouldn't be busy until harvest. She remembered how quickly Melva's house had been built at this time last summer.

So it was that a new addition—a two-story structure with two bedrooms upstairs—was begun, extending the Kristian house to the north. Anna and Sarah would share one bedroom, and Julia and

Nils would move into the other, leaving the big room above the kitchen for Peder and Henrik. The little room Peder had occupied would again become a guest room.

Mari and Anna were never far away from the carpenters. They brought out morning and afternoon coffee and with it jelly sandwiches and over-sized doughnuts. Mari was proud of her brother Iver, who, Nils said, was becoming a first-rate carpenter. Anna watched Peder and returned his frequent smiles as she thought of Sunday afternoon when they would go on their usual walk together. The sound of hammer and saw gave Julia assurance that adding to the house was indeed more than talk, and the smell of fresh lumber, the notion of a clean building soon ready for occupancy.

One day, however, everything in the town was interrupted by the necessity of attending a funeral at the church north of town. It was Sjur Hoffstad, a farmer west of town, who was to be buried. It never entered anyone's mind, except Anna's, not to attend.

"I'll bake the bread for you, Mama. Then you won't get behind with your work," Anna said, suddenly confronting her mother.

"That's not necessary, Anna."

"But I'd rather stay home. I don't like to go to funerals."

"You should think rather of the family, Anna. What if we all felt as you do and stayed home?"

"I know that, Mama. But it is just me, this once. Please let me stay home and bake the bread."

"All right."

Julia started her bread, no more fuss was made, and Anna remained virtually alone in the town.

Anna stood in her yard a mile away watching the hearse, drawn by Finseth's bay team, arrive from the west and turn north at the bridge. A large black cluster of carriages had gathered at the churchyard where mourners milled around the hitching posts. Soon the bell would toll! She must be ready for that, then she would go into the house and check to see if the bread had raised enough for baking. There was such finality in the tolling bell, as if the inevitable flaunted its triumph. Gong! Gong! Gong! No, the bell did not swing free and ring clear and clean from its vertex, it was merely struck by the hammer. Anna stood glued to her spot. She would not move until the tolling ceased, as if to run inside would leave some evil in its wake.

Once inside and attending the bread, she quite forgot what was going on a mile away. The fragrance of baking bread began to fill the kitchen. She went to the organ. There was a new hymn in English that had lately caught her fancy: "Lead Kindly Light." She began singing to her own accompaniment.

Lead kindly Light amid the encircling gloom,
Lead Thou me on,
The night is dark and I am far from home
Lead Thou me on.

The song struck a melancholy chord in Anna. Why was she singing such a sad song? She didn't want to feel sad.

She left the organ without finishing the song and decided to take a peek in the oven. She saw her hand grasp the oven door. Wasn't it a fragile hand? Delicate Anna! She drew her hand away from the door without opening it. She studied her hand feeling terror rising. She knew now why she never wore the sapphire ring. This hand was like the one in the easel portrait, wasn't it?

Premonition!

She remembered what people said about old Sjur Hoffstad. He had had a premonition he was going to die. He was perfectly healthy, they said, but he immediately began to prepare for his death. Think of that, and he was being buried right now up on the hill!

Premonition?

Hadn't she had a premonition, too, when the easel portrait turned into a mirror? No, no, no, no, that couldn't be, just couldn't be! She turned and ran out of the house, attempting to free herself from the grip of this terror. The town was deserted. Papa was not in his shop. The carpenters' sawhorses and ladders were idle against the unfinished wall of the house. A brisk wind roared in the trees and tore at her dress. Her hair blew in her face. Where was she anyway? There was a strangeness now in all this familiarity. I am here today, but won't be here next week? next month? next year? No, no, no, no, she must get ahold of herself and realize that there was no foundation for such a notion. But premonitions aren't supposed to be reasonable, are they?

She walked to the back yard and saw the chickens scratching indifferently in the loose dust by the barn door. She walked along the pasture fence where a little heifer lay asleep in the grass. It got up and approached Anna. Was it time for the pail of milk? Anna patted the creature's head. What was there to do but wait and see? Wait and see? To see if one is not to be? No, no, no, no, she must stop this foolish imagination! It made no sense and she was, after all, a rational human being. The sun is in the sky, the chickens go scratching and Tilly, here, thinks I have come to give her milk. And here I am. All's well with everything, me and the world.

The bread! She fled into the house, happy for the jolt back to reality. She took out the browned loaves just in time, and now she would cut off the end from one and eat it warm with butter and grape jelly.

The terror that had come to Anna this summer day was not resolved easily, however. It became like a traveler stalking her on the road. She tried to get out of his way by darting in and out among the crowd, falling behind, or racing ahead. But every so often the familiar figure walked beside her nudging her consciousness into turmoil. Sometimes she looked around for him in the morning, hoping he would have completely disappeared during the night. But no, maybe not too close, but he was there.

Shouldn't she tell someone—her mother, Mari? They were always sources of help. Why not? But she could never bring herself to do so. She was afraid that somehow this premonition would take on credibility if put into words. She was counting on its being foolish fantasy, and she hadn't convinced herself of it yet. But she thought she would eventually. Prayer? No, God was too awesome. He was, after all, in control of everything and if He willed her death now she would have to accept it. But she wasn't accepting death, not yet!

Peder? No, she need not tell him. When she was on walks with him, why should she even suggest another traveler who, at the moment, was so very far away. And with Peder she felt grown up; childishness had been put away and with it childish notions. It helped a great deal to label what troubled her as childish.

"It's your birthday soon, isn't it?" said Peder while out walking with Anna on the first Sunday in August.

"Who told you?"

"I was around last year on your birthday, and the year before, too, as far as that goes."

"But I wasn't your girl then, was I?"

"How lucky I am having a girl as nice as you." He reached for her hand.

"What would you have done if you hadn't come to America?" Anna asked as Peder helped her over a fence. They had crossed the bridge and decided to walk east along the Zumbro River.

"I might have gone fishing."

"Fishing?"

"Fishing is an important occupation in Norway, Anna. Many young men, especially the adventuresome ones, go fishing. And I don't mean only in the fjords, but out to the open sea up and down the coast. Some even go to the Lofoten Islands beyond the Arctic Circle."

"Really? Would you have gone there?"

"Perhaps. I was really interested in that for a long time, but my father encouraged me to go to America because he had your father to send me to."

"Are you sorry, Peder? Giving up on fishing, I mean?"

"Of course not. It was a childish dream only."

"What was it like crossing the ocean? Maybe you would have liked life aboard ship."

"That was no fun. But I'm sure that cannot be rightly compared to being on a fishing boat. First of all, we had a place to go and were anxious to get there; and second, we had women and children aboard. Danger was not adventure, it was terror for most of us. During storms we all huddled together longing for the safety of land and home. And when we did land we were hardly like boasting fishermen; we were lowly immigrants, not even able to understand the customs officers or make them understand us. Our trunks were tossed with distaste by those who handled them. I even saw one break open in mid-air and all the belongings fall into the sea. A woman cried, but the handlers paid no attention."

"Oh, those poor people!"

"How good it was for me to meet your father at last. Working for him is better than fishing."

"You're pretty good at English now, Peder," said Anna, sounding as if she had something new to bring up. "But I guess not quite ready to read a very good book."

"Yes, what book is that, then?

"*The Whale,* by Herman Melville. It's about a ship and crew going out after whales. It is one of the new books bought last year for the school library. Oh, Peder, it must be exciting to be on board a whaling ship! Let me tell you all about it."

Anna drew him down beside her on a fallen log near the river. She knew her power as a storyteller, and now she had a superb listener.

She started her story with Ishmael, all alone in the world, who had quite by accident joined a very strange crew. She described each of the harpooneers, those dark-skinned heathens, Fallahah and Queequeg, so mysterious, but having nobility unquestionably. Then the even more strange captain, Ahab was his name, whose face looked like he was being crucified, and who paced the deck on an ivory peg leg. Captain Ahab had only one thing in mind, she emphasized; he was determined to find somewhere in the waters of the world the whale that had torn off his leg. Yes, the crew members were scared of Ahab, but she thought they felt sorry for him, too, and searching for this big sperm whale became their adventure. Two mates, of course, thought he was kind of crazy.

Anna paused and studied Peder's face. Satisfied that he was caught up in the tale, she continued by describing the schools of whales, the terrible storm at sea, and the three-day struggle with the mysterious whale, Moby Dick. Fallahah's prophecy of the two hearses and it's fulfillment was emphatically recreated for Peder. Fallahah himself, who perished on the second day of the struggle, was discovered on the third day entangled in a rope fastened to the whale's back, the first hearse. But Captain Ahab would not have benefit of hearse—the second hearse consisting of floating timbers from the demolished ship, bobbing everywhere—because a rope in turmoil dragged him deep into the sea. Then she retraced her telling to include the coffin Queequeg made for himself which was covered with strange carvings. Naturally he never got to use his coffin, but (Can you believe this?) it was what saved Ishmael, the only survivor. It bobbed up right in front of him, as the ship sank, and kept him afloat many hours before a passing ship rescued him.

Before Peder came out of the trance he was in, Anna got up from the log.

"Come, let's go," she said, putting out her hand to draw him to his feet.

"I will certainly read that book someday, Anna. And I'll read it in English, thanks to you. But in the meantime you must read to me from it. Imagine those enormous creatures traveling the oceans of the world! It's so amazing!"

Still holding Peder's hand, Anna continued to draw him along.

"Look up there. I used to ski down that hill." She halted the two of them and directed his eyes up the Sande hill. "Papa gave me a pair of skis when I was ten years old, and I skied well all the way down to this very spot. I haven't skied since."

Peder knew the pain connected with that particular day in her life, and he dared ask no questions. They walked on as far as the mill pond. There they lingered in extended silence, watching the turning of the waterwheel. The best the two of them shared, neither seemed to put into words.

When it was almost time for harvest to begin and Nils and his crew were eager to go threshing, a spell of rain halted everything. One day of rain could be tolerated, but the easterly winds gave little hope of clearing weather. Jobs saved for rainy days were second-rate at best and soon lost their power to satisfy the working men. On the third evening of constant rain, as the Kristian family was finishing supper, Peder suggested that they all move into the new parlor and that Anna read to them from *The Whale.* Reading aloud was not an uncommon practice in the Kristian household, but it was usually done on winter evenings around the kitchen table. Quite willing now, the family members left their places at the kitchen table and filed into the room.

Anna sat down with her book at a little square table near the new bay window, while Sarah, bent on a spot close to the reader, came carrying her little stool. There was just enough light outside to be caught by the raindrops as they streamed down the window panes. When Julia brought a kerosene lamp to the table, the raindrops could no longer be seen but their pelting on the glass grew louder. What could better enhance the intrigue of the listeners on their journey out to sea with Ishmael?

While Nils wondered at his daughter's agility with such a multitude of English words, Henrik was swaying with the ship and hearing the clatter of the peg leg on the deck. Peder understood more of the English than he had expected, being taken vicariously on the ocean adventure of which he had stood in awe. And, curiously, the narrator, that frail little creature he called his girl, was involved in all the towering fury. Using lamplight to continue her knitting, Julia, at the mention of the word crucifixion to describe the face of Ahab, remembered Job of the Old Testament, as the Lord spoke of the mighty Leviathan: "Can you fill his skin with harpoons, or his head with fishing spears? lay hands on him; think of the battle; will you do it again?...whatever is under the whole of heaven is mine." Another moment was eternal for Julia, transcending the petty activities of the here and now to where her Creator was holding the Universe together.

This year, not only the beginning of the threshing season was hampered by wet weather, but also the end. In late October, with one week left to go, again came rain, and those easterly winds promising no letup. But what was worse, far worse, was an epidemic of fever which broke out suddenly, inflicting the children. It was diagnosed as measles, but no one in the town could remember any child's disease as severe as this one. Lars Mundahl was the first to be stricken, followed two days later by Gisle Veblen and Henrik Kristian.

Petra Haroldson was the consultant for the anxious mothers. *Dr. Chases's Information for Everyone* may have been in most homes, as it was in Julia's, but Petra had studied the procedures and rose to the occasion as the competent one. A mild laxative must first of all be given to keep the bowels open. The patient must be kept in a semi-darkened room, cool, but meticulously guarded from drafts. Feet must be bathed in warm water three times a day and a drink consisting of the juice of a lemon, a teaspoon of cream-of-tartar in a pint of water, sweetened with a sugar lump, must be made abundantly available when the patient indicates thirst.

Fever persisted hour after hour, far beyond the time it normally should have receded, and members of the stricken families took turns at the bedsides day and night. Running in and out of the rain, neighbors who had already been exposed to the contagion looked in on one another and compared observations. Melva had snatched Sarah away from the contagion of the Kristian house and said she could stay with Ellen as long as needed. Then came the hour Gisle Veblen died. The situation was indeed grave.

Henrik's fever broke, to the relief of his family, but a cough developed, leaving him weak and limp in his bed.

"Mama, I've got a terrible headache." Anna had moved toward the kitchen stove and stood shivering before her mother.

"Not you, my dear," cried Julia, feeling her daughter's forehead. "I shouldn't have let you sit with Henrik."

So Anna became Julia's second patient. Word soon came that Agnes and Josie at the Veblens, and Mari and Iver at the Mundahls were extremely ill. Who would have thought this child's disease would strike at young adults? Julia was confounded. Minneola Church buried the ten-year-old Veblen boy, and the rain continued.

Dear Peder, how good he was to help with Anna! Julia saw him as strength from God. He took the night hours at Anna's bedside, and some daylight hours, too.

Anna was aware of a cool cloth on her forehead. It was so good! But a steady windstorm kept roaring in her ears. A huge flock of gray, autumn birds from the field flew into the tree by the window and chirped fiercely. Soon they all dropped to the ground and pecked industriously, then all flew onto the fence and all back into the tree, their nervous twitter never ending. Anna's skin crawled and stung. No, it wasn't birds after all, it was a swarm of bees she heard buzzing, and they were stinging as well! She shook her head violently. Then a steadying hand touched her and laid the cool cloth again. Her eyes felt so thick she chose not to open them, but she knew someone was there. She kept thinking she was supposed to go somewhere and felt totally restrained. She imagined herself shouting let's go, let's go.

The steadying hand was Peder's; Julia was downstairs preparing supper. Suddenly the door opened letting in a spray of rain and a gust of chilly air. It was Petra. She shook the rain out of her scarf as a drop of water rolled off her nose.

"Julia," Petra's breath was short. She gasped once more. "Julia!"

"Yes, Petra, do come in, over here by the stove. You are shivering."

Petra entered and looked around like a frightened animal.

"Julia, Mari is dead," came a whisper.

"No, you mustn't say it. It can't be true!"

"A half-hour ago. It's true, Julia!"

The two women sank into chairs around the kitchen table laying their tired arms on the red-checkered tablecloth. Neither spoke.

Nils entered.

"You know, of course," he blurted, draping his wet jacket over a chair.

They nodded. He joined their silence, sitting in the chair that held the wet jacket.

"Poor Anna," whispered Petra, looking from one to the other. "How is she?"

"Not good, not good at all."

"So?"

"Out of her head with fever most of the time. Peder is with her now."

"She mustn't know this," said Nils earnestly. His clumsy whisper hung in the air.

After a long moment Julia rose.

"We must go and help Jenny Mundahl," said Julia. "We mustn't sit here like this when others need us."

"I am helpless, Julia," said Petra, not stirring from her chair. "Give me a hot cup of tea."

"Tea? Oh, of course."

Julia lifted her teakettle to check if there was enough hot water, then brought out the tea, sugar, and cream. Although the women preferred coffee, tea with sugar was considered best for quick strength.

"I'll make a mustard plaster for that boy," Petra responded to the cough she heard from the next room. "If we make it with egg white instead of plain water it won't blister that tender skin."

"I'll leave you to do that," said Julia. "I must go over to the Mundahls' right away."

That evening Julia took her vigil beside her daughter to let Peder have a full night's sleep. Toward morning Anna's fever broke. Thank God! Julia carefully removed Anna's wringing wet garments and sponged her tenderly, extremely apprehensive of any draft from that damp October weather just outside the windows and doors. Yes, there was a fire in the stove directly below, and Nils had seen to it that there was a full woodbox.

Anna smiled, feeling better in a dry bed. As she watched her mother nervously straighten the room around her, she was suddenly seized with anxiety.

"Mama, how is Henrik?"

"He is getting better every day. He coughs a bit, but that is natural with measles."

"I hear him sometimes."

"I know. Now try to go to sleep, Anna. You will be getting your strength back now that the fever in gone."

"I will." Anna turned toward the wall. She swung back suddenly. "Mama, how is Mari?"

Julia spun away from Anna. Why must she ask! Why must she ask! She knew the truth would come out sooner or later, Anna would persist, and persist!

Julia returned slowly and drew up a chair close to the bed.

"All of you have been very sick," she began, hesitating for a long, painful moment. "Mari died yesterday, Anna."

"Mari is dead?"

"Yes, Anna." Anna remained limp and expressionless. Her mother decided not to talk; she would answer questions if her daughter asked any. But Anna remained strangely silent.

Anna heard the question she had asked echoing and re-echoing in her consciousness. Mari is dead? Yes, Anna, Mari is dead. Mari is dead. So I wasn't to be the one to die—Mari was. Mari died instead of me. How stupid my premonition! Mari, I'm selfish, so selfish! I think only about myself. How could you stand me all these years? You were my best friend, Mari, my best friend—.

Anna felt hot, salty tears welling in the corners of her sore eyes.

"Mama, Mari was my best friend," Anna whispered.

"Yes, I know, dear. And you were her best friend. You rest now. Sleep if you can."

Her mother's reassurance brought calm to Anna for the time being. Because she was so very weak, she fell asleep.

One week later, as persistent northwesterly winds had dried the brown countryside, Nils and his crew left. They had to go to see if anything could be done with those remaining stacks at the Arneson place. Nils wondered, too, how easily the engine would start after all these weeks of corroding weather.

Anna hated to say good-bye to the men. On the day before they were to leave, Peder had carried Anna down the stairs to the familiar kitchen. In the days that followed, Julia began bringing her down and walking her slowly on her feet. Anna had certainly changed as far as Henrik could see. Her eyes were larger than usual and they had a distance about them which he couldn't reach no matter how hard he tried. Arne saw this, too, and got a smile, but not a return of the eyes. Her face was as white and fragile as a china tea cup, her hands limp, and her body listless. Arne carried pain back to the cobbler shop after seeing her.

But strength returned little by little as Julia encouraged movement and light activity. Then the day come when Sarah returned. Now, thought Henrik, her eyes are closer to all of us. Soon Henrik was back in school bringing home the world of books, things to talk about, stories to read. Julia, however, remained apprehensive. Anna did not utter a word about the thing that must have hung heaviest on her heart, Mari.

"Mama, I'm going for a walk. I feel strong enough now. Really I do." Anna was standing by the window looking out at the crystal-blue November day with sunshine whiter than she had ever known it. "I don't think it is very cold with all this sun."

"Fresh air is good for you. But don't stay out too long."

Anna was making the pilgrimage she had wanted to make all these weeks. And she wanted to make it alone, not with Henrik, Sarah, or even Peder. She started north toward the cemetery.

All I've done since you left, Mari, is get well, and it's taken so long. Otherwise you haven't missed much. You've lived what I've lived. We're still even, except—now you know what it's like to die. Anna suddenly realized that Mari had had the ultimate experience and, even if she was Anna's best friend, could not rush back to tell her how it was. She wouldn't be back, and that was a cold fact. An overwhelming sense of loss engulfed Anna, and she felt a weakness creeping into her legs. She stopped for a moment. She watched a bluejay fly from a tree down to a fence post. His handsome feathers had caught the colors of this beautiful day and he wore them regally. Why had he screamed at her, Anna wondered.

Anna started walking again. The dismal fact occurred to her that Mari's life was over, yes, over. No marriage, no children, no keeping house, no getting ready for Christmas. Nothing. Mari's aspirations, as Anna knew them, were so entangled with Anna's that she felt deeply that part of herself was gone—the other half of herself, her childhood self. It was as if a two-wheeled cart had lost a wheel and the merriment was gone.

She reached the church and walked along the south wall, searching across the dead grass for the fresh mound, the freshest one. Her heart sank. Yes, there it was! She approached, remembering how Arne had walked up to Inga's grave that Christmas Eve when she had been with him. She looked into the clods of black dirt. Frost was still visible on the shadow side.

"I'll see you again, Mari, but it might be a long time. We know so little about resurrection."

Standing here, Anna felt a kind of peace she hadn't expected. The grave lay under the sky, exposed to wind and weather. Snow would soon come, pure, clean snow. Spring would follow with sweet-smelling life in the clumps. Summer would flourish with abundance of green, scurrying little animals, nesting grouse, and singing insects. "Couch more magnificent"—*Thanatopsis* by William Cullen Bryant. She remembered a page out of the Sixth Reader. She revered the thoughtful man with the full, white beard, and because she liked his poem, she had memorized it. The lines came, not logically from the beginning like a stream, but in snatches like gentle rain.

> The golden sun,
> The planets, all the infinite host of heaven,
> Are shining on the sad abodes of death,
> Through the still lapse of ages. All that thread
> The globe are but a handful to the tribes
> That slumber in its bosom.

Nothing was so very wrong. The earth in its beauty and goodness had accepted Mari's body. That was all Anna knew, but it was good enough for now. She slowly turned toward home.

Nils and his crew were heading toward Wanamingo. It hadn't been easy threshing out the stacks at the Arneson place. The bundles, black and ill-smelling, stuck to one another by threads of pale-green sprouts, and the separator frequently clogged. As they came across the bridge over the Zumbro, Nils began pulling the cord of the steam whistle, letting it blast every few seconds over the last mile. The whole town would know that the threshers were coming home. Through the frosty air, engulfed in smoke and steam, the rig finally reached the vicinity of its seasonal shelter, the blacksmith shop.

"Papa and Peder are back!" Anna dropped her knitting and ran to the window. "I'm going out to meet them," she cried, quickly putting on coat, cap, scarf, boots, and mittens since avoiding a chill shouldn't be taken lightly.

She's herself again, thought Julia.

Anna was well, and Julia dared to believe it. It hadn't been easy, poor Anna. Julia had wondered if the sun would ever shine again. The first time Anna had gone outdoors, Julia had shivered, seeing the narrow shoulders of her daughter as she plodded toward the cemetery. Today's venture was certainly different. Restoration at last!

Chapter 4

On July 18, 1886, Melva Veblen had a baby boy. Julia had been fetched by the anxious husband just after midnight. It was an easy, normal birth, and Melva's radiant smile fell on her new offspring.

Seeing the cobbler's door open on her way home, Julia called the good news to Arne.

"This makes you a grandfather," she beamed.

"So all went well. I'm so glad." Arne rose and came closer. "You've been so good to her Julia. I shall be forever grateful to you."

"She's a special person, Arne."

Julia felt a warmth welling inside her toward this old neighbor. She marveled anew at his having brought Melva from Minneapolis to Wanamingo. He had a talent for loving people—who could help but respect him? And now his Melva had a decent husband and a beautiful baby boy; things just couldn't turn out better than that.

"You'll be over for coffee later?"

"I will, thank you, Julia."

Later that morning, Julia sent Anna, Sarah, and Ellen off to pick berries. As she gazed after them from her doorway, she saw her neighbor, Jennie Mundahl approaching the house.

"Do come in, Jennie," exclaimed Julia, opening the screen door and letting her in. "The men just left. They all but finished the cookies. Come and have some coffee with me. I haven't had mine yet."

Jennie took a chair at the table without saying more than thank you.

"Melva had her baby early this morning. Did you know? A beautiful boy, and everything went so well," Julia chatted as she filled coffee cups. Finally she looked at her guest. Jennie was a quiet little woman, but she seemed more so this morning.

"No, I didn't know. How nice that it is all over. A boy, you say?" Jennie smiled but her voice lacked enthusiasm.

"Yes, what else? And he has handsome people to take after. They haven't decided on a name yet."

Julia ceased her chatter as Jennie's thoughts seemed to be elsewhere. There was a short silence.

"Julia," Jennie began slowly. "Have you talked to Petra lately? I'm afraid I have offended her."

"No, Sigurd and I managed without her this morning. How so?"

"You know about the back room Clarence has, don't you?" Jennie's voice was mysterious without her meaning it to be.

Julia nodded. She and others in the town hadn't wanted to admit what was there, but certainly there was evidence cropping up all the time. Often farm wagons remained too long beside the store while their owners loitered within. It was almost suppertime last evening before she saw Axel Finnesgaard leave for home.

"Well, Melvin has been with Clarence too often lately. Sometimes he stays all day."

Julia set her cup in its saucer giving full attention to what was being said. Jennie looked into her coffee which was still too hot.

"When he does come home from there, he sinks into his chair and nods off. It isn't easy with him anymore, Julia."

"Oh?"

"No. If I talk to him, or even notice him, he becomes ugly and mean. I don't know him, then. I'm almost afraid of him."

Julia heard weeping in Jennie's voice but saw no tears in her eyes.

"I decided I would talk to Petra about it. Until then we both had pretended that nothing serious was happening and rambled on about other things, but I couldn't do that anymore. So I brought it up one day."

"I believe I would have, too."

"And she turned pale and began to shake all over. She told me I was blaming Clarence for making a drunkard out of my husband, and didn't I know that he was a sot all along and that was how it was with men like Melvin who couldn't leave booze alone."

"Petra can get very disturbed, I know."

"But things aren't any better with Clarence. Petra and her brother are really taking care of the store these days. When did you last see Clarence behind the counter? He's busy with his still, that's what he is. And don't you believe he is not drinking plenty of it himself!"

"I am vey sad about what you are telling me, Jennie," Julia responded, not knowing what else to say. Julia had faced adversity, but not this kind.

"Petra is such a good woman, Julia. Think of all she did for us when our children were so sick last fall."

"I know, I shall be forever grateful to her."

"And now, Julia, what now?" Tears spilled from Jennie's eyes as she groped in her apron pocket for a handkerchief.

"I don't think she meant to drive you away, Jennie. I'm sure she thinks as much of you as you do of her. She is undoubtedly as upset about Clarence as you are about Melvin."

Jennie wept into her handkerchief before speaking again.

"Things aren't the way they used to be, Julia. I watched Anna and the two little girls go off berry-picking, and Mari—Mari wasn't with them."

Julia rose, going to Jennie with a comforting arm. "Don't distress yourself so. Leave Mari in God's hands. She has it good now. Don't wish her back."

"What you say is true, Julia. It's only that I get lonesome for my girl. Now I have only my men. It's true Mari has it good, I know that."

"We'll just have to be patient with Petra," Julia continued. "I'm glad you came over. I can't do much good for you, I guess. But count on me as a friend, do that. More coffee?"

"No thanks, I must be off. Thank you, Julia, thank you."

"Come over any time, Jennie."

At noon Nils came in for dinner. He brought no client today, but Henrik, who had been working with his father, followed him in.

"Martin Mundahl was over to see me today," Nils began as he reached for a slice of bread following Henrik's table prayer. "He's not going threshing with me this year, he said."

"He's not?"

"He's going to stay in the harness shop. I wonder if he means it, or if he will change his mind. If he's not going to be with the crew, I'll have to start looking for another man."

"It's his father, Nils. It you stop to think about it, Melvin isn't himself anymore."

"So?"

"Yes. Jennie was here this morning. It's not good." Julia sent anxious glances at Henrik who shouldn't have been hearing this.

"So it's come to that."

"I'm afraid so."

Henrik had often wondered why Lars never spoke of his father anymore. For a while he thought Lars was more interested in farming than harnessmaking, but lately he sensed there was more to it than that. Henrik had seen Mr. Mundahl go to the back of the general store; it wasn't only farmers, leaving their horses and wagons on the side street who went into Clarence Haroldson's. Henrik knew the rumors, and the rumors were embarrassing to his friend Lars. And because of this Martin wouldn't be hauling water anymore, another crew member gone. He wondered when he would be old enough to fill a man's place.

"You'd better rest awhile this afternoon, Julia. You were up most of the night, weren't you?" Nils had finished his meal and was pushing his chair back under the table.

"It's hard for me to sleep on summer afternoons, but I'll try."
"Do that, Julia."

Nils had still another crew member he would have to replace this year. His reliable fireman, Peder, had left for the north country.

Peder had been in America three years now and thought it was time to see more of it. Furthermore, he thought he would like to acquire some land of his own, but there was no longer any available in Goodhue County. If he wanted a homestead, he would either have to go west into South Dakota or north to the Red River Valley. Since Nils and Peder's father had a friend who had left southern Minnesota with a party of Norwegians who took homesteads in the Red River Valley, Nils encouraged Peder to consider going there. "Write to Ole Hagen at Glyndon, Minnesota," he told him.

What Nils knew about Ole Hagen's party was that they left Houston County in 1870 and settled in Clay County along the Buffalo River. They had been delighted to find oak, ash, and basswood trees and a stream full of fish along side of the grass-covered prairie that would be their home. Nils figured that if Peder was unable to find land here, these people might know where he could claim land elsewhere in that open country. Of course, he could always come back and work for Nils. That was understood.

Ole Hagen responded that Peder would be most welcome. Right now he was in need of a hired man, he said, good help was not easily found, especially year-around. He had two boys of his own, but they were not yet old enough to carry a full load.

Peder had shared his dream of owning land with Anna. He never doubted but that she would be his wife some day and he counted her in on his fortune seeking. He had given her a chest before he left, a "hope chest," to be filled, in the meantime, with needlework furnishings for the home they would have some day. He would certainly make good somewhere in this great country, and she would be at his side.

Peder's first letter to Anna described how he had walked eight miles into town to get the mail. "I was so anxious to hear from you, Anna, and I knew that your letters were waiting for me in Glyndon. The roads here this spring are impassable. Wagon wheels become solid mud and won't turn. The people here call the stuff "gumbo." You can well imagine how heavy my boots got, and how I had to stop and scrape them often. But it was well worth it. There were five letters for me. I still read them over and over."

Letters from Peder came regularly, each lengthy and painstakingly written and as much in English as he could manage, to please his teacher. "We live in a small sod house here that was built in 1883 and hasn't leaked yet, although there are terrible cloudbursts. The walls are double sodded, the inside done after the sod-thatched roof was on, and whitewashed with white clay found in a nearby slough. It is fashionable here to paper the walls with pages from magazines, but Mrs. Hagen thinks that looks foolish. You might wonder where I sleep. The boys and I sleep in a bunk bed, myself on the top. Elsie sleeps in a trundle that slips under the bunk bed. The folks sleep on a spring that folds on hinges up against the wall in the daytime. It's really a clever arrangement. I wondered where I would sleep when I first came. Hired help, you know, don't sleep in the house up here, but I am treated like a son. I am very lucky."

In another letter Peder described the extent of Ole Hagen's farming operation. "Can any of you imagine how large a piece of land a quarter-section is, not to say a half, or a whole section? We're plowing all the time, it seems, and no one can manage more than two acres a day. It is new breaking. It means plowing twice with two month's time between. The second time is called backsetting. You just should see this prairie grass, and it must all rot under the breaking. Hagen's two boys, young as they are, plow with a sulky. Thomas is thirteen and Isak is only eleven, but they are big for their age. And Elsie, I must tell you about her. She does backset-plowing with a team of oxen named Thor and Sven. Elsie is sixteen, husky as any man and gets as much done as I do. Mrs. Hagen works outdoors all the time. I don't see how she manages to get all those good meals ready and all the clothes-washing done. One day a neighbor shot a deer and I cut it up. They think I'm a good butcher. Ole Hagen and I have been haying, putting up this prairie grass for winter fodder. There is certainly enough of it. One of our neighbors had tried growing alfalfa thinking that our livestock deserve something better. Besides the three horses and the team of oxen, the Hagens have six cows, four pigs and a flock of chickens. One problem we have is very poor fences. Our neighbor's cows and pigs roam around here and ours disappear, too, and have to be rounded up. Fencing is terribly expensive and most farmers around here can't afford it."

In July, Peder wrote that due to lack of rain the crops were meager. "The worst part of the summer has been dust storms. It is not fit for man or beast to be out in those black clouds of dirt. Hagen says he needs to plant more trees in his windbreak, and I agree with him, but it all takes time. Yesterday, when it was fairly calm, we plowed new firebreaks around the farmyard and also around the area where the grain stacks will stand. People here are scared of prairie fires, but I haven't had to fight one so far. Always be prepared, says Ole."

News from Peder was news for the whole town. Anna kept scarcely a line to herself. That others took such interest in her man, made Anna proud. But it seldom occurred to her that she would ever be a part of all that he described. She was quite content to be where she was and letting his experiences be for her, too, as it was for the others—a fascinating story, albeit a true one.

In August the Hagens' scanty stand of wheat was cut with a self-rake reaper, not the latest in harvesting machinery, but within the means of an operation like theirs. Through the long morning hours, Mrs. Hagen drove the horses before the reaper until it was time for her to go home and prepare dinner. Peder bound the sheaves with twisted stalks of grain as they fell from the reaper, his skill and speed increasing as he went along until he was almost able to keep up with her. While waiting to relieve her mother, Elsie taught her two brothers how to prop the bundles up into shocks. Ole was gone, as he so often was, either at the neighbors', or in the town. He was running all the time it seemed; if it wasn't tending to the needs of his own operation, it was tending to the needs of his neighbors in the settlement.

Peder was glad when Mrs. Hagen could leave for the house. Her shoulders drooped and she walked as though she had a pain in her back. But Elsie never looked tired. She managed the horses with the same instinctive skill she used on the ox team. There was something immensely attractive about this strong, healthy girl. Peder dared not smile at her; rather, he found himself avoiding her friendly glances. He had his own girl. Nothing must interfere with that.

After this week-long reaping and shocking, the grain bundles were put into stacks. Threshing in the Norwegian settlement would be put off until later in the fall, since Ole and several other farmers, with their own wagons, had hired out to work at the bonanza farm of Grandin. Peder, too, would have a chance to earn additional money during harvest by accompanying Ole to the bonanza. The wives and children would remain at home to take care of the animals. Although Elsie had pleaded with her father to let her join them, Ole stood firm. It's no place for you, girl.

Being a day late, Ole and Peder left long before dawn. The empty bundle rack began its rumble through the dimly lit morning as Ole slapped the rumps of his horses with slack reins.

"We've had quite a time in our settlement with that quarter-section of land over there," began Ole.

"How so?" Peder peered in the direction Ole was pointing.

"It has passed through several hands already, and the young couple there now don't seem the homestead type—too soft."

"Too soft?" Peder felt anxious.

"Life here is hard work. Some people aren't fit for hard work. If that is the case, they don't belong here." He kept staring into the horizon.

Peder wondered what he saw out there in the feeble morning light.

"See that sad-looking little sod shanty? That was built by a drifter who stayed for a year pretending to claim. Then he offered it to the rest of us for one-hundred dollars. That house hasn't been improved much since he built it, a lean-to on one side is about all."

"So this young couple you mentioned, they live in it now?"

"It should have been abandoned long ago. It leaks in the summer and lets in the cold in winter."

"The young man—doesn't he—?"

"He is a bit better than the man who lived there before him, I'll say that. With the help of all his neighbors, he is coming along."

"What happened to the man before him?"

"He went back to Norway. He told us he was sick and tired of sand storms."

Peder said nothing. Something hurt inside of him.

"This might be a place for you, if Victor Overvold gives up. It's a good farm. The land is as good as mine and quite a few acres have been broken."

Peder remained silent. Ole looked at him, wondering why he was so speechless.

"There is a chance further north at Bygland where land in a Norwegian settlement is still available. I should take you there and introduce you, but we'll have to wait now until the harvest is over."

Soon they would be crossing the river into Dakota. Peder had never been there.

"You are interested in a farm, aren't you, Peder? That's why you came up here, wasn't it?"

"Yes, oh yes." Peder supposed he had to talk about it. "I'll be wanting a farm eventually, yes."

"You ought to marry my Elsie. She's the woman for these prairies. Not all women are, you know."

Peder almost lost his balance as the wagon hit a badger hole.

"I have a girl," he said, hoping that would be the end of it.

"You have? Oh yes, you have been getting lots of letters. Nils wouldn't write that often, I'm sure. Who is she, if I may be as bold as to ask it?"

"She's Nils' daughter Anna."

"Not the one with spine trouble."

"How did you know that?"

"We heard about it from Hans Mentvedt who worked up here—let's see, three or four years ago."

"She's fine now," said Peder curtly.

"I'm glad to hear that."

They had crossed the river and were heading north into the vicinity of the bonanza farm. The sun had risen, throwing its gold across the vast, dry landscape. As far as the eye could see, were grain shocks, each casting its own wispy shadow ahead of the sun. Peder couldn't believe what he saw; such a stretch of cultivation was beyond imagination. Surely all this had been under the tugging plow, the harrow, the seeder, and finally the reaper with its measured swath. So many bundles to tie, eight to a shock. How many shocks? Who could count them? Men, horses, and, of course, machinery—how much it must have taken!

Soon they were able to make out buildings, square clusters on the horizon. The two men kept staring ahead now, tracing more and more of the gigantic farmyard. There was the house, apart from the other buildings, gleaming white with the morning sun mirrored in every window pane.

A well-worn road brought them into the immediate area of the farm, more like a town, a rural outpost. Peder looked through the open door of the blacksmith shop as they passed, and next to it was harness repair. Across the road a carpenter was shaking the curls of wood out of his plane. Extending in every direction were barns and sheds, men leading harnessed horses out toward wagons left on the outskirts.

"I'll go to the headquarters of the foremen over there. You wait here with the team," said Ole, throwing his leg over the rack and letting himself down on the road.

In the direction Ole had taken, Peder saw the bunkhouses in long rows. He wouldn't be sleeping in a haymow or a granary at this place. He grew uncomfortable at the thought of being surrounded by people other than Norwegians. He was glad he was not a totally green newcomer. He knew some English now, and he had his Anna to thank for that.

While Ole and Peder were away, Victor Overvold brought his wife to the Hagens not knowing what to do for her. Being with child was certainly not an illness, but Ruth was sickly pale and painfully thin. Mrs. Hagen hadn't seen Ruth since she became pregnant and couldn't believe the change.

"You're lonesome, my dear," said Mrs. Hagen, when Victor drove out of the yard. "You need womenfolk like Elsie and me. We'll take care of you."

So Ruth had stayed, sleeping on the spring bed hinged to the wall, and Mrs. Hagen had taken to the top bunk.

When the two men returned from their seasonal work at Grandin Farm, Mrs. Hagen introduced Peder to the young neighbor.

"This is Ruth Overvold."

"Pleased to meet you." Peder approached, having just put the horses away. He took off his hat and nodded. The woman extended a white, fragile hand which Peder hardly dared to reach for, his own being exceedingly rough and dirty. Not all women are fit for prairie living, Ole had said.

"Victor will be over after he finishes his chores," explained Mrs. Hagen. "He was here earlier today. We've all been waiting for you and expecting you any day."

Victor took his wife home with him that evening. Ruth said she was feeling a lot better and would get along fine now. Elsie promised to visit as often as she could.

"We'd better start the threshing run at their place," said Ole as he watched them drive out of the yard. "You girls will have to help her. And let's hope winter doesn't set in early. That house of theirs will need fixing, but it will have to wait until we finish threshing."

"You're considerate, Ole. No one can say anything else," replied his wife.

Threshing the farms on the settlement took until the first week in December. Since the crop was light and the snow came late that year, there was no hitch. The rig was not as efficient as the rig on the bonanza farm, nor as Nils' rig in Wanamingo, but it ran, and the only problem they had was getting water out of the frozen river. Peder figured he might have improved on the engine operation if he had been engineer, but instead he was put to pitching bundles off the stack.

Ole might not have been the best mechanic, but he was a good leader, and the little Norwegian settlement had him to thank. When the threshing machinery had been put away, his sense of urgency brought the neighbors quickly to their next job, that of repairing the Overvold house. Of course, nothing major could be done in freezing weather, but the sides were thoroughly banked, the chimney improved and the interior freshened with whitewash. After the job was done, the women came bringing food and cheer. Ruth smiled. Things were working out after all.

Ole decided the Overvolds should have a pile of fuel logs he had stacked by the river. He saw that their supply, in his estimation, was insufficient for winters such as were liable to come to this country. One sunny day in the middle of December, Peder and Elsie were sent to the woods with the ox team to bring back a load of logs for the Overvold place.

"We're lucky the big snow hasn't come yet," said Ole. "Otherwise those logs would be too far to fetch."

The big wheels of the ox cart rumbled over the frozen ground, the weight of the two people barely enough to keep on course.

"Do you like to chop wood?" Elsie liked lively conversation and tried her best with Peder.

"I don't mind."

"There'll be lots of splitting to do even if we give these logs away, don't worry. I'm no good with the ax, Papa says, and he usually has something else for me to do. You'll get that job whether you like it or not. Tom and Isak are pretty good at it by now, but they're too slow and can't do the whole job."

Peder wasn't listening attentively, but Elsie didn't seem to notice. She kept rambling on. Peder couldn't get his thoughts off the Overvold couple, that delicate little wife who wasn't thriving in this country. Maybe if people are born here, like Elsie, things would be different. Maybe one drew strength from the prairie if one got started from birth. It was a harsh environment, he decided, especially if the uprooted plant was tender in the first place. Was the dilapidated sod house adequately repaired for winter? The never-ceasing wind was really getting cold these days. Peder crossed his arms and tugged at the shoulders of his big coat. The oxen had begun going downhill now, and soon they would be at the wood-lot where exercise would begin to subdue the shivers.

While the oxen stood with drooping heads, the wagon was loaded, log by log. the larger ones Peder and Elsie lifted together.

"It's getting colder," said Elsie, slapping her mittens together to relieve the nail bite in her fingertips.

"It's cold all right."

"I'm really shivering, Peder." Her compelling voice forced Peder to stop and look at her.

"We should have taken the buffalo robe your mother offered us," Peder said, walking toward her.

"Take me with you inside your big coat," she said suddenly.

"I'll bet I'll be warm then." She pulled off her mitten and poked her hand between the buttons, into the sheepskin lining. "See how much room there is in here? Plenty of room for both of us."

Before he could muster courage to resist, she had thrown off her other mitten, unbottoned his coat, and moved in, her arms tightly encircling his waist.

"Now button us up and hold me nice and close."

In spite of Elsie's buttoned jacket, Peder felt those soft breasts, which he hadn't wanted to acknowledge, pressed against him. She had aroused him and he was mortified. Hot blood surged in his veins. He was so embarrassed he felt pain.

"Look," he said finally. "I'll give you my coat. You just sit down over here with it over you, and I will finish with the loading."

"You'll be cold then," she purred, showing no sign of relinquishing her hold on him.

"I'll keep warm as I work. Then I'll walk while you drive the oxen."

He tugged himself away from her as gently as he could. At last she dropped her arms and looked sadly into his face. She accepted his coat across her shoulders before she spoke again.

"You don't like me, Peder, do you?" she whimpered, drawing the big coat tighter.

"I gave you my coat, didn't I?" Peder was free again and renewing his effort to load the logs.

"You don't even want to put your arms around me."

Peder lifted one log after another and said nothing.

"I know you have a girl," she went on, putting her mittened hand against the side of big Sven.

"I do."

"I suppose she is very beautiful."

"Yes, she is."

"Could she handle a team of oxen?"

"No, I'm afraid not. But she can play the organ." Peder wondered why he told her that.

"Really? Then she is a fine lady like those that live on the bonanza farms."

"I wouldn't say that. Her folks aren't rich."

"Peder, why won't Papa let me work at Grandin? They hire both men and women there. I can do all kinds of things that are hired for. I could earn some money and meet other young people my age."

"I don't know," said Peder, beating the last of the wood chips out of his mittens. "I guess he thinks they would be bad company for you."

"Are they all bad, then?"

"No, not all, just some."

"Maybe next year. You could tell Papa he ought to let me go. I think he'd listen to you. He really likes you, Peder. We all like you, especially me." She caught his eye and smiled.

"Time to go. Get the oxen started and climb in. I'll walk. That way I'll stay warm."

He watched her head the oxen toward home. It was a heavy load for them, but on the home stretch they would always keep moving. He watched her climb on the load and wiggle in for the ride. He didn't miss his coat. No, he was angry to think she had aroused him. He was afraid he would have to hate her after this, and that filled him with dread. He wanted to run, but he stayed with the cart and walked home alongside Thor and Sven.

Chapter 5

With the coming of spring, 1887, a whole year had gone by since Peder left, and Anna had a pile of letters to verify it. She kept them in a "keepsake" box on the bureau in her room. With each one she filed away, she looked at herself in the small, oval mirror. No, she certainly wasn't getting any prettier; in fact, she had quit smiling at herself. And she felt less and less like writing. She pictured her pile of letters somewhere among Peder's belongings, most likely in that pigeonhole in his trunk. She wondered how much of penned sentiments reached the heart. There was a dryness settling in, an absence of flesh and blood. She was trying to conjure up for herself that smile of his, that smile that meant love, that all important smile. She didn't dare to think that someday she would fail altogether.

The "hope chest" had many items in it, for she had been busy. She had impressed the circle of womenfolk, among whom she lived, with three sets of pillowcases with wide crocheted edgings, two linen table doilies with an elaborate white solid embroidered design, and a cross-stitched wall hanging lettered "God Bless Our Home." She had also done knitting. There was a sweater, a muffler, and three pairs of stockings for her beloved Peder. She had thought of sending these to him but hated to risk his not receiving them—better to wait. And on top of all that was a piece quilt ready for the next quilting party. "Get it done, Anna, we want to get together and stitch."

But spring meant the out-of-doors. She wanted to close the "hope chest" lid for a while, even slide the cover over the organ keyboard. There would be seeds to plant, baby chicks to raise, and berries to pick. She would get along without Peder. In fact, she might do better this summer than she had last. Without him? Would it mean she would succeed less and less in conjuring up the smile? She grew anxious for a moment. No, spring and summer meant her letters would take on a freshness, no question about that.

A day in April before the farmers had gotten into the fields with their seed, Iver Mundahl received a letter from Peder. He took it, first of all, to Nils.

"Peder wants me to come and join him. He says he could use a carpenter. He has acquired a farm, he says, with very poor buildings."

"Well, now that sounds pretty good to me," commented Nils as he returned to the forge a piece of iron he had been shaping on his anvil.

"He says, too, that I might get a job doing carpenter work at the big farm." Iver followed Nils around.

"There are several bonanza farms up there that plant thousands of acres, employ a hundred men or more, and farm with the latest machinery. I can well imagine they would need carpenters. What do you think, Nils? Should I join him?"

"That, of course, is up to you, but it sounds good to me. Peder is not a foolish young man. If he thinks you might do well up there, most likely he's right. I'll have to look around for another man on the water wagon, I suppose."

"Give the job to Henrik and Lars. They are big enough now," Iver called back as he disappeared through the door as quickly as he had come.

He crossed the road and sought out Anna. He read the letter out loud to her so rapidly she could barely make it out.

Anna knew that Peder was now living on the Overvold place, as he called it, and that he had gone there to help out a young couple during January and February. He had written about how cold the winter was—drifts that covered the house—and how poorly the wife was, whose baby cried all the time. His last letter said he thought they might give up the farm altogether and return to Wisconsin. Peder felt very sorry for them because they scarcely had money enough for train tickets. But he hadn't mentioned that *he* might acquire the farm when they left. That was a new development!

"He's planning to build a new house on that place, Anna. He says the people in the settlement are anxious that he take over that farm. What do you think? Shall I take you along?"

A new house, that would be nice, but it wasn't built yet.

"You may bring him the new sweater I knit," she said brightly. "So you think you are really going?"

"Why not?"

"I think you will make Peder a good partner. He always liked you and admires what you can do. Go ahead."

As she watched Iver dash up the way to his own door, Anna wondered at her numbness. Shouldn't she be overcome with excitement if Peder had at last acquired the land about which he had dreamed so long? Would she have felt different if it had been Peder, instead of Iver, who just now stood before her with this news? Why, of course! Her misgivings were foolish.

In June, Julia's older brother, John Mattson, came for a visit. He was in the hardware business in Red Wing and until now seldom got away long enough to take a trip to Wanamingo. Lately, however, he had expanded his store and acquired a partner. Since he was a widower with no children, and not so young anymore, he sought comfort in his relatives.

Anna delighted him from the start. It was almost as if the rest of Julia's family counted for nought. Wouldn't a hardware man be interested in the blacksmithing Nils was doing, or in young Henrik, who Julia pointed out was the image of their younger brother? But no, it was always Anna. How bright she was, how talented!

"She has real musical ability, Julia," he emphasized one day as he sat by the kitchen table, watching his sister churn a batch of butter. "I think she should take more lessons. If she does well enough on the organ, then she should take voice lessons."

"I'm not against it should there be opportunity."

"Of course you've heard of Professor Schumann at Red Wing Seminary? His wife is Norwegian. She gives voice lessons."

"Yes, I believe I've heard that".

"She always has a schoolgirl helping her, beginning every fall. She has three small children, you know, and a big house to take care of."

"Doesn't she have a full-time housemaid?"

"I think she does, but she keeps a schoolgirl, that I am sure. I'll tell you what I'll do. I'll get in touch with her and see if she would consider having Anna and giving her lessons. I will pay for the lessons if the work only amounts to room and board. What do you think Anna would say to that?"

"I'm sure she would jump at the chance. I cannot guarantee but what she might get homesick. She hasn't been away from home at all, you know." The churn had not yet yielded butter, so Julia continued turning.

"You will talk it over with her?"

"I will."

Of course Anna would go. It was the opportunity of a lifetime, and she was sure Peder would be proud when he read her letter telling him all about it. Word finally came from Uncle John saying that the place was hers, and following that, a letter from Mrs. Schumann—such a nice letter—saying how happy she would be to have her come. She would be expecting her the first week in September.

Anna's summer passed rapidly as she anticipated her new life in the city.

"I'd rather have a new waist than these dreadful-looking aprons," said Anna as she watched her mother pedaling a long seam on the sewing machine.

"You'll need aprons if you are going to help out as a housemaid. This one will fit nicely. Of course you don't like wearing mine."

"That lace edging I crocheted, can't we trim a waist with it? I want something really attractive to dress up in."

"Of course."

Anna did the fine finishing stitches on all the new garments, but her mother still did the cutting and fitting. She would have quite a nice wardrobe to take in her little trunk.

"You're going away? When are you coming back?" cried Sarah when she had fully grasped that she would be losing Anna.

"I'm not going away forever, Sarah. This is my home." Anna sorted through her music portfolio, deciding what she would take. "You keep practicing. You'll be playing almost any song you choose pretty soon."

"Too bad the railroad isn't open yet between Zumbrota and Red Wing," said Arne, as Anna was climbing into Mattie Skaar's little rig. "You really ought to have a train ride."

"I've never ridden on a stage either," called Anna, starting the first leg of her journey with her music teacher who was going back to Zumbrota. Anna didn't take her eyes off the womenfolk and Arne waving in the doorway until the rig left them behind.

At Zumbrota she watched her little trunk being lifted into the carrier on top of the stage. She was helped through the narrow door into the enclosed interior. Because of the bright sun of this September day, she saw nothing the first moment she entered but felt for the seat and settled in. A wave of uneasiness swept through her; she had never ridden in an enclosed rig before. Why couldn't she see more of the world than these tiny windows allowed? And everything that lay around her would be strange. Could she do without the familiar? For a moment she thought she couldn't. She wanted to open the tightly latched door and run out, scare the birds, fly home. But the carriage was rolling faster than she had ever experienced. What kind of horses are hitched to stages? Yes, she knew they were the fastest that could be found. She wished she could see them; that would give her some comfort.

By now her eyes were used to the reduced light. The interior was all in red like Sophie's parlor. She sat on a red cushion, and a fringe of red tassels, together with a red rope to grasp should the road become bumpy, adorned the window. The ceiling looked like red satin and so did the walls. Someone could be sitting on the seat opposite her, she suddenly realized, but today there was no one. She moved from one side of her seat to the other, trying to look out the window. What she saw, as the stage flew along, was distorted and unsettling, so she decided not to gaze out anymore but just sit as in the parlor.

Uncle John met the stage, as he had promised to do, and he had a rig waiting to take her to the Schumanns'.

"How was the trip?" inquired Uncle John as he took hold of the little trunk being let down from the rack.

"It went faster than I thought it would," replied Anna, gazing around in all directions.

"Yes, these horses move. But wait until you ride a train."

She suddenly noticed what must be railroad tracks along side of the street on which she was standing, and beyond them the Mississippi River. And was that a train whistle? Sure enough, and it was like her father's steam engine whistle, but his was a toy in comparison. She looked up and down the street. Not only were there buildings bigger than she had ever seen, but there were so many of them. And, of course, there was Barn Bluff, which everyone talked about, rising so very close to the town. Yes, it was high up there. It even made the big buildings seem small.

"This town is full of bluffs. You'll find that out," continued her uncle as she sat beside him in the buggy. "We're going to climb one now known as College Hill."

They sped through the street among other carriages and suddenly were climbing up and up. Anna saw the river far below, flowing ever so slowly.

"I see a boat way down there," she exclaimed.

"That's a common sight this time of year."

"I think I shall like Red Wing," Anna announced to the pleasure of her solicitous uncle.

"I knew that all along."

Anna was surprised that Mrs. Schumann was an ordinary little woman who could have been a friend of her mother's. Her face seemed large, perhaps because the rest of her was so slight, and it was an expressive face with wide blue eyes that responded quickly to those on whom they were fixed. Anna liked her immediately and felt at ease. There were three children as Uncle John had said. The oldest was a boy of five who was called Eddie—no doubt his name was Edward, after his father—a girl of three named Lisa, and a baby boy, Richard. Anna did not meet Professor Schumann until suppertime, when he rushed in, dropped his valise of books, and grabbed his children one at a time and lifted them above his head. They shrieked with glee. Anna like him, too. There was somethng almost boyish about him which made it hard to believe he carried a professor's learning in his head.

There was a housemaid who served the evening meal to the family in the dining room, and she and Anna ate at the family table. Anna was relieved that these important people seemed no different from the people she knew.

Her first job at the Schumann household was to clean the pantry. Gudrun, the housemaid, never seemed to get around to it. Anna knew very well how to scrub shelves, climb high and low, but it made her tired. Was she, after all, delicate as her mother claimed? "I don't know when I'll get to the music lessons. I have spent the first three days here cleaning the kitchen," Anna wrote in her first letter home.

After that, Anna's duties became routine. She made the beds, dusted the furniture and tidied the rooms. When Ingeborg Schumann discovered how beautifully Anna could iron clothes, she was delighted. Up until now, this very particular woman had done the ironing herself, but now this new girl would relieve her of a few more hours to spend with her pupils. But Anna's main responsibility was being nursemaid to the children, and this turned out to be a source of delight. She rewarded their good conduct with extra stories, and they grew very fond of her.

Every Tuesday afternoon, Anna had her vocal lesson. She also had an opportunity to transfer her keyboard skill from organ to piano. Every Thursday evening, while Ingeborg was over at the seminary for choir rehearsal with the students, Anna had her teacher's studio all to herself.

That she was thriving in her new surroundings was reflected in her letters to Peder. "I have a room of my own upstairs with a view west toward Red Wing Seminary. As I sit here and write, I am enjoying the autumn leaves in a riot of color. You might not believe me when I say I have not been seriously homesick. Mama worried about that, you know. Oh, I think about my dear ones and look forward to going home at Christmas time, but that's not to say I'm in any way lonesome."

One morning, Anna lifted the usual flatiron off the stove and tested it with a wet finger. The sizzling told her it was hot enough. She brought it to the ironing table and clattered it into place on the metal guard. She unrolled a dampened, white, dress shirt. She remembered Ingebord telling her to be ever so careful not to burn it. It had been bleached and starched so many times it could easily scorch. Her mother had been particular, too, so Anna had learned to be careful. It went nicely.

"See the giant," said Eddie, lifting his slate in front of Anna.

"That's good," said Anna, going toward the stove for a hotter iron. "You'll have to draw his sword, too, and his big shield."

"Tell the story about David again," begged the little boy. Yes, there was a sword in the story. He must hear the story again.

"David killed a lion," exclaimed little Lisa, coming out of the corner where she had propped up her dolls.

Anna looked into the two eager faces. She had just finished the shirt and carefully folded it.

"Once upon a time in a country far away there lived a boy named David. He was very strong and brave. That is why his father let him take care of the sheep. David liked being out in the pasture all day and he often sat down by a little brook while the sheep were eating. There he made a slingshot for himself and picked up little pebbles to shoot. Once he saw all the sheep raising their heads at the same time as if they heard a noise—"

"Lions!" cried Lisa.

"That's true, Lisa, lions."

The story progressed and there were frequent trips to the stove as the irons cooled over dampened table linen, pillowcases, and aprons.

Suddenly Anna noticed Ingeborg in the doorway. How long had she been standing there? The storytelling stopped and the mother entered.

"They really love your stories, Anna," said Ingeborg. "Use Norwegian once in a while, why don't you? I want them to know my language, and it would be good if they heard it from others besides me."

"Of course." Anna wondered a moment at this. To her it seemed important to know English.

"Their father, as you have noticed, talks German to them. That, too, is good. People should know more than one language, and we learn best as children."

"What about the rest of the story?" Eddie was speaking as politely as he could. The children hadn't relinquished their places near the ironing table, but were waiting for their mother to leave.

"Mama wants to talk to Anna."

This meant they must leave the adults, with only a small hope that the story would eventually be resumed.

"I have another favor to ask of you. If you weren't so good at everything, I suppose I wouldn't be always asking you."

Anna had no idea what this could be. She couldn't imagine what else she would have time for.

"I need someone to accompany Halvor Bergum on the piano as he practices his vocal solo for the recital. I just don't have any more time in my schedule."

"On the piano? I'm not very good yet, I'm not sure of—"

"It will be good practice for you. You'll get the feel of it quickly enough. The songs are not difficult in the least."

"You really think I can do that?" Anna's hesitation turned to astonishment.

"Of course."

"I don't know Mr. Bergum. Is that his name?"

"Yes, Halvor Bergum. He's a second-year student. He won't expect more than you can do. He'll only be glad for the extra rehearsal."

"I'll try." Anna swallowed hard.

"Don't worry, Anna. I wouldn't ask you to do it if I had doubts about you. You'll do well. And Halvor might even like you." Ingeborg turned and left.

The two children returned with upturned faces. They waited a long moment. Anna wasn't ready to go on with the story; they could see that.

A weakness crept into Anna's legs. She returned the iron to the stove. What was about to happen now? She was terrified, but not altogether so. She was dazzled, too, by the possibilities she had often dreamed about but which she never believed could be hers.

"What happened when the little stone hit the giant?" called Eddie, thinking he could get the storyteller going again. It was taking her a long time to pick up that other hot iron.

"Yes, yes, Eddie." Anna looked at the eager children.

She continued where she thought she had left off. She had skipped part of the story, but they didn't mind. They had heard it many times before.

Chapter 6

Anna was practicing on the piano in the studio after she had gotten the children to bed. A knock was heard at the door. She knew it would be Halvor Bergum coming to rehearse his vocal solo; it had been prearranged so. Now she wished that someone might introduce them, it would be embarrassing to come face to face with a total stranger.

She opened the door. Yes, a young man stood there with a music portfolio in his hand.

"You're Anna Kristian? Mrs. Schumann said you would accompany my solos in her studio this evening."

"Oh yes, do come in," said Anna, suddenly realizing how awkwardly she had stared at him and kept him waiting outside.

"I'm Halvor Bergum. I'm pleased to meet you." He had taken off his hat and was waiting for her to hold out her hand.

"I'm happy to meet you, Mr. Bergum." Anna shook his hand and spoke with a smile. She was glad she had learned good manners.

"Come," she said, leading the way to the piano studio. Halvor hung his hat on the rack in the entry and followed.

"You must have had lessons before coming here," said Halvor as they moved through the sitting room. "You just came this year, didn't you?"

"Yes," she replied, turning around upon having led the way through the studio door. "I have had organ lessons before this. I'm not too good on the piano yet. The touch is different, you know."

"I can imagine."

Anna went to the piano stool and sat ready for what was to come. She hoped the music wouldn't have too many sharps. Suddenly a large piece of sheet music was placed in front of her. "The Holy City"—he sings that! She turned and looked at him.

"I'll try my best. I know this one—a little."

He smiled and waited.

Anna quite forgot her fears when she began to hear the music. Halvor was a baritone; she didn't suppose he would hit the high note at the end. He would know better if he couldn't handle it. She had heard soloists spoil this beautiful song because they foolishly believed they could reach the note by sliding up. That was so painful. His voice did have a rich quality, and he sang very well indeed—such clean enunciation—such breath control. She had reached the arpeggios now, an interlude for the singer. How well she was doing! She could scarcely believe it. Retard now, just enough to let him in again on the third verse. Yes, so she thought—an octave lower on that unbelievably high note, and how ably he held it. She mustn't rush him. What breath he had to sustain the closing note! She had never heard it so exquisitely sung, and she had actually accompanied. She was exhilarated.

She swung around quickly on the stool and beamed up at the young man. "Beautiful, Mr. Bergum. You sing very well, to say the least!"

He draped his arm over the corner of the upright piano. "Thank you."

"How long have you taken lessons, Mr. Bergum?"

"I'm a second year student. I began lessons last year just after Christmas. I was in the choir first, then Mrs. Schumann encouraged me to take voice."

"I can see why she would."

"You do a lovely job of accompanying. You surprise me, Miss Kristian. I don't think you missed a note."

"I may not be able to do as well on all your songs. You see I happened to like this particular song and have been playing it for my own enjoyment. So, you see, it is not entirely new to me," confessed Anna, knowing she could be stumped very easily by a piece she had never seen before.

"My other number is really a hymn which you probably know very well. It's *"Den Signede Dag Som Vi Nu Ser."*

"That one I can play." Anna, much relieved, reached for the hymnbook.

"This hymn is beautiful as a solo," Anna said wistfully when the song was finished. She turned slowly.

"Mrs. Schumann really likes Norwegian chorales, I can tell that. She's always encouraging me to sing them."

"Any others?"

"No, these are the two. Could we go back to the first one? I need to improve on the second verse."

When the session was over, Anna suddenly remembered Ingeborg's instructions.

"Come to the kitchen. Mrs. Schumann left some sandwiches and cookies for us. She thinks you fellows don't get enough to eat at the boarding club. Do you like hot chocolate? She gave me explicit instructions to make you some."

"Oh thank you. I guess I cannot turn down an invitation like that even if I do have lots of reading to do." He followed her to the kitchen, leaving his portfolio in the entry on the way.

"Reading? What kind of reading?" Anna got out the sauce pan and gathered her ingredients. She put another stick of wood in the stove.

"We have been studying the Greeks. Right now we are reading Plato."

"I've heard of him, but I haven't read anything by him. I read a lot though. Is it interesting?"

"Indeed. But it is hard to get everything read by a certain day."

"I suppose it's like that when you go to school."

"You say you read a lot. What have you read?" Having seated himself at the table, he watched her working at the stove.

"This past year I read *A Tale of Two Cities* by Charles Dickens. Do you know it?" She didn't turn around. She was stirring the hot drink for fear the milk would scorch.

"Oh yes. I found it in the library here and read it during Christmas vacation a year ago. It is one of the best books I've read."

Anna set a cup and saucer before her guest. With the little curls of steam came the aroma of chocolate. Anna took a chair opposite Halvor and pushed the sandwiches toward him.

"Vær så god."

"Thank you."

"It is one of the best books I have ever read, too," said Anna as she waited for him to swallow part of his sandwich.

"I was touched by Sidney Carton's dying instead of Charles Darnay," he said finally. "I could hardly believe it would happen, although there were hints of his intentions."

Anna suddenly realized she hadn't really looked at this young man until this moment. What wonderful eyes! They were hazel eyes—her mother had hazel eyes—and Anna hadn't thought that a very exciting color for eyes. But these were different. They were deep-set and had a kind of dark edge on them. They spoke now of the overwhelming generosity of Sidney Carton. There were deep feelings behind those eyes, she was sure, feelings that prompted that gorgeous rendition of "The Holy City," and much more.

"I have to confess I wept when I finished it," responded Anna with intensity. "I've never read a story with such a beautiful ending. I was lonesome for days after I had read it."

"Yes, I know very well what you mean." He smiled and took a sip. "What are you reading now?"

"Another very good book. It's a nice big one and will last me a long time. It was written in French and translated, but the title wasn't. It's called *Les Miserables*. Have you read it?"

"No."

"It takes place in France like the other book, only slightly later. I just love to read stories about Europe, particularly France."

"It's a good way to learn history, and more interesting than reading a textbook." He looked up from his cup.

She resumed her fascination with his eyes. Undoubtedly he would feel for the vagabond in *Les Miserables* the way she had. Here was someone worth knowing, worth listening to, worth, worth—.

"I must really be going," he said, gently moving his chair back from the table.

"You couldn't finish the last sandwich? Shall I wrap it for you? You could take it back to your room and eat it while you read."

"A capital idea! How did you think of that?" His eyes were merry.

"I sometimes eat when I read. Why not you?" She beamed back but rose quickly to find a napkin. "Here."

"Thank you, Anna. Certainly I may call you Anna?"

The eyes waited an answer. Anna studied them.

"Of course."

"And don't you go calling me Mr. Bergum all the time. I'll admit it is flattering to a green student to be addressed that way, but you, Anna, please call me Halvor." He stood tall now, lifting the chair and placing it under the table.

"I will. I feel I know you better already by calling you Halvor." She walked with him to the entry.

"And— Anna, please come to my recital," he said, hesitating a moment.

"This Sunday afternoon?"

"Yes."

"I'd love to. Thank you."

He was gone. She shut the door. She was stunned. He had invited her to come—a special invitation!

She ran with short, quick steps back to the studio. She wanted to skip, but she hadn't done that for a long time. She settled again on the piano stool. She looked to her right. He had stood just there, leaning across the piano. He had laid his portfolio over there on the table. She swung around on the stool. "Hosanna, hosanna!" had rung through this room. But she hadn't seen his eyes yet, that had happened in the kitchen. She ran with the same short steps to the kitchen. There were the cups. She would clean them up before Ingeborg returned. His cup—she lifted the cup and saucer and held it reverently—yes, his cup. She smiled to herself; she was being foolish, she knew. She grabbed the dishtowel in earnest and hung the clean cups back on their hooks. "Thank you, God, for letting me play so well for him. I'm so happy."

As she shut the cupboard door and hung up the dishtowel, Anna heard Ingeborg enter.

"So he invited you to the recital," called Mrs. Schumann from the hall. She removed her wraps and came closer, smiling.

"How did you know?" Anna looked like a child.

"Halvor told me. I met him just as I left the rehearsal."

"He did, that's true. But the children... I must take care of them while you are there. I'm not sure..."

"Mrs. Paulson might come over and watch them for us. She likes the children."
"Do you think she would?"
"I don't know why not."
"I guess I've always thought of her as your guest, not someone with whom you would leave the children."
"She's a dear old friend. She'll do it for you, Anna. She'll understand." Ingeborg winked lovingly.
"Oh thank you!" Anna rocked childishly on her tiptoes until she realized what she was doing then quickly shifted. "How was choir rehearsal this evening?"
"Very well, but I'm a little tired. It's bedtime."

Anna set her candle on the dressing table and closed the door to her little bedroom. She looked at the white bedspread and wondered if she would fall asleep. She wasn't a bit inclined, but she guessed it was late.

Soon she was under the covers. She tossed from side to side in an effort to settle. He wasn't just handsome, he was—well, she couldn't explain it. She thought she knew how Lucy had felt when she first saw Charles Darnay. It was recognition, it was a great discovery, a big yes. There was a world in those hazel eyes, a world she wanted to reach for, to explore, to come to know—a world in which she was sure she wanted to be. She was so sure!

She sat up. She looked out into the crisp November night. There was lamplight in several windows over at the seminary. Was Halvor still reading? He must have finished his sandwich by now. She wondered about Plato. Maybe he had written something she should read. There, one lamp went out. It was getting late all right. There went another. She remembered the Mississippi far, far, down between the bluffs. Boats weren't on it anymore; it was too late in the season.

She slid again down under the covers. It was getting cold in the house. All the stoves were going out. What one had to do was lock oneself within the quilts and find a little *fot hus* before toes got too cold.

Suddenly her heart sank. After the recital he would have no need to come and rehearse. The recital was the end; why hadn't she thought of that until now? Her evening was a thing of the past. But she wouldn't settle for that; she just couldn't. He wasn't going to quit taking lessons just because the recital was over, was he? He would continue to sing and would need someone to play for him, wouldn't he? And she had played well. He had said so, hadn't he? Maybe, just maybe she could count on other evenings like this one." The quilts had absorbed enough heat to keep her warm. She fell asleep.

She would wear the waist with the crocheted lace and her black wool skirt to the recital. She decided that the next morning. She hadn't worn it anywhere yet. She knew now why she had crocheted the lace and gone to such extra pains to sew it. Intuition.

Anna had been in the Red Wing Seminary chapel before, but never for a recital. She moved toward the front as close as she dared, looking around in case she saw someone she knew. She would get rid of her coat and bonnet at the reception in the dining hall which usually followed such recitals, but for now she would keep them on. Anna watched the guests arriving, the men moving to their side of the aisle and the women to the opposite. This was a chapel, after all, and that's how it was.

Someone came and moved away the pulpit, which stood at the center of the raised platform that was like a half dome with a front arch spanning the room. Another usher joined the first man and moved the piano closer to the center. Anna began to realize that this place was as much an auditorium as a chapel. The altar, far back into the crescent of the dome, was very inconspicuous; no one would pay much attention to it this evening. She gazed at the tall arched windows to her right. She felt exceedingly small sitting here; the ceiling was so very far above her head.

Soon the participants paraded in and took the front seats reserved for them. Halvor was among them. No, he didn't seem nervous. He was more dignified than she remembered him, and his hair was darker.

Finally Ingeborg Schumann entered, beckoned her first performer and proceeded up the steps to the platform. She was wearing a black silk dress with a white neck piece overlaid with fine lace, on which she wore a large cameo pin. Her hair was done high on her head, accentuated by a rhinestone comb. Anna had to admit she looked beautiful all dressed up, and she was proud she knew her. Anna admired more, however, the style with which she played the piano. She wasn't hunched and tormented by the notes on the rack, but she sat with a straight back, hands arched high, and her sharp chin forward. she swayed slightly, phrasing the music as if her body alone were doing the crescendos.

Among Mrs. Schumann's pupils was a mezzo soprano named Clarice Flatten, who sang "He Shall Feed His Flock like a Shepherd," from Handel's *Messiah*. Anna had never seen such blond hair. It shone like ivory. Maybe as a performer she should have worn black, too, but she hadn't; her dress was blue with elaborate tucking on the upper sleeves. Although the song was familiar—Anna had played it out of one of her organ books—she had never heard it sung like this. She felt drawn to this young woman and wished she were her friend.

Soon Halvor was on the stage and Anna vied with a bonneted head in front of her for a better view. She wondered if Ingeborg would be playing faster than she had. No, not really. How simple it seemed for her! Halvor reversed his two numbers, singing the hymn first. Anna found herself sitting with folded hands. The familiar melody carried her back to her own church, where Rev. Hanson with his strong voice had led the congregational singing. But this was more superb; a new luster surrounded the old chorale.

Soon she was following the crowd of guests to the dining area, where refreshments were served and where people could visit. She wouldn't feel as comfortable here as she had in similar social gatherings at Aspelund or Wanamingo. These people among whom she mingled now were educated and accomplished, at least so she imagined.

"I thought I'd find you. I'm glad you came." Halvor was suddenly at her elbow.

Seeing him at this moment was so unexpected that she almost tripped on the threshold, but she managed to feign composure.

"I enjoyed it all very much."

"I'm sure you saw how nervous I was."

"You didn't look nervous in the least. You sounded even better than the other night. A big auditorium suits you." she marveled that she could be so talkative, shy as she felt.

"Here, let me take your coat. I'll hang it up over here for you."

"Thank you," she said, conscious that at last she would be seen in her new waist.

"Thank you again for the other evening. You gave me more confidence," he said as they walked toward the refreshment table.

"You would like to meet Clarice, wouldn't you, Anna? I'll introduce you when we have opportunity," said Halvor, finding chairs after they had filled their plates.

"I would love to meet her. she has a beautiful voice. She must have taken lessons for a long time."

"Of that I am sure. She sings solo parts for cantatas at Christmas and Easter around Red Wing."

Quite unexpectedly the blonde girl came, her escort drawing up a chair for her next to Anna.

"This is Anna Kristian, Clarice," said Halvor.

"Oh yes, Mrs. Schumann has told me about you," responded Clarice amiably.

"How do you do?" Anna ventured. "I enjoyed your solo very much."

"Oh thank you. And, Arvid, meet Anna." Clarice drew her escort into the circle.

"Pleased to meet you."

Anna couldn't grasp what was happening just now. She was an actress caught here knowing her lines and saying them as graciously as she could. It wasn't unpleasant, however—quite the contrary. She had imagined occasions like this many times and knew very well how to handle them. Later she would have to figure it all out. In the meantime here was Clarice, more beautiful than one could imagine. How blue her eyes were! Maybe the blue of her dress made them bluer; Anna wasn't sure. And Arvid, another stranger, becoming an acquaintance.

"You're taking lessons from Mrs. Schumann, aren't you?"

"Yes, I am," said Anna smiling. "I just started this year."

"Your turn will come for this, too," Clarice chuckled.

Anna was included now in this circle. She felt elated.

The room became exceedingly noisy with conversation, and distractions were frequent. Halvor was so busy acknowledging all the kind remarks from friends that Anna found herself staring off at Ingeborg, who was the perfect hostess, missing no one. Anna imagined her parents somewhere in the crowd; she wasn't used to being without them. Her mother should just see what a good time her daughter was having. She wondered if her mother had ever heard such fine singing in Wisconsin when she was young.

"Let me walk you home, Anna," said Halvor as he helped her into her coat.

Anna looked at her escort. His eyes were asking a question.

"Thank you. I'd like that very much."

"It's still early and the fresh air feels good. Let's walk a ways along the edge of College Hill. I know a good place where you can see the whole valley."

"I haven't been out walking much since I came. I scarcely know the out-of-doors, except through the windows." Anna took the arm he offered. Was this real, or was she dreaming? The sudden crisp air felt good.

They passed the row of professors' houses and found themselves out in the country. The sun was about to set and the landscape was tinged with red. The trees, bare of leaves at this time of year, were dark silhouettes against the warm color of the sky. If it weren't for the crimson sundown, November would be a dismal scene, Anna figured. Now she was sure Halvor felt this, too, otherwise he wouldn't have asked her to go with him. She was now in his world.

"Did you finish reading Plato?"

"Oh yes, I managed to get it done."

"Was it interesting?"

"It's not exactly entertaining reading. Not as good as your Charles Dickens." He was smiling at her. They had stopped at the edge of the hill. "How do you like the view?"

"Oh, it is quite breathtaking, isn't it, looking down upon the river from way up here?"

They stood in silence for a long moment. Anna felt his arm around her waist. A strange sensation swept through her body. It was almost as if her soul had surfaced in a way she had never experienced before. This was being in Halvor's world. How exquisite!

"I often sit here on this boulder," he said, breaking the spell and walking toward a huge rock. "Want to sit a minute?"

"I'd love to. So this is where you come." She leaned into the rock as though she were sitting. It was too high for her. "I used to sit on one in our pasture, but that is pretty long ago now." Why was she telling him this? It was one of her guarded secrets.

"Where is your home?" He had chosen to lean against a tree.

"Wanamingo, in Goodhue County. Where's yours?"

"Rice County. My father took a homestead there."

"You are from a farm family, then?"

"Oh yes. And your father, is he not a farmer?"

"He's a blacksmith. We really live among farmers. My father has a threshing rig. Besides the blacksmith shop he has ten acres of land, pasture and garden. We have a few cows and chickens." Anna was saying more than she intended since his eyes kept asking.

"Threshing," he mused. "My brothers have been out all fall. It's an exciting season. I miss it."

"You do?"

"But I was chosen to be the one to study, to get an education."

"So?"

"My father is somewhat of a student—self-educated, you might call it. He's a lay preacher, a true Haugean. He is more interested in theology than he is in farming. He reads in all his spare time and all through the slack season."

"Really? That's admirable."

"He decided one of his sons must be educated, and it turned out to be me."

"Why you?"

"Because I'm inclined toward books and studying. My two older brothers aren't. That's why they are out threshing and I'm not."

"But maybe you're the lucky one."

"I guess so," he sighed. "My father wants me to study for the ministry. He wants me to have the kind of education he didn't get."

"Don't you want to be a minister, then?"

"I don't feel called, Anna." Halvor looked up and gazed intently at his new friend.

"Do you want to be something else?"

"I don't know really. I have thought about teaching, or law even. If I do that I would transfer after another year to the University of Minnesota." He picked up a little twig and twirled it in his fingers. "But I do think I would like to study theology."

"Then, why don't you? Besides, since you know it would please your father, maybe that is a kind of call."

"Do you think so?" He broke the twig and let it drop.

"I don't think you have to experience an earthquake or anything like that." Anna couldn't quite understand why she was saying all this, meddling even; it was his life.

"And I'm not one who gets up and talks about being saved." What he said sounded like a thunderbolt to him. There was a long, difficult silence.

"But you sing so beautifully," Anna said at last. "Maybe it is even better to sing what you feel than to talk long about things that are far too complicated to explain."

"Coming to think of it, my father wouldn't be half as successful if it weren't for his singing. In fact, he stops right in the middle of his preaching and sings a song and often everyone joins him."

"That's wonderful. I'd like to meet your father. He must be like Rev. Østen Hanson."

"That would be saying too much."

"He was a self-educated lay preacher, too, you know—and can sing."

"Anna, I love to talk to you. You—well you— kind of clarify things." He walked toward her and reached for her gloved hand.

"That's a compliment, Halvor, thank you," Anna responded as she was being drawn from her sitting position.

He held both her hands in his, reluctant to drop them. "I really meant what I said."

"Thank you," Anna repeated, not knowing what else to say. How was one to respond? She trembled to know.

"I'm afraid I've stayed away too long. I was supposed to take care of the children this afternoon. I mustn't keep Mrs. Paulson waiting. She has been good enough to watch them for me until now."

They started back toward the row of houses.

"If I need an accompanist, may I ask you?" He hung onto her hand long enough to ask it. She seemed suddenly in a hurry.

"Of course."

She ran up to the door. She turned and waved back at him before she went inside.

Anna dashed up the stairs to her room to change her clothes before looking around for Mrs. Paulson, the children or their mother. She looked absently out the window toward the seminary as she began undressing. She returned to the closet and hung up her new waist. She worked with a frantic kind of haste she couldn't understand. As she tied the strings of her apron, she caught sight of the keepsake box of letters in the secretary. Her heart sank. Peder, where were you just now? Where have you been? In that stack of letters, that's where. No wonder I don't see you!

She hurried out the door to her duties. She was in her apron now and the letters were unmistakably in their envelopes—nothing had changed much. She thanked Mrs. Paulson for watching the children, but noticed by listening to her own tone of voice that her gratitude wasn't the glowing kind. It was routine and flat.

How could she sort out her thoughts?

She welcomed her own bedtime, not because she thought she would sleep. Far from it. The first thing she did upon entering her room was lift the drop leaf, closing the secretary. Up until now it had always been open. Now, that looked better; an open desk looked untidy.

She summoned the ecstasy of this day as she pulled the covers over her head. What did she mean, nothing had changed? Everything had changed! A new life-luster stirred in her soul, and she wanted to take it out and examine it, completely unhampered. It had to do with music, the most beautiful renditions she had ever known. She reveled in it and wanted more. It had to do with being a part of all the music she had heard, yes, friendship with Clarice, the favor of Ingeborg, and—did she dare think it?—Halvor's world. She felt invited in, stepping ever so carefully and discovering things about herself, too. She was beautiful, capable, and intelligent—even she! Halvor had thanked her for—what was it now, exactly? Talking to him—listening to him? She guessed that was it. It carried with it a sweeping satisfaction she must, by all means, hold fast. It displaced all satisfactions heretofore. It devastated the "hope chest," with all its hours of careful work. It corrupted the English lessons, too. Certainly she hadn't succeeded in changing Peder's strong, ugly brogue. She wondered at herself for thinking she could improve him. Just now she couldn't understand why Ingeborg wanted her to tell the children stories in Norwegian. This was America, after all, and English was the language. How well people spoke English around here! She even discovered a brogue in herself if she wasn't watching. It was as if the language had been rendered refined in this new world, even as the music.

Oh, she would measure up, there was no question about that. She suddenly remembered her mother. Wouldn't she love to be here beside her daughter right now? She knew she would like Halvor. She liked to converse with intelligent men. And wouldn't she like Ingeborg? She was just as Anna imagined her mother's friends to have been. And finally Clarice. Beauty within as well as beauty without, her mother would say. Anna was a fortunate girl at this moment. She wondered if a dream could be sweeter.

Chapter 7

But the secretary could not remain closed forever. It was soon to be open with more letters to file away and more letters to write. Peder couldn't be ignored just because she had met Halvor. Anna had given a promise that she would write, and she wasn't one to break promises. It was a fact now that his smile no longer affected her; she had even ceased trying to conjure it up. But a promise she could keep, and she continued to write lively letters, pleasing to herself.

And letters kept coming. The winter of 1888 had been extremely severe up north. At one point Peder and Iver, surviving in the sod shanty another season before building the new house, had awakened one morning to find the dwelling completely drifted over with snow. They had to tunnel out to reach the shed where the horses and oxen were sheltered. Only the chimney stuck up, the letter said. Next winter will be different, Peder emphasized, because then the new house would be up. His letters continued to be written in English. In fact, she wondered if Iver wasn't a ready consultant, because they were improving.

Anna shuddered when she read letters of the cruel winter. She knew she had it good here in this professor's house, well-built, where floors were warm with carpets and walls tight against drafts. It was bitterly cold in Wanamingo, too. The news came from home that Axel Finnesgard was found a frozen corpse in his sleigh by the barn door. The horses, still wearing their blankets, had brought him home all right, but could do no more for their master. It seemed he had left Haroldson's store after dark, hadn't removed the horses blankets in which he could have kept warm, and headed home in weather twenty-five degrees below zero. No one had seen him leaving. That was the tragedy. He had been drunk and felt numb, she supposed, otherwise he could have managed the cold. Others did. What a shame for the family! Poor Matilda, she had put up with so much from him.

Anna reflected further on this disturbing news. Couldn't someone stop Clarence Haroldson from making his brew? Norwegians got drunk from their brew and made it terrible for their loved ones. How come Professor Schumann could drink his beer and not become surly and cruel? She guessed it was true; Germans were different.

And Anna wrote her news. She was now singing in recitals, as well as helping Ingeborg with accompanying. Clarice Flatten and she sang duets, occasionally appearing on programs throughout the city. Ingeborg had also encouraged four of her students to form a mixed quartet, she singing alto, Clarice soprano, Arvid tenor and Halvor bass. There were so many beautiful songs in English, most of them with easy harmony.

She attended St. Peter's Church, another parish served by her own pastor, Rev. Østen Hanson, who kept her in touch with the events and anecdotes of the home folks. Frequently he asked her to play the organ for the hymns or sing a solo as he would have if she had been home. He was deeply respected here, she wrote, and we were fortunate to know such a great and good man.

Work wasn't so bad at the Schumann household, since, after all, they did have a full-time maid. Anna often mentioned the children in her letters. Eddie had asked her once what language God spoke. She supposed he expected her to say Norwegian because Ingeborg wanted her to talk her language with the children. He's smart, that boy. She shouldn't wonder if he might become a professor like his father. Imagine a child knowing three languages already!

And, of course, Halvor was mentioned often. What she wrote to her parents about him, she wrote to Peder. There was nothing confessional, nothing startling. He was a friend among friends, like Clarice and Arvid, and she enjoyed playing for him. He had the best singing voice she had ever heard, and it was wonderful having such a talented and inspiring friend.

Thus one year went by. She spent June and July of 1888 with her family, but returned to Red Wing early in August. To be sure, her stay at home had been satisfying and reassuring. She talked long hours with Julia and found that her mother identified with all the aspects of her experience with culture and the city. With her father, Anna discovered that she had missed his sheltering all these months away from home, and she felt secure once again in his presence. Sarah hated to see her sister leave, since the two of them had shared so much. Sarah had indeed become a good little musician on the organ for an eight-year-old. Henrik had listened intently to all Anna had said about seminary life; perhaps he would go there himself someday. Arne thought she should stay at least through her birthday, but her plans seemed to be otherwise. Not the train this time either, the rumor was that the track between Zumbrota and Red Wing wouldn't be ready until late fall. So she was leaving again—for how long? She had no idea, why should she answer that?

On a day in early spring, 1889, in the season of Lent, Anna got a letter from Peder. As Anna drew the mail out of the box, happy that postal deliveries were made from door to door these days, she noticed the letter immediately. Having just put away the ironing table and the freshly folded clothes, she was quite ready to read. Leaving the rest of the mail on the hall table, she withdrew to a chair by the window in the sitting room. This time of year a faint smell of spring trailed in through doors.

Anna noticed something disturbing in the first few lines. She wasn't at all sure that she wanted to read what he had to say.

Dearest Anna,

I am getting more lonesome for you as the days go by. Now it is spring again and it is three years since I saw you. Can life go on like this?

The house that Iver and I built last summer has stood the test of a long hard winter. It is warmer and nicer than any other house in the settlement. We put in many windows on the south so that the sun would fill the kitchen and the sitting room with light. I knew you would like that. I can see you here sewing and reading. We'll have plenty of books, won't we? And, of course, there's a place for the organ and a cabinet for you portfolios.

Iver and I spent most of the winter making furniture. We did have enough sense to buy good tools before we started. That's why we have had such good results. The sitting room was a carpenter shop all winter. Just the other day Iver decided to move back outside. We have four chairs now and a very sturdy table. You should see all our shelves. We have a place for everything, just you wait!

Remember about the stove I said we bought last fall? Well, it makes awfully good bread. Elsie was here the other day. She says she'd rather bake bread here than at home. I think Iver likes her. He gets lively whenever she comes over, and how they jabber!

But I don't really want to write about them. I want it to be about you and me. When we get the seed in and another crop growing, I would like to come back to Wanamingo. We could have a June wedding. What do you think about that? Then I could take you back to our own home. Iver could take care of things for me when I'm gone. He can put up some hay and tend the garden. We haven't any chickens. We really should have some chickens. What do you say, Anna, dearest? Should there be a June wedding in Wanamingo?

Anna dropped the hands that held the letter into her lap. She couldn't go on reading. She get married and move up to that God-forsaken country? She? A wedding in Aspelund—she and Peder? Impossible! Why impossible? Wasn't that how it was all planned, once? Something had happened to her, she knew, and she wasn't the same girl she used to be. Could she simply turn around and be again what she had been? Right now, that was quite impossible. She wouldn't even try.

"Yoo-hoo!" Clarice called from the front hall. She caught sight of Anna sitting with her back turned. "Oh there you are, doing nothing. I knocked at the door, but I guess you didn't hear."

"Come in and sit down," Anna responded. An intruding friend now was most welcome.

"Letter from home?" inquired Clarice as she took a chair opposite Anna and removed her bonnet, exposing her exceedingly blond hair.

"From Peder."

"What's the matter, Anna?"

"The matter?" Anna forced a quick little smile. "Nothing, really. I guess he gets kind of lonesome sometimes." She folded the letter and put it back in the envelope. "I can smell spring on your clothes. What are you up to?"

"Anna, be prepared for this." Clarice got up and walked around. Anna was very suspicious of what was coming. She watched Clarice pace and tried to keep her composure; she would do that at all costs.

"All right, Clarice, what is it?"

"Halvor intends to propose marriage to you."

The letter on Anna's lap dropped to the floor. She picked it up without answering.

"Aren't you going to say something?"

"I'm flattered, really I am. Is that what you want me to say?" She was trying to keep her distance but felt she wouldn't succeed.

"You're a warm person, Anna. I know you like him a lot." Clarice's voice was full of emotion. She had her eyes on the letter.

"I have made promises, Clarice."

There was a long silence. Clarice returned to her chair.

"Does Halvor know about Peder?"

"No," Anna hesitated. "He knows we write letters. He doesn't know what you know."

"That you two are engaged?"

"That's what I mean."

"Shall I tell him, perhaps?"

Anna said nothing.

"Anna, Halvor is in love with you! He has told me so! He just worships you. He wants you for more than a friend. He wants to marry you!"

Anna remained silent as a stone.

"Anna, I'm not so blind. I know you are in love with him, too. It's written all over you. You glow every time he comes near you."

"Please, Clarice, don't torment me."

Clarice was overwhelmed by the anguish in her friend's voice. "I'm sorry," she whispered.

Anna got out of her chair and went to the window. She decided not to push aside the lace curtain for a look outside, or to turn back toward her friend. She couldn't bring herself to speak.

"Anna, dear. I'll tell Halvor anything you want me to tell him."

Anna turned slowly. Clarice was a beautiful person, just beautiful. Anna wasn't sure she deserved a friend like her. There had been Mari, once, but that was long ago.

"Shall I tell him what you told me just now: that you have made promises?"

Anna nodded. But she wanted to shake her head violently. She wanted to rush into her friend's arms and tell her that everything the dear girl had said was true—about being in love with Halvor and wanting ever so much to say she would marry him. Woe! Those promises!

"Peder wants us to be married in June. That soon for me is quite out of the question." Anna's voice seemed to come from a great distance.

Clarice understood without pressing Anna with further questions. She would tell Halvor Anna's secret ever so gently, ever so discreetly.

"We'll see you at rehearsal this evening?"

"Yes, of course."

Clarice reached for her bonnet and moved toward the door.

"Good-bye, my dear. I'll have that little talk with Halvor as soon as I find a chance. Don't worry, Anna," she smiled.

Anna felt the warmth of that smile coming through those honest, blue eyes. As she heard her friend's feet descend the front steps, as if immediately on this errand to Halvor, Anna was overcome with dismay. She wanted to dash after Clarice like a child after its mother. Don't, Clarice, don't! But Clarice would and that was as it must be.

Anna hung onto the doorknob for a moment hoping for the benefit of a little soothing spring air. Then she drew the door shut upon the dark entry. She hurried back to the work of tidying the sleeping rooms. She waved the coverlets; she would put Peder off for a while. He couldn't expect her to simply drop everything and say June was just fine. She would stall. That was the only thing to do. Wasn't it?

Would Halvor change when Clarice told him everything? That was the question she had to live with all day. Her heart sank as she pictured in her mind his simply turning his back on her. But she had turned her back on him; what more could she expect? He was, after all, a man and certainly had his pride. He certainly had the right to simply walk away. She plagued herself imagining him ignoring her in the company of their friends, never seeking her out, never fixing those wonderful eyes on her. Would the quartet come to an end? Dared she hope for a shred of friendship that might outlive such a crisis? She had had such confidence in him.

Of course no good could come of broken promises; she wouldn't let herself even consider such a sin against heaven. Promises were like links in a chain, they could bring pain, but at the same time they were what held one's life on course. She couldn't deny who she was, that girl of her past promised to Peder. If she denied that, where would be the healing for the broken link? It wasn't indecision she was suffering; the course was there, determined long ago, and that was all there was to it.

The tasks of the day, if they couldn't be done by habit, became sources of irritation. The story she had promised the children had to be accommodated at all costs. Like her life, even the day was linked together by commitments.

When the hour for cantata rehearsal was almost upon her, Anna's apprehension mounted. Clarice must have told him by now, she said to herself as she rummaged through her music folio, scarcely knowing what she was looking for. Might he come for her? He did sometimes, but not always—more often not. It would be unsettling to see him.

To her dismay Halvor was scampering toward the house as Anna opened the door on her way out.

"Anna," he called, "Such a beautiful spring evening, I just had to come and walk over with you."

"It is nice, isn't it," she responded mechanically as she came down the front steps. "I've been inside all day. What a shame."

He was half jumping along at her side as they went. He was acting boyish. She wasn't sure if it was just spring elation or if he was nervous.

"Anna?" he suddenly stopped in front of her. "Tomorrow afternoon will you walk up Barn Bluff with me? The trail may not be ready, but we might have fun investigating."

Anna was too startled to reply. He didn't know. Quite obviously Clarice hadn't had her opportunity.

"Please say you will?" He wasn't budging.

"I may have to watch the children."

"You always have Saturday afternoons off. That hasn't changed, has it?"

"Not really, but you can't tell."

"Say you will!"

He stepped out of her way and fell in stride. Maybe Clarice will get to talk to him before tomorrow, thought Anna, this was indeed awkward.

The rehearsal was held in the college chapel although the cantata was scheduled for Easter at St. Peter's Church. Seeing Anna sitting among the altos, Clarice dashed over, hoping for a moment or two with her before Mrs. Schumann appeared.

"I saw you arrive with him," she whispered.

"So you haven't talked with him yet," said Anna with noticeable impatience. "I thought by now..."

"I have talked to him."

"You have?"

Clarice was gone. The director was at her podium and everyone giving her full attention.

After the rehearsal Clarice and Arvid left quickly giving Anna no chance to get an explanation. Neither could she get rid of her perplexity by talking to Halvor, because Ingeborg walked home with them, talking about the cantata and how well it was going.

"She's not working tomorrow afternoon, is she?" Halvor said to Ingeborg as he escorted the two women to the door.

"No, she's free." Ingeborg looked from one to the other. "With you, I suppose, unless she has other plans."

"I'll stop by at one o'clock. Too early?"

"No that will be fine," answered Anna smiling, but she thought Halvor was beginning to recognize her perplexity.

He certainly seems sure of himself, thought Anna as she prepared for bed. What did he have in mind? Just what had Clarice told him? Could he have misunderstood her? Anna knew she should have told him about her promise to Peder long ago, but it just hadn't seemed necessary, an unimportant detail that never seemed to fit into any of their times together.

The next morning as Anna shook the rugs out into the freshness of the April sunshine, she lingered long enough to notice that green grass was beginning to flourish on the slopes that dipped toward the south. The trees had a lavender hue; life was returning to the trunks, branches, and to the remotest twigs. Leaf buds were plump. What an ideal day for a walk! Anna was losing her misgivings. Everything seemed so right on earth. She wasn't about to summon the cold realization that her life had heartache in it, or to mull over the details of her fate.

He came at one o'clock as he said he would, and they dashed off down College Hill. They would pass through the downtown before they would climb Barn Bluff. To be sure, people in the area, from the early Indians and explorers to later settlers and city dwellers, had climbed this bluff by various trails, but now a public walkway was all but completed. Barn Bluff was much more rugged and steep than College Hill; it was not to be a place for homes but was a massive rock formation nurturing only such hearty vegetation as will thrive in rock flake. A few trees were making an attempt, and grass, certainly, and a few brave spring flowers.

"Clarice talked to me yesterday."

At last he was going to talk about it. He had the same puzzling boyishness as yesterday. They were leaving the town and approaching the climb.

Anna didn't know how to respond, but ventured, "Were you surprised?"

"Well, I was, yes. Yet something she said made me very happy."

"Oh?"

"She said you liked me very much. She even said you might be in love with me."

"But you know I mustn't be in love with you," Anna retorted anxiously, "I have made a promise to Peder, and..."

"I know that, of course."

The path took them up and up. Soon the trail was so steep it demanded concentrated effort, and a silence fell between them. Hand in hand they edged past a cave-opening where water, dripping from the ceiling caused a little stream to flow in front of them. Scarcely had they stepped across it when a pair of huge wings flew out off the crevice, so close that the two of them struggled to keep their balance.

"We frightened an owl out of its sleep," cried Anna as they watched the bird land, heavy and docile, into a thicket.

"You're right, it's an owl."

They groped along out of the shadows to where the path leveled again, yielding a moment's rest. Anna caught Halvor's eyes as she and he dropped hands at the end of the steep stretch. They affected her, those hazel eyes. Could there be anything wrong in liking someone very, very much?

Before she knew it, he was speaking. "I want you to be my friend, Anna. You know what I mean, real friendship? Nothing should really stop us from that."

"I hoped you'd say that," said Anna with a warmth that surprised him. The bewilderment was over. "I do want our friendship to continue. I want it ever so much."

They resumed the trek. Anna walked sure-footed and confident at Halvor's side. They began to feel the sun on their shoulders, the warm sun that was even now enticing the dormant life out of the earth.

"Anna, I need to tell you that you mean a lot to me." He was getting a bit ahead of her now, as if he wanted to stop her again at some point.

"Oh?"

"It's the things you say sometimes. Maybe it's because you are so smart and wise." He didn't stop her yet, he simply walked a few steps ahead, frequently looking back at her.

"That's saying too much. I am neither."

"Oh yes, you are. I have a hunch you take after your mother, the way you describe her."

"Sometimes you make too much of what I say. You think you know my mother simply by listening to me describe her."

"Here's what I mean. Remember when you told me that a call to the ministry need not be an earthquake?" He stopped abruptly in front of her. "Well, that's what helped me decide to become a minister. That's what I needed to tell you."

"I had something to do with that?"

"You did, Anna, and don't laugh, it's true."

Anna didn't laugh, she dropped her eyes. She wondered how such a bit of conversation could have come to have so profound a meaning.

"And that is also why I wanted to ask you to marry me. I thought you would be wonderful to have at my side. You are always a part of the songs I sing and the thoughts I think. That's why."

Anna turned pale.

"Forgive me for mentioning something that you say cannot be," he said quickly, hoping to bring life back into her face.

She seemed to want to go on walking, so he stepped out of her way. She moved forward a few paces and then drew a handkerchief out of her sleeve. He sensed there were tears he was not supposed to see. Finally she turned and waited for him to catch up.

"I'm glad we decided to be friends if what you say is true," she said as he slowly approached.

"You're not unhappy?"

"No. Why should I be? Friendship is a very precious thing."

How he wanted to take her in his arms! Instead he touched her on the shoulder and they resumed the walk. The path was easy from now on. Anna suddenly spotted a cluster of violets.

"Oh look, these brave little flowers bloom even here," she cried, bending down to acknowledge them. "They won't be squelched. They dare to be the first of the season. Here's one for your lapel." She picked another for herself. "Here's to friendship!"

They were almost at the top now. Lake Pepin, widening toward the east, lay ready for summer's river traffic. Toward the west, far beneath them, was Red Wing's downtown bustling with trade on a Saturday afternoon. Birds flew about, indifferent to the height of the bluff or the distance down into the town. The sky was blue and cloudless. A ferry was crossing the river into Wisconsin.

"We made it! Hurrah!" exclaimed Halvor, pushing a fist into the air.

"Not a bad path either. Lots of people will be climbing here when summer comes."

The owl was not to be seen on the way down. He found it unnecessary, perhaps, to leave his crevice habitat. They crossed the precarious little stream and soon were on the decline into the town.

"The Salvation Army band is out. Let's go and hear them," cried Anna.

They were soon among the folks in the street. The band was approaching from the opposite direction so they waited with a little knot of people on the corner of Bush and Main streets. General Nilson halted the band in front of the little crowd.

"Let's make a joyful noise unto the Lord!" Major Dorothy stepped forward, speaking in a loud, clear voice. Anna admired the brave woman preacher; her high forehead beneath her Salvation bonnet was evidence of intelligence and ability. "Sing with us, all of you good folks. You'll all know the chorus, I'm sure. Sing along, Praise God!"

The brass band played "When the Roll is Called up Yonder," while the drummers remained respectfully silent. Then the band members lowered their instruments and took to singing the first verse.

"Praise the Lord! Sing with us now," the major called out just a few bars before the chorus.

Anna nudged Halvor and the two joined the singing. There was a lilt and vigor in Gospel songs that was immediately appealing to these children of Norwegian Haugeans, and their voices were heard.

Suddenly the woman with the Salvation bonnet approached Anna and Halvor with a songbook.

"Here we have a couple with beautiful voices. Praise the Lord! You look like newlyweds. No? Would you sing the second verse for us?"

Halvor accepted the book with a smile and the two sang heartily.

After Major Dorothy's exuberant message, the band struck up "Onward Christian Soldiers," and began moving down the street. Suddenly Anna felt a hand on her shoulder.

"So—you are among those disturbing the peace." It was Uncle John Mattson, who had momentarily stepped out of his hardware store.

"Uncle John!" exclaimed Anna in surprise. "What did you say?"

"Disturbing the peace," he repeated with a twinkle in his eye. He noticed her handsome escort. "The City Council has had numerous complaints about the noise the Salvation Army makes down here. And with them I find my niece."

Anna introduced Halvor. "You're not angry, are you, Uncle John?" she asked.

"Not as long as you are so well escorted," he replied, smiling at Halvor. "And so long as you don't start wearing one of those ridiculous bonnets and start preaching."

"It just wouldn't be ladylike would it, Uncle John?" laughed Anna.

Chapter 8

When Iver left for the north country to assist Peder, Nils gave Henrik and Lars more responsibility as members of his threshing crew. At first he used them on the water wagon, since he felt each by himself was not ready to handle a man's job. They did remarkably well. There was never a hitch in the operation that could be blamed to their lack of attention. When Henrik turned fifteen, Nils decided to make him fireman. Henrik had learned this job a long time ago by watching Peder read the gage and maintain an adequate amount of straw burning in the firebox. But it was only now when Henrik was older that he could be given this awesome responsibility.

As his engineer this particular fall, Nils had hired a conscientious young fellow, Alfred Solheim, from the South Prairie. Alfred had learned how to handle a steam engine from his father, who also owned one. He was a serious young man who was intent on becoming a minister and had two years left at Red Wing Seminary. He had decided to stay out a year, however, not only to earn money, for he was not well off, but also, as he put it, to witness for the Lord among farmers. The well-meaning youth, although respected for his ability to keep the all-important steam engine running, was not "one of the boys," but instead became the butt of the men's crass humor. Although Henrik would have preferred a more amiable partner after having worked alongside of Lars, he worked silently with Alfred.

On the grain wagon this season had been still another new man, a transient worker, Wilfred Barnes. He hadn't stayed long, however, but while with the crew kept the men merry with his tall tales. He was as loud and profane as Alfred was pious. He took pride in filling these men, whom he considered gullible, with yarns about threshing crews he had worked with elsewhere. One day, for example, this Wilfred Barnes told of two fellows who had gotten drunk at a neighbor's still, had come home late, and had gone to sleep in the straw pile. On the same farm were painters working on the farm buildings. This particular night they were awake enough to notice the drunken pair stagger in. As a practical joke, they took some green paint and smeared the faces of the two after they were dead asleep. When they awoke, feeling woozy in the stomach and head, they looked at each other. "You are green!" shouted the one. "You are green!" shouted the other, and the two toppled unconscious back into the straw. Henrik saw how all the men laughed at this story. But not Alfred, he never laughed.

Noticing that he had gotten no laugh out of Alfred, Wilfred retaliated a week later by putting on the appearance of a "newly converted." He had been to church on Sunday, he told Alfred, and all of a sudden his heart had been stirred and he had been "born again." Poor Alfred, vulnerable as he was, took the hoax for genuine and became the laughingstock for many days. When Henrik saw his father amused along with the rest of the men, he began to understand that menfolks, when out threshing, enjoyed crudity to which they would never stoop when with their families. He knew, too, that most of the men thought this practical joke cruel, even as he did, but justified it by saying young Alfred needed to learn his lesson.

But Wilfred Barnes soon left for parts unknown, leaving Nils to make do until another man could be found. In the meantime, the amusement had ceased and good humor at low ebb.

One morning, as the routine seemed extremely dull, Henrik got it into his head to compose a limerick. Often, as he pitched straw into the firebox, the rhythm of a certain poem would come marching in his brain. It stemmed from the admiration he had for elocutionists whom he had heard recite at county fairs and Fourth-of-July celebrations. He often imagined himself before an audience.

With his limerick he would captivate the crew around the dinner table, entertain them, there needed to be some fun these days. He even pictured the women who worked so hard over the stove as being part of his audience. With each forkload the rhythm of his own poetry was taking form, in Norwegian, of course. How else would his audience understand him? At intervals, after he had clanked shut the iron door, he looked out over the whole threshing operation. He saw the uniqueness of each crew member at his particular task, and each was woven into the framework of his rhyme.

"What's on your mind? Why are you staring off into space like that?" asked Lars as the crew was washing up at the bench outside the back door of the house. He was next in line for the towel after Henrik.

"Was I staring off?" Henrik laughed, letting his friend know he was feeling good-natured. Then he told him he had made up a poem to be recited for the men.

"A capital idea! I miss you now that you are not on the water wagon. We all need to laugh again."

The men moved without hesitation into the kitchen, grabbed at the benches, and slid onto them on both sides of a long table. The noise sent the women to their loaded platters of meat, potatoes, and gravy which they quickly passed along. Mrs. Torkelson was known for her good cooking and there was always more than enough food. No man along the table need wonder if he could have a second helping or even a third.

When the men fell silent working their forks and knives, Lars broke in: "Gentlemen, Henrik here, has made up a poem about us all. Haven't your ears been burning this morning as he has been rhyming you all into his verse?"

"Oh, so? We'd all like to hear it!"

Henrik decided to stand to make it like a toast. They'd all like that.

Threshing at Torkelsons (in translation)

A *Trønder* and a *Sogning* pitched from the stack,
Bundle after bundle into the track.
The *Sogning* is short, the *Trønder* tall,
Neither seems to grow tired at all.

The men all looked up and searched the faces around the table until they spotted the stack pitchers to see how each was taking the fun. It was true, the *Trønder* was much taller than his forkmate.

Back in the strawpile a *Kristianenser* stands,
He may be small, but has great big plans,
See him over there—he's wondering
How much money his grain will bring.

Mrs. Torkelson looked at her husband. "That's him all right!"

The grain box tender dares not turn about,
But always had an empty sack ready for the spout.
A seminary student at the engine works
Full of fear when the big belt jerks.
It's his to watch, it must not fail
Lest the wheels go spinning to no avail.

All eyes were on Alfred. His eyes were on his plate. He kept on eating.

The fireman struggles with bloodshot eyes,
Peering at flames and every spark that flies.

"Naw, Henrik," someone muttered.

That slick water-hauler with his horses so trim
Keeps all the barrels full to the brim.

Lars grinned at all his comrades.
Henrik looked over at his father.

> The owner of the rig must have our attention,
> For on him rests the whole operation.
> If the wheels, for instance, begin to slow,
> Quickly to the machine he will go,
> And the bewildered man from Telemark
> Will run around wildly as if in the dark.

"Jens, that's you!" shouted the *Trønder* as if he had a score to settle.

> While the men, as we break down, will gape and stare,
> The *Trønder* and the *Sogning* will laugh loud to the air.

Henrik bowed and sat down. A hilarious applause broke out. Eating had come to a standstill, except for Alfred, and the women who listened had almost forgotten their obligation to feed these men.

"You deserve the biggest piece of pie," said Mrs. Torkelson, quickly setting before Henrik a royal serving.

The mood of merriment had returned.

Although Henrik enjoyed the company of farmers and working with his father, he had often expressed a desire for an education as he listened to Anna's report from Red Wing. Observing how seriously Henrik had taken to reading, and how much he had already absorbed on his own, Julia and Nils determined to provide an opportunity for him. Therefore, in the fall of 1891, Henrik enrolled in the Red Wing Seminary Academy.

As Henrik lifted his little trunk into the waiting rig, he suddenly realized it contained all there would be of home for many months. As Lars sat ready to drive the trim team before the buggy, and Nils and Julia were near at hand with their good-byes, a wave of uncertainty swept over Henrik which reached panic proportions. He'd never felt like this before. All he knew was that such cowardly weakness didn't become a man. Julia noticed that his eyes were larger than usual and his uplifted hand forced. "He's going to be homesick," she said to Nils.

As he walked with his friend into the train depot to buy his ticket, Henrik knew that in less than an hour Lars would no longer be at his side. He never dreamed this parting would be so painful. After all, a few months wasn't forever. He tried to shrug off his feelings by keeping up a lively conversation. Suddenly the monstrous locomotive flashed beyond them as they waited on the platform. The door of a passenger car opened and the step was placed. Nothing could be done now but to move along with the crowd.

"I'll write to you, Lars." He had turned his back on his friend.

"I'll do my best to answer. You know I'm not much good at writing," Lars called as Henrik climbed the last step into the train.

As Henrik turned and waved once more, he saw his friend standing down there on the platform in the cold October wind. Henrik choked with emotion.

Settling in his seat, he directed his thoughts forward. He was an intelligent young man going off to school, and wasn't that worthy? And besides, coming back to practical considerations, Anna and Halvor would be at the Red Wing depot to meet him, have no fear. He suddenly wondered why the sweeping emotion of gratitude toward Lars was not as forthcoming toward his sister, who would certainly be on the platform when he arrived. He may have to depend on her more than he had once thought, if these feelings of uncertainty persisted. He shrugged back into the image of himself as the intelligent student and thus survived the trip.

Having had fears that students at the seminary were like Alfred Solheim, Henrik was glad when he met his roommate, a tall angular fellow with an easygoing laugh. Although this fellow was loud, it could hardly be said he had bad manners. He was well-intentioned, but quite without grace. Henrik felt at home with him immediately.

As the term began, however, Henrik discovered that there were more people like Alfred here than there were at home. In fact, Alfred seemed to fit in perfectly, being among the admired ones. It was fortunate for Henrik that his roommate, Oscar Sande, was of a different sort. During the first week, Henrik discovered that Oscar was a practical jokester, almost like Wilfred Barnes without the swear words. Of course, there were practical jokesters in every group of fellows, and Oscar found friends. Soon there was plenty of amusement going on, at least for a time.

As the fall schedule progressed, a series of evangelistic meetings were held. Evangelism at Red Wing Seminary, according to one of its leaders, was not commitment to pure doctrine, but a heart experience of sin and grace. "With the heart, man believeth unto righteousness, and with the mouth, confession is made unto Salvation." Students were encouraged to search their hearts and listen to the promptings of the Holy Spirit. Emphasis was further placed on giving expression to this heart experience in public prayer and testimony.

"I don't know about this business of testifying and preaching," said Oscar when he and Henrik were getting ready for bed after the first of the meetings. "You know, Henrik, I heard a story once about a barber who was often moved to speak to his customers about the condition of their souls. Well, one day this call to speak became so strong that he was sure he was supposed to talk this minute to the man covered with lather sitting in the chair. As he was strapping the razor for a sharp edge, he wondered how he should begin. Suddenly he spoke. 'Are you prepared to die?' The man lying in the chair, seeing the razor lifted, leaped up and ran out into the street, soap suds, apron, and all!"

"That's a good one, the best I've heard in a long time!" exclaimed Henrik, slapping his knees as he sat on the edge of his bed. They both laughed hilariously, tumbling backwards into their beds.

"We better not repeat that one around here," cautioned Oscar, suddenly sitting upright.

"Better not," agreed Henrik, not quite recovered from laughter.

Pulling the covers over his head at bedtime, Henrik drew a peculiar satisfaction from this admittedly crude story. It had some truth to it. "Prepared to die." How was one to understand a phrase like that? And there were other phrases that required a twist of the imagination. Henrik was down to earth; he identified with the man in the barber chair.

Two nights later, however, fun had taken leave of Oscar and he came home full of remorse for having told such a story. He had stayed after the evangelistic meeting for a prayer service for those wanting "to give their hearts to the Lord." Henrik, completely amazed; had returned to his room. Was Oscar feigning conversion, as Wilfred Barnes had? That just couldn't be—he felt embarrassed at the thought. But it was equally impossible to believe Oscar had turned pious like Alfred.

Again the phrases floated over Henrik: repent of your sins—washed in the precious blood—moved by the Holy Spirit—grieve not the Holy Spirit. The allusions to the Holy spirit were the most mystifing of all. What could they possible mean? Curiously they brought the dark chill he had experienced at the age of ten while talking to Sivert Lunde, the spike pitcher in Ole Bakken's wheat field. He did his best to shrug it away.

"I stayed after, Henrik. They prayed with me." Oscar walked in. His shoulders drooped and his voice was tight.

"I could have waited for you," said Henrik, not sure if sympathy was what he should offer at this moment.

"No, no, not unless you felt moved by the Spirit to get on your knees, too,"

Moved? Henrik shuddered, but said nothing.

"Henrik? I need your forgiveness. That ugly story I told the other night—I'm terribly sorry."

Henrik was astonished. He saw tears in the eyes of his roommate! "I didn't mind."

"But you should mind. You should have told me it was blasphemy!"

"You weren't serious, Oscar. I knew it was only a joke then and I think of it only as a joke now."

"My jokes are my undoing, Henrik. Think how much foolish talk I have to repent of."

"It can't be a sin to laugh."

"Maybe that is easy for you to say, but just think, idle words will condemn you. 'Every idle word that a man doth speak—.' His voice ceased in a choke.

"I forgive you, Oscar. I'm a grown man and I know what to take seriously and what not to. Now you can forget that you ever told it. Let's get some sleep, shall we?"

Henrik from this day felt a loss. The merriment was gone and a heavy gloom gathered. He knew, however, that Christian people were not supposed to be glum—Rev. Østen Hanson wasn't. And wasn't there plenty of laughter in his own home? He might have tolerated this sober atmosphere if it hadn't been accompanied by an underhanded kind of behavior on the part of his pious friends. They hinted they had been praying for him behind his back.

"I was baptized by Østen Hanson. I'm just as good a Christian as you are," Henrik had snapped out one day to hold his tormenters at bay. "You say no amount of Baptism water can save a person, but I tell you that Baptism is a sacrament. You cannot deny that!" And for quite a while they left him alone.

Henrik usually spent Sunday afternoons with Anna and Halvor. They noticed he was not thriving at school and attempted as best they could to encourage him. His one interst was debate, and they tried hard to capitalize on it. He never missed a single scheduled debate and was beginning to articulate his own opinions as well. They praised his clear-cut ideas, especially on two important issues of the day: temperance and women's suffrage.

One Sunday afternoon, however, they found him totally dejected.

"I'm going back to the farm," he told them. "I've had enough of all these pious people not minding their own business. I don't intend to become a minister, so why should I hang around here?"

"Who said you must become a minister?" asked Halvor.

"Everyone seems to, who comes here, that's all I can say. I don't believe you shouldn't. You're one of the better students, believe me."

"What will you do then?" asked Anna.

"I was getting somewhere before I came here," he said defensively. "I was reading my books in peace. I want to go back and read my books. I'll educate myself. There are many self-educated people in this country."

So Henrik returned to Wanamingo before the term was up. He had a dark ache somewhere deep inside him, and he wasn't sure how to eradicate it. He had shrugged at the ache often as a child, and now he found himself still shrugging. Someday he hoped to find answers, real answers, and until then would choose home and the open sky.

Poem found in translation in this chapter:

En Trønder og en Sogning på stakken stod
Og buntene tog de fod for fod.
Sogningen var av en særsjildt art,
Men på stakken tog ham altid sin part.
Trønderen nokså stor var,
En høg kjekk, kjempe kar.

Bak i halmhaugen en Kristianenser stod,
Liten av vekst men ful av mod,
Og der han stod og grunde på
Hvor mange penger han vilde få.

Gutten med traktoren er ikke så vest,
Han går på skole og skal bli prest.
Han sær at drivbeltet sitter på,
Ellers vil ikke maskinen gå.

Eiernen av maskinen må ikke bli forglempt,
For han bliet answaret først og fremst.
Når hjulene begunne ikke at gå
Til maskinen han hurtig må nå.
Telemarken springer rund omkring
Og ta på beltet med vær eneste fing.
Karene står der og gape og ser,
Men Trønderen og Sogningen står der og ler.

Chapter 9

The seasons came and went in the year 1892 and into 1893, each with its required tasks, seeding and harvesting.

Up north, Peder was breaking a few more acres each year with Iver at his side, keeping up his spirits. Although some of these years had yielded light crops because of drought, the people of the settlement were not giving up hope. Of course, Peder longed for the day he would have his Anna, but he would have to be satisfied waiting; there were, after all, things about women that no man could fully understand.

At Wanamingo, the traffic in and out of Nils' blacksmith shop never let up. With more tilled acreage in the area each year, machinery repair was no small operation. Nils was glad for the Tollefson shop; these two blacksmiths had never felt like competitors. Then, of course, he had his threshing rig and crew, and was off with them six weeks or more during harvest. He did without his son during the fall of 1891 while Henrik was away at school, but was mighty glad when he returned to his post beside the steam engine.

Julia, among her other worthy enterprises, was keeping bees. She was immensely successful at it, selling many pounds of succulent honeycomb to stores in Wanamingo and Zumbrota. She kept the hives in the cellar in the winter, where the bees survived docile and harmless. She still counseled the distressed in her neighborhood and gave food to the hungry without stint. Of course, she missed Anna, but she had Sarah, who was just as bright and industrious. Julia shouldn't have wondered if Sarah would become a first-rate dressmaker, she really had the knack.

Julia was more anxious about Henrik's future than her husband was. She didn't see him as a machinist like his father. It wasn't quite in line with his talent, and if he were to farm, more land would have to be acquired. It took her awhile to get used to the idea that he chose not to continue at Red Wing Academy, her mind restless as to what was disturbing him. He was as secretive with her as Anna was about what vitally concerned her. She felt impatient about her maturing children; she wanted so much to use her long years of acquired wisdom to help them solve their problems. At such times, she remembered what Rev. Østen Hanson once said to her: "You are so quick to decide things. You are like Job thinking you can understand everything. Can you command the morning or cause the sun to rise? Can you hunt the prey for the young lion?" Reflecting on this, she knew there were matters she should leave undisturbed.

Anna couldn't bring herself to give up her life in Red Wing, although she knew she would eventually have to make a break. She was still living with the Schumanns, but had fewer domestic responsibilities now that she was involved with choral groups and had become somewhat of a music teacher in her own right, tutoring several organ students. Halvor was in his last year of seminary and would soon be leaving Red Wing for a parish somewhere. Their friendship remained strong, and things they shared pervasive, but they both knew that there would be a parting, and both were willing to accept it.

One day in the spring of 1893, two letters come for Anna from Wanamingo. One was from Agnes Veblen, who, Anna knew, was engaged to Martin Mundahl, and the other from her mother. Anna couldn't remember ever getting a letter from Agnes before, although Josie often wrote, and she had a feeling all was not well.

> Dear Anna,
>
> Perhaps your mother has already written to you about the sad death of Melvin Mundahl. As you know he had been failing for a long time, mostly because of drink. He died rather suddenly after a night of severe pain. He was buried yesterday. Your mother is a big comfort to Jennie. Martin and Lars are taking it very hard mostly, I think, because of the shame connected with it. His death has sobered all of us.
>
> I am writing to you now because I wish you would come home and help us. A spiritual revival is stirring in the Wanamingo Church, not only among their members, but also among many of us in the community, no matter what church we belong to. People are giving their hearts to the Lord and witnessing, one after the other. Persons you would never expect to say anything get on their feet. It is a blessing to see this. Martin and I are among them—Praise the Lord! We need you, Anna, please come. Aspelund people are very much together with us. They are warm, Spirit-filled people like your mother, for instance, and I am sure you are the same. Our choir needs a leader and we are often in need of someone to play the organ. Please come, Anna. We are looking forward to a blessed

summer. The Holy Spirit is working mightily among us. Come and see.

Anna looked at the letter from her mother. She envisioned all that it would contain. But her mother never pressured her to come home. Would she now?

Julia wrote that Melvin Mundahl's drinking himself to death had stunned the whole community. Now everyone was aware of the still Clarence Haroldson had been operating, and it might well be the end of that. Jennie was taking it as well as could be expected; Martin and Lars were so good to her. And Iver was home. His father's funeral was held up for two days so Iver could be there. He, of course, brought greetings from Peder.

Julia mentioned too, the spiritual awakening going on in the Wanamingo Church. It had been heightened, she thought, by the sobering effect of Mundahl's death. The new minister, who lived in a newly-built parsonage near the church, was quite an evangelist. It was indeed heartwarming to see so many people giving testimonies. Could this be part of a nationwide revival? She had been reading in the newspaper about a certain Billy Sunday, a converted ball player who had become a powerful evangelist. The prayers of many are being answered. It would be a good summer to spend at home, she suggested. Might she be planning on it?

Halvor listened with intense interest as Anna related these developments from her home town.

"I'd like to visit for a few days among those people," he said. "To be in the midst of a revival would be a wonderful thing. Shall I go with you on my way home to Rice County?"

So Anna responded to Agnes' invitation by not only returning home herself, but also by bringing with her another who could certainly sing and speak.

Off the train at Zumbrota they were met by Iver Mundahl in what Anna recognized as her family's rig.

"I'm here to fetch you," called Iver as he came toward the only couple off the train. "Well, Anna, this must be you," he said accepting her hand. "I'd almost forgotten what you looked like, or have you changed? Welcome back. It's a pleasure to see you."

"Thank you, Iver. You're not a kid anymore yourself, I can tell that."

"This must be Halvor the student you have written about?" said Iver extending his hand toward Anna's escort.

"Yes, Halvor this is Iver Mundahl."

"Pleased to meet you."

"Everyone is pretty busy these days. The farmers are putting up hay. Since I am considered just visiting, I was selected to make this trip to bring you home," continued Iver as he placed the suitcases in the rig.

"You're doing us a great favor, Iver," said Anna. Before climbing into the buggy she hesitated. "I'm—I was so sorry to hear about your father."

"I wish to offer my condolence also," put in Halvor.

"Thank you," said Iver, suddenly losing his joviality. "It's been a hard time for all our family."

"I'm sure it has," said Anna.

"Well, climb in. Let's not waste time. Those Wanamingo folks are more than anxious to see you."

Zumbrota's main street was strangely familiar to Anna today in spite of its flourishing growth in the years since she was a child. There was Lett's Store and Sloan's Photo Studio, and there was the handsome elevator and bank fostering for her the image of Johan Ringstad, certainly more prosperous now than ever. Feelings out of her remote past began to stir. She was vaguely uncomfortable.

"Peder, of course, sent his greetings to everyone, especially to you, Anna."

The uncomfortable feeling turned to pain as she met Iver's glance in her direction. She should have asked about Peder right away. She wondered if Iver noticed that she hadn't and decided to bring up the subject himself.

"Thank you. He's well and all, isn't he?" Anna responded, trying hard not to seem flustered.

"He's fine, Anna. And he is mighty devoted to you. If he suffers it's because of that. It's been quite a few years now, you know."

"Yes, I know."

"If he breaks a new acre, adds more animals, builds a new shed, or buys a new piece of machinery, its's all for Anna, always Anna."

"He says so in his letters, too," Anna said weakly, knowing how little these demonstrative statements of his had affected her.

"He's a mighty fine fellow, Anna. I've never known anyone to match him."

"I know."

"He can make a go of anything. He makes money up there when no one else can."

"I'm sure what you say is true."

"Are you going to stay home for good now?"

Halvor, who had been watching the roadside, turned and looked at Anna.

"I may."

"I think you should. Everyone there thinks you belong to them no matter how long you've been gone. They feel the same way about me and Peder. And Peder, you can't make him wait forever."

The three people in the buggy fell silent. In the open country the warm smell of freshly cut clover rose and fell as they rolled along. They passed the shade tree under which Julia and her children had rested years ago on their way to Zumbrota, and Anna remembered her first English lesson. Finally they passed the mill on the Zumbro, a signal that they were less than a mile from home.

Although Anna had been home yearly, usually in the summer, since she had lived in Red Wing, there was definitely something different about this homecoming. It was as if the town thought she was home to stay; it was a thrust of open arms she had never experienced before. The Veblen women, Jennie Mundahl, Petra Haroldson, all had left their kitchens and formed a circle around the buggy as Anna stepped down. On the edge of this little crowd were the men out of their shops: Martin, Lars, Arne, Sigurd and Albin. Finally Anna saw her parents, Sarah, and Henrik with warm smiles. They had made their way through the circle, eager to greet her.

Anna was deeply moved. She looked from one to the other, not sure what she should say. Yet it didn't seem to matter. This audience was not expecting a performance. It simply wanted her to be among them again.

Finally she remembered to introduce Halvor. She told them he was on his way to Rice County, but had consented to visit a few days. He had just graduated from Red Wing Seminary and was looking forward to his ordination. No one seemed too surprised she had brought him. Perhaps Julia had prepared them in her own way.

As she mingled with these friends after Iver had taken the rig away, she heard that a prayer and song service would be held at the church this evening since this was Wednesday, midweek. They looked forward, they said, to having Anna and Halvor there with them.

At the church Anna discovered that her mother's description of the new minister was quite accurate. He was an evangelist. He had scarcely made the acquaintance of Anna and Halvor before he asked them to begin the singing while the people gathered. The Holy Spirit must be given entrance, and how better than through song? Anna kept losing her place, reading the organ music, as she threw side glances at the comers. On some of the songs she joined singing, but mostly she let Halvor sing alone; she knew how well received his songs would be.

The service opened with several prayers, freely offered by various people who had gathered. Anna tried to recognize voices as she kept her head properly bowed. Then followed the minister's Scripture reading. He flipped the gilt-edged pages from front to back, reading first a verse from Psalms, then one from the Gospel according to St. John, then another from Paul's letter to the Romans, and finally a glowing passage from Revelation, all of which he had carefully chosen to bear on this time and place. As he closed the Good Book by patting it lovingly, he called for people to witness as they were led by the Spirit.

Anna would never have believed what she saw and heard. Quiet farmers, old schoolmates, shy houewives rose one after another. It was not so much what they said—in fact, they all said about the same thing: they had been convicted of sin as the Holy Spirit had worked in their hearts, and they had accepted Christ as their personal Savior. Usually they quoted a favorite Bible verse.

Finally Martin Mundahl was on his feet. Anna scarcely recognized the boy who had infatuated her childhood.

"I have something to confess. The Holy Spirit lays this heavy on my heart compelling me to speak of it. When my father was dying, he used to cry for a drink. He was burning inside, he said, and must have a drink. I knew it would soothe him momentarily and yielded. I brought some to him. We had a container, a little kerosene can, Clarence would recognize and fill for us. I was torn between the demand of my father and what I knew I shouldn't do, give him that cursed drink. I grew weak and couldn't hold out against my father. I contributed toward his death. I confess it. Pray for me that I may be forgiven of this grievious sin."

He spoke so softly that Anna could hardly make out what he said. His final words trailed off into a kind of sigh.

A prayer followed, led by the pastor.

No sooner had the prayer closed than Petra Haroldson was on her feet shouting, "Pray for Clarence! Pray for Clarence! He must not be arrested, he is too ill, very ill!"

If the audience was startled, it didn't show it. The people bowed their heads again, waiting for the clear voice of their pastor.

A hymn was announced. It was a good time for a song, the pastor's voice continued. Anna fumbled through the pages—*Kom du Bedrøvede.*

Come ye disconsolate, where'er ye languish
Come to the mercy seat, fervently kneel
Here bring your wounded hearts,
Here tell your anguish,
Earth has no sorrow that heaven cannot heal.

"Now," said the minister, "Perhaps the Holy Spirit is speaking to others of you. Don't grieve Him. Speak what is on your heart. Today is the acceptable time of the Lord. Tomorrow may be to late!"

Anna's eyes fell on Henrik. He looked uncomfortable, yet she knew he would not get on his feet even if Lars had. Suddenly she felt a compelling emotion as she saw her family down there in front of her. Those dear people! She had deserted them for so many years now! She couldn't believe herself, what she was doing. She was leaving the organ stool and coming before all the people.

"I am one of those who is disconsolate," she found herself saying. She reached toward the organ for support as she began to feel a trembling in her legs. "I am convicted now of being away from all of you for such a long time. I have had vain notions about myself. Now I have come to realize where I belong—right here with you dear people. I need your forgiveness."

She heard his voice speaking before she realized that Halvor had stepped up beside her. She was too overwhelmed to follow completely what he was saying, but it was about her being a real blessing to him as he chose to become a minister. He thought they should all thank God for how He works in mysterious ways. This time Halvor led the prayer as the heads lowered.

The minister then suggested that these two fine people, who had surrendered their lives to the Lord, should sing for them. Halvor sang a Norwegian chorale he had practiced with Ingeborg. Julia had tears in her eyes.

"The Holy Spirit is continuing his silent voice among us. Who else will speak?" asked the pastor.

Emma Veblen rose to her feet. Anna was suddenly struck with remorse that she had ever gloated over Emma's being fat and ugly. Anna deplored that she had ever been among those thoughtless schoolmates who had tormented this girl.

"I am a sinner and need to get right with God. Pray for me," sobbed Emma.

Since this ourburst from Emma was a regular occurrence, many in the audience were visibly uncomfortable. Suddenly Melva got out of her seat and went to Emma and put a comforting arm around her shoulder. "Emma, you were baptized once. You have always been a child of God. Why should you feel forsaken now?" Melva spoke gently, but loud enough for all to hear.

"All we like sheep have gone astray," said a voice from somewhere in the church.

Unheeding, Melva led her sister-in-law back to her seat.

"Would someone choose a song?" said the minister.

After three songs, announced by individuals as their favorites, were sung, the meeting came to a close. Anna felt exhausted. Henrik waited for no one. He left the church and hurried home.

Sunday evening, the next scheduled prayer and song service, Henrik insisted on staying at home. "I've been to church once today," he said. "Tonight I want to read. You will have to pardon me."

His mother didn't argue with him. Neither did his sister. He was an avid reader and took seriously the books he had acquired.

As it began to grow dark, Henrik lit the lamp. Soon after, he heard footsteps outside the door.

"Come in, Arne."

"I saw your light. So I'm not the only one left at home this evening," Arne said opening the screen door and entering without hesitation. "I'm surprised to find someone at home in this house."

"Arne, I tell you, I think things are going a little bit too far. It pains me to see Emma Veblen get up time after time and cry over her sins. I just wasn't going to go and see that again."

"Melva mentioned how tormented the poor girl is. No, I couldn't stand that either."

"You've solved it all, Arne. You seldom go to church and you're better than the whole lot of them."

"No, no, no, and don't think me an unbeliever, Henrik. I guess I stay away because I'm not sure what some of those preachers are talking about. They talk as if they know everything, and I'm not so sure they do. And I can't stand them goading good people to tears."

"I think like you, Arne."

"Please understand, young man, I do believe in God."

"I know that."

"Do you think anyone will report on Clarence for illegal liquor?" said Arne, taking up another subject. "There is a forty-dollar reward in the county, you know, leading to the arrest of someone like him."

"I can't think of anyone around here being mean enough for that. He's no longer operating his still, and poor Petra has suffered enough."

"That's the way I feel," replied Arne. "But I was just worrying there might be a bounty-seeker among us."

Halvor stayed several more days in Wanamingo until he was able to catch a ride to Kenyon, the first leg of his journey home.

"You've promised to answer my letters," said Halvor as he and Anna walked toward the hitching post where his ride was waiting. No one knew better than he that a promise from Anna was a real commitment.

"Of course. And I will look forward to your letters." Knowing the moment for separation had arrived, she looked once more into the impressive eyes. He had seen her home where she belonged. He would be her friend by a special bond for the rest of her life. She was satisfied.

Iver returned to Clay County after a two-week stay in Wanamingo. He, unwittingly enough, reinforced two misgivings that his partner up north had had for a long time. The first misgiving Peder had wrestled for seven years—would Anna thrive in this sparse country? Iver seemed to be saying no, she wouldn't; she had become too refined. Maybe she had been that way all along, Iver couldn't remember. But she surely was polished now. Peder's second misgiving had begun when she wrote in the summer of 1888, upon his finishing the house, that she wasn't ready for marriage. After that, nothing in her letters led him to believe she was getting any closer to marriage. Perhaps she had another boy. She mentioned this Halvor in nearly every letter. Iver said that this seminary student had accompanied Anna to Wanamingo. They had sung together at church and certainly anyone could see that they were very close. As these misgivings began to grow unbearable, Peder decided to make a trip to Wanamingo. Iver assured him that Anna would be at home.

But first he must help his neighbor finish building a barn that had been started after the spring seeding. Peder was responsible for running the sawmill with the steam engine which was brought to the building site where timber would be cut on the spot from logs brought from the woods.

A week after Iver's return, sawing timbers turned tragic. Sawdust had been piling up under the spinning blade and it was necessary to stop and clear the accumulation, but Peder saw only one log left to be shoved through the line and decided to go for one more. Thinking he was at a safe distance, he pushed at the sawdust accumulation with his right foot.

Suddenly the men cried out in horror. Peder had fallen backwards on the ground. He had gotten his foot too close to the spinning blade. The saw had penetrated his boot and severed the toes of his right foot. The toe of the boot dangled crazily by a shred of unsevered leather.

How could such a thing happen to Peder, who always knew exactly what he was doing? This could have happened to anyone of them in their thoughtlessness, but not to the ever-cautious Peder. Someone stopped the engine as the men rushed to Peder's aid. Blood was spattered on the sawdust.

"Get me on the train to Goodhue County," he cried, getting himself up into a sitting position. "Dr. Grønvold must treat me!"

"That will take some days," protested Iver, remembering the train ride with the many station stops and the long wait in Minneapolis.

"It will take time getting to a doctor here as well."

Having been helped to the house, Peder ordered Iver to dress the wound. He winced but didn't cry out as iodine, the only remedy that they had for prevention of infection, was applied. The women tore sheets into bandages. They assured Peder that these white cloths had been boiled in strong soap.

"But you can't go alone!" said Iver as emphatically as he could.

"I'll be all right. Send a telegram as I get on the train telling the Kristians to meet me in Kenyon."

"But supposing...?"

"I'll be among people the whole way. There'll always be help around. You must take care of the place, Iver. You'll have plenty to do."

The neighbors stood around stunned. What could they do but marvel at this strong, young man who was taking charge of his own injury.

By the time Peder got off the train at Kenyon, he had acquired a pair of crutches. When Julia saw him through the foggy steam flushed from the locomotive she shuddered. He was the image of a brutally wounded soldier returning home to Wisconsin during the Civil War—those anguishing days!

Anna, standing beside her mother, watched the conductor help him down onto the platform. She was less concerned with the crutches and bandages now. She wondered, would she know him after all these years? She worried about her feelings. She wanted ever so much to love him, really love him, but seven years of separation had brought serious misgivings. No doubt about it, she knew what she must do, and it was even more urgent now that he was seriously hurt.

"Anna!"

It was his voice! He smiled! How could he smile like that! She ran to his side and touched his arm.

"So it's really you!" exclaimed that same strong voice.

"It's me. what a long trip! How terribly you must be suffering!"

"I've been wild with joy the whole way expecting to see you at the end of my journey!"

"Dr. Grønvold is here with us. We let him know right away that you were coming."

Grønvold, who was in the process of moving his residence to Kenyon, took Peder to his office. The dread of infection, which had tormented this good doctor for years, had refined his cautious procedures, and now Peder, in his youthful prime, was the beneficiary. Dr. Grønvold worked with extraordinary diligence, cleaning the tragic wound, removing flesh and bone which his skillful eye determined was threatening to the healing processes. From now on, Peder would be walking on the heel of his right foot, because that was what was left of it. The doctor told the young man it might have been worse; he could easily have been an amputee. He returned to the waiting women.

"You cannot move him for a few days. I must watch him. You had better check into the hotel," ordered the doctor with the same intensity that had surrounded the intricate task he had just completed.

Two rooms were engaged across the hall from each other. Peder was finally resting after all the awful days of travel and hours of excruciating pain. Anna and Julia took turns at his bedside, never leaving him unattended. Dr. Grønvold came twice a day for a week before he permitted them to return to Wanamingo.

During those hours at his bedside, Anna realized how much Peder was like her own father. Even in his helpless condition he was strong and capable, gentle and loving. He understood most things without being told; she was totally comfortable and at rest with him. She was beginning to understand why her mother had married her blacksmith father rather than someone more sophisticated. Love is being able to depend on someone; it is an instinct of trust. Strange it should be so, but love had turned out to be trust, something she had learned to feel long ago simply by being Papa's pet.

Chapter 10

What had happened to Peder was unfortunate, but he found immense consolation in that he was reunited with his Anna. Anna, too, was revitalized by his overwhelming approval of her. He was blind, she thought, no one could be as good as Peder thought she was. It was reassuring to say the least. All her anxieties concerning him were gone; Peder was no longer the paper figure, holding her fast by the commitment she had made as a mere child of fourteen. He was real. She thanked God sincerely. She was sure now what love was, and she loved Peder.

As the reality of his handicap began to dawn on him, Peder began to wrestle with the idea of giving up his farm. At first it was unthinkable. The farm was his own achievement: the almost unbelievable number of acres he had grabbed away from the relentless prairie, the respectable farm buildings he had designed himself, his machinery kept in running condition through his own skill, the animals he had raised—horses were old friends. His farm was what he was; he couldn't conceive of it being something he had not been. No, not yet.

How tired his right leg became as he wandered around town! He got out of the house as soon as possible, visiting the menfolk at their various tasks and telling himself that it would not be long before he would be able to work even as they. The fellows always encouraged him by saying he was lucky not to have lost his leg. He heard many stories these days of men without legs, but how his piece of fortune ached with fatigue! It occurred to him that Captain Ahab must have devised the hole on the deck to ease the terrible ache in his hips. He wished at such times he could devise something. He reflected, too, on Ahab's lashing out with terrible vengeance at the whale who got his leg. But how could he lash out at the inaminate saw, cold and still without steam power? Life had tragedies just as in books, he figured. But he, strangely enough, felt a subtle kind of strength within him; he wasn't sure if it was his own or Anna's, or the great family to which she belonged. He carried no grudges; it would indeed be unseemly to do so.

Letters arrived regularily from Iver. What Peder had suspected for a long time was about to happen. Iver announced he was going to marry Elsie Hagen at the end of harvest. He wouldn't spend a winter alone. In another letter, Iver wondered if Lars might be interested in joining him—there was a lot of work. He needed a partner, he said, at least until Peder was well enough to return. What did Peder think? Would he ask Lars?

Lars was quite ready for adventure. Why shouldn't he have his turn at something away from home? He would return, of course, and have his own stories to tell.

Now it was Henrik's turn to drive the trim team before the buggy and Lars' turn to say good-bye to his family. No, Lars wasn't having sick feelings, Henrik decided, as he helped lift the trunk into the buggy.

Henrik always felt a cloud hanging vaguely around when he knew someone was leaving. The cloud was there now as the rig headed toward Kenyon.

"I'll miss not being with you threshing," began Lars, feeling it awkward that Henrik was so quiet.

"I'll sure miss you too."

"Who do you think your father will find to replace me?"

"I think Peder will want to be around, but I'm not sure he can do a man's work even by that time," replied Henrik, his mind settling now as the quick team was clipping along.

Soon it was Henrik's turn to wonder at his friend's silence. He looked over at him. Lars definitely had something on his mind.

"Are you a Christian?" Lars' voice came out of another world.

"Am I what?" Henrik had heard, but needed time to put together an answer.

"A Christian? You see, you have never gotten on your feet and testified as most of the rest of us have. If I can be of any help to you spiritually—"

"No, no—yes, of course, I was baptized and—I guess I want to keep it my business." Henrik didn't want to sound on the defensive with Lars. He spoke as matter-of-factly as he could.

"I've sat and prayed that you would get up and speak. You are so gifted. You could make such a good speech."

"Not about something I know nothing about. Religion is something I cannot put into words. And when some people do, it sounds terrible to me."

"Words don't matter. It's what's in you heart that counts."

"I've heard that, too, Lars," said Henrik, feeling his ire rising. It must not get the best of him. "I just can't talk about something out of my imagination. If almighty God has saved you, hasn't he also saved me?"

"Yes, of course. I just wanted to hear you say it, that's all."

"I like to make speeches, Lars, but not those kind of speeches."

Henrik had silenced his friend too quickly, it seemed to him. Lars was the last person in this world he wanted to offend.

"I'm going to join the Temperance Movement, Lars. Now there's something I can speak about."

"Oh yes?"

"The sadness in your family has touched me deeply—really it has. Maybe you don't think so because I don't get up and speak at prayer meetings. I will speak, but let me speak in my own way."

"I know you have feelings," Lars said slowly. "But aren't you changing the subject?"

"No, I don't think I am. Everyone in this town has staggered under the evil that took your father. People have been turning to God, it is true, because they sense that evil is a terrible part of life."

"See? There you are beginning a speech."

"I want to talk about something real, Lars, not something out of my imagination, or about me at all. I want to take a crack at the liquor traffic before it destroys more of us."

The two friends looked at each other. Lars smiled at Henrik admiringly as he has done since earliest childhood.

"I'll do it for you," said Henrik.

Peder supposed Iver and Lars would do quite well together. For a while it was a comfort that Lars would be driving the bundle wagon, doing chores and perhaps even learning about oxen. But when he thought about Elsie being the "lady" of his house with Iver, he took pause.

At the same time he was watching his Anna. As weeks turned to months, he began to lose the hope that she would thrive where he had intended to take her. She was somehow frailer than he had imagined, a tiny little thing. The women of the settlement were plump and rosy, at least Mrs. Hagen and Elsie were; he remembered few others except, of course, poor Ruth Overvold with the sick baby that cried day and night. The memory of the winter with the Overvolds in the old sod house seemed to tell him, no, don't take Anna to Clay County. But the house he had built was better than the one her family was now living in, wasn't it? But Anna needed people; he saw that more and more. They stimulated her; she became wiry and alive when friends came to call. And the church was important to her for the same reason. She never missed a song service or a Ladies Aid Society meeting and was more than likely on the program for a solo or a reading. And people loved her. If he weren't so proud that she was indeed his, he might have been jealous.

Yes, people loved her. The mailbox was always full of letters for her, and often it took the better part of a day to read them, to say nothing of the time it took her to answer all of her friendly correspondence. Peder still had a streak of uneasiness when Halvor's letters arrived, but she always let him read them if he wanted to, and she had been very honest and fair with him regarding that promise of friendship.

As time went on, he began to realize that coming home to Wanamingo was not what he had imagined it would be. It was difficult to share with them his successes. That farm that meant so much now seemed remote and diminished; it was impossible for them to understand what his life up there had been. At first he thought his misery—he didn't like to call it that—lay in his disabled foot, but as it began to improve somewhat, a restless uncertainty came over him. At such times he would label himself impatient, telling himself that he was the luckiest man man in the world. What could be better than to be an integral part of the Kristian family?

When the threshing season came around, Peder was not ready to take a man's job as Henrik had suspected. He would ride old Prince out to the threshing operation and help awhile around the engine and then return home. Then there were jobs Nils left for him in the blacksmith shop. Who could be better to have around the place when so many of the menfolks were gone?

A new man, Olaus Strom, was found to drive the water wagon in Lars' place. He was thirty or so, but somehow seemed old to Henrik. He was a local farmer who tilled land with his father and two brothers. He was able to join the threshing this season because his youngest brother was now old enough to take hold and do a man's work at home. Olaus loved to sing, having a clear tenor voice, and soon began taking the liberty of visiting the Kristians on Sundays and joining Anna around the organ. He wore out his welcome with the menfolk very quickly, but Anna and Julia saw no harm in him; they really thought he was gifted.

One such Sunday, Nils, Peder, and Henrik had taken refuge in Arne's quarters as they very often did. Henrik sat with one eye out the window waiting for Olaus to leave.

"Excuse me. I'm going to have a word with our womenfolk. I see the windbag has left." Henrik hurried out, hearing a faint chuckle behind him.

"Anna, don't ever let that fool into this house again! I tell you he's a fool!"

Henrik's intrusion startled Anna, who was musing over a songbook.

"What do you mean by that?"

"I mean what I say. I'm sick and tired of your friends always monopolizing the house on Sundays. You're not the only one who lives here, you know."

"Henrik," said Julia, "Don't shout at Anna. Watch your temper."

"Mama, I am quite in control of my temper. I have something important to say and I intend to say it."

"Yes, say it then," said Anna, throwing the songbook down on the table. She wouldn't look at him though, not when he was in a rage.

"That man is not fit to come into this house! Listen to this: Last Thursday after Roy Anderson's funeral, Olaus went around saying that the man was not a Christian. And, wasn't it terrible to fall into the hands of Almighty God with unforgiven *sins* on your head? Then he had the audacity to say that the Anderson house was not only full of TB, but full of sin, and if they continued swearing and working on Sundays they'd all end up..."

"Working on Sundays, that I don't believe," said Julia.

"Oh yes. He insisted they worked in their machine shed all Sunday. No, they wouldn't go out in the field—they wouldn't want their neighbors to see them—but they might as well have for all the good it did them."

"He really shouldn't say such things. But you are always so hard on Christian people, Henrik. Not even Christians are perfect," said Anna, acting indifferent to her brother's tirade.

"He is so self-righteous it drips! Remember that awful humbug he came with in church the other night? It would be blasphemy to call it Christian witnessing. I'm sure you remember when he said if a steam engine ran over him, making him flatter than a pancake, he could only be glad because God would have taken him into the heavenly mansions! What kind of talk is that? The man is out of his mind!"

"I didn't like that either," agreed Julia.

"See, it didn't sit right with you either." Then he turned to his sister, who said nothing. "Anna, listen to me!"

"All right. But he is a good singer. We need good singers at our meetings."

"Not people like him, you don't!"

"You don't like my friends."

"There you said it! I don't. Why didn't you marry Halvor? Then you could have had these kind of people around you all the time. Peder is too good for you, Anna. He's a decent fellow. Why don't you spend Sunday afternoons with him for a change? But no, you have to entertain this ridiculous fool! We men have to put up with him all week—he makes us all sick—and you have to invite him over on Sundays!"

"She didn't invite him, exactly," interrupted Julia.

"You've said more than you should, Henrik," said Anna with a quaking rage in her voice. "And I hope some day you'll be sorry."

Henrik hurried out the door. Maybe he shouldn't have said she wasn't good enough for Peder. That was cruel. But someone needed to straighten her out on some of these people; Peder wouldn't and neither would Father, and womenfolk always stuck together. Besides, he was sick to death of all the self-righteous moaning that had gone on around here all summer. There comes a time when one can't stand it any longer.

Anna fled to her room. The tailor shop again, with the terrible mirror! Did Henrik really mean that she should have married Halvor? How many people believed that? Mama? Papa? (No, not Papa.) Arne? Melva? She knew her Red Wing friends thought she should have married Halvor, even, maybe, Uncle John. But here at home, where she felt safe?

Did Henrik really mean that Peder was too good for her? Anna had lived all these years by simply putting off the idea of living on Peder's farm. She had never thought of it as a real possibility; she succeeded better than most people at living in the immediate. Of course, she would have a house of her own to care for someday, but that was in the future, not today. The "hope chest" had more things in it, to be sure, but somehow it stood in her room as a reminder of her past rather than her future. He's too good for me—she yielded to Henrik's judgment—he really is! She put her face into the pillow. Peder is too good, too good for me! Tears came at last.

Julia remained in the parlor. She picked up the book she had intended to read, but it remained dead in her hands. Why was Henrik so sharp with Anna? Why was he so put out by Anna's "so called" friends? Was he fighting against becoming a confessing Christian, or was this a kind of persecution of those who were? No, no, didn't she know better than that? She felt ashamed of herself immediately upon having raised such a possibility.

Henrik hated sham, and wasn't much of what had been going on a kind of sham? Of course, there were many sincere people, most of them undoubtedly were. But this Olaus—what an unloving thing to say about the Andersons. She had to agree that was outrageous. She felt a little sick to her stomach, too, and proud of Henrik's revulsion of such talk; it showed he had feelings for people.

When fall was giving way to winter and frosty crisp weather seemed here to stay, it was time for butchering again. Peder was a master of this skill and made the most of it this particular season. He hired out to do the butchering for several households in the vicinity; he even incorporated in his services the making of sausage according to a special recipe he had worked out with Julia's assistance. Gradually his reputation spread, and farmers came into town asking for "Pølsa Pete."

As spring returned, Peder was in a better position to judge the extent of his disability since it was approaching a year since his accident. He spent most of his day now helping Nils in the blacksmith shop and had also helped Henrik put in a field of oats adjacent to the pasture. He hadn't realized before how many steps it took on the farm. The stretches of field were certainly greater than the confines of a shop, and he wouldn't be a farmer unless he could run the operation himself. Using the pitchfork wasn't easy either; it was a matter of balance. Peder discovered this as he helped Henrik put up hay for the few cows and horses kept by the Kristians. No, he must begin to think about a trade or business of his own; it would be unwise trying to run a farm again, to say nothing of returning north.

"There's plenty here for the two of us," Nils insisted more often than usual these days. "Maybe we should build a house for you and Anna so you could get married." Nils saw it was no use; Peder wanted to be more independent. "Of course, it's up to you."

Then one day an extraordinary thing happened. A man not wearing overalls, but dressed like a gentleman, came to Wanamingo looking for Peder.

"I'm Joe—Joseph Harstad from Kenyon," he said. "I want to go into the meat market business, but I can't do it alone. I need a partner. I have a building to start us off. The prospects for business are good. Kenyon needs a meat market. Mr. Olson, you already have a name for yourself. Someone with your skill is just the kind of partner I need."

This was the opportunity Peder had been waiting for. He recognized it at once. Butchering would be his trade.

"We will live in Kenyon, Anna. That's not very far away, only ten miles. If Iver's crop turns our well, he will send us our share again, and we'll build a house. We could get married, Anna, next June!" Anna wouldn't say no, this time.

"Pølsa Pete. You'll have to live with that name now," laughed Nils at the table one evening.

"I don't mind. Anna, how would you like to be married to Pølsa Pete?"

"Why should I mind if it brings you business?"

Sarah, who was now sixteen and a reliable seamstress, was delighted at the prospect of a wedding. She would sew the bride's dress, which had been discussed for almost two years now. And there would be bridesmaids—how many? And they would each have to have a dress. A flower girl? Oh yes, and that would mean another dress. she would be busy for months with her favorite project. And people would know that Sarah Kristian was the best dressmaker around.

After the Christmas holidays the women found the time speeding quickly toward June. The dresses, one after the other, were hung on hangers. The sewing machine was seldom silent; Sarah's energetic foot on the treadle never grew weary. Anna did the hand-finishing, making thousands of tiny stitches: hemming sashes, tacking facings, and attaching hook-and-eye closings. She seldom removed her thimble. To the in-and-out rhythm of her needle and thread she would count her guests, adding another and another until she had included all those with whom she corresponded. She saw herself in the gorgeous setting of a bride greeting each of them. How she hoped all those from far away would be able to come!

Julia and Nils felt a sense of relief that Anna and Peder would be married at last. The long engagement had not been easy; Anna had needed to grow up, and, best of all, she had remained faithful. Kenyon would be a good place to live. The Kristians knew quite a few Norwegians in that vicinity, and there was a Hauge church served by Østen Hanson, their own pastor. What could be nicer?

The wedding was as everyone had pictured it would be. It took place in Aspelund Church and was followed by a reception on the lawn of the Kristian home in Wanamingo. The trees were all in fresh leaves, and wild roses were blooming everywhere.

When Anna saw the table decked with all manner of good things to eat, she suddenly remembered Melva's wedding and how she and Mari had run back and forth with platters of food for the guests. So now the silly apple peeling had spoken the truth. It was "P" and "P" stood for Peder. She wanted to smile at this, but to her dismay it made her suffer a wave of melancholy. Maybe it was caused by the sudden memory of Mari, or was it the irony of that childish game, such flagrant innocence, surviving when everything else had changed with maturity? She looked at Peder now, remembering when she had seen him across the aisle so many years ago. He was the same handsome Peder, but he was older, and what mattered now was that she had learned to know him and had grown to love him.

Halvor was too far away to attend the wedding, and Ingeborg Schumann couldn't come either, since there was sickness in the family. She wrote a beautiful letter, however, sending her regrets. Maybe their not being here was just as well, thought Anna as she looked over her guests. Bringing her two worlds together had been painful, and even if she had integrated them in her own mind, she knew that bringing the various people together would be uncomfortable still. Only Uncle John came from Red Wing, and he had suddenly taken to Peder, who, like himself, would be a business man. Nils assured him that the groom was certain to succeed; he had such good judgment in all matters. He would be a good husband for Anna.

On the day after their wedding, Peder took his bride to Kenyon to a home practically furnished for her. Peder with the help of his business partner had found a house with an option to buy. It was owned by Jacob Swenson of the Swenson Lumber Company. Jacob Swenson was uncommonly wealthy; no one knew precisely how he had acquired his money, except through successful investments in stocks and bonds. He had built a huge mansion with a tower, bay windows, and encircling porches, all of which impressed the surrounding population into thinking that Kenyon now had its elite. His previous residence, a modest house by comparison, had been built by his father, in the lumber business before him. It was now available, and Joe Harstad was quick to snatch it for Peder. Since much of the furniture was for sale, Peder and Joe attended the auction and purchased many items that didn't need to be moved from the house.

"So you are the people who are going to live here," said a woman's voice from the front porch as Anna approached with her hat box and Peder with his trunk. It was as if the previous "lady of the house" hadn't left.

The stranger took them completely by surprise. Had she been there all the while they had been staring at their new home from a distance?

"Yes, we are," answered Peder. Seeing that the woman was old, he put down the trunk out of respect and introduced himself and his bride.

"My husband built this house and now my son doesn't want to live here anymore." She had a twitch on the left side of her face that caused her eye to squint unnaturally.

"We are fortunate to have found such a nice house," smiled Anna. There was nothing threatening about the woman. One could feel sorry for her.

"And the furniture was mine. My son sold all of it."

Peder and Anna looked at each other wondering whether to pick up the hat box and the trunk and continue to carry in their things. It didn't seem quite right.

"You must be proud of your son. He is admired by everyone," said Anna after the awkward pause. "He has certainly built a very beautiful home. Surely you must have a lovely room there with all those large windows both upstairs and down."

"Of course I have a lovely room—not only one, but several rooms. But I don't like to be there. It doesn't feel like home." She spoke with effort now, clearing phlegm from her throat. "And now strangers are moving into this house. It's heartbreaking."

"I hope we'll not be strangers for long," said Anna with kindness. "You must come and visit me."

"She means that," said Peder, meeting the old lady's look of astonishment.

"And now come in," said Anna motioning her toward the door through which she herself hadn't yet passed. "Be our first caller."

"You want me to come in?" the old woman was visibly pleased. "Then I'll show you around."

Anna and Peder smiled at each other. It was a bit irregular for the first caller to show the occupants around. What could it be but a good omen for their marriage?

"I left this fern," she said as she led them into the dining room. "I'm sure it would die if it was moved. It has stood here by this window for quite a few years now, ever since my husband was alive."

"It has had good care, I can see that," said Anna. "It's certainly doing well."

"Now it will have to be yours. I have refused to move it," she nodded with finality.

"I hope it will continue to do as well for me."

There was something about the green fronds, the way they spread out and reached over the sides of the wicker fernery like a funeral spray, that gave Anna a twinge of dread. Or had it been the mention of the deceased husband? The feeling was momentary, however. She told herself it could only be a good omen to have a live plant thriving in this, their first home.

"I must go now. I like you folks. You'll be good, won't you and take care of everything?" She wanted a commitment; this was not merely a departing gesture.

"We'll certainly try," said Peder. "Anna is a first-rate housekeeper."

"Do come again, Mrs. Swenson. Next time we'll have coffee."

"Good-bye, then."

Peder and Anna watched her walk away from the house. One hip sank lower than the other as she went along.

"It's kind of sad, isn't it?" said Anna.

"Yes, it is."

They resumed the task of bringing in their things. Anna, remaining in the house, decided where each item would go, while Peder made trips out to the wagon.

Finally Peder reached for Anna's "hope chest." Suddenly it came to him: People don't always live in the houses they build for themselves, do they?

Chapter 11

The train whistle blew.

"You four boys are getting off at the next station," announced the conductor, wetting the tip of his pencil and drawing another line across his notebook. The waifs were eight to twelve-year-olds still in his custody enroute to new homes in the middle west. They were large-eyed Jewish boys, evidently orphaned, who had been gathered off the streets of New York's east side. They had been riding for what seemed like weeks, their number steadily diminishing as a few at a time were being let off at depots in small towns along the track. The nation was in a depression. The year was 1894.

The four selected at random were hustled to their feet and led to the exit of the railroad coach. They carried nothing with them. The clothes they wore were several sizes too big and had the look of garments drawn from a charity barrel. That the four were next scarcely affected them; they were strangers to one another and to those left behind.

Outside the Chicago-Northwestern Depot in the Norwegian community of Kenyon, Minnesota, waiting for the train to deliver its passengers were Julia Kristian and her grown son Henrik. They had answered an advertisement in the local newspaper for persons interested in giving a home to a New York slum boy. They were standing in the early dawn of a June day together with three other parties who had answered the same ad. They looked each other over. Julia knew only one of the other parties, Mr. and Mrs. Olaf Hegvik. They would certainly be good to a child, but she had misgiving about the other two parties. Needing farm help could so readily be the main motive for such adoptions, since there was much a child could do in this busy rural world.

"Here they are, folks," shouted the conductor to the waiting people who had just been startled by the noise of the incoming train and felt the earth viberating under their feet. "Good luck to you!"

How small they were! Could they be older than six or seven? The train had scarcely pulled away when a man in a dirty overall grabbed the tallest boy and pulled him along. He was the farmer, all right, that Julia had eyed with suspicion and now eyed with disfavor. The other three boys looked around anxiously, more wary than innocent. Suddenly two of them came for Julia. What did this mean—she couldn't take them both? One of these saw Henrick beside Julia and took a hold of his hand.

"How small he is, poor little thing," said Mrs. Hegvik, looking at the child standing in front of Julia. Both women looked at him more closely.

"He's beautiful, Mrs. Hegvik. He has the face of an angel," said Julia. It was safe to say, the child knew no Norwegian.

"Let us have him, Mrs. Kristian. See, the other one has taken to Henrik."

The small boy willingly took Mrs. Hegvik's hand, and Julia watched the couple with their child go toward their buggy. The fourth boy must have left with the remaining party, for Julia and Henrik saw no one as they walked away from the platform. The train was now out of hearing range and on its way to the next town.

"What is your name?" asked Julia.

"He's already told me," interrupted Henrik, smiling at the boy. "He is David Ganz. Meet David Ganz. This is my mother."

"Happy to meet you, David," said Julia in her disarming English. "I hope you will like us when you get to know us."

"Why shouldn't I?" came the swift reply. No, he wasn't a bit bashful.

Julia saw his face now. He had the same large brown eyes as the little one who had walked off with the Hegviks. She guessed they all had those kind of eyes and were all thin and delicate. But there was something very alive about this boy. She liked the way he held his head; he had no apologies to offer anyone. He was oblivious to his rumpled hair and his ill-fitting trousers. He had no attachments which he regarded as anything—he was simply there with them.

"May I pet his nose?" the boy asked, hearing the gentle words spoken to the horses while they were being loosened from the hitching post.

"Sure. They don't scare easily. You have to be careful behind them, that's all."

The chapped hands stroked the moist velvet nostrils. Henrik and Julia looked at each other with mutual feelings. Certainly the best of the four boys had fallen to them.

As he sat between them in the buggy eagerly looking around, Julia glanced over at him as often and as long as she dared, wondering how infested his head might be with lice and his clothes with bedbugs. The first step to take upon arriving home would be to scrub. But certainly she would have to feed him before that; it would by inhuman to put him through the torture of a thorough bathing without first the benefit of food. The clothes she had laid out for him were perhaps a little too big, but overall legs could always be rolled up and shoulder straps readily adjusted. Julia was in the habit of giving away Henrik's clothes as quickly as he outgrew them, but she had succeeded in getting some of them back from Melva, things that young Selmer hadn't grown into yet.

David. That was the right name for him, Julia mused, remembering the little boy of ancient Israel who killed the big Philistine, Goliath, and later became a great king. His small, lean body was wiry, she figured, and he seemed capable. His smile was easy and his pride healthy. And then there was the New Testament Son of David, that little Jewish boy who grew up as a carpenter in Nazareth. One ought always to be vigilant, never know what angel one might be entertaining, as the old saying goes.

"How old are you?" Julia suddenly asked.

"Nine, Ma'am."

As Henrik and Julia entered their home village of Wanamingo, many eyes were fixed on them from windows, hedges, and doorways, but no one met them. This taking of a slum boy was, after all, a family affair and they had a right to privacy.

"There's our papa," said Henrik as he pulled the reins to stop the rig.

In the wide doorway of the blacksmith shop stood Nils, waiting. David was struck with awe. He saw a tall, dark-bearded man with whom he would certainly have to speak Yiddish.

"This is David, Papa."

Nils approached quickly now, and David saw silver streaks in his beard. He expected him to be wearing the *yarmulke,* but saw none. Papa was smiling.

"Welcome, David!"

"Hello, Sir." The small boy stood at attention before his elder.

"You've had a long journey."

"Yes, Sir." David thought this man's English sounded foreign—like who? He tried to remember who. He guessed his own grandfather's English sounded foreign like that.

"Our mother must give you something to eat. I'm sure you are hungry."

"Not very much, Sir."

"Come, David," called Henrik. "Help me put the horses away."

Surprised to see that Henrik had already moved the rig away, the new arrival nodded quickly at Nils and broke into a run toward the barn. Nils watched him go. It will be kind of nice having a small son around. It was like Julia to want to take a slum boy. This was another of her benevolent projects; she thrived on them. Who could come up to her, equal her in anything—anything in the world.

Julia began clearing the dirty cups left from Nils' morning coffee the minute she got into the house. She wiped the oilcloth. The clock said ten, hard to believe, but they had started out this morning at four, in time to meet the 6:25 train. Henrik would soon be coming in, bringing the boy. She would give Henrik his coffee and the boy a big glass of milk, and—lets see, there must be something more to eat than molasses cookies—some thick slices of bread and jelly.

"Mama's going to give you a good scrubbing, David," said Henrik, sitting with the child at the kitchen table, well aware of the torture that was in store for the small boy.

"I don't think I'm very dirty."

He was putting up a defense, but Julia thought it was too mild to worry about. She watched him drink his milk and was glad she had buttered the bread so generously.

"No one could be clean after riding on that dirty train all across the country," continued Henrik, knowing that his mother wanted him to do the talking. "I even saw a black smudge on the conductor's forehead. It must have gotten there from dirty fingers when he lifted his cap to scratch his head. You've seen those fellows do that, haven't you? Maybe those stiff caps aren't very comfortable—and they have to wear them all the time."

David kept his eyes on Henrik as they continued eating. He couldn't imagine a conductor being dirty, but if his new brother had seen it, it must be so.

The door opened.

"Here come the berry pickers," said Julia as Sarah, Ellen, and brother Selmer came through the screen door. "I thought you'd stay in the woods all morning."

"This is David Ganz," said Henrik, looking from one to the other of the three with pails hanging at their sides.

They had already spied the new boy and were looking him over. He was different, all right. They had never seen anyone with such dark eyes.

"I'm Sarah, your sister," said the girl who seemed to be in charge. "This is Ellen and Selmer Veblen."

"Hello."

"Hello."

"Do you want to see how many gooseberries I picked?" asked Selmer, bringing his bucket for the new boy's inspection.

"May I taste one?"

"Sure."

He crushed a green, juicy berry in his mouth while his audience waited in suspense.

"I shan't like your berries," he replied after spitting the green mulch into his hand. He went to the door to dispose of it and returned wiping his hand on his pants.

"They are sour, aren't they," laughed Selmer, setting his pail on the table.

"Otherwise you would have eaten all of them," Ellen sputtered at her brother. "We never took you along picking plums, because you'd have eaten all of them."

The overall was not much too big, and the fit of the blue shirt delighted young David, who came out of the scrubbing with no visible scars. Selmer had been patiently waiting outside, hoping that the new boy would be free to come out and play before his own mother expected him home for dinner.

"How old are you?" asked Selmer.

"Nine. How old are you?"

"Seven."

"You're just as big as me, aren't you," said the new boy. "Let's measure."

The two boys stood back to back and felt the tops of their heads.

"Pretty much the same," said Selmer as if an important issue had been solved. "Even if you're older than me, yet we're the same size. We can be friends then, can't we?"

"Sure."

Arne was standing in the doorway of his shop watching the ritual of two boys getting to know each other. He would wait no longer to meet the boy Julia had spoken for.

"So you have a new friend in this town, Selmer," said Arne.

"David, this is my Grandpa," Selmer responded with pride.

"Hello, Sir."

Arne nodded. "Bring him over sometime. He is welcome."

It was nice that the man next door was Selmer's *zayde*. David decided that the town had friendly ways. He looked up and down the road. How small the metropolis was, and how close the open country lay on all sides!

Arne returned to his shop as the two boys parted to their respective homes for dinner. Poor little fellow, but he'll pick up when he starts eating Julia's meals. He trotted off to his own kitchen. What remarkable eyes that child has! He was certainly different, as though he had come out of a story of long ago, a prince in disguise, maybe. Of course, he wasn't Norwegian or Swede, and those were the only kind of folks around here.

"Can't we take David threshing this year?" asked Henrik as he and Nils were getting the steam engine ready for another season.

"He's pretty small," replied Nils, wiping grease from his hand on to his overall.

"Of course not for the whole run. He has to be ready for school. I undertand that... but up until then... shock-threshing the way I did, remember?"

"Some men find kids a nuisance, and besides, he'd be another mouth for the women to feed."

"He ought to be permitted since I was, when I was a kid."

"You be responsible for him then. Remember how Peder saw to it that you never got in anyone's way? You do the same for David."

"I will, Papa."

"You really like that boy, don't you?"

"I do. He's very bright."

"I'm glad you get along so well. It's good for the boy. I'm glad, too, that you're still at home with us, Henrik. We could hardly do without you now, Mama and me. Bring the grease bucket and let's take a look at the water wagon."

Henrik would be the one to crawl under; it had been his job for years. He did it now, gratified by the words his father had just spoken.

The illusion that only a genuine Scandinavian could utter Norwegian words was quickly losing ground, as David gained acceptance among the threshers. Newcomers learning English had been a source of amusement for years, but here was a whole new twist: an English-speaking child learning Norwegain. And David learned quickly. He never became the butt of a practical joke in this regard, always clever enough to handle himself. Occasionally he would toss in a Yiddish word and have a little fun himself. "How's that?" they would say. He liked those boisterous men; he had often stood at a distance taking in the laughter and merriment of his grandfather's friends, but had never been drawn in like he was now; he supposed he had been too little then. These people had peculiar ways, though. They ate pork all the time, for every meal, almost, and didn't work on the day after the Sabbath.

And David wondered what it would take to make his new papa angry. As a matter of course, he identified this man as the one with authority like his own *Zayde,* but the blacksmith was so easy-going, had no deep furrows in his forehead, never frightened anyone with his eyes, had no moods of irritation to make a child wary. The new papa owned his own house and his shop, not having to worry that someone would put him out if the rent wasn't paid on time. "Where's the money coming from—*Gevalt!* I was cheated again—*Chas vessholem!*" Words such as these he hadn't heard in the three months he had been here. And he and Selmer never got into trouble. He wondered why? He hadn't brought sorrow to his new papa yet, and he hoped he wouldn't.

After a long, hot day threshing Ole Bakken's field, the men with their tired horses having set off for home, Henrik and David were left to put the engine at rest for the night. They saw to it that fuel was near at hand for the morning and stayed around while the fire died down in the firebox.

"Let's go to the swimming hole, what do you say?" Henrik looked at his partner; a smudge was on his face under the straw hat he himself used to wear.

"Sure."

They ran through the stubble toward the river, paused at the fence and straddled over onto the cool grass of the pasture. How wonderful it was getting off the hot work shoes! David was out of his overall by unfastening only one side and letting it fall. Henrik was already in the water.

"It's not deep," called Henrik, wasting words for his partner had already taken the plunge.

"I know how to swim," said David, paddling toward Henrik.

"You do?"

"My brother and I used to jump off the dock along the East River."

"Really?"

"But this is better. Nicer water."

"How so?"

"The boats that went along left oil on the water and we got all brown and sticky. But that wasn't the worst of it."

"No? what was?"

"*Goyim* threw rocks at us and chased us."

"*Goyim*? Who are they?"

"Other people—you and everyone around here are *goyim,* but not bad. Only some are bad like those who threw rocks at us because we were Jews."

With that David dove under exposing his extraordinarily slender legs, so seldom seen, and feet disproportionately large. Henrik took mental note of the word *goyim* and surmised it meant gentile. It made him feel vaguely uncomfortable. David, after all, was his brother.

"On hot days," said David as he turned upright again, catching his breath, "the water hydrants would be turned on to wash the streets. Then all us kids would dance naked in the shower until the policeman would chase us away. My brother didn't do that though, he thought he was too grown up."

The two sloshed out toward some rocks to let the water dry off their bodies before getting back into their clothes. The sun would be up for several hours yet, although the tree shadows were lengthening and the sunny spots fewer.

"He was a lot older than you?" began Henrik again, itching his ear with his little finger.

"He was twelve. He learned to be a *grifter*. And he was going to teach me, too, that was when we both got picked up."

"A *grifter*?"

"Someone who can pick money out of people's pockets, you know." David pushed a stone with his foot until it rolled into the water.

"You learned to do that?"

"I don't steal, Henrik," he said quickly. "The most I ever stole was fruit off the pushcarts. But most of the time I didn't have to steal, the vendor would give away the bananas when they got too black."

"Your brother did, though?"

"He brought grief to *Zayde* because he ran in the streets all the time. Then *Zayde* died and my brother took me with him into the streets. That's when we got picked up."

"Was he put on the train with you?"

"No, he was taken to court. They asked me if I wanted to go and live on a farm—but not him."

"What did you say when they asked you that?"

"I said sure!" He smiled at Henrik, proud of what was his own decision. "You see there was no one to go to. There was a good woman in the same building where we lived, but she couldn't take care of us. And my grandmother was dead. I told you that, didn't I?"

"No. Do you remember her?"

"Not much. She prayed—like Mama does—only we lit candles then. That's all I can remember." David had found it fascinating to throw stones into the stream.

While Henrik began pulling on his clothes, he wondered about the grandmother and her prayers. It made him feel more committed to the boy. He supposed the old couple had come from somewhere in eastern Europe. Sad it was about their grandchidren, citizens of the United States being destroyed by poverty.

"Come, David. We'd better be getting home. Sarah and Mama will have milked the cows and have supper on the table before we get there if we don't start moving."

As soon as Henrik said the word, David's clothes were on, all except his shoes. He would walk home barefooted.

Thus with David a new responsibility came into Henrik's life which was beginning to make all the difference in the world. It mattered less now that Lars had gone north, or that he found himself at odds with certain of his fellowmen, or that he felt lonely in certain areas of his existence; it was almost as if he in his early twenties had acquired a disciple. The boy had curiosity that probed often beyond the reach of both of them, and as time went on they conducted investigations, seeking answers, and, likely as not, finding them.

Among his books Henrik had a set of encylopedias purchased a year ago from a door-to-door book peddler. Julia had thought at that time that they were very expensive—who had such a luxury she didn't know—but her son convinced her they were infinitely useful, in fact necessary, if one were to be a real student of anything. Now Julia watched the two of them searching information on every subject imaginable. It was indeed a good investment. David was becoming advanced far beyond his years, and it was no small thanks to Henrik and those books. Julia would never begrudge Henrik his books, and certainly not now with a young mind like David's at his side.

Henrik's self-education drew fresh meaning from the boy being at his side. Henrik was discovering he could share his interest in history with someone else besides his busy mother. David's imagination was fresh and responsive. That the human race has a fantastic past easily won scope in the child's mind, and he eagerly listened to his brother.

As time went on Henrik began to wonder if science might not be the boy's real interest. More and more often a volume was placed before him with some aspect of zoology or botany. The boy wasn't among animals and growing things without practical questions about them, and he usually had the answers to the questions he put to Henrik before he asked them.

After supper on a November evening the kerosene lamp with its rose globe sat lit on the library table in the parlor. Next to it sat Nils, resuming his pipe after putting fresh sticks of wood in the stove. Julia sat with her reading and Sarah came with her knitting. Catching a beam from the lamp, David sat on the floor in front of the bookcase sliding open the glass door of the bottom shelf where the encyclopedias were.

Closest to the table, soaking up as much light as possible, sat Henrik with the book, *A Crown of Wild Olive,* a collection of lectures by John Ruskin. The first lecture was made to the Working Men's Institute at Camberwell, England, entitled "Work." Oblivious to those around him, Henrik took a pencil from the slot in the bib of his overall and began underlining. Julia had often called him on this habit, but her words went unheeded. Of course, he wouldn't deface a book, but he did want to leave a footprint to return to later—what was wrong with that? The pencil traced along several lines:

> The one Divine work... it is to do justice; and it is the last we are ever inclined to do. Anything rather than that! As much charity as you choose, but no justice. "Nay," you will say, "Charity is greater than justice." Yes, it is greater; it is the summit of justice—it is the temple of which justice is the foundation. But you can't have the top without the bottom; you cannot build charity. You just build upon justice, for this main reason that you have not, at first, charity to build with. It is the last reward of good work. You well-to-do people, for instance, will go to Divine Service next Sunday, all nice and tidy and your little children will have their lovely little Sunday feathers in their hats, and you'll think piously how lovely they look! Then you will come to the poor little crossing-sweeper and give him a penny and think how good you are. What does justice say walking and watching us? "Why shouldn't that

little crossing-sweeper have a feather as well as your own child?"

Henrik paused and looked around for David. He knew very well where he'd be. He was replacing one volume and taking another.

Chapter 12

Henrik saw Albin Veblen approach the house with the bills that must have just arrived from the printer. He carefully put down the sickle he was sharpening and dashed across the road to the house.

"Oh, there you are," said Albin. "These notices are pretty fancy. If the weather stays dry, I'm sure it will be the best Fourth-of-July celebration ever held in these parts."

"They're not bad," said Henrik, looking at the top one as Albin held them up.

"You're giving the speech, aren't you? How come your name isn't here? I'd think that's what would be the drawing card."

"No, Albin. I do have a streak of modesty in me. They'll find out soon enough who the speaker is, if they don't already suspect. Box social! That's what you'll be there for," said Henrik with a twinkle in his eye.

"Not that!" Albin looked more closely at the bill wondering what he had missed. "An old bachelor like me? I'm too old to bid on any young lady's box."

"Then I guess you'll just have to go without dessert. There'll be some mighty good pies and cakes in those boxes. It'll be up to you," laughed Henrik, taking the bills and moving toward the house. "Come in. How about a cup of coffee?"

"No, I must get back."

Smiling to himself, Albin returned to the store. Henrik is the one who wants to have the box auction; he's as fond of girls as he is of pie.

"What does the bill say?" asked Sarah, dropping her sewing. She heard the screen door slam and knew it was Henrik.

"See for yourself," repied Henrik, dropping the tagboard sheets on the table. "Don't mess them up. David and I intend to take them around today."

FOURTH OF JULY CELEBRATION

Otto Jenson's Grove, on the Zumbro
1/2 mile west of Wanamingo bridge.

PATRIOTIC PROGRAM: (starting at 11 a.m.)	A speech Music by Norway Quartet
SMORGASBORD:	Women, bring your delicious food!
BOX AUCTION: (benefit: War Relief)	Girls, get your baskets ready with those cakes and pies!
FIREWORKS:	Furnished for the occasion.

You are citizens
of a great nation,

CELEBRATE HER INDEPENDENCE

"I'm never lucky at box auctions," said Sarah mostly to herself as she read. "But there'll be lots of people from all over at this one, won't there?"

"We're tacking these up in the general stores all around the area: Roscoe, Bombay, Norway, Aspelund, and Hader. People will get to know about it all right. I haven't heard if Zumbrota is having a celebration this year or not. That might make a difference."

"How come you're taking these bills to all these places?"

"Hans Monset asked me. He's the chairman, you might say. I guess they figure I have less to do than most people. And I don't mind. I'll take Barney and the light buggy. David will go with me. We'll be back by supper."

"Ellen says you are going to give a speech. Is that right?"

"It is, if you don't mind," said Henrik indifferently. "Hans Monset and Eric Quam asked me last week when they stopped by to talk about threshing."

"There'll be lots of people, strangers, too. Aren't you scared?"

"Sarah, don't be foolish."

"I'm glad you're going to speak, Henrik. I'll be proud."

"Just see to my white shirt. I don't want any wrinkles, otherwise I'll have to say Anna does a better job than you."

"Stop teasing, Henrik. Of course I'll be careful."

"Where's David?"

"He was reciting the Gettysburg Address last time I saw him. I think he is outside by the barn somewhere saying it for the horses."

"I'll find him. We'll practice on the road," said Henrik as he folded a piece of newspaper around his precious bundle and tucked it under his arm. "Tell Mama where we've gone."

Ellen was the first to read the notice posted in her father's store. She waited until Henrik and David had left town, then she dashed over to see her friend Sarah.

"You've seen the bills about the Fourth of July, haven't you? Uncle Albin just put one up in the store." Ellen spoke rapidly lest someone walked in on them. "I want Henrik to buy my box, Sarah. Oh I hope he will be the one!"

"That's hard to say, Ellen. What if there are several hundred people there?"

"I know," Ellen sighed. "But maybe you could tell him what my box will look like and that I will have a berry pie, his favorite."

"You really are stuck on Henrik, aren't you?" said Sarah as if it were the first time she had noticed. "Ellen, if you want to know the truth, Henrik still thinks we are both just kids. He's in his twenties now and thinks he's much older than we are. It just hasn't dawned on him that we are young ladies. Why, even at Anna's wedding he made me feel like a mere child."

"I want a smart fellow. I haven't anything really against farmers, please believe me, but most of them are right out of the barn—no refinement. You know what I mean?"

"Henrik is a farmer, isn't he? He takes care of our few acres and the animals. He may acquire more land and make a living at it, at least I've heard he and Mama talk about it."

"But he's different, Sarah. You know what I mean. He reads books and recites poetry. And isn't he going to give the Fourth-of-July speech. You know he's no ordinary farmer."

"Maybe not."

"You haven't seen as many farmers as I have. I work in the store almost every day now since Papa and Uncle Albin are out building. Even some of the younger men we know have taken to chewing tobacco and showing off as they go spitting around. And they don't bother to talk English either, even if they have been to school."

"Don't fret, Ellen. Maybe you'll meet someone nice this time. I can't imagine anyone who is spitting tobacco will have the gall to bid on a nice lady's box."

"Sarah, do you think Henrik is too old for me?"

"No, I don't. But I think you might find someone better. Henrik is all right. I should say that since he is my brother. But he's so stuck on himself, and believe me, he has a temper."

"I don't care. I still hope he'll buy my box. I must hurry back. Uncle Albin wants to leave. He might even be waiting for me."

"Good luck, Ellen," called Sarah as her friend pushed through the screen door.

Mrs. Monset had expressed to her husband that a natural-speaking American ought to recite the Gettysburg Address. She said she was tired of hearing a Norwegian brogue when there certainly ought not be one. It's pretty hard to find someone around here wthout a brogue, her husband had told her, and they were not about to ask anyone from Zumbrota. Why not the New York boy Nils and Julia Kristian adopted, suggested the wife. He's awfully small, Hans had objected. Yes, but Mrs. Grimstad had told her the other day that she had heard him at church recite the Catechism in English. He was evidently reading for the minister in English, although they say he is smart enough to understand a lot of Norwegian, too. She said he had a loud, clear voice and held his head high. It was first any of the congregation had heard the Third Article in any other language but Norwegian. He had impressed them all. Thus David was chosen for the patriotic recitation.

He knew it by heart already as he sat beside Henrik in the buggy behind Barney.

"You'll have to say it very loud," said Henrik. "Being outside makes it hard. One almost has to shout."

"Four score and seven years ago..." David shouted into the clouds. "Like that?" His voice returned to earth as he looked over at Henrik.

"I guess you'll do," Henrik laughed.

"Do you know your speech?" David asked upon finishing his rendition of the famous American oration to his brother's satisfaction.

Henrik glanced over at the slight boy at his side. Might he not be a perfect audience? He saw the brown eyes, not many brown eyes around, not like these, yet the child was part of this great country where "all men are created equal." The emotion with which Henrik had written his speech surged forth toward the boy born in New York. Henrik had recited his speech enough these past few days, and each time a quality he labled "eloquence" swept through for him, in the words he had so carefully chosen. The convictions he had bestowed so fervently in his address now took new luster in the brown eyes that were asking to hear it.

"I suppose that is only fair," replied Henrik.

> As we have assembled today to celebrate the anniversary of this nation's independence, I thought it would be right and proper to speak about the state of affairs now existing between Spain and the United States.

"You mean the war?"

"That's what I mean."

> Not since the gloomy days of the Civil War has any president of the United States had a more grave duty to perform than William McKinley now has. Not since the time of the Emancipation Proclamation was issued, has there ever been given out a more important document from the White House than the ultimatum sent to Spain de-

> manding her to relinquish immediately her authority in the island of Cuba and to withdraw her land and naval forces from Cuba and Cuban waters.

"That's—what you read to Mama from the newspaper!"

Henrik nodded.

> Again the murky clouds of war are hovering over the nation. War is dark and cruel, we lament it, we deprecate its horrors; but at the same time we can also rejoice, for this is not a war for greed, conquest, or military fame; it is not a war of rebellion arrayed against our government, but it is a war for the despised, oppressed and downtrodden of another nation; it is a war for humanity. It is in the name of the poor, suffering, and starving people that our soldiers are fighting and sacrificing their lives.

"Are the people of Cuba starving?" asked David during the pause it took to direct Barney to make a ninety-degree angle on the road.

"They have a very unjust government, David. Spain, a country across the ocean, has ruled them and drained away what they had. Just think, the poor farmers work so hard, but their money is simply taken in taxes to make beautiful the palaces in Spain."

"We're helping them fight Spain, aren't we?"

"We are. We need to help them. A terrible Spanish general named Weyler herded the rebellious people into camps where awful things happened to them. We couldn't be so close to this little island and not help them when we know they were suffering so unjustly."

"Do all the people coming to the celebration know about how we are fighting with Spain?"

"Everyone knows there's a war. The newspapers tell of little else."

"Do they know why we are fighting with Spain?"

"If they don't, we'll tell them, David. And they will listen. They know what liberty means and they will want little Cuba to have a government like ours, where all men are treated equally and by elections choose their leaders instead of being ruled by tyrants."

"What's a tyrant?"

"A king who has complete power, who makes all the laws and doesn't need to worry about whether they are just or not, just so they please him."

"Does he live in a palace?"

"He does. He sees to that. In this country, David, the leaders can come from very poor circumstances. Remember what we read about Abraham Lincoln, who was born in a log cabin, yet became the best president we ever had?"

"Yes, and Edison, who was a poor paper boy in New York, became a great man, an inventor, wasn't it?"

"You are right, my boy."

They were pulling up to the hitching post outside Norway General Store. While Henrik tied Barney, David took a poster from the bundle. People around, for as far as the eye could see, would know about the celebration and would listen to Henrik's speech and learn what the United States was doing for the suffering people of Cuba.

"It's a box social auction at this celebration, Ragnild. If you want to go with us you'll have to prepare a box. Pies or cakes, it said. There is to be a smorgasbord, too, so the boxes must contain dessert." Melvin Vessedahl, the first tenor of the Norway Quartet made this announcement to his sister. "I just saw the bill tacked up at the store."

Ragnild was the accompanist for the quartet, two members of which were her brothers. They had done a great deal of rehearsing for this event, the other two members living on neighboring farms. The little settlement called Norway was near the two Lutheran Churches, Holden and Aspelund. The quartet members were from Holden. Wanamingo people were unfamiliar to them since few, if any, belonged to Holden, but they were nonetheless Norwegians like themselves.

"Most of the songs you sing well without accompaniment. Besides, did they say they would have an organ on the platform there in the grove?"

"No, they didn't say," said Melvin, "but I assume they will. They wouldn't ask us otherwise, would they?"

"I just don't know," said Ragnild, dreading the thought of her box being bid on by total strangers. "And now that I have to prepare a basket, I think I'd rather stay at home."

"Ragnild, you are too shy. Come along, we need you. And listen to this, I'll tell Leonard which box is yours, and you won't have to worry about a perfect stranger eating your cake."

The Fourth-of-July dawned clear as crystal over southern Minnesota. The grove, surrounded on two sides by the curving river, had a grassy clearing, cool and green. Several years before, trees had been partially logged off. Since the land was flat and fertile, it was considered for a field but flooding in the spring made it unsuitable for seeding. So it became a pasture.

Two wagons arrived loaded with lumber—thick planks, clean and sweet-smelling. Several men jumped off and began unloading, while others who had been waiting for the load moved in with shiny hammers. In no time the platform was up and draped across the front with red, white and blue bunting. The wagons on a second trip brought more planks and cut logs for benches; at least a part of the audience would have a place to sit. After the big event the lumber would be returned to the Jensen farm. Otto had lent it from the pile he had secured for building a barn. Soon a wagon carrying an organ slowly crossed the deep ditch leading from the road to the pasture. It was steadied by its owner, who felt proud about doing a patriotic turn, lending his precious property for this occasion.

Before long, rigs began to arrive. They were directed into a stretch of shade to the left of the entrance by Albin Veblen, who was wearing an official badge. The driveway was soon pulverized by hoofs, and clouds of dust rose with each carriage that entered the grounds. The ladies grabbed their full-length, white-voile skirts until they saw, to their relief, that the clearing was green with only an occasional pile of cow dung demanding caution. On the stage was a podium borrowed from the school house and a row of round-backed chairs for the dignitaries.

"This is our accompanist, my sister, Ragnild."

Henrik and David were below the platform waiting for the signal from the chairman to climb the step and take their places.

Before Henrik stood the girl named Ragnild—that's what he thought the spokesman for the Norway quartet had said. Her eyes were blue, very blue; he had never seen such blue eyes.

"Pleased to meet you, Ma'am."

"How do you do."

David watched his brother meeting this young lady. Henrik paused long upon being introduced to her. He scarcely looked at the other members of the quartet.

No sooner were they seated on the platform than David patted Henrik's sleeve.

"I saw her box through the fold in the dishtowel. It's blue, Henrik, blue." Afraid that he might have been heard, he quickly settled back into the far reaches of the chair.

Blue, was it? Henrik wouldn't forget blue.

Henrik Kristian. Was he a seminary student perhaps, or a young lawyer? Ragnild Vessedahl had heard of the Kristian Blacksmith Shop in Wanamingo, where broken machinery was taken when no one else seemed able to fix it. He must be the blacksmith's son. She knew also that the Kristians in Wanamingo had spoken for one of the New York slum boys who had come on the train a year ago. That must be the boy. He doesn't look like a Norwegian. Henrik Kristian. With his sandy red hair, a few freckles, and eyes a bit too close together, he wasn't really handsome, she thought. But his grooming was beyond reproach. She knew what it took to make a white shirt look like that.

The quartet performed its first group of songs and received enthusiastic applause. Then they invited the audience to sing "My Country 'Tis of Thee." This was what the children had been waiting for. Now that the song was over, they could leave their parents and go to the river to play.

All but David, who had yet to recite the Gettysburg Address. Swinging his arms and seemingly adding to his stature, he marched up, looked far beyond the people, and began. His voice seemed to come all the way from his feet planted firmly on the edge of the platform.

> Four score and seven years ago, our fathers brought forth upon this continent a new nation...

David saw a bank of pure white clouds above the trees.

> ...conceived in liberty and dedicated to the proposition that all men are created equal...

The people were listening all right. Mama and Papa were out there and his brother right behind him on the stage.

> Now we are engaged in a great Civil War, testing whether that nation or any other nation so conceived and so dedicated, can long endure...

For Julia the images of the great new nation's history merged with those of her own family. Her eyes were on Henrik. How he resembled his uncle, her brother, the Henrik wounded in "that Civil War." Her son would do well as a farmer, but it wasn't right somehow. Maybe he should run for office. Julia never doubted that young David would carry through to the end without a hitch. She had heard him recite the Catechism.

> ...that government of the people, by the people, and for the people shall not perish from the earth!

The people applauded. The boy's voice had articulated the great American address in the nation's language, as it should be articulated, emphatic and flawless.

The quartet followed David's recitation with two more numbers. Relieved that the most difficult of the songs had been sung, Ragnild returned to her chair, wiping her moist hands with her handkerchief. As she seated herself, she crossed her ankles to make herself more comfortable. Henrik Kristian was about to speak.

Surely he had more than an ordinary education. Words came so easy for him. Ragnild liked the sound of his voice. It was fervent; he believed what he said. He gestured with his hands, hands almost too clean to be those of a blacksmith. She looked around at the people. They were very attentive. She noticed one old man, not inclined to sit, who stood close to the platform with his hat held against his chest and his hand cupped to his ear. He was not the only elderly person in the audience, but he seemed to have a personal reason for the intensity with which he listened.

> Before I close I wish to say that we should be thankful for the fact that we are citizens of this great republic. It means something to be protected by the arms of a strong government that is ever ready to defend the cause of humanity. Let us therefore invoke the blessings of a kind Providence and pray Him who rules the destinies of nations to protect the privileges we are enjoying under this government and to aid us in pursuing this war (Spanish American War) to a successful end, so that the bright sun of peace, liberty, and happiness may also shine down on the desolate Island of Cuba. Thank you.

Ragnild was moved. He had captivated his audience with those closing words so that a silent moment prevailed before overwhelming applause. Patriotism was as noble a fervor as religion, and Henrik had touched their hearts. Our closing song will be fitting, she said to herself, as she caught the mood of the people.

The quartet rose and sang "Nearer My God to Thee."

"Congratulations on a very fine speech, Henrik."

"Thank you, Arne."

Ragnild caught these words as she saw the old man who had stood close to the platform shake Henrik's hand. Announcements were being made from the podium. The chairman was attempting to keep the attention of the people, just as they had begun to relax.

"Don't go away folks! The boxes will be auctioned as soon as we get them all up there on the platform. Don't go away, folks!"

The boxes, now with exterior wrappings removed, were placed in a colorful array on a plank spanning two chairs. Most of the boxes were square. Some, however, were round, unmistakable hat boxes. They were covered with cloth or paper tied with ribbons. There were elaborate bows on most of them. Some had incorporated a cluster of flowers, whose freshness had been threatened by the earlier wrappings and the long wait.

"See that box with the purple clover on top?" said Henrik to Melvin Vessedahl. "It contains an excellent berry pie."

Melvin nodded understandingly and smiled.

The auctioneer held up a blue box tied with many strands of ribbon which fluttered in the wind. At the end of each ribbon was a little paper flower. Henrik and David exchanged glances.

"How much am I offered for this beauty!" shouted the auctioneer.

"Two dollars!"

Henrik had produced another hush, but this time there were whispers. That much? Is he crazy? Whose is it? He won't be outdone!

"Sold —to Henrik Kristian for two dollars!"

Ragnild saw her box being handed to Henrik Kristian just below the stage. He must have mistaken her box for someone else's. This would be embarrassing. He was coming toward her. He knew it was hers!

"Blue to match your eyes. You were wondering how I knew, weren't you?"

"You paid too much for it," Ragnild smiled, trying to hide her astonishment.

"Not in the least. Besides, it's all for a good cause."

They watched the other boxes go to the highest bidders. Melvin was now bidding on a box with a cluster of purple clover tied in the ribbon.

"Sold to — your name? To Melvin Vessedahl!"

"She's a good girl," Henrik told Ragnild. "She works in her father's store. Her name is Ellen Veblen. Melvin is lucky."

"Everyone to the river! We are going to set off our firecrackers!" cried the chairman just as the last of the boxes disappeared into the crowd.

As the crowd moved toward the bend in the river, Albin Veblen, on a little sandbar, drew forth the firecrackers he had ordered. The children, barefooted and wet from wading, kicked water as they came. They were an eager flock, his first audience.

"Stand back!" he shouted. "We mustn't get them wet. Sit down over there on the bank!"

No child loitered. The bank became an amphitheater whose audience awaited sounds of war—harmless to be sure, but some little hands were already covering ears. The adults were gathering behind them, too slowly to suit the children.

And there were no mothers among them. They had stayed behind to untie the dishtowels that wrapped the casseroles and to lay out the smorgasbord on the long table of planks across several sawhorses. The sound of firecrackers didn't seem to interfere; the women visited as they worked.

As the last firecracker exploded and hissed into the water, the crowd returned to the clearing where the table stood waiting. The hungry saw baked beans, escalloped potatoes, smoked ham in huge slices, sausages, and shavings of dried beef. And there were potato dumplings, *lefse, kringle* and numerous kinds of breads with plenty of butter and a variety of jams and jellies. And there were pastries, too, pies and cakes, for only the unmarried men had bid on the boxes. Coffee was available in huge, white pots that were used during threshing, and lemonade was brought in milk cans from the stream, where it had been kept cool.

Having filled their plates, Ragnild and Henrik found a shady spot under a tree away from the crowd.

"So you live just west of Norway Store," Henrik said, ready to eat, with his legs pulled securely under him.

"Yes, that's right."

"My father threshes west of here almost that far." He began eating.

"I must tell you how much I liked your speech. You have talent. Where have you been going to school?" She lifted her plate toward herself for each bite lest she spill on her white dress.

"I'm entirely self-educated," replied Henrik between forkfuls. "A dirt farmer, I guess you might call me. I farm on a small scale, my parents' few acres, and help my father particularly during the threshing season."

"It's hard to believe that you are not a law student or a seminarian."

"No, I'm neither. Law interests me, though. And you? You play very well. Surely you have been taking lessons?"

"I have—a few. I've picked up much of it on my own, though. We live far from Kenyon, and getting into town for lessons is hard especially when everyone has so much work to do."

As Henrik listened, the food on his plate visibly diminished, yet he took his eyes off her only to refill his fork.

"You belong to Holden, I understand."

"Yes, and you to Aspelund?"

"M-huh, and that means we have been less than two miles apart on Sunday mornings for most of our lives."

Ragnild smiled easily at this. Although she was shy, she really didn't feel uncomfortable with this Wanamingo boy. Strange! Advances made by the young men she had known were always a kind of threat; she didn't want to lead them on; she hadn't met one yet that interested her. She preferred to be in the company of her brothers, with whom she felt safe. Henrik Kristian most likely talked to all new girls, she thought. He was being a good host, she coming as a kind of visitor to his community. She felt honored.

Soon they were sharing a custard cream pie from the blue box. It had a two-inch meringue, sweetened and browned to perfection. Henrik was not disappointed with the box's contents; he flattered her efforts with compliments.

In another part of the grove on the edge of the crowd, Sarah was sitting with the someone who had persistently bid on her box until it was his, and he didn't have much money either.

"Haven't I met you before?" Sarah began by speaking in her casual way to the short, stocky stranger before her. His head was round and sun-weathered, his hair thin and sand-colored.

"You have. But it was a very long time ago. My father has urged me to talk with you."

"Your father?"

"Sarah Kristian, I am your brother. My name is Oscar Monson."

How could she hide being astonished? It was true, then, what she had been told. Up to this moment it had seemed as remote as a fairytale. Now it all flashed forth.

She was told the story at age five as she stood naked in a wash-tub, her mother lathering her diligently with soap. "You belonged to a different family once, Sarah, my dear." Of all the voices the child knew, this one, above all others, she trusted. "You came to us bundled in your first mother's shawl. You were handed to me by your first father, a very kind man who thought you couldn't live in a family without a mother." The child interruped here. "What happened to that mother?" "She died and went to heaven." The soap got lost at the bottom of the tub and had to be retrieved. "So you came to a new family, my dear. You joined Anna, Henrik, Papa and me." That was all there had been to it, and it seemed so long ago. And everyone called her Sarah Kristian.

"My brother?"

"It's really not fair that I bought your box. Forgive me?" The last thing he wanted to do was to offend her.

She continued to stare at him. She no longer tried to hide her amazement.

"Please forgive me. You took me by surprise," she said upon regaining her composure. Her tight little smile was an attempt to put him at ease.

"So you don't mind?"

"Not at all. We should get to know each other."

A farmer with disheveled gray hair, who was wearing a clean work shirt and a new overall, stood next to Nils not far from the brother and sister.

"She's a respected young lady, Nils. You and Julia have been wonderful parents." The farmer, putting his hands into the bib of his overall and shifting on his feet, did not take his eyes off his children.

"She is that, a very fine girl," said Nils as amiably as he could. He thought he heard a catch in the voice of the *Vossing* who never seemed to have any luck.

"They should get to know each other. Don't you think so too?"

"I agree, Lars. It's right they should."

Chapter 13

No, she wouldn't go to Mrs. Johnson's coffee party this afternoon. She would have Peder stop by the Johnson house on his return to the meat market this noon and give Mrs. Johnson her regrets. Anna had just finished ironing an embroidered waist she had intended to wear and was sliding it onto a hanger when she made the decision. She wouldn't face those women today, those women who were always wondering when her dresses would become too tight. Yes, they had been wondering this for quite a while now, five years in fact. Could it really be that long? She resented the slim lines of this tiny garment and hooked the hanger quickly on the peg she had asked Peder to install on her bedroom door.

She returned to the kitchen and proceeded to put her ironing board away. She shoved the heavy flat irons to the back of the stove and drew forth the kettle for boiling potatoes. Anna, being methodical, always peeled her potatoes after doing the breakfast dishes. Her husband was still a farmer in many ways. He always wanted a full dinner at noon. Next she went to the cellar and brought up the package of fresh meat Peder always brought home from the market at closing time. Soon the pork chops would be sizzling in the cast-iron frying pan.

Five years she had been waiting! Not only she had been waiting, others, too, like Mama, Sarah, Papa, and even Henrik. Her friends, dear friends—could she really believe they gossiped behind her back, making up strange reasons about why she hadn't conceived?

But most of all there was Peder. How could she help but notice how he loved children. They were drawn to him. Seldom were they out anywhere but what a child would climb into his lap. He carried gum in his shirt pocket, handouts for the unsuspecting. Peder never mentioned her barrenness; he was too kind for that, but she knew he carried a longing within him that she wanted to brighten and fulfill. Who could ever know how much she wanted this!

She made another decision as she set the table for Peder and herself. She would ask Peder if she could take Blossom and the buggy and head for Wanamingo tomorrow morning. Of course he wouldn't say no, he would have the white mare harnessed for her whenever she was ready. Would he wonder? No, he wouldn't. She often spent a day or two with her folks during the summer, and now that spring had settled into early summer, favorable weather was assured for such a trip.

At seven the next morning Anna was ready to leave and Peder had the buggy waiting. A brisk breeze was tossing Blossom's mane and tail. No, it wouldn't rain today. The clouds driven by the wind were billowy white. But there had been a downpour during the night.

"If I'm not back tomorrow night, I will certainly be back the next day," Anna told Peder as she grabbed a hold and climbed the step into the buggy.

"Greet them all from me," said Peder as he watched her undo the reins. "The countryside is busy. I wish I were going with you. Have a good journey, then. Good-bye."

"Good-bye. Have it good while I'm gone."

The buggy turned on the next block and took her out of Peder's sight. He returned to the house. He would go early to the market today, and he would stay longer than usual; he would keep busy until Anna returned.

Anna was aware that Blossom's shod feet sounded her approach and passage through Kenyon's main street. There were shiny pools of water here and there, but horse and buggy left no appreciable tracks. Anna's eyes saw only one store front among the many, and that, of course, was the OLSON AND HARSTAD MEAT MARKET. It had prospered from the start and now there was talk of putting up a new building, a two-story, brick structure with living quarters on the second floor. It would be rather exciting living on main street, she had been thinking. All the newer business had living quarters above them, another aspect of city life to experience. But this excitement was hardly forthcoming this morning; she merely pictured a new store front replacing the one she saw.

She passed another row of houses. She vaguely wondered why she had skipped Mattie's coffee party, why the luster had gone out of her life, why being with friends had suddenly failed to lift her spirits. It couldn't be that she had lost faith in her friends—not that, she must dismiss such thoughts.

Five years. Wasn't that almost too long to be holding out hope? Soon she was out in the country seeing the steeple of a church in the distance. And now we all were in a new century. As 1899 ended, the church bells everywhere had rung for half an hour while the people sat in the pews silently praying. There was something touching about that, Anna thought. A future was unfolding, a new era of 100 years, certainly awesome; it held the rest of their lives in its grasp. That was a year and a half ago. Now the new century was moving on month after month, and where were her children? This she couldn't dismiss, but she had decided to do something about it. She would at long last talk to her mother.

Anna knew her mother had had problems with child-bearing, not quite like her own, maybe, but a secret was there; Anna's intuition told her so. Anna had often been inclined to bring up the subject, but each time she thought of doing so she had dismissed it, putting it off. Maybe it was a bit personal and could be embarrassing. But now Anna's distress had reached a point of no turning back.

The buggy rolled along through an area known to Wanamingo folks as the "South Prairie." Somewhere here Henrik had bought forty acres, a part of it meadow to keep his growing herd in hay and the rest a cultivated field for a cash crop. She didn't know precisely where it was—good fertile land though, she decided. It wouldn't be long before the timothy and clover could be cut.

There were times she had misgivings about her brother Henrik. Why was he buying fields and raising cattle—milking cows. What could be further from his dreams than that? If he didn't want to become a minister, he should have studied law. What a waste of talent! She remembered the last Temperance Rally at which he spoke. He could sway an audience, there was no question about that. And he could quote Scripture, too, that brother of hers, although he'd never given a Christian testimony. "Look not thou upon the wine when it is red, when it giveth his color in the cup, when it moveth itself aright. At the last it biteth like a serpent, and stingeth like an adder." How striking it had been!

But Anna had her own life to figure out, better let brother figure out his. Why are we so quick to decide how things should be? Anna remembered now what her mother often said: We cannot command the morning or cause the sun to rise. Let God be God.

Not only farmers were working, she realized, as she passed a crew of men laying railroad tracks. She had heard they were Italians who, for every meal, ate long stringy macaroni they called spaghetti. It was hard to tell at this distance what they looked like, but they were bending and lifting, pounding and pulling. It must be hard work.

She remembered how everyone was saying that the railroad was changing the location of the town. Since the railroad would make as straight a line as possible between Zumbrota and Kenyon, it would miss Wanamingo's present location by a mile. Anticipating the railroad, some businesses were already locating at a site close to the mill on the Zumbro and moving gradually south to meet the tracks. She couldn't feature her parents moving off their old premises, or Arne either, but the Veblens might very well consider it. Anna chose not to contemplate the change at the moment; she dismissed it quickly, since she was about to arrive at that comfortable, familiar place.

She waved at Arne standing in his doorway as she drove up to her old home. Even if it was a bit early for morning coffee, he and Papa would soon come over, knowing she had arrived. She was right.

"Peder must be about due for a new pair of shoes," said Arne, hardly letting the greeting take place. "No one can fashion such a special shoe but us," he continued, giving credit to Julia with a nod in her direction.

"That special shoe had done wonders for Peder. I can't tell you how much," said Anna with sober emphasis, interrupting the amiability of the meeting. "He will certainly come here for his next pair. Did you think he wouldn't?"

"Naw," laughed Arne. "But you know, times are changing everywhere and city dwellers...,"

"We're not city dwellers, we Kenyon folks, really we are not, although there are those who pretend they are."

The early coffee tasted good to Anna, as did the homely molasses cookies.

"What brings you if it isn't Peder's shoes?" said Henrik who had entered by the back door sensing that coffee was already available.

"Just to see you all again. It's been sometime, hasn't it?"

"Indeed it has. She needs no further reason," put in Julia as she set a cup before Henrik. She didn't like his tone of voice and hoped he wouldn't say any more.

"Come see the garden," said Julia after the men had left and the cups were stacked on the sink. "The potatoes are up beautifully. We should have a good crop this year, enough for you folks, too."

They walked down a lane east of the barn to an area known as "the slough," the wettest portion of the Kristians' ten acres. It was left for garden since horses and implements would bog down in the mire. When it became sufficiently dried out, Julia put in her seeds here because she knew the soil was rich and the small space would yield an abundance. Anna noticed that the seedling cottonwood tree of a former spring had grown considerably. Julia had decided to let it alone.

"How are you having it, then?" asked Julia as she led Anna up the last garden row and all the new plants had been duly recognized.

"We are doing fine, Mama. Peder and Joe are sure now that they will be able to build."

"Peder can be depended upon. He is truly remarkable. Want to sit a minute? It's rather nice under this little tree. I rest here. It's an oasis."

"It is an oasis," said Anna, happy to sit down beside her mother. "This is an oats field this year?"

"Yes, the barley crop is up on the forty." Julia wondered why Anna asked about the oats. She didn't seem too eager to find out. There was a wistful look about her. "You're not well, Anna?"

"Yes, I'm well enough. You don't think I'm...?"

"No, no. If that were the case you would have told me as soon as we headed for the garden. Is it that you never seem to become...?"

"Yes, that's it," Anna burst forth like the child she felt she was in the presence of her mother. "Why do you suppose I never seem to... conceive?"

Julia studied her daughter as these difficult words came forth. How hard it was, in spite of all the intermittent years, to think of Anna as anything but a child, but here she was at this moment a woman with a woman's problem. Julia knew the anxieties well, and she wept inside for her daughter.

"No one can know that," said Julia reaching for her daughter's hand. It was cool and soft, her own felt hot and dry. "Maybe the spine illness you had spoiled it for you." Julia didn't want to say this, but she honestly felt it was true.

Resentment crept into Anna's face, the usual resentment so familiar to her mother. It caused Julia to reconsider—of course it may not be that—and to hesitate with an alternative.

"Or, there may be a weakness in the family."

"A weakness?"

"I guess you might say it is a weakness." Julia hadn't wanted to bring this long-buried, painful perplexity to the surface, but now it seemed imminent. "It wasn't entirely right with me either, even if I did bring two children into the world."

"Oh? How is that?"

"I lost four of them. All of them were early miscarriages, except for one that I managed to carry for almost seven months. That one was the hardest to lose."

"You mean no one...?"

"Even Papa didn't know about them except, of course, for the one who almost lived."

"Papa didn't know?"

"He may have suspected. Yes, I believe he knew but thought it kinder not to talk about it. You know Papa."

"Weren't you very ill?"

"I was, but one carries on. But worse than physical illness was the sense of loss; the feeling that each was on the way to being born, each with possibilities one would wonder at. I was careful to bury each, none was simply cast out. They were like little birds, dead in their shells. I put each under a clump of sod."

"O Mama!"

"But that is long ago. And I have two grown children, healthy and intelligent, I seldom think about it anymore."

"You had one when I was in the cast."

"How do you know that?"

"You were so sad then. I believe, now, that you had more to worry about than me."

Julia was visibly moved. "You have always had deep feelings and you sense things like that, Anna." It seemed as though she meant to say more, but instead there was a long pause.

"And Sarah was put into your arms that spring."

Julia nodded.

Anna threw her arms around her mother. The sudden gesture stemmed from an overwhelming gratitude for the sharing of this secret which just now seemed so meaningful.

"And I also have David."

By the tone of voice Anna sensed that the stalwart composure she knew so well in her mother had returned. She released her arms and read her mother's face.

"You mean... we could adopt?"

"Why not?"

"I really don't know why not. I suppose there are orphaned babies, many of them, if one only knew about them."

"There are orphanages, you know."

"Yes, there is one in Owatonna. Many of the older boys there go out working on farms in the summer—mere children—and work as full hired men. Peder and Joe have seen so much of that in our area. It wasn't like that in the old days, was it? Sarah might have been carried off to an orphan's home rather than being offered to you. Is it not so? I remember the day you unwrapped that plump, red-faced baby and I sat on the bench in my brace and couldn't run to see her."

"Sarah was certainly welcome at that moment, I can tell you. And now you understand the reason why."

"I'll talk to Peder. He may even have considered this but never quite wanted to talk about it. Shall I, Mama?"

"I would say yes, you should."

The two women felt the warmth of a deepened relationship as they left the oasis and walked back to the house.

In the forenoon two days later, Peder caught sight of Blossom among the rigs coming into town and knew Anna was returning in time to get his dinner ready. If she only knew how lonesome he was when she was gone she would never leave—she was that good a wife. He was sure she wouldn't stop here at the market, she would go right home, leave Blossom at the hitching post and go straight into the house to fix dinner. He could see her lifting the cellar trap door and descending for the package of pork chops she was sure would be there.

"I see my wife is back," Peder said to his partner as he returned behind the counter.

"Gone two days. Long enough, is it?" replied Joe as he left for the cutting room at the rear of the shop.

Peder knew Anna would be watching for him at noon as he rounded the corner on his way home. Sure enough, there was Blossom hanging her head patiently waiting to be unharnessed. Anna was coming to meet him; she did that sometimes when she was excited about something. Now, he supposed, her visit had given her much to talk about.

"I think we should adopt a baby, Peder," she said after squeezing his hand and falling into step at his side.

"You mean us—doing that?"

"Yes, why not? Mama thinks it's a capital idea."

"So that's what you and your mother talked about this time. Was it her idea or yours?"

"Mine, really. We talked about how nice it was when Sarah joined our family and that made me think perhaps—?"

"If those are your wishes."

"They must be yours too!"

"They are my wishes, Anna, if they are yours. You're the one who will have to do with the children."

"You've thought about this before?"

"I have."

"You should have said something."

"No, not until you spoke of it."

"Oh, Peder, you'll make such a good father!"

"You'll make a better mother."

They reached the house and Anna ran in ahead of him, remembering the food she had left on the back of the stove and the serving bowls she had set out to fill. The table was already set.

Peder and Anna made their plans for adoption over the next few weeks. The State School at Owatonna was contacted. Peder and Anna would be notified when a baby became available; it was hard to tell exactly when. Stipulations were often made that families should stay together, or that a relative would take the orphaned baby in their good time.

Meanwhile, the new building was being raised on main street next door to the old market. It had been a good location, so why not continue there and tear down the old building in due time, leaving a small area for a lawn, a tree, and possibly a row of peonies. It would be nice to look out of the upstairs window at a tree; the lot was big enough.

While Peder was busy designing his new building, Anna was busy sewing a layette. She wondered about the sizes of kimomos; the baby could be several months old and they needed to be big enough—better too big, she decided. She knit sweaters, booties, and a cap, all to fit a year-old child. Pink or blue? She wasn't sure, so why not white? They had talked about a crib but hadn't brought it home; they might be in their new living quarters by the time they were notified.

In the middle of August just before Anna's thirtieth birthday, they moved their belongings into their new home.

"At last you're in a home I built for you," said Peder. "It took awhile. Sometimes there are some detours, but things eventually turn out."

In late September a letter arrived from Owatonna. They now had a child, a boy six months old, brought in only yesterday. If Anna and Peder were still interested, they were to wire immediately.

Forgetting to inform the furniture store that it was now time to deliver the crib and high chair, Peder and Anna set out for Owatonna. It was a warm late-summer day, not too bad for a journey except that the roads were dustier than usual and the days getting noticeably shorter and evenings chillier. Anna had brought infant clothes and blankets as she had been instructed to do. They were carefully stowed away in a suitcase under the buggy seat.

A curious little girl ran to the gate as Peder and Anna arrived. Off in the distance was a playground full of youngsters attentive to their games from which she might have wandered. The children must have been taught not to stare at visitors, thought Anna, feeling a bit uncomfortable with this child who was where she was not supposed to be. Once inside the gate, Peder stopped to acknowledge the little girl.

"I see you have a dolly," he began, bending down to her. She appeared to be about five years old.

"Just an old one," she said with a big grin. Then she tossed it in the air and caught it again. "See, it has only one leg. Her name is Tilly and I love her very much. They won't let me sleep with her, though. She must lie high on a shelf where she might fall down. But she wouldn't break, she's only stuffed."

Anna could see why Peder had stopped. She was an engaging little thing, the first orphan they had seen within the confines of an orphanage, parentless and homeless—for who could call the big white buildihg ahead of them with its straight rows of windows on three floors, home? It was, of course, and filled with dedicated people there to feed, clothe, bathe, comfort, teach, or whatever had to be done for helpless children.

"Maybe someone could stuff a leg for her and fix her all up," said Peder, reaching for the tattered toy.

"No." The child not only shook her head but twisted her whole body. "Then she wouldn't be Tilly, because Tilly has always had just one leg."

Anna, not having forgotten why they had come through this gate, began to move slowly up the long walk, expecting Peder to follow.

Peder finally caught up and the two climbed the flight of steps to the double door denoting the main entrance. To their right as they entered the front hall was a sign MAIN OFFICE. Anna, still walking ahead of her husband and carrying the little suitcase, stepped unobstrusively in.

"Yes, ma'am?" said a tall woman with an exceedingly slender waistline as she removed her glasses and approached Anna.

"We are the Peder Olsons. We were notified of..."

"Oh yes, come right in here."

They were ushered through the gate in the counter, and into a private office, where several high-backed chairs stood against the wall. The windows were higher than they had seemed from the outside and were practically covered by heavy green drapes. At a large desk, amazingly tidy, sat the matron, the one from whom Anna surmised they had received the letter.

"Miss Wilson, here are Mr. and Mrs. Olson, the Peder Olsons."

"Thank you, Mildred," said Miss Wilson dismissing the tall woman. She then looked at the childless couple from Kenyon. "Please sit down."

It was awkward to walk toward the wall to be seated, but they wasted no time.

"Now then," Miss Wilson said, clearing her throat. "I'm afraid I have to disappoint you at the moment. The child that was left here has relatives, an aunt, who wants it after she marries. It's the least she can do for her dead sister, she insists. So you may have to wait a bit longer. If you're lucky it may not be as long as you have waited this time." She smiled tightly, eyeing the little suitcase. "We do hate to disappoint anyone, believe me."

Suddenly Peder noticed the office door move slightly. Miss-whoever-she-was must not have closed it. What he saw next had no precedent. The little girl with the rag doll stuck a smiling face through the crack. Peder dared not look, but out of the corner of his eye he saw her wave a tiny hand.

"How did that child get in here?" Miss Wilson was on her feet, walking briskly toward the door. "Mildred, see to the child!"

"Wait a minute," said Peder, hesitating as if he didn't know just what to say next. "That little girl is a friend we met outside. She followed us up the walk. We are to blame, perhaps, because we talked to her."

"Our children know better than to barge in on adults. That child seems to have that yet to learn. Imagine being that bold!" Miss Wilson sat down again as if it were an emphatic gesture.

"Might someone adopt her?" said Peder, not knowing exactly where this conversation would take them.

"Children that age are not much in demand, Mr. Olson. Too young to be of much help to anyone and too old to start as one of your own, if you know what I mean. And she's Irish; there aren't too many Irish families around either."

Peder looked over at Anna, who was sitting rigid against the high back of her chair. He wondered why she wasn't talking. He guessed she must be very disappointed.

"Irish, you say?" Peder wasn't ready yet to get up and walk out.

"McCleary is the name. She is Emily McCleary."
"She has no family?"
"Only a sister someplace, given a home by a friend when the mother died. You, Mr. Olson, seem unusually interested in this child, maybe you would like to adopt her?"
With this remark the matron had expected a negative response, with a chuckle, perhaps, and the prospective parents making a move toward the door, willing to return when she would write them again. But it wasn't so.
"What do you think, Anna? She's not a baby, of course, and you had your heart set on a baby," said Peder, thinking that Anna's wistful expression meant this would be the end of it.
"You seem quite taken with her, Peder. Maybe she should be the one."
This alternative had become plausible enough in Anna's mind to utter those words, but nothing from within her really spoke. She had known many five-year-old girls, however, and several began rising in her consciousness. There had been Lisa Schumann. That child had been thoroughly enjoyable. But she was quite sure the little girl out there would not let her stuff a leg to help the poor dolly. Then she wondered why anything so foolish should ever enter her mind. Being Irish? No problem that she could see; David was Jewish and even that didn't matter. She would let the one-legged doll sleep with the child, that would be a first step.
"You are thinking . . . perhaps?"
Peder had an urgency in his voice he himself wondered at. Shouldn't there be long discussions on the many considerations of something as important as deciding to adopt a child? But now all seemed unnecessary. One either decided to do so, or one decided not to do so.
"You're people who listen to their hearts. They are the only ones who ever adopt children," said the matron, knowing what the outcome would be.
A slightly larger but much shabbier suitcase joined the one Anna had been carrying around, and three people climbed into Blossom's buggy.
"You're a very lucky little girl, Emily," said Miss Wilson, who had accompanied the family to the gate. "You have a brand new papa and mama. You need to mind your manners. Be a good girl, Emily."
"I will, I will. Good-bye, Miss Wilson," replied the child, more eager to see Blossom start moving than to register attention on her former authority.
"Thank you, folks, and good luck to you."
"Thank you and good-bye," replied Anna as the buggy began to move.
Emily settled deep between her new parents when Blossom began to draw. She was not quite sure what had happened, but she knew

she had made a staunch friend, the one holding the reins and saying "giddy-up" to the white horse.

Peder was struggling to justify in his own mind this impetuous move of theirs, but his logic was constantly overshadowed by the jubilation he had seen on that little face. Making that little creature happy seemed so right to him and fraught only with joy.

A kind of numbness settled over Anna. Their dream had taken a new twist, and she would have to make substitutions in the delights she had taken in having a family. Why shouldn't it be as much fun sewing little-girl dresses as kimonos? Much more fun, really. She wondered why she didn't feel that way at the moment. It would come.

But Peder and Anna had little time for the usual reverie they had been used to on long buggy trips. Emily's initial quiet moments deep between her new parents were short-lived; she suddenly became a question box. First questions about Blossom: Did they have a stable for her? What did she eat? Did she drink from a pail? Why were her ears flicking like that? Would she get tired pulling us? That led to: how far was it to home? Very few lapses occurred. At one point they heard her sigh and thought she might want to sleep. Anna suggested that Emily put her head on her mother's lap whenever she wanted to, but this only brought a new spurt of wiggles.

"We'll soon be home now," said Peder as Kenyon's elevator became visible on the horizon.

Anna felt a twinge of uneasiness as they passed Mattie Johnson's neat little house. People would certainly talk. Just what would they say? What could they say but nice things? It was certainly noble to give a home to an orphan.

Although it was after closing time, the furniture dealer was more than glad to deliver to the Olsons their furniture. Not the crib and high chair? No, a regular bed, that is, a single bed and—did he have a child's wicker rocking chair?

Emily watched wide-eyed as the men brought the new bed and chair up the long back stairs and put the new bed and chair into the almost bare room which she was told was her room. After the movers had left, she stood in the center of the room in complete astonishment. Hers, hers! Suddenly she spotted a small bureau off in a corner. It had been in the room all the time. She rushed to open the drawers. Diapers, tiny clothes—baby clothes. She turned around. There stood her new mother in the doorway.

"Do you like your room? After we've had some supper we'll be ready for bed, won't we?" Anna was trying hard but, seeing the look on the child's face, she knew she was making no progress at all.

"You wanted a baby, not a little girl!" cried the child, rushing toward Anna and slapping her with both hands. "I hate you, I hate you!"

Anna felt limp. She sank onto the bed that hadn't been made up yet.

"We thought Miss Wilson would give us a baby, Emily, so we got ready for a baby."

Rage turned to tears and Emily flung herself on the far end of the bed away from Anna. The convulsive sobbing shattered Anna. She wanted to stroke the little head but knew the child would not permit it—not yet. For the first time Anna noticed the red hair. Her daughter had red hair.

"We brought you home because we wanted you. Why else?"

Chapter 14

Ragnild Vessedahl wondered if Henrik Kristian wouldn't soon ask her to marry him. He was the suitor who was taking his time. All the other fellows she had known tried to rush her to a commitment on the first date, but not Henrik. He seemed too busy with a variety of interests to think about marriage. She knew, however, that she was his number-one girl. He always took her with him on his speaking engagements; many a Temperance rally she had attended with him, not to mention Young People's Society meetings in various churches throughout the area.

Ragnild was standing in front of the dresser mirror curling her hair. Although the room was full of daylight, her lamp was lit; she heated her curling iron by inserting it down the glass chimney and letting it hang by the spread of its handles. She combed each tress of hair she had curled and swept it back from her forehead as she waited for the iron to be hot enough to roll the next.

She laughed to her reflection when she remembered how Ole Peterson had imagined that she was flirting with him through the mirror on the organ at church. He had told her he always sat on the end of a pew by the aisle, five rows from the back, where she could be sure to see him. Being Holden's organist these past five years had had its anxious moments and its funny blunders, but this topped them all. Imagine flirting with Ole Peterson in the middle of a Bach prelude or during a communion chorale! She saw the whole room in her mirror now, and pictured how one's attention could be behind oneself—an interesting phenomenon. Suddenly she saw the door open, announcing the arrival of her sister Eva.

"He's here already. You are sure taking your time this morning," Eva said, waiting for her sister to turn around and eye her. "My goodness, aren't you getting clever with that iron."

"Does it look all right?" asked Ragnild before turning around. She had yet to blow out the lamp and comb out the final tresses.

"It's stunning, Ragnild. You'll have to help me with mine. I'd love to have a hairdo like yours when Alfred comes to see me next Sunday."

"You can do your own. You can start practicing right now, but don't let the iron get too hot. You can't replace scorched hair, you know."

Ragnild was ready except for her shoes. She quickly slipped them on, grabbed the button hook, and with nimble fingers worked her way up each shoe.

"Did you let him in? Is he waiting in the parlor?"

"No. I just saw a brand new rig with a team of dapple grays and decided who else could it be? Esther will let him in. She is in the kitchen."

Before pinning her gold watch to her bosom, Ragnild snapped it open and checked the time to assure herself that he had arrived early. Through the window at the first landing on her way downstairs, Ragnild saw Henrik talking to her brother. No doubt they were discussing the new buggy. Eva had not been mistaken. There it stood drawn by a team, no longer single Barney and the tiny carriage. The harnesses had shiny brass rivets and the straps on the horse collar were laced through gleaming-white ivory rings. Although she knew Henrik was too gentle to use check reins, the horses held their heads high. There was something different about today, she decided. Dared she hope it would be the day he would propose?

They were going to a Temperance Rally in Northfield, as much as two hours of traveling time. He had said he would arrive for her at ten o'clock. He was at least twenty minutes early.

"Sorry I'm early. I didn't mean to rush you," he said, leaving her brother and walking toward her.

"It must be your snappy team," she replied as she arranged the ends of the sheer scarf that held her wide hat firmly in place. "It's Barney. He has a partner."

"I'm glad you recognized him. He would have felt bad if you hadn't. I found this mare. A pretty good match, don't you think? I bought her from a farmer near Cannon Falls. Her name is Lady."

"A perfect match!" Ragnild greeted the horses with pats on their noses.

There was something striking about a brand new carriage, all right. One tends to forget how use and weather bring buggies to tatters. The wheels had shiny spokes with a line of red trim; the body was of the latest cast in unfaded black; the seats were soft with cushions, plump squares held in check by strong buttons in diagonal design.

"Vær så god," said Henrik, gesturing with his hand as he reached for hers.

Ragnild felt herself making the broad step with unusual grace today, her hand in his. As she sat in the new seat, she sensed the odor of clean leather, or was it the rubber mat at her feet? In a flash he was beside her.

"Barney really holds his head up," she began as the first lunge put them in motion.

"He was getting a little tired of pulling me around all by himself. Getting a partner to help carry half the load—you can just imagine what that means."

Soon they were speeding along well out of the sight of the brother left standing in the yard. Ragnild and Henrik were comfortable companions. Ragnild appreciated that, but got it into her head, sometimes, that he might show a little more of the affection she knew he had for her. He was solicitous always, but never quite close and warm. At such times she labeled herself impatient, knowing that in his good time he certainly would take her in his arms.

"How's your father?" Ragnild asked at length, remembering that he had been ill the last time she had visited. Ragnild was teaching in a rural school near Wanamingo, had been for the past three terms, and Henrik frequently brought her home to visit his parents, but several weeks had lapsed since summer vacation had begun.

"He's fine now. It was only a matter of a day and he was back in the shop. He's never sick—I guess that was why we all noticed it and wondered. He sold his threshing rig, did you know that?"

"No, I didn't know."

"He is getting on in years. He's over sixty. Last fall the threshing season got pretty strenuous for him. He held out this long because he thought, at long last, he might convince me to take over."

"You are hard to convince?"

"I'm not the mechanic he is, even if I grew up at his side and had the best opportunity to learn. I can manage as a farmer, but keeping steam engines in running condition is not for me."

"And your sister Anna, how is she getting along? I'm thinking often about the little girl they adopted."

"She's almost more than Anna can cope with. It's too bad."

"I felt so sorry for Anna after that tantrum Emily had at the table at your house. Remember that evening?"

"I do, and many similar times. Someone needs to show her the old switch, I'll tell you."

"There are times that is the only thing that works, I'm afraid."

"Peder is too kind. He does nothing but spoil her. He gives her everything her foolish little mind desires. I have always had a high regard for Peder, but when it comes to being a father, he is a flat failure."

"And Anna?"

"If she could have had the child from the beginning, as she so often says, things might have been different. But Anna doesn't have it in her to take the switch either. She nags and pleads and despairs that the child doesn't seem to have a conscience. 'You must ask God to forgive you'—what good is that if the girl doesn't understand? The latest thing is stealing, can you imagine that?"

A flock of sparrows fluttered into the air as they reached the top of a long hill.

"Stealing?"

"One morning while tidying Emily's room, Anna found the top drawer of the bureau full of dime-store items taken from Bresett's Variety. Peder wanted to take it all back immediately and save his wife and child the embarrassment. But I have to give Anna credit for insisting that the child be the one to return the things. So all three of them went. 'Ask forgiveness,' always 'ask forgiveness.' That is Anna's only quaking method, but it had something more to go with it this time, I believe."

"No bright spots? With any child there must be something bright."

"There is, coming to think of it. She is doing well on the piano. She is taking lessons from Mrs Newton. Anna thought it best not to try to teach Emily herself. It's funny, Anna found one thing that would captivate the little red-headed scamp, and that was piano music. How fortunate for Anna to have a new piano. You know that "fiddle-de-dee" piece, *Robin's Return;* you play it don't you? It proved to have the power of a fairy tale. You know, Anna couldn't even get her daughter interested in stories? Why I was completely taken with her storytelling when I was a kid. But that piano piece, that did it!"

"Wonderful! There had to be a joyous note somewhere."

"Ragnild, I admire your bright outlook. I think the women in my family have dark natures. Why should everything have to be such a struggle? It isn't, for you."

"We all have dark moments."

"But the clouds never seem to rise for us. We're always 'asking forgiveness.' We never walk with certainty. You do."

" 'God's in his heaven, all's right with the world.'—Robert Browning. He had a robust faith, did you know that?"

"Like yours, that I can imagine."

They reached the top of another hill from which they saw the grain elevators of Northfield.

"We're getting closer," said Ragnild. "What are you going to tell them this time?"

"Maybe include the plug for Women's Suffrage, is that what you are asking?"

"I like you for that speech, Henrik. You're so earnest and convincing."

"To please you, Ragnild, it will be included."

"You're the kind of a fellow who ought to own a bicycle. Want to try?" said David Ganz, walking in on the shoemaker next door. David, now a young man of eighteen, who was getting an education in medicine at the University of Minnesota, was home for the summer. He had brought his bicycle with him. It was certainly no novelty anywhere else, but it was a touch of the cosmopolitan in rural Wanamingo.

"No, no. I would if I was twenty years younger. You know you can't teach an old dog new tricks, that's expecting too much of an old man." Arne was standing at his workbench cutting heavy leather with a big pair of shears.

David laughed. "If you did, you'd be one better than Henrik, who is always fussing with those dapple grays."

Arne looked up momentarily. "This morning I saw him all dressed up, off somewhere in that new rig of his. Where did he go?"

"To Northfield, I believe. Temperance rally—but stopping on the way to pick up his blue-eyed girl."

"Do you think he will ever marry?" asked Arne, letting a piece of leather drop to the floor. "He spends a lot of time with this teacher friend of his. I believe she has taught three terms now at the Vangen School. Every week he's been bringing her here. Nice girl. Julia and Nils sure like her. Sit down, sit down."

David straddled an old chair and rested his arms on its back. "She's real nice, I agree."

"He needs a house, though. Maybe that's what's holding things up," continued Arne, the scissors snipping.

"With everyone moving to the new town there ought to be a house standing vacant." David watched the cutting.

"It's a funny thing with Henrik, though," said Arne, turning and pointing his shears with emphasis. "He'll never move out. I've never known anyone, even in the old country, so attached to a place as he is."

"Coming to think of it, he wouldn't stay with me a single night in Minneapolis. He said he had to help Julia with the milking, but that was just an excuse." David stretched out one leg as he continued to straddle the chair.

"He went away to school once, you know. But that didn't last long."

"No, I didn't know. Where?"

"Red Wing Academy, but only for a very short time. His learning has come through his own reading. And you, David, you have no trouble being away from home?" He returned to the task of cutting.

"No, but I am mighty glad to get back when the term is over. I might forget my Norwegian."

As if prompted by something, Arne put down the shears and turned his back on the workbench. The task at hand was being dropped for the moment. David knew by the abrupt movements of the old man that he had something serious on his mind.

"You certainly took to everything in this town, language and all, ever since you were a boy," Arne began in an off-hand manner.

"Why shouldn't I?" David was looking up at his friend. "I have never been treated here as anything less than a son."

"I know, I know." Arne fell silent. Finally he fixed serious eyes on David. "All the while I have watched you grew up, I have been wondering about this. Tell me: do you feel truly like one of us?"

"Of course, I have known all along that I was someone else, too, besides being the adopted son of the Kristians."

"Aha—there you have said it. How many of us have given you credit for that? I've watched you bear up under your secret."

"It's really not been a secret, Arne, only something we all, including myself, have chosen to ignore."

"I don't think it has been fair. We all should be allowed to be who we are." Arne was leaning against the bench now, his ankles crossed.

"I have always looked for answers about what it means to be a Jew: Henrik's books, school—the university is a great place. I don't mind telling you, Arne, that I am proud of being a Jew."

David saw the old man coming toward him with an extended hand. David rose, grasped it and smiled.

"Well, if you won't try the new trick of riding a bicycle, I'd better leave," said David, wanting to banter again.

"Where are you going?"

"I must see to Mama. Last time I saw her she was wearing Papa's gloves and had a cheese cloth over her hat. She was enticing a swarm of bees into her hive."

"It's dangerous business, but she's done it for years. No one can help her. You know that, don't you?"

"Yes, but being away makes me forget. I'd hate to see her lose her balance and fall. She could get stung severely. Bees are no joke."

"We don't need to have a medical student to tell us that, but we could use you to come up with a remedy." Arne was following the young man to the door. The boy was taller. Either that, or Arne was shriveling in his old age.

"I'm riding my bicycle into town after dinner. Can I get you anything?"

"Nothing, thanks."

"So long then, Arne."

"So long."

Arne left the sunshine of the doorway and returned to his leather. It was taking him longer to get a pair of shoes made these days, but they were better than ever. He knew that. He never took shortcuts now; every pair of shoes he turned out these days had integrity built into their very soles. And now people wanted store-bought shoes. He scorned boots and shoes handled in stores, and it saddened him that people settled for such inferior workmanship. Shoes were not simply a store item. They came alive on a man's foot like a hoof or claw to take the brunt of miles of walking. People didn't simply wear shoes; leather was not simply cloth. Shoes were grafted of living material made to adhere to every curve of each individual foot. How could people regard this so lightly?

Arne padded around in his shop—a tool lay over there, the machine was here, and the shelf was behind him. So David was riding into town on his bicycle. It was no longer a matter of going next door to Haroldsons for staples or for the incoming mail. The store was no longer there; it had been torn down after Clarence died and Petra and her brother moved away. Arne couldn't remember where. Veblens had moved to the new town near the railroad earlier. Could it have been five years? Arne missed Melva's running in to see him any old time. Now she came on Tuesday evenings and sometimes on Saturdays. Her four children were grown up now, at least so much so that his storytelling and antics ceased to engage them. They were lovely, her children, it wasn't that, and they were exceedingly good to their grandfather. Albin and his two maiden sisters Emma and Josie now lived in the house Sigurd had built for himself and his bride. Were there other homes left?

What was happening really was that the old town was becoming the Kristian farm. Although he owned his own plot and the building he occupied, he felt as if his establishment belonged to them. The only other business was the other blacksmith shop, its activity greatly reduced now that Tollefson had a flourishing livery stable in the busy new town. So the Kristians and he were pretty much what was left of the old town.

The school house would stay for the rural children. Arne was glad of that. He enjoyed seeing them walking from their farm homes, swinging their dinner pails. It was pretty quiet at the moment as the term was over, but during the school months a day would seldom go by but what he would answer a child's knock and admit two or three who would scramble for scraps of leather on his floor. The church on the hill would stay, too, for a while, at least, until expanding prosperity would begin to scorn its narrow modest structure. The dead were always left when people moved. There was no help for that.

And he was left, so were Nils, Julia, and young Henrik, who dared not stay away a single night for fear of being fraught with homesickness. As long as Arne was able he would fill orders, not so many for good boots now, but for shoe repair. He would improve on the store-bought shoes that came his way with tough new soles that would outlast the tops, and with sturdy seams where old threads had failed. This he would do until the fast-moving country had no need for a shoemaker like himself. His shop would stay around him as long as he needed it.

He returned to the sunshine of his doorway, sensing that it would be time to join Nils and Julia for forenoon coffee. It was a lovely day. He looked at the trees, their foliage thicker than ever this year. The trees had grown out of proportion with the years; his own maple seemed closer to the house with each new growth. Someone ought to take a saw to it and trim it a bit. The boxelders across the road weren't small any longer either. They had begun as little seedlings in the ditch; now they vied for the status of trees.

That gasoline engine has been running for quite a while now, thought Arne as he stood waiting for Nils to appear. What was Nils doing anyway? Had it ever run this long before? Maybe he was having trouble with the power belt again. Seeing his clock was well past ten, he decided to shed his apron and cross the road.

As he came through the wide door he saw no one. Entering out of the bright sunlight, he found Nils' shop as dark as his own. It would do no good to call out because of the noise the engine was making.

Suddenly Arne caught his pants leg on a sharp piece of metal protruding from a broken plow. As he bent down to free himself, he saw Nils lying on the floor directly in front of him. He'd been hurt!

Arne moved forward. Accustomed to the dim light by now, he saw no evidence of an accident. His friend simply lay huddled in front of the plow.

"Nils, do you hear?" Arne called, tapping the shoulder of the figure on the floor.

Caught in a frenzy, Arne turned the figure over. Can he be—is he dead?

Arne dropped to the floor to settle the matter. There was no heartbeat under the blue workshirt. There was no pulse to be found at throat, temple or wrist. He staggered to his feet in disbelief. The open eyes were dull and unfocused. Life was absent. Against the relentless rhythm of the gasoline engine Arne knelt down again beside his friend. With his forefinger he slid the eyelid forward closing one eye and then the other. It was a reverent act, closing the dead man's eyes. The distorted face became familiar again in sleep. Arne rose. He had let go of his friend forever.

The gasoline engine persisted. If only he knew how to turn it off! It was still furnishing power for Nils' complicated tools. There was nothing to be done but to let it run until someone came who could stop it.

Arne hurried across the road.

"Julia, come," he cried as he caught sight of her just inside her doorway. She had finished with the bees. "Is David around? David?"

"We're here, Arne," said Julia. "You're ill?"

"No, not me, Nils. I found him on the floor beside the plow, come!"

"Dear God, what has happened?" cried Julia, rushing out of the house.

They hurried together into the driveway in front of the shop. Julia ran in ahead, while Arne detained David.

"Turn off that thing, David. You must know how."

The two men watched the engine sputter to a stop. The fly belt began showing its seam and the wheels jerked a half-turn backwards before they ceased turning. Silence at last!

"Gone? You think he is gone, Arne?" came from Julia who was kneeling beside her husband and rubbing his heavy hand. "David would know. Tell us, David."

Down beside his mother, David spoke. "I think he is, Mama. I think he is."

Arne watched the foster son help his mother off her knees. They stood together. She wasn't ready to leave and he wouldn't rush her.

Arne came closer and stood beside Julia. How fragile this strong woman suddenly seemed, her shoulders so narrow and her arms so long!

"He was always so well and strong." she announced as if speaking in her husband's defense.

"He was," replied Arne. "And so easy-going, not a worry in the world."

"I don't understand," cried Julia.

Her words sank into the porous walls of the blacksmith shop. It yielded only the stale odor of the forge. There was no answer.

PART THREE (1906-1947)

AUTUMN WINDS

Chapter 1

"Coming to think of it, no one mentioned that this man was truly a born-again Christian. Certainly many wonderful things were said about him. He must have been highly thought of." A tall impressive stranger was speaking, looking from one to another of the menfolk in front of the blacksmith shop after the funeral of Nils Kristian. They had yet to partake of the food the women were laying out on a long serving table across the road next to the Kristian residence.

Henrik glanced toward Arne, his old friend. He needed encouragement for what he was about to say. Arne reinforced the young man with a sudden sharpness in his eyes.

"I don't want anyone to be passing judgment on the state of my father's passing into eternity. Only Almighty God is in a position to do that." Henrik approached the stranger now with well-calculated steps. "And don't you let my mother hear you casting forth such reckless doubts, my friend." Henrik's forefinger was too close to the stranger for comfort. "Remember, you didn't even know him."

David, standing now just behind his advancing brother, smiled in spite of himself.

The stranger looked away. He seemed to search among the womenfolk standing in small clusters across the road, hoping to see Sarah, his betrothed, as though he might draw strength from the mere sight of her. She must have told him that her brother had a temper, and this was undoubtedly what she meant.

Henrik studied the tall man intently all the while. Anyone who can't look a man in the eye is weak. Eventually Henrik, too, looked across the road. He saw Ragnild at his mother's side. For once in his life he had feared for his mother. He had never seen her look as frail before; she wasn't young anymore. And that remarkable Ragnild, how beautifully she was waiting on her at this moment! Finally it occurred to him that the women were waiting to serve the menfolk, and he became aware that in the absence of his father it behooved him to make the first move, seeing to it that the others would follow.

Halvor, sitting at his desk, had just finished reading a letter from Anna. Too bad he was so far away from those dear people; he wanted to have been at the funeral. The elevated train was hurrying over a trembling trestle on its way to the center of the city. He was glad this noise was at least two blocks from the parsonage. His church premises were situated on large lot, as far as city lots go, and set back from the busy thoroughfare. There was always activity on the street just short of the El tracks; horses forever drawing a parade of buggies, surreys, drays and brewery wagons in a clatter over cobblestone streets and letting their droppings fall wherever they may. The Reverend's position behind the window gave very little benefit of either their noise or their smell, but they were never far from his sensibility.

After having served a parish in Wisconsin for four years, Halvor had moved to this Chicago parish in 1897, already nine years ago. His parish was not far from the center of the windy city, what he thought might soon be the largest metropolis in the world. Although he thrived among the pocket of Scandinavians in which his church was located, much of what he saw and heard daily in his environment, whether he took the elevated train, or read the city's newspapers, was still alien to him. Now his mind was back in Minnesota, a June day, the grain fields emerald green, not yet headed, yielding to a breeze under a benevolent sun. And Nils Kristian was being laid to rest.

Anna. Poor, dear Anna! He had always considered her brave, yes, he supposed she was still brave, but somehow he detected a disturbing collapse of spirit.

Certainly she would be concerned for her dear mother, the letter said, and certainly her parental home wouldn't be the same anymore and naturally her brother Henrik would have to take his father's role. Of course, he wasn't one to fill his shoes, who could be? Then he was going to be married as early as December. Oh yes, his bride was a lovely girl from the Holden Congregation and a rural schoolteacher. Henrik had said he could not live through Christmas, the time departed loved ones are missed the most, unless she came as his bride to fill the void. She was really a nice girl, it wasn't that. And with Henrik married, her mother would no longer be the woman of the house, would she? Anna would like to take her mother into their home in Kenyon, but that, of course, would be out of the question. Mama wouldn't thrive without the garden, the chickens, and the cows; and besides, Anna had no peace of mind to offer her mother either with the child Emily around. Not that the older woman resented her granddaughter, far from it. But rows could easily break out and she wouldn't want her mother to be a part of them.

And there was news about her sister, Sarah. She had become acquainted with the Engeviks over by Faribault when she hired out as a dressmaker. He remembered the Engeviks, didn't he? Weren't they old neighbors of his? Last summer with the Engeviks during a series of evangelistic meetings under a large tent in Faribault, Sarah met the evangelist, Rasmus Hegge, a self-educated lay preacher who had a great gift as a speaker. Anna and Peder had been to hear him, too, and they certainly thought he was impressive. He stood tall and handsome before the people with his open Bible and literally brought tears to their eyes. Sarah had volunteered to play the hymns for him the first evening and after that attended every meeting. Soon Hegge was insisting that she be the one to play the songs; no one could play the way she did. If the Engeviks weren't to be in attendance, he would drive the five miles out in the country to get her. Early this year they announced their engagement. He was in attendance at the funeral. Brother Henrik, as he, Halvor could well imagine, didn't like Hegge in the least. That dampened things for poor Sarah and caused Mama to look indifferently at this young man.

Then Anna's news went back to Emily, who continued to be of immense concern. She had done well in school. In fact, she was very bright, no one could deny that. And she was making amazing progress on the piano. Who could have predicted that? But she couldn't be trusted. Anna and Peder wanted to believe her, but she came with blatant lies, told with such innocence it left them no recourse but to be wary. Yes, they had prayed with her, the girl even shed tears sometimes, but her repentance never led to any change. If anything, the things she would get into as she grew older became even more serious. Catechism instruction was fraught with problems. Since she took no interest in learning Norwegian—oh yes, she understood more than she let on—she had to be instructed in English. If all the children were being instructed in English, things might have been different. When the children were catechized on Sunday mornings, she refused to go up, remaining slumped in the pew between her parents. Of course the people of the congregation were charitable, yet Anna wondered if they weren't talking about them. They might well wonder why she and Peder were such poor parents! "Pray for us, Halvor," she wrote. "If her naughtiness is a cross we must bear, may we not bear it in vain."

Halvor yearned for something more from her letters. He yearned to hear that she was still singing or holding a choir together, or of hikes on summer days, or of books she had read, certainly she was on the way toward being self-educated as much as her brother Henrik. Halvor had waited, as had the rest, to hear of a child being born to Anna, a natural-born child; knowing her as he did, she would have received that as supreme joy, as no other joy. What he had read wasn't natural, somehow wasn't right, but how could he comprehend the distortion? Soon he would be picking up his pen and answering her letter. What could he say?

"Aren't you coming to dinner? Look at the clock. Need I call you?" Halvor's wife had entered. She caught sight of the letter on the desk; the size of the pages and the single fold betrayed personal correspondence. Ten or fifteen pages! She understood.

Ragnild was heading for the orchard as she caught sight of the dapple-grays coming into the yard. She wasn't expecting Henrik, not until tomorrow. She dropped her bucket for apples and ran to meet the incoming buggy.

"We finished threshing at Haugens this morning and since tomorrow is Sunday we did nothing more than move the rig to Petersons. And, as usual, Knute didn't have his granary ready. Barney and Lady prefer the buggy to the heavy wagon and I arrived here mighty fast. How's my girl? I couldn't stay away."

"I'm fine, fine. I was just about to make you an apple pie. You were to be here for Sunday dinner, remember?"

He fastened the reins as he jumped out of the buggy, then flung out his arms, receiving her as she rushed toward him.

"I'm glad Knute didn't have his granary ready," said Ragnild, resting her head against his shoulder.

"So am I, real glad." He was reluctant to let her go.

"Tie the horses and come with me to the orchard." She ran to the bucket she had dropped. "The Wealthys are the reddest they have ever been."

He obeyed, guiding the team to the hitching post near the gate. He easily caught up with her.

"They cling pretty high and are hard to reach," she continued now that he was walking at her side. "I don't like to shake the branches for fear more will fall than I can use right away. Windfalls need to be cooked up before they spoil, and I don't want to be stuck with canning sauce for the rest of the day."

Everything about this girl, smiling at him and swinging her bucket as she went along at his side, appealed to him. There was the sound of her voice; he scarcely listened for her meaning, he was fascinated by the lilt of her words.

Suddenly he found himself drawn down beside her on a makeshift bench, an old fence post on its side. Momentarily the bucket again stood empty, its bearer quite oblivious to its use.

"How's your mother?"

"She's doing very well. She's no different than she ever was—lonesome, perhaps, but she never complains."

"I can well imagine she gets lonely."

"Arne comes in for coffee every day as usual. They reminisce. He likes to have someone to talk to. He misses Papa as much as any of us."

"How's her potato crop? She was so proud of her hills this year."

"One of the best crops she's ever had. she works too hard, Mother does, but she won't slow down. Work is one of life's greatest blessings, she keeps saying. I believe the strenuous activity of this summer had absorbed the worst of her grief. She's an amazing woman."

"She is. I truly marvel at her."

"Ludvig Vangen stopped me on the road today," said Henrik after a moment, remembering the little visit on the corner near Jordahl's.

"Oh, so?"

"He told me I had stolen their schoolteacher right from under them. He said he thought you might have come back for the first three months anyway."

"I know, we talked about it. But I thought it would be easier for the board to hire a teacher beginning in the fall while the girls graduating from Normal School were still available."

"He was joking mostly. He said they had hired a young thing, and he wondered how well she would handle the big boys."

"There are no difficult youngsters in the Vangen School."

"That's what you say. No child would give you trouble," he teased.

"Stop it now." She bumped his shoulder.

"And you're the kind of girl satisfied with a parlor wedding." He was changing the subject again. "When you said that, I couldn't believe it. Neither Sarah or Anna would think that good enough."

"It will be beautiful, Henrik. You make it sound as if I am settling for something less than the best. It's the time of year you have to consider. Think how cold the church would be in December. Then think of how cozy our homes are at Christmas time. Well, we'll be ready for Christmas a week early and for a wedding. What could be nicer!"

"Nothing, if you say so. And another thing—"

"Yes?"

"How do you think you'll like living with my mother? There is not much chance that she will find another home for herself."

"We'll be family then, Henrik. Remember that. Families make room for one another." Ragnild studied his face for a moment, wondering what he wanted her to say. "I'm very fond of her, Henrik. Have no doubts about your mother and me."

He reached for her hand. "How can any man be as fortunate as to marry someone as wonderful as you are. I'm growing dependent on you already, imagine what it will be like in twenty years."

"And I need you. Don't you suppose that's what love is all about needing each other?" A rush of warmth came with the touch of his hand.

"You have said it well, my dear."

"And now for the apples." She was rising and drawing him with her. "See those red ones way up there?"

"I'll give the tree a shake. That ought to bring a few of them down."

He hadn't listened, she realized, but she did not stop him from this dubious harvesting method. As he shook the tree, a big, red apple hit the top of his head.

"Sir Isaac Newton discovers the law of gravity," she called to him. She was laughing merrily.

"Maybe, but it is a bit of a punishment," he said, rubbing his head.

"The apple got bruised, too," she retorted as she continued to laugh at him.

"Newton brought forth a very civilized notion, you know. Maybe I need not feel embarrassed?"

"So right you are. A lesser man might have considered it a bad omen, a superstition, you know, a thunderbolt out of the blue, perhaps?" She was still laughing.

"I'll accept the Newton theory." He stooped to retrieve the apple. "No bruise that I can see. I cushioned its fall. What do you think?"

"Don't admit to being soft-headed." With that she ceased her laughter and proceeded to pick up the spoils resulting from the onslaught.

"There are more here than needed for my pie. Maybe your mother would like a few of these. I believe your apples are Dutchess, she'll like these Wealthys."

"So that's how it is. I take the rest home. You've got it all figured out, all right."

"I have."

They filled the bucket together. Another apple fell late from the tree as if it needed to join the others.

"Come, I want you to see the grapevine we started from the sprig your mother gave me," said Ragnild when they reached the buggy. "Its over this way."

They walked again in the direction of the orchard but continued through it until they reached a little field road that ran the distance of the trees.

"How's Sarah and her preacher boy?" asked Ragnild, knowing it would take a few minutes to reach the grapevine.

"Fine, I guess. She stayed home for a few days after the funeral, but she's back near Faribault again. She seems to be quite in demand as a dressmaker in those parts."

"I'm sure of that."

"And her preacher boy?" There was a change in his tone of voice. "I believe I'd say he is your lesser man who would interpret an apple on the head as a thunderbolt of doom. He tries to put the fear of God into everyone."

"She's engaged to him?"

"Sorry to say, yes."

They were reaching the edge of the grove now, giving Henrik a perspective that surprised him.

"You are near the Holden parsonage, aren't you," he said suddenly.

"Very near. When we read for the minister we never walked the road. We used to cut through this way, crossing the field."

"An austere man, the late Rev. Muus. Is that right? Did he put the fear of God into you kids?"

"I was much more afraid of him than I ever was of God," she quickly responded as she stood beside Henrik and gazed with him across the field.

"Now that is quite a statement, my dear."

"It's true. I was never afraid of God, only of Pastor Muus. One Sunday, when we children were up before the congregation being catechized, the sun shone through the window directly into my face. I squinted and lowered my head. Before I knew it, I felt his hand under my chin, drawing my face up toward him. 'Look at me, my child, look at me when you answer.' I was petrified. Dear God, I whispered in my heart, help me not to make this man angry. See, that proves that he was more to be feared than God."

"My dear Ragnild, you continue to amaze me!"

They examined the grapevine. Ragnild also showed him the raspberry bushes her brother had started which should yield berries next season.

"I must get home in time for chores," Henrik said as they were returning through the orchard. "You know how mother insists on doing the milking. She would milk all six cows if I didn't get back on time, besides lifting those heavy milk cans. I always worry on days when we thresh late and mother goes ahead with all that work."

"I don't blame you. I'll be looking for you tomorrow. The pie will be ready. Good-bye. Greet your mother."

"I can't get back to you soon enough, believe me," he said, loosening the horses and climbing into the buggy. "So long, and thanks for the apples."

He was going at a fast clip before he knew it, having rounded the corner at Norway General Store, passing the residence of the late Dr. Grønvold, then the Holden parsonage, and finally catching sight of the church itself. Back from its tall steeple stretched the south wall with its four identiical windows, equally spaced. He noticed these now, calculating how a shaft of winter sunlight had bothered a little girl's eyes.

She had stood at attention among other girls in a straight line along the women's side of the aisle facing an equal number of boys standing at attention on the men's side. Up and down between the rows the venerable Rev. Muus would stride, flaring his long, black robe as he made sudden turns to call on the unsuspecting. Not only did he wear a robe, but also a white ruff collar which looked like bee's comb. All high church ministers wore them. Not only the children trembled lest they stumble over the sacred words, but their parents did, too, for weren't they responsible for having drilled the memorization? Henrik had been catechized in the same manner; however, Rev. Østen Hanson never wore a black robe or a white ruff, and he had a kind way of nodding approval, which Henrik doubted the venerable Rev. Muus had. Henrik smiled to himself. He guessed the rhetoric of the catechism wasn't too frightening; Ragnild wasn't afraid of God, she said. Everything in the catechism was prescribed so nicely, one need not be tormented. Baptism was the key, then must follow a willingness to frequent the Lord's Table with proper humility and reverence for the mystery. God was to be depended upon at every turn. Henrik wonderd why pietists like Rasmus Hegge made God seem so capricious. Clouds of doubt rose out of much of the preaching he had heard lately, a morbidity he refused to accept as legitimate Christian piety.

His mother—now there was an example of someone with true piety! No one, not even Rasmus Hegge, could threaten her these days. Her spiritual life remained stable, almost invincible. With the passing of Østen Hanson, Henrik concluded, his church had suffered a great loss; now his mother was the only one left, it seemed, with that deep abiding spirit. And now he was bringing Ragnild home. He was glad it was with his mother she would have to live, and not with either of his two sisters.

He glanced up the long driveway into the Peterson place as he passed by. Was Ludvig still working in his granary, he wondered? Not all farmers were equally adept; Henrik knew his own limitations when it came to mechanics of farming, and now he no longer had his father to depend on. He remembered his own granary with the efficient elevator, run by a sturdy little gasoline engine which Nils had installed just two years ago. No farmer he knew of had anything to resemble it. But as time went on, then what? There would always be a way; he supposed a person shouldn't borrow trouble, but deal with each problem as it arose.

He remembered the big yield of grain at the Haugen place, realizing that the farm land in Holden township was indeed unsurpassed. He wondered about the land he intended to buy adjacent to the original Kristian acres; a gravel knoll stretched through the middle of it. He had been reluctant to sell "the forty" on the South Prairie. It yielded extremely well, but the long haul with hay loads this past summer convinced him that having land that far away was impractical.

He turned the corner at the bridge finally, and looked toward his pasture to see where the cows might be. He caught sight of his herd moving in file on the cowpath on the sidehill leading to the barn. Mama must have gotten them started, he suspected, but she was nowhere to be seen. As the road skirted the little woods edging the pasture, he spotted her not far from the last little calf on the path.

She was stooping to pick up a fallen branch which she was about to drag home. She was always gathering wood to burn under the copper kettle, and since it was fall, there was so much to be accomplished. Something was boiling in it almost every day.

She had a firm hold on the branch now, the twigs raking the pasture as she moved along. Her shoulders were rounder these days and her muscles a bit stiffer, but her tenacious vitality was unmistakable. She would reach the yard about the same time he would. She wouldn't say much, but she would be glad to see him. He would show her the apples and she would say, "My, those are beautiful apples. Ragnild is so thoughtful."

Chapter 2

Not really knowing what she was looking for, Emily pulled open the top drawer of her bureau where she caught sight of her little red satin-covered book with the gold inscription, AUTOGRAPHS. She had gotten it last Christmas from Uncle Henrik; he and Aunt Ragnild had been the first to write in it. It had made the rounds of all her classmates. She had sneaked it across the aisle, back and forth along the rows of desks many times during school hours and never been caught. Occasionally it had met up with others like it, and always tucked out of sight under the cover of a geography book or shoved into a desk. A private time with autographs, that's what she'd have right now! She flopped face down into the middle of her bed, bent her legs upward across her back and began paging through the little treasure.

Printed on the opening page, each beginning with a floral capital letter, were two quotations:

A friend may well be reckoned the masterpiece of nature:
Ralph Waldo Emerson

You're my friend-
What a thing friendship is, world without end!
Robert Browning

When she first received the book, she studied these quotations as one would study a passage of scripture; friendship was indeed a very important part of life. No one must forget that. As time went on, the handwritten entries began to fill the pages; it was like gathering into a secret place, for all time, the friends of Emily McCleary.

Some pages she would return to more often than others.

Leaves may wither
Flowers may die
Friends may forget you
But never will I.

Your chum, Wilma

Emily wanted Wilma to have said, "Your Best chum," because that's who she was. But did she consider Emily her best chum? That was what Emily ached to know. She had written "Your Best Chum" in Wilma's book.

Yours until apples grow
On maple trees.

Your friend, Lillian

Lillian was nice but often hung along when she wasn't wanted. But then, Lillian liked Emily, and when other girls deserted her she could always count on Lillian.

It makes me giggle
It makes me laugh
To think you want
My autograph.

Freddy

Freckled Freddy, that's who he was, but naturally he didn't sign his name that way. One day he picked up her ruler when it fell on the floor. She had simply grabbed it away from him; she knew she should have smiled and said "Thank You," but she didn't want the other kids to think she liked him. But really she did, at least a little bit.

When you get married
And have twins
Please send to me
For safety pins.

Russell

He would say something like that; he wouldn't write decent, not Russell. She could see him, that fat kid, sitting in a desk that was too small for him. He would squeeze in and out of it as the occasion required, always taking his time and always being last.

In the golden chain of Friendship
regard me as a link.

Lovingly, Alice

Emily liked the sound of that entry. It was beautiful poetry. But then, Alice was always perfect; her stockings were never rumpled and her hair ribbon never drooped.

Roses are red
Vilets are blu
Suger is sweet
An so are you.

In your woodbox of memry
Put in a stik for me.

Your freind, Benny

Emily guessed Benny was awfully dumb. She remembered how long her book had stayed in his grubby desk. Finally, since he never dared to take it out during school time, he had stayed in a whole recess writing in it. And, of course, he couldn't think of anything else to write; he wrote that in every girl's book.

By hook
By crook
I'm last
In your book.

Stanley

Now he was the handsomest boy in school. Emily wished he had written something more personal. She knew he had scribbled it in a hurry and tossed it rudely on her desk, as if wanting to be rid of it. He'd never look her in the eye and smile. Oh well, boys were funny, always acting big and important, covering up for being bashful.

She began paging backwards until she was on page one and two.

Your hair is red
Your eyes are blue
What I wouldn't do
To a scamp like you!

Uncle Henrik

P.S. Remember me and bear in mind
A faithful friend is hard to find
And when you find one good and true
Change not the old one for the new.

Uncle Henrik liked Emily. When he called her "Scamp" it was always teasing, she could tell, because there was always a twinkle in his eye when he said it.

On the opposite page was Aunt Ragnild's:

Ten lively fingers
Practicing each day
Soon a host of people
Will listen to you play!

Aunt Ragnild

Aunt Ragnild had made up that little poem just for Emily; she knew because she had never seen it in any other autograph book before. And besides, Aunt Ragnild was always encouraging her piano playing. She wondered why she liked to have Aunt Ragnild listen to her pieces and not her mother. Both ladies were good piano players, and both said good things. It wasn't that; she guessed she somehow owed her mother something and never felt anything was quite good enough. She wished she knew how to love her mother more but resolutions to do so never amounted to anything. Emily paged in the direction of her mother's entry.

That you may live always
For love and truth
Is the sincere wish
Of your mother.

Anna Olson

Emily had problems with both living and being truthful; she only wished her mother weren't so anxious about it. She hurriedly closed the book. The time-worn, ugly resentment was searing anew as on the first day she resented the drawer full of baby clothes. When would she begin to love her mother? She rolled over on her back and looked at the ceiling.

The baby clothes had been given to Aunt Ragnild; that was nice because now she had a baby, a beautiful girl baby, so much lovelier than any doll. She had the tiniest fingers that reached out and grabbed ahold and a funny little smile that came with a little bit of coaxing. Emily wished for a baby like that in this house. She couldn't wait to go and visit again at Aunt Ragnild's because she always let her mind the baby. Now she remembered the last time.

"She's asleep yet, Emily," Aunt Ragnild had said. *Bestemor*—Emily used to call her Grandma, but since little Juliet was born she must always be called *Bestemor*—brought a plate of cakes into the parlor and passed it to her, first.

Bestemor was nice, more quiet, maybe, than Aunt Ragnild, and everyone gave her full attention when she came around, and Emily did too. Bestemor talked and laughed like the other ladies, but somehow, when she entered, the cackling stopped for more quiet conversation. By the kitchen window Bestemor had her high-backed, armless, rocking chair, upholstered with dark green cloth. Here with pursed lips she sat humming and rocking the tiny baby, too tiny yet for Emily to hold. Bestemor never told Emily to go and play. She would stand and watch as long as she wanted to.

But during the last visit, Juliet was bigger, eight months old and able to sit up on a blanket. "You can take her outside when she wakes up," Aunt Ragnild had said. As time went slowly by, the coffee cups were left standing on their saucers and the cake plate empty except for a few crumbs; the women went back to their handwork. Bestemor had a long coil in her lap; she was knitting a black stocking. The other ladies had embroidery hoops fixed in white linen into which they pierced threaded needles.

Finally came the signal that the baby was awake—not loud wailing, but a sound which seemed to push out with arms and legs as much as with voice. Emily followed Ragnild into the bedroom. She watched as the wet diaper was changed for a dry one, and the little, moist bottom dusted with talc. Once Emily had thought talc would make her doll smell like Juliet, but no, only Juliet could make talc smell like that. Finally Aunt Ragnild put a dress on Juliet, a white dress with white crocheted lace along the bottom. "There, we've dressed her up for the afternoon," said the mother, lifting her baby up in front of her. "Now you can take her." Emily paraded through the parlor, cheek to cheek with the precious doll; yes, the spread fingers of her hand was supporting the baby's back. Aunt Ragnild followed with a blanket that was spread on the lawn in the shade near the house. "Watch so she doesn't sit directly in the sun," Aunt Ragnild cautioned as she left to join the ladies.

That had been such a special afternoon. She and Juliet had looked at each other, listened to each other, smiled at each other. Juliet. That name ought to be in her autograph book. It was such a nice name for a girl. Named for her grandmother, she was. Juliet, a little girl's name for Julia. Julia, of course, could only be a grownup's name. "She is your cousin," her mother had said as brightly as her mother could when Emily had longingly expressed, "I wish she was ours." Emily's dolls didn't interest her now that she had minded her baby cousin; they were all left unattended in the corner. "Why do you leave your dollies lie without clothes on?" her mother had asked once. "You have so many nice dresses for them." Emily had never really thought about that, but her dolls were undressed most of the time, it was true.

Hearing Wilma and Lillian talking on the way up the back stairway soon to be knocking at the door at the end of the hall, Emily scrambled out of bed and returned the autograph book to the drawer. Lillian loved to dress dolls; Emily would let her do that.

"Can you play?" asked Wilma when Emily suddenly appeared in the doorway even before they knocked.

"Sure. Come in."

"Your mother won't mind?"

"No. Why should she? Come in."

"What are you doing?" Wilma always did the talking.

"Oh nothing."

"How come you weren't outside with us then?"

"I practiced my recital piece on the piano."

That settled it for the moment as the girls walked through the hall to Emily's room.

"My recital is the day after tomorrow and I must be ready for that, you must know." Emily tossed up her hands in a sigh and let them drop to her sides as she led the girls into her room.

"I'm pretty busy. Lillian, look at those poor naked dolls over there. You may dress them if you like."

With a sad little smile the girl who hadn't done the talking withdrew to the corner and dropped on her knees beside the doll box.

Now Emily's attention would be on Wilma. Yes, there was the recital. Strange how she could have been thinking about anything else. She remembered the shoes in the closet, still in the tissue paper lining the box brought from the store.

"See my new shoes?" Emily drew forth a shiny black slipper as the tissue paper trailed and crumpled on the floor.

"Patent leather?"

"Yep."

Wilma examined the shoes while Lillian crawed out of the corner to glimpse the latest wonder.

"Maybe I'll get a pair like this for Christmas," said Wilma in a matter-of-fact voice, unwilling to betray surprise.

Emily eyed her chum with calculation. Don't worry, Wilma was just as surprised upon seeing the new shoes come out of the box as Emily had been when the clerk uncovered them at the shoe store. Sitting on the fitting stool directly in front of her, he had rustled them out of the tissue paper. To find them, he had slid the ladder along to the far end of the wall of piled boxes, climbed almost to the ceiling and pulled out the patent leather slippers which just fit her feet.

"Mama is sewing my dress right now," Emily continued, wanting to reinforce the impression she knew she was making on Wilma. "I can't show it to you yet. She mustn't be disturbed."

"Your parents aren't your real parents, are they?"

The room suddenly whirled before Emily's eyes as the shoe box, with the left shoe still in it, slid from the bed to the floor. As if caught in a current, she dropped to the floor after it. Taking her time retrieving the box, she regained composure. She stood up and faced Wilma. "Why not? They are real, aren't they? And I don't have any other parents."

"You're mad, aren't you."

"No, not mad, only disgusted that you are so stupid."

"But you did come from an orphanage?"

"What if I did?" Emily felt like pulling hair and scratching flesh.

"Oh nothing." Wilma turned away with a tinge of triumph in her voice which seared a little deeper Emily's already ruffled temper.

"I have a sister older than me that lives in Oregon. We write to each other. Not many people have pen pals who are real sisters and I mean real!" Emily said firmly, but she knew that if she said anything more it would likely choke and tears would come.

Wilma had joined Lillian. She was into the paper dolls, busy bending tabs, putting a large picture hat on a lady. She made no reply, she may not even have heard Emily's last statement.

"Hello, girls." Anna stood in the doorway, an unfinished garment of dark green, silk taffeta draped over her arm and a tape measure around her neck.

"Hello," responded both girls at once. Only Lillian stood up to eye the dress.

"I need to try this on you, Emily. The waistline seam is only basted so be careful when you pull it down. I'll measure for the hem if the waistline is right and I won't have to bother you again."

Lillian watched Emily slip on the silk dress full of tiny ruffles. Emily wasn't skinny anymore under puffed sleeves. Her face was flushed almost purple against her vivid red hair. Lillian felt sorry for Emily; the kids called her carrot-top because of that hair.

Emily was standing in the middle of the floor now as her mother squatted around her, measuring and pinning.

"Look straight ahead," said Anna, sensing that Emily was conscious of her audience, "And stand still until I want you to turn."

Emily responded with pride, holding her head high. Wilma was certainly watching; Emily caught her glancing sideways from her seeming preoccupation with the paper dolls.

"May I come to your recital?" Wilma had left the paper dolls half-dressed on the floor and joined Emily and Anna as the final touches were made by the seamstress. Maybe in the presence of Emily's mother she wanted to reconcile the friendship.

"Of course. I did invite you, remember?" Emily spoke with the brightness of triumph, and she was sounding good to her mother, too. "Your parents will bring you, won't they?"

"My mother and I will come."

"And Lillian, you'll come too, won't you?"

"She can come with my mother and me," said Wilma satisfied that good feelings had returned at last.

Mrs. Newton had scheduled a recital for her advanced pupils for late August at the First Methodist Church. There were ten participants, among them Emily McCleary, foster daughter of Mr. and Mrs. Peder Olson. The stage was set as Mrs. Newton's grand piano was brought from her house, two doors away, into the chancel of the church, the pulpit having been removed from its prominent place at the center.

Mrs. Newton had an answer for anyone who might object to a secular performance occurring in this sacred place: all the music had been composed to the glory of God, composers like Handel, Bach, and the rest. Could applause be permitted? She convinced the Reverend without much argument that her pupils needed the benefit of applause, and furthermore, that they had been taught how to curtsy and bow; that was part of being a performer. How could he refuse such a request from his church organist? And he had to be mindful, too, that she was training future church organists. So it was decided that the Reverend would announce that, for this occasion, audience applause was in order. He doubted whether any of the Lutheran churches in the area would have been that accommodating.

The folks from Wanamingo came early enough to share a meal with the Peder Olsons; Henrik had brought a surrey full of womenfolk, his wife, his mother and the two Veblen maiden ladies, Josie and Emma. They would enjoy it so much. Ragnild had spoken to her husband, and Julia had agreed. And Little Juliet went where her mother went, content as a kitten. David, home for a brief visit, volunteered to do the evening milking, Arne keeping him company.

Just as Anna was bringing in the dessert, an angel food cake covered with whipped cream, Ragnild remembered the gift she had stuck in her bag.

"Excuse me? We have a little something for Emily on this important occasion." Ragnild went to the bedroom.

Bestemor, too, excused herself and went for her purse.

Emily sat up straight. This wasn't her birthday even, but, of course, one's first recital was important to one's life.

Bestemor returned and placed a silver dollar in Emily's hand. "We are happy you play so well, Emily," she said. "This evening you must do your best."

"I will, I will, Bestemor." Emily was out of her chair in a flash and threw her arms around Julia. A glow of genuine warmth flowed between them.

Ragnild, who had been standing behind Emily's chair waiting her turn, paused long enough to let the feeling between this good grandmother and the so-often-troubled little girl be realized to its fullest. After Bestemor had found her place at the table again, Ragnild handed Emily a rectanglar package in red tissue paper. Emily remembered how her autograph book had looked wrapped in the same way under the Christmas tree.

"Open it," said Uncle Henrik.

She slid the gold string to one side and worked through the wrapping. A book, to be sure, a diary. The covers were hard leather with a border of gold leaves, an inch from the edges, inside which MY DIARY appeared in gold letters. Across the opening gilt edge of the book was a strap attached to a gold lock; a key was attached to the lock by a rubber band.

"And what are you going to do with that?" asked Peder, beaming at everyone around the table, grateful for all the attention his little girl was getting. Misgivings about Emily must have completely faded at this moment, and he was especially glad Henrik had come.

"Write in it, I should think." Emily looked around the table. "Thank you, Aunt Ragnild. Thank you, Uncle Henrik."

"The first thing you must do tonight after the recital is to write on the August 21 page what happened on this day. This is a very important day for you, my dear." With these words spoken as a teacher, which indeed she was, Ragnild returned to her place.

"I know, Aunt Ragnild. I promise to do that."

While the guests were eating their cake, Emily undid the rubber band and put the tiny key into the gold lock. It worked. It would be secret, scrumptiously secret!

Anna was uneasy at the occasion of her daughter's display of musical achievement, in spite of the fact that she sat beside her good husband and was surrounded by her good family. Nothing could quell the constant anxiety she felt deep within her. She had held out hope that all the preparing she had done for this occasion would yield satisfaction, and it had to a degree. She was pleased with the dress; it wasn't easy to work on taffeta, to say nothing of rolling and stitching the yards and yards of hem on those ruffles. And she had let Emily wear the locket, that old keepsake from Anna's childhood. Emily had, for some reason, taken a fancy to the story connected with it and had begged to wear it, but the right occasion must arise, Anna had contended, and they both agreed the recital was the time. It did look lovely on that dress! And having her folks for dinner had gone so well! Henrik seemed to have his own reasons for calling Emily the "Little Scamp," which Anna didn't like very much, but, no matter, Henrik had his own way with people.

The participants were coming in now and taking their places in the front row. Emily's hair ribbon was on straight, thank goodness for that.

The closer Emily got to that piano the sharper Anna's anxiety became. It wasn't that she feared Emily would forget her place and spoil her performance, far from it, she would succeed without a flaw. Why then couldn't Anna rejoice in such dexterity? What is to become of this child? This perplexing question haunted every facet of Anna's experience with Emily. It frightened her now that the girl was so gifted. Certainly she and Peder had done right by giving her the best opportunity available to develop her talent, it wasn't that, either. It was a powerlessness that Anna felt, and it drained away all the joy. It was easy enough for her to take credit for the dress, the party, the fact that the child was even in this recital, but she could not, for all that, take comfort because she had no hold on the child, no eye-to-eye contact; there was always that evasion. But hadn't she set up the schedule for practicing, and an increasingly vigorous one at that, and hadn't it been followed religiously day after day all summer? But Anna could not attribute even that to any power she had over Emily. Emily loved the piano and cared to do little else.

So applause was permissible here; Anna clapped politely after each performance. Soon Emily McCleary was announced with Mozart's Sonata no. 1 in C. And there she was, sliding onto the bench, looking down for the pedal and finally raising her hands to begin. There were no pages to turn, the music was memorized, the Mozart creation was in Emily's head and in her fingertips. Anna had followed that piece from its inception when the runs had been taken ever so slowly, then gradually increased with each hour of practice all summer long. The result from those fingers was as precise as the sound from the throat of a lark, as clear as running brook water, as nimble as the movement of hummingbird wings. Emily resembled no one she had ever seen at the piano before, certainly not the mature Ingeborg who realized such deep reverence in the music she performed. Emily's music came from a remote world, a fairyland of glitter and color, and she played as if the fantasy could become real, through the ears, before one's very eyes. But Anna was afraid of this fantasy land, that was just it! What was to become of this child?

Anna looked over at Peder. He was pleased as a dutiful father should be; he showed none of the misgivings she had. Anna felt very burdened with the obligation to guide her child. Certainly there were precepts all people must learn in order to live, and Emily wasn't learning them. "Remember, Anna," he would say, "She's just a child."

The final crescendo was near. The trill. That trill had been practiced! It had invaded every crevice in the dining room and the parlor; it was almost as if crystal dishes in the china closet were set in vibration. Now the final three measures; there was still strength in those fingers. The final chord came hard, a unison note in three octaves, and Emily was off the bench in front of the grand piano curtsying like a princess. Then the applause; Henrik was to tell Anna and Peder later that it was greater for her than for any other performer.

Henrik took his womenfolk home after the performance as soon as they could break away. Barney and Lady drew the surrey along through the moonlight and fragrance of freshly cut grain fields. Little Juliet slept on, handed from one to the other of the women.

Julia's thoughts were on her daughter, Anna. She knew Emily was hard on her. It perhaps had been hasty on their part to take her home from the orphanage the way Anna and Peder had, but that was neither here nor there after six years. If only Anna could be happy! She had wanted a child so badly! And Emily, why was she so difficult? Julia had never in all her life run into a child like her, and even Ragnild was baffled. A haunting feeling disturbed Julia when Emily was around. That baby that had been Emily cried and cried hour after hour in her cradle, and no one came to pick her up. Julia had a vague but very real compulsion to pick her up and rock her, but, of course, it was too late. Then again, there was something so right about Emily, too. She was alive, fighting her way, perhaps, when all she really needed to do was to lean toward people eager to love her. She remembered the warmth of Emily's hug this evening. Anna should have had that, not she. Julia's heart continued to cry for Anna.

The surrey rolled on into the night. Weariness itched under uncomfortable clothes, and eyes that yielded not to the Sandman began to burn. But the horses knew where they were going and were surefooted in the semidarkness.

After the good-nights had been said and the horses stood without harnesses in their stalls, Henrik made his way up the stairs by the light of Ragnild's lamp on the dresser. Juliet slept in her crib.

"What do you think Emily will write in her diary?" said Henrik, wincing as he undid the button on his stiff. white collar.

"That's not for you to wonder at," replied Ragnild, removing her first petticoat. "She needs a place to store her secrets."

"I wondered why you insisted on getting it for her."

"My best friend when I was her age was 'Dear Diary.' "

Chapter 3

As Henrik stepped out of the barn after finishing his afternoon chores, he saw Jake Torkelson stopping on the road. Jake fastened the reins, jumped down from his wagon, and started walking toward the cobbler shop. He carried an old pair of shoes in his hand.

"Hey, Jake," called Henrik, hurrying toward him.

"Is the place closed? The shades are down and the door seems locked," said Jake when he saw Henrik.

"It's been closed for over a month, since the first part of September."

"I don't usually come through here these days unless I am in need of shoe repair. Is the old man sick or something?"

"He's going down hill, Jake. He may not live long. The doctor says it's cancer."

"Ah, that's bad news," replied Jake, shaking his head. "There's nothing going on here anymore." He looked across the road toward the empty blacksmith shop. "This must be the last place to close it's door." He lifted the tattered shoes he was carrying. "I suppose I'll have to take my business elsewhere."

"I'm afraid so."

"Cancer, uh?"

Henrik nodded.

Jake shook his head and slowly turned toward his waiting team. Henrik watched him toss the old shoes back into the wagon, climb into the seat, and slap the horses' rumps with the slackened reins. He was soon out of sight. Henrik continued toward the house.

It was plenty evident now that Arne was dying. Two weeks ago he had become bedridden, so weak that he could scarcely lift his head; he couldn't be coaxed into taking nourishment anymore, although Julia tried meat broth and fruit juice at regular intervals.

Henrik could never rid himself of the image of his dying friend. He saw him before his eyes wherever he went, whether he ground feed, carried hay to livestock, chopped wood, or filled the drinking-water bucket at the pump. He saw a skull covered with skin, yellowed by his disease and moist with perspiration due to relentless pain. (Melva had been instructed on how to use a syringe for injection of morphine, but he hadn't yet let her do it.)

There was no way of understanding suffering and death, however, so Henrik did his best not to dwell on it. He stayed longer than he needed to in town. The presidential campaign, that three-way race among William Howard Taft, Theodore Roosevelt and Woodrow Wilson, was a valuable distraction and yielded good discussion and argument at the Veblen General Store. Could Teddy Roosevelt possible be defeated? Being exceedingly vocal, Henrik did his best to keep the hope alive that the American voters would not turn to anyone else. The image of Arne did fade for an hour or two when he was in town.

Henrik reached the back door just as his mother was returning from Arne's bedside. He opened the door to let her in. Her shoulders seemed more stooped than ever under the shawl she was clutching tightly against the cold.

"Ragnild came to relieve me, since Juliet is asleep." Julia's voice was so low it was almost a whisper. "We'll now have some coffee." She threw her shawl across a chair and went to the shelf for cups.

The two sat at the kitchen table. Julia offered Henrik bread and jelly and ate some herself. Henrik sank his knife deep into the jelly glass and scooped out enough to cover a slice of bread. Julia swallowed hard; she had little appetite. There was silence between them for a long time.

"He doesn't have much money, but he wants to make a will. Just these last days he's been trying to talk. Strange—it's almost hard to believe! He wants to give all that he has left to the Santal Mission in India. He remembers that Skrifsrud visit, I suppose. He wants you to make a will for him and have it properly notarized. You can take care of that for him, can't you?"

"Now isn't that dandy?" Henrik intended to be jovial. "If I weren't more than a casual observer, I would say you talked him into it."

"Please, Henrik, this is not time for teasing." Julia simply couldn't go along with her son's attempt at lightheartedness although she knew perfectly well that this was his weapon against gloom. He was a tenacious shrugger of gloom.

"Sorry, Mama." He passed his palms over each other to get rid of crumbs. "What you say is quite extraordinary, I must admit. But, on the other hand, I'm not surprised. Arne is capable of it."

"Well, I must say I was completely surprised. I couldn't believe what he was saying."

"Maybe I know Arne better than you do."

Julia rose, reached for her shawl, and drew the wool over her shoulders.

"You'll see to his wishes then?"

"I will, today, as soon as I can."

She turned as she reached the door. "And—wait now in case Juliet wakes up. Ragnild will be back in a moment."

The cold October wind, whipping the dry leaves around, would tear at her the minute she got outside the door. Henrik guessed he had taken for granted that his mother would be the one to take charge of Arne's care, to arrange the bedside watches as neighbors volunteered. The sound of the closing door hung around a while in the quiet kitchen.

It was mighty interesting that Arne on his deathbed was remembering Lars Olson Skrifsrud and his Santal Mission in India. There was something about Missionary Skrifsrud, all right, that thoroughly appealed to both Arne and Henrik. He certainly didn't have the tone of voice nor the manner of behavior one would attribute to the clergy, at least the clergy Henrik and Arne knew.

Skrifsrud, a Haugean, who had been converted in prison, after which he resolved to become a missionary, was a native of Norway. Arne and Henrik met him when he was touring among Norwegian church folk in America, where he was receiving a warm reception and substantial gifts toward his work. He had visited Aspelund one Sunday—it seemed years ago now; Nils was still living—and had described most vividly his life among a primitive tribe in northeast India known as the Santals. It was rumored that Skrifsrud could speak twenty languages. His great gift as a linguist had enabled him to compile the oral language of the tribe into a written one so that the Bible could be placed in their hands. He knew the customs of these people and their mode of thinking. He composed hymns to the folk tunes he heard and worked in such a way as not to disturb their mode of life.

"Norwegian is not the only language the Word of God comes in," he reminded his Aspelund listeners. "And not all Christians wear stiff collars and heavy woolen suits to worship God, especially not in the middle of the summer." He had tugged with his finger to relieve the tightness around his throat. When asked to say Grace, as the women announced that the noon meal was ready, he looked surprised. "We've been praying all morning, now it's time to eat." He had stayed overnight at the Kristians' and Henrik had taken him to Zumbrota the following day as his itinerary required him to be in Red Wing next. Arne, who had not been present at church, met Skrifsrud during that brief visit, and Henrik hadn't failed to notice how taken he was with this man.

In the perspective of Arne's dying and the nature of his last will and testament, Henrik tried to put it all together. The two men knew the same places in Norway, the homeland; that kinship could not be underestimated. The four of them, Arne, Henrik, Nils and the missionary had been out walking all over town and out into the country. At the cobbler shop he had picked up a piece of leather and shared Arne's love for the material of his trade. At the blacksmith shop he had stroked the anvil and stressed the need for his Santals to forge better tools. He had taught them many skills, he said, which helped them to improve their lot. The four of them had looked over the fields, large beyond belief and tilled by such efficient machinery. Certainly not in Norway had he seen the like, and how small and poor were the plots of the Santal! He told how he had successfully moved many Santals, those with the most wretched soil, to a new area where they could start afresh on somewhat better land. Many lives had been saved, he said; starvation wasn't far from people in India. That was probably it—that terrible word, *starvation.* And here was a fellow native of Norway, not among people of plenty as here in America, but among people of the meanest poverty, and, furthermore, doing such great things for them. Arne's wonderful imagination had put together something unforgettable on that day.

"Why aren't you out in the barn, Papa?" Juliet was coming down the steps, momentarily stopping to look at her father. Her cheeks still had the flush of sleep.

"I've been waiting for you to wake up."

"Where's Mama?"

"She's with Bestemor over at Arne's. She'll be back soon."

The little girl finished her descent, a half step at a time, until she reached the bottom, then she rushed into her father's lap.

Henrik saw to the will that very day, got it notarized in town the next, and two days later his friend was gone. Julia mentioned she saw a smile coming over Arne's face a moment or so before his death; she said it must have been the release of the anguishing pain.

He was buried on the first of November, a blustery day with snow flurries, too sparse and infrequent to leave any evidence of moisture, but a reminder, nonetheless of the end of one season and the beginning of another. The people paying their last respects stood around the open grave, their backs against the wind and their faces hidden in coat collars.

At the foot of the grave stood the departed's daughter, Melva Veblen, wearing the appropriate black veil which lifted and jerked in the wind. *"You'd better come with me back to Wanamingo,"* he had said, *"I can't leave you here in this place."* She owed everything to this man. Anna was at the grave. She clutched her husband's arm. *"I always knew you would become a beautiful woman,"* he had said. *"But you must smile. That's what makes you pretty."* Henrik stood with his hat removed; he felt neither the frosty air nor the wind tugging at his trouser legs. *"No, no, no, don't think me an unbeliever, Henrik,"* he had said. *"I guess I stay away because I don't know what some of those preachers are talking about. And I can't stand them goading people to tears."* Julia looked over the bowed heads toward the leaden sky. She pursed her lips; she was done with weeping. *"Yea, though I walk through the valley of the shadow of death, I will fear no evil, for Thou art with me."* He had asked her to read the Shepherd's Psalm and to pray "Our Father." He seemed to have no need for the minister; an old friend like herself would do. And, perhaps, the ritual of Holy Communion was not appropriate to everyone's understanding. The words of the Psalm had been Eucharist for him. And on the other side of the world would come funds from an unknown donor just in time for better equipment to drill wells in the settlement of Santals at Assam. Lars Olson Skrifsrud had died the previous year, but his work was still going on.

The coffin, resting on taut ropes was soon to be lowered. The snowflakes that fell upon it were extinguished as quickly as they lighted. "...we therefore commit his body to the ground in the sure and certain hope of resurrection to eternal life through Jesus Christ our Lord..."

"So the old shoemaker is gone, rest his soul! I just came by to see if you folks had any rags, bottles, scrap metal—you know, the usual things I can take off your hands, and pay you for, besides?"

Speaking in an accent which was not Norwegian, was Cantor, the old, dark-eyed Jew, who drove up less than a week after the cobbler shop lost its occupant. How he caught wind of places to go looking for salvage, no one could quite figure out, but without fail he would appear. No one seemed to know, either, what town he came from or what town he was headed for; his hair grew unattended, as did his beard; he, people said, was the wandering Jew, wearing the dirty black skullcap and those ill-fitting trousers, filling his wagon, beyond the capacity of his aging horses, with heavy pieces of broken machinery, barrels of glass bottles and worn-out grain sacks, filled with old rags which stuck out of holes which defied patching. Julia had given him a meal on occasion, but he had never accepted an invitation to stay the night. Where he lay his head, one might wonder.

"We have several sacks of rags," said Julia, who had come to meet him out on the road. "And there is a box of glass bottles. Do you take leather bits? We found many boxes full, stacked in a corner. Why he saved them, I don't know."

The Jew nodded indifferently; there wasn't anything he would refuse.

"There isn't much metal this time. Not like the time we cleaned out the blacksmith shop."

Julia led the way into the cobbler shop. She was glad that she and Melva had gone through all the drawers and chests of clothes, towels and bedding. It was sad business sorting out garments of one departed, but it had to be done and there was no use putting it off.

Cantor surveyed the room with a quick movement of his deep-set eyes. Things were well boxed and sacked, but might there not be some choice piece of iron? The cobbler's machines had already been removed, to be sold secondhanded, he presumed. Suddenly he picked up a curious tool, a little hammer, not much metal there, but he might as well take it along.

"Not that," said Julia. "Funny it was left behind."

He handed the tool to Julia with the same indifference with which he had accepted the scraps of leather. Julia was used to seeing this hammer in Arne's hand; with a twinge of pain it brought him back to her as much as had the apron she found behind the door or the shoes under the stove. Of course, the apron and the shoes were nothing to save, but this little tool might come in handy some day.

"I will start weighing and loading. You say this is all?"

He reached for his scale and hung it at the back of his wagon. The scale was a spring with a rectangular face which would indicate the weight of a sack or box hung from its bottom. With a pencil, no longer than three inches, he wrote figures on a pad which he took from his shirt pocket.

"Each sack is worth ten cents. I'll give you one dollar for all you've got."

"What about the leather pieces?"

"I have no idea who'll want them, Ma'am. I may get nothing. But I'll take them off your hands."

Julia pursed her lips and nodded in agreement. She was not one to bargain, although old Cantor stood waiting as if expecting her to do so.

"Perhaps you're hungry? Our family has eaten dinner, but I have plenty left over. I could give you a meal."

"Thank you, Ma'am. Thank you. I will accept that."

Julia returned to her house carrying the little hammer while Cantor finished loading the boxes.

"So Woodrow Wilson is now our president. What do you think of that?" Julia set a plate of food before him. She remembered Henrik had found the old Jew interesting to talk to.

"You have Teddy Roosevelt to blame, if you don't like it, Ma'am," he replied, reaching for a slice of bread. He buttered the whole slice, he didn't break it in half.

"We're not Democrats, of course—most of us, that is, around here anyway."

He looked up and nodded. He cut the potato dumpling in half and discovered the tidbit of meat. "Pork?"

"Yes. The dumpling is only potatoes and flour, though. You don't have to eat the pork."

Again he looked up and nodded.

"Last time there was a young man here, David, I believe his name was."

"Yes, our son."

He looked at Julia as though he knew the whole story of the adopted child from New York.

"Where is he now?"

"He's a doctor now. He just got his degree in medicine. We're very proud of him. He lives in St. Paul."

Julia's guest smiled. He drank down the glass of buttermilk which had been set before him and licked the traces off his mustache.

"I must be going. The days are getting short and nights are cold." He shoved his chair away from the table and got on his feet. He reached for his overcoat that had been thrown on a chair.

"You could use a sweater under that coat, couldn't you, now that it is getting so cold?"

He stopped putting on his coat and looked at Julia once again. Without hesitation she went to a clothes basket which she had brought back from Arne's, clothes too good to put into salvage sacks.

"Here is a good warm sweater that fits no one that I know of. Take it and put it on."

"Thank you, Ma'am. I suppose it belonged to the shoemaker, rest his soul."

Julia nodded.

"You are a kind woman," said Cantor, straightening the sleeves and noticing how well the sweater fit. "You knit it, yes?"

Julia nodded.

"I'm much obliged to you, Ma'am," he said, reaching out his hand to her before putting on his glove. "I must go."

Julia watched through the window as he climbed into his tattered wagon. The docile team began to drag forward. Out of the rear of the wagon Julia caught sight of Arne's old blue shirt sticking out of a hole in a sack. She had removed all its buttons before discarding it. How painful to dispose of a dead friend's things! She let the curtain drop and went back to the table and began clearing dishes.

"Bestemor, we're home!" The back door swung open, admitting the little girl. She carried a little cardboard box in her mittened hand. "Bestemor, see what I got!"

"Let Bestemor take off your coat and bonnet first," said Ragnild, who came behind her daughter with a parcel she dropped on the table.

The little shoulders wiggled with impatience out of the red velvet coat her mother had made. The grandmother's hand smoothed the soft blond hair in disarray by the firmly tied bonnet.

"See? It's a doll. Papa says it looks like me. Mama says we will sew clothes for her."

Out of the little box came a celluloid kewpie doll no taller than six inches. The eyes were wide, the cheeks plump, and the mouth curved with a jaunty smile. The naked body was as rosy as the cheeks, the knees and elbows just as dimpled.

"My, my she is really something!"
"And she won't break unless I squeeze her. I mustn't let her get stepped on." With that she skipped away, giving her mother a chance at Bestemor.
"There were enough eggs to trade for groceries. And I bought some white muslin for the quilt backing. Now we can set up the quilt frame over at Emma and Josie's and get started stitching. Their nice warm parlor is a good place to work, they said."
After putting his team away, Henrik came in carrying the grocery-ladened egg case and set it by the pantry door. As he hung up his coat, he noticed Arne's hammer lying on the shelf behind the stove. *"I'll tell you a secret, Henrik, if you promise not to tell anyone,"* Anna, the story teller, had said. *"Arne's hammer is magic. It never misses. If you tell anyone, it will lose its magic. I perhaps shouldn't even have told you."*
"Where did you find this?" Henrik picked the hammer off the shelf and approached his mother with it.
"Cantor was here when you were gone. He took all the rags, the glass, and the leather scraps, but I wouldn't let him take that."
"What are you going to do with it?"
"I don't know. Why do you ask? I thought it would be handy to have a little tack hammer around."
Julia's attention was again drawn toward Ragnild's purchases as Henrik slowly returned the tack hammer to the shelf. When Anna had drawn Thor's hammer on her slate, it was always shaped like that, no claw opposite the head, just a tapered wedge.

Juliet had been asleep just short of two hours, waking up as the grownups were about to go to bed.
"It's an earache, I'm afraid," said Ragnild as she carried the child down the stairs. She sobbed relentlessly, holding her little hand over her ear. Her rosy face was wet with tears and saliva dripped from her open mouth.
"I'll rock her a while. Maybe she'll go back to sleep," said Bestemor.
"The cold autumn air must have been too much for her," said Henrik. "Maybe we should have left her at home with Bestemor after all."
Through the long night, everyone slept in fitful intervals of no longer than an hour. The pain in Juliet's ear grew worse and her sobbing became higher pitched and more piercing. Ragnild and Julia agreed to try putting a few drops of warmed mineral oil into the ear. It was worth trying and couldn't do any harm. There was no evidence that it helped much. It wasn't until chore time the next morning that Juliet fell into a deep sleep. When she awoke at noon,

Ragnild brought her downstairs and put her in the high chair. Juliet looked around and smiled.

"She's all right now?" questioned Henrik, looking first at his wife and then at his mother.

"The infection broke," said Ragnild. "Her pillow was stained with blood and matter."

"*Stakkars liten,*" said Bestemor.

Chapter 4

"Are those the people who are coming for dinner?" asked Emily as she came upon her mother looking at a picture of a family Emily had been told was living in Chicago. It wasn't the first time since that picture arrived last Christmas that her mother had lifted it from its place on top of the china closet. It was curious. There were many pictures sitting around the dining room and parlor, on tables, or top of the piano, but this one got far more attention than the rest.

"Yes. I expect they'll be here a little before twelve o'clock. They're coming from Faribault this morning. Stay around, Emily. I'll need you to help set the table. And you must dress up. We have to look our best."

"Will the kids come too?" Emily saw the sober faces of the two boys standing stiffly on either side of their parents.

"Don't call them kids. They belong to a minister's family."

"Boys, then."

"That's better. Yes, they'll all be here. We'll set the table for, —let's see—seven."

From the drawer at the bottom of the china closet Anna brought her finest linen tablecloth and her scroll of center doilies.

"First you can go to the back room and get another leaf for the table."

Emily did as she was told. Her anticipation upon seeing all the elegant china, crystal, and silverware to deck a proper table filled her with excitement. She could hardly remember when they had last eaten in the dining room. It must have been as long ago as last Christmas. Would the crystal goblets be used at last? She had never seen them on the table; they were always in their place on the top shelf of the china closet. "Be ever so careful, careful." One could scarcely open the curved glass door without that nervous call from her mother. And the sterling silver? Several times she had helped get the black tarnish off, but she had never seen those dazzling knives and forks next to a plate. The next best silverware was always used.

Anna, having memorized that picture, kept seeing it as she brought out the pad for the tablecloth. There was no trace of boyishness in Halvor anymore, but that was to be expected. After all, he had been married as long as she had. He met his wife in Wisconsin before he moved to Chicago. And he was the father of two boys, the oldest already twelve years old. His wife's name was Lottie, a large heavy-set woman; her wedding picture showed her as being as tall, if not taller, than Halvor. His letters said she kept a spotless household and laid down strict rules for him and the boys to follow in the keeping of it. She cared little about church work; she didn't sing in the choir, teach Sunday school, or help with women's activities; however, because she wanted to do her duty as a minister's wife, she attended Ladies Aid meetings and served, when her time came, as meticulously as she kept house. Was he happy with her? He never really complained, but Anna thought she could read between the lines and wondered.

Emily helped her mother pull apart the table to insert the leaf. Together they placed the white, quilted pad; then, making sure their hands were clean, they spread out the pure white, linen tablecloth. From the scroll of embroidered doilies, Anna placed one which Emily had scarcely seen before, one with snow-white molded leaves of solid needlework in a circular design interspersed with eyelets. It lay at the center of the table without a crease or wrinkle, adhering to the linen cloth as though it were a part of it.

"Go downstairs to Papa and bring up a pound of butter. It's so hard right out of the cooler. It needs to sit out a while."

Emily hurried down the front steps. She and her mother always entered the meat market from the front; the cutting room was off limits to the ladies.

Anna began taking out her tableware by counting in sevens. Halvor's oldest boy did look like his father, that was for sure. The letters said he was musical and had been given lessons on the violin. He sang well, too, a boy soprano, but his voice would soon change, Halvor suspected. But unlike the older one, who loved school and all kinds of sports, was Joseph, nine years old, puny with asthma and hopelessly spoiled by his mother who always favored him.

There it all was as Emily had suspected: the best china, the crystal goblets and the sterling silver! And there were the napkins, the largest ones, starched and immaculate, ready to be put around.

"Here's the butter." Emily hurried into the kitchen. "Now do you want me to set the table?"

"You must be ever so careful," cautioned Anna, as if it might control the pace of her impetuous daughter, who was now almost fifteen. "You know how to place the silver, the knife blade facing the plate."

"Of course I know, and I'll be careful," called Emily as she left her mother behind in the kitchen.

Having made sure her mother wasn't following, she flicked her fingernail against a crystal goblet—that exquisite ting! And once again, ting! She placed the stack of plates over her forearm and set them, one at a time, as she walked around the table. She made the same circle with the silverware, and with the napkins, placing them on the left of the fork as she had been taught. Then the crystal! Hearing her mother opening the oven door, Emily flicked her fingernail at another goblet. Ting! The oven door closed and the aroma of roasting pork drifted into the dining room. Food! There would be a sumptuous meal; Emily remembered the two lemon pies, meringue two inches high, cooling on the table in the back room.

Anna, having pulled the roasting pan out of the oven momentarily, poked at the roast with a fork and basted it thoroughly. She wondered how it would be to see Halvor after eighteen years. How could she have imagined they would be separated for so long? She dreaded the feelings that she suspected would clutch at her, and she felt self-conscious of what he might be thinking at the sight of her. Vague memories stirred of how an owl was disturbed and flew out of a cave, almost into their faces, as they climbed Barn Bluff. *"I want you to be my friend, Anna,"* he had said then. *"You know what I mean, real friendship."* That vow of friendship had been kept. There were more than a hundred letters to vouch for that, six to ten letters a year, arriving not quite once a month. But shouldn't there be celebration now that two old friends were about to see each other again? She was trying her best to make it a celebration. She lifted a spoon of juice from the roast and let it fall back in large drops. There would be good gravy, the juice was amber brown. She put the roast back into the oven and shut the door.

Emily had finished setting the table and gone to her room to change her dress. Anna was already dressed and needed only to remove a large, gingham apron to be presentable for guests. She surveyed all the serving dishes she had set out on the kitchen table; everything was as ready as it could be. She looked nervously at the clock; it would be only a matter of minutes now. She felt hot. Her face must be red as a beet and her hair-do, reinforced earlier by the curling iron, wilting.

The doorbell rang. Off came the apron, landing on a hook behind the pantry door. Nervous fingers poked at Anna's hair in the mirror of her dresser in the bedroom, then swift steps brought her to the bottom of the long front stairs.

"My dear Anna, at last we see each other," exclaimed Anna's guest the moment she opened the door. He clasped her extended hand into a sustained hold. *"Takk for sist."*

How familiar was that voice! She hadn't counted on that; it was the eyes she had carried in her imagination.

"Halvor! How glad I was to hear you were back in Minnesota and would some day come to Kenyon." Anna squeezed his hand; she abhorred limp handshakes. "Come in, come in, all of you."

They stood around her in the entry at the bottom of the stairs. Anna had closed the door, blocking out Kenyon's main street.

"My wife Lottie."

Anna shook the hand of the large woman and smiled.

"This is Halvor Jr."

Anna extended her hand toward the taller of the two boys. She noticed he was carrying a violin case.

"Call me Hal, for short," said the boy who looked exactly like his father.

"Im happy to know you, Hal," smiled Anna. In her role as hostess all her misgivings were gone. "And you brought your violin. How thoughtful! I wrote your father how anxious I was to hear you play."

"And this is Joseph."

"Happy to meet you, Joseph." Anna received a limp, little hand and gave it a warm clasp. "And now you must come along upstairs."

She led the way, turning her head back toward them.

"Did someone bring you into town?"

"Elmer Engevik gave us a ride in his surrey. He had several errands in Kenyon today, he said, and he will pick us up again at four o'clock."

At the top of the stairs was a foyer where coats and hats could be removed and hung up. Since June required little in the way of wraps, it was no use lingering there, long enough only for Halvor to hang up his hat and Lottie to catch a glimpse of herself in the the mirror of the hat tree.

They stepped into the parlor.

"This is Emily."

The red-headed girl, Anna and Peder's foster child stood before them, a full-grown lady in a bright blue skirt and a puff-sleeved waist covered with lace. Halvor was amazed. But, of course, she was going on fifteen; she had been confirmed last month, Anna had written. She went into a slight curtsy, rather than extending her hand, as she was being introduced to the four dinner guests. Halvor, however, reached out his hand toward her.

"Im so happy to meet you, Emily," he said as she responded in a handshake. "Your mother is a very dear friend of mine."

Emily smiled. He was certainly nicer than the minister she had seen in the picture, and so was the tall boy. The mother and the little boy were more like the picture.

"You play the violin, Hal? I play the piano. I'll accompany you. I'd love to hear you play." Real enthusiasm swept over Emily as she caught sight of the violin case. She led him to the piano in the corner of the parlor. Joseph followed his brother.

"I'm so happy to find you in such a lovely home, Anna," remarked Halvor as he walked around the parlor. "Peder has done very well, I can see that. You haven't mentioned his disabled foot in a long time. It's no problem anymore?"

"Not much. He gets tired, but he doesn't complain. Please be seated. Emily, let's get the food on the table."

Emily looked at the woman guest, expecting her to offer to help, but she wasn't offering. "I'll be right there."

"I hear Peder coming up the back way. He'll soon be joining us," said Anna, seeing her people comfortably settled before she dashed off to the kitchen.

After freshening up, which included putting on a clean shirt, Peder entered the parlor.

"Velkommen!" Peder extended his hand to Halvor, who stood up to receive it. "Anna has been looking forward to this day. You are making her so happy by coming."

"How do you do," responded Lottie upon being introduced to the man who married Halvor's Anna. She had heard from acquaintances around Faribault that his business was so successful that he was actually wealthy. And all these elegant furnishings seemed to bear it out. He looked like a working man with heavy hands and ruddy cheeks.

"Vær så god." Anna invited her guests into the dining room.

"You have gone to a lot of work for us," said Lottie, in the routine words she used as a guest in parishioners' homes. Suddenly she realized that her words weren't idle ones. She hadn't seen such a table in a long time, if ever!

When everyone was properly seated, and the Reverend having said grace, Anna and Emily began passing bowls and platters from which guests helped themselves. Not until all the plates were ready for forks and knives, were they seated.

"We met your sister, Sarah, yesterday while visiting the Engeviks," began Halvor. "She says she's going to be married in two weeks."

"Yes, finally," replied Anna. "They've waited quite a while. He wanted to finish seminary, that is, Bible School, first. I guess you understand that. And then he has done extensive traveling, preaching as an evangelist, even as far as the West Coast. But Sarah has kept busy with her dressmaking and organ playing. She gives lessons now, you know."

"All I've heard from the women we've been visiting is how beautiful this wedding is going to be," said Lottie. "They say your sister has sewn all the dresses, that she's having two bridesmaids besides the matron of honor, and also a flower girl."

"Juliet, my cousin, is going to be the flower girl," blurted Emily before thinking that perhaps she should let her mother do the talking.

"Henrik's little girl?" said Halvor.

Anna nodded vaguely. She was taking a quick survey of the plates. Everything must be tasted by her guests and second helpings urged upon them.

"Did all of you try the pickles? They're made from watermelon rinds. And the jelly—you must taste that. Mother still has her own grapes. *Vær så god.* Emily, pass the meat and potatoes again, and there is more hot gravy in the kitchen. Hal, more bread?"

"They'll make a good-looking pair, those two," remarked Peder, thinking it was time to pick up the conversation again. "Rasmus Hegge is a handsome man."

"And she's stunning," added Halvor, glancing toward his wife.

"Tell them, Halvor, what Sarah asked you to do." Lottie met her husband's glance. She would move the conversation quickly in another direction.

"We've been asked to the wedding," began Halvor.

"Naturally," said Anna. "Since you folks are around, it would be..."

"And she wants me to sing."

"What could be nicer? A friend of the family such as you are!"

Anna uttered the word, friend, with such casualness it surprised her. The floating cloud which had held the two friends, once lovers, over decades was dissipating in the sweep of present events, the ebb and flow of normal living. It wasn't loss exactly, it was change. Halvor was smiling. He was about to eat the lemon pie with the two-inch meringue.

"May Hal and I be excused? We're anxious to try some music." Emily was too impatient to wait for everyone to finish.

"Certainly," said Peder. "We're all anxious to hear you."

Before long, the young man's violin sang in the room. It responded to long bow strokes and quivering fingers firmly on the strings. Grasping the instrument with his chin brought intensity to his face, the eyebrows lifting, the forehead creasing. Such concentration changed him; he was putting a great distance between himself and those who watched, to be filled only with shimmering sound. Emily, on the piano, was creating a background not to be taken for granted, a landscape behind a soaring bird or a quiet lake beneath a sailboat.

A sudden wave of joy swept over Anna with a freshness that hinted strangely of the first time she had played for Halvor back in Ingeborg Schumann's music studio. The performance soared far beyond her expectation, yet here were the two children, Emily and Halvor's boy. Halvor looked at Anna. He recognized her at last.

Sarah's wedding would be among the largest that ever took place in Aspelund Church. Through the years, as they frequently appeared before audiences, Sarah and Rasmus had acquired a considerable following in the extended community. There were those who doted upon the marriage of the handsome evangelist who had won their hearts and his bride-to-be who was no ordinary girl, but had the look of a queen. Her beauty was aristocratic, they said, tall and stately, just the kind of wife for Rev. Hegge. And Aspelund now had a brand new church building with an extraordinary four-pointed tower and gothic windows. The congregation had a new minister, too, the oldest son of the late Rev. Østen Hanson, Rev. Martin Hanson, a tall engaging man, much like his father, many expressed.

"Since my sister has chosen you to be her husband, I give my consent." Henrik had responded as formally as he had been asked, when Rasmus approached him on the subject to being given Sarah's hand in marriage. With the same aloofness, Henrik had consented to give away the bride at the ceremony. That this arrogant, self-righteous man was to marry his sister, however, was an irritation to Henrik which he could not easily cast off.

Julia took this occasion to remind the couple that they must not forget to invite Lars Monson and his son Oscar; she seriously doubted whether they would attend, but then again, the old Vossing might like to see his daughter wedded. Since Nils had passed away, she hadn't seen either of them.

Ellen Veblen, who was now Mrs. Melvin Vessedahl, at last got her opportunity to be the matron-of-honor for her childhood chum, Sarah Kristian. Sarah had already fulfilled her part of the bargain made in girlhood by being Ellen's maid-of-honor when Ellen married Ragnild's brother; their romance, like Ragnild's, stemmed from the Fourth-of-July celebration in 1898 at the Otto Jensen grove. Ellen's enthusiasm for her role in this gala event was as warm and exciting as Henrik's was cold and indifferent.

And Juliet was to be Tante Sarah's flower girl. (As the word *bestemor* had been introduced into the second-generation child's vocabulary so had *tante*.) Juliet had turned four in January and had a full imaginative appreciation of what her role was to be although she had never seen a wedding. All the details had been conveyed to her when Tante Sarah had spent several days at her house sewing her dress. "You're going to look pretty," Tante had said, "prettier than the bride." Bestemor hadn't liked that remark; "You needn't make the child vain, Sarah." Everyone talked about this wedding and little Juliet listened. One day a letter came that said *Onkel* David would be coming from Minneapolis and that made Bestemor and everyone happy.

The reception would be at the Kristian home, out of doors, as Anna's had been and Melva's had been. Julia and Ragnild, although bearing the responsibility of hostesses, were given all kinds of help, particularily from Melva and the Veblen maiden ladies, and, of course, Ellen. Ragnild, pregnant, but scarcely noticeably so, was coddled and relegated to the less strenuous tasks.

Shepherding her child became Ragnild's role. The girl needed to be dressed, combed, and quietly encouraged. And the mother was good at it. Together they practiced marching down the aisle, tossing imaginary flowers onto an imaginary white carpet, standing quietly for a time, turning gracefully, following Maid of Honor Ellen, and above all smiling. It was a companionable venture for mother and daughter.

But on the day the event was about to take place, Ragnild felt something was wrong. The child wasn't herself; there was a sober listlessness about her. Did she have a stiff neck? It wasn't noticeable to anyone else, the mother surmised, and it could be that the little girl was merely apprehensive.

At the front of the church during the ceremony, when all members of the wedding party were facing the altar, Ragnild noticed that her child, in discomfort, kept lifting her left shoulder and tilting her head against it. Maybe it was just an itch. It was a hot day.

When the service was over and Juliet was returning down the aisle among the bridal party, she carried her head slightly back and far to the side all the way down. Certainly now it became noticable to everyone that something was definitely wrong.

"She has an ear infection, Ragnild," said David, who was quick to reach the child's mother.

"It was her left ear that gave her trouble last winter." Ragnild had drawn Juliet up into her arms. The little head lay against the mother's shoulder.

"Can Uncle David see?" coaxed the young doctor, gently touching Juliet's head and trying to explore the region behind her ear. It was red as he had suspected. "Does it hurt here?"

Tears came as she nodded at her uncle.

"I'll take her," David said to Ragnild. "Go and find Henrik."

The child willingly went into his arms and Ragnild made her way through the crowd toward her husband.

"We must take her to the hospital as quickly as we can," David announced to Henrik. "She has a serious ear infection."

"Ear infection?" Henrik questioned, looking first at Ragnild and than back at David.

"There's inflammation in the mastoid bone. Mastoiditis it's called. She must be carefully watched. She may need an operation."

"An operation?" Henrik was astounded.

Ragnild stared down into the flower basket left sitting not two feet away. Something had happened to the flower girl.

"Ragnild and I can manage to get her into Faribault if you'll let us take the dapple-grays. You must be at the reception."

"No, no. I'll go with you."

"Henrik, please listen," said Ragnild. "Bestemor cannot be the only one at home. You must be there to help her. Getting a ride shouldn't be hard. There are so many rigs here. We'll be just fine with David."

If anyone else had spoken thus, Henrik would have fought. But now he saw only too clearly his dilemma. It was no use arguing.

"All right, David. It's up to you."

Juliet opened her eyes and watched her father walk away.

Chapter 5

Few noticed Henrik's dapple-grays leave the church premises, but the word spread quickly when people got wind of where the flower girl was being taken. It was uppermost in the conversation of the cluster of friends gathering at the Kristian residence for the wedding reception. "She's in good hands with David," more than one person said, and soon the mood seemed normal again as platters of food began to move.

While the people were around, Henrik's anxiety became secondary. There were many old friends to talk to, and Old Wanamingo was lively once more. Lars Monson and his son Oscar did come, and Henrik hosted them as his father would have done. The three men went into the old shop for a look around; of course it was a bare shed, but not quite; the forge and the bellows were still there, and the heavy anvil. The familiar shelves and hooks still hung on the walls, but with few things on them. And the gasoline engine was still there. No one knew what Henrik would do with it; such a shame how it sat there unused. "He was so good to fix things," Lars kept saying over and over again. At last Henrik drew them back across the road; he was feeling a vague pain; he felt his own ineptness. He didn't have his father anymore either, even as Lars had lost the blacksmith who could fix things. Once again surrounded by the many guests, that pain sank away.

Soon Henrik was surrounded by the ladies who hung on his words hoping his usual entertainment would be forthcoming. He was trying his best until he heard his mother being told, "How nice it is here since that old cobbler shop is gone. Why, you can hardly tell where it stood. It does give you more room, doesn't it?" And Julia answered, "The Veblens took it away in a hurry. It was very considerate of them. They are certainly people who get things done." Henrik returned to the table for a refill of coffee and picked up another *fattigmand*. He hoped the ladies wouldn't follow him.

When the time for chores rolled around, most of the people had left. The previous half hour had been feverish with good-byes and well-wishing for the bride and groom. And in a short time they also were gone; Anna and Peder took them to Kenyon where they would stay until the day they moved to Kasson where a parish awaited Rasmus. As the echo of departing guests gradually receded in Henrik's consciousness, anxiety about his daughter returned with accelerating intensity. Things weren't right. Even the immediacy was altered by his missing horses and no Ragnild to help him, nor his little girl to play with the cats. Suddenly Albin Veblen showed up to help, wearing overalls. Henrik was disturbed by his intrusion. Why was Albin here, who so seldom set foot in the barn? "In the morning," Albin was saying, "Emma and I will help your mother do the milking so you can leave before dawn." Where was Henrik going before dawn? Of course, he must go to Faribault, yes, to Faribault.

"I'm praying that all will be well," Julia spoke in the early dawn as she clutched a tattered shawl. In another hour she would arouse the cows who were still asleep in the little woods on the edge of the pasture.

"It may rain. The wind is from the east," said Henrik as he climbed into the old single buggy drawn by his only other horse, old Ned.

"Good-bye then, Henrik."

"Good-bye, Mama."

The old buggy hadn't been used for a long time. Henrik found the cracked leather seat hard. And he wasn't used to looking down at the back of a single bay horse. Neither was old Ned used to pulling a light buggy on a public road; he was a farm horse hitched between the dapple-grays used for pulling the plow. Certainly Henrik was not riding in his usual style, but what did it matter? The top of the buggy seemed adequate to hold off rain and the bay reliable enough to get him there.

There! What would he find? He shuddered. His lungs seemed to swell with the dust shaken from the old buggy as it creaked along. He sighed deeply, gasping for the fresh air the late dawn seemed to be withholding from him.

He was getting used to his ride now as the day was becoming lighter and he realized he had a long ways to go. Hegvik's cornfield was really looking good; he must have been out cultivating yesterday. Henrik's field would have to wait a day or two. By rights he should be in it today, but then, of course, it might rain; the wind seemed to be picking up.

Spring had been late this year and the corn was just now getting a healthy start; the young sprouts had been yellow so long. And he had had trouble with gophers. They had gone down the rows on the north end of his field near the pasture and eaten the sprouted kernels just below the surface. Those contemptible gophers! He had bought himself a .22 rifle and had picked off quite a few as he came upon them in the pasture. During the pause before they would duck safely into their holes, he had taken aim. He had repaired his corn rows with a second planting by hand. Juliet had been with him, watching the old hand planter make the little hole, drop the seed, and cover it. She had been fascinated—Juliet.

How was it going with the little one? David had seemed alarmed. Henrik knew his brother so well, and he knew what that look meant. But David was also so competent; he always had answers long before most people comprehended the question. It wasn't surprising that he had graduated from medical school with the highest honors. He had marvelous powers of concentration. Henrik remembered the encyclopedias on the bottom shelf behind the glass door; they hadn't been used much since David left, and Henrik, too, had become preoccupied with the pressing needs of running his farm. He wondered now how the other boys who had come off the train that morning had fared—it had been this time of the year, hadn't it? The only one he knew anything about was the little one picked up by the Hegviks, who had taken sick and died; everyone had felt so bad; he was such a beautiful child.

Beautiful child. How was his child? He was in the town of Faribault now and it was going on seven o'clock. He had made good time, considering, he said to himself as he snapped closed his gold watch and returned it to his vest pocket. It hadn't started to rain after all, he discovered as the grayness was lifting from this June day. He knew the hospital was on this end of town, although he had never had reason to come here before. He had no trouble finding it, and there were ample hitching posts close at hand. He tied old Ned and turned toward the long concrete steps leading to the double doors of the main entrance.

David must have been watching for him from some window because he was at the front door in no time. A terrible dread clawed at Henrik when he saw his brother's face. He knew immediately what he was going to say, but was struck with disbelief and reached out desperately for the words.

"You have come a long way and it is still early," began David, pulling him into the dark entry and closing the door.

"Henrik," began David again with difficulty, fixing a pair of serious brown eyes on his brother. "We couldn't save her. We failed."

"Couldn't save... failed?"

"She died at 5:10 this morning. We tried. We operated almost immediately upon our arrival. We penetrated into the bone pocket and drained out the accumulation, but the infection had gone too far. At first she seemed to rally, but then the fever rose and..."

Henrik sank into a chair beside the hat rack. He stared intensely at his brother even after the words had ceased, but David had lowered his eyes as if there was nothing more to say.

"Come, we must go to Ragnild," said David finally. He took his brother's hat from him and hung it up.

"Yes, Ragnild, poor Ragnild. How is she?" Henrik was groping in a strange world. He was lost.

"This way," said David guiding his stricken brother with hand on the shoulder. "I left her in the waiting room here on first floor."

He and David were undoubtedly going some place as they were walking together down this long hall. But where? He longed for familiarity. He would see his wife, but she would be a stranger, too, even as David had suddenly taken on strangeness.

She rose from her chair the moment she saw the two enter the door.

"You can't see her, Henrik. They have taken her out of the room. But how could you know that you would be too late?" Ragnild fell against his shoulder, needing to feel his arms around her.

Failed, David said. Too late, Ragnild said. Now he knew, he had been told. What remained for him was to open up his consciousness to this painful truth. He felt Ragnild's fingers clutching at his back; sob, my dear Ragnild, sob, for both of us, sob!

Henrik sat in the front pew of the church staring straight ahead. The altar was there with its statue of Jesus reaching his arms down to the suffering of earth, and the altar railing upholstered for kneeling communicants moved in a perfect semicircle around the source of bread and wine. The high pulpit was to one side of the chancel and the organ on the other. He saw none of these things. Neither were his eyes fixed on the short, white coffin on the catafalque he and Ragnild had followed into this sanctuary. He was numb.

But there was the baptismal font. "We must remember," Ragnild had told him, "she was baptized. We placed her in the Lord's hands then. She is safe now, forever in His bosom." Ragnild could say it so well, couldn't she? Under that elaborately carved cover was a basin for water. He remembered looking into it the day he and Ragnild, together with Peder and Anna, had stood there and seeing the drops fall off the minister's hand onto the head of that precious infant. The minister's voice had gone on, "Receive the sign of the Holy Cross... the power of His resurrection and the fellowship of His suffering." Suffering, who can understand it? Please, who can understand it?

And there had stood the Christmas tree, precarious with all its lighted candles, and his little girl had recited her Christmas piece. She had shouted at the top of her lungs because he had whispered to her to say it loud. "I'm just a little girl, I can't say much, but a Merry Christmas to you all!" Why that was two Christmases ago! Last Christmas she had crawled over the piano bench and chorded for herself what her mother had taught her, and sang "Silent Night." She had held a nickel, her offering, in the fist of her left hand as she played the bass note with her index finger. And only last Thursday she'd been a flower girl here at a wedding. It just couldn't be that this child of theirs was lifeless inside of that white coffin.

Lifeless: young shoulders cramped inside the satin-lined walls, eyes glued shut forever, and hands too heavy to grasp at anything again, but yet she was so much like his little Juliet—everyone thought it was appropriate for her to wear the flower-girl dress. Infection of the mastoid bone—drilled through bone—Henrik felt cold waves of pain. He drew a long breath of air into his lungs, but it was only stifling. There would be fresh air outside; he shifted in the pew and bumped Ragnild's shoulder. Pardon me.

In the midst of his restlessness Henrik was suddenly jarred by an unforeseen interruption. Rasmus Hegge was on his feet, moving out of the pew directly behind Henrik and out into the aisle.

"I am a new member of this family, as of last week, as you all remember, and I feel very close to them now in this hour of their bereavement. While sitting here, God's Spirit has moved me to say a few words. Dear friends, if the Lord is speaking to you in this hour of grief, harden not your hearts, accept her death as being His Holy Will and as a sign that we must repent of our foolish ways and yield to His wise authority. Surrender to him now, you that still haven't done so. Taste and see that the Lord is good. The Lord giveth and the Lord taketh away, blessed is the name of the Lord."

Julia was jolted out of her meditation. Quickly she turned and fixed her eyes on her new son-in-law. Not only she, but there was a sudden turning of heads, together as one, in the first two pews. Why does he think he needs to say anything, thought Julia, an intrusion, that's what it is! Henrik will be very offended; she dreaded what might come of it.

Again people gathered at the Kristian residence, not as many as at the wedding, perhaps, but all the close neighbors who through the years had come to love and respect Julia and Henrik, and, of course, his capable and lovely wife. Every family brought food of some kind. The pantry shelves were lined with cakes, some layer cakes with egg-white frosting covered with coconut, some loaf cakes with chocolate frosting as thick as fudge. Plates of *krumkake* and *rosettes* were there, too, and *lefse* rolled up in scrolls with brown sugar in between. Sandwiches were brought to the kitchen table; some had dried beef fillings, some cheese, others ham loaf, and still others a layer of canned salmon. Some women had made buns—nothing was too good for the Kristians—and had arranged them as open-face *smørbrød.* In the cellar, crowded on the butter shelf, were several bowls of red gelatine salad filled with sliced bananas and heaped with whipped cream.

"Dear me!" Ragnild stifled nervous laughter as she and Julia walked from their kitchen into their pantry. "Who's going to eat all this food?"

"I have no appetite either," said Julia, glancing around for fear they would be overheard. "People try so hard to be kind at a time like this. Certainly it is far too much."

"You ladies go into the sitting room. We are prepared to do the serving. The table is ready outside and there are so many here to help." Melva Veblen had suddenly arrived behind them; she put one arm around Ragnild and reached out her other hand to Julia. "We'll bring your plates of lunch. You don't have to come outside."

The two women did as they were told. It was best that way. The people could come through the house with their offerings of condolence. Sarah and Anna, having left their husbands outside with the menfolks, were already in the parlor. Emily was there, too, as lifeless as a Grecian statue. Soon plates of food were brought to the women; the servers wore sedate smiles and spoke warm words. Each bite chewed, became as a tasteless lump hard to swallow, and when the women returned to gather the plates, most of the food was left.

Soon Ragnild's tears were flowing as neighbor women embraced her. It just couldn't be helped when members of her own family came through, her mother and her three sisters. "You have another coming. Take comfort in that," one of them dared to whisper. Many had thought to say that, too, but had remained silent.

Finally as the friends and neighbors prepared to leave, the men also came through, most of them with awkward handshakes and eyes reluctant to look at tearful faces.

No one took food home. The women would come for their plates, pans, and bowls at some other time. It never entered their minds what the three of them would do with all the leftovers. Who would dream of taking anything back?

After the buggies had left, Henrik returned to the house looking for Ragnild. She was still in the parlor, surrounded by the rest of the family. Peder and Rasmus, too, had come seeking their wives. David sought out his mother, who was giving attention to Emily. Suddenly Henrik broke the unnatural silence.

"Rasmus, I wasn't going to say this to you in front of our friends, but now that we are here as a family I am going to speak."

Julia caught these words in her corner of the room and drew closer. David followed her while Emily hung back.

"You had no business getting up the way you did today. You preachers always think it is your prerogative to speak whatever the occasion. You say it is the Holy Spirit's promptings. I say poof, it is just arrogance."

"Please," spoke Anna, moving close enough to touch her brother's arm. "Don't say now what you will be sorry for."

"Anna!" Henrik's eyes flashed in her direction. "I am in my own house and it was my child we buried. I have every right to speak."

"Harden not your heart, Henrik. We have been praying that you would come to know the Lord." Rasmus said with the quality of persuasion he had spent years developing. "Anna, Sarah, and I are concerned for your soul's salvation. You have beautiful sisters praying for you."

Again Henrik's eyes flashed at Anna. So it had come to that, had it? Anna shrank back to Peder. Was it shame she felt or was it fear of Henrik's wrath? No one could be sure, not even she.

"How dare you imply that I am hardening my heart? What do you know about me, you who know too well that you are not to judge your fellowmen? You preachers wrap up everything so nicely for us that we don't need to think for ourselves. That's it, isn't it? You in your pompous judgment have the audacity to say that my child's death was God's will! That just shows how little you know about it. The child died because human life is fragile and subject to infection. Sickness and death are enemies, any fool should be able to see that!"

David left Julia's side and went nearer Ragnild. His mother could take care of herself.

"How God deals with his enemies is far beyond our understanding. Admit it, Rasmus, that you don't know anything. And please stop deciding for the rest of us!"

"I forgive you for your anger, Henrik. I will say no more." Rasmus linked his hands behind his back and rocked on his heels.

David drew Ragnild into the kitchen. "Don't let Henrik upset you, Ragnild. He's right, you know. When he gets it off his chest he'll calm down. He always does. Are you all right?"

"I'm fine, David. Thank you." replied Ragnild as she sank into a kitchen chair. It was good to get out of the parlor.

Julia followed. Henrik was right. Who dares to think he can explain the ways of the Lord? She remembered what Rev. Østen Hanson had told her years ago when she had thought she had an explanation for Anna's illness: Who are we to decide such things? Each day we trust that the sun will rise. He restrains the vast universe by His might. How we are led astray when we think we have answers! How puny are our human answers! Humility, that's what was lacking in her son-in-law. She wondered if he would ever change. Julia sat down beside Ragnild at the table. They both hoped the outbursts were over.

As suddenly as he had begun to speak, Henrik walked away. He climbed the stairs to the bedroom. Sooner than anyone had expected, he returned, having changed from his Sunday clothes to his overalls. He left the house without a word to anyone.

"It's too early to go for the cows," said Peder, bewildered. "We are all here to help him."

"He's still angry," cried Sarah anxiously.

"He's so touchy. I'm so sorry he had to attack you so," said Anna to her brother-in-law.

"He is very unyielding, God help him." Rasmus hadn't moved. He was still standing with his hands behind his back, staring above his newly acquired family to where the wall met the ceiling.

Sarah, in a state of agitation, went to the window and pushed aside the lace curtain. "He's going down in the pasture. He's carrying a gun! Dear God, what he might do to himself!"

Quickly Anna joined her sister at the window and verified what Sarah saw. "How sorry we must be for what we have done. We've provoked him!" She glanced at her brother-in-law, who still had his eyes on the ceiling.

Peder joined the women at the window.

"You must follow him," cried Sarah, looking at Peder. "Hurry, hurry!"

"Wait a minute, calm yourselves." David suddenly appeared in the doorway. "He's going to check his cornfield. He's had trouble with gophers."

"How can you be certain? I know my brother, too. He can become very angry." The pitch of Sarah's voice was rising.

"But he's over it now. Who can blame him for wanting to get out of the house?"

The lace curtain dropped back into place.

Henrik tramped along his familiar fence line. Praying for him! What was the matter with them? Or, what was the matter with him? This nagging had been going on ever since the revival of 1893! He remembered his friend Lars telling him he prayed for him to get on his feet and testify. He had forgiven Lars and accepted it as rather naive, but now, his sisters! Didn't they know him? He wasn't ready to forgive them, no Madam! The old familiar ache clutched at him, the strange return of an emotion surrounding an ominous doubt he thought he had resolved years ago.

A gopher stood tall beside his burrow. Pow! Henrik rushed forward; he must have gotten him. That should teach him to leave my corn alone, Henrik said to himself as he kicked the striped creature with his boot. He suddenly felt better.

He set his rifle carefully against a fence post and proceeded to bend his way through a barbed-wire fence. The corn he and Juliet had planted was coming up, all right, and the rest of his corn was looking good, almost as good as Hegvik's—it's amazing how much change comes with a day of hot sun.

Henrik was tired. He couldn't remember the last time he had felt this strange fatique in his legs. He sat down on the side of the plowed furrough edging his field. He rested his arms over his bent knees. How good it was to get out of the house away from—away from everything. The sun, which would ordinarily have made him drip with discomfort on this June day, warmed him against that strange chill which was a kind of pain. The smell of cultivated soil relieved his lungs of the stifling feeling he had carried around so long. A meadowlark lighted on a fence post near him and rent the veil of silence with brilliance that startled joy.

At his side was a wild rose bush still attempting to grow in spite of his attack on weeds. It had three blooms and several little buds still tightly bound. A bumble bee nursed at the center of the largest flower; a petal dropped to the ground. Having seen the roses, he became aware of their fragrance.

> As for man, his days are as grass,
> he flourishes like a flower of the field;
> for the wind passes over it, and it is gone
> and its place is known no more.

In the bib pocket of his overalls he found his watch. It was time to bring home the cows. He rose, slapped the dust off the back of his pants and slowly stooped through the fence back into the pasture. He saw his gun with the barrel pointing up, just as he had left it. Oh yes, he mustn't forget it here down in the field.

The cows saw him coming and began to let up eating the tender grass. They knew they were soon to drink of the water at the tank and then to enter the barn to be relieved of the milk in their heavy udders.

It had been more than half an hour since those at the house had heard the shot and there was no sign of him. Sarah tried hard to control her agitation by joining the women in the kitchen. David was in charge now, and he had decided that Henrik was entitled to be left alone. If he wanted to check his cornfield, he should be given that prerogative.

Later Julia had quietly disappeared and changed into her barn clothes. She was going out the door carrying a milk pail before anyone noticed her or realized what time it was getting to be.

"He's coming," she said, retracing her steps into the house. "He's bringing home the cows."

Chapter 6

Emily was on the train, returning home to Kenyon. It was the last thing she could have imagined, all by herself like this, occupying a red plush seat for two, no one speaking to her except the conductor to whom she had shown her ticket. She had started out without a suitcase; now she had a brand new one full of clothes she scarcely dared to claim: a frilly party dress, high-heeled pumps, a sheer black nightie with a matching negligee—and expensive pearls, too. They belonged to the coquette she had been for one elegant night; now she was Emily again, ordinary Emily, foster daughter of Mr. and Mrs. Peder Olson.

Outside the coach window the farms, fields, hills, and wooded ravines moved by at an unbelievable speed. The steel wheels beneath were rolling so fast she wasn't sure the engineer with all the levers he had to pull could slow them down, to say nothing of bringing them to a stop.

She wished Conrad Welch had let her stay and ride back with him in his Oakland automobile; that would have been ever so much nicer. But she must get back before she was missed by too many people, especially by her folks, who would certainly worry; Conrad had been right in saying that, but she couldn't help resenting him for it.

The whole thing got started back in the drugstore on the day Conrad Welch, the pharmacist, got his automobile, an Oakland, not a Ford—he could afford the best. Emily had teased him for a ride, and when she heard he was going to drive to Minneapolis on business, she begged to go along, nothing less.

Emily had been a salesgirl for the pharmacist for almost a year now, working after four o'clock and on Saturdays during the school year and regularly during the summer months. Not only was she quick and efficient, but she also had a friendly way with customers; Conrad Welch had discovered she was an asset to his business. But more than that, he had taken a romantic fancy to the girl—he, forty-one, married and the father of three children. It was an infatuation he allowed himself; nothing would come of it; no one need know; she was innocent, to be sure, but she was also astute and sly. And she was a little flirt. It flattered him that this alive little female could be taken into his arms.

The time and place for a rendezvous such as theirs was always a problem; it wasn't easy in a town such as Kenyon. The first time he had kissed her had been among the medicine bottles off limits to customers, but this was far too risky. Finally they decided on a place, an overhang on the steepest part of the Zumbro River bank as the stream approached the city park. She could reach this spot by pretending to walk out to see Adelaide Thompson, a girlfriend she often visited in the last house before the park. He could reach it by simply going out his back door and pretending to investigate a patch of herbs he was known to be growing near the water's edge. Considering how diligently Emily's parents kept track of her, it was even more difficult to settle on a time. Nevertheless, Emily would work it out with unbelievable stealth.

But riding with him to Minneapolis would indeed be a spectacle! In fun he had bantered with her about it, never dreaming she would work out such a thing. Her mother was spending a whole week with the Hegges at Kasson during a series of evangelistic tent meetings, and she wouldn't be home until Wednesday, or Tuesday at the very earliest. Her father was often out in the country these days, buying animals for slaughter and leaving Joe at the market to wait on customers. She would tell her father that Adelaide had invited her to stay overnight and as long as it took for Adelaide's parents to return from St. Paul, where they were visiting relatives. She would then walk her usual route beyond Adelaide's house and down the Helgeson Road, which was lined with trees, and descend well out of anyone's view. There he would have to pick her up. It would be a mile or two out of his way, but it could easily be done, getting onto the Minneapolis road without returning through town. Who would mind the store? That was his to figure out. Violet Arneson might do it; she had worked for him last winter. And why wasn't Emily on the job? She had asked for time off to visit her uncle in Wanamingo. It wasn't completely without loopholes, but it seemed safe enough if everyone stayed where he was supposed to be and didn't ask certain questions.

Thursday morning, supposedly before going to the drugstore, she, with her little crocheted bag, was leaving the house. "I'm going to Adelaide's now. I'll leave my things there this morning and will go directly there after work. Good-bye, Papa," she had said. "I'll be spending the day at the Kinseths, don't worry about me," Peder had replied.

They were pretty sure no one had seen her beside him in his grand automobile. It was early in the morning; the farmers were busy in their barns milking cows; and the meadows were deserted, too wet with dew to allow haying. One farmer, however, had caught sight of the oncoming automobile and came closer to the road for a look. Emily quickly dropped out of sight, hoping the man wouldn't compel Conrad to stop for a visit as farmers so often did. He didn't; the two men simply waved at each other. "Come on up. It is safe now," Conrad had said. She knew he didn't like this close call and hoped he wouldn't resent her for it.

By noon they had reached Minneapolis where the Oakland was no longer a novelty. There were more automobiles than Emily could count with horns blowing and engine motors roaring on every side. How frightening it must be for the horses drawing their wagons in the middle of it all! Emily had imagined tall buildings but hadn't quite considered them so close together. They walled away the sky.

Then Conrad had driven under a canopy, and, to her surprise, a black man in a red uniform opened the door for her. "This is Nicollet Hotel," Conrad said. "We'll get a room here." Then the Negro climbed into the car and drove away to what she imagined was like a carriage house.

"You poor little thing with nothing but the dress on your back!" said Conrad as she was walking around staring wide-eyed at the room they had acquired. "Now we must go out to the stores and get you some new clothes." He softened her embarrassment by taking her into his arms and kissing her.

That moment had been sweet. There was nothing to fear in far-off Minneapolis on the sixth floor high above the town. But now that she was being swept along over steel rails against her will, she was filled with remorse. Conrad had been decent and kind, it wasn't that, it was—it was being alone now. The red plush seat was too wide for one. And what if Mama were home? It was Monday, she could be. What if Papa had found out she wasn't at the drugstore? That could have happened, too; it was one of the chances they had had to take. She dreaded who might be meeting the incoming train. Crowds seldom gathered anymore, but there were always one or two people, and they might know her. She decided that she would not walk up main street, but go up the alley leading to her back door.

She wondered how long it would take to get to Kenyon. Going this fast, not long, but it was beginning to seem long; the moving panorama out there was becoming monotonous. She found herself staring at the curved ceiling of the coach. It had a kind of elegance, embossed designs, gilded borders. She remembered the high-ceilinged rooms of the Nicollet Hotel. She saw again the stage on which there had been a performance. A very black Negro had sat at the piano; he was not swaying with the phrasing as she was used to, but bouncing lightly up and down on the bench with the heel of his shoe keeping time at the pedal. She was hearing his music again as the wheels beneath her hit the evenly-spaced splicings on the rails. She could play that, sure she could! The chords weren't complicated; it was a matter of rhythm and coming on after the beat. You felt the beat first and then heard the note. How interesting! It had a carelessness about it she liked immensely. It scrambled, galloped, loped, and leaped. It told her not to worry about a thing. People had really clapped for him, too; she had seen him bow several times, smiling and showing a row of gleaming white teeth. The room had been dark and crowded, people laughing at the comedian whose jokes she only pretended to understand.

She had worn the frilly dress and the high-heeled pumps. "You look the part now, Honey," he had said at the big department store called Daytons, as she came out of the fitting room and stood before him. "You look older." He tilted his head. "You know what I mean, mature—grown-up. Honey, you look beautiful!" Honey, he had called her. You are beautiful, he had told her. But now it was all over. Oh yes, he would come back to the drugstore and she supposed she would be there as usual, but things would never be the same. No, she couldn't blame him; think of all the money he had spent on her, giving her anything she desired: French perfume, genuine pearls, and a gold bracelet. She couldn't believe how little they meant to her now, but she had to admit he had spent a lot of his money.

Sending her home alone, that was cruel!

"Kenyon!" the conductor called out as he came into the coach where Emily was. He stopped at her seat. "It'll be ten minutes, ma'am." At last!

Emily stepped down onto the rubber-padded foot rise the conductor set at her feet, then received the suitcase he handed her. She hadn't counted on the noises with which incoming locomotives announced their arrival, and now all these noises announced that she had returned home. She jumped as the belated emission of steam hissed forth a hot cloud. She didn't enter the depot. Instead she waited for the train to move on, freeing her to cross the tracks and to find her alley. She didn't think Emil Stromme, the depot agent, had seen her; he seemed preoccupied with express boxes coming through sliding doors way down the track.

She found the back door locked as she arrived panting on the landing. She hadn't stopped running; she had come across the tracks, three blocks, and gone up the long flight of stairs. She sat down for a moment on the top step. She supposed she would have to go down to the market and see if Papa was there. Mama wasn't home yet, thank goodness, otherwise this door wouldn't be locked.

"She's here, Peder. Emily is here!" called Joe to his partner in the back room.

"Hello, Joe," said Emily nonchalantly.

"Hello. What a scare you gave us all!" Joe glanced across the counter at her.

"A scare?"

"Why no one could find you. You have been lost, kidnapped, murdered—or something like that."

"Stop kidding, Joe. Where's Papa?"

"Emily!" Peder came around the counter and grasped both her hands. "Thank God you're back!"

"Back? Why—I've been—"

"Come, we'll go upstairs. Mama isn't home yet, but you and I must have a talk." Peder was nervous. Emily had never seen her father so nervous.

As they passed the mailbox at the bottom of the front steps, Peder remarked, "A letter came for you today."

"A letter?"

"From your sister, by the looks of it."

Emily ran up the steps ahead of him.

"Emily, read your letter while I make some coffee. Then I want to talk to you." Peder saw that she had already picked up the letter from the table in the foyer.

"She's coming to visit us, Papa. Amanda is coming to visit us!" Emily rushed into the kitchen.

"She is? When?" Peder rattled the stove plate as he poked up the heat for the coffee pot.

"Let's see. July 26—that's next week. Yipee!"

All was quiet again as Emily finished reading her letter. Peder sat down on a kitchen chair and waited. Finally, when he thought she had finished, he rose and went to find her. She was sprawled in the rocking chair, the letter still before her face. She sensed his footsteps and flopped her arms on the chair's high rests.

"Emily, I want you to tell me where you have been," Peder began with difficulty. He preferred to stand. He walked toward the window.

"Been?"

"The Thompsons weren't in St. Paul. Mrs. Thompson dropped by the market while shopping. And you haven't been at the drugstore either. Violet Arneson has been there since Thursday."

"All right. I've been in Minneapolis."

"Minneapolis? I want the truth, Emily." Peder's voice was devoid of threat. His words wanted to catch in his throat.

"I did go to Minneapolis. I went with Conrad Welch in his automobile. Did you know Conrad Welch is in love with me? Well, he is." She pulled forward in the chair and eyed her father. "You don't have to believe me if you don't want to, but it's true!"

Peder looked out the window without moving the lace curtain.

"Papa, he has taken me in his arms, he kisses me, he calls me 'honey' and tells me I'm beautiful!"

She looked at her father's motionless profile. She must make him turn around.

"We stayed in the biggest hotel in town. He took me through the big stores and he bought me three dresses and many other beautiful things. He took me out to entertainment and..."

He was turning around. "Emily, don't you realize he is a married man? He is not for you. You shouldn't have let him..."

"But we didn't commit adultery, Papa!"

Peder swung toward the window again. What was she saying now, this child? And she was about to cry. He knew so well that quality in her voice.

"Papa, I haven't been bad like you think. He wanted to see me dressed up nice. He wanted to see me wearing a black georgette nightgown. He stroked my hair, he kissed me over and over. He said he liked to touch my soft skin. But he left me when he said goodnight. He kept calling me his child, then, like he was putting me to bed. He had a room somewhere else. I didn't ask, and he always came back in the morning. He's kind, Papa. But I know it isn't right. I guess I'm a bad girl after all." She paused to expel a sob, and wipe out her eyes with her fists.

"I guess you know this shouldn't have happened." Peder came toward her, his voice so low she could scarcely hear him.

"Yes, Papa," she whimpered.

"You came back on the train?"

Emily nodded.

"Alone?"

"Yes. But please don't tell Mama any of this," Emily burst forth. "She doesn't need to know, does she? Please, Papa, don't tell anyone. Please?"

"There's no need for me to talk about it to anybody. If you want to tell Mama yourself, that's up to you."

"I'm such a bad girl. I make you so unhappy, Papa. I don't like to see you so unhappy. Forgive me, Papa."

"It's all right."

Suddenly Emily caught sight of the letter lying on the floor. "And don't tell Amanda what a bad girl I am, that I steal, that I tell lies, and now this. Oh, Papa, Amanda must never know this. She thinks I'm good. Please don't change her mind. Please?"

Emily fastened large eyes on her father now; she was indifferent to the tears that ran out of them.

"Don't call yourself bad. Don't say that. I don't think you're bad, neither does your mother. We try to help you learn, that's all."

"Thank you, Papa."

Peder felt her hot tears against his cheek as she embraced him. This poor child; who would ever have thought life could be so hard as it was for her!

"Papa, I'll never forget how good you are, never!" She clung to him a moment longer. "You're a saint. I'm calling you a saint!"

Now that Amanda was coming, Peder told Emily she must quit working at the drugstore and spend her time with her sister. Emily welcomed this suggestion; the anguish could now be forgotten.

The next noon, a day earlier than she was expected, Anna returned just as Peder and Emily sat down to their dinner. The anguish on her face startled them; the usual greeting upon returning after several days of separation was not forthcoming.

"I've heard such terrible things!" Anna took off her hat and stuck the long pin back into the straw fabric.

"Terrible things?" Emily whispered, her mouth dropping open.

"People are saying that Conrad Welch is unfaithful to his wife and it's all because of that Emily McCleary he has working for him in the store."

Peder got up from the table and drew out a chair for his wife. She was trembling.

"Who told you that?" Emily fixed a pair of frightened eyes on her mother.

"The Johnsons were at the tent meeting last evening. Mattie told me. She said it would be better to hear such bad news from a friend than to learn it from gossip."

"I'm not working at the drugstore anymore." Emily's voice had regained its composure. "I'm sure glad now that I am not, if that's what people are saying."

"Not working there? Then something has happened!"

"Don't disturb yourself, Anna," said her husband. "Emily got a letter from Amanda. She is coming here for a visit. Naturally Emily doesn't want to be working when she comes, and she needs time to get ready."

"Amanda is coming?" Anna repeated the words she heard, scarcely noticing what she was asking.

Peder nodded as she looked up at him.

"How can we go into the street—to church—to visit friends?" Anna's anguish continued.

The three of them sat motionless for a long stifling moment. Anna's words reverberated in that hot kitchen on second floor. It was becoming another sweltering July day.

"We'll just have to forget that, Anna," Peder said finally. "Gossip eventually goes away. It will this time, too."

Emily sent a grateful glance toward her father. She got up and filled a cup of coffee for her mother.

"Didn't you hear what we said?" Peder continued. "We have something else to think about now. Amanda is coming for a visit. We have a guest to prepare for."

Anna looked at Emily as she received the coffee cup. Emily was smiling; her sister was coming, that pen pal who had corresponded with her for so many years, and whom she had never seen. Anna drew the cup toward her.

"So you got a letter saying she is coming? When?"

"July 26. That's next Tuesday!" Emily sparkled. Her mother had shifted in her direction.

Peder picked up his fork and finished his dinner. He left the women at the table and returned downstairs to his meat cutting.

Emily's sister Amanda impressed Anna and Peder, to say the very least. What they had expected they couldn't quite say. Could there have been some mistake and this was someone else? When she stepped off the train, she greeted them in Norwegian.

Soon they learned that the family that had raised Amanda were Norwegians who had come to America on the same boat as the McClearys. And both families were headed for the West Coast. Although they couldn't understand each other very well, the two women befriended each other. When the Norwegian woman took sick and couldn't nurse her infant daughter, the McCleary woman fed a second baby along side her little Amanda. "I will repay you someday," the Norwegian woman had tried hard to make the Irish woman understand. "You have saved my child's life." When her Irish friend died five years later bringing Emily into the world, she kept her promise. She took the child, Amanda, into her home and raised her as a daughter.

Emily was destined to be raised by a stepmother. Since McCleary moved the family to the Midwest shortly after his second marriage, Amanda became separated from her own father and sister. All she knew was what she remembered, together with the kind things her Norwegian mother told her about her Irish mother. Then, when she was ten, she learned that her father was dead and that her stepmother had put five-year-old Emily into an orphanage at Owatonna, Minnesota. The correspondence from there gave word of Emily's new parents in Kenyon, Minnesota, and thus a lively pen-pal relationship began.

Emily had mixed feelings when she first saw her sister. She wasn't quite as Emily had imagined. She had neither brown, blonde nor red hair—she was somehow plain, not even looking like the pictures that had arrived in letters. Everybody likes her better than me, Emily thought to herself, as Amanda got along so famously with her parents. But this ugly feeling disappeared when she began to realize that this person with so much charm had come not to see her parents, but to visit her, and better yet, she was her real sister.

Soon her feelings became admiration. Emily studied her sister's face—could her own be like Amanda's? The eyes said so much; she guessed they were gray, but color didn't matter, it was the way they sent and received messages. They laughed together with her voice and her ready smile. They wept, too—not tears, that is, but they had a seriousness that came from deep inside. Emily hoped that her own eyes were like that. And Amanda's nose. Emily hadn't really noticed it at first, it was just small and ordinary, but soon it began to pronounce a kind of pride, especially when she tilted her head back. She did this when the two of them were silent together, during that pause before serious thoughts took words.

As Emily lifted her own head, she became astonished at herself in the presence of her sister. Never before has she known anyone with whom she could be truly serious, never before had she known the importance of her own thoughts. There was a hidden Emily that scarcely anyone but Amanda knew. How great it was to make such a discovery!

Peder watched with amazement the new Emily who began to appear as the sisters continued to be together. The child they had struggled to raise was maturing, getting a self-confidence of her own. Peder remembered his own youth; there had come a time when he knew he could handle himself even when it came to leaving home for a distant land. He was sure this new Emily wouldn't fall into the traps of folly that had been so prevalent in her life up to now; and it had been only a matter of weeks since she had sat like a child in the rocking chair telling about her trip to Minneapolis. Things work out, strange as it seems.

Anna saw another Emily, too. It was certainly an answer to prayer that Amanda should be such a good, capable girl and such a fine example for Emily. She hadn't dared to believe this could be true; she had been apprehensive of the older sister's arrival. Anna had not let herself imagine what this girl might be like, it may be too painful. Who could have thought the girl would be so sensible?

During the month-long visit, Anna wondered what the two sisters were talking about. They were always disappearing somewhere: into Emily's room, out of the kitchen and into the parlor, or out on the street shopping. She wasn't worried, only curious. She, too, was convinced that Emily was growing up and that Peder had been right all along—the girl was all right, she just needed to grow up. She only wished she didn't feel so left out around them. But she supposed that was the way it was when parents finally see their children as adults. She had been secretive with her own mother,too, not as secretive as Emily, perhaps, but secretive. She wondered now if Julia had felt left out; there must have been a time when she did.

On the day Amanda left, Anna wondered about that beautiful lady's suitcase. Where had Amanda gotten ahold of that? She hadn't had it when she came, Anna was sure of that; she must have bought it somewhere in Kenyon, but she couldn't imagine where. It had caught Anna's eye as it went into the train together with Amanda's old one. They were secretive, these two.

But the mystery was to be solved for Anna on the last day of August, a hot, humid morning, when she feared, as she had done all summer, that moths might be invading Emily's closet. Emily hated the smell of moth balls and wouldn't have them around. But neither did she remember to hang her woolen things out for airing, and she had such careless ways like leaving things folded for months in boxes. What moths couldn't be doing in that back closet on such a hot day!

"I'll hang those things out like you said, Mama." Emily, sensing what her mother was up to, stopped playing the piano and dashed to her room.

"And these things in boxes." Anna had slipped off the cover of a large, white box she had found on the closet shelf. "Silk, silk isn't safe either. Where in the world did you ever get this dress?"

"Amanda didn't want it."

"So she gave you such a dress?"

"No, Mama." The words came slowly, but Emily resolved quickly not to lie. "Conrad Welch bought it at Dayton's in Minneapolis. He gave it to me as a gift. I shouldn't have accepted it. But it's too late to return it now, since I don't work for him anymore."

Anna let go of the dress and it fell back into the box. Dear God! But she was convinced now that her daughter was telling the truth.

"The suitcase—that was a gift, too?"

"It was. And I gave it to Amanda. It made her happy. She had more things to take back with her than she brought. You know how that is."

Anna stared.

"And I won't ever wear that dress," Emily went on, wanting her mother to smile. "Maybe we can make it over into something. Wouldn't it make a beautiful waist?"

Anna nodded faintly; she had to admit it would. Then together they assessed the amount of material in the long, full skirt.

"And, Mama?"

Anna was still holding onto one end of the skirt. Finally she looked up. What else now, Emily?

"When I get to be eighteen and on my own, Amanda wants me to come and live with her. She says we could rent an apartment or something."

Anna dropped the dress. "You mean—move away? Papa and I, we'd be—"

"Not as if I'd never come back, of course." Emily hadn't counted on feeling sorry for her mother. "I'd come back as often as I could. And I'd write to you, you know that."

At this moment Anna's child slipped away altogether. Anna felt a flush of heat reddening on her neck and rising to her face. For years she'd tried to tell herself that she had a daughter, but Emily had never been her daughter. Now she was ready to go home. Home? Where? Anna didn't know. She only realized that it must be near someone Emily felt was her own, and this would be her sister. It wouldn't be right to object. One could only pray that all would be well.

Emily waited. Finally she understood that her mother would say no more. Again Emily would try to soothe those feelings she knew she had hurt.

"But I'm not eighteen yet. I don't know why I am talking like this."

Chapter 7

Four months after the loss of their little daughter, Ragnild and Henrik had a son, whom they named Henry after his father. He was a healthy baby, bringing comfort and healing to his parents even as Henrik had done thirty-eight years earlier to his distraught and melancholy mother. On this June day, in 1916, he was almost three years old, proving himself to be a bright child and adding words to his vocabulary every day.

And Henrik's crops were promising; it had been a congenial spring both for his small grain crop and his corn. He had just mowed the alfalfa and hoped by the signal the sunset gave that rain would not touch it until he could rake it together.

Although no one was busy in his own blacksmith shop now, there was activity in the other one still standing in the old town. Lars Mundahl was tinkering there. He had returned, the old boyhood friend of Henrik's who had gone up north to the Red River Valley to join his brother, Iver, years ago—was it twenty years? Lars had bought the old Tollefson house, too, deciding it was in better condition than his old boyhood home. Just why he had chosen to return wasn't clear; it wasn't that he hadn't been successful up north—he had plenty of money to fix up these old buildings. It must have been desire for family. Iver was married and had a family; Lars was not. When he settled in Old Wanamingo again, he took his mother into the newly remodeled house to keep it for him. Jenny, who had felt quite useless while living with her oldest son, was happy to return to the old neighborhood, back to Julia, the Veblen maiden ladies, and the familiar air.

Lars' return raised Henrik's spirits greatly; he had missed the fraternity of the town. The two general stores, which were no more, used to be lively with people more eager to talk than to get their supplies bought, and his father's blacksmith shop, it had been his nurture in childhood—how could he do without the fellows? And Arne—how many things had been clarified for Henrik in the exchanges with that old friend! How he missed them all! No wonder Lars' return was a boon!

It was not that his present mode of life failed to yield contentment—not at all. He was sure that no married couple could match them for sheer happiness and compatibility. Being a farmer had its tedious side, so many hours alone with field work and chores, but he had learned to fill them up by playing with the backlog of ideas from his reading. Speeches and poems which struck his fancy he had readily memorized. Now he recited them over and over again to imaginary audiences that loomed up over the backs of horses as he plowed, or in the vast corners of the barn loft as he pitched down hay for his cows. Not that he lived in fantasy all the time, he didn't. He took interest in his farm, growing crops gave him great satisfaction, as did tending his animals. He realized his limitations, too, his lack of interest in machinery and in weighing options when it came to investing his small returns. But he ambled along; he wasn't doing badly.

And he had become vitally aware of another issue besides women's suffrage and temperance: the plight of the farmer. His own struggle gave concrete evidence of what a farmer was up against in this country, and he combed with scrutiny all sources of information available to keep himself posted on this issue. He was convinced that agriculture was the basic industry, the ultimate source of all material good; even now the conflict in Europe proved that starvation is imminent when agriculture breaks down. But there were big businesses in this country thriving on agriculture, growing fat on profits from it, and robbing the farmer of his due. Government existed to see that justice was done, and, since the citizens were the government, the electorate must be enlightened. This was a great country with limitless resources, but there must be wisdom in handling them, otherwise ominous clouds were on the horizon. It was strange how Henrik's mind constantly took him out *there,* when at his feet were practical decisions to be made. Should he build a silo? Then he could keep more cows. That would mean enlarging his barn; that could be done. But there's where it broke down; he failed to envision it. Ragnild would help him with such decisions. Together they would succeed.

Having Lars as a neighbor had an added advantage: he owned an automobile. Now the two of them could go to town in the evenings after Henrik had finished his chores and Lars had hung away his tools. Lars had bought a Ford; he wasn't pretending to be swell, although Henrik knew he had enough money to own one of those bigger cars. Henrik might own a Ford, too, but he was not in a hurry, yet.

"So Henrik went to town again this evening," said Julia as she drew from her sewing basket the shiny ball needed for darning stockings. "Have you noticed how little he expects of us these days when it comes to talking politics?"

Ragnild had joined her mother-in-law at the kitchen table, where the two of them were tackling a basket of mending set between them. Lamplight wasn't the best for sewing, but June days were too filled with gardening, berry picking and helping with farm chores to ever get next to a pile of mending. Yet they mustn't get behind.

"It really has made a difference around here since Lars came back from up north," Julia went on. "And now that Lars has that car, it doesn't take long to get to town and back."

"No one discusses with Henrik the way you do. None of those men are that smart," replied Ragnild, licking the tip of her sewing thread before putting it through the needle's eye. "You're the most remarkable woman for knowing what's going on in the world. No wonder he is so convincing when he talks about women's suffrage, knowing his mother!"

"You're exaggerating."

"No, I'm not. Remember a year ago," Ragnild went on, "when he spoke at the Commercial Club banquet? Wasn't he good? There were all the elites of Wanamingo Village listening to him tell them why women should vote." She folded a shirt which had had a missing button. "I wish he'd run for the legislature. I think people would vote for him."

Julia nodded her agreement, but not quite sharing the enthusiasm of the young wife. Julia had wished this for years, but little ever came of her wishing.

"There is Ole Sagang, who campaigned for William E. Lee for governor, he's a farmer who got himself elected. Remember when we heard him in Zumbrota? He sounded just like Henrik, but Henrik could do better. He has a better command of English."

"I thought the same that day."

"Hasn't he ever thought about being elected to office?" Ragnild was now putting a patch on the knee of Henrik's overall. "Whenever I mention it he is evasive. He says he has a farm to take care of, a family to support; he can't just be running around the country."

"He will never leave this place. How could he go to St. Paul or even Red Wing and stay for weeks at a time? Henrik is that way, I don't know why. If you could change that I would certainly hand it to you." Julia rolled the darned sock together with its mate and put the pair alongside the folded shirt.

"I'm beginning to believe it too," sighed Ragnild. "For a long time I thought this was all foolishness."

"But he does a lot of good with his talent. Whatever he reads he tells to someone and there are many who listen to him. Why, even now, at Sjur's Cafe there's a crowd of men ordering doughnuts and coffee just to stay and listen. And he's not a rabble-rouser at all. They do well to listen to him."

"That's true." Ragnild was making a scraping sound with her thimble as she worked the needle through the heavy cloth.

"And all the temperance speeches he has made? Why, just see what progress is being made! Forty-three of Minnesota's counties are now dry. Soon prohibition will be statewide—than a national amendment!" Julia had another sock in her hand, but she finished what she had to say before searching for the hole to be darned.

Ragnild looked up to meet the eyes of her mother-in-law, who was so proud of her son. Ragnild smiled. She was proud, too.

"There will be a better world for your children, Ragnild." Julia now had yarn in her needle, ready to tackle the next hole. "Maybe young Henry will be the one to be elected to office. I wouldn't be a bit surprised. There is always hope come the next generation."

As Julia had assumed, Sjur had a full house in his little cafe this warm, June evening, but it wasn't coffee and doughnuts that were so much in demand as it was that beautiful treat none got at home—ice cream. And Sjur served it in generous glass bowls.

Sjur had furnished the town its restaurant from the beginning. He had had competition from time to time, but he always survived. He was short of stature, scarcely five feet tall, dwarfed and hunchbacked; no one knew what illness might have caused it, or if he had simply been born that way. But what may have been grotesque about him to an outsider never occured to any of the townspeople, least of all the children. Standing at their level, he was like no other adult. From his large hand, surprisingly larger than theirs, they would receive oversized ice cream cones if they were fortunate enough to have a nickel. He persuaded the women of the town to furnish him with homemade doughnuts and pies, for which he paid them generously with cash and compliments. And on evenings such as this he was the perfect host to the men who had gathered for the confabulation. Could an eighteenth century coffeehouse host have been more discerning and adroit than he? Even as he scooped deep into the bulk ice cream containers, filling the glass dishes, his mind was on what was being said. His imput was always forthcoming as if he hadn't more to do than his customers. He kept the discussion lively; the men argued and the listeners cheered on their favorite spokesman, but if the little restaurant owner sensed that insults were about to fly, he would change the subject so cunningly that scarcely a person knew that the conversation was taking a new turn. Little of stature he was, but there was a commanding strength in the set of his mouth, in the exaggerated length of his arms, and in the bigness of his hands and feet. Even his ears, somewhat too large, had a prestige about them.

"But now they are saying Wilson kept us out of war," said Sjur, placing two dishes of ice cream on the counter and picking up his customer's change.

"How can you argue with that, Henrik," said the editor of the village newspaper, a sparse man among these robust farmers, and a Democrat. "You know that the submarines have been quiet for quite a while now after the president served notice on them following the sinking of the *Sussex*."

"You think that is going to last?" said Henrik, straightening in his chair and looking from one face to another as if each was a part of an audience. "If Britain isn't persuaded to give up the blockade that is starving Europe, the submarines will soon be at work again. Consider for a moment: is death on a ship carrying war cargo any more inhumane than the starvation of Europe's children? What business have American citizens risking passage on such boats? I say the *Gore-McLemore Resolutions* should have been passed, keeping us out of the war zones."

"But we're not the ones at fault, Mr. Kristian," retorted the editor. "Germany is the one breaking the law of the high seas, not us. Why should we put restrictions on our citizen's rights to be where they please on our oceans?"

"Of course people don't rush into a burning house, but some are that foolish, as we have seen since the sinking of the *Lusitania,* and if they are that foolish, is it so unreasonable to pass a law that would save them from themselves, and the rest of us from being sucked into the war?"

"I believe you are right on that score," said Sjur, having come around the counter with a cup of coffee for himself. His clients were listening now; there would be a slack period before another round of refreshments.

"Of course. If Wilson was running a neutral course, why did William Jennings Bryan resign his post as Secretary of State, answer me that, Mr. Editor?"

"Bryan has proved himself a fool. He's no good to the party anymore." The editor's voice was as thin and pinched as his face.

"Most of us here think pretty highly of Bryan," put in the host. "Calling him a fool is uncalled for." A pause followed.

"No entangling alliances," Henrik began again. He was not aiming at the editor this time—Sjur had made him quiet for the moment—but at his audience. "Hasn't that been our policy in this country? Why get entangled with the quarrels of Europe that our fathers came here to get away from?"

"Henrik, recite the poem, you know, the poem!" Lars looked back at his fellows after his insistent words with Henrik.

Another spoke up. "Yes, the poem. We want to hear the poem!"

"It's not mine, you know," responded Henrik, injecting a bit of modesty. "Jens Grondahl, the editor of *Red Wing Republican,* wrote it. I found it on the front page of his paper some time ago."
"We know that. Let's hear it!" someone urged.
"With the editor's kind permission," said Henrik, looking over at his adversary.
"I won't dispute the sentiments of that poem," the editor sighed, as if he had heard the recitation a hundred times.

'Tis the madness of the monarchs
'neath whose lash the nations groan!
And humanity, obedient rushes on to slay its own—
Marches on, in servile millions, to appease the royal wrath
Oh, what a feast awaits the vultures in that dark and bloody path!

T'is the madness of the monarchs bound by some Satanic spell,
That invokes the help of Heaven to perform the deeds of hell—
That implores the Prince of Peace and cries, "Thy will be done, not mine,"
While the madness grasps the saber to destroy by "right divine."

From the funeral pyre of nations, from the drenched and reeking sod,
There shall rise the soul of freedom to proclaim "One King, one God;"
But the king no maddened monarch of the crowned and sceptered birth—
Nay, that king shall be the Manhood and Womanhood of Earth.

Then the weak and strong shall prosper and the warrior earn his bread,
For the sword shall turn to plowshare when the dynasties are dead;
Then the olive branch and dove of peace together shall be seen
On the coat-of-arms of nations that profess the Nazarene.

The audience cheered as Henrik relaxed back into his chair. They had cheered him before in this same reading. It was no less now. He looked over at Lars. The two friends smiled at each other.

"When do you think this will come about, what your poem so aptly predicts?" The editor was speaking. "When will the kings topple from their thrones and men and women of earth rule themselves?"

The men were quiet again. A legitimate question had been raised.

"That's hard to say." The host was the first to respond. "We never had any thrones to topple in this country. Most of us came here knowing this land had freedom. What about it, Henrik?"

"History will solve that for us if we live long enough."

"Might the thrones topple as a result of this war that is raging?" The thin voice seemed to have more depth. "If that's the case, maybe our aid is not altogether uncalled for."

"Those are cheap assumptions, Mr. Editor," replied Henrik. "Shipping arms must be one of our worst misdeeds."

"Wars of liberation are cruel wars, nobody denies that—our own revolution—our Civil War—"

"But how can we be sure that victory for either side would liberate Europe? I can't agree with you until I am assured of that."

"That is true."

A thoughtful hush fell over these citizens of the United States. Vague uncomfortable feelings began to stir. If only the election this fall could solve things. Every man would vote. Henrik would vote against Wilson; he had stated his reasons; the editor would vote for the President because he was a Democrat. What could a Charles Evans Hughes, the Republican candidate, do if he were elected? He was a respected man, there was no quesion about that since he wore the robe of the High Court. He must be discerning about justice, and justice would somehow bring peace.

On November 7, Wilson was re-elected. Submarine warfare was resumed in February; Henrik had been right, those deadly covert invaders of the sea were raising their ugly periscopes again. On April 6, the United States declared war on Germany with loud pronouncements that this was a war to end all war, the world would be made safe for democracy. Henrik could wish that this would be the doomsday for the monarchs of his poem, but he was far from sure. He was moved by the courageous vote of Wisconsin's Senator Robert M. LaFollette against United States' entry. Now the country was indeed entangled, the most one could hope for would be that the Allies wouldn't go beyond requiring of the United States money, munitions and ships. But scarcely a month had passed before Congress had put through a draft calling for all men between the ages of twenty-one and thirty to register for the military.

Wanamingo proudly contributed its share of able-bodied men to the United States Armed Forces and Henrik watched them go, each willing and loyal, each loving his country. David enlisted and became a commissioned officer in the Medical Corps. "If Selmer Veblen and others like him are going into the battle and getting wounded, I want to be there to help them," he had told Julia on his visit home before he left. By June troops were landing in Europe; it was all moving so quickly.

Soon a busyness settled over the populace. Liberty Bond rallies and solicitations were held, children saved their nickels for war stamps, women knit sweaters and stockings for soldiers, and farmers concentrated on their yields. There were evidences of shortages; many commodities were rationed. How was one to bake bread with these flour substitutes? But one must not complain when men were dying. Julia, however, was more disturbed over the treatment imposed on Germans in Minnesota: their loyalty was suspect, their group actions monitored. They were told they couldn't use their language even to worship God; they must use English. She sensed that foreign tongues of any kind were quickly dropping into disrepute; she spoke more often in English herself nowadays when she went anywhere. English was the language of this busy country and its fast-moving transactions, especially now. The old languages, if they remained at all, occurred where it didn't matter much: in conversations among the old, in memorized hymns and catechism, and in prayers to God.

Henrik's crops were good in the summer of 1918. The thought that the American farmer would feed Europe's needy gratified him. When one worked hard for a cause one would begin to believe in it more fervently. A victory for the Allies would mean that this country could share its abundant good, and yes—why not?—aid in self-determination for oppressed peoples. That was a beautiful word, self-determination. Maybe it could mean something if men died for it, if a war was won in its behalf.

Then on August 10, came the shocking news that Capt. David Ganz, Medical Corps, AEF, had died in action near an evacuation hospital during the battle of Chateau Thierry.

The telephone rang out in the kitchen of the Kristian home while Julia was knitting a sweater that she had promised the local Red Cross would be ready by the end of the week. Ragnild was pouring melted paraffin over several jars of raspberry jam. The two bells, side by side on the box attached to the wall, signaled the Kristian residence by a short and two long rings.

"There's a telegram here for Mrs. Kristian."

"Yes, I'm Mrs. Kristian."

"No, Ragnild, I mean for Julia," said the local operator.

"Yes, Nettie. I'll get her to the phone. Bestemor, it's for you."

"For me?" Juia disliked the instrument on the wall. She got up from her chair more slowly than usual and folded the sweater before she moved toward the phone. It was too high up for her; she had to stretch as best she could and put her head back to speak into the mouthpiece. At eighty-one, she was not as tall as she used to be.

"Hello," she hollered into the protruding mouthpiece. "Hello!"

"Hello, Julia?"

"Yes, this is Julia."
"There's a message here from the War Department."
"What, where?"
"The War Department."
"The war?"
"Yes, do you hear me now?"
"Yes, I hear."
"It's about David."
"David, you say?"
"Yes. The telegram says he was killed in action."
"He's dead?"
"Yes, Julia. I'm sorry to give you such bad news."

Julia said no more into the telephone. She caught the receiver back on its hook.

Ragnild, sensing something was wrong, reached out to her mother-in-law and guided her back to her chair.

"She said David is dead." Julia's voice was flat, no less unnatural than the loud one she had used into the phone.

"I'll go see if I can find Henry. He was playing just outside the door. I'll send him to fetch his father. Henrik may very well be on his way home from the field." She looked at the clock as she went out the door.

Julia sat in disbelief, looking at the box on the wall. That black piece of machinery called the receiver had told her David was dead. Yes, she had recognized Nettie's voice, but it was so far away, and she had been forced to holler.

Julia shifted her eyes to the folded sweater. It wasn't done yet; two rows were left when she was interrupted. How she had prayed that her boy would be safe! With each stitch that clicked along throughout the entire garment had trailed her prayer, not only with this sweater, many sweaters and stockings for the Red Cross full of her prayers.

"Dear God, what has happened?"

David is dead, the telegram said. He is dead. He became one of those who would die. She wondered how he could die in a hospital. That wasn't as dangerous a place to be as in the trenches. She wondered how it had happened. Was it instantaneous, or did he suffer a mortal wound? She saw again the ugly wound in her brother's shoulder, he, the Civil War soldier. How horrible, war!

"Papa's here, Bestemor," said little Henry in Norwegian as he led his father into the kitchen. "I got him for you."

"They told you David—" Henrik stammered as he walked toward his mother.

Julia nodded fiercely. Tears were breaking through her tightly closed eyelids. Henry retired into his mother's skirt; Bestemor was going to cry. Ragnild patted the little boy's back as she drew a handkerchief from her apron pocket to blow her nose.

"I'll go to town and find out exactly what the telegram said. Lars has his car outside." Henrik took refuge in immediate action.

Ragnild, as her eyes followed Henrik through the door, felt a familiar movement in her belly. Her third child was becoming active. David, that competent doctor, had been around to encourage her with her other two. *Dear David, you won't be with us this time—or ever again!* She sank into a chair beside Bestemor.

Five-year-old Henry slowly turned around and walked outside.

Chapter 8

While doing some last minute Christmas shopping, Anna saw it, just as she stepped out of Jorgenson's Dry Goods Store directly across the street from the meat market. It was a rectangular box the size of a coffin carried by four men, two in front and two behind, moving slowly up the long, outside stairway leading to her back door. The slant of the box startled her, as did the way it responded to the lift and pull of the bearers. In an unexplainable way, she knew what it felt like to be lifted and carried like that; it stemmed from an ancient place deep in her consciousness, as from a dream she had had a thousand times. After the lifting would come the long drop, down, down! Here it was again, that *dread*, that old, all-too-familiar dread! Extending from a red Christmas bow fastened to the slanting surface were two ribbons fluttering willy-nilly in the wind. They were wide ribbons, wide enough to extend from a floral casket spray with gold letters: our beloved father—or mother—or brother. She watched the box as it leveled on the landing, as it paused momentarily while the door was being opened, then finally as it disappeared inside.

"I'm sorry, Mrs. Olson, I didn't mean to bump into you. I guess I wasn't looking where I was going," said an acquaintance about to enter the store. "Merry Christmas to you."

"Thank you, same to you," nodded Anna, scarcely seeing who it was. The woman disappeared into the store.

Anna looked again at the long, open stairs going up along the brick wall of their meat market. So Peder had chosen a time when she was out of the house to have her Christmas present delivered. It was too large to gift-wrap, but the furniture store had tied it with a huge red ribbon. Peder must have been delighted.

Anna crossed the street. She became aware again that she was carrying parcels; she had them all. It was so easy to leave one behind somewhere. She stopped at her front door on Main Street; she never went up the back stairs in winter.

She had no sooner removed her overshoes and hung up her wraps in the foyer than she moved with deliberate speed into the dining room. Fiercely she set to work with the task at hand. She found her scissors, rustled red tissue paper across the table and unrolled yards of glittering green string for tying. She would make such a momentous activity out of wrapping Christmas gifts that it would drive away the dreadful fantasy. Assembling her articles, she adroitly avoided the back room, where she knew the retangular box had been left.

So Peder had bought her the cedar chest he had been talking about for so long. "The hope chest has never been big enough for all your beautiful things," he had said. "And the woolens are never safe there. I know how careful you are about moths. A cedar chest, Anna, that's what you must have." And now it had arrived, proudly donned with a bow. She wouldn't let on that she had seen it delivered; she would let him have the pleasure of leading her to the surprise.

Picturing to herself her husband's delight at indulging her, she grew full of self-reproach. Why was she always robbing herself—and yes, certainly him—of joy? She was letting her mind play tricks on her, ugly tricks. Or—could it be really be true *she was being stalked by something evil*? This had been going on most of her life. It was as if her fear had wary eyes which caught glimpses of the dreaded *thing* when she least expected it. She hurried into the bedroom with an armload of wrapped gifts thinking how unsettling it was never to learn. Nothing ever came of these glimpses; they invariably vanished before anything dreadful really happened. She pulled open a deep drawer and deposited her load. But the fears aways came *afresh*, even as the first time: that was the trouble. She must make herself to understand that there was no one. NO ONE! She closed the drawer with finality. And Christmas would soon be here!

This year for the holidays, Peder and Anna drove to Wanamingo in their new automobile, an Essex. Peder had had his car only since April, and it still amazed both of them how short a time it took to get to Anna's old home. Roads in winter normally would be impassable, but as yet no snow had arrived, just hard frost. The back seat of the sedan was loaded down with the contents from Anna's bottom drawer. In addition, Peder had for his little nephew Henry a wind-up train, the largest on the market, complete with miniature stations and dray wagons. He had bought it the first year Emily was gone, before the war and those shortages on the shelves. But Henry was too little then, Anna had told him; he must wait until the boy became at least five. Now Henry had just turned six; the time had come.

This year, in spite of being pregnant, Ragnild had spared nothing in her preparations for Christmas. She and Bestemor had accomplished all the intricate pastries, all the finished products of butchering, and made the rooms as sweet and clean as the freshly starched curtains. The tree stood in front of the kitchen's south window, the shiny balls catching the light of the winter sun. Long strands of strung popcorn draped its branches, and candles in clamp-on holders stood waiting on the boughs for the guarded moment when they would be lit. The kitchen range with its wood box close at hand was as much the center of attention as the tree. In its oven succulent spare-ribs, the choice part of the hog, were roasting together with rings of sausage seasoned according to Julia with a spice combination used in the family for years. The largest of the kettles stood in waiting prepared for boiling lutefisk, that special *Julaften* fish, the odor of which would announce that it was Christmas again. And the kitchen table had received another leaf, a fine linen tablecloth, and the best dishes drawn from the remotest corners of the buffet. The Bible lay at Bestemor's place; Henrik preferred to have his mother read the Christmas story and offer the family prayer.

No Christmas would be quite like this one for young Henry, for never again would he be six years old. His anticipation reached an unbearable pitch when the meal was over, as he waited for his mother, Tante and Bestemor to clear the table, wash and wipe the dishes, and finally scrub the numerous kettles. Would they ever get done? No presents could be opened until the cleanup had been completed. He had looked at the heap under the tree now, for what seemed like hours. There were all Tante's presents wrapped in red tissue paper; one box was extraordinarily big, and had his name on it. Then there was the package from Portland, Oregon, which the mailman had brought about a week ago. Since it had been around longer than the rest, his curiosity toward this box in brown mailing paper was the greatest.

"This will be the first one," said Henry, bringing it from under the tree to the table after the dishes had been cleared.

"You'll just have to wait," said his mother. "Don't touch anymore packages. Do you hear?"

"Do you know who sent that box?" Anna was quick to notice which package Henry had selected as number one.

"Cousin Emily."

"Do you remember her?"

"Nope."

"No? She had a lot of fun with you when you were little."

Henry sensed that Tante wanted him to remember, but he didn't. She looked sad. Quickly he ran to his toy box and took out a huge red and yellow top the size of a dinner plate and brought it to her. "See what she gave me last year."

But Tante had already turned away and was talking to Mama and Bestemor. "Of course he wouldn't remember her," she was saying. "This is the third Christmas since she left."

Mama and Bestemor looked as sad as Tante. Were they sorry, too, because he couldn't remember? When he finally got her attention, Tante nodded and smiled. Then he pumped the top vigorously, tighter than it had ever been wound, and let it scurry where it would across the kitchen floor. It swooped in among the women busy with the dishes and nearly tripped Bestemor.

"Please, Henry," said his mother, turning from the dishpan to look at him.

Finally the wet dishtowels were being hung on the line behind the stove. Henry ran to his father for the jackknife. It was time to undo the string around the package on the table.

For him there was a wind-up toy, a mounted clown who danced vigorously, tossing long arms and legs. He scarcely noticed what else came out of the box—ordinary things like aprons, socks and handkerchiefs— except for what Tante got: a box for jewelry, beautiful like his mother's china dishes, which played a little song when the cover was open.

"It's a sad little song, isn't it, Ragnild?" Tante said.

"I wouldn't say sad, exactly. It's lovely." Mama smiled.

Then came the moment when the big box with his name on it was opened, and from the red tissue wrapping emerged the train. Wasting no time, Uncle Peder drew him into the parlor where they dropped to the floor. The two of them put the pieces of the track together by inserting the pins of one into the holes of another. When all was assembled, the locomotive ready to pull the string of railroad cars, Henry called everyone in to see the magnificent toy in operation.

But the evening of enchantment was not over yet, even if all the presents under the tree had been opened. There was a knock on the door. Neighbors. Lars Mundahl and his mother had come. More presents? Jennie was carrying a wrapped box which she handed to Ragnild. "Some cookies," she said. Lars was taking his time fiddling with something big outside the door.

"Henry, maybe you can help me," he called.

A sled! A little bobsled just like his father's was out there, complete with a double-box painted green and trimmed with red! When the two finally got it over the threshold so the door could be closed against the cold, they all could see it was a sled that had been crafted in Lars' shop. Everyone was impressed. Papa and Uncle Peder inspected it with scrutiny, all the carefully forged iron pieces that held the whole thing together, and exclaimed about Lars' skill. "Have you ever seen the like?" they kept saying while Lars stood by and smiled.

"It's nice to have a small boy here in Old Wanamingo," said Jennie to Bestemor.

Peder and Anna stayed in Wanamingo for several days. During that time there was no need for the women to help with chores. The two men, such old friends, would have long intimate exchanges as they milked the cows, distributed hay, poured measures of ground corn, and cleaned the manure out of the gutters.

Henry was on hand, too, following the men around and helping when they would let him. He stayed until the cows had devoured the ground corn. He liked to watch their moist noses become covered with the coarse grain, which was licked off with long, thick tongues. Then he would disappear outside the barn, where he had parked his new sled. Already he had begun breaking a trail for himself encircling the farmyard. Around and around he went, carrying in the little double-box sticks of wood which in his imagination could be almost any kind of cargo he wanted them to be.

The third morning after the morning chores were nearly done, Henrik looked over at Peder as they were spreading straw for bedding under the cows. "You say you are not always feeling so well? Maybe you shouldn't be out here doing all this lifting."

"I have to get up many times at night, and I have pain sometimes, low down. Don't worry, Henrik, it's just that I'm getting older. I remember my father standing longer than the rest of us boys when we went outside before bedtime. You're ten years younger. Just wait, you'll feel quirks sometimes, too."

"I'm losing my teeth, Peder. It's no fun having them pulled, I'll tell you. Soon I'll have false teeth, but until then, I'll be grinning like an old man. Toothaches were becoming unbearable. I had to have something done."

Each cow had golden straw beneath her, and some had nestled in for the day. Henrik led the way to the house, carrying the cans of fresh milk while Peder followed with the empty milk pails and the strainer funnel.

These past few days Henrik had been watching Peder. For the first time he thought his brother-in-law was older. Although he had been painfully aware for some years now of his mother's aging, Henrik saw Peder as the first of his generation to grow old. But this fact robbed neither his mother nor Peder of the warmth they had always shown. Every moment while he was in the house now, Peder would be on his knees in the parlor beside the train and his delighted little nephew. They took up all the available space on the nine-by-twelve rug. The uncle winked at his nephew clicking the winder key; he smiled at the tongue protruding from the side of the little boy's mouth.

After the holidays were over, the pain in Peder's abdomen grew worse. When he could no longer conceal his distress from his wife, he consulted a doctor. He was told the problem was an enlargement of the prostate, a blockage of the urinary tract. Surgery was arranged immediately, and he was taken to the city hospital in Faribault.

Anna remained amazingly calm. She knew that Peder was, and always had been, strong, never sick a day in his life, and had overcome, long ago, whatever handicap his injured foot had inflicted on him. Besides this, his doctor was one to be relied upon. Dr. Adolph Hanson had earned an excellent reputation for himself as a surgeon, giving Faribault's hospital a good name. He was the grandson of the late Rev. Østen Hanson and known to the family. Anna secured lodging in a rooming house across the street from the hospital.

The day Peder underwent surgery was long and bleak with a blizzard raging outside. Anna kept herself busy. First she took care of her correspondence: a letter to Emily thanking her for the music box and Peder's monogrammed, linen handkerchiefs, another to Halvor, and finally one to the folks in Wanamingo. Then she took up her knitting, alternating it with reading. She had been told she could be with Peder when he was brought back to his room, and here she had began a long vigil. Nurses came and went; there was scarcely a moment when he was left unattended. Dr. Hanson stopped by with assuring words. "He was badly in need of this operation, Mrs. Olson," he said. "Now we must pray that he heals without infection." It was a long wait until Peder stirred after the ether, and after that, he kept falling back to sleep. Finally she was told she could go to her lodging for the night and return again in the morning. She crossed the street through gusting wind and whirling snow.

"Mail for Peder Olson," someone said, handing her a letter as she walked through the main lobby the next morning. It was from Emily, forwarded from Kenyon.

"Thank you."

She continued down the long, wide corridor. The smell of ether wafted her consciousness back to yesterday; this would be another day steeped in the inevitable odor of the hospital.

He smiled at her as she entered. He was himself again, her dear Peder; the gray pallor she had seen on his face yesterday had entirely disappeared. Instead he was bright-eyed and pink, not ruddy as usual, but that would surely come.

"You must be feeling good this morning," she said, moving rapidly toward the bed. She kissed his forehead and grasped his hand.

"I've had tea already," he said with enthusiasm. "The effect of the ether has left. What a relief."

"Do you feel pain?"

"No, not much. They give me medicine for pain. I really feel pretty good."

"A letter came from Emily this morning. Shall I read it to you?"

"She doesn't forget us, our dear Emily. Yes, please read it. But first take off your coat and stay awhile."

Surprised that she had to be told, Anna quickly removed her coat and hung it on a hanger in the corner. She peeled off her overshoes and set them directly under her coat. She pulled up a chair beside the bed, the letter in her hand.

> Dear Mother and Father,
>
> I was so glad to hear from you. When I have to wait for a letter I think you have forgotten me. Thanks a million times for your letter. Thank you, too, for the beautiful material you sent me for Christmas. It will surely make a lovely dress. Amanda has a pattern. She said she would help me sew it. Thank you, Papa, for the lovely stationery. It makes me think you really want me to keep writing. Oh Papa, you are such a dear!
>
> I'm sure you had a good Christmas with Uncle Henrik, Auntie Ragnild, and Bestemor. How I miss you all! Sometimes I wonder why I left you dear people. I was never a good girl. I am a good girl now, really I am. I didn't know how much I loved either of you until I had left. I have your picture right by my bed and I look at it every day. And I do go to church, Amanda and I always go. We never miss a Sunday.
>
> I have met a fellow who is ever so nice. His name is Chester Hale, and he has a band that plays entertainment in restaurants and hotels. He likes the way I play the piano and I have a part in his show. Now don't misunderstand—I am a proper girl and all that. He might be falling in love with me. And I do think he is awfully nice.
>
> I suppose Henry is quite a big boy by now. Did he enjoy the clown with the dangling arms? I thought it was cute. And Papa gave him a train? Dear Papa, how much he must have loved you for it!
>
> Oh I hope you are well, Mama and dear Papa! I don't want anything to change, I want to get back and see you soon. Oh, do take care of your health.
>
> Lots of love and hugs and kisses to you both,
>
> Emily

"She's like herself, isn't she, Anna?" said Peder, catching with the back of his hand a tear that rolled out of his eye.

"Yes, that she is," replied Anna, slowly putting the letter back into the envelope. What more was there to say? Soon she rose and put the letter away in her purse.

It was a good day full of assurances that things were going well. Peder received nourishment, smiled, and talked during his waking hours, and slept peacefully when he was told it was time to rest. He won the nurses; they couldn't do enough for him: baths, clean linen, back rubs, pillow fluffing, and fresh water. That smile of his had captivated them, too. While he slept, Anna took her meals. She crept back and forth in this spacious building as if she'd been here for a much longer time. Again she was told she should go back to her lodging. *"God Natt, sove bra kjære Anna,"* Peder said as she put on her coat and overshoes.

Five hours later, shortly after midnight, a knock on Anna's door aroused her from sleep. Wondering how long the knocking had been going on, she quickly drew on her robe and made her way to the door.

"Mrs. Olson, the hospital is calling for you." The landlady, a hefty, hale woman, stood in the dim light from a single bulb hanging at the end of the narrow hall.

"I'll get dressed right away. Thank you for calling me. Sorry you had to be awakened on my account."

"It's part of my job running a rooming house so near to the hospital. Don't fret about that. Dress warm. It is very cold outside—way below zero. I'll leave the light on in the anteway for you."

Anna struggled into her clothes. Garments tended to go on inside out or button out of line. How long it was taking her! At last she had pulled on her overshoes. She scarcely realized where she was going, or why, until she felt the frigid cold touch her face and saw the hospital across the street, looming larger than she had known it to be. The night was perfectly clear; the blizzard was over.

Having watched for her at the huge double doors, Dr. Hanson himself let her in.

"Mr. Olson has suffered a relapse. We're hoping for the best. He's fighting a flareup of infection and his temperature is rising." His voice was low. His family resemblance was more pronounced than ever to Anna at this moment, and she felt close to him.

"I'm glad you called for me. I want to be near him."

"I thought you would."

"Will he pull through?"

"That depends," he said, leading her down the hall toward Peder's room. "If his heart doesn't weaken. He seems to have a strong constitution."

"Yes, he does."

Anna saw immediately the change that had come over Peder; she didn't need to be told. It was distressing to see how his eyes tended to open, enough to show how they rolled in their sockets. The dream he was in tore at him with a covert kind of violence; Anna felt the tumult, too. She began to tremble. To relieve her shaking, she busied herself by removing all the winter wraps she had pulled on only minutes before. She found the chair she had occupied for the last two days, and composure gradually returned.

In the room the lights were turned down, coming strangely from spots low on the wall at the head of the bed. It made the faces of those who attended him graver than ever. The shadows of the two nurses who came and went made it seem as though a host of people were around. Anna wished for more light, but, of course, it was better for Peder this way.

"Could we bring you a cup of tea?" A nurse surprised Anna, who was quite sure no one knew she was around.

"Well yes, that might be very good," Anna replied after a short pause.

The tea was brought and she let herself become preoccupied drinking it. The hot cup warmed her fingers.

This was not the first time she had sat at Peder's bedside, although it certainly hadn't been often. She remembered the hotel in Kenyon, Dr. Grønvold coming and going as she kept vigil over Peder's injured foot. Infection. Peder had fought then and won; he would win again. Under the white bedclothes lay that foot, calloused and sinewy, evidence to his strength.

He loved life more than she; there had been so many things in which he had delighted throughout his lifetime. She tried to picture him as the small boy who thought he wanted to be a fisherman and go to the Lofoten Islands. It wasn't hard to picture; he still had that boyish enthusiasm, perhaps not as often nowadays, but certainly he hadn't lost it. Less than two weeks ago the toy train had been unwrapped and there was Peder setting it up and making it go. *P is for Peder.* There was that young man she had discovered at Melva's wedding, smiling at her across the church aisle. His smile. How she had responded to it through the years! That smile opened his world to her. Her beloved Peder! From her chair she tried to peer up at him on his elevated bed. She saw his receding hairline and the long sideburns, bushy in front of his ear. She decided that was enough to satisfy her for now. She would see his smile when the battle with fever was over, even as he had smiled when the effects of the ether had disappeared.

Then there was Herman Melville's *The Whale,* the story they had shared during courtship. He had been so intrigued by those awesome whales that couldn't be conquered, the dark mystery, as if it were not altogether impossible to get to understand them. Who can understand such tumult under the surface? There was an ocean under Peder now; he was being thrashed around in the waves. The white bed stood serene in the dim light—how deceptive!

A nurse came and checked his pulse. She hurried out. Before Anna expected it, three more nurses came. "We better call him," a voice spoke. The last to enter turned and left immediately.

Dr. Hanson seemed to appear out of nowhere. Wasn't he home asleep in his bed? Suddenly she felt the good doctor's hand on her shoulder.

"Come," he said, guiding her out into the corridor. "His condition is grave, Mrs. Olson. It's his heart. We've been hoping all night for a break in the fever. If his heart is weakening—"

"Is he dying?" Anna blurted. How awkwardly the words rose from her throat!

"It's extremely critical."

"You mean—"

"He's in God's hands, Mrs. Olson. That's all I can say to you."

Yes. *Kjære Gud, bevare oss!* Together they returned to the room. Anna was surprised to see traces of daylight around the edges of the drawn shade. She had been here all night. There was something calmer about him now, Anna thought, as she and Dr. Hanson stood looking at him. The eyelids no longer were agitated. They remained closed and serene, but he was pale, almost yellow.

"He may be conscious now," the doctor whispered.

"May I talk to him?"

"You may. I'll be right outside the door."

"Peder," she whispered as she bent near him and reached for his hand. "Peder, it's Anna. I'm with you Peder. I'm Anna."

She felt a slight pressure from the hand she was clasping. He'd heard!

"God is with you, Peder." She wanted to scream—don't leave me! Don't leave me! But she wouldn't disturb him now with such childish outcries. "Rest in the Savior's arms, Peder. It's Anna who is talking to you, your Anna."

She felt pressure again in the hand clasp. She heard a slight murmur. The jaw that had drooped under his open mouth rose to meet the upper lip. Anna bent closer, sensing he would speak. "*God natt*, Anna."

She had heard. Her name had been spoken. But it would not have been audible to anyone but her. A wave of pity for him touched her; he didn't know it was morning. The rising sun was sending a golden shaft into the room.

The hand grew lifeless. It frightened her. Dared she leave him to go for the doctor? Just then a nurse came. Quickly she returned and brought the doctor.

"He is gone, isn't he?" said Anna.

The doctor nodded.

During the extremely cold night which followed the long blizzard, Ragnild in Wanamingo had her baby, a girl. It hadn't been easy getting the doctor all the way from Zumbrota across the drifts. Henrik had gone with horse and cutter to a point in the road where the doctor could no longer travel by car. Bestemor had been up all night keeping the stoves going and giving comfort to her daughter-in-law. Bestemor had delivered babies, Ragnild knew, so if the doctor didn't arrive on time, they could work it out together. Just before the crucial moment, however, the two men walked in the door.

As the early morning sun was shining through the east window of the downstairs bedroom, Henry got his first look at his little sister. Bestemor had tied a large handkerchief over the tiny head; she wasn't sure if the room was warm enough. Henry looked into the little face under the kerchief. She was a tiny little old lady who looked like Bestemor.

"We'll call her Ann," said Ragnild. "Anna and Peder will be her godparents."

"She should be named for your mother," said Henrik. "You said yourself you liked the name Ellen."

"Henrik, listen. Poor Tante. I've been thinking about her all night. It's only right, isn't it, that one of our children should be her namesake?"

Chapter 9

If Anna had yielded to her emotions, she would have gotten rid of the cedar chest. It was the most painful object in her house, more painful, even, than the dining-room clock which had been the only thing audible as Anna began to stir in the haunted quiet of her rooms.

How the ticking clock mocked her! Time was no longer moving, only the clock said so, and worse, its striking the hours jarred the quiet Anna was struggling to establish in her soul. Each time it struck, it came as a piercing reminder that she was alive and that she must get on with the business of living. But, of course, she must get on with living. Resenting the clock wouldn't help; it was faithful to its duty, salutary. She would do well to profit by its discipline.

But the chest, no salutary value could come of it; it had provoked her fantasy, hidden in it was the troll, the incomprehensible dread that had lifted its ugly face. Sell it! Take it back to the furniture store! What a husband buys doesn't always suit his wife; that would be plausible enough. Don't be foolish! Such a beautiful chest, what she'd always wanted; besides, it was the last gift from her beloved husband! Anna clung to what she conceived as reasonable; she refused to give her fantasy any validity; she was a sensible person; just why her emotions played tricks on her she couldn't understand, but she knew how to apply common sense. She would deny the troll his existence. So the chest remained. She contiued to do what Peder had envisioned: storing all her fine needlework, gifts for others now, however, only waiting there for the appropriate occasion to be given away.

Even before Peder's burial, Anna's family had mapped out a plan for her. They couldn't conceive of her being alone for any length of time after Peder's death, at least not to begin with. For the remainder of the winter her mother would come and live with her. Julia somehow felt that Anna had wanted her ever since Emily left, but had hesitated then; she loved the farm too much. Besides, Ragnild and Henrik needed her to help with the children. And Peder took such good care of Anna; that had been so nicely settled long ago. But now things were certainly changed; she would hesitate no longer. Who wouldn't thrive in that beautiful home, always warm on the coldest winter nights, and all kinds of time for reading? Julia would read now to her heart's content; her hearing was bad now, but not her eyesight.

Then with the coming of summer Anna would visit her sister. The Hegges now lived in Fargo, North Dakota. They had two daughters, Mabel, almost five, and Dorothy, two. Anna, seeing Sarah's delight in this prospect, certainly couldn't refuse. Rasmus, an evangelist, was traveling so much, and Sarah, as long as the children were small, couldn't go with him.

After the winter, both Anna and her mother welcomed spring. Although they had many callers in their home together, and life could be lively at times, the days began to drag. Julia was no woman of leisure; Anna's mode of living was not hers, and she longed for her grandchildren and the activities of the farm. At last Henrik came for her in is new Ford, and Henry ran ahead of his father to greet her. It was April; she had insisted on returning home in time to plant her little garden in the "slough." Anna would be leaving for Fargo in another week, and she would be busy getting ready for her trip and could fare for herself. Friends would see her off on the train.

Rasmus had moved his family often, too often for Sarah to put down any kind of roots. They had lived longest in Kasson, but since then they had lived in Minneapolis, Fergus Falls, and now in Fargo, with a possibility of moving to Grand Forks. The Lutheran parishes in North Dakota welcomed Rev. Hegge and his "seasons of spiritual refreshing" since they were isolated in rural areas and several served by a single pastor who had difficulty reaching them all as travel was subject to the weather.

When Anna walked into her sister's house in Fargo, she found it unbelievably drab. She couldn't understand how this could be the home of a minister. Fresh wallpaper was long overdue and the carpet had certainly seen better days, but the drabness could not be attributed to careless housekeeping; even what was threadbare was clean. Anna, however, didn't occupy herself long wondering about it; this was Sarah's home.

"Welcome to our home," the evangelist said. "Who could we welcome more than Sarah's dear sister? You have borne up so well under affliction, Anna. The Lord loves those he scourges. What a beautiful Christian spirit you show."

"Thank you," said Anna, failing to be moved by his words. She didn't even wonder why; it was over when he released her hand.

Sarah had set the table with fine linen, beautiful dishes, and silverware—all wedding presents, as Anna remembered them—but the meal was frugal, very little butter for the beautiful homemade bread, small meat balls, dainty if there had been more than one for each after the head of the table got his share, and no frosting on the cake served for dessert with half a peach, fruit Sarah must have canned last summer.

"We've quit using cream in our coffee," Rasmus announced as Sarah brought the pretty china cups with the steaming liquid. "But I think you'll have to bring a little for our guest."

"Take some yourself. You always liked lots of cream just like father," exclaimed Anna when Sarah handed her the little cream pitcher that matched the cups.

"No, she quit cream long ago," broke in Rasmus, glancing first at his wife. "She's not on the farm anymore where cream is free and abundant."

"I believe I will," said Sarah, returning his glance with a touch of defiance. "Just for old time's sake."

Anna watched Sarah pour a generous amount into her coffee.

"Your next series of meetings, where will that be?" asked Anna at length, noticing that he had retreated somewhat.

"To Crosby, North Dakota."

"Quite far from here, isn't it?"

"Not so bad. I have a clergy pass on the trains, you know. It doesn't pay for me to own a car."

"In that case, I suppose it doesn't."

Anna was shown to a tiny room that had no closet. The bed, though the mattress sagged into the middle, was made up a with snow-white bedspread and embroidered pillow cases. Home-loomed scatter rugs, as bleached as the bedspread, lay across the once-painted, wide boards of the floor. Starched curtains made the single window a cheery one, and the neat towels hung above the wash stand completed the simple decor.

"I know this is not quite what you are used to," said Sarah, setting down Anna's suitcase. "But it's the best house Rasmus could find for us here in Fargo."

Anna didn't sleep much that first night. It wasn't the strange bed, although it was none too comfortable; it was the sadness she had seen, which Sarah wore as the lady of this house, and he a completely different sort of Rasmus who sat sullen at the table, a total absence of the usual charm he held out to the world. Could it be that he was a stingy husband? It was an appalling thought to be sure. Anna hadn't ever met such a man; such men had existed only in gossip, rumors, or hearsay. While helping with dishes, Anna noticed no larder; there was little in the pantry, certainly not what Sarah had been used to. She stingy with butter? It couldn't be believed! The little girls looked sad, too. Children who were that small should be happy and full of life. Sarah's weren't. Why? Tomorrow he would leave again. Maybe things were easier when he was gone. Never before had she felt sorry for her sister. Anna turned restlessly back and forth until morning.

On afternoons when Rasmus was away, Anna and Sarah frequently took the little girls for a walk. In the neighborhood was a little corner drugstore that had a soda fountain. Here Anna insisted on stopping and bought ice cream cones for everyone, and here they sat on wire-backed chairs around a little marble-topped table and ate quietly. The treat was preoccupying.

"Rasmus would say we are spoiling them," Sarah said the third time this happened.

"He needn't know," replied Anna. "Or if he should, I'm the aunt, and don't aunts have a right to spoil children?"

Sarah laughed quite naturally now.

One day they walked farther and came across a little millinery shop with a profusion of hats in the display window. The girls, running ahead of the two women, stopped to look.

"Let's go in," said Anna. "You always liked hat shops, Sarah."

Sarah hesitated, standing sober-faced before her sister. Finally Anna grabbed her by the arm.

"Do you still make your hats? You used to make some dandies. It won't hurt to look."

All the hats were on sale. Although Easter had passed, there were many to choose from. Before Sarah could comprehend what happened, Anna had outfitted the two little girls with wide-brimmed, soft straw hats, the crowns of which were circled with lavish ribbon. "Mother, too, must have a hat," insisted Anna, getting the happy, little creatures on her side.

"I have just the hat for you," said the saleslady, looking at Sarah. "I've been waiting for someone like you—stately. Do you know what I mean? You'll look like a duchess."

The curtain to the back room dropped for a moment, then came the hat carried high. The crown was soft with blue feathers—they must have been real peacock feathers—and the wide brim held in its circular crevice, pink flowers interlaced with more feathers. One feather reached over the rest toward the top, almost touching the crown.

Sarah smiled at herself in the mirror as she tilted her head adorned by the hat. With enchantment she reached up and touched the feathered crown.

"We'll take it," said Anna before Sarah would come out of her trance.

"Mama, how beautiful you are!" exclaimed Mabel. "Throw away your old hat. Burn it up in the stove!"

"Why, Mabel, how can you say such a thing?" A look came over Sarah which didn't become the hat.

"I'm sorry."

"We'll take the hat," repeated Anna.

They walked home with two hat boxes. In one were the two little-girl hats carefully guarded with generous folds of tissue paper; in the other the magnificent hat for a duchess.

After the girls were put to bed and the women found chairs in the parlor, Sarah sighed heavily and looked intently at her sister.

"He'll be very angry about the hats, Anna," she began. "Both the girls and I wanted Easter bonnets this year, but he said it was an extravagance. Last year's hat would do. He didn't seem to know I had worn mine for the last five years, changing it as best I could with scraps of ribbon. He'll be angry now, just you wait."

"I wouldn't have believed that. I always thought..."

"Everyone thinks he's wonderful, but they haven't seen him in his home. He's such a saintly, Christ-like man when he blesses little children out in the congregations, but he never notices his own, except to reprimand them."

Sarah's eyes were becoming moist and shiny. Anna was afraid there would be tears.

"You have good, little girls."

"I do, I know, and I am grateful. And they are both healthy. I had trouble bringing them into the world and I was fearful they might be sickly. The doctor told me I'd better not conceive again."

"You never wrote about that," said Anna in surprise.

"No. There was no need to worry you and mother." Seemingly unconfortable, Sarah got off the limp pillow deep in the armchair and moved to the organ stool. "There is so much I would like to do for them. How I could dress them up in pretty dresses! But he only says, 'Do you want to make our daughters vain?' And there is never enough money for anything. You see how it is. Scarcely enough food! It isn't that we are poor, Anna. It's simply that—" Sarah lowered her head and reached for the handkerchief in her apron pocket.

"Your house is spotless. I've never seen such snow-white dishtowels."

Sarah looked up and laughed a little. "It's a mania of mine, isn't it?"

" 'As white as Sarah's dishtowels,' has become a saying of mother's."

There was a pause. Sarah began twisting the corner of her handkerchief. "See this rug? We had a nice one, as you remember, in our home in Kasson. But when we moved to Minneapolis he sold it to a second-hand store in exchange for this one and all this delapidated furniture. I really don't know what's gotten into him."

"I would love to buy you a new rug. If I stay on here it is only right that I..."

"He'll soon be asking you for board and room."

Anna grew uncomfortable. Perhaps she shouldn't have come. Sarah had that look about her, too, that said so.

"That's not as unreasonable as it seems," said Anna without conviction. "You see I've never stayed away like this for any length of time, so it never entered my head..."

"Of course not, Anna. I'm so unhappy!"

Sarah broke down and sobbed.

Anna met with some success in standing up to her brother-in-law's anger over that hats.

"Why should you deny me the right to give my own sister and my two lovely nieces gifts? Perhaps we women do have little vanities, but of what harm is it if it brings a little joy? And giving makes me happy. It's a way to show love, don't forget that."

Rasmus retreated into silence. The issue wasn't resolved, of course, but Anna felt better.

The next move was a new parlor rug. Sarah didn't fear her husband's wrath as much this time since she was bolstered by her sister's presence. "She's more than paid for her keep," Sarah announced to her husband before he had a chance to bring to Anna the subject of board and room.

The old rug came apart when it was taken up. The rotten threads couldn't withstand the pull.

Henry was happy to have Bestemor back. Never before had she been away that long. Sometimes he had sat in the green, upholstered, rocking chair by the window, since it was always empty these days, but it only filled him with longing. Sometimes, as he sat, his mother would put baby Ann in his arms, especially after her bath. He tried to rock her the way Bestemor did, but he felt clumsy and was afraid he might drop her. And sometimes when out pulling his sled around the yard, he found himself singing one of her songs. Last fall he had discovered, coming home from school, how nice it was to find her there waiting for him with a big jelly sandwich and a glass of milk. Then she would sit down beside him at the table and listen to him. Talking to her meant shifting his words back into Norwegian, to translate the happenings in his world of English into her world. "The children must be taught to speak Norwegian. If we don't teach them, it will soon be forgotten," she had told his father with the authority of a parent. No, he wouldn't forget Norwegian; his grandmother put such value to it. Now that she was back, he could run home from school and find her there.

When summer vacation came, he never was far from all her outdoor activities. He would go with her to her little garden in the "slough" where the giant cottonwood tree stood. In his wagon he carried her tools. Sometimes the handle of the hoe became unwieldy, but he always managed. She told him how new plants would grow out of the eyes of cut-up potatoes which she buried in hills, and sure enough, it was true. She told him how little the cottonwood tree had been, that tree which stood tall in the middle of his father's oats field and near Bestemor's tiny garden. Yes, he believed her; he supposed it had been little once, but it was hard to imagine, just like so many things in her world.

Once, when she was planting flower seeds in a bed on the south side of the house she said, "See these stones? A house used to stand here. A shoemaker lived here. His name was Arne." "He made shoes?" the boy asked in surprise. "Yes, he cut them out of leather and sewed them together the way your mother sews shirts." How Henry would have loved to see that!

Another time, when they had gone to the mailbox, she had wanted him to cross the road with her. He loved the old blacksmith shop, but he couldn't quite understand why a lady would care about it. But, of course, this was his grandma. He ran ahead of her up to the anvil, that invincible rock of iron which couldn't be moved in a million years. He grabbed a sledge hammer and give the anvil two or three mighty blows. He loved the sound it made, and now he was showing off for Bestemor. "You must inherit that anvil," she said then. "I will speak to your father." He tried to imagine what he would do with an anvil, unless he set to work in an old shop like this, or like the one Lars Mundahl had. "Your grandfather was a tall man with dark hair and beard. He spent most of his life in this place. There was always a fire in the forge, and he was always fixing broken machinery. Every day our little town was full of farmers." This part of a town? And he had had a *bestefar*? It was hard to imagine. Nonetheless, she made him wish his bestefar were still here. That would be better, even, than visiting Lars, since the one he visited would be his very own grandfather.

On most days during the summer, Bestemor wanted to be the one to go to the pasture and bring home the cows. Henry resented this. It was his job. But his mother had told him, "We'll let Bestmor get the cows. She likes to do it. And don't tag along, she likes to go alone." He had felt left out. He watched her pull her walking stick from under the bench where the milk pails were turned over to dry; it was not a real cane but simply a two-foot-long branch stripped of its twigs. She always opened the gate; she never went over a fence the way he and his father did. He followed her with his eyes as she sank below the hill. He wondered why she wanted to get the cows and why she wanted to go alone. This he couldn't imagine; it was a complete mystery.

He liked to have Bestemor put him to bed. They were close to each other then, and he could look at her face for a long time. Those gray eyes had puffy wrinkles under them and often a redness around the lids, but they were her windows. One had to look into them to understand her, and with them she received him and cared about him. She pursed her lips often; she seemed to have more flesh than most people to purse them with, and that pursing always meant something; she seemed to be thinking then, or remembering, and he would wait, for soon she would tell him something. If she remained silent at such times, it was disappointing because what was there would remain a mystery forever, and her silences were frequent.

The Bible stories she told him were out of her world, too, and also hard to imagine. She would tell him that those stories came out of the Bible, that big, black book of hers which was terribly old, and although he could read a little English, those words were Norwegian and the letters hardly resembled the alphabet which he knew. Then they would say prayers. She always prayed for missionaries in countries far away. They were another thing in Bestemor's world who were hard to imagine, but he wished he could go to some far-away place and see one. Then she would sing the song about how angels watched over him while he slept. He knew he would never see them because, in order for them to be there, his eyes must be closed.

Thus two summers were spent.

The small boy would grow up, but never would this world of his grandmother be lost on him, and he had it all in the language of the land from which she had come. The mystery of that world trailed back into remote reaches where imagination would fail, but the reality of it all was there, and a nostalgia would seep into the emotions. It would be quite another world where he would live out his life; the language would be English in a country that was coming of age.

When the second summer came to a close and Bestemor was putting her things into the old, brown suitcase, Henry thought she looked sad. He knew better than to get in her way, so he went to the kitchen, where he found his father waiting to take her to Kenyon. The Ford was waiting outside. Finally she came and appeared to be ready.

"Here's your cup of coffee before you start out," said his mother.

"Mother, do you know your bank account is dwindling? I can't figure out where it is going, unless you are giving it all to missions," said his father, holding one of those little books from the bank.

When she didn't answer, his father closed the bank book and looked at Bestemor. He didn't know that she was sad already, and now he had made her cry.

Henry hurried to his grandmother's side. "I think it is good of Bestemor to give lots of money to missions," he said with conviction. He climbed into her lap.

This was the last time Bestemor was to be in her old home. In late November she took sick with a severe bladder ailment. The doctors suspected cancer, but the body of this woman of eighty-five was diagnosed too frail for an operation. She and Anna did not come to Old Wanamingo for Christmas; Henrik managed to come one day just before the new year, but he didn't bring either Ragnild or the children. Ragnild was expecting a baby some time in February and

Henrik thought it wisest not to take her out in the cold for such a long trip. Henry had wanted to come, but his father convinced him his mother needed him at home. On February 26, Ragnild had a baby boy. He was named Neil Peter, for his grandfather and his late uncle.

During her illness Julia said very little. Sometimes Anna suspected that her mother had pain, but she never heard about it. At other times a mysterious calm came over the sick woman. Certainly she didn't feel pain then. Until early April she managed to sit up for short periods during the day, and it always had to be by a window. She held her head up then, for long moments, and looked into the sky. Rev. Okerlund came frequently and together the three of them took Communion. At times her mother's silence distressed Anna, but there was always that terse *"Takk"* coming from her which could only mean love and sincere gratitude toward the one caring for her. Nothing trivial interested her. She showed no interest in Anna's knitting or crocheting. She was courteous to callers, but she never mentioned them after they had left. She nodded when Anna opened her mail and read cards and letters to her. Only one thing she wanted and that was to see her new grandson.

Traveling with a tiny baby was too hazardous to be risked. March had one snowstorm after the other and no automobiles attempted the roads; the farmers all reverted to sleighs. It wasn't until the first week in April that Henrik and Ragnild arrived with their children, and only after the Ford had gone through miles of slippery mud, ugly, deep ruts, and awkward detours.

The family gathered around the woman in the chair by the window.

"Your grandson," said Ragnild unwrapping her bundle and uncovering a tiny face. She put the child on Bestemor's lap. "His name is Neil. He's named for Nils."

While watching this, Anna whispered to Henrik. "She's weak. She may not be able to sit up much longer. Yesterday she was in bed all day. Today she insisted on getting up after you called and said you were coming."

Not far from his father and his aunt was Henry, whispering to his little sister. "She's Bestemor. Say Bestemor."

"Bestemor."

"That's right. Bestemor." For his sister's benefit he pointed at the woman in the chair.

Ragnild picked up her son who was beginning to squirm. She acknowledged Bestemor's smile. There was no need of words.

As his mother lifted Neil away, Henrik saw his chance. Leading his little sister by the hand, he approached his grandmother.

"Bestemor, *vi har kommet.*"

"Bestemor," said two-year-old Ann, pointing as her brother had taught her.

"You remember your grandma?" The voice was husky.

Henry nodded, and his little sister nodded.

"Your grandma has been longing for you. Come."

The two children drew closer. Henry felt her tired hand on his shoulder. He looked steadily into her eyes; he knew her, all right. She patted his cheek and he patted hers. Ann learned the ritual quickly and knew what to do when it was her turn.

This was the last day Julia ever sat up in a chair. On the morning of April 22, when she most likely would have been hoeing open her potato hills, if it had been as other years, she died. She had been given Communion the previous evening. Words from the Lord's Supper trailed across her lips in the hour of her death. *"Jesu blod."*

Chapter 10

When Sarah received the telegram at her Grand Forks home telling that her mother had died, her husband was as far away as the West Coast. The prospect of seeing her family again took precedence over the grief she felt through the loss of her mother. Now she had reason to leave Grand Forks, at least for a while, and she would make it a long while, for a visit with Anna and the dear folks at Old Wanamingo. She sent a return telegram immediately, saying she was arriving by train with her two girls. Rasmus was somewhere in the state of Washington. She stuffed two old suitcases, not debating long what to take and what not to take. She decided against taking a hat box; they would wear the hats bought two summers ago in Fargo. Maybe she could get some sewing done at Anna's; there might be garments there to be made over for her girls.

Sarah was pregnant. She suspected she was now in her fifth month, but she couldn't be sure. In her letters to Rasmus she had withheld this rather distressing news for some time—why should she worry him? Finally she decided that if anything happened to her it would be worse for him if he didn't know. To tell the truth, she was surrendering to a feeling of loneliness and need for her man to share the responsibility of their children. Certainly there couldn't be anything wrong with that! In his reply he scarcely expressed joy over the prospect—he might well have, he always wanted a boy—but said rather that he would pray an additional petition in her behalf, and she shouldn't worry since everything was in God's hands.

Henrik and Anna met their sister at the platform outside the depot. Henrik scarcely recognized his sister as she stepped out of the train. Maybe his immediate grief clouded his eyes, but he thought she was older; she looked tired and certainly sad. And he wished she weren't wearing such a ridiculous hat! Anna immediately recognized her sister's condition, although Sarah's figure scarcely showed it. What was not supposed to happen evidently had, but then Anna could be wrong. Let's hope so! Mabel was taller than Anna expected her to be, but, of course, she was seven years old now. Dorothy's hug was warm and refreshing; Anna hadn't counted on this kind of joy, not at this time.

"She will be buried tomorrow," began Henrik. "You're the farthest away. Uncle John is coming from Red Wing, otherwise all those attending the funeral are from around here."

Her brother's words brought to Sarah the sudden realization of why she had come, and she felt herself trembling as she followed him toward the car.

"She passed away so peacefuly, Sarah," Anna was saying as she led Dorothy by the hand. "She was ready to meet her Lord. During her last days I could see how she was waiting, how she longed to go."

Sarah saw Mabel up ahead, slowly following Uncle Henrik; she felt an impulse to catch up with her and put an arm around her, the child who had grown tall so suddenly, who looked awkward and desolate.

"I wish my girls could have known their *bestemor* better. That's what comes of always having to be so far away," Sarah said to Anna as she watched Henrik direct her daughter into the back seat of his touring car.

"The roads are greatly improved. You should have seen them earlier this month. I left the side curtains on. The air is a bit chilly yet. We don't want to catch cold." Henrik was being talkative while the rest climbed into the car.

The women were glad for the side curtains. The isinglass windows were sufficient; they really didn't want to be seen.

The earth was turning green again on the day Julia Kristian was buried, and everywhere there was evidence of stirring growth. The small grain was up, violets and blood roots were blooming along lanes and under hedges, and even the soil heaped on the side of the open grave was fragrant with nourishment for new life.

Standing beside his cousin Mabel and surrounded by his family at the gravesite, Henry quite understood what there was to understand about death and burial, albeit this was his grandma who was being put away. As far as he was concerned, his *bestemor* had left; it was hard to imagine but was not unlike so many questions that have no answers. The old lady he had seen in the coffin was supposed to be his grandmother, but he didn't recognize her; he saw a stranger. If he couldn't look into her gray eyes, it was impossible to know her, and the mouth was not pursed, but flat, making a long straight line. Now everyone stood looking at that coffin. Soon they all would be going home; funerals were almost over when the people were out by the grave. He would be glad when the people started moving. His house would be full of company for a while, and Mabel would be around for a few more days. He glanced at his cousin. She wasn't very much fun, but she might cheer up when they got home and feel like playing with him.

Now that their mother was buried and life should be settling down, Henrik saw that his sisters were in no hurry to depart. One day after another they moved around in his house, the two of them, talking in monotonous voices about this and that; it was almost eerie, as if they were searching for the folks who were not around anymore. Invoking ghosts, that's what they were doing—why couldn't they let the dead rest in peace? Why couldn't Anna and Sarah be enjoyed like normal guests? He supposed he missed Peder; a visit from Anna was not the same without him. He wanted a man around. Henrik despised women prattle, and he was getting more irritable by the day.

He wanted badly to get on with his corn planting. He was increasing his acreage this year because by fall he would have the new silo ready to fill. The building plans, which included an extension on the barn for additional cows, had been delayed by the war, and it wasn't until now that they could see it clear. No, his sisters weren't delaying him exactly. He went out in the field every day trying to ignore them. But each day he wished he could crank the Ford and get rid of them. Were things different when his mother was around? He thought so, but of one thing he was sure: his sisters really irked him. And Sarah's poor little girls; he knew he should give them more attention, but the mood seldom struck him now, to spoof around with them as he could so readily do with children.

The only thing that gave him comfort was his new windmill. It whirled in the brisk, spring wind, drawing the well rod up and down in persistent rhythm. Fresh water gushed forth for cooling the milk and watering the stock. Fresh water, lots of it! He could see his windmill from any of his fields; he could hear its rhythm around any of his buildings. It soothed his soul.

"There are things your sisters are talking about that you should know," said Ragnild one morning as she slipped in to milk the cow alongside the one Henrik was already milking. "It's women talk, Henrik, you know... things that could be embarrassing to talk about in front of a man."

"How's that?" He was eager for her next words, but the noise of the first squirts of milk into her pail was interfering.

"Sarah isn't well, Henrik."

"You say she's not well? She is thin and pale."

"She's five months along."

"That could explain it."

"The doctor said after Dorothy was born that she shouldn't have any more."

"Rasmus came home once too often, is that it?"

"That's another thing. Rasmus should come home. Soon it will be her time. He shouldn't be away, especially since things may not be exactly normal."

"Satanskap!" Henrik got a cow tail in his face.

"They're afraid to talk about Rasmus in front of you, too, because they know you don't approve of him."

"That's a new one!"

"Your sister is suffering on account of that man. She needs your sympathy."

"So?"

"Neither of your sisters has her man, you know that. They need you, Henrik. They are trying to make plans, and they don't want to carry them out unless you agree."

Henrik said no more. He had finished his last cow. He stood up and tossed his milk stool into its place in the corner.

Ragnild hadn't expected an audible response from her husband, but by his behavior she knew she had troubled his conscience, reached him.

Plans for Sarah began to take shape. Although there were few words between the two sisters and their brother, because of Ragnild's go-between, they began to feel they had his tolerance, if not his sympathy, and that was important. Sarah and her girls would stay with Anna at her home in Kenyon until the child was born. They hoped Rasmus would return in the meantime. It would be unthinkable to send her alone on the train all the way back to Grand Forks.

After Henrik took his sisters to Kenyon, things began settling down. He got his corn in while watching the beginnings of a heavy yield of alfalfa in his hayfield. Before long he would by haying. Ragnild nursed her infant, took care of her family, and helped with the morning and evening chores. Henry was capable now of small chores, but more important was the reliability with which he watched Neil and Ann, freeing his mother to do her tasks. He wasn't a bit sorry to see Mabel and Dorothy leave.

Sarah found Anna's closets to be treasure houses of little-worn clothing. With zeal she set to work at the sewing machine making over garments into wardrobes for her two girls. And, further, Anna insisted on buying soft, new flannel for the baby layette.

Letters were mailed and letters were received. Anna finally returned to her correspondence, which she had neglected for some time. There was so much to write about, so much had happened. She got a letter from Halvor saying that he would be coming back to Minnesota in mid-September, and he hoped he could visit friends around Kenyon then. Rasmus said nothing in his letters about returning. He was having a "blessed time." The Lord was "working mightily" among the folks on the Pacific coast. Sarah was content; she didn't particularily care if he didn't come, since she was comfortable with Anna. He would only worry her.

And Sarah had seen a doctor. Anna had finally persuaded her to do so, although Sarah had seemed reluctant. Either she feared the worst, or was resigned that all would be well; Anna couldn't tell. The doctor prescribed pills to build up her health, told her to lie down and rest every day, and cautioned her against heavy exertion.

Both women were diligent about following the doctor's orders. Anna saw to it that the pills were never forgotten and that rest time would be undisturbed. But, for all of that, on July fourth, just as the four of them were ready to go down into the street to watch the Independence Day parade, Sarah was struck with labor pains.

"You go. I'll be all right. It isn't time yet. It's a false alarm, maybe." Sarah looked at Mabel and Dorothy, then at Anna.

"I'll leave the girls with Mrs. Harstad. She said she was coming to watch the parade out here in front of the meat market. I'll come back as soon as I can," said Anna, moving toward the front door with the two girls.

It was a hard day and a harder night. The child was coming; there was no question about that. The doctor was called immediately when Anna returned. He came and went, always saying, "It will be some time yet." Anna got in touch with Mrs. Harstad again and made arrangements for the girls to be away for the night and the next day, sending their nightgowns and toothbrushes. Finally the doctor brought a midwife, whom he often engaged for just such times, to sit with Sarah to help her cope with the rhythm of her labor. As the hours dragged on, Anna became more and more horrified by her sister's screams of pain. Always there was the hope that this would finally be the last one, but not yet. Anna had decided she wouldn't call the Wanamingo folks until the child was born, but she was having serious misgivings now; she wished Ragnild were here. Finally there was a change. Anna heard an infant cry; it seemed unreal. She slipped into the bedroom and stood in a corner. A little girl, a month premature. Anna saw that Sarah was exhausted. The doctor was working with her now, quite oblivious of the newborn, whom he had handed to the mid-wife. He kept using his stethoscope. Anna's feet became glued to the floor; to move would have been an impossibility. Sarah was dying. Anna could see she wasn't going to pull through! *Dear God, in your mercy, help us!*

The doctor withdrew the stethoscope and put it slowly into his pocket. He walked toward Anna.

"What we feared has happened. It was too much for her."

"She is dead?" Anna whispered, knowing what the answer would be.

The doctor nodded.

"We must see to the child. She has a chance, I think." The doctor was talking as much to himself as to the two women with him. "If we could find a woman who is nursing a child, that, of course, would be the very best, otherwise..."

"I know someone," said Anna quickly. "My sister-in-law. Her child is four months now. She always has enough."

"She must get here before too long," said the doctor, glancing toward the midwife, who was wrapping the newborn.

Anna hurried out to the telephone. Yes. Ragnild would drop everything and come. Lars Mundahl would bring her; Henrik was out in the field. She would send Henry to tell his father where she had gone, and she would take Neil and leave Ann with Josie and Emma Veblen.

"She'll be here in less than an hour," announced Anna to the doctor and the midwife, who had moved into the kitchen.

They had closed the bedroom door. It looked awkward that way; Anna always kept it open. Anna opened that door and stole inside. They had drawn the sheet over Sarah's face. Anna lifted it carefully. There was no screaming now, no screaming. Yet in Anna's ears those agonizing sounds were still so immediate and so audible. The only evidence of Sarah's late agony was her rumpled, tangled hair, damp at the temples. Anna stroked that thick, brown hair, which once had made her sister look like a queen.

"Your baby will live, Sarah. Ragnild is on her way."

Anna lowered the sheet as respectfully as she had lifted it and returned to the kitchen.

"Could we move into the front bedroom? There are plenty more diapers, blankets and kimomos there," said Anna, scarcely daring to look at the infant who was now in her basket. There were other things to attend to.

In response to another of Anna's telephone calls, the Kenyon funeral director came for the body. Anna met two men at the back stairs and let them in. She pointed at the closed bedroom door.

No sooner had she done this than Ragnild and Lars were at the front door. She ran down the long stairs to welcome them. Lars, the good escort, nodded and left.

"How good of you, Ragnild, how good of you!" exclaimed Anna, embracing her sister-in-law. "Let me take Neil. The doctor is waiting in the front bedroom."

"The child is doing fine," the doctor told Ragnild as she joined him near the basket. "She has a healthy heartbeat and fully developed lungs, even though she came some weeks early. I don't think she will have trouble sucking. It's no hurry now that you're here. Have a cup of tea and relax a bit."

Having seen to it that the infant was taking food, the doctor and the midwife went, leaving Ragnild alone. What a tiny little thing, scarcely five pounds! But she was alive and hungry, and she knew how to get what she needed. Ragnild marveled. She had thought of weaning Neil some time ago; how glad she was now that she hadn't! She had heard of nursing mothers feeding a child other than their own, but she never dreamed it would happen to her. Sarah's baby would live! That Sarah had died a tragic death hadn't yet broken in on Ragnild, but it would, and in its wake would come the overwhelming satisfaction that she, of all people, was the one who could nourish the life for whom Sarah had given hers.

When Henrik arrived the same evening, Anna was relieved she had her brother to consult with. She had already telegraphed Rasmus by using the address she had found on his last letter to his wife.

"What a man! See how he takes care of his family! That's one for you," Henrik lashed out at Anna as they sat eyeing each other across the kitchen table. "I always knew he was no good."

"Please, Henrik, don't let Ragnild hear you. She mustn't be upset." Anna's voice was surprisingly firm. "And what good does it do to complain about him now? He is the husband, that we can't change."

"We'll plan for a burial at Aspelund, that's what I say. Why wait for him to make any kind of arrangements? We've waited for him too long already."

"I've thought the same. This is the only home she has known."

"That's right."

"I needed to hear you say it. I'm glad we agree."

Four days later Rasmus arrived. He was met at the train station by his daughters and their uncle. He fell into the plans that had been made for him, offering no objections or suggestions. His little girls responded to his coming with sober faces; he was an awesome stranger. If there were to be any comfort to be found for Sarah's little ones, it was not forthcoming from their father; they leaned against the shoulders of their two aunts, Anna and Ragnild. Henrik sheltered them, too. It pained him to see them, one on each side of Rasmus Hegge, as they walked behind the coffin of their mother. At that moment he resolved that when this was over, he would take them both on his lap. Whether it was before or after the funeral, Rasmus seldom spoke, and little was said to him. Anna waited to learn what his wishes were regarding the girls; finally he asked, "Will you take care of them until I can make other arrangements?" Anna had simply nodded.

Since Rasmus didn't bring it up, Ragnild did. "Won't you baptize the child before you leave?" He consented. This seemed to bring him back somewhat, and he immediately assumed his role with his usual demeanor. As the family stood around the library table in the parlor, he began by speaking the usual, "What will the name be?" while he poured water from the porcelain pitcher into the washbowl. Ragnild looked from one to another before answering. "Ruth Louise." It was the name they had chosen for Neil in the event that he had been a girl. The little ceremony concluded with a prayer, bringing the long day to a close. Tomorrow would be another day, and he would be gone.

> Dear God in heaven, may this child which Thou hast received in Holy Baptism always remain in her baptismal covenant. May we all present here renounce anew the devil and all his works and all his ways.

Henrik's resentment welled up in spite of the decency to which he had committed himself this terrible day. Why was it up to Ragnild to insist that he perform this baptism? It was appalling to imagine his leaving without first doing this for his little daughter who had miraculously survived.

> Thanks to Thee for the life of our dear Sarah: wife, mother, sister, that she was faithful even to her end when Thou, according to Thy Holy Will, took her from us to Thyself.

Henrik wanted to shout! Here this man stood attributing God for his wife's death! Wasn't he to blame? Oh no, he was a servant of the Lord, his family came second—if at all! He had said that to Sarah, yes he had. The Lord must always be first in his life—his ridiculous meetings!

> We thank Thee also for the life of Sarah's dear mother who is now with Thee in Glory. Grant that the circle be unbroken as we all come to the end of our days.

Now what does that mean, growled Henrik under his bowed head, "circle be unbroken?" He had heard it many times, sung if not spoken, and each time it irked him. He didn't consider himself part of any "holy circle" here below, and therefore was sure he was not entitled to be a part of the circle in the sky. Yet, a haunting fear trailed these words now that his departed mother was mentioned. An icy stone formed in his chest; he rubbed his palms together. It was as if he weren't sure but that people like Rasmus did, after all, have a monopoly on the hereafter, and if that were indeed the case, then he, Henrik, would be left out.

> Grant us Thy protection as we sleep, and, if it be Thy will, may we wake to another day ready to serve Thee. In Jesus' name we pray, Amen.

"So we keep the child, is that it?" said Henrik to his wife when they were ready for bed.

"He didn't bring up the subject. He perhaps hasn't a plan yet. Don't be hard on him, Henrik. A man like that is to be pitied, not condemned."

If Peder had been around, it would have been easier to care for Sarah's little girls, but Anna did her best. She took them with her whenever she visited friends, she sought out playmates for them, enrolled them in Sunday school, and gave each a lovely doll—every girl is entitled to a nice doll. She vowed she wouldn't spoil them, but she did want them to be happy. They were quiet little girls.

When September came, Mabel enrolled in second grade; she brightened somewhat on becoming a schoolgirl. And Anna had plans for music lessons. Dorothy reminded Anna of Sarah, and Dorothy was the more outgoing of the two; it was easy to favor her. But Anna was committed to treating each as fairly as she knew how.

Then came the week Halvor Bergum was in the vicinity. He came three afternoons in a row. The first afternoon he came to chat. Anna and he visited about many things, serious and otherwise, that had been a part of the correspondence between them. They both had lost their spouses. It was now four years since Lottie died and soon three years since Peder passed away. Emily was living with her sister out in Oregon, and she wrote regularly. Hal was attending college, his second year; his father hoped he would go to seminary after college. Joseph was finishing high school this coming spring and was thinking about business college. He had outgrown his asthma to a certain extent, although he wasn't as robust as his brother.

The second afternoon Halvor seemed to be assessing the recent events in Anna's life. Naturally she would miss such a good man as Peder. Anna described how well the business was being handled by his partner. If he should decide to sell, that might be a problem for Anna, but she had her brother; she could always count on him. And it certainly must have been hard to lose first her mother and then two months later, her sister, both of them here in this house under her care. Anna admitted that it was hard, but said strength came when she needed it most. Now she was busy with the two girls. That was nice, she had something to live for. "Anna," he said that afternoon, "You are as strong as I always thought you were. You've had it hard sometimes, but you've always shown your true courage." Anna appreciated being assessed thus; she had good friends, but perhaps none quite as good as this one. "You'll come again?" "Tomorrow, if I may? You'll be home?"

After this second afternoon, Anna's intuition told her that he had something in mind. She tried, in the meantime, to prepare for it.

"Would you marry me now?" asked Halvor.

The words came in such a matter-of-fact way that Anna was startled in spite of her preparation.

"I'm not the same girl I was when you knew me, Halvor. I was young then, and thought I was gifted enough to be a minister's wife. You'd find me quite different now."

"I've followed you through hundreds of letters. Of course I know the years have changed both of us."

"I have two little girls."

"We'll take care of them. We'll adopt them if we may."

"So much of what I am is invested here, Halvor. I'm not sure I could start all over again somewhere else."

"You could," Halvor said without conviction. "It's just a matter of putting the past into the past."

"It's not that easy. It isn't that I am now always living in the past—not that. It's that I belong to what has gone before, and I must somehow see it through."

"There is always wisdom in what you say, Anna. This I will have to ponder."

"I guess I have the same answer for you now that I had way back then. I'm committed to where I belong."

"Anna, I shall always care for you. I respect you deeply."

"Our affection is true friendship, Halvor. May we always be good friends."

"Devoted friends."

Even after she had seen him to the front door and climbed up the long stairs again, she continued to hear his words echoing in the walls. She had turned him down. Suddenly she felt desolate. She was quite alone; it was true. Peder was gone, her mother was gone. She did need someone to depend on. Could she deny that? And now the only one who remained for her, as she saw it, was her brother Henrik.

Chapter 11

Mabel would rather not write letters to her father, but Anna was persistent. "You two are not orphans," she told them. "You have a papa." Finally she took them to the drugstore and let each pick our a box of stationery on which to write their letters. It worked. Mabel took pride in her penmanship and Dorothy printed her name, drew pictures and wrote the numbers from one to twenty. Anna might have wished that their father were more kind and considerate, but he was a Christian man and in the end would do right by his daughters. Sometimes patience was required in such matters; circumstances were not always within one's control, and people were not all alike in how they perceived things, not even Christians. Although his letters were few and far between, Anna made the most of them by reading the latest one aloud, often two or three times. Then on the last day of Mabel's first school term in Kenyon, a letter came saying he was coming to see them and that he had a wonderful surprise.

The surprise turned out to be a new mother. Rasmus had married again, a maiden lady he had met while conducting a series of meetings in Grafton, North Dakota. She was a rural schoolteacher, but for the last two years had cared for an aging mother until she passed away. Upon the suggestion of the parish minister, Rasmus proposed to her; she was now ready for another kind of life.

Their arrival was exceedingly distressing for Anna. To begin with, she was given such short notice. There was no time to write a letter inviting them to a meal or to be overnight guests. They arrived at nine o'clock and were gone by noon. No, they couldn't stay for dinner; they had another engagement. Anna and the girls had to set to work immediately rounding up all their belongings—nothing must be forgotten—all their winter woolens, books, pictures, dolls. And all was done under the eyes of the heavyset, new mother, who was certainly a stranger, and there was no time to get acquainted.

"You'll be going to Wanamingo?" said Anna as they stood around the baggage that had been put together so rapidly.

"No, not this time," replied Rasmus, taking hold of two suitcases. He was ready to descend the stairs.

"No?"

"I'm writing them a letter, Anna. That child is Ragnild's. She is the one who has given it life. I feel I must make a sacrifice even as Sarah did."

"Sacrifice?" Anna didn't understand at all! She wished he'd put down those suitcases.

"God moves in mysterious ways," he replied, not looking at anyone in particular.

"And the little girl's sisters, must they make the sacrifice, too? Ruthie is their sister, not their cousin."

"It's all the same, isn't it? Sister, cousin?"

"Where are we going?" blurted Dorothy, looking first at Mabel, who perhaps understood this better than she.

"Home."

"Where's home?" she persisted, risking impertinence.

"We're a family now," hesitated the new mother. Rasmus seemed to be expecting her to answer the child's question. "Your papa has come for his little girls. He's been lonesome for you for so long. At last you are reunited with him."

"Now we have a new mother," put in Rasmus in the role of Jesus blessing little children. The suitcases were waiting beside the trunk; he now had his arms around his girls, his voice rich with assurance.

The new mother beamed at her acquired family while Anna stood by, still wondering about Sarah's other child in Wanamingo.

Mabel and Dorothy embraced their dear tante, but not with a full realization of what was happening. Dorothy's question, scarcely answered, became suddenly suspended by the action of going away, and, when one goes away, one says good-bye.

The new family descended Anna's long front stairs. Anna stood in the street and watched her girls climb over their baggage into the back seat of a strange car parked in front of the meat market. Rasmus never owned a car; he must have borrowed this one from a Christian friend in this vicinity. Soon it became part of the other traffic on Kenyon's busy main street.

Anna wasn't ready to re-enter her empty rooms; all she would hear would be the dining-room clock ticking and striking the half-hours. Instead she pulled open the meat market door.

"Joe, I have a roast in the oven. Why don't you come upstairs for dinner? I'll call Lucille and tell her to come, too."

"Your company left?" said her late husband's business partner in surprise.

"I really don't know what the hurry was," replied Anna, trying to sound casual.

"Well, I'd say they don't know what they are missing. Sure, why not? Lucille was coming down town this afternoon anyway. Now she can come a bit earlier."

He picked up the phone to verify his assumption. "Fine with her, Anna, we'll be up shortly," he announced as he replaced the receiver.

Anna returned upstairs and set the table for three.

Henrik and Ragnild could understand no better than Anna what Rasmus meant by "sacrifice" and how "God moves in mysterious ways," but they were relieved that their little Ruthie, now soon a year old, would continue to be a part of their family. Anna was the one who was losing out again, Ragnild perceived; those two girls had become very precious to their aunt. Ragnild's heart cried for Anna.

For want of a role in her household of one, Anna became more and more involved with her brother's family as the person everyone called Tante. She was somehow more than just another aunt; (Ragnild had many sisters and therefore her children had many aunts.) she was in a sense a kind of bestemor. Henry was the only one of the children who could remember the original bestemor, and he was the one least impressed with Tante. He realized that it was good she encouraged Norwegian, that was important. But, although her stories were many of the same ones his bestemor had told, she was nothing like her. He saw her as a usurper; it couldn't be helped.

But with Ann it was different. As the children grew into their middle childhood, Anna and her namesake became fast friends. That Ann had the same name as Tante might have set it off for the child, but certainly it would have happened anyway. When she was seven, she spent weeks at a time during the summer at Anna's home in Kenyon. She slept by herself in a great big bed, bathed in a shiny white bathtub, ate Puffed Rice instead of Oatmeal, although both cereal boxes had the picture of the Quaker, looked at pictures through the mysterious stereoscope on the parlor table, and explored every cranny, finding ever-stranger objects from a block of ice in the ice box to a floating ball in the white tank behind the toilet.

And she learned embroidery, cross-stitch at first. It was important because she accompanied Tante once or twice a week to the house of a friend where the women would visit while doing fancy work. Then she and Tante would wear pretty, summer dresses. Getting ready for such an afternoon was as much fun as visiting. Tante would curl hair with an electric curling iron, first Ann's then her own. Into Ann's newly made curls Tante would tie a ribbon that matched her dress. At the lady's house would be a frosted cake, which Ann hoped would be chocolate, as well as several kinds of cookies. A big glass of milk or nectar would be served to her even before the coffee cups were filled. And they would brag about her, Anna's little niece who looked so pretty and could cross-stitch so nicely; they were sure they hadn't done as well when they were her age. And wasn't it wonderful that this little girl could speak Norwegian? There weren't many children learning the language of their grandparents these days;

parents just weren't teaching it to their children anymore. Tante's friends always spoke Norwegian; they were all as old as grandmothers. Sometimes they would say they were sorry they didn't have any little girls for her to play with.

But this didn't mean Ann never had anyone her own age to play with when she stayed with Tante at Kenyon. There was Rosella, who lived across the street above her father's grocery store. From her Ann learned to play jacks, to jump rope, and to maneuver new forms of hopscotch. Rosella came every morning, wanting Ann to come out to play, and Tante usually let her.

But what Ann liked the best about staying with Tante was listening to stories. Some stories Tante read aloud from a magazine called *The Friend*, stories which continued from one issue to the next, and Tante had saved then all. Other stories she told unlocked secrets about the old blacksmith shop at home, about the town that had once surrounded them in the old days, and even about the one-room school which Ann attended now. The little girl couldn't imagine that there had been as many as thirty pupils, some of them grown-up, even, who had just come from Norway. The best story of all was about the funny, little shoemaker who lived in a house next door to her home, and about whom Ann continued to ask questions. The more Tante told about him the more fascinating he became. How she wished he still lived there—this would make her world a storybook world!

When school started, the visits to Tante at Kenyon came to an end, but one could always write letters. Ann had seen all the letters, some from far-away places, which Tante got in her mailbox; now her own would be among them.

One day in early December of this same year, while Anna was out Christmas shopping, she fell on Kenyon's slippery, main street and broke her hip. People out on the sidewalk came swiftly to her aid; the doctor was called out of his office, and a stretcher soon brought her into her house. Of course, she could go to the hospital, the doctor said upon diagnosing her fracture, but he thought he could set her hip as well at home. He would rig her bed with a solid board and attach a sandbag weight on the injured side to keep the reset bone in place. He would come every day to check her and see how things were going. She must have a nurse living in, at least to begin with, and, as she got better, maybe she could engage a woman companion who would do what needed to be done. Anna accepted the doctor's judgment; it was certainly distressing, but being at home was vastly preferable to being in the hospital.

Responding to the doctor's telephone message, Ragnild arrived by train from Wanamingo, bringing Neil and Ruthie with her; the last snowstorm had blocked the roads. She stayed for three days until she was satisfied that Anna was in good hands: Beatrice Moland, the special nurse who was procured, was of excellent reputation and knew how to enter the home of an invalid with competence and good cheer. And Anna's many friends sought out what they could do; one of them, Selma Nelson, volunteered to be the live-in companion.

"We've come to say good-bye for now," said Ragnild as she brought in to Tante her five-year-old "twins."

"In the top drawer of the dresser is a billfold. Take some of that money for Christmas presents for the children." There was a sad urgency in Tante's voice which Neil and Ruthie were never to forget.

"You shouldn't bother about us," said their mother. "You need your money yourself now."

"No, no. Take two ten-dollar bills. You and Henrik will have to buy the children's presents for me."

"You are so good to us, Tante," said Ragnild as she pulled open the drawer and found the billfold. "It hurts me to think that you will be laid up like this through Christmas. We'll write to you though, and come as often as we can."

Henrik's family left after Neil and Ruthie had patted Anna's cheek and she had patted theirs.

Anna had lain on a board before, more than forty years ago, and in a dream had been carried by four bearers across a pasture. Soon they had slanted her rigid bed and brought her up to the roof of a house. Now this was happening again! She was being carried at the mercy of others! Finally the roof was reached and the bearers put her down. Then, to her dismay, she heard their footsteps shuffling back toward the steep stairs. They were going away! She called to them to stay, but no one answered. She listened again; she heard droning voices far down a long hall. They had left her now; she was all alone!

Suddenly hot wind began to tear at her hair. With it, out of the darkness, came a whirling, flashing, buggy wheel. It was on fire! Sparks were landing in her hair! As she threw up her hands to protect her head, she saw a face in the center of the spinning disk. It was Peder.

"Catch hold of the rim of the wheel, Anna, and you will be lifted into my chariot. Don't be afraid. Reach up, Anna, catch a hold!"

Anna grasped into the air but caught a hold of nothing. It was as if the whirling wheel had no substance. "Peder, Peder!" she screamed, her words echoing as if she were calling into a tunnel.

"Don't worry, Anna. I'll come back for you another time," Peder called as the wheel ascended and disappeared.

No sooner was the fiery buggy wheel gone than another wheel rolled toward her. Again sparks began spilling into Anna's hair. Again, as she raisd her hands to keep her hair from catching fire, she saw a face in the spinning disk. It was her mother, Julia.

"Catch hold of the rim of my wheel, Anna, and you'll be lifted into my chariot. Don't be afraid. Reach up, Anna. Catch a hold!"

Anna tried harder this time, clasping her hands so tightly that her fingernails dug into her palm. "Mama," she called. And again the curious tunnel echo mimicked Anna.

"Never mind, Anna, my dear. You'll have a chariot of your own someday."

No sooner had this fiery buggy wheel disappeared than still another rolled toward her. For a third time sparks were spilling into Anna's hair. Even before she had a chance to protect her hair from burning, she saw the face. It was her sister, Sarah.

"Don't try to grab my chariot, Anna. You will get burned, I tell you!"

Anna remained rigid.

"Anna, listen to me. I can't take you with me because you must take care of my girls, Anna, you must take care of my girls!"

Anna's tongue became wooden when she tried to answer. She spit consonants, but no voiced vowels would come. Finally she shook her head. Mercy no, that wasn't right! Then she began nodding vigorously. Sarah wasn't understanding about the girls. In desperation Anna reached up her hand.

"No, no! Stay, stay!" the frantic woman in the spinning disk screamed.

Suddenly, as if caught in a whirlwind, the third fiery buggy wheel spun itself upward, growing smaller and smaller as it rose, giving Anna the sensation of falling.

"Sarah, Sarah!" Her sister's name began to reverberate from every direction.

"Wake up, Anna. There, there, now. You've had a bad dream."

Anna caught herself thrashing her head as she awoke. She must have hollered in her sleep and brought Beatrice to her bedside.

"I was dreaming. I'm so sorry I woke you."

"Never mind that. Here have a drink of water. I'll sit with you for a while."

"You are kind," said Anna after a refreshing swallow of water. "You know, I had the strangest dream. I saw wheels in the sky, just as Ezekiel did."

Patient and nurse laughed a little.

In early February when Henrik was seeing his sister, Dr. Morgan brought his son, a recent graduate from University of Minnesota

Medical School, to examine his patient. As the busy doctors hurried away, Henrik detained the young man until he had stated his diagnosis of Anna's condition.

"She will walk again, for that we can consider ourselves fortunate. Many with this kind of a fracture remain invalids in wheelchairs. But she will have a bad limp. One leg is almost three inches shorter than the other."

"Would she have been better off if she had gone to a hospital?" Henrik thought this a fair question.

"Perhaps. There are new procedures for fractures these days. As you know medicine is making great strides. But my father had done remarkably well. Who can say if a hospital team could have done any better."

Standing at the top of the stairs, Henrik watched the young man's light-footed descent. In a matter of seconds he was gone.

Limping for the rest of her life—she was fragile enough without that! He should have seen to it that she had gotten into the hospital. What does old Dr. Morgan know!

Powerless now to change things, Henrik moved back from the stairway. His knees were quivering. Pity for her surged through his sudden helplessness. She's suffered enough already! A vague pain began to surface at his temples. Why had he always treated her so surlily? He hadn't been a very decent brother, never gracious; he had often been cruel. Would he find it in himself to treat her differently in the future? He must! By making this resolution he was reaching for strength.

Selma Nelson lived with Anna for two years. Henrik, Ragnild, and the children made frequent visits. During this time, Anna moved from crutches to a cane, and finally she got around in her house fairly well with neither. But her home of many rooms was a burden to her now. She seldom had a house full of guests anymore and so much of what she had was never used. Then, there were those long stairways both front and back. She could go up and down now, a step and a half at a time, if she hung tightly to the banister. She hadn't considered trying the back stairs, and wondered if she ever would.

Then came the day when Joe Harstad, after thirty-two years, gave up the meat business, but not before he had found a new butcher who was eager to rent from Anna, not only the market but also the upstairs living quarters. Although this marked the end of a long, compatible business relationship, which she and Peder had shared with this good friend, she saw in this circumstance an opportunity. Now she would find a more suitable place to live.

Almost immediately she found a one-room apartment in a downstairs duplex occupied by the aging Mrs. Østen Hanson, wife of the pioneer Haugean pastor of Anna's childhood, and her daughter Elisa. These were respected friends Anna had known all her life; she would not be alone here. Elisa, a nurse, would see to Anna's needs as well as she did to her mother's. It mattered a great deal to them the kind of person who rented this room so close at hand. The last tenant the landlord had put there was a retired railroad man who they suspected smoked in bed.

In the spring of 1929 just as school was out, Ann visited Tante for a week. Since Ann was older now, Ragnild pointed out to her ways she could be helpful. For two years, Ann had watched how small and thin Tante was becoming as she herself grew taller. She had seen her struggle with crutches, with a cane, and finally with a raised shoe, which turned out to be more bothersome than helpful, and Ann's heart cried out for her aunt. She wanted to be helpful—it wasn't that—but somehow the joys of visiting Tante had lost their luster. To be sure, Tante had the sewing machine out, and together they made a new wardrobe for Ann's doll; Puffed Rice was still available from the little kitchen cabinet that served as a pantry; the cedar chest at the foot of the bed was as full of beautiful things as ever; the glass china closet with its beautiful dishes and crystal graced a corner, and the bottom shelf of the secretary housed all the back issues of *The Friend*. Yet nothing was the same.

Elisa had a coffee party one day and Ann once again sat among Tante's friends, yet she felt strange and caught herself wanting to answer them in English. Although she could embroider better now—French knots and lazy-daisy stitches—she found herself caring less. Then they had gone to church. Tante left behind her cane, which she always used away from home, and depended entirely on her niece. Ann loved her tante, it certainly wasn't that, but it became loathsome always to be hung on to, always to be clutched for support, and always to move so slowly especially up steps. It was better when they were at home, but one room was a small home, and Ann missed all the nice things Tante had sold or stored away. When, at last, her family came in the familiar Model T, Ann was very happy knowing the time had come to go back to her own home. She consoled herself that soon Tante would come to them for the summer months. She loved to have Tante stay with them on the farm; that was entirely different. Ann had more freedom, then, to do other things she liked to do. Tante would share the many goings-on.

From the middle of June until the end of August, the confining, little duplex in Kenyon was deserted. Not only was Anna gone, but also Elisa and her mother who returned to their old country home near Aspelund. Ever since she had undertaken the care of her mother, Elisa had devoted herself to the project of preserving the old home as she remembered it when her father was alive. Before bringing her mother out to the old homestead, Elisa went there alone for several days of scrubbing floors, airing rooms, ironing curtains, and putting in a little garden. Here on the farm, the two Hanson women entertained members of their extended family from far and near—bedrooms always ready for guests, vegetables from Elisa's garden and homemade baked goods from the old oven graced their table.

Anna's escape from her one-room apartment was no less rewarding than that of her two winter companions. Soon she was involved in many of her brother's family tasks. She baked bread, hemmed flour sacks into dishtowels and embroidered on them, patched overalls and peeled potatoes. Although as the children grew older numerous new interests captivated their lives, Tante still held her place. She delighted in their delights, she listened to them, and laughed with them. One day Neil and Ruthie acquired a new puppy, and soon it was as much Tante's puppy as theirs. "What shall we call him?" Ruthie wanted to know as she came carrying the soft, little creature to Tante. "You name him," insisted Neil. So the dog became Philox, after a neighbor's dog of long ago.

And they looked at the Sears Roebuck catalog together. Wouldn't it be fun to have bathing suits? The Zumbro River was the children's favorite place on hot days; what they did they called wading, although, most of the time, it ended up as a long dip with their clothes on. Now, with the new attire, it could be called swimming, and they would look like the children in the catalog. Tante went for her pen and with the children—all but Henry—picked out the suits they wanted. The order letter was ready for the mailman. A week later, after the delightful package arrived, Henry and his father, harvesting the oats, were to see, without warning, Ann, Neil and Ruthie donned in swimwear, running through the pasture, rolling under a fence, and finally disappearing in the cornfield on their way to the river.

The summer Ann was eleven years old, she and Tante paid a memorable visit to the old Hanson homestead. Although the men were busy with field work, Henry reluctantly consented to drive them there after he had eaten his dinner and to pick them up again just before milking time. Elisa and her mother had urged them often to come for an afternoon visit and were overjoyed to see them.

"Velkommen," called Elisa as she hurried toward the car. "How good of you to come."

Ann suddenly realized that Norwegian would be the language of the afternoon. She was stepping again into the old world she had known before with Tante's friends: niceties of china cups, loaf sugar, and old memories related in great detail.

"I don't know how long it's been since I was here last," said Tante, responding to the greeting. "Nothing has changed much, has it?"

"Of course, some of the trees got too big and had to be taken down, and the hedge is a bit overgrown. Otherwise, I imagine you can recognize it," chatted Elisa as she gave Tante her arm to lean on. "And we must get the old lawn swing fixed."

Ann, upon the mention of the lawn swing, began to imagine that it would be fun to play in this yard. The slanting cellar doors, and the rain barrel offered other interesting possibilities.

Entering the house, they were met by Grandma Hanson. She was wearing the same little cap she always wore around the house.

"Velkommen. Takk for sist!" she said, the handshake held long.

"I'm glad we finally could come," responded Tante.

Elisa stood smiling while waiting to escort them farther. "Before you sit down, I want to take you through the house. I believe there are many things about it you will remember, Anna. And your niece had never been here before."

The first room they saw upon leaving the entry was what Elisa called the study. It had lots of books, old books with heavy leather bindings, all of them on shelves behind closed glass doors; nevertheless, Ann was sure she could smell them. On one wall was the familiar picture of Martin Luther she had seen in old books and on another wall the famous painting of Jesus in Gethsemane. The one big piece of furniture was a writing desk—not a secretary, but a big desk—on which lay an open Bible and a pair of reading glasses. There was also an inkwell and a pen. Not quite in the center of the room was a potbellied stove, which kept the room warm in the old days, and beside it was a rocking chair under which a pair of slippers were waiting.

"This room is exactly the way it was when he left. There has been no need to change anything," Elisa was saying.

Suddenly it dawned on Ann that the occupant of this room had been dead for many years, and there on the wall hung his hat!

Ann became even more uncomfortable when she was taken into the parlor. Here, encircling the room, were life-sized portraits in heavy glass frames leaning against easels on the floor. Each portrait subject had a story which Elisa told in great detail. In the most prominent frame was the Rev. Østen Hanson, the occupant of the study they had just seen, and beside him, in a matching frame, was his first wife and mother of his three oldest sons. As they moved from picture to picture, Ann got the impression that all of these people looking out at her from their gilded frames were dead, although she didn't know that for sure.

Still uneasy, Ann climbed the steep staircase to the bedrooms on the second floor where thick braided rugs lay on the floors, pieced quilts covered the beds, and pillows with cases edged with embroidered ruffles rested up against high wooden headboards. Each of the rooms had washstands with towels put out for the next guests and a chamber pot conveniently placed under each bed. The illusion that the people of the portraits still occupied this house followed Ann wherever Elisa took her.

They came down another stairs to the kitchen, where a pan of cinnamon rolls was cooling on the table. In the context of the illusion and the old kitchen, Ann wondered how long they had been there and if they were actually going to eat them.

Finally they were led into the dining room, where an old wall clock was ticking away the hours, where old china gleamed white and blue from behind glass cupboard doors, and where a linen lunch cloth, elaborately embroidered, was spread under a sugar bowl and a pitcher of cream. Grandma had been busy here putting out cups and saucers.

"Vær så god," she said with a gracious little gesture.

Shortly, Elisa returned from the kitchen with the plate of cinnamon rolls and another of *krumkake* and *fattigmand.*

Outside of what etiquette demanded, Grandma Hanson usually spoke little; her daughter could do ample talking for the two of them. But today she surprised her guests while they spread their napkins on their laps.

"On Resurrection morning won't we all be busy greeting one another? I've been thinking about that. The very first thing I will do is say 'Good Morning' to the first Mrs. Hanson." She bowed a firm resolution.

Ann looked at Tante and Elisa. They were smiling.

Chapter 12

As he carried a can of evening milk from the barn to the cooling tank in the milk house, Henrik caught sight of Andrew Haugen's cattle truck coming into the yard. He quickened his steps to put away the milk. This morning, one of his cows had been shipped to South St. Paul, and now Andrew was returning. Henrik wasn't expecting a big check this time, since he knew farm prices had dropped to an all-time low, but Andrew was here bringing what the market would bear.

"The cow didn't bring enough to pay for the haul," said Andrew Haugen. It was awkward to approach his client without the green envelope containing the coveted check.

"What are you saying, Andrew?"

"The bottom has dropped out of the market."

"You mean...not...?"

"It didn't pay to ship her, Henrik. In fact you owe me two dollars."

"Has it really come to this?"

"Forget about the two dollars, Henrik. It pains me enough to have to tell you this. I really must be on my way." The cattle hauler returned to his cab. "Times are hard for everyone these days," he called as he went, as if this could be of any comfort.

Lifting his hand, Henrik acknowledged his caller and the message he had brought. He stood watching as the truck turned around in the barnyard where only this morning he and Andrew had coaxed the unwilling animal to its fate. He continued to stare even after the truck was out of sight.

Shipping this cow—Min was her name—to South St. Paul had been a decision involving the whole family. She had been Ann's little dairy calf:

> I have a little dairy calf
> She is all black and white
> I have to laugh at her sometimes
> Because she is so bright.
> I give her milk out of a pail
> And as she drinks
> She wags her tail.

His little daughter had won a prize for her poem on the "Junior Page" of *Hoard's Dairyman* magazine. "Don't sell her!" she had cried. Ann was no where to be seen this morning. "I wouldn't sell her," Henry had spoken to his father man to man. "Let Min go?" Ragnild had questioned.

Henrik had never had a better cow than Min. Not only had she let down more pounds of milk in her day than any other of his herd, but, what was more, she was almost human, an animal having an imposing dignity and a handsome demand of respect. Almost from the start she became the herd's leader, bringing the long line of cattle behind her on the cowpath across the pasture and up to the barn. One would need only to get her started, when it was time to bring the cows home, and the rest would follow. But this noble creature had developed udder problems; she wasn't producing anymore; better to sell her than to keep her on for another winter. Good farmers had to make decisions like that; he supposed it was foolish to get so attached to his animals, but he had to admit that his love of animals had gotten him into farming in the first place. But Min hadn't been worth the haul; she had brought no price! Prices the good farmer couldn't ignore. They meant well-being for his family; they meant paying building costs; they meant money for taxes and money for interest on the mortgage. Prices were all important; they meant survival, if not impressive success. With these low prices what was a farmer to do?

Money for the interest payment was imperative; delinquency meant losing one's farm to the bank which held the mortgage. This had already happened to one of his neighbors who had purchased land and incurred a mortgage the same year Henrik did. There was something so terribly unjust about that, the law being rigged against the hard-working farmer. Help for this could be forthcoming from a young man running for governor of Minnesota, Floyd B. Olson, who was advocating a moratorium on farm mortgages, but he had to be elected first. Henrik was speaking out strongly for him these days as the November elections were approaching.

Little help was coming from Washington. President Coolidge had twice vetoed the McNary-Haugen bill designed to boost farm prices, legislation which Minnesota's senators had worked hard to pass. And Herbert Hoover's Federal Farm Board had turned out to be worse than a joke. In the 1928 election, not wanting to vote Republican because of the farm issue, Henrik had no one to vote for; he couldn't vote for the Democrat candidate who favored the repeal of the temperance amendment Henrik had supported so vehemently. It was frustrating to say the least.

Henrik was learning that it was not enough to scrutinize the moves of government as a sovereign citizen and influencing public opinion whenever possible in one's own little sphere. He looked in the direction of his barley field covered with stubble; the grain had been clipped and threshed. His barley crop had always yielded his interest money and more. But now, the bottom having dropped out of the grain market, it wouldn't yield nearly enough, and he hadn't yet come up with a plan to supplement it. In his granary, the rich-smelling grain was stored; it was inconceivable that it was worth so little! Soon it would be time to plow the stubble under, getting the field ready in the fall for seeding in the spring. At the prospect, a feeling of futility gripped him. And Ragnild, practical as she was, couldn't come up with a plan for raising more interest money, either. She said she was praying; the dear girl would do that, but moving the Almighty seemed incomprehensible to him.

Finally he turned from the spot where he had been standing so long. He released the windmill lever, which let the wheel face the wind. Soon water gushed into the cooling tank. He returned to the barn and dismissed the remaining two cows by unloosing their stanchions. It was still warm enough at night to let them stay outside; he wasn't looking forward to the time when he would have to house cows in the barn. Before closing the door he grabbed a shovel and cleaned away the dung left behind.

Would he have to resort to borrowing money from Anna again? It pained him to do that. He didn't want to owe her anything and vowed each time he was forced to borrow that he would never do it again. Last year she had paid the taxes; there had been no other way out of it. And she was so eager to help. Could that be the reason he was so repulsed by the idea? She always come limping toward him, that frail, little woman, handing him her savings book, saying "Take what you need, Henrik." At those times he was forced into an encounter with her; she was not to be ignored then. He had vowed many times not to be short with her, but she always quickened ugly feelings inside him. He wished this wouldn't happen. It was far too complicated and painful to examine, so he did what he always had done: shrugged the bad feeling aside. Having an agonizing pity for her, he would, at all costs, control his temper. He owed that to her; she had been hurt enough in her life.

Anna hadn't returned to Kenyon yet this fall. Elisa and Grandma Hanson were surely back from their summer homestead by now since it was becoming colder and necessary to have heat in the house. Henrik had to admit he was glad when Anna left for the winter. She could have a life of her own then, he figured, surrounded by her friends. Yes, her friends. What a miserable lot they seemed to him! Henrik had to admit he despised certain kinds of people; there was no help for it. Could it be she was waiting to pay the interest for him?

The long handle bounced as he set the shovel up in its corner. He hooked the door through which the cows had gone and grabbed his jacket. He walked the length of the barn, pushed shut the sliding door, and stood again on the spot where he had watched the cattle truck leave. He suddenly realized that Ragnild had left for the house quite a while ago, and supper must be on the table. He moved reluctantly toward the house. Soon he would have to deliver to the rest of the family the distressing news Andrew had given him.

Henrik hadn't sold his barley yet, otherwise Anna would have returned to Kenyon earlier. It wasn't difficult for her to figure out how hard times were becoming on the farm, and she was sure she would have to help Henrik when interest on the mortgage came due. When she and Ragnild talked about such things it was always, "We will wait and see." She knew that last year the barley crop hadn't been enough either; the interest had swallowed a whole month's milk check as well. She could have helped then, too, if she had known at the time how tight things were. Today she had seen the cattle truck and knew that he had shipped a cow. He said the cow had developd a complication and that was the reason for shipping her, but Anna wasn't sure of that. She knew her brother had an immense amount of pride—that was good in a man—but it made it difficult for her. It would be so much simpler if he would let her know how she could help. Peder had made all his money in good times. Why couldn't it now be used to help her dear ones when times were so hard? Last year she had managed to help him pay his taxes; she had found opportunity then. She had simply said, "Here is the bankbook. Now you must see to my taxes. And take enough to pay your own, Henrik." And he did, but made it clear it was a loan, and that was all right if it made him feel better.

This same day, Anna was mulling with these thoughts as she sat darning woolen stockings in the kitchen, the warmest place in the house on such a chilly morning. Ragnild had found this handwork for her, practical work because winter was surely coming.

"A letter for you Tante," said Ann, who had been the first to spot the mailman stopping on the road.

It was a business envelope postmarked from Kenyon. She stuck the large needle upright in the sock, laid aside her work and opened the letter with her scissors.

"Ragnild, see what it says here," she said after a long moment.

Ragnild was making a pungent relish out of the remains of the garden: green tomatoes that the cool autumn sun failed to ripen, onions not selected for storage, and the smallest of the cabbage heads. The room was fragrant with pickling. Ragnild put down her wooden spoon quickly and came to Anna.

"My renter. He's decided to give up," Anna said, handing the letter to her sister-in-law. "I thought he was having a hard time paying the rent. His checks have been coming later and later each month."

"Such a good butcher? Should his business be falling off?" Ragnild laid the letter on the table in front of Anna as she spoke. "Maybe he..."

"Times are hard everywhere, Ragnild. I suppose I'll have to find another renter. That might not be so easy."

"Henrik will see to it for you," said Ragnild with warmth. "It's easier for him to get away these days, too, since most of the fall work is done."

When Ragnild helped Henrik with the milking that evening, she thought she should say something to Henrik about Anna's new situation, but she had found no opportunity. It would be best that he see the letter for himself; the cold fact there.

The family waited for Henrik to come in for supper. For some reason or other he was taking his time, but before anyone was sent out to him, they heard his heavy feet on the back step. They all watched him hang up his jacket and cap. They heard him fill the washbasin at the sink, splash wather over face and hands, and finally jerk the roller towel toward his face. No one would go to their chairs before he was ready.

"Andrew had no check," Henrik announced as the silence that faced him became unbearable.

Each member of his family stopped eating and looked at him. Only with their eyes they questioned him.

"She barely paid for her trip to South St. Paul. There was nothing left."

Eating continued. No one spoke for a long time. What father said was sinking in painfully.

Tante suddenly broke the silence. "I got a letter today, Henrik. I have lost my renter."

Henrik was taken by surprise. She had changed the subject.

"It may not be easy finding another renter, and I guess I'll have to depend on you. If you haven't enough from the barley and the cow for the interest, take from here." She drew from somewhere in her lap the bankbook and passed it on to Henry who was sitting next to his father.

"But if you lose your income from rent, you'll need your money," Henrik said without conviction as he watched his son lay Tante's wealth at his plate.

"There's enough."

Ragnild and Henry were as one with apprehension; the moment was tense. They had witnessed such encounters between this brother and sister before. Ann watched from her place, looking at Tante, then at her father and then back at Tante. The cow hadn't been enough, she had heard. How much money does it take? Min had been sold and still there wasn't enough. Only in Tante's little bankbook was there enough. Neil and Ruthie were the only ones eating. They sensed the distress of the moment, to be sure, but they would do what they had come to the table for.

"We'll go to Kenyon tomorrow," said Henrik as a matter of course. "This doesn't surprise me. The whole country is hit by hard times. Everyone will begin to feel the pinch sooner or later."

The next day Anna was ready with her suitcases to return to Kenyon. She was convinced that Henrik would accept her offer; he hadn't given back the bankbook. If Anna's business should keep her brother away beyond the hour of chores, Henry and Ragnild would do the milking.

As Henrik and Anna stopped briefly at the duplex to be rid of the suitcases, they were greeted by Elisa and Grandma Hanson and didn't get away before they had drank a cup of coffee. Next they consulted with Anna's insurance man, also an agent for real estate and rentals, who assured them that he would do the best he could. Then they climbed the long, familiar stairs to the living quarters above the meat market. Anna expressed her regrets to her renters; everything was in such fine condition, she told them. Before leaving Anna took a key from her purse and opened the door to the back bedroom which she had reserved for storage. She searched in a dresser drawer for an old picture album she had promised to show to Grandma Hanson. Henrik shuddered as he saw all the furniture, which once had been so grand, shoved into this tiny room. She really should have gotten rid of it long ago. He waited while she purchased some items at the grocery store and some doughnuts at the bakery, and finally he brought her to her winter home. He knew she had bought the doughnuts for him, and he dared not leave before he had been served at her table.

With the coming of spring, as good fortune would have it, Anna had secured a new renter who occupied the upstairs as well as the meat market. Things seemed to settle once again.

"Sit down, Henry." The superintendent was offering a student the oak chair with arms directly across from his desk. "I have called you in this morning to congratulate you. You rank highest in your class. You are valedictorian for the class of 1931."

Henry's hands clutched the arms of the awkward chair. "Thank you, Sir."

"You're not surprised?"

"A little bit," Henry replied shifting his weight from one hip to the other and trying to smile.

"You'll do well making a speech." The superintendent reached for a folder he had previously placed on his desk. "I have a speech for you here."

"What?"

"Your speech. It is a rather nice one, I think. We'll make this as painless for you as possible. Here."

Henry's fingers didn't budge from the chair arms. "I prefer to write it myself, Mr. Jacobsen. I want to deliver my own speech."

The superintendent laughed. "Get your dad to write it, is that it?" He continued laughing heartily for a moment then suddenly spoke. "Maybe that would be better than this after all. Your father is a very intelligent man."

Henry was impatient to reply. "My father will have nothing to do with it." He lifted his hands and let them fall back on the oak. "Since I am the valedictorian, am I not the one to make the speech? And isn't it right that it should be my own?"

The superintendent leaned across his desk and stared at the young man. Henry stared back, watching the peculiar back-and-forth movement of the eyes fixed on him.

"All right, then," the superintendent said finally. "Bring it to Miss Johnson when you have it ready. She will look it over." He rose from his chair, signaling the end of the conference.

Henry descended the three steps that led from the superintendent's office to the hall.

"A canned speech?" said his father with distain as chores were being done that evening.

"That's what I thought," said the son.

"What are they teaching you in that school? I have a feeling that elocution is becoming a lost art."

"What's elocution?"

"Speech-making, my son, good, old-fashioned speech-making."

Being the highest ranking student in his class, Henry was now in possession of a tuition scholarship to any Minnesota college, and certainly he wanted to go to college. Of course he would work out during threshing or at any other job he might get among the neighbors, but what little they had to pay him wouldn't go far. Tante had said she would give him as much as he needed. She had been so proud of his speech the night of graduation. "The boy has great talent, Henrik. We must do our best to see to it that he goes on with his schooling," she had said. But he disliked, almost as much as his father did, taking money from her. "I have given the girls music lessons. Isn't it only fair that I do something like that for you, too?" Her words softened his resistance, and plans were made for college in the fall.

Ann ran away from Neil and Ruthie. She got tired of them, sometimes, and wanted to be alone. Anyway, it was time for Ruthie to practice her piano lesson; Ann had already practiced hers for the day. And Neil could carry lunch to the men in the field; he liked to drive the horses and would beg his brother to let him try cultivating corn.

She took refuge in the old blacksmith shop, one of her favorite haunts. These old walls were a hideaway. They had given cover for Ruthie as she got over the chagrin of having cut her own hair, comfort for Neil who had been scolded for mistreating a cat, and a private stage for Ann who would act out her private fantasies. She didn't climb into the old buggy seat this time; she would leave such antics to Neil and Ruthie—they liked the way they could make the old seat bounce. Instead, she dashed around the machinery her father stored there these days until she reached the stairway to the second floor. The bottom step was rotten; one had to watch it. The floor upstairs was none too secure either; it was pretty good by the stairway, but on the other end porous boards sagged, and one could see right through to the machinery below. Neil had played the acrobat at one time and let himself through one of the holes, frightening Ann to the point where she threatened to tell his mother. But soon he proved to his sister that he was so agile he would never hurt himself.

At the top of the stairs she looked out of a window. The panes which were left were exceedingly dirty, one could scarcely see out of them. She wondered if anyone ever thought to wash them. She had removed some of the panes for an art project in school, painting on each a black, lacquered silhouette of a bird, animal or child, and framing each with a background, a piece of foil from a cereal box. She had given one of these pictures to Tante, and now it hung in her room in Kenyon, and another to Emma and Josie Veblen, who had expressed such admiration for her talent.

The carpenter shop up here hadn't been used for a long time. Only once could Ann ever remember anyone up here, other than she and the kids, and that was when Anton Anderson had enclosed the front porch of the family's house and built a railing on its flat roof. Then she had seen him clamp pieces of wood in the vise and plane away curls which dropped to the floor. She and Ruthie had scrambled for them.

But what attracted Ann lately to the second floor was not the old carpenter bench; it was rather, the old boxes and trunks that were stored there. In one corner were old school books. Her father, who was the clerk of their district school, found it repugnant to burn books so all the discards were brought here. The primers had been fun; she had taught Neil and Ruthie to read out of them before they had started school, she being only in second grade herself. She had discovered that they were smart, those two scamps. The geography books were fun, too. The pages were much bigger than the ones at school now, big, so maps could be big. One day she had found a map of Europe and thought it was all a mistake until she had shown it to her father, who told her it was how Europe looked before the World War. Her Uncle David, whom she had never seen, died in that war. At this point she was happy because now there would be no more war, the world was safe for democracy.

Today she decided against looking at books. She would look through old magazines instead; there was a deep trunk full of them. There were many old copies of ones she recognized, such as *The Friend, Saturday Evening Post* and *Hoard's Dairyman.* The pictures opened for Ann the world of yesterday. She studied the advertisements that showed women in long dresses and big hats, men in shoes with pointed toes and stiff black hats. There were magazines in Norwegian with fewer pictures, and those only of ministers in clerical collars who had been important long ago. The bannerheads of the periodicals interested her; she was fascinated by lettering of any kind. And any blank pages she would save for her own scribbling; paper just to write on was scarce in her house. Nothing here, however was as good in that respect as the *Congressional Record,* which her father got in the mail, the old copies of which seemed never to be stored here. Many of those issues were graced with a perfectly blank page at the back which could easily be removed without harming anything.

Suddenly in the shuffle a strange pamphlet appeared; she'd seen nothing like this before. It was an old catalog of machinery parts, with lots of pictures, but nothing she understood very well. She gave the pages a quick flip, meaning to toss the pamphlet back, when she saw something green between the pages. She paged for a second look. Money! She had thought it was money the first time. A five-dollar bill? It said "five" and had a picture of Lincoln, but it was larger than the bills she had seen before. Could she be sure it was real money?

She raced back to the house.

"Your grandfather must have been paid by some farmer and didn't take time to put the bill away in his cashbox. Instead he put it between the pages of his catalog." Her father said this, and Tante agreed. Both of them were amazed. Ann was amazed, too. She had never known her grandfather, yet here, before she was even born, he had left a five-dollar bill between the pages of an old catalog. She tried hard to imagine it.

That same summer in the midst of the big drought, another windfall occurred that Ragnild interpreted as an answer to prayer. A truck with a highway department insignia on the cab door drove into the yard.

"We think you have a valuable vein of gravel on your farm, Mr. Kristian," said the stranger. "We would like to survey that knoll." He was pointing in a northeasterly direction toward Henrik's dried-up oats.

"That may well be," Henrik replied. "It's been too sandy for good crops even when there has been plenty of rain. Certainly, go right ahead."

Although Henrik agreed with his wife that the discovery of first-rate gravel on his farm was Providential, it proved to be a mixed blessing. A part of a field and a portion of his pasture was stripped of topsoil, which came to lie in mounds covered with weeds. And there was nothing to be done with the large rocks, which came up with the huge shovel, but to dump them at a comfortable distance, taking up more space from his pasture. But he was paid by the square yard for the gravel that rolled out in trucks three yards at a time. The gravel, he was told, was rich in clay, the best possible road surfacing, and this made him proud. And best of all, the checks were yielding money for interest; no more need to borrow from Anna.

But the gravel trucks, too, turned out to be a plague. The dust they stirred up hung as a thick cloud over the farm and no rain fell to bring relief. Ragnild would try to get her washing done and her clothes dry early in the morning before the worst of the dirt billowed against her loaded clotheslines. And Henrik, not convinced that this was entirely good fortune, made this observation to his wife: "Our farm is being hauled away by the yard."

What was Ann to do with her five-dollar bill? She had a choice of keeping the large, old bill as a souvenir—the longer she held onto it, the more valuable it would become—or she could cash it in at the bank for a crisp, new bill. Naturally she chose the latter, although her father had given it a long look, as if there were no choice but to make it a keepsake.

First she began studying the Sears Roebuck catalog. There were so many things there she could order. White shoes. Wouldn't it be nice to have a pair of white sandals to wear with summer dresses? A camera. Imagine her, a mere child, owning a camera and lining up people to have their picture taken! A shiny, yellow raincoat. That would be it! There was a hat that went with it, too. She hurried to find a pen and then began to fill out the order blank very carefully. The slicker, as it was called, cost $3.98. She would have a whole dollar left for something else. A fountain pen $.59, and, oh yes, there must be something left for postage. The order was ready. She folded it properly and put it into the yellow envelope. She didn't seal it or bring it to the mailbox, however; instead she put it inside one of her books.

Now that money couldn't be spent for foolishness! She would look funny, wouldn't she, in a slicker, especially since her chums wore nothing like that? And the teacher hadn't let Willis write with a fountain pen in school, so why should she have one? What would be worthy of five whole dollars which she had found almost like a miracle? She could put it in the bank, a savings account, her mother had suggested. Then she wouldn't have to decide right away, and besides, there would be interest. It would certainly be better than a yellow raincoat! It was so much money, more than Henry earned in several days threshing, and Henry needed money now, too, since he was going to college in the fall.

Give it to Henry! That would really be worthy, yes it would. Her heart jumped at the thought. It might be embarrassing though. She wanted her family to think it would be nice of her to do this, but, at the same time, she could conceive of it as being rather startling. But what more important use could she think of? None.

On the campus of Augsburg College, Henry opened the envelope Ann had given him just moments earlier. In it he found the crisp, five-dollar bill. He looked up. Just now the family had driven away in the old familiar car. Finally he climbed the stairs to the third floor of the big, yellow dormitory, and he was alone in a strange room. He suddenly felt weak. It couldn't have been the effort of the climb. He sank into a chair. How could she do it?

Weeks later, Ann's father began to wonder what she had decided to do with her five-dollar bill. "I gave it to Henry," she told him. He almost said, you needn't have done that, Ann, but he didn't. "I hope he will be as good to you as you have been to him," he said instead, drawing her close to him. Ann smiled. It felt good to have her father say that.

In May of 1932, Ann finished rural school, the eighth grade. For two-hundred or more graduates from the 196 rural schools of Goodhue County, gala graduations exercises were held in early summer at the magnificent Sheldon Memorial Auditorium in Red Wing, the county seat. Ann had been there when Henry graduated from the eighth grade, and she never forgot the sight of all those boys and girls sitting on the big stage with the floodlights on them, the girls in pretty, pastel summer dresses and the boys in shirts, ties and white, duck pants. Of course it meant that she, too, would someday be sitting there.

Not only did the Kristian family see Ann graduate that summer, but they saw the new courthouse. Henrik led his family up the long, marble steps.

"This building belongs to us," he said in the manner of a guide.
"To us?" said Ann, catching up alongside him.
"We, the citizens of Goodhue County, own this magnificent, new building." He stopped and looked back at his family. "Now we'll see if the clerk of court is home."
The clerk of court greeted with enthusiasm his friend Henrik Kristian, who had helped elect him. He shook the hands of each member of the family as Henrik introduced them.
"And this is Ann, our graduate."
"Congratulations," he said, holding onto her hand longer than the others. "Now would you all like to look around?"
Ann liked this man. He wore rimless glasses which made him look impressive. The duties of county officers, Ann could readily list, but now she didn't bother remembering that, as she walked down the hall, looking at the beautiful architecture; suffice it that this man did important work in government. She wondered how much all this grandeur cost, and she wondered, too, how poor people like themselves could afford such a building. But here it was! Maybe they weren't so poor after all.

Chapter 13

"I'm so sick of this dress I'll never wear it again!" exclaimed Ruthie as she came downstairs dressed for church one Sunday morning. "Mama, when are people going to see me in something else?"

Ragnild was gathering her music off the piano. She took a quick look at herself in the kitchen mirror to see if her hat was on straight. Her Ruthie was almost thirteen this March morning, 1935, and things like clothes meant a great deal.

"Hurry or we'll be late. Papa's got the car out," cried Ann with her hand on the back-door knob.

Sunday mornings were always like this. With the motor running, Neil and his father sat in the car with exaggerated forbearance, waiting for the women.

The Kristians had joined the church in town when the children were old enough to go to Sunday school. The church on the hill north of the old town had been torn down and a beautiful, new building erected in Wanamingo.

Although Aspelund, that church of Henrik's childhood, had the departed Kristians in its cemetery, it seemed right to him, as times were changing, to leave the little, rural congregation for one in the more immediate community.

On Sundays they left home shortly before ten o'clock, the Sunday school hour, with the regular church worship to follow at eleven. While Ragnild and the children were in Sunday school, Henrik spent the hour before church at Sjur's Cafe, where he and its proprietor would look over the Sunday paper.

Henrik wondered when Ragnild's activities in the church would let up. She had been Sunday school superintendent for several years, and now, even though she wasn't that anymore, her help was always being sought. Last Christmas, when the person directing the Christmas Tree program became ill, Ragnild dropped everything in the middle of butchering and went to rehearse with the children. And now, this spring, when the sixth grade teacher complained about incorrigible boys in the class, Ragnild consented to finish the year. Then, she was one of the two people in the congregation who could play the church organ, a beautiful pipe organ installed in the sanctuary well ahead of the depression. Albeit she was assistant organist, she spent much time practicing on it. And, of course, Henrik had to realize that she enjoyed this instrument immensely. And she wouldn't be doing any of this if she didn't enjoy it and weren't so superbly able.

This spring, to top it all off, she had organized a youth choir. Having worked with children over the years, she had come to know the talent latent among the teenagers of the congregation, not least her own three. So this latest of projects was off the ground, and transpiring was an engagement to sing at the Spring Southeastern Minnesota District Luther League Convention in Rochester two Sundays hence. No, there was no let up with Ragnild, and she managed it all with poise and optimism.

Wondering why they were still so poor, Ruthie pushed in beside her mother at the opening service of the Sunday-school hour, just as the first hymn began. Here was her mother wearing the same dress and hat she had worn last year. Would they go down to the convention in Rochester, both she and her mother wearing these tiresome dresses?

Ragnild found the hymn being sung and shared the book with her daughter. As the singing progressed stanza after stanza, Ruthie began letting go of the ugly mood she had dragged in. Because she was close to her mother, a warm, singular feeling came over her. In her fancy she carried the image of the moment—her mother and she standing there singing out of the same book—into a kind of limbo, isolating it from its immediate context. She didn't want anything to change; she and her mother must go on singing even as they had done since Ruthie was very little. She was proud that her mother was directing the youth choir, and she was glad for her own singing voice.

Why should anything change? It was a foolish feeling, she supposed, but she didn't mean anything by it, really. It was just a fancy. Of course, her mother would become older; there was no help for that. She glanced at her mother now. No, she wasn't old; she'd perhaps be around for a long time. What about herself? Would she be an outstanding singer some day? But she thought she'd outlive her mother; that was logical. She wondered how it would be when her mother was gone and she was left in the world. They were singing the last stanza of another song now, and soon they would break up, mother to her class, which everyone, but her, thought was unruly, and Ruthie to hers, the Confirmation class, taught by an old man, where she could continue dreaming. Bringing a Bible and sitting quietly while he taught was all he ever demanded of them.

Ruthie watched his stiff, old hand write "P" behind her name in the attendance record. As soon as she had found in her Bible the scripture lesson for the day, she was free to let her fancy move where it would.

Ruthie knew of the other mother way back there when she was born; Tante had told all about her. It always came up when the old Vossing showed up, that old man who never rode in a car but walked to see his neighbors. He didn't come very often, either, but when he did appear on the road, she was reminded, even as she was told from the start, that she had a grandfather. There were no other grandparents, only she had a grandfather, and he was this man. She had two sisters, too, and a father whom she had never seen, Tante always said, especially after she had gotten a letter from Everett, Washington. Ruthie had known this all her life, but she never felt different from Neil or Ann, she and Neil being uniquely twins. Tante made a lot of that, too. She was Ruthie, yes, Ruthie, who was going to sing at Rochester next Sunday, and she wanted a new dress, and she wanted her mother to have a new dress.

"Ruth Kristian, verse six," prompted the teacher, his eyes fixed on her.

She was called back. The class was reading the scripture aloud, a verse each, going from one to the next around the circle. His eyes were immensely patient; that's how she always saw this old man of the congregation, those tired eyes. She was sorry she had been inattentive.

"Ruthie, come let's take a look upstairs in the closet and see if we can find something to make over," said Ragnild after the Sunday dinner dishes were done. "We should be able to sew you a new dress to wear next Sunday."

Through the depression years, when there was little or no money for clothes, Ragnild with her sewing machine had kept her girls looking respectable. She ordered cotton prints from Sears Roebuck catalog at ten cents a yard and made from them perky, summer dresses. The dressy silk and woolen fabrics were harder to secure. These she got in the form of used clothing from several of her sisters. One unmarried sister, who did special nursing in the homes of rich folk in Chicago, sent little-worn garments which were offered to her before they were given to charity. Another sister, who had daughters older than her own, sent dresses and suits needing little, if any, alteration. Nothing arrived from these sources which Ragnild couldn't convert into the lastest fashion.

"I like this blue one," said Ruthie, pulling at the skirt of a dress as they nosed among the garments on hangers. "These tiny prints—do you think it's too old for me?"

"No, I don't think so. We could trim it with white. How about a white ruffle collar? Here is a white ruffle on this blouse. See how nicely it is edged? It would make a beautiful collar."

"But maybe you could wear this dress the way it is? It looks like it might just fit."

"I don't need a new dress just yet."

"You do too, Mama! Next Sunday you'll be up in front of a lot of people."

"But they won't have seen my dress. It's not as if the program were here, you know. The dress I have is just fine."

Ruthie wasn't so sure, but she guessed what her mother said was logical. Inside she cried for her mother, though. She deserved the best dress in the country! Nothing in any of these dumpy closets was good enough! "Maybe a new hat then?"

"Isn't my hat all right?"

"It is. I forgot. It is, really." It had been a problem, but at last she and Ann had found a hat that did suit their mother. They were still trying to convince Ragnild that she should have a bob. Many women were cutting their hair these days, and why shouldn't mother get rid of that pug which unraveled so easily and always interfered when she tried the more stylish hats?

"Really, Mama, you look beautiful. All the time you look beautiful!" cried impulsive Ruthie, throwing her arms around her mother. Ruthie did this often, and every time it warmed Ragnild's heart.

The blue dress with the wide-ruffled, white collar became the sewing project of the week. Tante, who just returned from Kenyon that very day, could always be counted on for handwork. She carefully ripped the seams and pressed the pieces ready for Ragnild to lay on the pattern and cut. Ruthie was put to work basting seams after which Ragnild let her stitch them on the machine. When the dress was together, Tante sat for a full day with the prize on her lap. No one could do the hand stitching the way she did!

The clothing projects of womenfolk had always been close at hand in the environment of Henrik's house, be it his mother at the spinning wheel or his wife at the sewing machine, but not until his daughters demanded of him an observation had he ever paid much attention. Yes, indeed, Ruthie certainly looked lovely in that dress! He noticed, too, that she was no longer a child, and he remembered that she and Neil would be confirmed in the fall.

Anna, arriving for the summer earlier than usual this year, came with the question: where would she go next fall? With the passing of her mother, Elisa Hanson had given up the duplex and moved away. Likewise, Anna had given up her one room and stored her household things among the other items in the back bedroom of her own building. The day she locked the door upon what she owned, Anna caught her limbs shaking. She steadied herself upon her brother's arm.

"Are you all right?" asked Henrik.

"I'm all right."

But he wasn't so sure. She seemed to cling more to stop the trembling than to lean for walking. For a fleeting moment he wondered what was to become of her.

"We must ask her to make this her home now," said Ragnild as she and Henrik were out repairing a fence. The cows had been hard on fences during these years of drought, and a new corner post was needed.

"She'll be away from her friends," said Henrik who didn't seem to want to talk about it.

"What friends? You're always talking about her friends. I don't know who they are anymore. Times change, you know. Some people move and some people die. Selma Nelson has asked Anna to come and live with her, but Anna doesn't seem to go for it."

"Selma Nelson, you say? Why should she turn her down?"

Ragnild did not like the sarcasm in his voice. "It wouldn't be her home, Henrik. She feels that this is her home. Can't you understand that?"

"I never wanted you to live with either of my sisters. At the time we were married it was my mother."

"What was wrong with that?"

"She was easier to live with than my sister."

"I never said that."

"It's no good, two women in the same house."

"Henrik, how you talk! If it happens that in a family there—"

"All right, all right!" Henrik dropped the post auger on the ground and reached for the post he had brought for the corner. "Here. Be sure to hold it straight now while I tap in the dirt around it."

The two of them were succeeding at the task at hand. That's how it went; they worked together.

"She bakes good bread, Henrik. She helps me a lot."

"Maybe she does what the girls should be taught to do."

"I wouldn't worry about that, if I were you."

With echoing hammer strokes, Henrik drove in the staples that pinned the barbed wire firmly to the post. Soon they would have the job done.

"We should settle it with her soon. It would ease her mind."

"All right, you do that."

"No, you must do it, Henrik."

What Henrik had been dreading ever since Anna broke her hip had now come to fruition. Anna had come for good. And with her came all her furniture. Not all at once, but gradually, so that everything was slowly altered.

The downstairs bedroom, which was to be hers, she furnished with the elegant bird's-eye-maple bedroom set she had had in her own front bedroom. She put up her own curtains. Then the bed which

Ann had loved on her visits to Tante came and replaced the one in which Ann and Ruthie slept. Soon chairs in the parlor were replaced by better ones of hers. "How nice," they all said except Henrik; with each replacement his resentment grew. For want of a better place to store the cast-off pieces, the old chairs and beds were carried out to the granary. "I won't let you throw out my chair!" he cried out one day. Seeing his temper flare up, Anna was hurt. "I mean no harm," she later told Ragnild, who quickly consoled her. "He thinks that chair is comfortable, rather like an old pair of shoes." Ragnild said. "I'm sure that's what he meant."

Times began to improve noticeably after Franklin D. Roosevelt took office in 1933, and Henrik saw hope for the nation again under what was called the "New Deal." By 1936, a huge majority of the electorate shared Henrik's hopes by voting FDR into office for a second term, every state except Maine and Vermont giving him their electoral votes. Ann, following her brother's example, enrolled at Augsburg College that fall with the same tuition scholarship, but she lived off-campus, doing the work of a domestic for room and board. Henry, having prepared himself for secondary teaching en-route to higher education, was on his second year as a high school instructor in a small town in western South Dakota. He considered himself lucky. There were many unemployed among recent college graduates, not the least those who had prepared themselves for teaching. Although no one could take the place of Henry in his father's eyes, Neil proved to be a better farmer than his brother. Even if Neil didn't have it in him to be companionable, he was a far better mechanic than his father and had an adroitness upon which Henrik was beginning to draw heavily. The twins had two years left of high school; Henrik was glad of that; there was something disconcerting about having one's children grow up.

Then one day Ragnild announced that she had better see a doctor. She reported that she had tried several kinds of laxatives and that all had failed to help her. Upon seeing their family doctor, she was referred to the hospital in Faribault where she was immediately taken into surgery. It was discovered that she had cancer of the colon, which caused a blockage of the digestive track. It was successfully removed and, as things were explained to Henrik, if no complications set in, her chances for recovery were excellent. The dread disease had not visibly spread.

Upon learning the outcome of the operation, Henrik immediately sat down and wrote to Henry and to Ann, letting them know their mother's condition.

Since she had asked to see the twins, Henrik brought Neil and Ruthie to visit their mother on the third day after her surgery. Never having been in the hospital before, they both fell silent as they moved along with their father into the medicinal odor of the long corridor, where nurses all in white hurried back and forth.

They knew their mother would be lying in bed, but what they saw was foreign to anything they had imagined. The bed was narrow, so very high, and dazzling white. The mattress was raised at the head so their mother could see them as they entered by letting her head roll slightly on the pillow. That she would move so little, had never occurred to them.

They watched as their father bent over to greet her.

"I'm well taken care of here," they heard her say. Her voice was more familiar than the rest of her; they were glad to hear it.

"I'll go and find the doctor and see what he has to say today," said Henrik finally. "I'll leave the twins here with you."

"Come, my dears," she said when their father had left. "How good of you to come. Out of school?"

"No, this is Saturday," answered Neil, shifting on his feet.

"You want to sit down. There's a chair."

Neil sat.

"My hair is untidy, isn't it Ruthie?"

"No, Mama."

"Want to comb it a bit? There's a comb in the stand."

"All right." Ruthie found the comb and worked the strands off her mother's forehead with short little strokes. She dared not tackle anymore; most of her mother's long hair was in a braid.

"How's Tante?" Her words were spoken slowly. It was perhaps hard to talk when one is lying down.

"She's fine. She wanted to come and see you, too, but she said she'd wait till you come home. She wants everything to be in order. You know how she is." Ruthie kept stroking with the comb.

"Henry and Ann?"

"We thought they might come this weekend. They're not here yet." Ruthie kissed her mother lightly on the cheek. "There now."

"Is it better?"

"Yes, lots better, Mama." Ruthie put the comb away. She lingered. Finally she walked toward the window and looked out. Nothing out there registered; all she saw was the woman on the bed behind her. She thought of sitting somewhere, too, when she heard her mother speak again.

"Do you remember your catechism?" Neither of them dared ask her to repeat this sudden request. They would settle for what they thought they heard.

"Yes, Mama, I think so," answered Ruthie, returning to the bed.

"You, Neil?"

The urgency in the voice made him rise to his feet. "Yes, I hope so," he hesitated.

"I want to hear the Third Article. Come, let us say it together."

They had never felt compelled by their mother before; this was utterly confounding! It had been two years since Confirmation; certainly it couldn't be a check-up to see if they still remembered what they had memorized. She said she wanted to hear the third Article. What kind of a place was this to say the Third Article?

Neil walked toward the bed, but as he did so, he eyed the door. "Please, Mama—" Neil couldn't find it in himself to oblige. Would his father have?

She took his hand. She smiled at him out of eyes larger and brighter than he had known them to be.

"Ruthie? You and I will say it then?" She took Ruthie's hand. Now she had one on each side of her.

After looking across at Neil, Ruthie nodded. Neil would want her to, even if he couldn't.

> I believe that I cannot of my own reason or strength believe in Jesus Christ, my Lord, or come to Him, but the Holy Ghost has called me by the Gospel, enlightened me with His gifts, sanctified and preserved me in the true faith. Even as He calls, gathers, enlightens, and sanctifies the whole Christian Church on earth and preserves it in union with Jesus Christ in the one true faith.
>
> In this Christian Church He richly and daily forgives me and all believers all our sins, and on the last day He will raise up me and all the dead and will grant me and all believers everlasting life. This is most certainly true.

After the first phrase Ragnild's voice became less and less articulate, and soon Ruthie was saying it alone. The words came as fluent and sure as on the day of Confirmation. Their mother's eyes closed and her mouth dropped open; it seemed easier for her to breath that way.

When Ruthie's voice punctuated the final period, Ragnild's eyes opened again, searching the two of them before her. She brought her lips together before she spoke. "Thank you. God bless you both," she whispered, squeezing with little strength the hands she held. Her hands were warmer than theirs.

As a nurse entered the room, the clasped hands were dropped; the intrusion was a signal for the visitors to retreat from the bed.

"Perhaps we should leave and let her sleep?" Ruthie questioned the nurse.

"There's a waiting room to your left. You'll see the sign." The voice was low and matter-of-fact.

The twins slowly moved toward the door. Their heads were hanging.

"Do you think she's going to die?" said Neil.

Ruthie was startled. "Of course not. Don't you say such a thing!"

...raise me and all the dead...

"Then why did she . . . ?"

"Neil, can't you understand? It was like . . . family devotion. You know how Mama never forgets family devotion."

Neil said no more. They found chairs in the waiting room and remained there until their father came.

"Neil, you drive the car home. Ruthie, go with him. I'm staying here."

They did as they were told. Neither spoke the whole way home. They kept hearing, over and over again, their father's instructions.

After a sleepless night, Ruthie joined her brother in the barn as she had done the evening before. The words her father had spoken had all but disintegrated with bombarding repetition in her head, but the context of fear surrounding them had not gone away.

Neil made two trips to town on Sunday morning, first bringing Ruthie to her Sunday school class and then returning for Tante in time for the church service. For Sunday dinner, Ruthie set the table for three. Tante filled a serving bowl with meatballs and gravy, the last of the home-canned meat. There were more potatoes than they could eat. For dessert they finished the cake Ragnild had stirred up and baked before going to the hospital.

After dinner Tante went to her room. She always took naps then. Neil decided against turning on the radio—he thought it best not to disturb Tante—and went out to the granary to tinker with the gasoline engine which had given up on the last day of threshing. Ruthie did the dishes and sought out her homework.

She should have studied her chemistry but instead opened her American literature text. They hadn't gotten to Emily Dickinson yet, but there was something about her picture that reminded Ruthie of a picture they had of Grandma Kristian. Funny, women must have all looked like that in those days. To Ruthie's scanning, the woman's poems were short.

> Safe in their alabaster chambers
> . . . lie the meek members of the Resurrection . . .

Ruthie felt an arching in the pit of her stomach. That's who she is—will be—we all are—*meek members of the Resurrection. He will raise up me and all the dead*—Ruthie saw the dazzling white bed and the graying hair of her mother on the pillow.

It was terribly quiet here in the kitchen! No one around, NO ONE AROUND! No one was standing by the stove, no one sitting in that chair with the newspaper! The clock with the carved pharaoh crown on its head made the only sound!

A car was turning into the yard. Someone must be bringing Papa home. She ran to the window. It was Pastor Nesvig, and he was alone.

As Ruthie invited in their guest, Neil came through the back door and Tante limped her way to the kitchen table.

"Please sit down, Rev. Nesvig," said Ruthie. "It's warmer in here than in the parlor. Shall I take your coat and hat?"

He removed his hat, but didn't relinquish it, and sank into a chair with his coat on. He placed his hat on the table in front of him.

"Henrik, your father, wanted me to stop here and tell you," he began, fingering the rim of his hat. He looked at each of them before continuing. "Your mother has passed away. About ten minutes after one, it was. I left here right after church and got there just a few minutes before she died. The doctors said peritonitis set in and her heart failed."

Unable to concentrate further on the three faces before him, the minister lowered his eyes and stared at the figures on the oilcloth on the kitchen table. A long moment passed as his words hung in the walls.

"Just before I came, she had blessed your father with the words of the "Priestly Benediction." How she had voice enough for it so close to her death, he couldn't figure out."

Neil and Ruthie looked at each other. Neither spoke.

"We mustn't wish her back," the minister continued. "Oh, how we're going to miss her! But at those times, instead of grumbling, we'll just have to thank God that we had the privilege of knowing her, and you, that you had such a wonderful mother."

"Could we offer you a cup of coffee, Rev. Nesvig?" asked Tante.

"No, thanks." He lifted his hat as if it were time to go. "Henrik will be back as soon as he gets arrangements made. Someone will bring him home."

As the family arrived in the narthex of the church, Ruthie couldn't believe her eyes when she saw the crowd which had gathered for her mother's funeral. The sanctuary was full. Most of the poeple were familiar, but Ruthie hadn't seen some of them very often. Sitting there with cherries on her hat was a lady who had said to Ruthie once, "Your mother was the best teacher I ever had." Yes, many had told her that.

As the family was forming a line to walk behind the coffin, the door, which someone had just closed, opened and a tall man with heavy, gray hair let himself in. Tante left her place at Ann's side and went over to talk to him. Finally he came over and shook hands with Henrik. He was ushered inside and someone found him a chair.

"Who's that?" whispered Ruthie, turning back to her brothers.

"I know him," she heard Henry whispering to Neil. Facing her he informed them both. "Rasmus Hegge."

"Who's he?"

"Never mind."

Rasmus Hegge—Hegge—my real father! Lightening flashed for Ruthie and the resulting thunder kept rolling as she walked beside her father who had adopted her and behind the coffin of the mother who had made her live. The spray of roses, riding on the closed lid, trembled. When the family was finally ushered into the reserved church pews, she was glad to sit down. She glanced at Henrik as he laid his arm along the pew behind her shoulder. His mouth was closed and set, his cheeks showed how he was clamping his teeth. It was good to be near him. And Neil, it was good to have him sitting at her other side.

Ellen Vessedahl, one of Old Wanamingo's children, married to Ragnild's brother, was busy with two other women in the pantry of the Kristian home, putting sandwiches and pieces of cake on platters. The people were returning from the cemetery and soon the serving would begin.

"So the evangelist is around again. I haven't seen him in years," said one of the women. "I heard he's conducting a series of meetings in Minneapolis. He drove down by himself, by the looks of it."

"If he'd cared at all for Sarah's family, he would have been back a long time ago," said Ellen.

"You were bridesmaid at their wedding, weren't you? I remember that very well. He's still just as handsome. He hasn't lost a bit of his hair, and now it is turning white."

"Do you think Ruthie knows he is her father?" asked the other.

"What difference does it make? He can't mean anything to her," replied Ellen.

"He didn't bring his wife and family," continued the first.

"He always travels alone," said Ellen, feeling the pain suffered by her childhood friend, Sarah. It was too painful to talk about.

"I suppose that's the way it is with evangelists away from their families so much of the time." "I wonder what he thinks seeing Ruthie, his own flesh and blood," persisted another.

"No thanks to him. Ragnild and Henrik have brought up a beautiful daughter." Ellen's voice was emphatic. "Frankly, I wonder why he came."

The platters were carried to the kitchen table. The house was filling with guests.

There was still one automobile left in the yard when Henrik in his overalls stepped through the back door, ready to join his boys doing chores. It was a Chrysler Rasmus Hegge drove. Henrik returned to the kitchen. He looked around.

"Where's Tante?"

Ann, who was putting the good dishes away in the buffet, looked up in surprise. "Tante? I guess she is out in her room. Ruthie is there, too."

"I must talk to you, Anna," said Henrik outside the bedroom door.

"Come, then."

Ruthie was helping change the bedding. The room was evidently to be a guest room again.

"I see you have invited him to stay."

"I have."

"Where do you think you are going to sleep?"

"On the couch in the living room."

"Well, I didn't invite him." Henrik's anger was visibly rising. "Why did he have to come anyway?"

Anna reached out to the dresser for support. "He thought a lot of Ragnild. He's a friend of the family, and not being further away than Minneapolis, he—"

"Friend of the family, you say?"

"Well, your sister's husband, then."

"Was, not is!"

"And don't you think he might not have wanted to see Ruthie?"

"Me?" Ruthie let her elders know she was there.

"He baptized you, Ruthie," said Tante.

"Do you know what he wanted me to do just now? He wanted me to ride to Aspelund cemetery with him to see Sarah's grave," replied Ruthie, fixing serious eyes on Tante. "I told him I just couldn't."

Anna's body gave a twitch. She leaned more heavily against the dresser.

For fear a flood of tears would begin again, Ruthie walked toward the window. "See, he's on his way now."

Together the three of them watched the car drive out of the yard.

"He could have been on his way back to Minneapolis," said Henrik bitterly.

"I thought we must show hospitality. This house has always shown hospitality. Bestemor and Ragnild were always hospitable. It's a long ways back to Minneapolis starting so late in the day."

"Anna, can't you understand?" Henrik was pale. His voice was strangely mellow. "This has been a hard day. Must it end with the likes of him around?"

"He'll be gone tomorrow."

Not even as Henrik climbed the stairs and undressed for bed, did he really grasp what had happened. He had moved through these distressing days displaying for his family the dignity which must become someone in this situation. He had even found it in himself to exercise a decent tolerance just a few minutes ago when Rasmus proposed leading family devotion before bedtime. Why this man always showed up at family funerals and always got in his word about "God's will" and "harden not you heart" lest the "circle be broken" Henrik would never know, but he had been civil, handled it all with dignity. Tomorrow, after that car was finally out of the yard, everything would be back to normal.

Since an autumn chill gripped the room, he quickly got under the covers on his side of the bed. *Soon back to normal*—but Ragnild wasn't on her side of the bed! Ragnild was gone now; she would never come back. He tossed his arm across where she used to lie. He touched her pillow. Not many nights ago—the bedding was even the same—she had been here. He buried his face in her pillow. Ragnild! Ragnild! You are gone!

Chapter 14

"Tante, I have to run. Neil's waiting for me. Leave the dishes. I'll do them later," said Ruthie on her way out the door.

"Where are you going now?"

"4-H meets tonight."

"I'll do the dishes."

"Please don't, Tante. You must be tired. I'll do them. Please leave them."

Seconds later, Anna heard the motorcycle leave the yard. She shuddered for Ruthie's safety, hanging on the way she did behind her brother. Again Anna was left sitting alone at the supper table. It was always like this, the family running off somewhere and she seldom, if ever, with them. Henrik's habit of going to town every evening hadn't changed, in fact he needed the fellows at Sjur's Cafe more than ever now. "I forget my troubles," was how he put it. And Neil and Ruthie always had some excuse to run into town with him. All winter there had been basketball games, school play rehearsal, weekly choir practice, and now 4-H club.

It was different when Ragnild lived, then Anna went out more. She and Ragnild would go to Ladies Aid, not only in their own church, but as visitors in neighboring churches as well. All her life Anna had enjoyed such gatherings, but now she seldom went anywhere except to church on Sunday mornings, and then it was to rush home. Visiting after church was always cut short; it wasn't like the old days when no one hurried away. Ruthie was always there to take her arm and trot her off to the car.

Leave the dishes? What kind of housekeeping was that? Of course she was tired, but she would take her time. "Leave the work to Ruthie," Henrik kept saying, but Anna couldn't live in an untidy house; it wasn't Ruthie's fault if Anna found herself tuckered out at the end of the day.

She set together the dishes she could reach before rising from her chair. Then she began her tedious trips back and forth to the sink in the pantry. She could carry only a few dishes at a time and keep her balance as she limped along. Next she scratched a match and lit a burner under a kettle of water. Heating water wasn't as convenient as having it available when the wood-burning range was going, but May had brought warm weather and that meant using the kerosene stove. She put the table scraps into the saucepan, containing the morning's left-over oatmeal, and carried it out the back door to the dog.

Philox, the puppy that the twins had asked her to name, was soon ten years old now. And Anna always fed him well. Since table scraps were seldom enough, she boiled extra oatmeal in the morning to add bulk to his evening meal. And she was generous with milk, too. Philox, no special breed, just a sand-colored farm dog, stood by his dish wagging his tail. He knew it would take time for her to get down the steps, to reach his bowl and to balance herself as she scooped out what she had in the saucepan. She was to be depended upon, though. Every day she would come through that door. And she was always home; very seldom was he left alone these days. Anna found satisfaction in watching Philox eat what she had brought him. Giving his head little jerks with each bite, he tossed the food to the back of his mouth for swallowing. Anna was sorry there wasn't a bone this evening. She was reassured that he would soon be lying on the front steps; he always lay there when she sat in the wicker rocker on the porch.

She returned to the kitchen. Her most treacherous task was getting the hot water to the sink; she was careful never to fill any kettle too full. Running water and electricity would certainly make keeping house a lot easier. Think how nice it would be to have a refrigerator! She dreaded the coming of hot weather, which meant trotting up and down the cellar steps before and after every meal with the butter and the milk. She let the stacked plates sink into sudsy water. Each glass, cup, and dish was meticulously washed, rinsed, dried and placed on the shelf behind her.

Of course it was impossible for her to fill Ragnild's shoes. The family didn't expect it of her, and she didn't expect it of herself, so always there was that appalling void. The twins needed their mother. Oh, how Anna saw this, yet when she tried to reach out to them she sensed resentment—even anger—that she was around in their mother's stead. And Henrik needed his wife. The best that Anna could do was to see to his meals, wash and mend his clothes, and have a meticulously laundered, white shirt ready for Sunday. No, she had no claim to being the lady of the house either, yet in an apparent sense, who was, if she wasn't?

After having wiped the kitchen oilcloth and hung up the dishtowel behind the stove, she decided against walking over to Josie and Emma Veblens'; although it was only a stone's-throw away and they would walk her home. They had asked her to come to see their bed of tulips, but that could wait until tomorrow; she had been on her feet enough today. She dropped into the wicker rocker on the front porch; its high back gave her a rest for her head.

As they had been doing all day, the faces in a dream of last night fluttered at the edges of her consciousness. Relaxing as she was, with nothing demanding her attention, she let them enter for fanciful examination. She had responded to the front doorbell of her home above the meat market by running with exceedingly light steps down the long stairway. It had been almost like flying except she did feel each step under her feet as she flew. Upon opening the door, she saw Lars Mundahl standing beside Ragnild, who was holding baby Neil in her arms, just as she had seen them the day of Sarah's tragic death. As she was about to admit Ragnild and to see Lars retire into the street, Anna suddenly heard someone on the steps behind her. It was Lars' mother, Jennie. "Come in, Lars," she cried. "Come with me. Hurry! You shall live, Lars, you shall live!" Anna had known Jennie Mundahl as a serene woman. She had had many sorrows in her life, always bearing them with quiet patience. This was indeed Jennie, but now she was alert and decisive, on a kind of rescue mission. Before Anna was able to move her sister-in-law up to the urgent mission of Sarah's newborn child, she saw Jennie and Lars climbing the stairs far up ahead. At this point Anna had awakened.

Anna brought her head forward from the high wicker back. She thought about Lars. He really had been the best of the Mundahl boys, so good to his mother. And he had given his heart to the Lord during the revival of 1893. And poor Jennie with that drunken husband of hers! No wonder she counted on Lars to live, almost as if it was in his father's stead.

Anna let her head fall back against the rest. Seeing people so vividly, those she had known long ago, gave them a renewed immediacy. It had been so long since Jennie left this world, almost as long as Anna's mother had been gone, and here only last evening she had seen her. And kind Lars, he, too, she had seen so unmistakably. He, too, had been gone a long time; he had died of pneumonia the winter after the death of her mother. Now his shop was gone, torn down, and the house stood empty, the bay window boarded up. That a house could stand empty for some twenty years was inconceivable; much more real was her dream. She had seen those dear people only last night.

How she wished she could have detained Jennie for a visit; she had seen that lovely, familiar face for such a short moment! Wouldn't it be nice if people would enter one's dreams on demand, having cozy visits which one could go around thinking about during the day? But people of the past came when they would and could never be detained. Where did they keep themselves? Surely dreams took place in a world beyond one's reach, timeless, in a sense, and yet so full of the stuff of real living.

Suddenly Philox jumped off the front step and began to bark. Someone had driven into the yard. It was probably someone looking for Neil; whoever it was could come to the front door. Anna remained in her chair.

"Well, hello there! I thought no one was at home here." It was the hearty voice of Selmer Johnson, a bachelor farmer who lived along the river road.

"Come in, Selmer," said Anna, bringing the rocker to a forward position and attempting to rise.

"No, no, don't get up." He let himself in the screen door. "I am bringing you folks some rhubarb. I always brought rhubarb when Ragnild lived. And this year there is so much of it."

"That is certainly thoughtful of you," said Anna. "Sit awhile, can't you? There's a chair over there."

He put the bundle of red stalks, still with their wide leaves uncut, beside the door and pulled up a chair beside Anna. "How are you folks getting along, then?" he asked.

The three Johnson bachelors were helpful neighbors, but Selmer was the only one apt to stay and visit. Anna was glad he had stopped by.

"We do all right," replied Anna. "Naturally we miss Ragnild."

"That we can all understand," said the good neighbor. "We all miss her. She did so much for everyone."

"It's hard for Henrik to take all the responsibility alone, especially with the children. She was such a good mother."

"That you can say."

"He worries himself sick about the twins riding around on that motorcycle. He thinks they are getting wild, don't you know. Neil put that machine together mostly from parts he found. Just like his grandfather, good with machinery. It's hard for Henrik to put his foot down."

"Young people like to have something smart to be riding around in. In our day it was horses and fancy harnesses. Henrik had those dapple-grays, remember?"

"That's so. But I don't think Henrik considers that the same thing."

"I suppose Ann will soon be home for the summer?"

"In another week. She has three years of college in now, and she has kept herself, you know, by working for her board and room."

She'll be good help for you."

"Maybe then we can clean house and put the garden in. And Henry is married, you know. He may not come until later on in the summer."

"So? I hadn't heard that."

"Just a simple home wedding last fall shortly after school started. He married a South Dakota girl. Her father is a minister."

"A Norwegian?"

"Oh yes. Her name is Solveig."

"She must be a nice girl with a name like that."

"I'm sure Henry thinks so."

Philox was back on the front step, his chin on his forepaws; there was comfort in hearing voices.

"Aren't the twins finishing high school this year?"

"That's so."

"My, Henrik certainly can be proud of his children all doing so well!"

"He's anxious about the twins, though. It isn't so easy getting the children started in life. Ruthie wants to become a nurse, and he hopes he can go along with that. We do need her at home, too, but how can we stand in her way?"

"She'd make a good nurse, I'm sure."

"And Neil. He says very little. He takes ahold of farm work very well. Ragnild always said he would be the farmer and carry on here. Henrik misses Henry, though. He and Neil don't get along as well. I know Neil is different, but he's a good boy."

"So Neil will stay home?"

"So far it looks that way, fortunately for us. I don't see how we'd get along without him. How are the fields?"

"They've never looked better. The small grain is up six inches. Does Henrik have his corn in?"

"Tomorrow, I heard him say. He was dragging today."

"I must be going, Anna. It was nice talking to you." He picked up the straw hat he had dropped beside his chair and rose.

"Thank you for the rhubarb. It was so good of you to come and talk for a while." Anna leaned forward in her chair, but felt she need not get up.

"Take care of yourself. Henrik is fortunate to have a sister like you. Good-bye then, Anna."

Philox had to move to let the neighbor out the door. He didn't bark now; he permitted the good man to get into his car.

Henrik was fortunate, he'd said, to have a sister like her. It was kind of Selmer to say that. Anna rocked longer, listening to evening sounds. A robin was still singing; soon it would be frogs. As she turned into the house, she glanced briefly at the rhubarb bundle tied with twine. She would ask someone to carry it in for her in the morning. She would be busy tomorrow boiling up the rhubarb with sugar and filling Mason jars. And Henrik might like a pie.

As Neil began farming with his father after graduation, the dreadful war raging in Europe clouded the horizon. It was talked of constantly at Sjur's Cafe, Henrik stressing, in no uncertain terms, that the United States must not get involved. No, he guessed the nations of Europe would never settle their differences. The munition makers, furthermore, wanted war, he said, and as long as there are huge profits to be had while young men die, he supposed there would always be war. But as December, 1941, brought in the Japanese attack on Pearl Harbor, such talk was useless and abandoned.

"We must apply for an agricultural deferment for you," Henrik told Neil. "I can't run this farm without you." Neil was silent at first. He wasn't quite as ready as his father to decide a matter which came up in such a hurry, and nothing was done immediately. In the meantime, Henrik found it hard to live with uncertainty.

Then one day in early June, Ruthie, home for a brief vacation from nursing, carried coffee and sandwiches to her father. He was cultivating corn, the tiny stalks just beginning to reveal themselves in rows. He caught sight of her coming along the edge of the field, but he dared not take his eyes off the fragile sprouts. So nice to have her home again, but how lonesome for Ragnild it made him.

"Neil has plans you should know about, Papa." she began immediately upon setting the lunch bucket on the ground. "He's twenty-one now and says he's going to enlist in the Air Corps."

Henrik drew off his gloves and threw them on the ground. "He told you that?"

"Yes, when he met me at the bus yesterday. He said he hadn't talked to you. I told him he must, right away. But you know how he is. By enlisting he thinks he might become an airplane mechanic. No doubt he'd be a good one."

Henrik sat down on a grassy mound near the furrow, but he didn't take his usual sip of coffee Ruthie had poured for him. The sandwiches lay before him on waxed paper. "That boy never talks to me. I never know what's up. He's not like Henry. I always knew what was on that boy's mind. If Neil leaves now, I'll have to start figuring out what I'm going to do. I'm too old to run a farm alone. Doesn't he know that?"

Ruthie turned around, grasped the top of a fence post and stared off in the opposite direction. She had told her father now. He needed to know this so he could remain reasonably calm during the upcoming distressing encounter with Neil. Her father was a very reasonable man, but stupid Neil didn't dare to talk to him.

"I'll have to rent out the land. Wayne Bakken, who boasts of his deferment, should be happy to take on a few more acres. I'd have to sell some of the cows." Henrik had begun eating now and Ruthie sat down beside him. "We must try to hang on to some of them, though. What would we live on if we didn't have a milk check every month? It won't be easy, Ruthie. Your Papa is getting old." He held out his empty cup for her to fill.

"I don't think you're old," said Ruthie. "But you don't have to run the farm. Rent, like you say. Let the pushy farmers with the putt-putting tractors do the farming." She reached for one of the cookies she had just taken out of waxed paper.

"I was thinking of getting a tractor before the fall plowing. Neil has been after me for a tractor for a long time."

"Now, don't. Rent." Ruthie began putting the lunch things into her bucket.

"It's easy for you to say, Ruthie. It's harder for me, but I guess you aren't far from right." He and Ragnild had made many decisions, sitting here like this.

Ready to head for home, Ruthie watched the horses raise their heads as Henrik reached for the reins and climbed onto the cultivator seat. She caught a whiff of the black, moist soil as the delicate operation began, the horses moving gingerly between the rows. How carefully her father guided them so that none of the tender plants would be disturbed! She supposed a tractor could be made to do that, too, but not with such quiet grace. Ruthie knew her father wasn't happy, and it made her sad.

Renting out his land and cutting down his herd was an exceedingly distressing thing for Henrik to do. Wayne Bakken's tractor was a mere mechanism going forth and back in his fields. Seeing empty stanchions in his barn bothered him, too. Certainly things were going backwards, things were falling apart. But he must hang on until the war was over; then Neil would be back and all this would be his. He never entertained the thought that Neil would do anything else; he had the knack that he himself lacked. He took comfort in the thought that Neil could make good as a farmer.

All his misgivings, all his uncertainties, all his lapses of desire to pick up the tasks of each new day stemmed from the loss of Ragnild. As the years went by, he became accustomed to this loneliness and fatigue, but there was always that search for her, unconscious though it usually was. He searched for her in his daughters and found glimpses of her there, but they never remained home long enough, always running off with their own affairs. He never found her in Anna, although he perhaps should have; she was always near at hand waiting on him. Instead, he ate so much pain with the food she fixed and found only misery in the cleanliness of his house. Even among women out side of his own household with whom he chanced to converse, he searched for morsels of satisfaction such as Ragnild had given him. And the search never let up, and life's luster never returned.

Shortly after Neil had left for the Air Corps, Henrik got a letter from Henry. Certain that he would eventually be drafted, Henry had joined the Navy where he hoped, with his kind of skill, to be assigned clerical work. His wife and two-year-old son would live somewhere in the vicinity of bootcamp as long as basic training lasted. Then, could she live near them until the war was over? Would Henrik look for an apartment for them in Wanamingo? Solveig wanted her own place. She had decided against living with her own parents, who had made another of their frequent moves and there was nothing for her in South Dakota.

Although Solveig had been around very little and Henrik scarcely knew her, he was overjoyed at the prospect. He had tried in vain to keep Ann and Ruthie around. He had wished Ann would have gotten a teaching position nearer home, but instead she was as far away as Brainerd, Minnesota, and couldn't be expected home until Christmas. Ruthie was in her last year of nurse's training at Swedish Hospital in Minnepolis, and worked on the floors now with no time to get away. In the back of his mind Henrik hoped she could work in Rochester upon completing her training. Then she might even drive back and forth as long as the weather was nice. But now, all this mattered less; finding an apartment for his daughter-in-law and his grandson, Henrik III, gave him more pleasure than he had had in a long time.

"You know why we have come here, don't you?" said Solveig as she poured coffee for him the day he helped her move into their modest household. "Henry wants Ricky to know his grandfather." Those words went a long way toward restoring life's lost luster.

Solveig was sunny and optimistic, and he needed that. Every morning he brought fresh milk to the apartment and in return he got a cup of coffee and a chance to talk. They read the same magazines and followed the war. And it surprised him how much Henry had told her about the family home, and Henrik certainly had to give her credit for listening and taking a genuine interest. She was intelligent and attractive. This daughter-in-law he was proud to introduce to his friends.

She got along equally well with Tante. Anna always blossomed around cheerful people; gloom gathered without them. Solveig was cozy in a way Ragnild had been, not quite, but almost. And Solveig was helpful. There were so many things Anna wanted done which her limited strength couldn't manage; now she welcomed eager hands.

But of greater benefaction was young Ricky. He followed his grandfather around the farm, responding with wonder to the routines that had grown drab for Henrik. He reawakened in his grandfather something long buried under layers of wontedness and treadmilling. Old Blossom, the only horse Henrik had on the place, got added attention, not to mention the six cows that were routinely recognized as they took their stanchions. "You can be in front of them," his grandfather cautioned, "but never behind them." And the boy complied. Philox hadn't played since his puppy days, but now with a small boy around, he permitted himself to be tussled for short periods.

And Tante had an ardent listener; everything she told him took on story proportions. One day, to keep him from being under foot while she washed the kitchen floor, she set him on a chair and proceeded to tell him the story of "The Last Morning," when the sky would fill up with angels bringing Jesus back to earth. He was coming to get all the people who belonged to Him. He would give them all wings so that they could fly back with Him into heaven. A loud trumpet would raise all those who were dead, and they, too, would have wings with which to fly with Him through the sky. The story dazzled with wonder! Why had Anna chosen to tell this story? Perhaps she needed to make it alive for herself once again.

Suddenly it occurred to her that he had never seen anyone wash the floor the way she did. Before she set him on the chair, he had wanted to try wringing the mop, but she told him he'd get himself all wet. She couldn't wash a floor on her hands and knees the way his mother did; Tante had no choice but to use a mop and pail. It never occurred to her that this tedious procedure could hold any kind of fascination—more so, even, than a story? This she wouldn't decide. She released him when she had wrung her mop for the last time, and he scampered out the door.

Christmas, 1943, was enhanced, too, by the presence of the child. It was the first time that the tradition of Santa Claus had been introduced into the Kristian family observance. Ricky had had his picture taken at age one with the white whiskered man, when he visited a department store in South Dakota. Ricky treasured this picture. Although he was too young then to remember the occasion now, he recognized himself sitting there in the lap of this Christmas fantasy, and the story grew ever more delightful as he contined to ask questions about his mysterious friend. "He'll be here tonight," his grandfather told him.

Henrik surprised himself. How could he now be giving credence to this mythological figure who could conceivably take on the exalted position of the Christ Child? He remembered an old minister, a long time ago, threatening that if he had a gun he would shoot Santa Claus because he didn't belong in Christmas. Henrik chuckled now; he felt a part of a conspiracy, time was allowing him. And even Tante seemed to have no qualms. She was like a child herself. He even sensed a glimmer of the Anna who had recklessly drawn Thor and Balder for him on her slate.

"Will he come down the chimney?" asked the small boy.

"Sure will," said his grandfather. "Right through the stove into the living room!" There needn't be a fireplace, although one would have been convenient just now. The door of the coal-burning space heater would have to do.

The child had no reason to be skeptical of his grandfather. Seeing the boy's dazzling eyes, Anna understood what was there; she, too, had been capable of conjuring up Arne's *Julenisse* one Christmas long ago.

Even as Peder had set up Henry's toy train, which really didn't seem so many years ago, Henrik set up a miniature farm, complete with buildings, fences, and animals, over the living room floor. The door would remain closed on this wonderment until the right moment. First the dishes from the festive Christmas Eve meal must be done, then all the family gifts under the tree be opened.

As the right moment arrived amid the delights of inspecting presents, Grandfather startled everyone into silence. "I heard the stove door rattle in the living room. Were any of you just there?"

Ricky tore toward the closed door as anticipation mounted behind him.

"He came!" announced the small boy in a matter-of-fact voice as he returned to the doorway. "See, Santa brought me a farm!"

During the winter that followed Henrik discovered a vexing problem while tending his animals in the confinement of his barn. As he reached high across the front of Blossom's stall with a bucket of water, he rubbed against a sore spot in his chest. Henrik knew he had a lump there, but he had shrugged off any anxiety about it; as long as it didn't hurt, it was easy to forget. As this happened more than once, he began making adjustments in his habitual way of watering his horse. Soon he was favoring the source of his pain more and more until it was interfering with all his work. Finally he decided the prudent thing to do would be to see the doctor.

It was imperative that the lump be removed, and quickly, according to the doctor, as it might be malignant. He had surgery in Faribault, where the trusted grandson of the late Østen Hanson was still practicing.

"Papa, I have come," said Ann approached his bed. "I came last night."

Ann had wasted no time getting herself on a bus upon receiving the message that he was in the hospital. The agony of her being absent from her mother's side seven years ago was still strong in her.

"So it's Ann! I didn't expect to see you." Henrik was visibly moved. "You're like your mama. Who else would I rather see?"

"I couldn't stay away."

"What about your school?"

"I hired a substitute for a week."

"You think a lot of your old dad, don't you?"

"You look a lot better today. I was in last evening, but you were fast asleep."

"I feel pretty good. Have you talked to the doctor? Has he told you it was cancer?"

"Oh, no!"

"He told me this morning. He pulled up a chair right there and sat down as if he had all day to talk to me. My, how he resembles his grandfather!"

"He told you it was cancer?"

"He did. But it's gone now. He said I was lucky I came when I did. He peeled it right out. He's a good surgeon, Ann. They couldn't do better in Rochester."

Cancer. Ann had wrestled with this worst of possibilities on the bus from Brainerd. Last evening there was some comfort; she had seen him, and he was stable and resting well. Now she knew. She was surprised at her father's optimism. It's gone, he said. She supposed that was so, something really to feel fortunate about.

"Come closer, Ann. I must look at you. Sit down in that chair. Now we can talk."

"Maybe you should rest. You've talked a lot already."

"Naw. I'm fine. I rest plenty right down in bed. You know I've never been sick, Ann. Resting in bed day and night is something I've never done. It's good of you to come to see your papa in the hospital."

Before sitting in the chair, Ann clasped her father's hand and kissed his cheek.

"My depression child. My, you have done well! You got yourself through college during the worst times."

"I guess I did count my pennies," laughed Ann. It was strange to be talking about such things now, but if he wanted to, it was pleasant. Ann felt close to her father. "I have money now. I could pay your taxes for you. Have you paid your taxes?"

"I'll bet you would, too," he chuckled.

"I would," she bantered back.

"Tante will be glad to see you. You'll go home with Ruthie, won't you? She's got the car and should be here any time now."

"Won't Tante come?"

"She always thinks there has to be someone at home, you know how she is."

"That's true. She always has things ready and in order. She treats me like a princess when I come, always a bed made up with clean sheets, and always fresh cinnamon rolls because she knows I like them."

"She's partial to you."

"I don't think so. She does a lot for us all."

"Bless you, Ann. You sound like your mother. Of course, Tante had always done a lot for us."

Henrik's elated mood continued throughout the day. He introduced Ann to each and every nurse, orderly and cleaning woman who came through the door. When Ruthie and Solveig arrived, he had three daughters to introduce to those caring for him. For a short period he allowed them to leave him. "I must have my afternoon nap," he said.

In late afternoon, when Dr. Hanson arrived on his routine visit of patients, the exchange between the two men became a hilarious uproar. Henrik began telling stories the daughters had heard a hundred times, and the doctor countered with his "one better." "So like your grandfather!" Henrik would say over and over again.

"We've missed you around here," said his friend, Sjur, as Henrik showed up again at the cafe. "The place wasn't the same without you."

"Well, you know you can't keep a good man down. Yes, it was cancer." Henrik nodded at the questioning faces of the men who had come in. "You might as well know it. But it's gone now. The doctor peeled it right out."

Chapter 15

"Neil, look at that beautiful living-room set," exclamined his bride of one week. "Let's buy it for our new home."

Neil had met Gloria, a southern belle, while stationed in Huntsville, Alabama. Being a mechanic, he remained behind in the country longer than most Air Corps personnel, plenty of time to fall in love. When the war was over, he delayed his return home to Wanamingo long enough to marry his girl who had waited faithfully for him during his ten months overseas.

"The house we will live in is full of furniture already," said Neil, trying to move her along the street past the department store display. They had arrived by train in Minneapolis with a four-hour stopover before catching a bus to Wanamingo. New merchandise was beginning to appear in shop windows, causing considerable excitement; for so long there had been a scarcity of almost everything.

"We have our wedding money to spend. We really can afford it, you know," said Gloria with irresistible pleading in her eyes.

No girl had ever interested Neil until he met Gloria. She was exquisitely beautiful, different from any girl he had ever known. Her eyes were brown, but lighter than chestnut, and her hair a rich brunette, auburn, you might call it. Her smile came easily, bringing light into those eyes and revealing beautiful teeth beneath her supple, rouged lips. She had the figure any young girl would covet and looked like a model in whatever she wore. She had class, that's how Neil put it. She was no "hussy" who hung around canteens; no, she had charm, and it existed just for him. Everything about her charmed Neil, not least her accent. Her manner of speech was music. He felt fortunate; no one, absolutely no one, could compare with her. Unable to put it off any longer, he had written to his family in late spring that he was bringing home a bride. He knew this would be startling news for them, but he had been away so long it was hard for him to picture exactly what their reaction would be. He dismissed whatever misgivings he felt by telling himself: how could they help but be taken with her! She was exceptional.

"We needn't be in any hurry to spend it." He pleaded, too. "You should really see our place first. And it's not as if there weren't others living there. My father and..."

"I know that. But wouldn't it be fun to have something in the house which would be ours, our very own?"

"It would be, Honey," he replied, clasping her closer as they continued gazing into the display window. "But the house is small, quite a bit smaller than yours. Your house had very large rooms compared to ours."

"Come, let's go in anyway and see how much it costs." Although he was unwilling, she drew him into the furniture store.

"This is the first we've gotten in since the war," said the salesman. "It's the very latest." Neil shuddered when he remembered how tiny the parlor of his Wanamingo home was, with too much stuff in it already. Certainly such massive furniture as this didn't belong there. But he tried his best to accommodate such a possibility. In the summer, when the space heater was gone, perhaps the davenport could sit along the north wall. But what of the chair?

"I love it, Neil, I just love it! Let's get it. They say they'll ship it anywhere. We have the money. Let's buy something really nice with it."

Unable to withstand the persuasion in the brown eyes, Neil reluctantly consented.

When they were seated on the crowded bus, assured that their baggage was duly checked and that freight would yield the rest of their belongings including the new davenport and chair, Gloria took out a cigarette, holding it ready for Neil to light.

"Another thing I must tell you, Honey," said Neil, anticipating a bit more realistically, now, introducing his bride to his family. "You can't smoke in our house. None of us have ever smoked in front of our father nor our aunt, and I don't want you, of all people, to be the first."

"I can't smoke in our own house?"

"If Ruthie or I want a fag, we go somewhere in the yard, either behind the granary or in the barn."

"Oh, Neil, really? You have no courage to be yourself."

"It's not a matter of being myself, it's a matter of not hurting them. My father has never smoked a whiff of tobacco in his life. Neither has he ever taken a drink. We kids haven't succeeded in being that pure, but we respect him and wouldn't, for the world, light up in front of him."

"So you sneak."

"Yes, I guess you could call it that, but I'd rather think of it as having respect for the old man."

"Neil, I must say I love you precisely because you're that kind of a guy. Strange, now isn't it, that consideration for him should come before consideration for me—and stranger yet, I don't really mind."

"Gloria, you're great!" Neil smooched. All G.I.s smooched with their girls. It was a common sight.

Finally by autumn of 1945, the war was over. That there would be no more casualty lists brought an immense relief to every city and small town in the land, and not least to Henrik, who would be permitted both his sons again, alive and unmaimed. Steadily the G.I.'s were filtering back, a few at a time, and Henrik grew expectant that Henry and Neil would be returning any day now.

Since he had been engaged in the European theater, Henry returned before VJ Day, in time to enroll in the graduate school at the University of Minnesota under financial aid to veterans. He moved his family into a crowded, student-housing project consisting of rows and rows of quonset huts. These were not far different from what he had known in the service, but with all the difference—he was reunited with his wife and son and, at long last, back to work at his chosen career.

That Henry was about to fulfill his desire for higher education gave his father deep satisfaction, too. Through the years, an uncomfortable conviction had been plaguing Henrik Kristian: he should have prepared himself for law or politics, but now, be that as it may, he had a son who would realize these dreams. Although he would miss companionship with Solveig and Ricky, they would be no farther away than Minneapolis, a two-to-three hour trip in Henry's prewar Model A Ford.

Henrik knew he would have to wait a bit longer for his second son, who had been in the Pacific for the past ten months, yet he held out hope that he would be back before winter. Henrik felt himself unable to carry silage and hay another season, to his herd sheltered in the barn; the chores had become just too much. But the months dragged on. Ann, helpful as she was, had gone back to her teaching job up north, leaving only Ruthie. Although Ruthie drove back and forth from home to Rochester, as Henrik had hoped, she was gone most of the time, it seemed, working unpredictable shifts at St. Mary's Hospital. Henry was helpful when he came home, as occasion would permit for a visit, but when winter set in for good, his trips home were less and less frequent. "Why don't you get a schoolboy to help with the chores?" Anna kept saying, suffering her own kind of fatigue, always doing more than she should so that Ruthie could help her father outside rather than do housework indoors. But Henrik saw it as no solution. It was more of Anna's nagging which was not to be taken seriously, but to be endured, a woman harrowing a man's patience.

Subtly, a new kind of fatigue was taking grip on Henrik. At first he didn't distinguish it from the weight of what was demanded of him every day. He found himself sighing deeply as if the air were stifling and, he out of breath. Ruthie, burdened all winter with the conditions at home, grew more and more apprehensive as she watched her father's frequent pauses for rest when he did his work. She had tried for three years now to convince her father to go for a medical check-up. "Don't nag," he always retorted, "I'll see a doctor when I need one." To her more gentle attempts at persuasion he would simply say, "Your papa is worn out, Ruthie, that's all." And Ruthie's heart would cry out for her father, but she was quite powerless to help him.

Finally, on that day in late spring the letter came from Neil. He was married and bringing home his bride. That's what all this delay had been about, thought Ruthie. She was angry at her brother for his all-too-familiar way of dealing with his father—this long, cruel silence.

"This farm hardly supports us," Henrik exclaimed. "How does he think it will support a wife and family at this stage with only a few cows, worn-out machinery, and no tractor. What's he thinking about, anyway?"

"They must have the downstairs bedroom." Tante was figuring out the sleeping arrangement in the small house. "And I will move in with Ruthie. Neil's room isn't big enough. It will have to be a closet from now on, or a room for Ann when she comes home."

Henrik scorned this display of hospitality on Anna's part, sacrificing her room, always self-sacrificing. "Neil must take care of his own wife. It's not for us to decide for him."

"You said it, Papa! It's his problem," exclaimed Ruthie. "But at least he's coming home!"

True. Neil was coming home at last. In spite of Henrik's initial outburst, a tremendous sense of relief came over him. Now the responsibilities he had carried so long would be lifted from his shoulders. And no one interfered when Tante set about making the downstairs bedroom the bridal suite. Anticipation sparked enough energy for her tedious trek, a half step at a time, up the stairs, bringing her own things to other quarters.

At first sight, Gloria impressed everyone in Neil's family as he had thought she would. Her impeccable manners dealt with all awkward moments so that even the coming of the huge davenport and chair was not as overwhelming as Neil had figured it would be. Her fascinating southern accent, the slackened pace of her language, gave Henrik and Anna the feeling she has lots of time for them and was in no hurry to flit away somewhere, that annoying trait of the young. Although one might judge it to be shallow, her friendliness was reassuring.

In the wake of Henrik's feeling of relief that Neil had finally taken the burden from him, Henrik consented to do as Ruthie had begged—to go to the doctor. The fatigue he felt wasn't merely the result of overwork or advancing years, it had, as he had begun to suspect, its own cause. The cancer was reoccurring, this time in Henrik's lungs. It had shown up on a chest x-ray.

His family marveled at the optimism with which Henrik lay hold on the hope held out to him by his doctor: radiation treatments. Not only did he talk of it at home, but he also described graphically to his friends at Sjur's Cafe the miraculous procedure being dealt to him behind the hallowed walls of the Mayo Clinic. He reiterated feats beyond belief that were happening in the advance of modern medicine, not least at Rochester, Minnesota, practically next door.

Neil hadn't been home long before he realized, as never before, how his father, now ill, and Tante, for that matter, hadn't been around in the world the way he had. They didn't know the world the way he did, and he grew more and more dissatisfied with the living arrangement. It wasn't that he was unhappy at home, but things had changed in ways he had not expected.

"Let me find a job," said Gloria one evening as she lit a cigarette in the barn after her father-in-law had left for the house.

Neil was tossing a forkful of hay to the calf being fattened for fall slaughter. "My wife working? Hardly."

"Why not? I'm of no use here with you gone all day."

"You can keep house. Tante is old and tired. She shouldn't be doing half the work she does."

"She doesn't let me do very much. I guess she thinks I don't know how and maybe I don't. At least I don't know how to take hold of things she had done so long. I'd love to get away all day the way you do."

"What kind of a job?"

"I could ride with Ruthie into Rochester."

So Gloria got a job as a salesgirl selling dresses at Massey's. Ruthie assured her father that it was a job in Rochester's finest fashion shop, and being qualified meant having Gloria's charm.

Henrik's daughter-in-law continued to please him, it wasn't that. If Ruthie sensed an erroding of her father's peace of mind it was due to worry about Neil's future as a farmer. Now, after six months, there were no additions to the herd filling the empty stanchions, no mention of taking back fields, of getting a tractor, nothing that indicated to Henrik that Neil was even interested in all that was to become his. Instead, his son was taking jobs to his liking elsewhere. Now he was driving back and forth to Cannon Falls, working at auto repair. There was no question about it, for Henrik, that Neil had other plans for his life not disclosed to his father.

While they finished milking one evening, Henrik confronted Neil. "You're not interested in the farm?"

"There's not enough here for me."

"What do you mean, it's not enough?"

"Now a farmer has to have lots of acres, lots of cows to make it pay. This farm has a mortgage. It isn't clear, small as it is. How could we buy more land. With what?"

"Not enough?" Henrik's heart sank. Yes, the mortgage, there was still the mortgage.

"You've always said your fields were gravel knolls good only for road surfacing, and you are right, they are. Where could I get more acres? And all we have is old machinery—no tractor. Even if we filled the barn with cows, we'd never get ahead."

"Your mother and I managed here through the worst depression."

"I know, and it wasn't easy."

It was no use to push the issue further. His son had seen the squalor of those days. It wasn't strange, at all, that he saw no future here. No doubt Neil was right. Times were certainly changing.

So Henrik carried on as before. He continued to rent out his fields to Wayne Bakken, and together with Neil, who felt it was his duty to stick by his father, milked the six cows and collected a milk check. Only now there were more mouths to feed and money for the household had to come from each of the wage earners in his family. There was something very awkward about this. Things were going further adrift from anything he had ever anticipated.

Even as he was confronting Neil about the farm, he was confronting the massive formation of abnormal cells in his lungs, which were robbing him of his breath. In spite of the ingenuity of radiation, what was happening to him could not be controlled. There was no wisdom in outbursts of anger; time had taught him that wrath, which seemed a hero's strength, had questionable results when applied indiscriminately.

He rose early. He needed so much time now for whatever he set out to do. He chose to be the one to arouse the sleeping cows and bringing them to the barn for milking. He found the morning air more potent; what little of it his lungs would permit him was rich and clean. The stops for rest forced on him by exertion seemed natural pauses for contemplation.

This was a morning in June, the most beautiful of months, when cows could wade in the ample green of the pasture, grazing as they went. Now, most of them were lying in the dew even as the sun was bursting through the rain clouds of the past night. Clouds did have silver linings. "This is the day the Lord has made," his mother used to quote from somewhere. She would be picking up her hoe and going to the little garden in the "slough." The cottonwood tree was still there; he saw its shiny new leaves twinkling the sun's light as they moved in the morning breeze. Year after year he had skirted the slough with his farm implements even as Wayne did now during planting. He had never taken the tree down; it had just grown bigger and bigger. It was foolish shade for whatever one wanted to raise. Why hadn't he removed it? One didn't live by logic any more than one lived by outbursts of wrath. Life held mysteries. it was full of complexities.

The Lord hast commanded the morning. He searched around for the bitterness, the shattered pieces of his anger. He found them, all right, but they had become strangely devoid of meaning. Was hope at work again? Hope had picked him up countless times as he quoted for himself something from Alexander Pope:

> Hope springs eternal in the human breast,
> Man never is, but always to be blessed.

He wasn't sure it was hope he had now. *Why did God create man?* A catechism question which he had always thought was loosely related to what Pope had to say. The answer: *that he might be blessed forever.* Was this hope or a statement of truth?

He wasn't sure, but the Lord's new day, pure blue and so rich with life, seemed to establish evidence of something for Henrik as he moved from a reststop closer to the sleeping cattle.

That summer Ann took her father for rides. It was part of a tight routine Henrik wove for himself as he tackled the living of each of the days left to him. "Drive in here," he told her one day as she was about to pass the grove near the Zumbro River. It was still used for picnics, but today it was accommodating a 4-H softball game. He likes to watch young people, she surmised. "Over there." He pointed toward the far end of the parking area. "See that tree? It's been there a long time." His breath would permit him to say no more, but he had succeeded in having her look with him. One Fourth of July he and Ragnild had had their first talk, their first meal together under that tree. Funny how trees outlast us, he thought. It even had healed a gash inflicted by a lightning bolt.

"He must have the downstairs bedroom now," Gloria told Ruthie on their way to work one morning in August. "It's taking him ages to climb the stairs. You know how he has to rest between every step. It's getting worse. He mustn't do that any longer."

"He certainly hangs on hard to his routine. He simply permits himself more time to make the climb."

"Neil and I want to trade rooms with him."

"Maybe he'll consent if you suggest it."

"I will."

Henrik had climbed the steep stairs for the last time; he consented willingly now to whatever was planned for his comfort. It seemed to him that he was surrounded by helpers. His daughters and daughter-in-law blended into willing, smiling entities; he scarcely knew one from the other. Sometimes he thought them all dressed in white, as he saw his Ruthie so much of the time. Only Tante was different. Only Tante was real.

"You must not leave me, Anna," Henrik said one morning as the cars drove out of the yard, the girls to Rochester and Neil to Cannon Falls. "You and I are the only ones left."

"Where else would I want to be?" A lump arose in her throat.

"The others just run here and there."

"They try hard, all of them."

"I don't complain about the children. They are all very considerate. But we've been sister and brother together for many, many years." Henrik seemed miraculously blessed with breath for this flow of words.

"We have, Henrik," Anna replied. Tears spilled.

"What are you going to do when I am gone?"

"Emma Veblen has asked me to share a room with her at Sunset Home."

"Who would have thought Emma would survive Josie?"

"We don't know those things. Remember how badly we treated Emma when we went to school? 'Fat and Funny' everyone shouted."

"I do. We can only regret such foolishness."

As more and more things were done for Henrik he became less and less aware of time; hours melted into one another and morning could as well be evening, or mid-morning, mid-afternoon. But Anna never left him. She knew instinctively her brother's need of her. She took to sleeping on a downstairs couch, always with an ear alert to his faintest appeals. And Henrik knew she was always there. His mother had watched over Arne, and now Anna was watching over him.

She would slip with him into his memories and laugh over little oddities. Although talking became more and more laborious, he never felt rushed with her. "Bestemor inherited Arne's *Mjolner,* did you know that? She used it as a tack hammer for years and it brought her nothing but good luck." "And she never knew the reason why," Anna responded with a chuckle. "We gave Juliet a little kewpie doll one day. Ragnild made a dress for it just like Juliet's. The two looked just alike." Anna remembered and smiled. "We had a handsome tomcat that used to hang around the barn. Ann called him Barbara. Can you imagine a tomcat called Barbara?" "That's your Ann," Anna said. "So full of fantasy."

Occasionally a neighbor would stop in, but none would choose to sit on the new davenport. The minister came often. He sat in the chair to the set; he made himself comfortable.

As summer ebbed into fall and Ann, who had spent most of her vacation at home, went back north to her teaching position, Henrik lapsed into silence. It was the silence Anna had seen in her mother the last days of her life. His eyes were out the window where leaves were blowing willy-nilly in the wind until they caught somewhere. He asked the minister to pronounce the Priestly Benediction whenever he left. "He remembers Ragnild," was Rev. Nesvig's usual aside to Anna on the way out.

One cold, October afternoon, Philox announced a caller. The minister had just left, and Anna, feeling the chill of the gusty wind let in as the good man departed, was warming herself by the stove. Now an unfamiliar car had driven into the yard. When Anna reached the window for a look, she saw a tall man closing his car door. Rev. Rasmus Hegge! She glanced over at Henrik who again seemed to be asleep. She must keep this visitor out of the house at all costs! If she had been helpless to prevent the tragedy of her sister Sarah at the hand of Rasmus Hegge, she would spare her brother yet another of this man's unwarranted intrusions!

She must hurry before he reached the door! She was wearing a sweater but took on a coat. While doing so she concentrated on her cane; she would need it. It was hanging by the back door.

She managed to get herself out the front door before the man reached the steps. As she made two quick half steps down from the porch, the wind nearly toppled her. She trembled against her cane.

"You can't come in. He mustn't see anyone. He is very ill. You've come at the wrong time, Rasmus." The words came like a torrent even as the wind that pushed her off balance.

"I have heard he is dying. That's why I've come."

"He's found peace, I tell you. There's nothing you can do. Please go. I beg of you."

"I'm sorry, Anna. I came to—I never felt he was—"

"It's all right, I tell you."

The evangelist turned slowly. There was nothing more he could think to say. He looked back at her once, as if he should have supported the frail woman out of the wind. As he walked along, he looked at the bay window as if there were someone there he should have seen. Then he climbed into his car. Philox remained at Anna's side and ceased barking only as the car door closed. Upon hearing the raised motor, Anna discovered new strength in her limbs. She would have the courage to tell a lie, too, if Henrik was alert enough to ask. She re-entered the house.

"Was it Charley Otterness?"

Anna caught Henrik's question as she returned to the living room. "No, it wasn't." She waited anxiously.

"I sold him my horse."

"Yes, I know. Blossom will have a good home," Anna replied with quiet relief.

"Charley's good to his horses." He had more to say, but it would come after a long lapse. "When he comes—"

"Yes?"

"Don't take—his check."

Two days later Henrik died. It happened during a brilliant sunset on a copper, Indian summer day. There was no wind. The leaves were all resting where they had fallen.

The farm was sold, as everyone thought it would be, and the mortgage finally resolved. Five of Henrik's cows were picked up quickly by a cattle buyer; one was too old, good only for a few dollars when shipped to the stockyards.

The first Saturday in November was chosen for the auction. It was pretty late in the year, liable to be blustery and cold, but Indian summer, as it did some years, might hold out until Thanksgiving. The weather turned out tolerable; no rain fell, but neither was there a strong, comforting sun.

The disorder in the house during the routing out of all the auction articles disturbed Anna. Neil had wanted to take her to Sunset Home in Kenyon, before the auction, but she felt she should be around. It was somehow the last of her duties to see to it that the new generation understood about the things on the old place. Of course, this was impossible, but she would try. "The spinning wheel must be kept by someone," she insisted, "Also the big, copper kettle, and Bestemor's bureau." But how could young people know the value of these things which had outlasted the people who used them?

After the long tables set up in the yard had been ladened with countless small items, Anna wrapped herself well in her old, winter coat and knitted cap, took her cane and limped out the door to survey what was there. The yard was cluttered. Before she could reach the tables, she moved in and out among the pieces of furniture. Her heart sank when she saw Henrik's chair under a tree. How dilapidated it was, how like a discarded pair of old shoes! Who would want to buy it? Rather, it should be lovingly burned—let to collapse in flames. But how could she insist on that? She didn't want to be bothersome with her suggestions.

She pivoted in the direction of the tables. Ragnild's eggbeater. It was no one's now, just another eggbeater. The leather strap which sharpened Henrik's razor—the kettle which had boiled the Christmas lutefisk—the lefse rolling pin— the wooden spoon worn away on one side from years of stirring sauces and stews—a china tea set. It was Ragnild's tea set; wouldn't you think one of the girls would have wanted that? It was a gift from some church ladies in appreciation for Ragnild's efforts in Sunday school. Anna grasped her cane more tightly and moved on. She couldn't be guardian of all these things; what was she thinking about? Suddenly her eyes sharpened as she caught sight of the little tack hammer among the tools. *Mjolner!* She quickly grabbed it up. She must persuade one of them to keep this! Gloria! Anna was inspired. Yes, Gloria, she'd be the one to believe its magic. Her nieces and nephews had become aloof now, no longer the children they used to be, but Gloria, her eyes still danced. This one item she would rescue; that would have to be enough.

After the tour of the auction site, Anna returned to the shelter of the house. The rest of the day she watched from a window. The people who tramped around the premises were not the neighbors who had crowded there for weddings and funerals in the old days. In fact, they weren't neighbors at all. Most of them were total strangers. And they somehow lacked respect. They laughed hilariously when the auctioneer held aloft the milkstool Ragnild had asked Lars to make for her. The old washtub was cast aside with disdain, since no one cared to bid on it. She was glad when the noise was over. She saw things being loaded as people began leaving with what they had won on bidding: pitchforks, milk cans, harnesses—and sometimes, getting it all along was a problem. Anna was amazed. When one sheds his earthly possessions, they are grabbed up by others and become again what they originally were: simply wood, stone and metal.

It was not feasible for Anna to stay any longer; the house would be vacated at the end of another week. Since Neil worked every day except Sunday, she agreed to be taken to Sunset Home the day after the auction. Anna had been carefully selecting her keepsakes, and these she stored in her cedar chest. It was the only item of furniture she would consider bringing with her; Emma Veblen had brought a favorite chair. All her clothes fit into her suitcase.

As she took her dresses off hangers and folded them neatly, she wondered if she was really Anna Kristian; maybe she was just another stranger, like the ones she had seen yesterday, grabbing up what was worth taking. After a long glance around the room in the event that she had forgotten anything, she slipped for a moment into absentmindedness. Coming to, she bent forward and latched down the old suitcase. Was this the last trip it would be making?

A gunshot cracked and echoed from somewhere down by the barn. Anna knew what it meant. Philox was dead.

"Couldn't Wayne Bakken have waited?" Ruthie rushed in, taking refuge where Anna was. "He promised to wait until we were gone from here. Couldn't he find something better to do on a Sunday afternoon?"

Neil was waiting in the doorway. "Are you ready, Tante? We'd better go."

"Yes, I'm ready."

EPILOGUE

"Something to read today, Mrs. Olson, a book or a magazine, perhaps?" At Sunset Home a library cart had stopped outside Anna's door.

"I don't think you have the book I want. I've never seen it among those books you keep bringing." There was a quiet resignation in her voice.

The volunteer entered and bent over Anna's chair. "I'd be happy to bring you any book you name if we can find it." She had to speak loudly to these old folks.

Anna lifted her head and fixed her eyes on the kind woman. "Could you bring me *The Whale* by Herman Melville?"

"About Moby Dick?" Could that be it?

Anna nodded.

"That's a classic. We ought to be able to find it." She eyed Anna questioningly. "It's called *Moby Dick,* isn't it?"

Anna smiled. "Yes."

"I'll have it for you this afternoon, if not then, tomorrow."

"Thank you."

"Good-bye, Mrs. Olson. I'll soon be back."

The cart began to roll again.

Anna spent many days with the book. She didn't start at the beginning; she knew her way around. She read to put vivid color again on the old familiar images: the livid scar on the copper face of Captain Ahab, the ancient tatoos on the body of Queequeg, the eerie amber light on the swinging lanterns in the utter darkness aboard the Pequod, brilliancy on the burst of sunlight across the deck at the moment of dawn, and over the water ethereal purity on the whale-spout clouds as the giant leviathans came up for air. Sounds, too, she read to make vivid: wind and wave creaking the tiny ship, shouts and curses of frightened, angry seamen, and the crisp tap of the ivory peg leg on the deck boards as the sinister captain moved about. And silences: the morose numbness of men endlessly waiting, the doldrum of the looking glass when the ocean lapsed as though time had come to an end.

The book was lying at her side as much of the time as it was in her hands, but its presence was all-consuming. She hiked with Peder along the Zumbro; he had wanted to become a fisherman, he said. She sat with him as his injured foot healed, listening to him read his adopted language. She read for her family on a rainy October evening before the distressing epidemic of measles swept the little town. And her mother had talked about the Leviathan described in the book of Job, the very largest of God's creatures, rising and receding in the depths of the sea. "None is so fierce that he dares to stir him up," she quoted, and furthermore, "What is under heaven is mine, saith the Lord. Hitherto shalt thou come, but no further, here shall the proud waves be stayed."

One afternoon in her chair, in the manner of the very old, Anna nodded into seeming sleep. There had always been that unfathomable ocean under her in which the great whale was. Sometimes he slept on the bottom, far, far down, almost forgotten in the deep. Sometimes he would rise at a great distance away and spout a fountain of mist. And sometimes he would rise directly under her, lifting her willy-nilly on troubled water, blinding her eyes with the poisonous mist of his spout. At such times, awake or asleep, would come the repeat of a dream. Down, down, she would fall into a depth she was never able to comprehend. When she was young and tender, she had quaked with terror: a portrait of a girl her own age, a sapphire ring, a full-length mirror. As she grew older, these moments settled into a sober dread, a chest carried up an outside stairway along a brick wall, then coffins, one after another, of her loved ones. She alone was left. She, the delicate one!

Neither she nor Peder had sought revenge on the whale. That was wise. Peder had lived with his stump of a foot so conscientiously, task after task, and she had endured limping for nearly thirty years, but the whale hadn't destroyed them; that mysterious leviathan, in spite of the peril he caused, was restrained. He is kept within bounds by the Creator. Likewise, the sun, which one must let go at the end of each day, will surely rise again at His bidding. The Lord who restrains the great whale also commands the morning. The dawn has not yet failed.

Anna opened her eyes again and remembered the visit of her niece, Ann, just yesterday, or was it the day before? The buildings are gone at the old place, was the news she brought—the house, the barn, the silo, everything except the windmill. She hardly recognized the old farmyard, she said, except for two old cottonwood trees and the lilac bush. Gone.

Anna's head drooped again. She was the lone survivor, she, the delicate one. She had sat at the bedsides of four of her loved ones and watched them die, and she was still here. Now the place where they all had lived was gone; she was Ishmael, surviving as he, with a chest. Yes, she had hung onto the cedar chest! It was the last

Christmas present from her beloved husband, and she would keep it at all costs. They had said it was too big to go into this tiny room where they had moved her when Emma Veblen died, but they had finally complied. Her niece would have the chest and all its contents when she left this world.

Anna opened her eyes again and looked at the chest with the familiar grain in the dark red wood. The book was lying there on top of it. Her niece, Ann, had picked it up. She had acted so surprised. She had never known that her Uncle Peder wanted to become a fisherman before he came to America. Of whales? Why not? He was strong and brave, her Peder. Norwegians were never afraid of the sea in the old days. Ann had agreed. Strange how Ann didn't know that her Uncle Peder had wanted to become a fisherman. But, no matter, she supposed it was Tante's fault, maybe he had never told her in the first place.

Anna's head sank once more. No, it wasn't that the great whale had destroyed her home. No, it wasn't that. Nor had he destroyed her loved ones. They had prepared themselves, not for death but for resurrection. And she, too. She would sleep in the earth even as they were doing now, under sky and wind. The Lord was in charge. He would command the morning. Grandma Hanson used to talk about resurrection morning; it was good to think about.

"It's bedtime, Mrs. Olson. My, you seem asleep already."

The nurses talked so loud. Anna supposed it was because they thought she was deaf. But it wasn't that either, exactly. It was that she had diminished and her surroundings were all out of proportion.

"I'll get you ready for bed." The nurse was tearing aside the bedspread. "Here, let me take off your shoes."

Anna consented.